I0699032

CONTESTS OF STRENGTH

A Novel

Melissa Slager

TRUTH & STORY

Copyright © 2025 by Melissa Slager

All rights reserved. No part of this book may be used or reproduced in any manner whatsoever without written permission except in the case of brief quotations embodied in critical articles and reviews. For information, address Truth & Story, P.O. Box 2782, Everett, WA 98213.

The characters and events in this book are fictitious. Any similarity to real persons, living or dead, is coincidental and not intended by the author.

Maps © 2025 by Aaron S. Parker

Chapter illustrations © 2025 by Ross Jimmicum

Whaling canoe illustration from T.T. Waterman's *The Whaling Equipment of the Makah Indians* (University of Washington Publications, 1920), public domain.

Library of Congress Control Number: 2025900922

Publisher's Cataloging-in-Publication Data:

Names: Slager, Melissa, author.
Title: Contests of strength : a novel / Melissa Slager.
Description: Everett, WA: Truth & Story, 2025.
Identifiers: LCCN: 2025900922 | ISBN: 979-8-9915435-1-4 (paperback) | 979-8-9915435-2-1 (e-book)
Subjects: LCSH Makah Indians--Fiction. | Indians of North America--Northwest, Pacific--Fiction. |
    Northwest, Pacific--History--20th century--Fiction. | Whaling--Fiction. | Family--Fiction. |
    Olympic Peninsula (Wash.)--History--Fiction. | BISAC FICTION / Historical / General
Classification: LCC PS3619 .L34 C66 2025 | DDC 813.6--dc23

ISBN 979-8-9915435-1-4 (paperback), 979-8-9915435-2-1 (e-book)

Set in Brill Latin

Praise for *Contests of Strength*

"A masterfully crafted tale—rich in detail, immersive in its storytelling and unforgettable in its impact." —*Meredith Parker (Makah)*

"A cinematic and involving historical novel... riveting..." —Foreword *Clarion Reviews*

"The natural disaster that waylaid the tribe is a real one, with her research into it and scholarly command of all the relevant source material nothing short of magisterial. ... However, this book is, first and foremost, a novel, and it tells an engrossing story. ... A historically rigorous and emotionally riveting period piece." —*Kirkus Reviews*

"Slager skillfully balances the history with a fundamentally human story..." —*BlueInk Review*

"Contests of Strength is rich with battles, murders, whale hunts, slavery, spirit quests and secret love, climaxing in the massive subduction zone earthquake that devastated native Pacific Northwest communities on January 26, 1700. It is also a hypnotic portal to a lost indigenous world of fogged forests, smoky longhouses, and waves crashing on America's northwest tip, told with careful research and real empathy." —*William Dietrich, author of the bestselling Ethan Gage series*

"Most books on Pacific Northwest history are set after the arrival of European colonizers. *Contests of Strength* is delightfully different by presenting a well-researched and fascinating story of the people of the Cape; people we know today as the Makah tribe. Through an achingly impossible romance between a chief's headstrong son and a proud slave woman, and immersive depictions of lives lived as one with nature – even when the usually life-giving sea turns against them – this must-read novel captivates the reader right to the very last page. I look forward to more from this author." —*Kelli Estes, USA Today bestselling author of* Smoke on the Wind *and* The Girl Who Wrote in Silk

"Melissa Slager's *Contests of Strength* is an intensely emotional and captivating read. I was instantly drawn in by the dual perspectives of Amuun'a͟xsum and Dushuuw—their troubled pasts and secrets, hopes and yearnings, and the danger that erupts and threatens their lives and

world in the tsunami of 1700. Slager's elegant prose, complex characters, and meticulous research about the Makah people of Washington state are evident throughout. Her portrayal of every aspect of everyday life in a small whaling village in the American West Coast, and most especially in the song, dance, and folklore of the Makah Tribe, is told with reverence. Readers will think about the trials and heartbreaking journeys of Dushuuw and Amuun'a_xsum long after the last page. A must read!"
—*Adriana Allegri, author of* The Sunflower House

For Rob and our girls, with love.
For the Makah individuals who encouraged me, q̓atiqšiƛ̓ʔits ʔuktiˑp duˑb.
And for Jesikah, for everything.

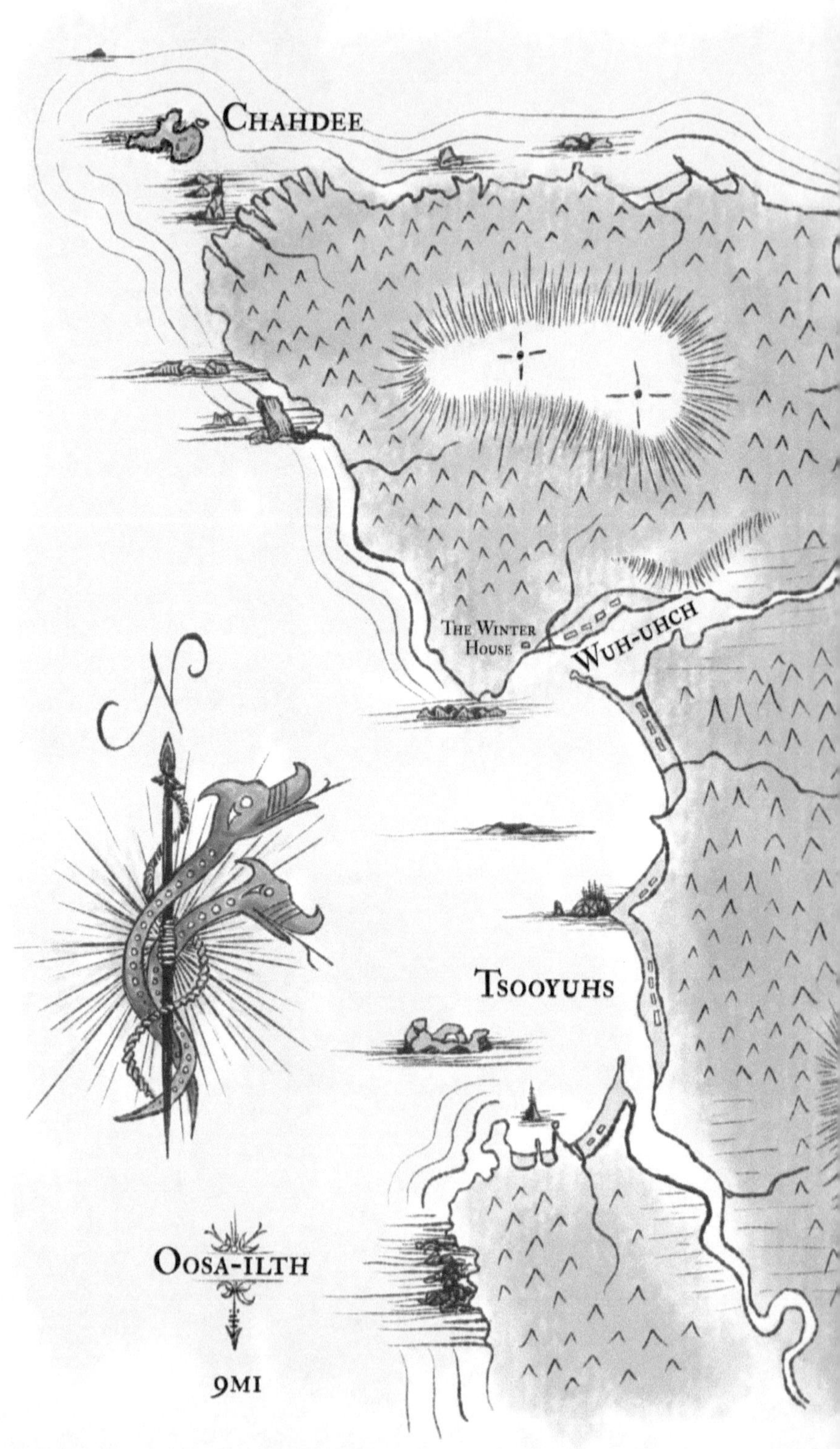

CHAHDEE
THE WINTER HOUSE
WUH-UHCH
TSOOYUHS
OOSA-ILTH
9MI

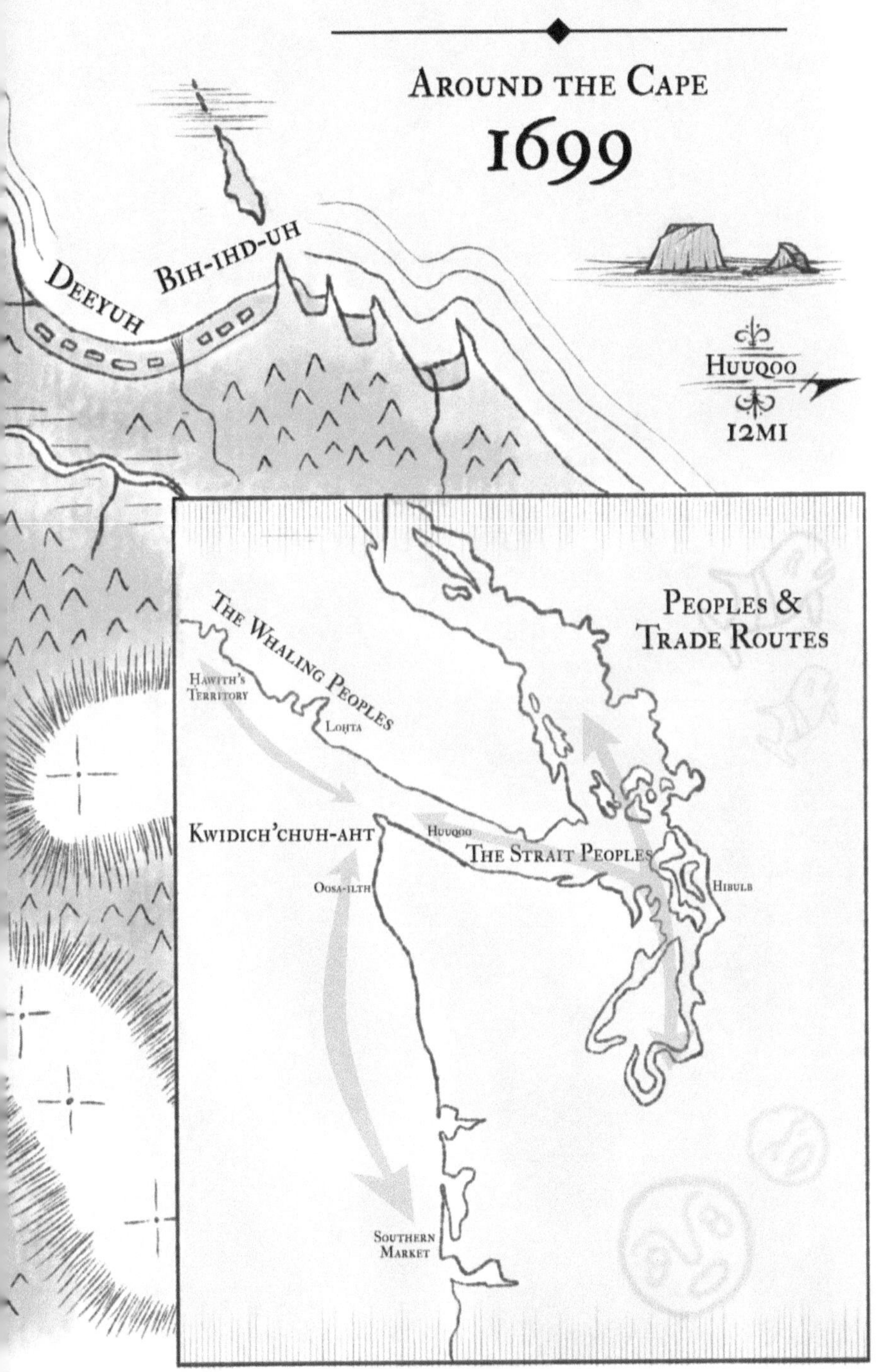
KWIDICH'CHUH-AHT
LANDS & WATERS
AROUND THE CAPE
1699
DEEYUH
BIH-IHD-UH
HUUQOO
12MI
PEOPLES &
TRADE ROUTES
THE WHALING PEOPLES
HAWITH'S TERRITORY
LOHTA
KWIDICH'CHUH-AHT
HUUQOO
THE STRAIT PEOPLES
OOSA-ILTH
HIBULB
SOUTHERN MARKET

Author's Note

This book is based on a real historical event and on real places, but the characters and story are fictional. I aim to depict life in a whaling village on North America's West Coast at a time when Europeans knew nothing of these shorelines; this unexplored area was simply (and perhaps appropriately) filled in as sea on their maps. The book is primarily set in the territory of the Qʷidičča?a·tx̌ (written in this book as Kwidich'chuh-aht)—more widely known as the Makah Tribe—which encompasses, in part, the Cape Flattery area of Washington state. Wa?ač (written in this book as Wuh-uhch) is one of five traditional winter villages that formed the Makah confederacy in the years before and into European and U.S. contact and colonization. I am a descendant of Dutch immigrants who benefits from that colonization. And while I diligently sought to make this book reflective of its time and its cultures, there is inevitably no true window to the past in these pages. This is a novel, a novel that I hope inspires you to appreciate in particular the Makah Tribe as well as their First Nation cousins on Vancouver Island's west coast—but also to visit their territories for yourself and learn more about their incredible living histories. Much of the proceeds from this book go to support those voices, including the Makah Cultural and Research Center, as I seek to give back in appreciation of all the time and expertise shared with me over the course of this project.

—M.S.

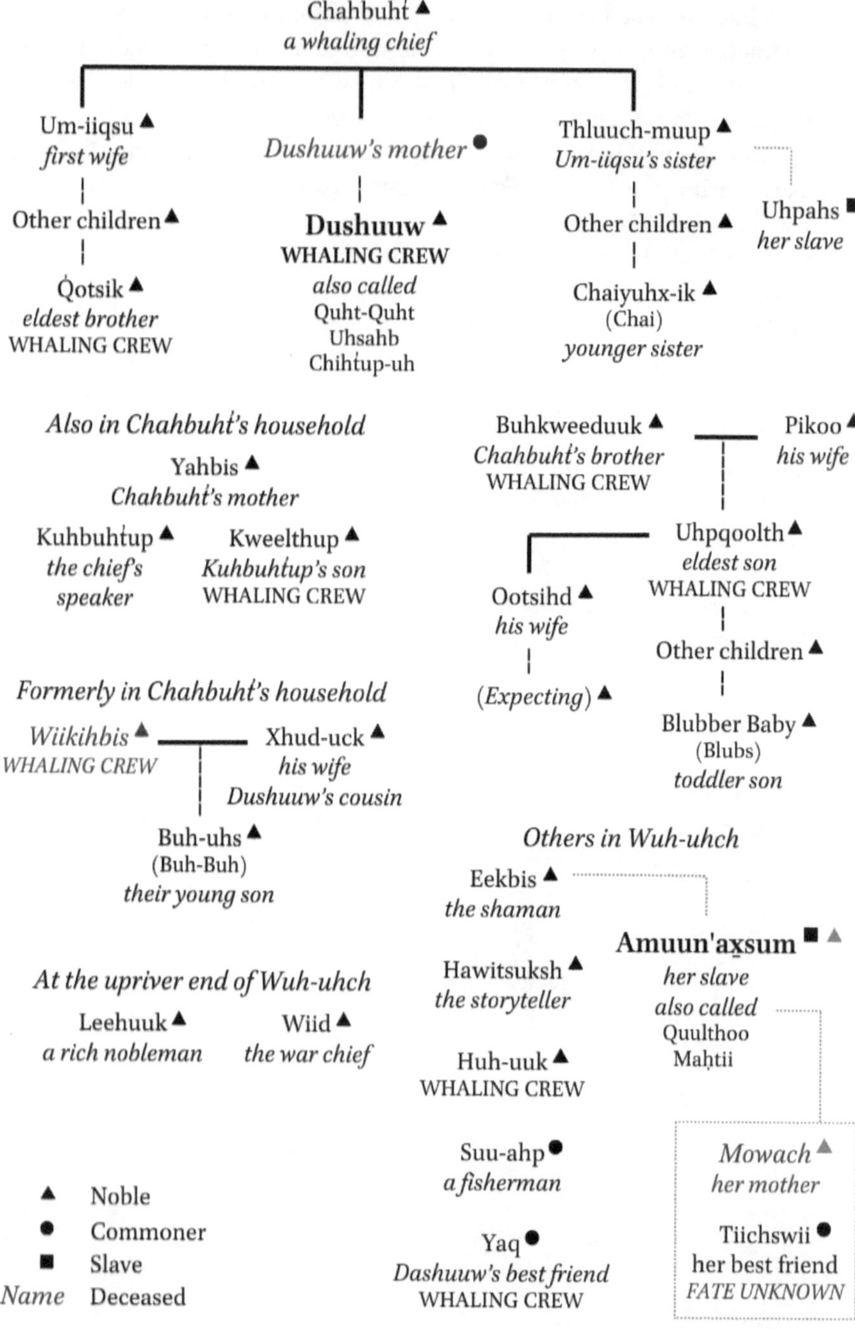

The Kwidich'chuh-aht confederacy
Wuh-uhch

Chahbuht ▲
a whaling chief

Um-iiqsu ▲
first wife

Dushuuw's mother ●

Thluuch-muup ▲
Um-iiqsu's sister

Uhpahs ■
her slave

Other children ▲

Dushuuw ▲
WHALING CREW
also called
Quht-Quht
Uhsahb
Chihtup-uh

Other children ▲

Qotsik ▲
eldest brother
WHALING CREW

Chaiyuhx-ik ▲
(Chai)
younger sister

Also in Chahbuht's household

Buhkweeduuk ▲
Chahbuht's brother
WHALING CREW

Pikoo ▲
his wife

Yahbis ▲
Chahbuht's mother

Kuhbuhtup ▲
the chief's
speaker

Kweelthup ▲
Kuhbuhtup's son
WHALING CREW

Uhpqoolth ▲
eldest son
WHALING CREW

Ootsihd ▲
his wife

Other children ▲

Formerly in Chahbuht's household

(Expecting) ▲

Wiikihbis ▲
WHALING CREW

Xhud-uck ▲
his wife
Dushuuw's cousin

Blubber Baby ▲
(Blubs)
toddler son

Buh-uhs ▲
(Buh-Buh)
their young son

Others in Wuh-uhch

Eekbis ▲
the shaman

Amuun'axsum ■ ▲
her slave
also called
Quulthoo
Mahtii

At the upriver end of Wuh-uhch

Hawitsuksh ▲
the storyteller

Leehuuk ▲
a rich nobleman

Wiid ▲
the war chief

Huh-uuk ▲
WHALING CREW

Mowach ▲
her mother

Suu-ahp ●
a fisherman

Tiichswii ●
her best friend
FATE UNKNOWN

▲ Noble
● Commoner
■ Slave
Name Deceased

Yaq ●
Dashuuw's best friend
WHALING CREW

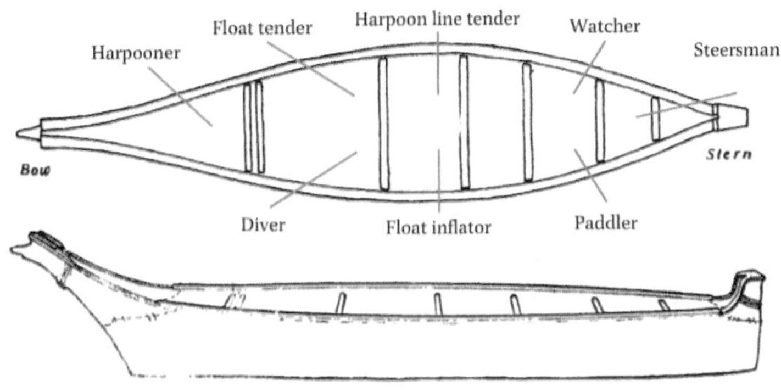

WHALING CREW

Ẉotsik Uhpqoolth *Wiikihbis* Kweelthup Buhkweeduuk

Yaq Huh-uuk Dushuuw

Other villages in the confederacy:

Oosa-ilth

The largest village, south of the cape

Deeyuh

Neighbor upriver of Wuh-uhch, on
the strait side of the cape

Oodahk ▲ Ṫoopuuk ■
whaling chief *his slave*

Tsooyuhs

Neighbor south of Wuh-uhch,
across the bay

Shuchkuk ▲
warrior

Bih-ihd-uh

The smallest village, east of Deeyuh

Across the strait

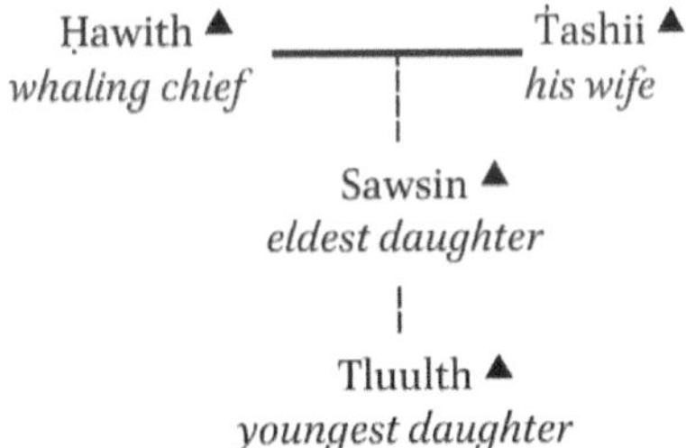

*Hear names
pronounced*

For a complete guide to names, including original Native spellings and meanings,
see the back of this book. An audio pronunciation guide can be found at
melissaslager.com/reader.

Foreword

MANY LIFETIMES AGO, in the ancestral lands of the present-day Makah, in the maritime paradise of Cape Flattery, where the Pacific Ocean and Salish Sea converge, a love story is born. It unfolds amid a lively culture, which flourishes among old-growth forests. And yet, voices from the present, which seems so far removed from the historic setting, resonate through the book you're holding. My people still guard and carry allegiance to ancient legends. We still live with the bones of our ancestors, on the shores they knew as well as we do.

My hereditary name is Xaʔwiłeyatuk. I'm a lifelong artist, fisherman, hunter, educator, and proud Makah. A number of elder knowledge-keepers from our community, some of our living treasures, shared precious narratives with Melissa, and in part from these sacred teachings, this story was born.

Contests of Strength carries the essence of who we are and where we come from, as it has been passed down by our elders for generations. Melissa immersed herself in a number of our people's important oral histories, which she has expertly woven into the backdrop of a tale of immortal love first shared in the times of our ancestors. She researched traditional nuances with an ethos of respect and reverence for the sanctity of our legends, which we've kept alive in what is now Neah Bay.

Melissa pulls the reader back in time, into the folklore of the Makah people. Her ethnography blends authentic oral histories with a fictional narrative reminiscent of both Makah family histories and tribal historical teachings. From these timeless stories, she carefully crafted a love story, a reincarnation of ancient connections, like a pearl emerging from an old-growth bivalve.

The story takes place in a culture exotic to most. The ancient Egyptians built pyramids; we hunted whales. Two souls drift in the generational river of our people, in a particular setting that echoes in the modern age. The pyramids still stand; so do our legacies.

I read Melissa's work at several stages, and I was struck by the candor and openness of my elders. She probed ancient knowledge and the vast wealth of living oral histories among not only the Makah but also our Nuu-chah-nulth relatives, and she spent invaluable time with people who know what it means to live with the ancestors. The glimmer of this living flame burns through the book. Her characters' names called to mind titles and names I was familiar with, and she shaped their identities in a recognizably Makah context. Her authenticity in portraying a surviving pre-Columbian civilization demonstrates the highest respect for our heritage.

The saga features situations both universal and particularly important to our people: the quest for mental fortitude and self-improvement, and the struggle between dueling aspects of human nature. This book, imbued with the trust of our people, embraces these themes of our storytelling traditions.

Part of my career has been to safeguard the essence of who we are and where we come from. We hold common core values that require knowledge and discipline. I'm an artist who's made a living from the sea. I preserve our traditional foods. I know some songs, some dances; I know more stories. I learned our modern system of governance. The Makah fortitude and leadership Melissa describes is still evident today. While serving on the Makah Tribal Council, for example, I helped pass national legislation, the Coast Guard Reauthorization Act, to enhance maritime protections, as our territory has suffered the worst oil spills of our region. The Makah manage a world-class fisheries agency and steward one of the world's beautiful seascapes, a realm rich in culturally important living resources. *Contests of Strength*—its name and the story it holds—embodies the leadership of our people and our sacred relationship to the ocean. As a chief said during the writing of the 1855 Treaty of Neah Bay, "The sea is my country." Every setting in the book reflects this immortal connection.

Contests of Strength incorporates various perspectives among the storytellers of our people and a wealth of stories, rich in interpersonal nuance and high drama, that have reverberated through generations. It's an introduction to the universe of the Makah, where we are the living breath of our ancestors.

I implore the reader to appreciate that the book's natural splendor is still the habitat of our living culture. The timeless, raw beauty of our rugged seaside cliffs and their forested, emerald edges is fundamental to the Qʷidičča?a·tx̌, or "People of the Cape." For many lifetimes, the great houses of our people have sung, danced, and told stories woven through many marriages and generations. *Contests of Strength*, with its drama and romance, is reminiscent of a blockbuster movie, but perhaps more awe-inspiring is that the story grew not from fantasy but from real legends that we, through love, fortitude, and knowledge, have kept alive.

Micah McCarty
Olympia, Washington
January 2025

When we sing our songs,
when we show our masks and headdresses,
we invoke the presence of our ancestors.
We are collapsing time.
— from *Out of the Mist: Treasures of the Nuu-chah-nulth Chiefs*

From a human-shaped world
you are about to step into a terrain
dominated by other forces.
The sea makes the rules.
— National Park Service sign at Cape Alava trailhead

The Long Ago

SMALL ONE SLUMPED against her grandmother's fleshy side, her gaze fighting sleep, her mind intent on the dancing and on the music that mingled with the smoke of many fires across a vast room and the ever-present scent of the sea. The girl reveled at the rhythmic turns of the skirts. The puffs of eagle down tumbling through the air. The pound, pound, pounding of sticks on plank drums. The shaking rattles. The calls of the singers. A steady murmur from low conversations filling the tiny voids in between.

yay ah ay ay ah

Her mother twisted and dipped among the dancers, arms rising with the others. As she swished past, she cast Small One a surreptitious smile. Strings of thin dentalia shells swung from the woman's skirt. The shells, clicking together, sounded like rain. Small One tried to pluck the sound of one shell meeting another—but one gentle touch was both lost in and amplified by the gentle touches of thousands of shells that danced on the dresses of the dancing women. A beautiful storm.

ay ih yah ya ah ah

Beyond the open doorway, the sea pulsed on the beach, as the last orange remnants of the setting summer sun washed away.

As the night wore on, the groups of drummers, singers, and dancers gave way to individuals and pairs. There were family songs, family dances, coarse jokes. And there were always stories.

Grownups chatted and laughed. Children squeezed under and around benches in an overtired frenzy. Slaves wended through the throng with more food. Amid the din, Small One heard only the words of the story. She was as captivated by its dark imaginings as she was by the light of her mother, and perhaps more.

"...And she cried and cried." The storyteller's voice rose and fell and rose, like an infant's swinging cradleboard. "The mother cried so hard, so hard, that mucus fell from her nose, fell into a clam shell."

Small One shifted in her grandmother's lap at the edge of the clump of children. Friends and cousins fidgeted in a tight circle at the storyteller's feet. Outside, the sea pounded, and Small One breathed in the sweet fullness of the wind. Her grandmother stroked her hair.

"One of her tears fell into the clam shell. And that mucus began to change, change into a baby. This baby grew, and grew—grew into a young man right before her eyes. And he looked at her face—so red from all those tears—and he asked her, 'Why are you so sad, Mother?'"

Small One hid a yawn behind her palm.

"'Oh,' the mother says, 'oh, it is that Wild Woman of the Woods. She has stolen your sister, and the other children too—stolen them. They went farther than where their mothers and fathers said they could go, and now she has them. That giantess, she goes around chewing on pitch, and she rubbed that pitch on their eyes. She put the children in her basket, and she has carried them to where we cannot find them. I do not know where she has taken my daughter, your sister.'"

Small One shifted, and her eyelids fluttered.

"He says, 'Don't worry, Mother. Stop crying... I will find her... I will bring her home...'"

The storyteller's voice grew hollow in Small One's ears. The woman's words broke apart, tones floating up before winking out, like tiny sparks, popping from the warm fire and swirling in the building breeze...

Small One woke near dawn next to her sleeping grandmother on their shared bedding. Rain battered the roof planks. Most of the fires were still banked, and it was quiet except for the rain, a retreating grumble of thunder, the squawks of gulls, and the loud gossip of slave women foraging for shellfish that filtered in through the open doorway. The rain lessened. The gulls left off, and the slave women suddenly hushed. Small One's body quivered. She scrunched her eyes closed, drew her cedar blanket up to her shoulders. Light brushed her eyelids, but she did not want to get up yet. One of the slaves outside shouted. Small One continued to shake, despite the blanket. And she wondered why, since she did not feel cold.

The girl blinked, sat up, and looked around. Her grandmother frowned in her sleep and sighed. A large loom rattled against the wall beside them, then banged and fell to the floor, kicking up dirt into Small One's face. The girl gasped.

The house trembled. Hundreds of objects clattered and crashed. Partitions fell. Racks of dried fish tumbled. Seal-skin floats spun wildly by their strings from the rafters. Shouts sounded. An infant cried. A burst of wind blew across Small One's head. Her grandmother started to wake. Small One looked up. A roof plank skidded out of place, and started to tip. Small One thought she must be screaming as the heavy plank fell toward them, but all she heard was the rumbling of a thousand drums, the incessant pounding of countless dancing feet.

You know of the great Thunderbird. Thunderbird beats his massive wings, and the beating makes thunder, louder than any of our plank drums. He brings the rains. Thunderbird, he takes off his serpent belt and whips it through the clouds

> *—whips it like that*

>> *—and it makes the lightning.*

Thunderbird is very important to the people. So important, so honored, that one day, Whale becomes jealous. Whale tells the people that they must decide, decide forever who is greatest.

> *Whale or Thunderbird?*

>> *Thunderbird or Whale?*

And the people, they are afraid, afraid of making Whale angry, afraid of making Thunderbird angry, afraid of them both.

And so, they go to Owl. They ask, 'What should we do?' And Owl thinks and thinks—and then decides. He says, 'Thunderbird has served you faithfully. He is good and means you no harm. His anger is loud, yet he shows restraint. But Whale rules the sea. He can do great harm to the people of the sea. This you know. He wrecks your canoes. He drowns your hunters and fishermen. He beats your shore, threatens your homes. You have suffered at the hands and feet of Whale, yes. But nothing can compare to what he might do if you offend him now.

> *'Above all,' said Owl,*

>> *'above all, I advise you,*

> *keep peace with Whale.'*

1699
SPRING

HE WAS A WARRIOR, not a whaler, and this was a fight he could never win.

The whale's flukes towered above his head. All around was the gray sea. Above, the gray sky. And here he crouched, in a cedar canoe with a paddle raised in his hands, dwarfed by the massive span of gray skin that rose higher and higher, seawater sluicing off in sheets, pelting the bow of the canoe like a deluge. Men shouted. The canoe rocked as they jumped overboard. But Dushuuw was planted to the hull, trapped in the whale's shadow. He could not jump, not yet. He must protect—

The tail started to come down.

Dushuuw tore his gaze away, looked down the length of the canoe toward the bow. His brother's name rose in his throat. But his brother was no longer there.

He dropped his paddle. He bent his knees. He—

A splintering crack like lightning split the air.

Dushuuw's stomach lurched toward his toes, then his throat, as he sailed through the air. There was no above, no below. He was flying, falling. He crashed into the sea with a painful blast. The sea sucked him down with icy tendrils. The men's shouts, the whoosh of the sea air, his hammering heart—the roar of the sea overpowered them all, joined by the reverberations of the whale's tail slap and a high-pitched call that sounded like a distant song. Dushuuw's mouth opened in response.

By the time he thrashed to the surface, coughing up seawater, the waves had carried him far from the other men. He heard their shouts but struggled to see beyond the churning surface of the sea.

Swimming toward the sounds, he hefted himself atop a seal-skin float thrown from the canoe. With the bit of elevation, he could spot the overturned canoe—shockingly far away. His uncle and others treaded water in another direction. Beyond them, two support canoes sliced through the waves to assist. But still he did not see his brother. He looked the other way, and saw only the sea, the gray sea that surrounded them on all sides. Land had been lost in the distance long before this hunt went wrong. A swirl of wind chilled his back and caressed the sea, shrouding the damaged canoe in a veil of mist.

It had been Dushuuw's first time in that canoe. His first time on a whale hunt. He had not wanted to come at all. Had not wanted to enter the realm of his brother, a place permeated with secrets and unknown forces. Had not wanted to replace the crew member who had died—the man he had killed.

Fighting back panic, Dushuuw pushed away the float and swam toward the canoe. He needed to keep moving. He pumped his legs and pushed aside floating debris. A wooden bailer. A paddle. A woven mat. His wet hair lay plastered over his shoulders and back, his top knot undone, his hat lost. He reached the damaged canoe and brushed his hand down the hull as he swam toward the submerged bow. He sucked in a breath and dove. The view below wavered before his eyes. The prow piece that had crowned the bow was missing. The bow itself was split. And there was no sign of his brother. He resurfaced, panic building again. He gathered his breath, but it was another voice that called out.

"Brother! Over here..."

Dushuuw turned and drank in the sight of his brother, Q̇otsik, who leaned over the side of one of the support canoes.

"I thought you—I thought..."

"Perhaps I waited a bit longer than I should have." Q̇otsik shrugged. "But I wanted to save the harpoon."

An old man sat panting behind Q̇otsik in the canoe, shivering under the dry cloak someone had placed over his drenched body. "Only you were fool enough to stay put," Hawitsuksh said, as Dushuuw hooked an elbow over the side of the canoe. "If I didn't know any better, I would think you were just giving me extra grease for the fine story I will make of this adventure." But by the old man's haunted eyes and trembling smile, Dushuuw deduced the storyteller's good humor was more like his wagging finger—intended to cover up a stronger emotion. The old man drew the cloak tighter.

Dushuuw started to look about. "The others..."

"They are all accounted for," Q̇otsik said. "And now you, so are you. You had me worried, brother."

They clasped fists. Q̇otsik's grip was strong, full of a brother's love but also a whaler's power. A power that had brought him several whales already for one so young. But there would be no fin tip to dry and add to his string from this hunt. Dushuuw followed his brother's gaze toward the north, where a distant plume of mist shot skyward from among the migrating herd.

"The whale's spirit called to you," Dushuuw said, "but I—"

"No," Q̇otsik said. "I was too eager."

Dushuuw shook his head.

The old storyteller coughed, and Q̇otsik turned to pat him on the back. Hawitsuksh was not meant to be in the whaling canoe either. He had wheezed much of the journey as it was. Dushuuw's heart weighed him down, pulling him back into the water.

None of this would have happened if it hadn't been for Dushuuw—it was his paddle that had clipped the submerged whale, a whale they had not seen as Q̇otsik pursued another.

The man he killed had joined all of his brother's hunts until this one. That man would never have made such a mistake.

End it...

He couldn't get the woman's voice out of his head.

Be stronger...

Another woman's voice, far older and familiar, that he clung to like a float on a rocking sea.

Dushuuw burst through the water and started retrieving supplies, shoving them toward the men in the support canoes.

"I think we can save the canoe," a voice called out.

Dushuuw turned toward the voice of his best friend. Of all the men there, Yaq alone seemed buoyant; his ever-present smile was more strained, but he spoke with his usual energy.

Yaq swam away from the damaged canoe, which other men were flipping upright. "The split is not large. Our lines are lost, but we can use other canoes' gear. In any case, the canoe is holding on, like it's waiting for us to figure it out." Yaq swam over to Q̇otsik, wiping away blood from a cut on his forehead. "I remember how some of the old whalers talked about what to do, because I remember thinking it was pretty much like tying up the whale's mouth so it doesn't take on water. Except this time, it's two sides of a split canoe, and I don't have to poke any holes anywhere." He dragged the back of his hand under his nose. "I figure if I can do the one, I can figure out the other."

Q̇otsik considered the damaged canoe. "My father would at least want us to try," he said.

Yaq drummed his hand on the hull, then shoved off.

Dushuuw continued to retrieve floating debris with other men fit enough to stay in the water. One by one, most of them got into one of the support canoes and wrapped blankets around themselves. Dushuuw handed a few more items up to his uncle, Buhkweeduuk. "I hope Yaq is successful," Buhkweeduuk said. "These canoes are riding low with our crew added in. It would not take much of a wave to send us all beneath the sea." They watched as Yaq dove to wind a rope around the canoe, its bow still dipping below the waterline.

"Now say," Buhkweeduuk said, his voice rising, "see what we have here." He pulled up a hat, seawater dripping off its brim. The conical hat of woven cedar was topped by a knob that had drooped before the whale strike and now positively sagged. Seeing Dushuuw's expression, his uncle laughed.

"I cannot be rid of the thing," Dushuuw said. His uncle settled his own hat atop his head in response, its knob expertly wrought and erect. Dushuuw left his hat behind and kept swimming.

Short of drowning, Dushuuw would not accept his brother's proffered hand again, not while other men remained in the water, especially their cousin, Uhpqoolth, who had been shooting him disgusted looks the whole journey. The cold pricked. But Dushuuw had been raised to know it well. And as he reflected on their situation, grateful that no one had been seriously harmed or worse, his mood lifted. He had his best friend, his uncle, his brother. And here was a set of tasks. Here was a plan of attack to which he could contribute. Here was something he could do.

Meanwhile, a heavyset whaler made a lumbering effort to roll himself into a canoe. Dushuuw couldn't help but laugh.

That was a mistake.

"You find this whole thing humorous?"

Dushuuw cringed as his cousin swam closer.

"The storyteller wouldn't be out here if it weren't for you," Uhpqoolth said.

Dushuuw swam up to the end of the line that Yaq tossed him. He grabbed the rope with both hands. Uhpqoolth swam up behind him and took up the slack.

"He should be hearing about this story, not be in the middle of it," Uhpqoolth said. "Then struggling for breath," he added, and spat.

On the other side of the damaged canoe, Yaq and another man took up the other end of the rope.

At Yaq's signal, both pairs of men began to pull.

Dushuuw's mind was not on the work, however. Nor the whale. It was back on the dead man, as his cousin intended. That death loomed. It was a shadow that would never leave.

End it...

Dushuuw twisted and squeezed the rope.

In between Yaq's calls to pull, Uhpqoolth spat insults at Dushuuw's back in bitter whispers.

"He was a better man," Uhpqoolth said.

They pulled.

"A better man than you."

They pulled.

"You've changed everything," Uhpqoolth said, and the cousins pulled a final time. A wave swept over Dushuuw's head; salt water slid down his throat.

He gasped, and coughed.

But his heart now pounded from something other than the lingering terror of the whale strike or mysterious forces he preferred to avoid, and any remorse he had felt in the moment was doused. He vividly remembered the day that the man had died at his hands. And though Dushuuw's guilt remained like the stench of smoke, always greater was the same hot fury that had flared right before he broke the man's neck—and changed everything.

Night fell as the men finished salvaging the damaged canoe. They found the prow piece floating at a distance, its deer-like head shorn by the slap of the whale's tail. Q̓otsik kept the piece close, as he did his harpoon. The split bow of the whaling canoe rode low despite Yaq's patchwork. They would attach floats to prop it up. It would make the paddle home slow going; but they would closely follow another canoe that would cut through the waves for them.

For now, Dushuuw knelt at the back of the canoe with two others, levering the bow up enough that Yaq could better caulk the split with strips of cedar matting. At the first pair of thwarts, the split lessened to a crack. The crack ran along the surface of the hull in a straight line to the canoe's midpoint. Dushuuw knelt just beyond the spot. He shivered at the thought of the whale—of any whale, now. But he shivered more, and his grip on the side of the canoe tightened, as the crack grew a bit longer, as if reaching for him.

There was no better feeling for Dushuuw than being in a canoe. Out on the sea with his best friend Yaq—dropping their fishing lines over the sides while sharing jokes and memories—Dushuuw could forget his problems, both old and new. He was not a warrior, with the constant urge to fight. He was not a son, missing a mother and avoiding a father. He was not, this day, even a young husband who couldn't seem to please his wife. Being with Yaq on the water, for no higher purpose than a baited line, helped pull the broken pieces of himself back together.

"I can tell you are thinking about a girl."

Dushuuw turned to Yaq with a start, his fingers still playing with the shiny abalone lure.

"No," he said, putting the lure away. He reached for a spear-like pole.

Yaq laughed. "I worry about you," he said, pulling out a large lure that looked more like a game piece than something to attract a big-headed bottom-feeder.

"No more than usual, I trust."

Dushuuw took the large lure from Yaq—three fins of cedar attached to a cone—and fixed it to the point of the pole, using the pole to push the lure to the ocean floor. When he hit bottom, he jerked the pole away, pulled it up, and set it aside across the thwarts.

The two friends peered into the water. The lure, free of the pole, floated upward—revolving and slowing as it went. And the shadow of a curious cod followed.

"I don't know why you don't just spear it," Yaq said. "Or better yet, drop a baited hook."

"Where's your sense of excitement? This is far more fun." Dushuuw tossed a rock into the water toward a small shark, sending it dashing after a fake morsel rather than stealing his prize.

Yaq crouched, net in hand. As the lingcod rose to the surface, Yaq scooped up the massive fish and grunted as he brought its thrashing body into the canoe, its giant mouth open to reveal sharp teeth. Dushuuw raised a club and brought it crashing down onto the cod's head, and it was still.

"And we're full," Yaq said.

Dushuuw almost threw the giant fish back overboard, just so they could catch another. Now that Yaq was on the whaling crew and gone more often, Dushuuw craved these trips together even more.

Their people were whalers before they were anything else, be it sealers, halibut fishers, traders, carvers, weavers, or warriors. Whales fed a glut of house construction. Whales bought more slaves to keep up with the needs of a booming population, fattened on whale flesh and whale oil. Whales cloaked their nobles in furs and finery. Whales lavished attention and toys on their children. Whales secured their status among coastal tribes hundreds of miles in every direction.

There was no glory associated with his and Yaq's mindless trolling. Hook. Club. Gut. But Dushuuw chased the warmth that welled inside him, when doubt subsided and left space for relief.

And there were more reasons to doubt himself back on land, confined by cedar walls. His father's expectations for him had increased in the past year—as if the older man suddenly remembered his youngest son. It was no longer enough to be Young Son, goofing off with his best friend and building his family's wealth with a bloody club. An exalted name. A strategic marriage. Only just past his eighteenth summer, Dushuuw felt squeezed between two lives—the old one that fed him, and the new one he had to feed. Dushuuw recalled his wife's expression, unusually happy, as he had left to fish.

Yaq picked up his paddle.

"We could stay out for the night," Dushuuw said. "I got the firebox."

"I noticed. But man, I need more than fish to eat. And no offense, but I need more than your company. I need a woman."

"You always need a woman."

"You used to be the same, my friend." Yaq smirked. "Has marriage made you weak?"

"If it has, it is because I exert myself so much in my wife's pleasure," Dushuuw lied.

"At least I can entice the next willing woman, if the first isn't in the mood," Yaq said with a laugh.

Dushuuw turned and dipped his paddle into the water. "There is that," he murmured.

They followed the meandering line of the cape, wending around towering seastacks. Oyster catchers, cormorants, murrelets, and gulls called from their perches on the cliffs or as they took wing overhead.

"So, when will your brother get a wife?" Yaq asked. "He cannot much appreciate his younger brother enjoying the pleasures of a marital bed before him, especially being so close as to hear the evidence..."

Dushuuw shrugged. "Father has said there is time, that this first whaling season with Ọotsik wielding the harpoon can only improve his prospects," he said. "Uncle is more direct: 'Weddings are expensive.'"

"Well, Ọotsik has already proved himself capable as a whaler," Yaq said. "Seems your father should let him prove himself capable as a man."

Dushuuw sighed in agreement. Yaq had a better look at Ọotsik's capabilities, being the diver on the whaling crew. But Dushuuw didn't need to be in the whaling canoe to see his brother's success, which was on display with every plate of every meal after he took a whale. Ọotsik was young for a harpooner, his move to the bow coming quick, but not only because of their father's injury. Ọotsik's name was beginning to be whispered among the region's more senior whaling chiefs, who spoke of the young man as one uncommonly blessed—even without the spiritual aid of a wife. So far it was only whispers. Most were holding out to see how the next whaling season would go. But Dushuuw knew it was not chance. Ọotsik was born to be a whaler.

An uncomfortable twitch moved through Dushuuw's shoulders. He flicked his paddle and splashed Yaq in the face. Yaq splashed him back.

"If you think you have cooled my passion, you are wrong, my friend," Yaq said. "When we get to shore, I shall lure a far prettier catch."

Dushuuw laughed and shook his head.

They rounded the point, and the view opened wide as the friends caught sight of the cove. They paddled across the expansive bay, then up between the lines of rocks of a canoe run. Leaving the fish for slaves to process and cook, Yaq ran off, and Dushuuw made his way more leisurely toward the lines of houses facing the sea. On the busy beach, he walked into a din of laughter, chatter, and the myriad sounds of hundreds of people at work. Fires dotted the area and warmed his legs as he passed. The hot smell of smoke melded with the cool whiffs of seaweed, salt, fish. Women lined pits with fern fronds for cooking. Other women sat on mats, weaving baskets. Small white-haired dogs yipped and begged as they shivered, freshly sheared. A parade of children playing chase crossed Dushuuw's path, kicking up sand. A boy toddled after them, giggling and dragging a broken piece of kelp, its bulbous head bouncing along behind.

Dozens of large houses stood in rows along the bay and up the riverbank. Buildings were staggered so that most doorways faced the sea. Dushuuw walked toward the largest of them. Its cedar-plank wall towered over his head. Inside, old women sat at hearth fires, and slave women kept busy weaving or cooking or minding children. Dushuuw headed toward his own dedicated living space. He still smiled at that. Not just a workbench that doubled as a bed. A proper living space, with its own hearth, surrounded by partitions for the kind of privacy desired by a newly married couple. Dushuuw hesitated at the thought of his wife, desire mixing with anticipation of another argument. Yet the space was empty. The fire was banked. Yaq's comments burned in his mind as he stored his fishing gear. He trudged away.

A young boy bounded up to him.

"Did you catch many fish, Quht-Quht?"

Dushuuw crouched and shook the boy by the top of his head. Only Buh-uhs used this pet name for Dushuuw—the closest the boy could get as a toddler to the familial term his parents taught him, then repeated so often it had stuck.

"What do you think, Buh-Buh?"

Buh-uhs twisted out of his grip and pretended to club fish head after fish head. He pounced left and right, adding dust on top of the dirt that smudged his skin. "Lots and lots!"

Dushuuw laughed. "Yes, Quht-Quht must keep his little cousin fat and well-clothed." Buh-uhs smiled at the first of those promises, but shot Dushuuw a disgusted look at the mention of clothes. "Well-clothed only for feasts, of course," Dushuuw added. "And maybe when it is very cold." The boy smiled, placated. "But I think your father needs to teach you technique, little man."

"He is not here right now. Anyway, mother says I can bash anything I like, as long as I do it outside."

Dushuuw swallowed his laugh and nodded at the boy's mother. Xhud-uck was kin. In this case, that meant they were cousins through his brother's mother's aunt, who had married a nobleman from Oosa-ilth. They could each recite the lineage. But like other relations, close and extended, they were simply family—a large one in this case, with many of them living under his father's roof.

Xhud-uck smiled up at Dushuuw and her son from where she sat, her legs crossed to cradle a bowl of halved sea urchins as well as to cradle her pregnant stomach. She brought a pinch of bright roe to her mouth, then checked on a box of boiling seal flipper, giving it a stir. "Yes, son, now go and let your tired mother work."

Buh-uhs hollered and shot off.

She shook her head. "ʔe·ʔe·, to have his energy..."

"So where is your husband?" Dushuuw asked.

"Getting more planks for our new house, most likely."

"Making room for more sons."

"Yes, and I wonder when you and your young wife will make one," she said. "My new boy will need a friend."

Dushuuw managed a half-smile in return. She had no idea how much he wanted to make hundreds of sons with his wife, if only the young woman allowed him the opportunity.

"And I can only hope you and Wiikihbis have a daughter," he said. "She can teach Buh-uhs a thing or two."

Xhud-uck laughed, and Dushuuw left the house.

He turned the corner, walking between his father's house and his uncle's house. Already the sound of the sea was muffled by the walls of cedar. The sounds of people were distant as well, everyone working at sea, on the beaches, or up in the forest. Before him, his cousin's house stood under construction. Dushuuw was about to head past it in search of his brother, or maybe the war chief, when a sound coming from within made him pause. He crept closer and stifled a laugh. Groans and pants filtered to his ears, and he wondered at Yaq's audacity, not to mention quick powers of persuasion. Dushuuw shook his head and started to move toward the hillside again, then stopped. He decided his friend deserved to be interrupted. Besides, he demurred, his cousin may not appreciate Yaq's presumption. Better to save his friend some trouble. He smiled to himself as he pivoted and jogged to the doorway.

"I did not think it possible for you to exert yourself so long," he called out.

But it was not Yaq whose sweat-covered body joined with a naked and willing woman against a post. The man looked over his shoulder, and startled.

"Dushuuw, I thought you were out fishing," Wiikihbis said.

Dushuuw did not look at the man. "I was," he answered, absently. He had registered the man as his cousin Xhud-uck's husband. That betrayal was enough. But it was the woman he studied. Her eyes did not betray fear. They were not filled with guilt. Instead, his wife looked on him with disgust. Dushuuw looked away, dizzy.

Blackness came to the edges of his vision. Wiikihbis's hair was in a topknot as if for a job that required focused effort. The man's hands shoved at the area below his waist.

Dushuuw uncoiled.

He was tackling the man before he knew he had moved.

They rolled across the matted earth. Dushuuw sprang up and collided again with Wiikihbis, who had barely stood up in time and now skidded on his feet across the dirt as he pushed back. The fight circled the house. Dushuuw punched, kicked when he needed to, clawed his fingers into the man's flesh. His wife shouted, then others, but they sounded far away. A stray thought of accepted wrestling techniques brushed past his mind out of habit. But Dushuuw banished all distractions. He let other instincts kick in. He sent the rage that crackled inside him into the body twisting in his grip.

Until that body collapsed, limp, to the ground.

Dushuuw fell down with it, still gripping the man's topknot.

When the man did not move, Dushuuw let go and sat back. The man looked out toward a back wall, the neck twisted at a grotesque angle. Dushuuw scrambled backward across the ground.

Crying out, his wife tried to crawl past him to the body. He blindly shoved her aside.

Dushuuw's chest heaved as he looked behind him. A crowd had gathered, spilling through the doorway. His uncle stood among the onlookers, but closer, as if he had been about to break up the fight.

Hands squeezed his arm. He looked down. His wife was on the ground, pinned there by his hand at her throat. He startled, began to pull away. But she grabbed at both his hands and pulled them back to her neck. Her face was flushed and wet with tears. Her lips were still red and plump in ways they had never been for him. But it was her furious expression that stirred his own anger again.

"Go on. End it," she whispered.

Dushuuw's fury surged, his fingers twitching against her skin.

She hugged his hands against her neck, urging him on, a twisted smile on her face. "End it…"

Dushuuw ripped his hands free and moved away. He pressed his palm against a pole as he stumbled up.

She laughed.

Dushuuw roared as he turned away. The crowd's shock gave way to dismay, and disgust, all eyes on him. Men and women clogged the doorway, and Dushuuw's shoulders sank as he scoffed. The meaningless doorway. In this half-house, which might never be a house now. Light shone all around, with no roof to block the daylight. Shoulders slumping, Dushuuw turned away from the crowd and stumbled over to the back wall. He shoved aside a loose wall board and stepped outside, as if he were a child fleeing invaders—or a corpse being removed. He headed for the dark shelter of the forest.

As he ascended into the trees, a woman's wail echoed off the cliff.

Dushuuw stayed in the forest for three days. In truth, he would have stayed away far longer, if not for his brother.

"You left an easier trail to follow than a bear," Q̇otsik said.

Tired and hungry, Dushuuw glanced up from where he sat slouched against a tree. He thought he could remain emotionally blank, but shame filled him anew at his brother's look of disappointment.

"You could not smash his canoe? Have her whipped?"

Q̇otsik asked more rhetorically than in earnest.

The brothers were just three summers apart in age. But, though the larger by far, Dushuuw shrank in his older brother's shadow. Q̇otsik settled beside him, and Dushuuw took the container of water shoved against his chest. He tipped the kelp stem high and drank deep.

"We needed that alliance," Q̇otsik said.

The water felt like a rock going down Dushuuw's throat.

"So she is gone?"

Q̇otsik nodded. "Back with her people," he said.

Tension seeped out of Dushuuw's shoulders. If he had been required to see her again, to live as if nothing had happened...

"She is not the only one gone."

Dushuuw's fingers tightened around the stem. Q̇otsik recited a long list of names of those who had defected.

Now a widow, Xhud-uck also had left; she returned south with Buh-uhs to her kin in Oosa-ilth. That, in turn, sparked a further exodus of those who followed her along favored family lines. They took their possessions and their slaves with them. A few skilled artisans followed—among them, a master carver and a weaver known for her quality loom work.

Dushuuw leaned forward and swallowed. "Are you here to tell me to leave Wuh-uhch too?"

Q̇otsik shot him a look. "What? Of course not," he said. "Father had a ṗačiƛ with the families. Your shame is erased." Q̇otsik reached out and gripped Dushuuw's shoulder. "Even so, I need you brother, now more than ever."

Everything Q̇otsik had told him buzzed in his mind. As he connected names and roles, he swallowed. "The whaling crew..."

"I already have a plan."

"I have ruined—"

"You will help make amends by getting in the whaling canoe."

Dushuuw whipped his head up to stare at his brother. Q̇otsik may as well have suggested Dushuuw take up basketry. "You cannot be serious."

Q̇otsik looked back in confusion.

"I am no whaler," Dushuuw said. "And do you think the others would welcome me in that canoe now?"

Q̇otsik looked away. "Father has agreed. And I will bring peace to anyone else who questions the decision too."

Dread filled Dushuuw.

"I will," Q̇otsik said. "This will be good, in the end. Don't you see? It is what I have long seen. You and me, in the whaling canoe together. You made a mistake. If uncle had gotten there in time to break up the fight, it never would have happened. Anyone with common sense can understand. Now, think only about your good name, and how to keep it clean. Banish your anger. Learn. Prepare. And when spring arrives, get in that canoe—show them your heart. Do that, and all will be well."

Dushuuw clenched and unclenched his hands in fists, aware of the blood of the dead man that remained caked under his fingernails. No amount of wealth could smooth over the wound to his heart. But neither could the blood.

A few days after the whale strike, the damaged canoe was tucked away in the forested hillside above their village for repairs.

Their father had not been as upset as Dushuuw would have thought when they had returned from the failed hunt. A whale strike with no lives lost was a testament to Q̇otsik's power, the older whaler said. And the canoe could be repaired, a further sign of blessing. Besides, the chief had already commissioned the building of a new canoe for Q̇otsik; the tree had been identified last year and was to be felled soon. The old whaler, leaning on his walking stick, said nothing about Dushuuw. But his silence was as calculated as his praise, both aimed at the other old men who had crowded around the fire.

No, there was no anger. In fact, there would be a celebration.

Now, Dushuuw stood outside the doorway of the great house at the front of a long line of dancers. Sunlight warmed his back as he squinted to see the crowd inside, waiting for the signal to begin the dance.

Locals, kinsmen, and neighbors sat on benches, or stood against the walls, waiting for the men of the cove, the men of Wuh-uhch.

Wuh-uhch was the oldest of several villages spread across the cape, a ragged expanse of rock and evergreen bounded by strait, sea, and river valley. The village was tucked inside the cape's rocky embrace on a warm cove that faced the crashing sea. Intertidal rocks gave way to a modest beach, which was cut through by a burbling creek. Houses lined the beach all the way to the mouth of the river, with still more houses tracing the river's shoreline inland. Ragged hills rose all along their backs, building up to a modest peak. Beyond the river to the south, a wide sandy beach continued to trace the bay's arc, and other forested hills rose and fell, hiding lakes and prairies and streams. Blue plumes of smoke pierced the canopy miles beyond, rising from the fires of neighbors with their own longhouses. Together, the people of the cape villages were known as the Kwidich'chuh-aht—the people who live by the rocks and seagulls.

Dushuuw peered again through the doorway, impatient to begin the dance. A fire burned near the back-right corner, the house's seat of power. His father, Chahbuhł, sat on a fur-lined bench there with a bear skin draped over his shoulders. The whaling chief's black hair, streaked with white, was oiled down. His cheeks and chin were plucked clean of stray hairs. His nose was pierced with a large ring. The chief sat with his two wives, his elderly mother, and his youngest daughter. The women were draped in sumptuous sea otter furs and wore their largest abalone ornaments. The girl stole a glance toward the doorway, knowing how much her half-brother itched to move. Chaiyuhx-ik let the barest smirk slip, and in response Dushuuw widened his eyes and puffed out his cheeks, like some deranged sea creature. She started to laugh, like she always did, then pressed her fingers to her lips as if to swallow such an unladylike urge.

Dushuuw turned his attention back outdoors. Nearly every house in the village had dancers waiting in this line. His gaze connected with that of Wiid, the war chief, farther down the line with others who lived upriver. The man shot him one of his challenging looks, and Dushuuw smiled in response. Between them were as many slaves as nobles and commoners. His father had enlisted anyone he could, to ensure the dance floor was as filled as years past.

A few long rib bones from a whale were left just beyond the reach of high tide. The whale had drifted to their beach before the failed whale hunt—brought there by Ḍotsik's prayers, the same as those who fell to his harpoon the previous year. The brownish bones would bleach white like the older bones stacked around the great house. A songbird perched atop one curve of bone. At the sound of drumming from inside the house, the bird flew away.

The dance began. Dushuuw lifted a spear over his shoulder, crouched low, and stepped across the threshold. As he entered the house, he thrust the spear at the roof—first over one shoulder, then the other. The other dancers followed, while a group of women swayed in a row off to one side, palms turned out as they sang. The men continued to move in the low crouch, skimming the packed earth. Step, thrust. Step, thrust. On and on, Dushuuw led the crouching dancers, the dance floor filling as more men stepped through the doorway. Whenever he spotted Wiid, he made sure to crouch even lower than his old mentor—a friendly competition. At last, all the dancers entered the house. They raised their spears toward the roof. Then, as the women built to a loud wail, Dushuuw and the other dancers sprang high in the air, holding their spears aloft. As he jumped, Dushuuw felt weightless. But he quickly crouched low again, to step and thrust, step and thrust, on and on.

By the time the dance ended, the men were slick with sweat. The house was stifling, filled with hundreds of bodies along with the heat of the fires. Dushuuw followed Ḋotsik back to their family corner. Slaves handed the brothers containers of drinking water, which they emptied in great gulps.

The house grew loud with conversations and laughter.

Dushuuw eyed the women of his family. Yahbis, the elderly mother of Chahbuhł, sat at one end of the bench. His grandmother's familiar crinkled smile was absent—even her wrinkles seemed to offer a challenge. Beside her sat her daughter-in-law Um-iiqsu, gray-haired and regal, comfortable in her position as first wife of a whaler and mother to a whaler such as Ḋotsik. Um-iiqsu's sister and sister-wife sat on Chahbuhł's other side. Thluuch-muup was his father's third and youngest wife, and she tilted her head toward their daughter, the youngest of Chahbuhł's children. Pride prickled across Dushuuw's skin as he regarded his half-sister. Chai was flush with excitement. The opportunities for an unmarried young noblewoman to be seen in public were few. As she entered her fifteenth summer, she was nearing the age to marry. The frontlet of shells draped over her chest rose and fell as she traded quick smiles with her girlfriends around the room.

Dushuuw thought of his own mother, his father's second wife, who had died giving birth to a stillborn girl when he was a boy. If his mother had lived, would her hair be starting to turn gray? Would she have given his father more sons? Would the sister he lost have married and brought her husband here, or followed Chahbuhƚ's other daughters who, each in their turn, had married at their parents' pleasure and only visited their childhood home on feast days like this? The corner of the house felt bigger with every departure.

He took another slug of water and wiped the sweat from his brow, trying not to think about all the recent departures.

Despite his father's efforts, their village's diminished numbers were evident. Dushuuw scanned the room and read the looks of the visitors toward their family. The desire for Chai. The admiration for Q̇otsik. The respect for Chahbuhƚ that seemed, in some expressions, to be mixed with uncertainty. Gossips were busy this day. And they found their juiciest topic when they turned their eyes toward Dushuuw. He read their doubt, and he glared back. The men turned away. The women whispered more furiously.

Q̇otsik walked by and handed him his hat. His father nodded at him meaningfully, and Dushuuw shoved the hat—with its sickly knob—atop his head with a sigh.

Woven knobs protruded from the hats of several of Wuh-uhch's nobility, like the putrid blooms of yellow *tibu·t* that studded the swampy areas this time of year. The knob-topped hats were a new distinction of class for the cape. Only nobles could wear them or, indeed, afford them. The shaman's slave, acquired the previous fall from across the strait, now made them for Dushuuw's family. That saved them the expense of the hats' exorbitant prices. The slave was certainly the cheaper bargain. Dushuuw's hat had been her first for them and, seeing it, his uncle worried they were swindled. Still, she quickly improved. The next ones were as finely wrought as any they had seen across the strait. But Dushuuw was stuck with what he had for now.

If his father didn't insist, he wouldn't wear the awful accessory at all.

Chahbuhƚ cleared his throat and turned to Kuhbuhƚup, the man charged with speaking for the chief at such gatherings.

Like all feasts, this one held a purpose beyond bringing together allies for decadence, frivolity, and flirtation. Chahbuhƚ used the first whale hunts each spring to formally celebrate the hunting and gathering seasons on the vast tracts of forest, river, and sea to which he held rights. After a long winter of mostly dried food, it was a time to remember the joy of fresh meat on the tongue—and perhaps as well, the hand from which it all came.

"This is the house of Chahbuhƚ," the speaker called out. "We welcome you beneath this roof to share our dances, share our songs, share our food, and share these words."

Kuhbuhṫup launched into the speech. The speaker delineated Chahbuhṫ's territory: portions of whale and seal feeding grounds; sections of the far shoal with its halibut; the river to its bend with its salmon; the surrounding forest and its many resources, both plant and animal; the point of land above, with its ocher and fresh-water spring; the broad intertidal area below, with its many delicacies, such as the butter clams and periwinkles that were passed around at that moment in ornately carved bowls. Guests slipped the briny, sweet results of his words onto their tongues.

The speaker took a step forward and began the next phase of the speech: the authority behind Chahbuhṫ's claims on the territory, passed down through generation after generation of Wuh-uhch whalers. When he called out the name of Chahbuhṫ's father, Dushuuw, some men turned their eyes toward the deceased whaler's namesake. Eventually the list of names gave way to other lists. Kuhbuhṫup was sure to point to prominent guests around the house, indicating their connections, often by marriage, that granted access to resource areas as well as promises for support should any of them be threatened.

"We are all related," Kuhbuhṫup said, "we who call the sea home."

As night fell, the substance of those words took other forms. The privileges on display belonged to Wuh-uhch. But mixed into that identity were dances from neighbors around the cape, stories from allies across the strait, and songs from kin beyond the river. The feast tied together all those whose doors faced the sea.

Dushuuw took the floor for an ancient dance his father had given him the rights to years earlier, before Dushuuw's mother died and the older man seemed to forget his son for a time. Dushuuw had practiced the dance since childhood, his warrior-trained body taking to the moves like a seal to water. The slow lift, the quick descent. The drum pummeling an incessant beat. He didn't often present the dance before crowds like this, and he knew his father was putting his skill front and center to cast him in a positive light. As he walked back to his family, several older men nodded their heads in appreciation.

Then Q̇otsik prepared to sing a song on behalf of their father, who held the right for its words to be uttered at all.

Yahbis hobbled over on Chaiyuhx-ik's arm and they sat next to Dushuuw. The elderly woman leaned toward Chai. "It is one thing for a man to sing," she whispered. She pointed toward Chahbuhṫ, then pointed to Q̇otsik as the young whaler stepped forward. Dushuuw leaned in and finished their grandmother's familiar lesson: "It is quite another to have someone sing to him his own words."

Q̇otsik stood in front of a large wooden screen. The outstretched wings of the carved Thunderbird stretched over the whaler's head as he lifted his voice.

we are proud of our cove

Their uncle drummed to accompany the song.

this cove is our home

Slaves piled the family's possessions on the floor around Chahbuht.

all are astonished at our dancing

As Q̇otsik sang the lines over and over, the pile at their father's feet grew and grew.

Skin upon skin of whale oil. Baskets of dried berry cakes. Seal hides. Otter furs. Decoratively carved bowls and platters. Cedar blankets. Rattles made from pecten shells. Abalone pendants. Ornamented bone combs. Fans made with eagle's feathers. And other treasures, too, acquired from distant tribes. Yellow dye made in the south. Baskets of giant clams dried far to the east. Lengths of oddly hollow wood that drifted from unknown groups beyond the horizon. Surrounded by sea, the people of the cape stood at the crossroads of a vast trade network. More important, they knew how to leverage their position, and it showed in the pile of objects at Chahbuht's feet.

The trove did not reach the number of gifts given in *pačiƛ* at Q̇otsik's and Dushuuw's naming ceremonies and at Chai's womanhood celebration. Still, nearly everything the family owned would go to others' hands. The guests would fill their stomachs with Chahbuht's food—in his house, and on their way home, and in their own large houses weeks later. It was a gift, and it was a message.

"There is a confidence in it." Yahbis leaned close to her granddaughter. "That he can give away so much because he had no trouble acquiring it."

And the guests would owe Chahbuht at least as much in return for the honor.

This wasn't just a spring feast. This, too, was *pačiƛ*. One to celebrate Q̇otsik's drift whale, as well as the protection experienced in the failed hunt. Those who helped salvage the damaged canoe would be given special gifts. But everyone in attendance would receive something. The gift-giving would highlight what was important: Q̇otsik's spiritual power, Chahbuht's generosity.

Dushuuw looked away from the pile of gifts and down at the packed earth. With enough wealth, you could do almost anything. Give your son a powerful name, to lift him above his mother's low birth and make him a worthy match for a noble wife. Remove that son's shame, after he murdered a man and lost that marriage alliance. With Dushuuw, a *p̓ačiƛ* always meant something to fix.

The celebration continued, the pile of gifts growing smaller. The guests would raise their hands in appreciation. They would add their own voices in speech and song. And they would forget, at least for one day, the village's recent troubles—and their source.

~

Late that night—when most of the guests were asleep or gone, and the rain droned on the roof—Q̓otsik sat near the fire, receiving wisdom from the visiting whalers. In return, Q̓otsik circled the fire as he shared a ritual he used to call on the spirit of a whale. Dushuuw watched from the shadows against the wall. The smoke shrouded Q̓otsik, then released him as he moved around the flames.

Q̓otsik was gifted with a *łume·nuwis* for whaling. Reenactments of the young man's first whale hunts had taken up a bulk of the previous winter, alongside the stories of Thunderbird himself who first showed them how to hunt whales.

Dushuuw glanced up at the dance screen that was back against the wall behind him. The wood was dark with age, but fresh paint made the carved lines stand out bright. Dushuuw stared at the space where Thunderbird's talons disappeared into the back of a whale, seeing the image with new eyes now that he had experienced a hunted whale up close—too close. Black lines shaping talons melded into the black line of the whale's back. New paint for an ancient image. The whale in this carving was a gray, a whale that could be ferocious when struck, the kind of whale a man grasping a harpoon needed spiritual power to face. There was little room for error. The Thunderbird stared out toward Q̓otsik, absorbing the man's shadow as the whaler passed in front of the fire.

All around the walls, guests and kinfolk slept, warm and secure.

Q̓otsik made his spiritual transit of the fire, bathed in its glow.

Paces away, an abandoned hearth darkened the ground like a bruise.

Dushuuw rose from his bench and crept out into the wind-whipped night. He walked toward the bay, feet pressing into the wet sand. Rain pelted down. It pattered the brim of his hat. The tide was at its lowest, and Dushuuw walked out to meet the water's edge. Soon the houses were far behind him. When he looked to his right, the cliff that jutted into the sea loomed black. Tiny circles of light bobbed against its backdrop as slave children held torches for slave women, who gathered among the exposed rocks at the cliff's base. When the tide is out, the stomach is filled. And there were guests to feed come morning.

Dushuuw watched the moving lights. Drops of rain slid off the brim of his hat, making the lights seem to dance.

Seawater slid over his feet, wet his ankles, and slipped back under his heels. The tide was turning. He waited, waited until the sea tugged back and forth at his knees, then set his legs apart to feel its pushes and pulls for a while longer. Waited until the rain stopped. Until the torchlight stars winked out, one by one.

THERE WAS A LOUD CRACK, a giant moan, and then the forest reverberated with the crash of a large cedar tree.

Amuun'aẖsum, kneeling among ferns, felt the ground tremble. She guarded her eyes from the small bits of dirt and leaves that reached her even at a distance. The fronds of the ferns bowed and swayed. For a brief moment, in the wake of the tree's collapse, the world grew still—a whispering through the boughs, a release of pent-up breath. Then a young man cheered, and Amuun'aẖsum shared a laugh with her friend Uhpahs, and the sounds of wedges and hammers began to knock again. Woodpeckers answered.

The sap was running.

Groups of women and men were deep in the forest, children at their sides. The sound of the sea didn't reach here. But the large cedar the men had worked all day to fell would taste the sea's brine; in a year's time, it would be a canoe, plying the waters, seeking whales.

Most of the people in the forest, however, including Amuun'aẖsum, were not here for a canoe. They would instead shape strips of cedar into far smaller creations. Cedar was the base for most woven items, from the clothes the people wore, to the blankets under which they slept; from the mats that caught cooking grease, to the sails that sped long canoe journeys. Gathering and preparing the material for its various uses would occupy several months. And it began here.

Amuun'aẖsum watched a man notch the bark near the base of a cedar. He tugged, and teased, and tugged. The bark peeled away in a long, thin swath so high up the trunk that Amuun'aẖsum had to crane her neck to follow its path. The tree's smooth flesh shone beneath. Similar stripes ran the length of other cedars. The pale wood shone against a landscape of browns and greens. Larger trees whose bark had been harvested in past years bore their striped scars.

Soon, Amuun'a̱xsum would help bundle the long strips and pack them back to the village. For now, she foraged for roots with Uhpahs.

Amuun'a̱xsum dug her fingers into the loose soil around the base of the feathery fern, feeling for its root-covered rhizome. Her knees were damp and muddied. She coaxed the fern up, then cut the stocky rhizome free of the earth's grip with a whack of her digging stick. As she shook the plant, bits of dirt fell and pattered the shredded cedar strips of her work skirt. Bugs fled up and out of the hole left by the plant; they skittered on tiny legs, their shiny, flimsy armor rocking back and forth. Amuun'a̱xsum tossed the fern into her large gathering basket. She brushed aside a dew-covered spider's web as she bent over to dig again.

She paused and tested her memory of Uhpahs's latest cooking lesson, which anticipated the upcoming gathering of salmonberry shoots. Amuun'a̱xsum tallied what else she would need to prepare the shoots—leaves of alder; alder sprouts, too; and the young leaves and stems of white aster—then she set her hands to the fern again. Later, she would lay the fern and alder leaves over hot stones. They would make a bed for the other ingredients and balance the sweet with a subtle spice. If she didn't burn it all.

Amuun'a̱xsum yawned, feeling the lingering effects of the late night gathering food for all the guests as they had slept. She shoved the soles of her rock-scarred feet into the dirt, and considered all the names in all the languages she now knew for shellfish. She breathed deep and lifted her chin, thinking again about the sweet sleep of a fur-lined bed... She would have that again. She would take from the bowl rather than fill it.

"Anything is possible in spring," she said, unsure if she was conveying the depth of her thought with words that still felt oversized on her tongue, despite their similarity to her mother's language.

Uhpahs blew a stray hair from her face. "Very good! You are well beyond 'which way to the urination spot.'" Amuun'a̱xsum simply smiled as the slave woman recovered from her laughter. Uhpahs blew again at the stray hair, scratched her arm. "I like that it is warmer. But this work always makes me so itchy."

Amuun'a̱xsum set her uprooted fern next to its neighbor in her basket and went over to Uhpahs. Uhpahs, who had taught her so much, including the nuances of the local dialect and how to cook—passably, anyway. Uhpahs, who snored as loud as the shaman, as Amuun'a̱xsum had discovered when Uhpahs came to share her sleeping space in order to eke out more room for guests in the whaling chief's house.

As she knelt beside her only friend, Amuun'a̱xsum glimpsed a clutch of blush-hued blooms in Uhpahs's basket. The soft, cupped petals extended in pink bunches from dirt-caked roots. Uhpahs shook a plucked fern and added it to the basket, gingerly lifting the flowered plant out of the way before setting it back atop the pile.

Amuun'aẖsum snorted back a laugh.

"What?" Uhpahs feigned surprise. "The vetch? It tastes so good with salmonberry."

Amuun'aẖsum laughed and shook her head. "If you say so. All I can see is, you are being careful with those roots. And even I know that those have nothing to do with steaming salmonberry." She poked at the plant. Uhpahs shooed Amuun'aẖsum's hand away. Amuun'aẖsum sat back, triumphant. She may not be able to put the deepest matters of the heart into the local language quite yet. But she had mastered the joke. Uhpahs made that all too easy.

"Come to think of it," Amuun'aẖsum said, in mock clarity, "those roots are used for a certain balm. Now, what was that balm for again?"

Uhpahs blushed and turned her head away.

Amuun'aẖsum reached over and pretended to rub balm onto her friend's neck. "I remember. To get a man..."

"Well," said Uhpahs, batting away Amuun'aẖsum's hand again. "We will see." A smile flitted across Uhpahs's face, then disappeared. The slave cleared her throat, popped to her feet. "Looks like they are ready for us, Quulthoo," she said.

Amuun'aẖsum turned away, as if to check the contents of her basket. But her smile disappeared too. She reflexively adjusted the cedar band that wrapped her wrist, making sure it covered her scars.

This, too, was her only friend. Uhpahs, who knew enough of Amuun'aẖsum's history to know she hated the slave name she had been given, but called her by it anyway. Amuun'aẖsum cringed again at having given in, for thinking Uhpahs would understand, for telling Uhpahs what she had told no one else. That she was meant for more.

Still, they remained friends. This also was Uhpahs. A woman who could keep a secret.

Amuun'aẖsum and Uhpahs folded bark and added the bundles to their gathering baskets. Gradually, the forest grew quieter as people returned to the village. Basket filled, Uhpahs swung her basket to her back, then swished between ferns to the trail. Amuun'aẖsum donned her own basket, bearing its weight through the tumpline that crossed her forehead. She sliced a path on the diagonal, cutting in front of Uhpahs to take the lead on the trail back to Wuh-uhch.

The sheltering stands of cedar, spruce, and hemlock gave way to the forest's edge, with its dense undergrowth of crabapple, elderberry, salal. The muffled sound of the sea grew louder. On the path, a cougar's print was pressed into the mud. Above, an eagle perched near the top of a spruce, looking to the sea as it fluffed its wings out, taking advantage of the break in the rain to dry its feathers.

Amuun'axsum slowed as she passed an old woman. The woman murmured coaxing prayers to the green leaves that bent beneath her gnarled fingers. Likely, the woman put off her morning meal each day until she had bathed and prayed, making herself clean in spirit as well as body. Amuun'axsum adjusted her burden basket and resumed her quick pace. She still repeated the gathering prayers she had been taught, but the words had become rote in the absence of the rituals that went with them. Mostly, the words had become like other private, hidden rituals—a way to remind herself of that past, to hold on to it.

~

Amuun'axsum sat beside a fire on the beach in front of the great house, cooking salmon for the shaman, but her focus was on the bay.

Several men waded through the high tide, flanking a massive cedar trunk. The trunk was the second and last to be floated over from trading partners across the strait. The village's leading whaling chief, Chahbuht, together with his brother, Buhkweeduuk, would spend the coming months directing the architecture of a massive winter house on the high ground. The two trunks would become support posts for the house, ensuring its front wall loomed over the tallest man. From now on, the brothers of Wuh-uhch would spend their winters under one roof, as they combined their efforts in one whaling canoe.

But it was the younger men who would do the work.

Amuun'axsum practiced the young men's names as she did the patriarchs, committing to memory the village's power structure. Splashing through the water was Huh-uuk, a man large even by local standards. Displacing nearly as much water though a fraction of the size was energetic Yaq, another low-ranked individual she mostly ignored but could not avoid since he was always with Dushuuw, the chief's youngest son and an accomplished warrior, who sauntered along behind. Quietly following them was Kweelthup, whose timidity was surprising, given his father Kuhbuhtup's prominent role as the whaling chief's speaker. Where Kuhbuhtup was booming, Kweelthup was hushed when he spoke at all. The young man was nothing like Uhpqoolth, who charged toward shore on the other side of the trunk. The brusque man's father was Buhkweeduuk, though Uhpqoolth so far did not share that patriarch's savvy trade pursuits.

All of them came willingly under the arm of Chahbuhł. And now, they also willingly came under the arm of the chief's eldest son, Q̇otsik, who rested a hand on the lead end of the trunk as he walked through the water with ease. The talented young man now led the whale hunts, and one day he would take over for his father in every other matter as well. Perhaps soon.

Amuun'axsum swelled with pride seeing Q̇otsik wear the knob-topped hat she had woven, with its scenes of a successful whale hunt. Amuun'axsum recalled her disappointment when he had taken the hat without remark, looking at the images—a figure in a canoe, harpoon poised, a tow line extending from the struck whale—as always, his eyes on the whale. He seemed to think of nothing else.

The smell of smoked meat brought Amuun'axsum's attention back to the fire. With a burst of panic, she reached beneath the cedar mat to check the salmon fillets.

"A bit of entertainment while you cook, I see," said Uhpahs, eying the young men as she joined Amuun'axsum.

"Gulls are very entertaining." Amuun'axsum let the mat fall back over the fish and the salal leaves on which they lay.

Uhpahs snorted and crouched beside the fire. She gave Amuun'axsum a skeptical look, then tipped up the mat. She looked back with arched brows.

"Not burned," Amuun'axsum said.

"Yet."

On shore, other men raced about, adjusting small logs in parallel lines on the beach. They would roll the trunk over the run as far as they could, then drag the trunk by ropes uphill over a ramp of flat boards.

The wind rustled the lengths of Amuun'axsum's skirt. The scent of the cooking salmon deepened.

Q̇otsik strode out of the water and toward their fire. The young whaler pushed his long hair back as he adjusted the hat. Amuun'axsum found herself standing to face the nobleman, and she raised her chin, if only to encourage herself. Then her head dipped. She saw her greasy palms. The globs of fish scales that clung to her dirty work skirt. Q̇otsik glanced at her as he walked toward the great house. His look carried the hint of vacant recognition, as if he were glancing at one of the dogs. He gave the fire a wide berth.

Amuun'axsum dropped to her knees, her cheeks flushed. She poked at the overdone fish with a stick, trying to banish the twisting feeling behind her ribs.

"What were you thinking?" Uhpahs whispered.

Amuun'axsum just shook her head.

Uhpahs sighed. "Quulthoo, you need to let go of this. Do you honestly imagine yourself to be a whale hunter's wife?"

"Stop."

"Filling those holes in your ears with shell ornaments again?"

"Please—"

"It is not going to happen," Uhpahs said.

The stick in Amuun'axsum's hand snapped. She turned away and pressed her palms onto the sand. Her friend pushed on.

"You will be hurt, or worse," Uhpahs said. Her tone was flat, using words she had already said many times before. "You are not what you were before, my friend. You are a—"

"I am *not* a slave."

The words spilled out in Amuun'axsum's native tongue, but Uhpahs understood.

Amuun'axsum ground her fingers into the cold top layer of sand to the trapped warmth below. The grains slid out the sides of her palms, leaving her gripping nothing. Scars and fresh scratches crisscrossed the tops of her hands from days spent gathering in the forest. The cracked skin over her knuckles bled.

Uhpahs sighed and was silent. She pulled the salmon onto a tray, then covered the fire with sand to douse the low flames.

Amuun'axsum stood to take the meal to the shaman, but Uhpahs held up a finger. "Wait," she said, her voice gentle. Uhpahs pulled out a clam shell from a pouch attached to her hip and held it out to Amuun'axsum. A perfumed film covered the bottom of the shell. "Thluuch-muup threw this away," Uhpahs said. "I thought you might like it, so I retrieved it from the fire's edge when she was not looking."

Amuun'axsum felt greedy looking at the balm. She glanced up at Uhpahs's anxious face, then smiled as she accepted the shell. She drew the shell close to her nose, closing her eyes as she chased the faint scent of the perfume past the stronger scents that surrounded them, of fish and smoke and seaweed. Amuun'axsum murmured her thanks, took the balm and the salmon and turned to head toward the shaman's house.

"Quulthoo," Uhpahs called.

Amuun'aẋsum grit her teeth at the slave name, but turned back.

"I will try to get you more." Uhpahs twisted a strand of her skirt.

Amuun'aẋsum smiled as she nodded in farewell.

Hiding the shell in a pouch at her hip, Amuun'aẋsum entered the shaman's house and set the platter of salmon in front of Eekbis. The old woman eyed the burnt meal. "I think I have lost my appetite again," the shaman said. "It is a good thing I do not keep you for your cooking."

Amuun'aẋsum grabbed the platter and slid the fish into the flames.

Eekbis raised an eyebrow, then pointed to a pile of split spruce root. "The chief wants another whaler's hat, this time for Dushuuw."

Amuun'aẋsum ran her fingers through the fibers, calculating. "It could take a year with everything else that needs to be done," she lied. She expected the shaman to argue, but Eekbis only mumbled and nodded, fluttering her fingers in Amuun'aẋsum's direction.

Ignoring her rumbling stomach, and the regret of what now lay in the fire, Amuun'aẋsum sat on a low platform and unpacked weaving supplies one by one. As she organized the tools, the last scent of scorched salmon wafted away through a gap in the roof. The small house's familiar odors of vacancy settled in its place—dust, must, and aged wood, a thin veneer of smoke overlaying it all.

Only the shaman lived in this small cedar house now. The far corner, where the man who built the house had lived with his family, loomed in its emptiness. It was empty of the things that fill a house, as well as the warmth that accompanies those things. The smells of sweat, dirtied diapers, a hundred meals. There remained only shiny grease stains on the walls, gaps chinked with seaweed and moss, and dust-covered hearths. The shaman stayed here year-round, so the little house did not even receive the occasional freshening that comes with being disassembled and transported to a summer fishing site or whaling encampment. It was as if the walls had put down roots.

Amuun'aẋsum felt the frail weight of the shell of balm hidden in the pouch at her hip. Though she itched to bring it out, she instead splayed the basketry fibers across her lap and started to separate the roots into groups. Her first attempt at a hat for the nobility here had been a sad, pathetic thing. Its knob wanted to part with the rest of the work—and she did not blame it. That the chief did not throw the hat away, but instead gave it to his youngest son and asked her to make another, was a sign of the family's eagerness for the mark of stature. Thankfully, her subsequent hats were much better. Memories of time spent with her mother had returned, and practice proved itself through patience.

Chahbuhɫ and Q̇otsik wore her hats daily. So did Buhkweeduuk and Uhpqoolth. Amuun'ax̱sum had woven those over the winter, when there was little else for her to do. Now that the busy seasons were underway, she could justify going slower. As much as she wanted to see a new hat replace the failure on the head of the chief's youngest son, she needed to draw the project out in order to stay in one place. Any hat could be her last for the noble family, and she was unsure what would happen next. Amuun'ax̱sum tugged at the cedar band wrapped around her wrist.

On a mat near the hearth, the shaman sat facing the fire. The old woman's long, ash-colored hair pooled on the ground.

As evening fell, the fire's bending and flickering light grew brighter. The empty parts of the house slipped further into shadow, while the cluttered corner where the shaman lived came alive.

Amuun'ax̱sum put away the weaving tools and the bundles of roots.

The shaman stretched, bones creaking, and hobbled toward the wall and cleared her own work from a raised bench to make it into her bed for the night. Amuun'ax̱sum helped the old woman lay down several layers of mats, with cedar boughs tucked between to ward off fleas, then topped the pile with beaver hides. Eekbis sat with a grunt on the edge of the bench, then lay down atop the prepared mattress. She pulled up to her chin several blankets, each made of softened cedar woven all over with either yarn made from the dogs' wool or the downy feathers of duck skins. Sometimes, when the shaman was away, Amuun'ax̱sum would place one of the soft hides or blankets against her cheek.

Despite the abundant space, the shaman abided by strict boundaries of class. "Slaves sleep by the doorway," she had said that first night. "Soon enough this house will be full again. So you may as well get used to it."

Stepping away from the comforting heat of the fire, Amuun'ax̱sum unrolled her bed mat on the other side of a privacy partition, and settled near the doorway. A hide was tacked away from the opening to let in the breeze. It was one of those unseasonably warm nights that hinted too early of summer, like a trick.

Already the shaman started to snore.

Amuun'ax̱sum relaxed as she sat on her bed mat and drew blankets over her lap. With a shaky sigh, she pulled out the shell from Uhpahs and breathed in the scent of the balm. She ran two fingers down the shell and brought them to her forehead, massaging upwards. She swept up more of the thin remains of the balm. The shell rested in her palm on her lap. She closed her eyes and tilted her head to one side. Her loosed hair slipped over her shoulder. She slid the balm down her neck, then tilted her head to the other side. Her hair followed, brushing across her back, and she spread what remained of the balm down the other side of her neck. Her fingertips ended, dry, atop her pulse, which beat, beat, beat.

Amuun'axsum reluctantly hid the shell again inside the pouch, then tucked the fragile package beneath her mat. Easing down onto her side, she glanced toward the vacant house corner, lit by the fluttering light of the banked fire. The wall of overlapping rows of boards seemed to shift in the light, like slats of armor on a giant warrior. Sucking in a breath, Amuun'axsum rolled to her other side. She tugged at the blanket, and focused on the surface of the water that wavered in the moonlight. It reminded her of flames. She shut her eyes.

Fall 1692
Seven years earlier

Amuun'axsum rested her hands on her father's shoulders as he lifted her at the waist and set her atop a raised platform. He looked on her with pride, and Amuun'axsum basked in the glow of his approval. She wore a dress and fur-lined cape. Her hair was divided into two parts, each folded up inside shell-studded cedar bands that rested on her shoulders. Long strings of dentalia shells draped over her chest. A weighty headdress made of the shells crossed her forehead. Still more of the shells were stitched in fringes to her dress. A bone ornament pierced her nose. Abalone earrings dangled from her ears, an extravagance worthy of a whaling chief's daughter.

As the day wore on, she stifled her smile—tried to reflect the seriousness of the occasion as her father instructed—and peered down her nose at the long procession. Each person stopped, looked up, and spoke her name to her face.

Old women.

"Amuun'axsum."

Old men.

"Amuun'axsum."

Children.

"Amuun'axsum."

It was a name that, repeated time and again, tied not just her new name to their memory, but the village itself. The village her father had created from nothing. The village he had named Amuun.

The abalone earrings and the new name compensated for the fact that she had to wait so long since her first blood for this womanhood ceremony, only to share it with another young woman. She glanced across the house to the platform that reflected her own, at the girl similarly adorned, but with dentalia earrings. That young woman was nearer her first blood. Her wrist was still red from the tattoo. Her tired features reminded Amuun'axsum of her own recovery from her first blood, when all she wanted to do was curl into a ball and try to sleep.

Not this day. Amuun'axsum was eager to remain awake far into the night. She had been whispering her new name to herself long before it was officially given. She had been practicing the song even longer.

Her eyes left the sagging skin of the ancient woman in front of her and flitted to the side, seeking the smooth and oil-brightened face of her mother. This night, her mother would officially give her the right to sing the song. Her mother graced her with a smile, then nodded back toward the line of well-wishers.

The name and the song. These were her gifts to bring with her into womanhood. She glanced at the other girl again. And perhaps the earrings too.

She looked down and saw Tiichswii. He looked up at her, ready to say her name. But a clump of his hair stuck up from his forehead, as usual, and she eschewed formality to grin at her friend. Tiichswii took it for mockery, and grew stern. He gruffly said her name and moved on. She quickly wiped away her grin, and wanted to catch his eye. His voice echoed inside her mind. She wanted to hear him say her name like he had always addressed her when they were children—full of mischief, joy, curiosity. But her mother looked at her reproachfully. Amuun'axsum lifted her chin, and turned back to the next witness.

~

It was late. The house was mostly empty. But being on the smaller side, with the fire built up, it was cozy. A few of the village's elders remained, along with the other girl and her family as a courtesy, and Amuun'axsum's parents. A select audience. Amuun'axsum was full and happy. Pieces of herself were falling into place. Tonight would complete her transformation into a woman, a woman with property, a woman worth something. She sat up straight and leaned forward.

Her mother got ready to pass on the right to the song. The woman smiled at her daughter, then looked at those gathered, giving special consideration to those who would be paid as witnesses. The fire cast a golden tone to her skin. When she moved her head, her abalone earrings shifted and caught the light, like submerged rainbows.

"There is not much I can share with you about this song," she said.

Amuun'axsum's father shifted beside her on the bench.

"Its words are in a language from a people who face the sea from a different beach. But more than that, it is a song for dark times. A song that remembers the power of Daylight. A song that calls on that power to light the way home." The woman's face clouded for a moment as she recited the words. But then she grew insistent, and warm. "But I sing it tonight, to let you all witness that it is mine to sing, and that this right will now also belong to my daughter, Amuun'axsum."

For any other song, a narrative of its lineage would fill time. Her mother simply prepared to sing. Amuun'axsum took an eager breath.

The woman nodded at the slave man who would drum for the song. The man had come from the same distant village as Amuun'axsum's mother. Besides Amuun'axsum, he was the only one familiar with the song. Certainly, no other slaves were allowed in the house this night. Yet he seemed not to notice that he differed from everyone else, clad only in a waistcloth. A plank lay across two boxes. The man sat behind it, facing Amuun'axsum's mother, and waited for the signal to begin. The woman nodded and turned her eyes toward her daughter.

The slave struck the plank to an incessant beat, his eyes never leaving the singer as she made her mental count. She started with sounds alone. A *hu, hu, hu* to signal a coming chorus. And as the chorus spilled forth—words Amuun'axsum had recited time and again, that she thought she knew—Amuun'axsum leaned forward, drawn anew.

Daylight is found on the mountain

The words started soft. If Amuun'axsum had not already known the words, she would have missed them beneath the drum's clamor. Her mother's hands formed fists with the effort to sing against the drum.

feathers dance on the echoes of wolves

Amuun'axsum's heart raced, understanding now what her mother meant about a song finding its true form inside cedar walls. Trees reshaped by the hands of men cupped the words, amplifying them. Even so, the drum sought to overpower the words.

we touch lightning

The last line echoed off the rafters, as her mother's voice filled with power. Amuun'axsum's eyes flitted to the drummer. But, no, he had not stopped. He still slammed the sticks down to the plank, again, and again.

And the beating filled the space once more.

Her mother repeated the words, over and over, against the backdrop of the plank drum that marked its own path. The drum beating loud, as if to drown the words. The words winning, in the end.

Then nothing.

The singing and drumming both stopped at some unspoken cue that both singer and drummer understood. The air pulsed with remembered sound. Amuun'axsum did not dare budge, did not dare breathe. And she was afraid.

That mix of love and fear was reflected back in her mother's gaze, locked with her own. Her mother started to step toward her—then collapsed beneath a pile of debris.

Splintered roof planks and a large weight stone lay atop the woman's body. At the same time, the silence that had followed the song was filled by cries of panic and alarm. Screams. Shouts. Rattling wall boards. Rumbling roof planks. Flaming torches started to rain down through the hole above.

Amuun'axsum could not make sense of the cacophony, could only stare at the mound on the floor, disbelieving. A lax hand poked out from beneath the planks. A stream of red glistened in the firelight.

The tiny hairs atop Amuun'axsum's head raised, and she pressed her hands over them, wondering if fear alone could rob one of her soul. Yet her fear only increased. Amuun'axsum brought her hands to her ears, clamping them tight.

Suddenly, her father was pushing her to the floor. He slid off the lid of the storage bench she had been sitting on. Amuun'axsum shoved her back against the box, raised her knees, and looked around the room as she kept her hands pressed against her ears. Some people tipped buckets of water over the multiplying flames. Others huddled in confused knots. Flaming torches no longer fell from the roof, but arrows did. She looked toward the doorway, and choked. Two bodies lay over the threshold, spiked with arrows.

She should move, do something. Yet her body refused to respond. Panic clawed at her skin.

Over a fiery mass in the middle of the room, Amuun'axsum saw the other girl standing in shocked stillness. The two girls looked at each other, and it was as if Amuun'axsum looked at her own wavering reflection in a pond. Hair folded up in bands. Pierced ears. Eyes brimming with questions and fears. Then the other girl seemed to shift her gaze through Amuun'axsum. Her expression relaxed, and the fear left her eyes—but nothing rushed in to replace it. No relief. No bravery. A blank nothingness. The girl's body crumpled to the floor. An arrow stuck out of her back, a flower of blood blooming around its stem.

Amuun'axsum vaguely heard someone calling her name. But she could not tear her eyes from the girl. Flames flared at the edges of her vision and died back beneath splashing water. As her hands fell from her ears, the air filled with screams of different pitches, as if the villagers had all turned into gulls whose wings were no good for escape.

"Amuun'axsum!"

Her father's hand was at her face, turning it toward his own. He held his war club in his other hand. His spear rested against the bench. Sweat gathered on his forehead. He looked down at her, and she could tell he was trying to tamp down fear, which caused her heart to race more.

"Mother?" she asked.

He closed his eyes briefly, put a finger under her chin and raised it.

"Who are you?" he demanded.

She tried to speak, but she was strangled by confusion.

Her father's face burned in the firelight. The din of terror faded to the background. His eyes, full of fear and possession, fixed on her own. There was the familiar stirring in her stomach, that effort to please.

"Who are you?" he demanded.

"I am Amuun'axsum."

"Where are you from?"

"I am from Amuun."

Her father did not smile, but nodded as if her answer was not only the correct one, but the necessary one, the only one. He drew a great breath as his hand slipped to the back of her head. He pressed his lips to her forehead. The kiss gained pressure, as if to seal her identity, then he nodded to the bench. "Get inside," he said. Amuun'axsum stumbled up and did as she was told. She lay among the objects within, looking up at her father. "Stay inside until it is safe," he said.

Fear scrambled up her spine again, but she nodded. The lid was replaced. Her father's face slid away, and she was cast into darkness.

Amuun'axsum lay trembling. Time dragged on. In the dark, each crack of burning wood was like a thunderclap. Each scream like a lightning strike. In a panic, she grabbed at her chest, feeling for an imaginary arrow. Instead her fingers ripped through the strings of shells. They scattered by the hundreds, striking wood and rolling like tiny insects over her skin. She was drowning.

Suddenly the lid was pulled aside.

"Father!"

"Maḥtii, keep quiet..."

Amuun'aẋsum sat up. This was not her father. This was the slave man, the one who drummed for her mother. He crouched beside the box and reached for her arm. She looked over his shoulder. A lingering flame spreading up a loom. Scattered embers. Motionless bodies. Smoke, and more smoke. She coughed, but forced words out.

"My name is no longer—"

"We do not have time for that."

Amuun'aẋsum cried out in pain and he put his hand over her mouth to stifle the scream. She stared down at her wrist, at the bloody slash across her tattoo. The cut was not deep, but it stung.

"Silence," he said in a fierce whisper. "They will come for you."

He lowered his hand, and she tried to keep her rattled voice to a whisper. "What are you doing? Where is my father? My mother?"

"Can you keep quiet?"

"Where—"

"In time, Maḥtii, please!" He glanced over his shoulder. "Put your hand over your mouth. I am not finished yet."

He grabbed at her wrist again and poised the knife over the tattoo in a different spot.

She wrenched free.

He grabbed her again, gripping her so tight she whimpered. He gave her an anguished look. "Maḥtii, I am doing what your mother has asked of me," he said, pleading. "Please."

"She's alive?"

"You remember what she said, Maḥtii?" His voice was like the surf, a powerful surge then a gentle shush.

Amuun'aẋsum's throat constricted and fresh tears pooled. She nodded. She covered her mouth with one hand, and held her tattooed wrist up to his knife. He slashed at her skin—bloody streaks crisscrossing over the undulating, wave-like pattern that circled her wrist—and though she shook with tears, it was not because of the pain. Expecting what was coming made it easier to bear, but only physically. He wiped the blood, then wrapped her wrist with a wide strip of softened cedar.

"I don't understand," she said through restrained sobs. "How does this help me get to my grandparents?"

He ignored her as his hands fumbled at her hair. He ripped out the hair bands, tossing them aside into the box. He took out her braids and tousled her hair into messy knots. He nervously met her eyes as he withdrew her earrings and the nose ring. "They aim to kill all of you," he said, as he slid the bone out of her septum. "But if they see her"—he nodded over his shoulder at the dead girl—"they will think the deed done." He looked at her. "We will disappear."

He started to take off her dress. She batted his hands away in shock.

"Of course," he said, dipping his head. "You are a woman now." He handed her a skirt made of shredded strips of cedar bark. A slave woman's work skirt. "Put this on—quickly." He turned to let her change.

"Where is my mother?" she moaned.

His shoulders slumped as she stepped into the rough skirt and pulled it up, tying it by the cedar strands to fit her waist.

"She is gone, Maḥtii. We must let her go."

She almost missed the answer, his voice was so quiet. Though she knew, still she hoped. Gone, escaped? Or gone…

He turned and saw the question. He shook his head in answer.

Amuun'axsum felt her world unravel.

The slave spread dirt across her cheeks and down her arms. "Your mother was a strong woman. You are a strong woman, too."

An edge came to Amuun'axsum's voice. "And what of my father?"

The man closed his eyes and hesitated; his jaw stiffened as he stepped aside and gestured toward the doorway. Amuun'axsum looked, then wished she had not. A pile of bodies filled the doorway, blood running in streams to pool in the dirt. On the ground lay a club, a spear. On top of the pile, a body with lax arms bearing familiar tattoos…

"No," she whispered.

"We must go."

Screams and chants came from houses farther up the beach.

"He did not even make it past…"

"Maḥtii, we must go. They will come back here."

A lingering tongue of flame started to climb the far wall.

She shifted out of his grasp and clenched her fists, staring him down.

"My name is Amuun'axsum."

He held her arms. She tried to wrench free again, but he gripped her tight. She looked at him in challenge, and he did the same in return.

"Your name ties you to this place," he said. She gasped as he shook her. "They will know who you are and you will be cut down!"

"But I have no reason to be ashamed."

He shook his head with pursed lips. "You cannot keep your father's name for you alive—not if you are dead, Maḥtii." He clenched his jaw, then shook the tension free. "And everything your mother entrusted to you would die with you too." His hands relaxed on her arms. "All we ever wanted was to protect..."

Amuun'axsum started to cry again, her confusion building.

He gently rubbed her arms. "Do you trust me, my lady?"

Amuun'axsum was breaking apart from the inside. But she remembered the way her father had pressed his finger beneath her chin and raised her courage. She remembered how her mother sang for her. She nodded.

The slave stood, bloodied knife in hand, and led her to the back wall. The screams outside were growing fewer. The tongue of flame was growing higher. He cut the straps that held a wall plank in place and pulled the wood aside, then another. War chants started to draw closer again. When the gap was large enough, he turned to Amuun'axsum. "Be quiet. Stay close."

Amuun'axsum resisted the urge to turn back, to hunt the bodies that littered the ground for that of her mother. She followed the man through the wall like the dead never would.

The chill night air crept over her exposed skin and through the thin skirt. An orange glow wavered across the dark tree boughs, making them seem to dance. Amuun'axsum flinched at the sound of a distant scream, at the sounds of men's shouts and chants.

The slave man held his hand out and she took it. His hand was large and warm. His fingers threaded through hers. He hunched over and she mimicked his posture. She followed him into the dark fold of the forest.

They had only gone several paces when he suddenly stopped. She stifled a cry as he gripped her hand even tighter, as if to crush her fingers.

A man in slatted armor blocked their way. And Amuun'axsum was so afraid of the club that the man raised high, that she fixed her gaze on the spot in the sky where it pointed. The club fell. Amuun'axsum felt wet droplets splash against her cheek. The slave's fingers loosened and fell from hers as his body fell away. Bone and flesh met again and again, and Amuun'axsum stood rigid as she kept her eyes trained upward, at the crowns of the trees bending and swaying.

Finally, Amuun'axsum's mouth opened in a scream, but she could not hear herself. She screamed harder, chest tightening, unable to move. Something pinned her arms to her sides and ripped her legs from the earth, whipping her around to face the reflecting sea. She fought, driving her heels into grass, then rocks, then sand. Shards of shell and carapace tore at her soles. She was taken with splashing steps into the sea and tossed into a massive canoe. Another man was waiting, ready. His arms clamped around her to prevent her escape. Still, she fought. Crazed ideas ran through her head. To find her mother's body. To sing it back to life.

As the canoe pulled away, glimpses of shore passed in and out of view as she pressed her body against the arms that continually wrenched her back. Amuun'axsum watched her village burn.

The shore slipped out of sight, blanketed by night and by the dark silhouettes of larger promontories. Sparks from the unseen fires floated above the treetops.

~

She awoke on a beach, disoriented. For a moment, she believed it all to have been a nightmare. Then she registered the rough scrabble of sand beneath her cheek, the chatter of people whose language she did not know, and she rolled onto her back. She blinked at the clouded daylight. In the sky above her head, a raven banked into a tight circle, joined by another, and another. At the edges of her vision: dark round shapes, held aloft like half-wrought totems. Amuun'axsum heaved herself up on an elbow and turned to take in the scene. A phalanx of spears rose up like a fence. Each spear driven upright in the beach. Each spear topped by a severed head. The highest among them—swollen and purple, glassy eyed and slack jawed—was the head of her father. Ravens took turns alighting on the head, pecking. The highest would be the first to fall. Amuun'axsum spun away, and scrambled onto her hands and knees. But she retched before she moved much farther. Around her, men shouted, and women sang, and Amuun'axsum did not need to know the words to understand their jubilation.

That same day, she was bound with others and put in another canoe. If the other captives recognized her, they said nothing. She sat listlessly in a small pool of water in the hull, bent over, cheek against wood, too shocked to move. Through the cedar, she listened to the roll of the sea, and felt its vibrations. The hull rocked side to side, as the paddlers propelled the canoe forward, forward, forward. The sound of the sea being pushed back by the paddles was louder than the lapping of the waves against the hull.

They traveled south down the vast, mountainous island and sold her to another tribe, her worth defined by the sum of bulbous containers of whale oil and string upon string of dentalia.

Amuun'axsum woke with a start, choking on imagined smoke. The shaman crouched over her, rubbing Amuun'axsum's head as she sang a soft prayer. Amuun'axsum's face was damp with tears and sweat. She tried to slow the racing of her heart as she came out of the fitful dream, in which the words of her mother's song spilled from a burned and bloody face. As Amuun'axsum caught her breath, Eekbis ceased her ministering. The old woman peered down at Amuun'axsum.

"Just an ordinary nightmare," Amuun'axsum said.

Eekbis pursed her lips, squinting a bit, but returned to bed.

Amuun'axsum sniffed and looked out the doorway. She reached under her bed mat and felt for the shell, bringing it out. Under the cover of her blanket, she inhaled the sweet scent of the balm, as if to heal the burns and wipe away the blood from the face that still lingered in her mind. She tried to see the face of her mother—that smooth, oil-brightened face. But she could not. Why did memory have to cling to the moments that hurt the most? A severed head. A boy's scowl. A broken toy. She longed for the softer memories. A hand pressed to her heart. A soft kiss on her cheek. A babbling creek's song. But she could remember none of the details surrounding those wisps of time. The bad memories were louder.

Still, she clung to them. People could take her freedom, her comforts, and her choices, but they could not take her memories. She refused to forget who she was and where she came from. An act of remembrance would become an act of defiance.

Soon, dawn bathed the clouds above the far hills in a yellow glow.

Blue mist rose between the trees on the blue hills.

Amuun'axsum rolled up her blanket and bed mat. She tucked the pouch that contained the balm inside the bedroll. She slipped on a simple cloak to ward off the cold, started a fire outdoors, then walked toward the bay. A fisherman handed her a bass, and she brought its slick body back to steam over the hot stones in the fire. Slowly, the cold morning air, the cold ground beneath her feet, and the cold fish in her hands started to dispel the heat of the nightmare and the scorching memories it had reignited. Along the way, she passed the place reserved for women's baths. She heard laughter and splashes beyond the sheltering willows. Amuun'axsum caught glimpses through the branches. The whaling chief's daughter bathed with assistance from her mother and Uhpahs in a pool carved into the river's bank. The girl lifted her arm. Steam rose from her skin like the mist in the hills.

At the fire on the beach, Amuun'axsum stared at the flames and breathed in the warm scent of steaming bass. The fresh meal had always brought comfort, and she held her breath, holding onto the feeling, trying to stem the tide of grief.

"Quulthoo," the shaman called from inside the house.

Amuun'axsum ignored the old woman. For the moment, she instead looked off toward the bay, watching the small silhouettes of sandpipers as they plied for morsels in the smooth, wet sand. Slowly, she pulled the fish from the stones, and turned toward the house.

qitap—bass.

pa·sak—damp, misty air.

qutu·—slave.

These were words she heard every day, as much a soundscape of the place as the cries of gulls, the crash of the surf, the wind through the creaking boughs of trees. One of those was now more than a word, though, directed at her so universally that it had become her name—because she could not give them her true name.

Seven years carved away at a person's intentions. A doorway for a bed, for seven years. A tumpline imprinting itself on her forehead, after seven years. Her father's language fading even from her dreams—seven years for new words to amass and overwhelm the old. A dozen villages, in seven years, and none of them her own. No lips uttering the name Amuun'axsum. No mention of any village called Amuun. No ransom offered for her redemption. For there were few left alive to pay for her life, if they even knew she lived. And how to let them know? When she didn't know where they were. When she must pretend to be dead.

Sometimes Amuun'axsum wondered if she were already dead. There were days she did not seem to know herself. The days passed in a blur of tasks and sweat, meals scarfed down. No decorum here. No sign of a woman of such a stature as to be entrusted with an ancient song and an honorable name. It was as if to be silent, to give words of power and worth no voice, no chance of a witness, was to consent to decay.

Seven years would seek to erase the twelve that came before.

The shaman appeared in the doorway, gesturing. "Quulthoo!"

Amuun'axsum slowed her steps further.

She bent her head to look up at a sky that shone blue, at least for the moment. Clouds were blowing in from the sea. One long, dark cloud hung lower than the others, like a canoe weighed down for war. Amuun'axsum entered the shaman's house, but kept her chin raised.

DUSHUUW SLID HIS PADDLE through the water. He avoided looking at the coiled sections of line at his feet.

Not only had his father not thrown him out of the whaling crew, he had moved him to the line-tender's spot on the killing side of the canoe. There were eight men in the whaling canoe, with his brother in the bow, his uncle in the stern, and the rest sitting in pairs on the thwarts between. Each played a role. His father and brother had demonstrated many of the positions over the winter. In the past week, there were more focused lessons—and prayers—with the old storyteller Hawitsuksh. Still, the others looked askance at him, and he couldn't blame them. They didn't have a choice. But neither did he. Let them rest in that.

If he felt uncertain before with only a paddle, Dushuuw now felt downright daunted. But there was no way Hawitsuksh could go out again. And they were short of men. They would already pay Leehuuk, a nobleman from the upriver side of Wuh-uhch, to borrow a canoe. They may as well also hire one of his men, his father said.

"But he can just sit there and paddle. It will be you with our lines." The words carried authority. Chahbuhi had glanced at Dushuuw, then back down to the shapeless carving he was whittling. "You are my son." It sounded like an accusation.

Dushuuw looked over his shoulder to the spot where he had sat before, closer to where his uncle worked in the stern. The paddler from Leehuuk's household glanced back at him. Dushuuw's father would be paying a handsome price—from whatever whale Qotsik took—for the use of both the canoe and the man. And to the household of Leehuuk, a man his father did not admire.

In the distance, Leehuuk's crew followed in their own whaling canoe, ready to support Qotsik's hunt. The nobleman worked a paddle near the back, his sleek hair tied up in a topknot with a sprig of greenery.

Leehuuk was becoming well known for his growing wealth, if only because he gave away just enough to be socially acceptable. Dushuuw knew his father did not approve of Leehuuk's tight fist. But the nobleman came from a respected family, and his investments made it possible for another whaling crew to take to the water. In addition, the man's cousin, who headed a household beside him, served as the village's leading war chief. Dushuuw had followed Wiid on many raids, even as his father complained that a growing number of them benefited Leehuuk. They couldn't avoid Leehuuk and his family's influence before, much less after the people with ties to Oosa-ilth left them.

Dushuuw had spent plenty of time near the nobleman's family, learning under Wiid—sometimes sleeping under Wiid's roof when the battle stories went late. Leehuuk had always been generous with food and comforts. Dushuuw wasn't sure this new partnership was so bad. But he knew better than to say as much to his father.

Dushuuw squared his shoulders and sat up straight as he looked ahead again, only to face the back of his cousin Uhpqoolth, whom he now sat behind. He settled in for another tense journey. He tried to look like he knew what he was doing.

But there would be no time for getting the feel of things.

"There is spray there," said Kweelthup, the crew's watcher. "A gray."

"I see it too," Buhkweeduuk said.

The crew was barely beyond the mouth of the strait.

"That was quick."

"Pay attention now..."

From the stern, Buhkweeduuk steered the canoe to come alongside the whale as it dipped below the water. Dushuuw gave his head a shake, trying to bring his mind up to speed.

"Here we go."

By the time Uhpqoolth shouted for Ǫotsik to strike, Dushuuw was fumbling to remember his role, hurriedly reaching for next section of the line. But Ǫotsik was shouting and leaning precipitously over the bow of the canoe, still holding onto the upper harpoon shaft, which remained stuck in the whale. Uhpqoolth grabbed at Ǫotsik's waist to prevent him from going overboard.

The men shouted in a confusion. The canoe began to tip with a creaking groan. The diving whale was dragging the line down and—with no one feeding the line out—the canoe with it. Panicked, Dushuuw grabbed his knife, leaned forward and slashed the line. It slapped the surface of the sea, then was sucked under. The canoe righted itself, and rocked on the waves. The whale retreated.

"What did you do?" Uhpqoolth shouted.

The men looked in the direction of the whale, paddles frozen.

Uhpqoolth slapped the side of the canoe.

Dushuuw sat back, keeping his eyes on the hull. Uhpqoolth picked up the cut end of the line and flung it at Dushuuw's lap.

"What were you thinking?"

Dushuuw gripped the strip of wood fixed atop the canoe's side, as if to rip it off—wanting to, if only to remove the tell-tale mark of the blade where he had cut the line.

"I told you he wasn't ready."

Qotsik cleared his throat. "This was my fault," he said, holding out empty hands.

"What happened?" Buhkweeduuk called.

"The shaft did not disengage. I struck the whale too deep. It was embedded in the flesh. I tried to dislodge it, but..."

"A killing strike for sure," Uhpqoolth said, gesturing toward Dushuuw. "One wasted because this one didn't tend the line."

Dushuuw closed his eyes, but only to bank an urge to send his cousin over the side of the canoe. He was fairly certain he wasn't the only one who failed in their usual roles, trying to protect his brother.

"If you boys are done with useless talk, perhaps we can pursue the whale now," Buhkweeduuk said.

The crew plunged their paddles into the sea, heading up the strait.

They spent considerable time tracking the whale. With no float attached to the line to track the whale, one or another of the men would call out when he spotted its speckled back. But its path was unpredictable, the time between its breaths inconsistent. They could not get close enough to strike again. And soon, they were well beyond their territory, or that of any of their allies—and daylight was fading.

"The season is long," Buhkweeduuk said after Qotsik called an end to the pursuit. "It takes practice with a new canoe and a new crew."

They returned home, drawing a curious crowd.

"The loss of the sinew line is a blow," said their father, as he conferred with his brother and his oldest son. "It was a powerful one. And the harpoon has been in our family for generations."

"There will be other hunts. It is early," Buhkweeduuk said.

"With new equipment, we can go out tomorrow," Qotsik said.

Chahbuht shook his head. "We older men will have to prepare a new sinew line. That will only take an afternoon with all of us working together, but the prayer and song cannot be rushed. And you must straighten and treat the other harpoon. We will need time. And we need more practice—yes, Dushuuw?"

Dushuuw stood with his hands on his hips and nodded.

And so, after only a short rest at home, they followed Leehuuk's crew that same night out to sea to serve as a support canoe and help with any quarry his harpooner caught.

Dushuuw was grateful to leave the lines behind.

"Think you can handle that at least?" his cousin said, flicking a glance at Dushuuw's paddle.

As they pushed out to sea, Buhkweeduuk had the crew repeat their practice drills for timing issues, focusing in particular on Uhpqoolth and Dushuuw as they pretended to throw over phantom floats and lines.

~

The next day, Yaq and Dushuuw met up outside the great house and headed toward the bay. Dushuuw saw his own smile echoed on his friend's face. But they never got to the canoe. Chahbuhi held up his hand for Dushuuw to wait.

"Before we start on the sinew rope, I think I will check the halibut station at Huuqoo. You will help paddle us there, Dushuuw," the chief said. "We will leave at first light. Bring what remains of the whaling line. You can become intimate with it there—without the usual distractions."

Yaq took the cue and slipped away.

And so Dushuuw, chafing under his father's comment, did not wait; he spent the rest of the day with the plaited cedar line. He coiled each of the three remaining sections of increasing length and decreasing width. If joined and completely stretched out, the assembled line would run the length of the vast house five times over. It was incomplete without the power-imbued sinew cord that led it and entered the whale. But these were the sections for which he was responsible. So he uncoiled them and coiled them again. He practiced bending one line on to another, tying, untying, and tying again. He practiced hefting sections of line over the side of an imaginary canoe, tying on, heaving over, tying, heaving, faster, then faster still. His palms formed blisters, which burst. He started again. Still, he wasn't sure if was a desire to improve driving him, so much as a physical outlet for his anger and frustration.

Later, as he walked outside near dusk to relieve himself, he passed two old men. They sat on a drift log near the side wall of the house, sheltered from the wind and the bustle of village life as they pushed peeled tree boughs into the hollow stems of bull kelp. Making rope occupied the waking time of many of the village's elderly. The shell of one of the cape's smallest creatures—the mussel—was used to fell the cape's largest creature—the whale. But the old men were fond of reminding everyone that a successful strike didn't mean a thing without a cord strong enough to carry the quarry home.

The two old men nodded to him as he passed and then shared a look with each other. Dushuuw stopped around the corner of the house and inclined his head to listen.

"Well, he does not have a wife pulling out a piece of hair to blame for that gaffe," one said.

The other man groaned and laughed at the same time.

There was a moment's pause. Dushuuw almost left it at that—it was bad enough—but there was more, and he felt a particular need to punish himself.

"Qotsik, though, we will be all right with him in the bow."

"I fully agree, of course. Still," the first man said, "the one who sat in the line-tender's spot before—he would never have let that happen."

"Yes. We lost a good one there, it cannot be denied. Yet things are as they are. He is young."

"'He is getting over his grief.' 'He is learning a new role,'" the man said in a sing-song voice. "Our chiefs are full of empty reasons to push him up the canoe—much less into it. Enough, I say. He attracts trouble."

Dushuuw slipped away. He rammed his knuckles against a tree as he entered the forest's edge.

~

The next morning, Dushuuw maneuvered a small canoe up the strait, heading for the river at Huuqoo. He had dreaded the talk his father had certainly crafted to give him along the way. But then Thluuch-muup had opted to come along for the excursion. Dushuuw felt a hesitant sort of relief.

Dushuuw appreciated his stepmother and the comfort she gave his father, staying by his side as he aged despite her relative youth.

Thluuch-muup was unlike her sister—loud where Um-iiqsu was quiet, heavily adorned where the chief's first wife was more restrained. She wore her status loudly. Even for this errand to a fishing camp, Thluuch-muup wore countless pieces of jewelry and one of her best cloaks, lined in luxurious sea otter fur.

Thluuch-muup chattered on about courtship plans for Chai. Dushuuw had escaped one unwanted conversation only to be trapped by another. At least he would not be expected to contribute.

"You see what I mean," Thluuch-muup said.

"I know how you feel," Chahbuht said. "But we also have to think about Deeyuh. Oodahk's family is strong."

"Oh, always Deeyuh. Don't we have enough ties to that village?"

"You can never have enough. They are our strongest neighbors."

"Well, my people are strong, too."

"They are."

"It is settled then."

"No. It is not settled." An impatient edge crept into his father's voice.

Dushuuw tried to paddle more forcefully, but instead he had to ease off to match his father's slowed pace.

"The arrangement was with Oodahk for one of his sons," Chahbuht said. "True, the boy will not be a harpooner. But he is from a strong family with the ties we need. And he already shows a generous bearing."

"I do not see how you can pair our daughter to anything less than…"

"Our daughter is a bright star," Chahbuht said, his voice soft and stroking. Dushuuw closed his eyes with a grimace. He knew without turning around what kind of look his stepmother must have given his father to elicit that response. "But I need a stronger alliance with your peoples, to maintain what we have going forward. No, it will be Qotsik. Qotsik is the one."

Thluuch-muup gasped with delight.

The chief picked up the pace again. Dushuuw matched his father's pace and tried to nudge it a bit faster.

"Oh, this is perfect," Thluuch-muup said. "Of course, it will be to a daughter of Hawith and Tashii. So he will marry Sawsin, correct? We will have to move fast. I am surprised no one has arranged for her hand. Tluulth is fine, of course, but a bit young and flighty."

"There is more than one?"

The canoe veered again as Thluuch-muup fixed her husband with an exasperated look. Dushuuw at this point turned to see for himself, there being no other option unless he—well, yes, that is what he would do. He shifted farther forward and started to trade sides of the canoe with his paddle. Huuqoo was too far today.

His stepmother sighed. "Sawsin is the older one of course."

"Ah. Well, yes, her hand is arranged for," the chief said.

"Oh, how awful. To whom?"

"To our family."

"Wait, when…"

"Ḥawith and I arranged this when she was a babe," Chahbuhṫ said. "Nothing is ever a done deal. But the fact that he has not married her off to another probably means he is still open. Frankly, he and I have not talked about it since Dushuuw here was getting out of diapers."

"Chahbuhṫ!"

"We are here," Dushuuw said, never happier to see the mouth of a small river.

Soon, they were ashore.

Huuqoo was one of several seasonal camps the Kwidich'chuh-aht confederacy accessed up the strait. With no significant rivers of their own, they spread far and wide to gather enough salmon and other foods to feed their thousands of people—and raided for it when they still ran short. Most of Dushuuw's earliest battles were with strait peoples to maintain spots like these.

Beneath a sheltering roof of overhanging rock, slave women cleaned and filleted halibut atop beds of kelp or fern. Others steamed mussels. Fishermen headed out as a group into the strait. Others stood by their canoes, stretching their legs, while slaves unloaded baskets full of the fish and delivered them to the women who paid the men no heed but, flinging hair out of their eyes, continued their work with slick hands.

Dushuuw returned to the canoe to fetch his parents' bedrolls. Baskets containing some of the line for the whale hunts sat in the hull as well, waiting for him. He looked away.

Two fishermen chatted nearby.

"…lost by some hunting party. Harpoon was still in it! Imagine the strength of the man who thrust that one," one of them said. "Must have died of the initial wound and washed up on their beach."

Dushuuw turned toward the men. "A lost whale?"

The man who had been speaking turned to him. "Yes, drifted onto the shore of a village east of here. A gray whale."

"And you're sure about the harpoon shaft?"

"Yes, it was pretty thick. About so much around," the man said, using both hands to form a circle. "One of yours, you think?"

Dushuuw's heart pounded. He brought the bedding to his father and told him he would be back soon. Thluuch-muup's hands were wrapped around Chahbuhṫ's arm tightly, in seeming proportion to the speed at which words flowed out of her mouth to the couple with whom they conversed. His father looked at him in question, or possibly with a plea for help. Dushuuw hurried away.

He grabbed a slave boy, and soon they were pulling into the strait.

They approached a mighty river before Dushuuw spotted the village. A gray whale lay on the beach, half carved. His brother's harpoon was still lodged in its body, the prized sinew line snaking out. The people paused their butchering to look down the beach to where Dushuuw anchored his canoe well away from the site. He further dispensed with formality by wading directly into the water, taking sloshing steps onto shore. A man approached, upset, and Dushuuw raised his hands to show he came with no ill intentions.

"I heard about the whale that washed up on your shore," Dushuuw said, in a mix of the trade language and the local words he did know. He pointed his chin toward the carcass. "It was my brother's good aim that brought it here. I come for his whaling gear." The man's look of disgust deepened, and Dushuuw took a step forward. "You know the whale was ours. You know the look of our gear."

The man folded his arms across his chest. "The whale came to our beach. Now I think you should go. You have not been welcomed ashore, and I have no intention of doing so now."

"All I am asking for is the gear."

The man turned and signaled the men who watched from the edge of the butcher site. Dushuuw sloshed through the water and onto the sand, his irritation growing. His people's warriors were known all along the coast—this man should fear him.

"I just want the gear."

The man stood with back turned and said nothing. Dushuuw reached for the man's shoulder, turning him. "Listen to me—"

Dushuuw's head whipped back from the force of the punch. He put a hand to his jaw and tasted blood. With a shout, Dushuuw tackled the man at the waist, and they fell into the surf. The man reached for a dagger, but Dushuuw reached his own first and thrust the blade into the man's throat, ripping upward. Blood sprayed as the man briefly flailed, and Dushuuw scrambled to his feet. The other men shouted, running faster now, and Dushuuw's gut sank. Was there so much death inside him that it overflowed to make its own claims on life? The retreating surf pulled at the dead man's legs, and Dushuuw leaped over them to race back to the canoe. He felt the death behind him like a weight on his back. He let the dagger fall to the hull as he scrambled inside, heart pounding, but not with any thrill of battle.

"Get us out!" The slave boy, his face pale with fear, dropped the anchor stone he had already been furiously pulling up, then dug his paddle into the water with Dushuuw. The men chasing them splashed into the water. One of the men came close, club raised. Dushuuw swung his paddle into the side of the man's head and sent him staggering sideways. The other man was farther behind and stopped his pursuit as Dushuuw and the boy took the canoe into deeper waters.

Dushuuw kept looking over his shoulder as they paddled back down the strait. The canoe veered left and right.

Back at the encampment, his father was livid.

"Rash. Foolish! Why did you go alone to make such demands?"

Dushuuw looked away.

"We all have to watch over our backs now."

A fisherman's wife sat nearby, putting a mashed bite of food into her child's mouth. She glanced at them nervously.

"Why did you go alone?" his father said again.

Chahbuhɬ was shorter than his son, and he was growing frail, but his voice was as full of authority as ever.

Dushuuw tried to contain the breaths that came in heavy surges.

"It was not your place, not your decision to make. Your brother does not need your help," Chahbuhɬ said. "Not this kind of help."

Dushuuw dug his hands into his hair. The people of the strait would not ignore what he had done. They had not followed Dushuuw to Huuqoo. That left an open question on where and how they would seek to balance the death on their side. "We could position a slave hunting party near their village to provide—"

His father cut him off with a shake of his head. He motioned for Dushuuw to follow him closer to the river's mouth, away from the listening ears of slaves and foreign wives. Chahbuhɬ took a deep breath, tongue pushing at his cheek. He stepped close to Dushuuw and dropped his voice. "We will go back to the cape," he said. "We will gather the household leaders and urge Wiid to deploy our warriors, along with any who will join us from Deeyuh and Tsooyuhs. We will plan. We will prepare. We will attack."

Dushuuw was silent, trying to tamp down his eagerness.

"You were wrong to go alone. But you are right that they are thieves. Besides, we could use the slaves. Qotsik must marry soon, and we will need far more currency to achieve a betrothal in so short a time."

Dushuuw's pulse quickened with the familiar rush of anticipation of a raid, and a better chance to set things right for his brother. But his father clamped a hand around Dushuuw's arm and shook him. The older man's nostrils flared as he looked at his son.

"More than that, I am Chahbuhḷ, a whaling chief of Wuh-uhch, whose father and forefathers were whalers, and who have held sway over much of these waters since the mists of time. You are my son. Your words are not your own." He roughly released Dushuuw's arm. "This summer, you will finish what you started."

"I could do it sooner. I know Wiid would be willing. We could—"

"No. As much as I look forward to one of your battles finally benefiting your own family again, we need the whaling crew back on the water. And that includes you. There have been delays enough, including this one. Leehuuk's crew has been active, and we're on the beach? No," his father said. "Now, time to practice with those lines."

THE SKY WAS STILL its dawn shade of blue, brightening to white. A light rain fell as Amuun'ax̱sum and Uhpahs set off in a small canoe. Another canoe with two women, a baby, and a young girl paddled alongside them. The girl held a miniature gathering basket. Together with a third canoe of women, the group paddled across the bay toward a hillside known for its plethora of salmonberry.

Villagers were gorging on the young sprouts. Each tart, juicy bite was a welcome burst of change after months of dried fare. Everyone hankered for more.

As they neared the salmonberry spot, prayer songs shifted to gossip.

"Too little patience from some of them."

"Can you blame anyone? Such a long winter."

"Yes, but we needed that week of warm weather. Otherwise we would come back with puny stalks, and then how they would complain—especially in a moon or so, when there should be berries but they ate them before they could grow."

"Well, the shoots here should be tall enough by now. Enough to take, enough to leave. It will not be a wasted trip."

"If the elk have not gotten to them."

"Or if they have not grown so eagerly that they're woody and tough."

The women laughed at their own pessimism.

They pulled the canoes up onto a small, rocky beach. After picking their way over the drift logs that shored up the steep terrace, they entered a moist thicket. The leaves of the salmonberry beckoned, bright green against a backdrop of a dozen greens—of grass, of spruce saplings, of salal. Pink blooms flashed, precursors to the orange berries that would come later. For now, the women sought the shoots: straight, pink-hued, and defiantly bearing their spiny armor.

Two older women pinched off sprouts, avoiding the myriad thorns.

"Tough as elk tongues," Uhpahs whispered. Amuun'axsum giggled.

Several of the younger women used folded pieces of mat scraps to guard their fingers. Working quickly, the scrap slipped in Amuun'axsum's hand. She sucked at the round orb of blood from a thorn and continued on.

Wrens chirped in the growing daylight. The women drifted apart. The little girl carried her baby sister strapped to her back. Holding her own tiny gathering basket high, the girl tried to follow her mother. But the salal became thick, the baby fussy, and instead the girl meandered back to the beach, swaying to lull her sibling to sleep as she paced the beach and studied its rocks.

Since the salmonberry was not yet mature enough for its bark to be useful, Amuun'axsum picked some nearby lady fern and wood rush. The shaman anticipated a few births. The former would be used with laboring mothers to encourage easy passage of their babies. The latter would be given to infertile women who would look on in envy. Amuun'axsum put the plants in her basket. She looked up, a snide comment about some noble mothers itching on her tongue, but Uhpahs was too far for conversation. In the moment of disappointment that followed, Amuun'axsum felt ashamed. Had she worked as a slave for so long that she now began to think like one?

Soon, the women had filled their baskets with salmonberry stalks, and they prepared to go back. The little girl sat on the rocky shore, her legs splayed out as she sang to a doll she had crafted out of a smooth oval stone, sticks, and dried shreds of kelp. A familiar story ran through the girl's mind. "I look for you," she trilled, her foot swaying back and forth. The baby slept, its fat cheek smooshed against her back. Her mother tapped her on her shoulder and she hopped up, abandoning the faceless playmate and peering at the canoe's bounty.

The sun was near its midpoint by the time the women returned. Older women who had stayed behind to build the fires now greeted them from beside the kelp-lined pits they had prepared, hot and ready to steam the sprouts.

While they waited for the sprouts to cook, a woman struck two sticks together and several other women started a celebratory dance. As Amuun'axsum watched the women sway like the tree tops, Uhpahs tapped her shoulder.

"Thluuch-muup wants me to get the salmon eggs. Come with me."

Amuun'axsum followed Uhpahs across the creek to the great house.

The sounds of the striking sticks and the chatter and the children's laughter faded as they stepped into the shadow of the tall structure.

Amuun'axsum paused inside the doorway, her pulse quickening. She had forgotten the effect it could have, walking into a home filled with the signs of superior rank. The carved posts and the massive screen depicting Thunderbird tugged at her heart. But so did the fur-lined beds. Rafters so full of food the sun could barely peek in through the gaps. Toys strewn everywhere.

Everyone else was outdoors. Uhpahs ambled toward the far corner, looking over her shoulder as she went. "You can come in, you know."

"How you can be this close and not want some of it for yourself?"

Uhpahs shook her head. "I am here to please the noble lady. And for that, I have more than I could want."

"But maybe you could at least understand why I want it back," said Amuun'axsum, striding farther into the whaling family's corner. She traced the edge of the whaling chief's bench, inlaid with pearlescent ovals of snail opercula. Uhpahs eyed her nervously. Amuun'axsum grinned and continued to draw her hand along the bench.

Uhpahs looked around, then back to Amuun'axsum. "Please don't."

With a sigh, Amuun'axsum dropped her hand and sauntered over.

Uhpahs climbed atop a box and reached for a seal bladder hanging from a rafter. "This has been fermenting for almost a year." She handed down the bladder, then jumped to the ground. "It should be ready."

Amuun'axsum stiffened as she opened the sack that contained the roe. The friends winced as the pungent odor slammed their senses, laughing at each other's expressions.

As the pair walked back to deliver the treat, Uhpahs paused in her steps. Amuun'axsum followed her friend's gaze toward a fisherman who held a massive lingcod over his shoulder by its gaping, fanged jaw. He walked out of sight. Uhpahs let out a tiny sigh.

"I see what the vetch was for," Amuun'axsum said.

Uhpahs startled and started walking again. "You think I woo a fish? I am not sure I want to be that wet." She smirked.

When they returned to the beach, Chahbuhi was gratifying the children who surrounded him with a story. The little girl who had accompanied the women to the salmonberry hillside bounced on her knees. The baby, now on her hip, giggled in glee. Other conversations continued in the background as the chief sang part of the story.

are you lost?
i shall be a salmonberry shoot and look for you
i shall be a salmonberry blossom and look for you

As he finished, the old women withdrew the sprouts from the pits. The pink color had drained away and the stems were green. They were limp, juicy. Several of the women who had helped to gather the sprouts collected their bundles—wrapping them in cold strips of kelp—to take home to their families. The chief and several others ate on the spot.

Amuun'ax̱sum and Uhpahs stood together, waiting for their share.

There was a shout in the distance. Everyone looked toward the bay.

A man stood on one of the house roofs and gestured toward the sea. As he began to beat at the rooftop, those gathered around one seasonal delight knew before they followed his pointing hand that hunters had returned with another sure sign of spring—a whale.

Thluuch-muup pressed her palms together. "Oh! They are home, Chahbuhɫ. They are safe."

"Safe? Of course they are safe. That is my son with the harpoon," Chahbuhɫ said. He struggled to his feet. He waved off Thluuch-muup's help, telling her to get his robe and her sister, Q̇otsik's mother, who had lay prone in bed to help draw the whale.

"Wait, is that Leehuuk's canoe?"

Chahbuhɫ squinted.

Most of the other women had already hurried off to help celebrate.

Uhpahs stepped toward Thluuch-muup. "I will get—"

"No, I will," Thluuch-muup said sharply.

Chahbuhɫ looked over his shoulder.

"You have no place in these matters," Thluuch-muup said. She included Amuun'ax̱sum with her gesture.

Chahbuhɫ raised his eyebrows, and limped away to find out whose harpoon head was in the whale.

Uhpahs flushed. "I will get the rest of the salmonberry stalks. That is what I was about to say."

"Well, of course you will." Thluuch-muup hurried off.

Uhpahs stood for a moment. Then she came back to attention and turned to Amuun'ax̱sum with a smile. "You will help me, Quulthoo, won't you?" Uhpahs turned to the thin waft of steam trailing up from the hole at their feet. She knelt in the sand and started lifting out the remaining bundles of sprouts, laying them in rows on a mat.

Amuun'ax̱sum regarded her friend. The arms of the whalers were raised in song in the canoes in the distance. The words of the hunters' song were nebulous across the stretch of sand and dancing and wind between. She stepped forward, and her shadow fell over Uhpahs. She looked away from the celebration, crouched beside her friend, and bent over the radiant heat of the pit.

~

She was lost.

Amuun'axsum set the basket of cedar bark bundles down and rubbed her forehead. She had followed a small group to gather more bark. Basket quickly filled, she had set out on her own to return to the village. But the errand had taken them off the well-worn trails. Amuun'axsum followed what she had thought was the right path—until it faded to nothing. Now she listened, and heard the faint sound of steadily rushing water.

The river.

Amuun'axsum sighed with relief. Too far east. But that sound was all she needed. Picking up the basket, she headed toward the river's call. She could follow its path and end up right outside the shaman's house.

Yet with no trail, the going was slow. Amuun'axsum wove around fallen trees and prickly salmonberry. Tough salal scraped her shins.

A downed cedar blocked her steps. Looking up its girth and down its vast length, Amuun'axsum surmised the tree once punctured the upper story of the forest. Its top had tasted the open sky. Now, it lay in a sodden heap. The tree had fallen long ago, either from storm or fire, some of the only forces strong enough—besides men—to tear down a tree that sent its roots down deep and spread them wide, anchoring itself to the earth. Yet in its death, this cedar still gave life. The trunk sprouted with a miniature forest of salal, moss, lichen. Even a few young cedar saplings drew on its nutrients, rising toward the sky in a long line. Amuun'axsum followed the trunk, expecting to come across its root wall. Instead, the trunk ended in a collapsed and rotting tangle on the ground near its stump, which remained firmly rooted in the ground.

The stump was massive. Amuun'axsum rested her hand for support on its moss-covered bark. She looked up toward its ragged top, crowned with spindly huckleberry. She started to walk around the snag, dragging her fingers over the rumbling ridges of its aged bark. She traced its curve with several large steps, then suddenly the bark gave way to a charred expanse. A short section of the stump had collapsed and rotted away, revealing a cave-like interior—blackened by the fire that had eaten it away from within.

Amuun'axsum set down her basket and stepped into the hollow.

She had not been the first to find this place. Portions of the blackened bark inside had been scraped away to reveal the uncharred wood beneath, and on these makeshift canvases were charcoal drawings. A smile played on her lips as she took in a child's crude depictions of a snipe and a bear—the sketches were old and faded. As she stepped closer, something broke under her foot. Kneeling, she found a hole carved into the ground at the snag's base. She brushed away layers of cobwebs to reveal shiny sea rocks and a broken toy spear intermixed with a large accumulation of dirt, leaves, and other natural debris.

As she turned to leave, a small fluttering motion near the snag's opening drew her attention. A hummingbird staggered amid bits of bark, twigs, and dirt. The feathers on one of its wings stood on end, as if the bird were not in a muffled shelter but in a thick sea wind. Amuun'axsum crouched and held her finger out to the hummingbird. It did not fly away—could not fly away. "Poor bird," she whispered. Its needle-like beak gaped with a silent cry of alarm. She brushed the back of her finger over its iridescent feathers.

With a sigh, Amuun'axsum left the cozy hideaway, grabbed her basket, and continued on toward the river. She followed its overgrown edge at a manageable distance until she spotted a marked trail again. By the time she reached Wuh-uhch, she was dirty, scraped up, and tired. But she trudged on through the day, soaking and peeling and pounding bark. Her hands and fingers grew blisters, which broke. Aches settled in her shoulders. Fibers flew and invaded her nose and throat. For the bulk of the day—the sea going out, the sea coming in—all she could smell was cedar, slipping down her airways in tiny ragged bits.

Amuun'axsum wiped sweat from her brow. She twisted her shoulders as she straightened, stretching out her back.

Returning to the shaman's house, she thrust the prepared bark into a mound on the floor. Then she made trip after trip to the river to fill a large box with water. She plunged the prepared bark into the box. A few days of a clean soak, and the unpleasant edges of the bark's odor would disappear. Amuun'axsum would then split them into strips more suited to weaving a nobleman's hat.

Other pieces would be needed. She would bury grasses in wet mud to dye black. Those would become the geometric canoes, whaler, and prey on the hat for the chief's younger son. She would bleach other grass, and paint some of it red using masticated bits of red alder. Those would become the whale's blood.

But there were other tasks to complete. She made multiple trips for firewood, then helped other women gather nettle for twine-making. She hurried through the work. Red scratches formed across her palms and fingertips, inflaming the open blisters on her hands. Even lifting her fingers to her mouth to eat thimbleberry sprouts later elicited stings of pain. Her hair stood in frazzled fringe about her head.

Sun sinking, village life swirled around her as she replaited her hair and thought on the next day's tasks. They would be like this and many other days in recent years, and it would seem her life now was to haunt the forests, haul its bounty, and crawl onto her bed mat aching for sleep.

Children darted here and there around her at play. They dotted each other's cheeks with mud, pretending to be whalers and shamans.

A pair of elderly women played a betting game with beaver-teeth dice, laughing as they vied for each other's spoons.

Beyond them, the sea was dark and full of chop in spite of no wind, carrying the anger of some distant storm. The waves crashed down in white-tipped towers, rolling and roaring over top of each other in their greedy chase for the shore, where they abruptly succumbed into a flat, foamy sigh. Gulls swarmed over the water in great swirling vortexes.

Dusk was about to fall when Amuun'a̱xsum found herself back at the hollow, shorn tree. She was so weary, she did not know at first why she was there, what prompted her to take those extra steps, to find the snag again. She looked down at the injured hummingbird, now laying down, its green breast puffing in and out, wing pointed outward in a mockery of flight. Amuun'a̱xsum knelt in the coarse detritus; the sea was a distant rumble, barely noticeable over the closer rushing of the river. She gently scooped up the bird's pulsing body, and twisted its neck.

WHEN THE NEXT WHALE hunt had come, Dushuuw was better prepared—logistically, if not mentally; his mind was on war plans. But he still stifled a sigh of relief when Leehuuk's crew came up with a strike first, and Q̓otsik instead directed their crew to support their neighbors. A whale was a whale, and there would be food and oil for their assistance. Still, the disappointment in the canoe was palpable. It had been moons since they had taken a whale. The men working behind Q̓otsik were largely silent. Uhpqoolth sat as rigid as a plank.

As they helped tow the whale home, the whaling crews crossed over a trench, where a different kind of whale hunt was underway. Tall black dorsal fins sliced through the water, heralding a pack of killer whales, their sleek black and white skin glistening. Amid the pack, a speckled arm rose above the water—a small gray whale trying to breathe. The killer whales battered and dove over the calf to prevent it from surfacing. The gray whale mother's tail came up and slapped down, but the pack knew how to avoid her strikes. Some members harried the mother, while others took turns biting the calf or leaping out of the water and landing atop the calf's back. In the back of Dushuuw's mind, he imagined snarls and howls, as if the slick haunches of the killer whales had revealed the fur of their wolf forms.

Back ashore, they hauled the whale in and marked off their sections.

Children ran about, helping where they could. An older man instructed the most curious, pointing out the different parts of the whale's anatomy.

"See how he avoided striking the belly sack? You think it stinks now. Imagine if that had been pierced!"

Dushuuw looked over the whale carcass. He had been one of those curious young people, intrigued by the ways a dead whale and a dead man were both similar and far different. Hands. Feet. Intestines. With the best whalers, they would be carving the harpoon tip out of a whale's heart at this stage.

"But ah, see here. See this piece? At the very end, the man with the lance missed the brain stem. He tried to go for the brain itself. Cannot do it. Too much in the way."

The village delighted in the taste of blubber. They smoked the meat.

Dushuuw was on his way to meet with Wiid, when he came upon the same old men he had overheard days earlier. The men slurped periwinkles, sucking out the meat, then tossing the emptied shells at a rock. A small pile had gathered at the base of the rock, with a few tiny shells scattered farther away. Dushuuw muttered a respectful greeting as he passed.

He stopped behind a house. He glared at the sky, then edged back to listen in. He peeked around the corner. The backs of the two men were to him. They were still snacking and flinging shells, and Dushuuw felt embarrassed. He was about to walk on—suddenly aware of every small twig that could announce his sudden reappearance—when one of the men spoke up.

"So, is your opinion of him the same?"

His friend dragged a cloak over his shoulders. "What do you think?"

"I think they helped bring home a whale. A good one."

"The sun can still shine on a dog's anus," the cloaked man said. He flung a shell and it bounced off the rock. "And 'helped' is the word."

"He is a good warrior." The words came out slowly, like a question.

"That is true. And perhaps that is the problem." The cloak shifted on the man's shoulders as he turned to his friend. "A man who takes that much human life—perhaps the spirit of the whale cringes from it, you see? Is there really a way to get rid of so much human stench, such darkness of heart?"

The other man waved his hand, as if to swat away a pesky insect, but he listened.

His friend drew a satisfying breath and gave the edges of his cloak a tug. "I say move him back to the support side, at the very least. Acquire someone new who is better trained for the line-tender spot. In fact, move Leehuuk's man into the slot. That nobleman seems blessed lately."

"This hunt went well enough." The man's tone, though, was hesitant. He drew a shell away from his lips and let it fall to the ground.

"You will see."

Dushuuw slipped away, walking into the shadows of the forest, his own shadowed thoughts filling him.

Days passed. Dushuuw woke late one morning to dusty light tickling his eyelids. Maybe if he kept his eyes closed, he could forget the last hunt.

If it could be called a hunt.

Dushuuw had fallen asleep at his latest prayer spot. He missed the call to shove out and so had delayed their departure. When daylight arrived, they were too far to overtake the whales. That was more than enough for the whispers to find their target again.

He squeezed his eyes shut.

You will see...

In the days that followed, it felt as if the spinning disc of the world was tilted a bit farther off its axis. Yahbis kept trying to beckon him over, but Dushuuw always managed to be looking elsewhere or to be on his way out the doorway. It was easy to avoid his grandmother—and everyone else—with so many hours spent in the company of Wiid again. The bear-like war chief drew him to one-on-one planning sessions day and night, to prepare for the coming raid. But they also recalled old battles. The origins of various scars. Dushuuw eased back into a familiar role, one both comforting and demanding under the gaze of a man he had long admired. The war chief's eyes were alight with eagerness, both for the fight and for old times.

"Where have you been, hey? What are they making you into? I barely recognize you anymore. You are a whaler now? I need your club."

End it...

At home, Dushuuw eyed the basket of lines as he oiled his weapons.

The next whale hunt neared as Dushuuw knew it would. His skin prickled like the day before a raid. He wished it were for a fight. He tried to pray. He tried to care.

The day before the hunt, Uhpqoolth emerged from the great house after a talk with Q̇otsik. When he spotted Dushuuw, he marched over. "You going to be ready?"

Dushuuw sighed and nodded.

"Are you sure you are going to be ready?"

"Yes." Dushuuw let the word drop like a rock. But his cousin did not leave, as would a shark after a fake morsel; he was not fooled.

"Because your brother always believes that you are ready, always takes the blame on himself," Uhpqoolth said. "But I am thinking maybe you want to move back to your old position, you know?"

Dushuuw breathed in, breathed out.

"Or swap with another of Leehuuk's men," Uhpqoolth said, "and join a support crew instead."

Dushuuw wasn't sure what he was more upset about: his cousin's spite, or the fact that he agreed.

"Or ditch the hunt altogether?" Dushuuw offered.

Uhpqoolth looked back at him straight-faced. "Not my call."

Dushuuw looked off, working his tongue in his cheek.

"You should not be the one in that seat." Uhpqoolth shook his head.

"Right," Dushuuw said. Images of sweaty bodies and a blank stare and blood-stained fingers flooded his mind, along with war plans, old men's chatter, and dark thoughts. "You are right. It should not be me. So maybe I should be home. While you go off to whale." From the corner of his eye, he saw Uhpqoolth shift. "Keep an eye on your wife." Dushuuw let the black void grow, spill into his heels. "See if it's her to blame for a broken line when she breaks a strand of her hair." He turned his face toward the punch he had invited. He let his cousin pummel him, telling himself each rock-like taste of blood in his mouth, each splotched field of vision, was a cleansing bath. The greater fight was within. It was harder not to fight back when he could easily send his cousin to the dirt, but Dushuuw was still winning. Uhpqoolth shrieked.

By the time shouting relatives had separated them, Dushuuw had a bloody nose, a half-shut eye, and the kind of aches that would be worse the next day. He looked up at his cousin's enraged expression, and smiled. He stood up—only to be shoved back to the ground by his uncle.

"You have gone too far," Buhkweeduuk said.

"Me? I did nothing."

But his uncle was not fooled either.

Q̇otsik spun Uhpqoolth away to walk off his anger. "It's not right to fight," Q̇otsik said. "Don't think about him anymore." Dushuuw watched them stride away, Q̇otsik's arm over Uhpqoolth's shoulders. Dushuuw bent over, as if struck. His uncle kept talking to him—about bringing down a good name, about bringing shame on them all—but Dushuuw soon shut out the angry words. His palms stung, and he held them up. Sand had ground its way into tiny puncture wounds; he had clenched his fists so tightly in an effort not to use them, that his fingernails had sunk into his flesh. His father stood near the house; he gave Dushuuw a cold look, and turned away.

The next day, the cousins were sent out together in a small canoe. Old men took inventories of their scars to ensure any new ones would stand out. It was rare for men to fight. Rarer still for family to fight. Uhpqoolth's limbs were loose, his shoulders slumped, the weight of shame sucking away his anger. Dushuuw simply felt resigned.

The pair paddled into the bay, though in nothing resembling unison. The canoe veered one direction, then the other. Uhpqoolth shoved the anchor over. They sat in determined silence, bobbing together over swells. They pressed themselves into bow and stern. By unspoken agreement, they took turns stretching out their legs to avoid touching each other in the tight confines.

The cousins returned to shore that night, still silent. Their fathers sat them down for a lengthy talk. About family. About community. About the whale.

The young men directed their gazes toward the ground.

In the end, Dushuuw gave in to his cousin.

~

When Q̇otsik came to nudge him awake in the pre-dawn darkness, Dushuuw rolled to his side, facing the wall. In part, to turn his brother away. In larger part, because he could not look at his brother and not want to follow him, no matter the path.

Q̇otsik tried a couple more times to urge Dushuuw to get up, then he left. A long silence followed. Dushuuw drifted back to sleep.

He awoke with a startle, his face wet. He choked and gasped at the smell of urine. He looked up at Q̇otsik, who held the bucket and looked away. Their father glared at Dushuuw.

"The other men have sacrificed much to be in that canoe," said Chahbuhḷ, trembling as he forced the words out. "They have spent their whole lives to be where they are. They bathe, pray, sleep apart from their wives—abstain from whatever desires tug at them."

Dushuuw's stomach roiled with anger. He drew his hand down his face, then flung the moisture to the dirt.

Q̇otsik murmured uncomfortably. "Father..."

"No, there is no excuse for him this time." The chief turned to Dushuuw again. "If you cannot act your rank, or your name—at least act like a man."

Dushuuw responded by laying back down. He turned toward the wall again, this time to hide the tears that would seal his father's opinion. He refused to budge. Perhaps this time they would cast him out. But at least he would not be in that canoe—unable to harm his brother, unable to bring down his family any further than he already had. Q̇otsik mumbled something low, and his father answered angrily, as the two men left the house.

Several hours later, in full day, Dushuuw emerged from the house, ignoring the looks cast his way. The whaling canoes were long gone. Men fished in the bay. Women sat on drift logs on the beach, weaving or eating. Dushuuw went uphill, followed the burbling creek farther into the woods. He washed, then spent the day walking here and there, anything to keep moving. His father would see now, would see it was better this way.

As he walked in the cool shade, emotions as familiar as anger swept in—regret, loneliness.

He returned as the whaling crew approached empty-handed.

Dushuuw shaded his eyes with his hand. His father was sitting in the stern, where Buhkweeduuk usually served as steersman. Instead, Buhkweeduuk sat in the line-tender's spot.

As the other men brought the canoe ashore, the chief limped heavily toward the house. Dushuuw turned to find his father's walking stick.

"Young Son!"

Dushuuw stopped at the sound of that name. He half-turned, wondering if it was an aging father's mistake. It was a name he had turned to for most of his growing up years, after all. But it was diminutive, a child's name.

When he saw his father's face, Dushuuw knew it was no mistake. The name burned worse than the thought of banishment.

"Young Son," his father repeated, drawing closer.

The words that Dushuuw had rehearsed turned to dust in his mouth.

"You will go to a secluded place. You will pray. You will make peace. For however long it takes," Chahbuhṫ said. "And then you will get back in that canoe. You will do this—if not for yourself, then for your brother."

"Why do you think I refused...?" Dushuuw despised the pleading tone, a weakness he couldn't contain.

The chief put a hand on Dushuuw's shoulder. It weighed heavily, and Dushuuw was unsure if it was for emphasis or for support. His father looked away for a moment, catching his breath, then glared into his son's eyes. There was a tightness to old man's face, as if he had battled something but was not yet sure if he had won. "You must be in that canoe." There was something deeper behind the declaration, something the chief almost tried to express, but instead he pursed his lips.

Chahbuhṫ squeezed his shoulder, and it was not a comforting

gesture. "You are dancing on a cliff's edge, Young Son." The chief withdrew his hand; Dushuuw felt its imprint. "You must decide to move on from what was, toward what must be."

"You called me..."

"Yes. And others will too."

"For how long?"

His father drew his shoulders back. "When you are worthy of the name again and can keep it clean," he said, speaking so that the others could hear. "When you are strong like the generations of men who bore the name before you—and you no longer persist in being a careless boy."

Dushuuw's face burned.

Um-iiqsu handed her husband his walking stick, and he hobbled with her back into the house. Dushuuw felt the other men's watchful eyes on him. He wanted to run away again, but that would not help. He walked over to Q̇otsik in a daze. His brother eyed him. Dushuuw helped him stow the gear and supplies. They worked in silence.

The sun dipped toward the sea. Soon, Dushuuw would remove himself to the forest, to go through the motions his father required. For now, he simply kept busy.

A call came from down the beach, but he did not think anything of it at first. The call came again, louder.

"Young Son!"

Dushuuw turned and saw Yaq, looking apologetic. His friend winced and gestured at a tangle of fishing line. "Help me out here?"

"Even you?"

Yaq held up his hands. "I do not go against a chief."

"But you will go against a friend."

Yaq shoved the tangle of line with his foot. "You would have me put up for discipline? How is that, for going against a friend? I do not go against you. Do not put that on my back. You know me. We were Young Son and Yaq for many years, and maybe they were better years anyway."

Dushuuw fixed him with a look, then angled away.

"I should not have said..."

Dushuuw waved his hand to stop Yaq from speaking and trudged toward the forest.

~

Dushuuw spent four long days and nights in the forest, fasting and scrubbing his body. The pain spoke for him better than any prayer, and so he didn't bother singing. His half-hearted searches for spirit help came up empty, time and again, a gap as large as his loneliness. But he at least emerged from the forest a quieter man, his rage a rumbling but distant storm.

Whaling continued through the rest of spring almost daily, as weather allowed.

Dushuuw settled at the back of the canoe again and paddled once more on the thwart beside Kweelthup, the ever-quiet watcher.

They borrowed a different man from Leehuuk's crew, their line-tender's son, who ably moved into that role in Q̇otsik's canoe, drawing even more of the family's resources in compensation.

Dushuuw answered to his boyhood name with cringes, though mostly the men avoided using any name for him at all. He took some comfort in being closer to his uncle again. Buhkweeduuk was quieter around Dushuuw, but still never failed to offer him an encouraging smile. Dushuuw was relieved to simply hold a paddle, and with relief came a fragile peace in the canoe. The added distance between Dushuuw and Uhpqoolth didn't hurt either.

There were the usual abandoned hunts, like the gray they had to let go as it pushed farther out to sea. And there was another hunt where they helped a Deeyuh crew dispatch their quarry.

Q̇otsik's crew notched just one successful take, though it only drew haggard expressions and muted celebration by the time the long travail was done. The crew's more seasoned members said it was one of the toughest whale hunts they'd ever had.

"We are done hunting for now," Q̇otsik told them.

Dushuuw would have rejoiced, if his brother had not disappeared directly afterward, off to spend time in prayer. Q̇otsik looked at the ground on his way uphill, eyebrows drawn, his teeth scraping his lower lip with worry, not even seeing his brother.

A spring squall seemed to match the mood, keeping everyone else indoors while the whaler was away.

But when the weather cleared, Q̇otsik had another successful take anyway—an aged whale drifted dead onto their shore. Q̇otsik emerged from the forest to the sounds of celebration, and smiled.

By the time eagles descended in their droves to the treetops, three whales had come to Q̇otsik by harpoon or by drift—four whales, if one were to count the lost gray, though that went unmentioned. And the richer fall runs were still to come. Q̇otsik said they would wait until then, to give him more time for prayers. Once again, remarks over the young whaler's blessing circulated the villages, and nearly displaced the whispers about his blighted brother.

~

One morning, Dushuuw walked out of the great house toward the river's mouth. His father hitched up the beach, leaning on his walking stick, and handed off a bass to a woman. Though his father's bones seemed to settle inside themselves more each moon, the old man never neglected to cast a line each morning the weather allowed. Chahbuhť's mouth hung open with heavy breaths. He took off his hat by the knob and looked inside it, brows drawn. He spied Dushuuw and motioned him over with the hat. He held it out to him.

"Young Son," he said. "Take this to the shaman's house for me. The inner band, something is not right." The chief shook his head. "See if the girl can fix it."

Dushuuw took the hat and held it at his side. His father continued on toward the house, not waiting for a response. It hurt, hearing his boyhood name; but more, it hurt to be sent on a boy's errand. Perhaps this also was part of his punishment. Or perhaps it was his father's way of forcing him to go to a place he had avoided. The shaman's house was where his ex-wife had spent most of her days, learning under Eekbis.

Dushuuw's feet slid over slick rocks as he eschewed the bridge and sloshed through the creek. He wandered over sand, grass, clover. Eagles cried out in swooping droves overhead and in congregations along the opposite shore.

The shaman's house marked a kind of transition point along the village's length. The small house was near the spot where bay and river met in a meandering swirl. Dushuuw slowed as he neared the familiar doorway. He regretted avoiding the old shaman who, with no children of her own, felt a special bond with the chief's sons. Yet she seemed to understand. When offered, she had turned down the open living space in the chief's house. Or perhaps Dushuuw thought too much of himself and she simply desired privacy, like many shamans.

Dushuuw took a step into the musky house, calling for Eekbis. His voice seemed too loud in the odd emptiness.

The old woman's face popped around a partition. Her wrinkles were more pronounced in the low light. Her long hair covered her like a gray cloak. She opened her mouth, then shook her head as if correcting herself. "Young Son..."

Dushuuw looked down at the ground with a half-smile.

"I am so happy to see you, my boy."

He took her hands in his own, giving them a squeeze.

"It has been a long time since you filled my doorway." She held up her hand to indicate she didn't need a reply. "Do you need something?" She eyed the hat wedged under his arm.

Dushuuw gestured toward the slave woman. "My father says the band needs to be fixed."

The slave cast a worried glance at the hat. She held her chin high as she approached. "Let me see it," she said.

Dushuuw handed it over and watched with disinterest as she poked and prodded. "I think I see the problem," she said. "It is an easy fix, if you want to wait."

Dushuuw shrugged and sat near the shaman, who patted his knee and asked him how his stepmothers were faring, how his father was doing. She knew already—she was no stranger to their doorway, even if he was a stranger to hers. But he appreciated the easy conversation.

"And you," the old woman said. "That is a nasty mark. Aster is good for that—the white one—and easy to come by."

Dushuuw looked down at his arm at the purple bloom of a bruise he had not noticed. It was not the kind of thing that deserved attention, even if he knew what plant she was talking about—which he didn't.

The slave handed him the repaired hat. "We have some," she said to the shaman, "left over from what was gathered for the salmonberry."

Dushuuw started to raise his hand to wave off the offer, but the women ignored him.

"Ah, well, give him some. Mash it, too. Save him the trouble."

"I am fine," Dushuuw said.

Eekbis wagged her finger. "You need to take care of yourself." She turned away again. "Get him extra roots, too, my girl. To use tomorrow. I will get a pouch for that. Oh, and there is a new aromatic blend I have been thinking Thluuch-muup would like. If I can find where..."

Dushuuw watched with a mixture of impatience and curiosity as the slave ground roots into mush. Her technique was different than his... He looked away, hating that for a moment he saw the woman not as a slave, but as a noblewoman worthy of a shaman's guiding hand—too close to the woman who haunted his thoughts with her scorn.

When she was satisfied, the slave walked over, and he held out his hand for the ointment, trying to hurry things along. But the woman looked at the hat, at him, and shook her head.

"I will do it," she said. "It stains, you know. The chief's hat should be kept clean." She eyed the hat, then him. He sighed and sat back down.

She knelt in front of him as the shaman sifted through baskets and bowls and who knew what else beyond the partition. The women talked back and forth in an easy way, the slave reminding the shaman where this herb was kept, or that they were out of that plant.

The slave held his arm and rubbed the ointment over the swollen bruise, her fingers moving in firm circles. Perhaps because of the setting and its reminders, Dushuuw suddenly felt her touch to be a most intimate gesture. He tensed. The woman noticed, and apparently took it for pain—her eyes flicking to his face—because she massaged the poultice in more gently.

"Just a little more." She scooped up a bit more of the mashed roots with two hooked fingers.

"It is fine," he said, worried she would think him weak to feel pain over something so minor.

She traced the contours of the bruise once more. A cedar band was wrapped around her wrist; it poorly hid a scarred tattoo. So, he had not been far off, seeing in her a noble bearing. But a once-noble who was unwanted.

The slave stilled and looked up at him. He looked away.

The shaman was still mumbling and banging around on the other side of the partition. "Oh! There it is..."

Dushuuw stood, and the slave's fingertips ran down his arm as he rose. She stood and reached for his arm again. Annoyed, he placed his hand on her shoulder to stop her.

"It is fine, truly," he whispered. "The old woman coddles."

He paused. The slave's skin was warm, and soft. He withdrew his hand, as if burned. But as he stepped past the woman toward the shaman, he still felt the warmth of her skin on his palm.

OUTSIDE, AMUUN'A̱XSUM EYED the whaling chief's youngest son as she cleaned her hands and the bowl in the river. He had lingered, talking to an older woman the next house over. She eyed the hat in his hand, which he drummed against his leg—and she blew out an angry sigh.

The chief's hat was the best she had made yet. The band was fixed; yet if it loosened itself again, would the old man think her skill insufficient? She needed to stay in one spot if she had any hope of finding her mother's family. Each move had taken her farther and farther south. Now she was across the strait, at the edge of the world she had any chance of understanding. She turned her attention back to the river. She gripped the bowl and held it under the water, pushing it into the gravel. Tan swirls of sediment rose and raced down the current.

The chief's son walked down the beach with a pair of children. A girl stood on his feet, wrapping her arms around his waist as he gave her a walking ride. The boy trotted along beside him, hands on hips. Amuun'a̱xsum slid glances their direction until the trio strolled behind where she crouched. He did not wear his own knob-topped hat. It was not raining. But she would not blame him if he doffed it in a downpour. An embarrassing first attempt—she cringed still. It was not just the lack of a status symbol, though. There was something in how this man often carried himself, confirmed by the snippets of gossip she had overheard and, most of all, the fight she had witnessed—with his own cousin. This man was noble, but he did not seem to care to act the part. His father sent him on fool's errands.

Amuun'a̱xsum dipped her head to look over her other shoulder as he continued down the beach. The girl was twirling with arms outstretched now. He tousled the boy's hair. The children scampered back up the beach. Amuun'a̱xsum looked down into the water. Her fingers were turning pale in the cold currents, against the hard curve of the bowl. She cleared her throat and raised the bowl, shaking the water out. Her hands trembled.

He was gone, crossing the creek on his way to the great house. Amuun'axsum dipped her hand in the river once more, then brushed her dripping fingers over her shoulder.

"Quulthoo," the shaman called.

Amuun'axsum took a fortifying breath and stood. She batted the bowl against her leg as she eyed the slow current for a moment. She pushed her shoulders back and walked to the house. Eekbis stood in the doorway waiting. The shaman took the bowl.

"How long does it take to wash a bowl?"

Amuun'axsum moved past the question into the dusk of the house. "You wanted to go upriver? I will pack us some water and get a canoe."

"Well, bother the tides and do let me know when *you* are ready."

Soon they were on the water, moving upriver with the flow of high tide. They passed house after house on the north bank of the river as they reached the farthest end of Wuh-uhch. Slaves from Leehuuk's household cooked or sat weaving against the house walls. One of the house's elders watched the river, and his gaze idly followed the women as they passed. Amuun'axsum started putting a bit of extra strength into the paddle, thinking of the distance to Deeyuh. Soon they were out of sight of Wuh-uhch. River and land met head-on here, with neither side giving way enough for human habitation. Tree branches dipped low to the water, their leafy tips floating and dragging in the current.

"Bring the canoe close to that copse up there," the shaman said.

Amuun'axsum looked where the old woman pointed. She wondered at the odd destination, but she angled the canoe through the current.

"Is this really where you want to be?"

Eekbis grunted her assent, and as Amuun'axsum maneuvered the canoe into the overhanging branches, the shaman tossed a stone anchor over the side. "Close enough. You will have to wade to it. It is that spruce, there. You see the growth?"

The shaman held a knife out to Amuun'axsum.

Amuun'axsum took the knife and slipped over the side of the canoe. She winced at the cold water that tugged at her legs. Sharp bits of gravel pricked the soles of her feet. The shreds of her bark skirt floated on the water as she waded over and picked her way through the tangle to the tree. She reached up through the branches to carve away at the burl. Her arms began to ache. She shivered in the cold and looked back. Eekbis was gazing upriver. Overhead, a pair of ravens harried an eagle.

As the tide shifted, the river tugged the canoe in the other direction. Amuun'axsum's arms ached; she carved as quickly as she could. At last, she cut off the last bit of the growth. She waded back to the canoe.

"Good, good," the shaman said, taking the burl and knife and tucking them inside a basket. "Come, come. Tide is with us, and we will be home in no time."

Amuun'axsum hefted herself back into the canoe. It was the last her arms could handle; they hung lax at her side. She would be glad for the tide, to worry about little more than nudging the canoe a bit one way or the other to avoid the banks. The shaman was already pulling up the weight line. "Give me a moment," Amuun'axsum snapped.

Eekbis's hands stilled on the weight line; she slid a look at Amuun'axsum as cold as winter.

"Take up the paddle, Quulthoo."

Amuun'axsum took the paddle in both hands as ordered, but she stuck its point into the rocks of the river bottom, and held the canoe in place. Leaned on the paddle, more like, glad her weight and not her arms were enough to hold the canoe in place. The current tugged at the hull, and her sore arms burned as she willed the paddle to be an anchor. She tried to catch her breath.

Eekbis finished pulling up the weight line, and placed the rope-bound rock in the hull with a deliberate thud. Her eyes flitted upriver, then back to Amuun'axsum with a glare. Amuun'axsum glanced upriver, seeing nothing but ducks and eagles and ravens. She looked back at the shaman, realization dawning.

"We are trespassing," she said. "This part of the river, you do not have gathering rights here, do you?"

Eekbis winced, then scoffed. "Who owns the river? Look at it." She motioned at the falling current that tugged at them. "It is already gone. There it goes."

"Yes, but..."

"And the sun? The moon in the night sky? Who owns them?"

Amuun'axsum stammered.

"The power is in the place, girl, not the men who have no earthly idea how to use what is here," Eekbis said.

"The power is in the words placed over them," Amuun'axsum said.

The two women stared at each other across the small canoe.

"You taught me that," Amuun'axsum added more softly. She had become familiar with beatings. And though the shaman had only ever struck her once, Amuun'axsum still cringed. She clutched the paddle, angry with herself and yet forcing herself to appear meek.

Eekbis gave a tight smile. "Yes. That is right." She casually looked about, then back to Amuun'axsum. "The tide has been ready for some time, Quulthoo. Are you ready yet?"

Amuun'axsum swallowed and lifted the paddle. The canoe drifted, freed to follow the eager current that raced back to the sea. Amuun'axsum made minor corrections to coax the canoe along the near shore. The shaman watched her along the way, hands folded on her lap.

"The power is in the words..."

The shaman's voice was soft. The old woman gave a short laugh, and flicked a finger in the direction of Amuun'axsum's scarred tattoo.

"Do you hide any words from that past of yours? Beyond prayers for clover that I already know..."

Amuun'axsum stopped breathing as she focused on keeping herself expressionless. But she started to pick up the pace. She shook her head.

The shaman's gaze was like a flame.

When they returned to the house, Amuun'axsum built up a fire. She was still damp, and she sat close to the warm flames, rubbing her hands. Eekbis took the burl and placed it on a workbench, slicing into its gnarled girth. She paused and looked over at Amuun'axsum, as if considering something. "Come here, Quulthoo. I will show you the use of this thing you have gathered for me."

Amuun'axsum went still, then shot up and edged over to the shaman's side, heart pattering. Mud lined her shins, and she wiped her hands on the shredded lengths of her skirt—she would need to make a new one soon.

The shaman reached for her hand and guided her fingers over the knife, then proceeded to detail how Amuun'axsum should make the cut, what to add and how much of each plant, how hot to make the water, the steps to pound it all into a consistency such that none of its distinct parts could be recognized, even by the best nose. The task took a long time. But Amuun'axsum did not notice.

They put the resulting concoction into a small box with a tight-fitting lid. The shaman wrapped the rest of the burl in cedar, and tucked it and the box into the bottom of her storage bench. Amuun'axsum watched as the shaman closed the lid and turned toward another task, as if it were a normal evening. Clattering bowls together. Tossing leftover stems into the fire. Mindlessly humming.

"What is it for?" whispered Amuun'axsum, aware of the frantic greed pushing out the words but not caring.

Eekbis looked at her with a blank expression. "What is *what* for, Quulthoo?" She gave the barest of smiles, then turned away.

Flustered, Amuun'axsum grabbed a box and headed outside toward the river for water.

Down the beach, a man crouched, watching an assemblage of eagles at the river's edge, waiting for one to leave behind a feather, which would elevate his own song in the long nights of winter.

The Long Ago

SMALL ONE SHIVERED now with actual chill and wondered how she came
to the beach from her bed. But was it her beach? This one was so vast.

Far off, in a waterlogged stretch of sand—that had never before felt
air—a lone man faced the sea like a miniature totem. She looked at him
over the absence of sea and wondered at this strange tide. Had the
rumbling earth caused it to run and hide? Or had the passing summer
storm blown it away? She tried to discover why it was not the absence of
the sea, or even her aching leg, that set her on edge. No, it was not just
the absence of shushing surf. It was the other sounds that were absent.

No birds, anywhere.

She looked up, at the wide stretch of blue sky and piercing sun. They
did not beat their wings there. She turned in a slow circle, seeking them
out to no avail.

She turned and turned, until she again faced the sea, which had
changed again during her small orbit. A white line shone in the sun,
stretching all the way across the horizon.

"The sea is coming..."

Small One tilted her head, curious, as others started to shout.

"The sea is coming!"

She looked down as water started to trickle up. She balanced on the
sides of her feet, inspecting the swirling sand beneath her soles. When
she looked up again, a wall of water was above the totem man's head.
Small One stumbled from her unbalanced stance and felt her heart rap
its knuckles against her rib cage.

The totem man disappeared.

The people choose Whale. They do as Owl said, heeding his warning.

They choose Whale.

Thunderbird...

When Thunderbird learns of this he is deeply wounded in spirit. But more than that. Thunderbird is angry, too. He shoots up in the air, so high—so high, that he looks no bigger than a raven.

Circling...

Circling...

From high in the sky, Thunderbird starts to stir up a great storm.

1699
SUMMER

THE MILD WEEKS SETTLED in, one atop the other, as the sky held back its rain, shaved clouds from the sky, drew the winds down to breezes, and increased the warmth of the air on their arms by minute degrees. The days lengthened as the nights grew shorter and shorter.

In the dark, Dushuuw looked out over the bow of the canoe.

The first canoe introduced to the people of the cape was a war canoe. It was carved from the body of the world's largest cedar. Its stern was as high as a man, its bow higher still. The idea had come from Q̇watee, in that shadowy time when animals and humans were nearly one and the same. Q̇watee's own canoe was small, but he did not need to propel it with any paddle. His word and its name were enough. "Go, *Hupidu·wa·š*"—and the canoe surged forward.

Always when planning and preparing before a battle, Dushuuw remembered this story. There were many Q̇watee stories—about as many as there were sides to Q̇watee, who may be a hero in one story, only to act the buffoon in the next—but this story had been Dushuuw's favorite since he was a boy with a black eye and scraped knees. The story was a visceral connection to his warrior calling. Even as a young man, he took a stupid joy in floating a leaf on water, recalling how as a child he pretended it was a toy canoe, blowing on it with a whisper: "Go..."

Forty paddles propelled this canoe, sliding through the waters of the strait at the hands of forty men. The canoe slid silently through the water—its hull burned by fire, smoothed by bone, polished by stone. The upper part of the canoe was painted gray, with a wide black stripe beneath, then a red hull. The colors blended and cloaked the craft like fog. Carved and painted eyes on the high prow piece searched the darkness ahead.

The men, too, became shadows. Charcoal coated their skin from head to toe, a reflection of hearts ready to take human life.

Hemlock branches filled the hull. Moonlight played off the bile that coated their weapons. The carved Lightning Serpent on Dushuuw's war club glistened.

From the bow, Dushuuw looked back over the heads of the warriors with him. Theirs was one of four similarly outfitted canoes. There was a canoe of warriors from Deeyuh, another from Tsooyuhs. The canoe directly ahead of him was led by Wiid.

As they departed Wuh-uhch, the men in each canoe had sang slow songs of preparation, to make them strong. But now they were silent. They beached the canoes a fair distance from the village, careful to stay out of the line of sight of a redoubt, where men would be scanning the waters for signs of danger. Some of the warriors would stay here and paddle the canoes to the village beach once they heard the fighting underway. The fighters edged into the spare cover of the trees. The few who had armor put it on. Dushuuw slid on an elk-hide vest, weighted down by its vertical slats of wood; it pressed on his shoulders as it fell over his chest. He looked around at the other men with him, then slipped a masked hood of partly tanned hide over his head. A slit across the front of the hood allowed him to peer out. They were ready. Together, they ghosted between spires of alder and dogwood, each man holding the weapon of the man in front of him as they crept to the back of the village.

Dushuuw and Wiid had already scouted the village to divide the houses among the war parties. Dushuuw and his men would target the main house.

The warriors paused in a loose line near the edge of the village. Dushuuw looked to his left and to his right, making sure everyone was ready. Most of the warriors carried clubs made from the heavy jaw bones of whales. Others held bows with poison-tipped arrows. A warrior from Deeyuh grasped a long spear, fingers curling and uncurling over the shaft. A Tsooyuhs fighter stood nearby with a whalebone club in one hand and twirled a short dagger in his other hand—the same weapons Dushuuw gripped. Dushuuw took a last sweeping look over the backs of the dark houses.

His gaze froze at a gap between two houses. A lone man stepped into view, lit by an unseen fire. The man stretched and then turned back toward the fire, disappearing behind a house. There would be no surprise attack with that lookout.

Dushuuw signaled the others to wait and then crept forward. He crouched in the shadow of a house, and let his war club dangle by its cord tied to his wrist. He waited, waited for the right moment—when the man's back was turned, his eyes briefly filled with the fire's light—then burst out, grabbed the man from behind, and slammed the dagger into his throat before he could call out.

As he carefully lowered the body to the ground, he glanced around at the still-sleeping village. He paused long enough to spread the fire apart, taking one of the burning logs and placing it under the hull of one of the village's overturned canoes—if they couldn't steal it, they could at least prevent it from being used in pursuit. Pulsing light outlined the canoe as he slipped back into the shadows.

After one more check of the village, Dushuuw gave a deep, throaty *kraa*. The other war party leaders echoed the raven's call. Warriors flowed between the houses onto the beach.

Dushuuw led his men toward the far side of the village. They edged along the shadowed walls of the houses—large groups cut away at intervals, slipping through doorways.

Ahead, Dushuuw spotted movement. Another lookout appeared from the shadows, his gaze toward the canoe, its hull now licked with flames. Dushuuw was too far to prevent the man's call of warning. But it came too late anyway. Already, cries of alarm sounded here and there from inside the longhouses where many residents had already been killed in their sleep.

The lookout shouted and raised his bow.

Dushuuw shouted and ran ahead, spurning the shadows.

An arrow sailed through the air, narrowly missing Dushuuw's head. In the houses they had not yet reached, several local warriors emerged, armed, drawn by the lookout's shout. More of Dushuuw's men peeled off to deal with the new threats. By now, women, children, and elders would be making holes in back walls to escape to the woods—where the rest of Wiid's men waited.

Dushuuw and the few warriors who remained with him neared their goal, the village's largest house. Resistance intensified as they went. Around them, a Deeyuh warrior fell to one knee, an arrow protruding from his thigh, before hobbling forward again. A Wuh-uhch warrior collapsed on his back, a spear protruding from his chest. Yet another Tsooyuhs warrior paused, aimed, and fired an arrow, taking down the lookout. Dushuuw ran onward. His breath pulsed hot against his face inside the helmet, his eyes on the carved eagle that loomed atop an entrance pole over the house's entry.

A man appeared in the doorway, and before Dushuuw could move to the side an arrow flew at him and lodged in his wooden armor. As the man nocked another arrow, one of Dushuuw's warriors thrust a pike through the man's gut. The man cringed, and Dushuuw swung his club into the man's head to finish him off. He jumped over the body into the house, eyes darting as he searched for the next blow.

It came from his left. The dying archer's body prevented the enemy from getting too close, and the blow to Dushuuw's head was a glancing one. But it shifted the helmet on his face. He growled as he peered with one eye toward the man, lunging to take advantage of the man's missed thrust. He jabbed his dagger into the man's side, wrenching the blade upward as he swung the club in his other hand into the man's head.

Behind him, the sounds of battle reached a fever pitch, then started to ebb. These were a strong people. Dushuuw and his men needed the advantage of surprise, and it made all the difference. The local men had weapons ready, but no time for armor, so every wound went deep. As soon as their families were safe, they would flee to join them. Dushuuw ripped off the helmet as he scanned the house, dagger and club held at ready. This was the farthest house to reach. Its inhabitants had time to flee. There were no signs of any more men here; still, he did not dare relax. He knew what that cost.

One of his men came to report, filling the doorway. "Their warriors are leaving too. We are catching the stragglers."

Dushuuw started to lower his weapons.

But not everyone had escaped.

A slave girl darted out from beneath a bench. One of Dushuuw's fighters grabbed her by the wrist. She fell and tried to pull her arm from his grip. But he held on tight, and she began to cry.

Dushuuw again scanned the house, which still appeared empty, except for the weeping girl.

Satisfied, he sheathed his dagger and gestured with his bloodied club at other warriors, ordering one to build up a fire for light, and another to gather their wounded while others secured the captives in the canoes, which would have arrived by now. "We will want to leave quickly, before they regroup." As he untied the club from his wrist, he looked down at the arrow that still protruded from his armor. He had forgotten about it. The point pierced the wood right next to a gap. He wriggled it free and tossed it to an archer for reuse. The girl kept crying, and Dushuuw waved for the warrior holding her to leave the house.

As the girl's cries faded, Dushuuw swept his eyes around the house again. He searched, though not for potential threats this time.

"Where are you...?"

Every house had its own feel. A house spoke of the people who lived within its walls—there was the weaver's loom, here the curls of wood shavings from a master carver. A house also spoke of its own home—coiled basketry made from nearby grasses, the overwhelming scent of salmon pulled in droves from the wide river. Dushuuw sorted through the foreign, seeking the familiar. Light from the growing fire built behind him as he approached a corner, drawn to a large storage box. Dushuuw slid the lid aside. The harpoon lay there, as if waiting.

The shaft was warped. Dushuuw ran his fingers over the wrapping of wild cherry bark that overlaid the braided cord of cedar fibers, binding the shaft's jointed parts together as one. He lifted the shaft—so heavy he had to use both hands—and set it aside to search the box for the harpoon head. He found it, the sinew line, and the following length of line he had cut free.

"Canoes are here," a warrior reported. "We lost one man. Injuries to the others are manageable. We are binding the captives—I count more than a dozen."

Dushuuw turned and nodded in acknowledgment. "Take one basket's worth of their salmon here, then we go."

The man cut short a frustrated sigh. Dushuuw could not bar the other war parties from pillaging other houses—it was part of their payment. But his father had said slaves, and so it was slaves they took. As for himself, Dushuuw had come for one thing—his brother's whaling gear—and now that he had what he needed, he saw no need to prolong their stay. A bit of salmon. Well, perhaps more than a bit... Dushuuw smiled as the man found the largest basket available in the house: a woman's burden basket.

As the man pulled fillets of dried fish down from the rafters, Dushuuw sat on a nearby bench and gathered each piece of the whaling equipment. He lifted the harpoon head and ran his finger over the edge of its mussel shell point. The blade, and the barbs that had held it fast in the whale's flesh, were still smooth from the pitch coating they had been treated with to ease their passage through the whale's flesh. He ran the sinew line through his palm, the piece his father and brother described as holding great power—the sinew of a whale, to enter a whale.

Dushuuw balanced the heavy harpoon shaft over his legs. He reattached the harpoon head. He coiled one end of the sinew line and fit it into a special groove at the tip of the harpoon shaft. And it was a weapon again. His hands hovered over the length of yew, then rested on it. Before this night, he had never touched a whaling harpoon. Dushuuw recalled how Q̇otsik wrapped the shaft in kelp and heated it to make the wood straight. How he kept his harpoon heads and the sinew line in special spots on the wall in his living space. How he joined them together in prayer. How his fingers curled around the grips as he practiced lifting the harpoon for a strike, testing its balance.

Dushuuw stood and lifted the harpoon experimentally. Embarrassed, he looked about. But the other warrior was already gone.

With a shake of his head, he confirmed that his weapons were in place and folded the helmet under his belt as well. He hefted the long whaling harpoon onto his shoulder, then hesitated. He grabbed his war club from his belt. Silly though it might be, it felt better holding the familiar in one hand to balance the unfamiliar in the other. Dushuuw started toward the doorway.

A shadow that had been creeping at the edge of his vision suddenly bolted toward him.

Dushuuw barely deflected the man's club with his own, and buckled to one knee, thrown off balance by the harpoon's weight. The man's strike at him had been wild, and he careened past Dushuuw. This was no great warrior, perhaps no warrior at all. But Dushuuw was still the one on the ground as the man shouted again and ran for his back. Dushuuw dropped his club and grabbed the whaling harpoon with both hands. He swung the harpoon around, taking the man down at the shins. As the man thudded onto his back, Dushuuw hefted the harpoon upward and then fell with it onto the man's chest. The man stared up, eyes full of wrath, but his face wet with tears as he choked. The harpoon sank deeper. Dushuuw felt the point pierce through flesh and bone to meet the earth. The man shuddered. His breath was a wet tangle. His hands sprang open. Dushuuw closed his eyes against the odors that sprang from the man, then forced himself to look. The man's eyes were barren.

The face was youthful. Likely the young man used a weapon that didn't belong to him. Perhaps his father was among the dead near the doorway. Or the slave girl had been a lover he failed to protect.

Dushuuw straightened. The harpoon shaft fell free of the body as he sat back. The sinew line snaked out of the man's chest, channeling the seeping blood to the floor. Dushuuw turned the body over. The point of the harpoon head stuck out, but not enough to grip.

Shouts of victory sounded from the beach. Wiid's voice rose in a song of exultation.

Growling at the delay, Dushuuw took his knife and carved into the man's back, then tugged the harpoon head free by the sinew line. Blood dripped off the harpoon head and line, and from Dushuuw's hands. And he recalled something else about his brother's treatment of the whaling harpoon. How Qotsik would never refer to it as a weapon.

With a grunt of disgust, Dushuuw raised his club and brought it down against the man's neck, again and again. He put the harpoon head and lines in a basket under his arm, hefted the harpoon shaft, grabbed the severed head by its hair, and strode through the doorway.

Captives sat bound and gagged in the now-gathered Wuh-uhch canoes, except for some of the younger boys who would be put to immediate work paddling for warriors who had been wounded.

At the water's edge, the Tsooyuhs fighter waited with a severed head. Wiid was there as well. Their helmets were off, and Dushuuw saw a reflection of his own face, blood mingling with paint. Dushuuw recalled the Tsooyuhs fighter was the one who carried the same weapons as he did. As he drew closer, Dushuuw shook off his agitation and pulled his shoulders back. He sifted through his memory, matching the man's reputation to his name. "You are Shuchkuk."

The Tsooyuhs man nodded slowly.

"Do you look in their eyes, Shuchkuk? To see death come?"

Wiid looked at them askance.

But if Shuchkuk detected the bitterness in Dushuuw's tone, he ignored it. The warrior squinted for a moment, then shook his head. "I do not," he said. "They are already dead when I decide to strike them."

Wiid barked out a laugh. Dushuuw's shoulders relaxed, the last shred of his rattled nerves easing instead into appreciation.

"I heard we have you to thank for this raid," said Shuchkuk as he put the head into Wiid's canoe.

Dushuuw nodded. "When we can aid Tsooyuhs in the same way, I will be glad to follow you."

"You both fought well," Wiid said. "And you will see each other again soon enough. We should leave."

Dushuuw would return to Wuh-uhch. He would help Wiid place the severed heads of the enemy warriors on the beach, and let the vacant eyes face the sea for four days. Then they would mount each head on a spiked pole. They would drive the pikes into the ground in front of the homes of those who had taken the heads.

It was Qwatee who taught them this. They were the instructions Qwatee laid out on the threshold of his death, after being so audacious as to steal the box containing daylight. As a boy, Dushuuw had liked that story nearly as much as he did the one about Q̇watee's canoe. Dushuuw took his first head soon after his fifteenth summer. That first time, he had not felt as he had always imagined Q̇watee would have felt—strong, brave, triumphant—but instead he felt confused, angry, fearful. In his nightmares, the head came to life, opened like a mask, and morphed into the hollow-eyed visage of a ghost. But as more men died by his club, and as his club was stained deeper shades of brown, the act became a rite. Too long without a fight, and he would itch to start one.

He had recovered his brother's whaling gear, and he had procured slaves for his brother's gain. Satisfaction filled him.

As they shoved off, the burning canoes of the village cast wavering hues of orange and red over the swells of the waves. Their enemy's losses would linger long beyond this night.

Dushuuw swatted the side of the canoe near its eye and looked over his shoulder at the men holding the paddles.

"Go."

~

Dushuuw returned from the raid full of adrenaline—and pride in returning the gear to his brother—only to run into a cliff.

"The time is short," the shaman counseled. "And the sun is only a messenger."

Dushuuw chafed under the woman's attentions. He felt like a slug. Such a crash after the high of a raid wasn't unusual. Usually, he would work through the low by fishing with Yaq. Or commiserating with Wiid.

Not this time.

For four days, whalers, hunters, craftsmen, and others seeking spiritual strength spurned their houses and set out—on sea-sprayed outcroppings, on forested hillsides—lips murmuring prayers through the brief nights. In years past, Dushuuw watched them go with no more than a passing thought, his mind intent on fall battle plans. Now, he was one of them, and at war with himself.

That his father had sent him to Eekbis for advice on spiritual preparation only rankled him further. He had never needed a shaman's spiritual guidance in preparing for battle; his physical training and capacity to endure pain were all he needed. What rituals did exist were opposite those for whaling—they weren't to get clean.

Dushuuw clenched and unclenched his fists. The shaman's slave flitted worried glances his way—as if he were a cougar poised to pounce—making it harder for him to concentrate on the shaman's words. Memories of the slave's fingers brushing his arm and her skin beneath his palm didn't help either. He heard about half the old woman's advice. Most of it seemed to line up with what he already had been attempting.

The next morning, Dushuuw trudged through the forest's damp edge without destination. After watching his brother trek up the mountain above the village, he decided to stay low. He traced the curve of the river at a distance, following no marked trail. Instead, he let the stiff stems of salal scrape his calves and thighs as he hacked them aside with a club, let the needles of nettle bite his ankles as he marched through them. These things had never bothered him. It was the silence that hounded; the silence—and the flies. A deer fly settled on his arm with a stinging bite and he slapped the spot.

Along the way, he marked guideposts for himself. First, a tree with a massive white mushroom bracketed to its trunk. Then, tucked into another tree, a leaf-lined cavity abandoned by nesting martens. Later, a dirt-encrusted wall of roots, dislodged from the earth some years ago when the spruce fell; fern and lichen made homes in its tangled mass that towered above his head. Finally, there was the large snag. Ragged at the top, it appeared to be a stump from the back side. But the other side gave way, retreating in on itself in a blaze of alternately scorched black and raw red bark. Dushuuw ducked inside and regarded the overarching boughs of living trees above, and the old, crude children's drawings. This would be his final marker. He exited, and cut a more or less straight path with his club to the river.

Burbling water greeted him. A thicket of moss-covered vine maple arched over the river's edge. Downed trees and drift logs clogged together nearby in a slick mound. The blockage had allowed water to pool. The surface of the pool was still, dotted by the feathery feet of water insects. Beyond, through the branches, mist drifted over the surface of the flowing river as the day started to warm. The shaman had mentioned clean water.

"As good a place as any," he mumbled.

Dushuuw patted the side of his leg with the club, then propped it against a log on the bank. Only his body as aid, the shaman had said.

"Well, now that that is done..."

The nettle stings around his ankles and on the arches of his feet started to needle their reminders. So did the growing number of insect bites. Dushuuw stepped into the pooled water. It lacked the cold bite of the sea. Trapped in the pool, the water here was warm. He felt a tickle and slapped his neck. He regarded the crushed mosquito on his palm as a dozen more descended on other parts of his skin. *Slap*. Another of the shaman's pieces of advice came to him.

"You help me deprive myself?" *Slap*. "How thoughtful..."

Dushuuw swiveled and fell backward into the pool. The rocks were slimy beneath his body. He sat up with a grimace, wiped his hands over his face, and flicked the water from his fingers. Sitting in the pool, he took a deep breath, and closed his eyes.

Water trickled over a nearby rock. The steady flow of the river droned. Beneath the pooled water, tiny fish brushed over his legs. Above, insects hummed. A light breeze shook the alder leaves. A sapsucker drilled. And away toward the sea, gulls squawked their greetings. The air was chill, and his breathing came slow, came easy, in, and out, in a rhythm, a lonely rhythm. And it came—as it always did now, but sooner this time—the heavy rhythm of his wife's pleasured breaths, beneath the thrusting arc of another man's body.

His eyes shot open, and he drove his fist into the water. A brown cloud plumed beneath the surface, shrouding his arm. Standing, water sliding off him in dripping sheets, Dushuuw told himself he trembled because of cold air on wet skin. His shoulders sank with the weight of four days stretching before him. He had dreaded one piece of the shaman's advice above the others—to go alone.

The insects finally prompted him to move. Itching hills of flesh dotted his skin. He dug a hole halfway into the water, shoving aside rocks. He coated himself with the mud, and found some relief. He settled against a log on the rocky shore beside his club and reminded himself that he did not care. That his talents as a warrior had not diminished. That he could at least use a paddle. That this idea of obtaining spiritual power was unnecessary.

"Greedy, even..."

A salamander sashayed over a rock, spotted him, and skittered back to its hole.

It was no good. He needed that elusive power. To protect his brother, above all. But also to have confirmation he belonged in that canoe, as his father and brother so staunchly insisted. He wanted to silence the gossips and have a taste of what blessed his father with wealth and his brother with... everything. But there was no hand appearing from the ground, no pool of cosmic sea foam, no indication at all that he was worthy.

Early on, Yaq tried to convince him his troubles really came down to sexual frustration. His friend roped him back into old exploits, finding their way past willing girls' skirts at the forested edges of the adults' feasts. And he had tried. In a low after a raid, he had forced himself to flirt with a girl who fancied him. He led her into the woods, slipped his hands over her skin, fondled her breasts, tasted the salt on her skin with his tongue, and took what she gave. But he did not do it again. He could only hear his wife's taunt in the woman's breaths. *End it...*

Not for the first time, Dushuuw wondered how his life might have fared if his mother had not died. He remembered her smile, but not her eyes. *Be stronger...* He was stronger than any man he knew. It didn't seem to make a difference.

Dushuuw slumped until his head rested on the log. His stomach growled its own complaints.

"Well, at least there is that," he mumbled.

Fasting made some things easier. Soon enough, he would put his worries to sleep with his body, to awake and try again.

~

Dushuuw returned hungry and ripped a piece of dried meat between his teeth. It was the winding-down time of evening in the great house. Some of the elderly were already asleep. A young mother sat on the floor weaving; she rocked her foot in an even rhythm, swinging her sleeping baby's suspended cradleboard by a string tied to her toe. Slaves were sent off on final errands. Q̇otsik was still up on the peak, praying. Dushuuw gave the tough meat an aggravated tug and it flew from his hand down the gap between the wall and his bench. With a grunt, he stretched his arm down the gap to retrieve the food to throw in the fire rather than attract pests. But his eyes were drawn along the wall to something else that lay in the dirt, behind the benches and storage boxes used by his father and brother.

Pieces of whaling equipment lay amid the bits of trash and forgotten toys. It was a dark spot, but the shadows could not hide the brown splatters of blood that still coated the yew wood shaft, the barb and the blade—even the prized sinew line. Dushuuw thought back to the moment when he had proudly placed the equipment back in his brother's hands. How Q̇otsik had received them quietly, chin held high. How he had basked in Q̇otsik's approval. And, now, how he had been utterly wrong.

Fog enveloped Chahdee but did little to obscure the island's vast bulk, rising out of the sea. The passage would have been ominous on a clear day. Amuun'axsum gripped the side of the canoe with one hand and held her supplies close to her chest with the other.

A raft of murres floated nonchalantly on the bobbing waves. Amuun'axsum glanced at the men working the paddles, alert but at ease. She wanted to trust their confidence, and the knowledge that people had been coming to this island ever since First Daylight. But with no beach in sight, she could not help worrying. Would they drive themselves into the rocks? Or would they pass straight through its mass, like the sea?

She had heard stories about the island from Uhpahs. Caves that went under the entire length of the main island, the sea rushing beneath, causing the earth to shudder. On top, salt-drenched earth, and winds so powerful that they could blow you straight off the edge. Hidden crags and gaping joints between rocky landmasses. Bloody tales from the past about invasion and war.

Uhpahs leaned against Amuun'axsum with an encouraging smile.

Amuun'axsum let go of the side of the canoe, embarrassed. She tried to exude calm like the seal hunter's wife in front of her. Still, she re-checked her basket of tools and drew it close again, as protective of its contents as the hunters were of their harpoons and giant halibut hooks. Inside her basket were the weaving tools and the surfgrass from the southern coast she had been waiting for. If there was time between helping with the halibut catch, she would continue weaving the hat for the chief's younger son. She had tried to leave it all behind, to prolong the work as well as to keep it safe. But the healer insisted.

Red plumes of kelp kissed the surface of the water as they neared the island. There was a beach, after all, tucked inside a cove of sorts. The men at the paddles, still unfazed, waited for the right moment. When the canoe lifted high on the crest of an incoming wave, the men propelled into the inlet, shouting, and ran the canoe up onto the sand. Amuun'axsum pitched forward at the abrupt landing, then sighed with relief that the journey was over.

Dozens of other canoes already filled the beach, most with plain hulls, others brightly painted. Many families came to Chahdee each summer. Others went to other summer encampments. They packed up their homes—from bed mats to the wall planks themselves—and ferried them off in large traveling canoes. Still others chose to stay in the permanent winter village sites and send along family members and slaves to shoulder the hard work. In Wuh-uhch, the whaling chief's wives were skipping Chahdee. The shaman had no reason to go, and claimed bones too frail anyway. But their slaves would contribute to the intensive labor. The work of summer would carry the village through winter. Work-filled days aside, Amuun'axsum and Uhpahs looked forward to weeks together, out from under the older women's noses.

Amuun'axsum tried to avoid running into anyone as she craned her neck to look this way and that. Butted up against the cliff were smokehouses, surrounded by tiny huts as well as canoes turned over for more expedient sleeping spots. Most of the houses and structures where people would sleep were located atop the island. A series of ropes led up a steep, winding incline to the island's wind-shorn top. Amuun'axsum was pushed along by the crowd that made its way to the path. Then Uhpahs's hand was at her elbow, pulling her aside.

"We will go up later," she said, setting their belongings aside. "For now, it's off to get dinner."

The women climbed over the sloping rocks and skirted the island, farther and farther, seeking a spot that wasn't already teeming with women. Their baskets flopped against their backs. Now and then, the sea crashed on the rocks beside them, spraying them with salty mist.

"You will learn the way the waves break here," Uhpahs said. "So that when there's a shift, you will know to look over your shoulder—or better, just start running. Even in areas that seem calm, you can be tasting saltwater pretty quick."

Amuun'axsum tightened her grip on her basket strap.

"Be careful to watch for floating debris out there, too. A drift log can get tossed up here and pin you as flat as a bottom-feeder," Uhpahs said, springing over a tiny chasm. "Of course, you might also want to keep an eye out above. Rocks are known to fall quite frequently. Watch in front of your feet for sharp rocks, sticks," she added, flicking one such roadblock aside with her foot. "And if you come across a fur seal, turn and leave. Those things can be nasty—and quicker than they look."

Amuun'axsum's head spun as she cataloged Uhpahs's warnings. Out to sea. Up the cliffs. Down to her feet. Over her shoulder.

Uhpahs stopped abruptly in front of her and turned.

"I was here one summer when a woman was caught by a wave that deposited her halfway up the cliff," Uhpahs said. "She clung to a ledge there all day before someone finally noticed she was missing. They found her, and put a rope down to haul her up, and she went back to work."

Uhpahs giggled and walked on.

Amuun'axsum remained rooted where she stood as she watched her friend patter over a narrow plank that spanned a wide surge channel. Uhpahs reached the sloping black rock beyond and looked back.

"Well, come on then," Uhpahs called.

Amuun'axsum took a step forward. The algae was slick beneath her feet. The water in the channel below boiled and surged. The bridge seemed as frail as a bird's bone.

"Careful you don't fall."

Amuun'axsum spun and saw a man smiling down at her. His face bore a long, old scar that cut across his eyebrow to his cheek. A small harpoon was strapped to his back.

"Fall into one of the crevasses here," he said, "and it's likely no one would hear your cries for help."

"Is this supposed to encourage me?"

He laughed. "No, but this is." He held out his hand for her basket.

Amuun'axsum eyed the bridge again. Her eyes traveled across it to Uhpahs, who beckoned her impatiently. Amuun'axsum's embarrassment overrode her fear, and she handed her pack to the man and stepped onto the bridge before doubts overcame her again.

"Nothing to it," he said. "One foot in front of the other."

After a hesitant first step, she skittered across. Safe beside Uhpahs, she blew a sigh of relief, and adrenaline pushed laughter out of her lungs. Uhpahs laughed with her.

The man was across before she caught her breath. "See? No death today." As he handed her the basket, their fingers brushed. Amuun'axsum's breath hitched for a moment, a memory of a man's touch on her shoulder wafting across her mind. Before she could respond, the man walked off with a smile to whatever task he had aimed for in the first place.

Uhpahs hooked her arm in Amuun'axsum's. "Come, brave friend."

The climb to the top of the island later was not as steep as it looked from below. Still, Amuun'axsum gripped the ropes tight and watched her feet. As she crested the edge, the wind sucked her clothing to her skin and blasted over her ears.

"We will have to walk a bit to a free shelter," Uhpahs said. "There's only one crevasse to steer clear of along the way—that I know about."

Amuun'axsum groaned and laughed at the same time.

Soon, they entered a small house that reeked of damp and guano. Amuun'axsum put a finger under her nose.

"Oh, do not worry. We will not be here often." Uhpahs gave a sarcastic laugh.

"Especially if we are kicked out." Amuun'axsum pointed to a corner.

A pair of crows shouted from around a nest. The nest was tucked into a corner of the house on the ground. Three nestlings craned their blue necks; the start of feathers poked through their wrinkled skin. The women called over a passing slave, and he prepared to take away the nestlings, which also would draw out the mother and father.

"Where will you put them?" Uhpahs asked.

"Toss them toward the edge, probably," he said. "Wherever I can dump them quick to avoid having my head pecked full of holes."

Uhpahs gave him a brief, apologetic smile.

"But won't the gulls kill the little things?" Amuun'axsum said.

The man shrugged. "These ones," he said, nodding toward the adult crows, "eat the gulls' children before they're even hatched."

The women unrolled bed mats to claim spaces.

"I saw your fisherman," Amuun'axsum said. "Has the vetch worked?"

Uhpahs gave a slight shrug. "Perhaps it is working even now. We shall see. With any hope, you will have to find another bed at least one night." Uhpahs gave Amuun'axsum's hand a gentle squeeze. "That is, if you don't claim the hut for some fun first."

Amuun'axsum threw off her friend's hand. "You know that will not happen," she said, though she found herself blushing. She pushed Uhpahs out the doorway into the summer day that was bright with sun and a blaze of green. "Now, how to get your mind off your man?"

This time, it was Uhpahs's turn to groan. "That is easy. Let me introduce you to our bottom-feeding friend the halibut—and all his many, many friends."

~

Amuun'axsum's gaze passed over the ogling eyes of yet another dead halibut. On the beach, she washed the wide body and wiped it with a fern. Then she hefted it onto a drying rack.

Chahdee was crowded, and it was easy to see why. There were abundant reasons to draw so many people to the island. Sea lions barked from their haulouts. Murres and cormorants fluttered off and back to their nests among the rocks. Each type of animal would feel a harpoon or arrow point over the summer. Sea lion was bitter to eat, but its hide was useful and the stomach made a prime storage container for oil. Sometimes their whiskers were used in dance headdresses. Bird bones were used for awls, fish hooks. Their feathers served many uses, and the meat was not so bad either. Some groups used Chahdee's beach as a closer base for whale hunts.

Yet for Amuun'axsum and Uhpahs, the primary reason for being on the island was halibut, and more halibut—and more halibut.

Dozens of other women labored in the same way. One man dropped off a load of the fish, only to soon be followed by another fisherman.

Off came the head. Then the tail. Amuun'axsum split the flat body in two and pulled out the back bone. Off came the skin. She filleted the flesh into thin layers, using a knife designed to cut again and again without gumming up. She placed the slices on a mat, placed another mat atop, and set a large rock over all, her biceps tightening into their own hard masses as she leaned into the rock here, then there, squeezing the moisture out in blooming splotches. When satisfied, she draped the fillets over a wooden rung to dry in the sea wind. At night, the racks would go into the smokehouses. In about three days, if the women were attentive, the white flesh would turn a golden tan.

They would save the skins to wrap the cured fish. The bones, heads, and tails would be dried for soup stock. Only the entrails were discarded, but even they helped by keeping the scavenging birds satisfied. Small boys practiced their shooting to scare off the more brazen fowl.

Soon, rack after rack was strung with hundreds of banners of halibut. The racks were set against walls. On rooftops. From a distance, the encampment appeared covered in snow.

Despite the fog that had blown in, Amuun'axsum's back dripped with sweat from the constant work.

Near day's end, she caught Uhpahs's attention. They smiled, as if they had both forgotten the other's existence in the litany of tasks.

"Shall we go up top and get some salmonberries?" Uhpahs said.

Amuun'axsum's mouth watered, her tongue craving the tart sweetness—or anything to replace the smoke and salt.

As they headed toward the uphill trail, mist dampened the tiny hairs on their arms. Amuun'axsum knuckled the small of her back.

Once again, they were greeted at the top of the island with a punch of wind. The friends found some stunted salmonberry. They drifted apart as they picked. Amuun'axsum filled her palm with the orange berries, then funneled them all into her mouth at once—only to cringe with surprise. They were coated in salt. Amuun'axsum choked the berries down as she turned to Uhpahs. A wide smile crossed Uhpahs's face as she tossed her uneaten berries to the ground, her laughter carried away on the wind.

Fog swirled, and Amuun'axsum's hair loosened further from its braid. Uhpahs's own hair tumbled about. Hitching elbows, the friends walked back to the cliff's edge.

DUSHUUW GAZED UP at the large mountain that loomed over the village on the shoreline. It surpassed Wuh-uhch's modest peak. It had been a long journey across the strait and tracing the large island's shoreline—all along the mountains on one side, the sea on the other. In the large traveling canoes, the children craned their necks, dusting off their sleepiness as they sensed their destination near at hand. The older villagers by contrast settled more deeply in their perches on padded thwarts, in anticipation of rest. They banged sticks on the hull to join the song of greeting. From the beach, women and men walked into the surf, singing their own song, confirming what already was communicated by their hands held open in welcome.

Protocol and pleasantries filled the allotted time, but already several households had started to gather with items for trade. The village's leading man of stature, Ḥawith, came to welcome them and take first barter. His hair was thick, though streaked with gray.

"I hope you are not here under false pretenses, to see only how good my salmon tastes," said Ḥawith, with a droll smile. "I assure you, the salmon here is terrible compared to that of our neighbors. You would be better off raiding there again, I should imagine. Although I hear perhaps your tastes have shifted to the salmon of the strait peoples." His gaze flitted to Dushuuw.

"We are known for our war clubs as much as our whaling harpoons," said Buhkweeduuk, gesturing to Dushuuw, then to Q̓otsik. "But the salmon supply at Wuh-uhch is sufficient."

Dushuuw wondered at the last statement. They had a river, and blackmouth salmon could be found there. But it was no great river.

"In fact," his uncle said, "we have food in such abundance that we are building a larger house to store it all this winter."

"And here I thought some had left your arm, Chahbuhṭ," Ḥawith said. He smiled, but held his head at an angle, waiting for a response.

"Rather, more are seeking to join him," Buhkweeduuk said. "They hear of our great young whaler." He put his hand on Q̇otsik's shoulder.

"Yes, I have heard." Ḥawith settled his eyes on Q̇otsik, then smiled. "Your reputation as one who can call whales even without harpoon in hand is well known here, Q̇otsik."

They traded their best items with Ḥawith. Then, at his uncle's invitation, Dushuuw helped set out baskets of dried halibut, boxes of oil, and large bundles of their local swamp grass for weaving, among other goods, to barter with the other households.

Ever since Dushuuw had accompanied his uncle on a big trading mission the previous summer, Buhkweeduuk had been giving him brief lessons in the art of trading. Dushuuw had only been brought along as extra muscle for the journey to the great southern trading market, located near a massive river a week's paddle or more down the coast. He remembered the exotic mix of smells and sights, so many languages crisscrossing each other. He had been hooked. And seeing his interest, his uncle had been eager to share what he knew about identifying partners, the art of haggling, honing the language of trade, and knowing when to pull back too.

Now, Dushuuw himself measured out whale oil using a pelican's beak. In return, he sought the local grasses for Wuh-uhch's weavers, extra strings of dentalia to supplement their more meager supply, and—for the steepest price, adding several boxes of dried halibut—a small pouch of opercula.

Beside him, Buhkweeduuk measured out oil as he bartered with another man about the return in slaves. Not liking what the man was offering, Buhkweeduuk shrugged his shoulders and turned away toward another household. The man quickly relented and called him back, and a deal in Buhkweeduuk's favor was sealed.

By a fire on the beach, and another inside the house, Chahbuhṫ and Ḥawith discussed a far different deal, but the most important deal of all.

Later there was a feast, and the Wuh-uhch families finished the night as guests rather than traders alone.

Um-iiqsu and Thluuch-muup sat with Ṫashii, Ḥawith's wife. The women were childhood acquaintances from neighboring villages, and they acted like girls once more. They lost themselves in fits of giggles and whispered gossip. Ṫashii brought over her daughters, Sawsin and Tluulth, who showed off their jewelry and basketry. In turn, Chaiyuhx-ik held out her cloak, lined with sea otter fur, to be petted.

Dushuuw walked over with a small bowl to where his brother sat. Qotsik rolled his own bowl between his palms, looking over the women. Platters of food circulated the house. Dushuuw scooped a bowlful of berries from a passing dish and sat beside Qotsik. "See something you like, brother?" He popped several of the berries into his mouth.

Qotsik startled at being caught, then smiled, cheeks warming. Dushuuw poured some berries into Qotsik's dish.

Beyond, in the cluster of women, Sawsin leaned forward to see past her sister, as if searching for something, though her gaze fell on Qotsik. Upon noticing Dushuuw watching, she spun back to the women.

"Looks like you are not the only one." Dushuuw nudged his brother. "Come. Let's go sit by the old men and fall asleep to their droning."

Dushuuw made sure they walked by Sawsin.

They joined the cluster of leading men and advisers. Their father and uncle chatted with Ḥawith about fishing runs, whaling, weather.

Dushuuw settled into a shadow against the wall. The conversations held no interest for him. He scanned the room, reflexively searching for his ex-wife's face even as he feared finding it among the crowd. She was from another village and was not here—his stepmothers had done some whispered reconnaissance—but still his eyes darted. He looked over at his brother, who also was barely engaged in the men's conversation. Instead, Qotsik's gaze continued to stray to the group of women.

"You have fought them back?"

The edge in their father's voice drew the brothers back to the older men's conversation.

Ḥawith took a bite of salmon as he nodded. "It has been a long time, but the northerners never stay away for long. We made our peace years ago, and it is quiet—yet too quiet. We have heard nothing from our women who live among them, carrying their loads or bearing their children—not in a long time."

"They have not come as far south as us in my time, but we have all heard the stories," Chahbuhł said. Chahbuhł looked at Buhkweeduuk, and something passed unspoken between the brothers. "You have our support," he said.

Ḥawith wiped his mouth with his fingers, a false smile playing beneath them. "I doubt it would mean much."

Chahbuhł bristled.

Buhkweeduuk motioned toward Dushuuw. "The cape has the region's best warriors. This one alone has taken hundreds of heads."

Dushuuw sat straight. Self-doubt plagued his mind—another

exaggeration among calculating friends—yet he met the local chief's appraising gaze.

Ḥawith squinted at him. "Perhaps we can test this some day," he said, his tone momentarily jovial. He turned back to Chahbuhṫ. "I know your peoples' way with the war club. Yet it is not your skill in battle that I question, but your ability to make it to the battle in time to make a difference. This is not one we would start. Not with the northerners."

The men were silent. Dushuuw thought of the day-long paddle to this village—even at a rapid pace it would take a good while. Laughter burbled up again from the women. Loud conversations came from other parts of the house. Platters were refilled and passed among the crowd.

"Well, we will hope your people get you the message ahead of time then," Chahbuhṫ said, "so that you also can get a message to us in time."

"And hope that the need never arises in the first place," Buhkweeduuk added.

Ḥawith wiped his lips, rubbed his palms together, and smiled broadly. "Or perhaps I will drop hints of some easy marks I know of a bit farther south."

The men laughed, and Dushuuw smiled to himself. It was a troubling thought—the idea of their village being attacked—but no one had dared invade their territory in generations. Most of the time, it was the cape warriors who brought the battle.

Ǫotsik shifted on the bench. Sawsin approached the men—her mother at her elbow—cradling a small basket in her hands.

"I thought Sawsin might show her work to our visitors," Ṫashii said.

Sawsin kept her eyes downcast, as was proper. But decorum could not dim her confident grace. Shells adorned her dress. Her face was bright with the heat of the house. Dark jagged lines ringed her wrist, echoing the innumerable mountains that watched over them all beyond the planked roof.

For the first time, Dushuuw looked over at the woman's younger sister, Tluulth, and wondered. The memory of a woman's smooth shoulder beneath his palm lingered. But the girl's skin was still bright around her tattoo, and he turned away.

"Meet my eldest daughter, my pride," Ḥawith said. "This is Sawsin."

Tluulth bounded up, eyes bright. An older woman scurried behind. Tluulth draped her arms around her father's neck. "And me, father."

"And my youngest daughter," Ḥawith said with begrudging bemusement. "This is Tluulth." He pulled her tight to his side and his smile turned genuine.

"Your joy," Tluulth finished.

"And as beautiful as her sister and mother," Buhkweeduuk said.

Tluulth looked miffed but had been raised well enough to avert her gaze. Dushuuw smiled in spite of himself, and her gaze suddenly found him in the shadows. He sobered and looked elsewhere. If she would not, he would have to.

Sawsin approached Buhkweeduuk, handing him the small basket.

Buhkweeduuk turned the small twined basket in his hands. Even from his seat against the wall, Dushuuw could make out the fine, tight weave, unlike any made by weavers in Wuh-uhch. Dyed grasses created geometric patterns around the bowl. In a dramatic flourish, Sawsin produced a lid from behind her back and placed it on top. A small spiraled shell served as a handle.

"Remarkable," Chahbuhⱡ said, leaning in close.

"Crafted by the hands of a master weaver," Buhkweeduuk agreed. He rotated his hand, eying the basket from several sides, before returning it to Sawsin, who looked at the ground but smiled broadly.

"Remarkable," Chahbuhⱡ repeated. He turned to Q̇otsik, whose eyes were on Sawsin rather than the basket. "Do you not agree, Q̇otsik?"

"She is amazing," Q̇otsik quickly answered, then flushed.

Sawsin's chin jerked upward as she looked at Q̇otsik. She blushed as she dipped her head again. No one's eyes but Chahbuhⱡ's were on the basket by that point. Sawsin's mother hurried her back to the other women, where Buhkweeduuk's wife Pikoo took a turn admiring the basket, her gaze intent, as if imagining what trinkets could be special enough to store within. Tluulth meandered after the women with her relieved chaperone.

Laughter and conversation filtered over the rest of a casual night.

Dushuuw watched his brother watch Sawsin. Worry tinged the edge of his mind at his brother's increasing lack of guardedness. Sawsin looked over her shoulder at Q̇otsik once more that night, and his brother sighed without thought. Dushuuw sensed Tluulth trying to catch his eyes in the same hidden way, so he avoided looking her direction at all. Instead, he studied the lines of Sawsin's shoulder blades, the straightness of her spine, searching for deception.

~

After the first night's festivities, Dushuuw had tried to disentangle himself from any expectations Tluulth might have formed. Yet it seemed he was unable to avoid the girl. Every time he looked off for something, she was there, waiting in his field of vision, smiling that knowing smile that knew nothing. Dushuuw was sure to pointedly turn his back to her each time. It didn't seem to help. In fact, it seemed to make things worse. Dushuuw hoped his brother soon achieved Sawsin's promise of marriage, before their family's lingering necessitated a second wooing.

Late each night, Q̇otsik had risen from his bed under their traveling canoe and sat outside a wall of Ḥawith's house—at the spot where he knew Sawsin's bed to be—and softly sang. Afterward, he would leave oil, dried halibut, and other valuable items outside the family's doorway. Yet each morning, the growing pile of gifts would still be outside, unmoved, gathering tiny dunes of windblown grit.

By the third night, all of the other guests who had filtered in and out for feasting and trading had left for their homes. Only the party from Wuh-uhch remained.

Q̇otsik sat hunched over beside a fire on the beach, rubbing the top of his nose as he waited for their hosts to retire to their beds to feign sleep. Dushuuw and Uhpqoolth kept him company. They were joined by their fathers. Q̇otsik seemed to take the older men's presence as reason to be worried. He stared at the fire, brow furrowed.

"Nephew, you look more worn out than after a week preparing for a whale hunt," Buhkweeduuk said.

Q̇otsik hunched over and rested his elbow on his knee. He dug his hand deeper into his hair. He looked up from his troubled reverie at his uncle. He tried to smile, then slouched and shook his head. He turned to Chahbuhł. "Was this what it was like to woo my mother?"

Dushuuw tried to disregard the sting of offense that, though not as intense, was still his first reaction to mentions of rank and their mothers. There had been no grand ceremony preceding Chahbuhł's union with Dushuuw's mother, whose family was of such low rank no exchange of wealth was necessary.

Chahbuhł surprised them both by laughing. "You have it much easier, my son," he said. He raised his eyebrows and shook his head. "My marriage to your mother was not arranged as most noble unions are. Not as we have done for you boys and all your sisters." The chief threw up his palms and shook his head. "Smitten," he said. "It is my only defense. She was a beauty, your mother. But I had to convince your grandparents that I was worthy of their daughter's hand. No easy task there. So I was outside her bed—like you have been—for ten long days."

A groan escaped Q̇otsik, and he buried his head in his hands.

Chahbuhɫ laughed. "Your mother always joked it was my stubbornness that finally made them give in; though, in truth, she had taken a fancy to me and convinced her parents I was a catch." The old chief's eyes sparkled. "I did marry above myself. And her union to me went a long way, I am proud to say, in helping our family rise—that access which our marriage brought me, some of the rights and privileges you have as a result." He grew thoughtful. "I eventually married her sister, too, to cement that access. Their father was a fair but hard man. And Thluuch-muup is special, above me in rank as well, I am sure. But," the chief said, looking at Ǫotsik, "your first wife is first in everything."

Dushuuw tried to squelch the twin sources of his anger—at his mother not even worth a side note, and at his own failed marriage. He tossed bits of wood into the fire, trying to calm himself.

Ǫotsik sat up, only to deflate with worry again. "Ten days, father?"

Chahbuhɫ waved his hand. "Do not worry."

"You have already won her," Uhpqoolth said. He sat bent with his arms on his knees and smiled easily.

Ǫotsik still looked nervous.

"As if she had any other choice," Dushuuw said. He had meant to add to the encouraging words, but his bitterness tainted them, twisting the meaning.

"A woman always has a choice," Chahbuhɫ said.

Dushuuw didn't look up, but felt cornered by the older men's gazes all the same.

"But you had no trouble, father. Your wives came to you, and stayed with you," Ǫotsik said, as if to reassure himself, oblivious to the tension.

Their uncle laughed.

Chahbuhɫ nodded at his brother. "Keeping the affections of your mother was little issue. But Thluuch-muup..." He blew out his mouth and raised his eyebrows, then leaned toward Ǫotsik. "You must please a woman if you wish to keep her, and do not think she does not work that to her advantage."

Dushuuw shifted to the edge of the log on which he sat.

"She will let you know what she requires, though you may have to hunt around a bit," the chief said. "And sometimes a marriage cannot be helped. I've known men whose wives left as soon as the wealth was exchanged that made the marriage official. Others become old and marry a woman too many years their junior, and she leaves for a younger man who can still satisfy. Other women who leave, it is a complaint that the husband spends more on the feasts than on her."

Even Q̇otsik cracked a smile at this one, knowing Thluuch-muup to fawn over their father whenever he bestowed some trinket—as he was sure to do with regularity.

But Dushuuw was done feigning mirth. He walked away.

He had not gone far, though, when he heard footsteps behind him.

"Wait up, brother," Q̇otsik called.

Dushuuw stopped only because it was his brother. Q̇otsik put a hand on his arm. "Please, come with me tonight," he said.

Dushuuw looked away for a moment. How could his brother ask this of him? But he followed.

They walked toward the shadowy form of the big house. They rounded the back corner, and the slosh of the sea and the rush of the wind were instantly muffled behind the cedar walls. The brothers sat outside Sawsin's living space. She was hidden behind the wall of overlapping planks. But one plank had been tied higher than usual, creating a small gap. Q̇otsik began to softly sing, but Dushuuw cut him off. He shook his head, and whispered in Q̇otsik's ear.

Q̇otsik sang anew...

i cannot forget you

you are in my mind

these words are my attempt to see you

He sang the song's repeating refrains, soft yet earnest. The way a man sings a song when it is the right song.

It was a song the boys had heard from their house corner often. Dushuuw's mother liked to sing it to herself—a reminder of the way their father had wooed her. It was one of the few things Dushuuw remembered of her. She was not carried in a canoe to her husband's doorway. She offered no alliance, no access to desirable hunting areas. She did not even own the right to a dance. Yet she was worthy of a song, composed in a burst of infatuation. She sang that song often, and Dushuuw now wondered just for whom the reminder was meant.

Q̇otsik softly finished the song and sat with his side pressed against the wall. He whispered with Sawsin through the chink in the wall. At a silent pause, Dushuuw gently thwacked Q̇otsik on the shoulder. He gestured toward the gap, stood, and turned to go.

As Dushuuw stepped away, he heard Q̇otsik take a breath. The sound of the loose board pushed higher. A feminine laugh. Dushuuw looked over his shoulder, saw Sawsin's hand reach through the gap to rest in Q̇otsik's hand. Q̇otsik leaned his forehead against the wall, and Dushuuw imagined Sawsin doing the same from the other side. He knew how smooth a noblewoman's skin felt—thin bones and veins forming ripples, a man's rough thumb rubbing over the soft skin like waves in ebb and flow.

It began to rain as he walked toward the canoes. The drops pattered the hull of the canoe he lay beneath. In time, they lulled him to sleep.

~

At dawn, Dushuuw came slowly awake. He rolled his head, stretching his neck. Above him, Ọotsik held out a hand to help him up. His brother was smiling. Dushuuw glanced over at the village's main house to confirm what he already knew. The pile of gifts was gone. In time, Sawsin's family would bring their own gifts that would equal or outshine what Ọotsik's family offered, and nearly all of that would be given away at the marriage feast. For now, everything was tucked away inside the house.

They entered the great house for a morning meal and farewells. Sawsin avoided looking at Ọotsik directly—at least, not too often—but a broad smile never left her face. Ọotsik barely ate, stealing glances at his beloved. His smile grew to a grin as Ḥawith and Ṫashii stood in front of their daughter and told him in mock disgust to come back later. By admitting they knew of his attentions, they gave their consent.

Outside, Dushuuw checked over their canoes. He made sure his father's pouch of opercula did not get crushed beneath the other goods. Then he looked out over the bright blue waters. If he closed his eyes, it felt something like Wuh-uhch. The sound of the surf. Salt on the tongue. The cries of gulls. These similarities were as much an affirmation of alliance as a bladder of oil, a bloodied club, a woman's hand.

People milled outdoors, though Sawsin and her sister were conspicuously absent. Ọotsik flitted glances to the house doorway so frequently that the local nobles took note. Dushuuw shook his head. His brother had the sickness bad.

Their father and uncle were caught up in conversation with Ḥawith and other men near the house. Dushuuw knew another payment of goods had been given toward Ḥawith's bride price for Sawsin. He wondered how long it would go on—year after year, as sometimes happened? He wasn't sure he would be able to bear that much pining from his lovesick brother.

Nearby, Ṫashii and his two stepmothers had one last conversation. Dushuuw set down the box, worked up some courage, and approached the noblewomen.

Ṫashii eyed him inquisitively.

"May I present you with an offer?" he asked.

His uncle cast a look in their direction.

After some awkward pleasantries, Dushuuw promised to procure for Ṫashii a basket's worth of the clover available only from Chahdee, some prepared beauty treatment, another skin of whale oil, a basket of dried halibut, and a full basket of Wuh-uhch's renowned ocher—all in return for a few of Sawsin's artful baskets. Ṫashii looked away, as if to consider, but more to hide her pleasure. Dushuuw glanced at his uncle, and noted Buhkweeduuk's worry. Dushuuw was giving away far more than the market would say the baskets were worth, no matter how gorgeously wrought. As the woman pretended to consider, Dushuuw gave a pointed look in Ọotsik's direction, then looked back at his uncle. Buhkweeduuk quietly laughed. He slid Dushuuw a look of approval as he returned to his conversation. Dushuuw let a smile brush his lips as Ṫashii acquiesced to the deal and brought the offer to her husband.

The deal in product was made—and Dushuuw managed to gain the unspoken part of his deal, as well.

As he pulled out the promised goods from the canoe, Dushuuw patted his brother on the back. "Look behind you, brother, and enjoy the sights one last time, hey?"

Ọotsik looked at him quizzically, then turned—and grinned. Sawsin stood in the doorway. She wore a cedar dress, pinned at one shoulder, leaving her other shoulder and arm exposed. She did not wear the jewelry she wore at the feast, though her beauty did not require such help. She handed off three of her baskets to her mother, as agreed upon. As her mother walked back toward the men's canoe, though, Sawsin lingered under Ọotsik's gaze. After a time, she tipped her chin and glided back into the shadows. Dushuuw slapped his brother's shoulder again.

Dushuuw held the tiny basket Sawsin had shown his family their first night, about to pack it with the others, when Buhkweeduuk called him over. Dushuuw strode over to where his uncle stood with his father and Ḥawith.

"Your uncle tells me that you did well at the southern market last summer," Ḥawith said.

Dushuuw kept his eyes on the basket and shrugged away a nervous twitch. "I enjoyed it. I would love to return." He spared a quick glance at his uncle, who smiled encouragingly. "I have much to learn from my uncle. I am thankful so many of our own words are at the root of the trade language."

Ḥawith waited to hear more. Dushuuw's father was equally still. Buhkweeduuk angled his head, encouraging Dushuuw to continue.

Dushuuw cleared his throat, heart pounding—but with more than nervousness. "There is more to learn in barter, and how to better steer it," he said. The conversations he had with his uncle churned in his mind. "Demand grows for dentalia. A trader there had tattoos on his arm to measure off the different lengths. 'So I won't get cheated,' he says." The men laughed, but Dushuuw shook his head. "Dentalia is the definition of wealth. And it comes from our shores."

Ḥawith nodded and gestured toward the large bay. Men in canoes lowered long poles, one after the other—one pole lashed to the next as they descended farther and farther—until the specialized spear reached the sandy depths. "You will not get better quality dentalia than here."

Dushuuw glanced around at the men. "We coastal peoples dictate the direction of trade over thousands of miles with a thin shell. I wonder if we can leverage that advantage even more. They talked at the southern market about an even grander market in the far interior, up their river, where all this dentalia floats. And from there, even farther, to places we can only imagine. I think there is more we can get for the other goods we offer—not just canoes, oil, slaves." Dushuuw ran his finger around the lid of Sawsin's basket. "There could be many beautiful pieces of your family's artistry turning up in a round tent surrounded by nothing but grass."

Ḥawith laughed. Dushuuw's finger paused on the basket.

"What did I tell you?" Buhkweeduuk said.

Dushuuw's father squinted, as if considering something new.

"I think you still have a lot to learn," Ḥawith said, putting a hand on Dushuuw's shoulder. "But I will enjoy having you visit more often." They started walking toward the canoes. Ḥawith shook his head in thought. "Nothing but grass. Can you imagine?"

"And yet they still wrap their feet," Buhkweeduuk noted.

"You have heard about the herds of animals they hunt—I forget the name," Dushuuw said. "But I felt its fur on one of their robes. You have seen it? Heavier than that of a bear. The man said it was only a third of a hide, and the animals are hard to kill. He was quite proud of this."

"I have seen this, too," Ḥawith said. "I have one such hide in my collection, and it is quite impressive."

"I told him one thing," Dushuuw said.

"Oh?"

"It's no whale."

AMUUN'A͟XSUM GRAZED her fingers over an anemone, smiling as its soft arms clamped around her skin, thinking it prey.

In the late-afternoon fog, she and Uhpahs sat eating a meal overlooking a still pool of water left behind by low tide. The ocean surf crashed in the distance. The pool was calm. It was only when Amuun'a͟xsum withdrew her hand that the surface rippled.

All around them were rocks that for most hours of a day were underwater, battered by the sea. Now, once-flowing strands of green-brown algae lay plastered against the base of rocks, giving way to broad splotches of red algae farther up and knobby green bladderwrack. Higher still, the rocks were capped by hard white barnacles and jagged spires of black mussels. It was the world in colorful miniature, from sea to mountaintop.

The women had filled their gathering baskets. Around them, others continued to gather mussels, or dig on the beach for steamer and butter clams. The shrill *wheep-wheep* of an oystercatcher carried over the sounds of the surf. The bird stabbed its red beak at a limpet.

"Have you had a chance to get intimate with your man?"

Uhpahs talked around a mouthful of halibut. "I do not even know if he likes me."

"So that would be a 'no,'" Amuun'a͟xsum said.

Uhpahs finished her bite. "There has not been much opportunity—as you have seen."

"So 'not yet,'" Amuun'a͟xsum teased.

Uhpahs looked away, but then inclined her head. "Maybe."

Amuun'a͟xsum looked back down into the pool as she ate. Purple urchins left grazing marks. Green anemones opened like flowers. Starfish lined the rock walls by the dozens—orange, purple, yellow—hovering above bright pink hydrocoral, red-brown sponges, and the purpled skeletons of coralline algae. Color reigned and revealed a world as malevolent as a rainbow. At the water line, an orange starfish hungrily wrapped itself around a mussel.

"Your tryst is bound to happen," Amuun'axsum said, wiping her fingers on her skirt. "And then I will be without a friend, for she will spend all her time with her husband making babies, all of them demanding her attention."

"Is that what you think? It is enough to hope for a bit of a fun tussle," Uhpahs said. "Marriage? I can only dream."

"Why should that be?"

"For one, he is above me. Would he want to marry a slave? For another, he would have to ask permission anyway. I have been at Thluuch-muup's side since I was a child—I know what she prefers, what she abhors—and I do not see her allowing me to move from that bed near her hearth any time soon."

Amuun'axsum snorted and shifted to a higher rock nearer her basket. "So, she is selfish and lazy. Is that it?" She rested her hand on the basket's rim. "I have seen slave women with children in tow. If you are so desirable, it seems Thluuch-muup should at least allow you to breed."

Uhpahs had been rinsing her hands in the pool. Now she flung the water up at Amuun'axsum's shins.

"You actually wonder why, at times, I am as bitter toward you as the others, Quulthoo?" Her voice was loud, and she looked at Amuun'axsum with equal parts wonder and anger. "You would think of me that way? As nothing more than a dog—useful for its fur, for its litter?"

Amuun'axsum's shoulders slumped and she looked away. She gripped a cold mussel inside the basket.

"At least I accept that I may not have a proper husband," said Uhpahs, standing up and hoisting her own basket. "Unlike someone else, who will still be saving her body for a man she does not deserve until she is a shriveled old woman. The kind of man who would never want her, because she is a slave."

Amuun'axsum hurled the shellfish toward the sea. Uhpahs marched away. Amuun'axsum looked up to the sky in an effort to send her tears back inside her eyes, regret and anger making their competing claims. An eagle soared over her head, a murre chick in its talons.

The water in the pool started to pulse. The sea was creeping back.

A starfish's arm reached out and touched the edge of an urchin, but it was too late—in its hunt, the starfish had chased the urchin straight into the waiting mouth of a giant green anemone. Amuun'axsum pulled her basket close, as a cold wind built with the rising tide. The anemone curled its tentacles inward with its paralyzed meal, and the starfish instead turned its attention to a pair of sea snails. Amuun'a̱xsum stood and turned away from the pool, not waiting to see how that chase would end, when the pool itself was submerged once more.

~

Songs filled the house where the summer village's highest-ranked residents packed themselves for a bit of entertainment.

Fires dotted the ground outside the house for those who could not fit inside but who wanted to listen. Amuun'a̱xsum joined one of the groups. Uhpahs was presumably asleep back at their own shelter, away from the ruckus. Or perhaps finally getting her dalliance.

Amuun'a̱xsum watched the comings and goings. The chief's youngest son, Dushuuw, laughed with his friend Yaq as they elbowed their way inside the house. The pair had spent a day off Chahdee fishing. Amuun'a̱xsum cringed again at the sight of the shabby appearance of the nobleman's hat. She wished she had brought her weaving to work on beside the fire after all, but the thought of going back near Uhpahs at this moment made her content to fold her hands instead.

"Another day put to rest."

A man slid down beside her, seeming to draw the warmth of the fire with him. Amuun'a̱xsum recognized him from her first day at Chahdee.

"Let me see if I remember," she said. "Your name is Ṫoopuuk?"

"Very good," he said. "I, on the other hand, have found out enough about you from your friend to know *not* to say your name."

Amuun'a̱xsum blanched, and wondered what else Uhpahs had told him. But his mood remained jovial, and so she pretended to be the same.

"I see you got over your fear of bridges," he said.

"Yes, I have not died yet," she quipped.

Ṫoopuuk held his hand out. She cupped her hand and caught the tiny waterfall of red huckleberry, blueberry, and blackberry.

"Deeyuh's finest berries," he said. "A little soft now, but still tasty."

"No salt? Then they are the best," she said with a laugh, thinking of the island's berries. "And what brings you from Deeyuh to Chahdee?"

"Mostly seals and halibut. Whatever task my chief assigns me. Mostly, I guard his back—except, of course, when it is a select crowd." He gestured toward the house, then tipped his head back and funneled the rest of the berries into his mouth.

112

Behind them, the drum beats and the calls of the singers grew louder and faster. Amuun'axsum imagined the dancers spinning.

A coal popped in the fire before them as a man pushed at the logs with a stick. Ťoopuuk stood and walked over to grab another length of driftwood to add to the fire. The flames leaped.

He glanced at her as he circled back. She quickly turned her attention to the berries still in her hand, slipping a huckleberry into her mouth. Ťoopuuk sat in the scrub and leaned against the log on which she sat, near her leg. He stretched his feet close to the fire. His face glowed in the warm light.

"Did you get that scar while defending your chief?" she asked.

He turned and looked up at her. The pale line of the scar faded into shadow, and the firelight no longer danced in his eyes.

"Tlukwaali judgment some years ago," he said.

"Did you lie?"

Ťoopuuk slowly shook his head.

Amuun'axsum slid the rest of the berries into her mouth, then drew her cloak tight and held it there.

"You really want to know?" he asked.

She hesitated, then nodded.

He tapped her leg with the backs of his fingers. "Killed someone."

"And that is all they did to you? Scarred you?"

Ťoopuuk was pleased by her reaction. He was toying with her. He flicked a coal back into the fire ring with his toe.

"No, it was for a lie, as you guessed," he said. "I hid some of my catch for myself. Although another slave was similarly charged alongside me. He was held down by four young men. His mouth was forced open, and an awl was inserted that a strong man pounded through his head to the ground. His blood pooled all about like a little lake."

Amuun'axsum knew he was giving her all the details, and perhaps embellishing them, to spark a reaction. Still, she shuddered. "What a mercy, to only be scarred. Thanks to your former rank?" she said. Nobles captured into slavery often retained a modicum of respect, if only for their potential monetary value in ransom. Scarred slaves like Amuun'axsum—whose noble status had been rejected—were the exception rather than the rule.

"No, not rank," Ťoopuuk said. "I am the lowest of the low: slave, born of slaves." His lips parted in a soundless laugh at her expression. "That other man was worthless. Me, I am good for many things."

Ťoopuuk turned his attention back to the fire.

Amuun'axsum tried to keep her attention on the other conversations that carried on without them around the fire. But her attention kept flitting back to his joyfully smug demeanor. She sighed loudly, but he did not bother to look over. Finally, she settled onto the ground beside him. It was warmer there, near both him and the fire. She looked at his profile and waited. "Well?"

Ṫoopuuk glanced at her in feigned query.

"What kinds of things can you do as a slave, that you would be treated so lightly?"

Ṫoopuuk leaned toward her and grinned. "You can come to my bed and I can show you one of them."

Amuun'axsum blushed furiously and looked away.

He leaned closer. "Maybe it was a noblewoman who saved me." His breath was hot on her neck.

It took everything in Amuun'axsum not to give him the satisfaction of pulling away. Instead, she looked him straight on. "You speak too boldly," she said.

Ṫoopuuk laughed loudly, and a few conversations paused around the fire as others regarded him briefly. He ran his hand over his mouth and dipped his head toward her again. "Says the woman with empty holes in her nose and ears." He drew up a knee, dangling an arm over it. "Maybe other places, too...?"

Amuun'axsum shifted away. "You *are* the lowest of the low."

"And the happier man for it," he said, his tone softening.

"Happier—when any day it could be the awl through your throat?"

"All men die someday. And not quietly, if they are men."

Amuun'axsum looked up to the cloud-shrouded moon. Inside the house behind them, someone was singing—it sounded like the chief's son. She turned toward the house. But the words and the voice were indistinct behind the walls and under the wind.

Ṫoopuuk drew closer.

there is too much forest here

Amuun'axsum smiled as he softly sang in her ear, thinking about the nearly tree-less island.

there is too much forest

She turned toward his voice, soft and sincere.

there is too much forest
between you and I
and I must see you

She blushed as he edged closer and sang through the song again. He kept angling his body to look her in the eye, and gauge her expression, but she dodged his gaze—not wanting him to see how the melody, and his attention, pleased her in a way she could not suppress.

The song ended and Amuun'axsum bit her lip as she felt his regard. Their bodies nearly touched, and Amuun'axsum was acutely aware that they did not.

"Let those men think their songs mean something more than mine," he said, his voice low. "But do they even know what they sing? Words so old they've lost their meaning. But my song is for a moment, for the living, for the present in which we breathe and move and work and—"

Amuun'axsum grew cold even as he drew closer. "You are wrong." She faced him. "They know. And those songs—they mean everything."

He would scoff at her now, and this confusing encounter would be over. But Toopuuk looked concerned. And he brushed a finger over the broken lines on her wrist. Somewhere along the way, the wrap that hid her tattoo had fallen away.

"I am not like you," she said, voice catching as she clutched her wrist.

Toopuuk did not laugh this time. He rubbed the back of his neck.

"No, you are not like me," he said, with a shy smile. "You are better than me, I am sure. And I do not lie to beautiful women." He reached out and ran the back of his finger down the curve of her face from her eyebrow to her cheek, a whispering touch that nonetheless sparked the heat of a knife's cut. For an exhilarating moment, Amuun'axsum found herself wanting to lean in to the touch. He seemed to wait for it.

Instead, Amuun'axsum fumbled up and stepped over the log. The world snapped back into focus. People chatting and drums beating and the chief's son singing and the wind whistling. After walking a bit, she dared to glance over her shoulder. Toopuuk had not followed her, and she sighed, though whether in relief or disappointment, she was unsure. In the building wind, though, the cool air seemed not to touch where he had stroked her face.

She wove between fires, the flames spinning and diving in the wind. Inside their shelter, Uhpahs was asleep, alone. Sheltered by the walls, their small fire burned low. Amuun'axsum sat on her bed mat and regarded her scarred, fading, unfinished tattoo. She took a new strip of cedar from her basket of weaving supplies and re-wrapped her wrist, around and around.

Twisting pain swirled inside her, like a storm, like a monster. Maḥtii wrapped her arms around herself, as if she could hide the pain and make it disappear. This was the passage to becoming a woman? This is what she had to endure before she could receive the name of Amuun'axsum?

Maḥtii shifted on the cushion of tree limbs and moss, refusing anymore to look at the thick globules of blood they soaked up. Her back was against the wall, her knees drawn up to her chest. Her feet started to tingle again from the long hours she had kept this position. It was the second day, and her mother said there likely would be two more days. Four days on her passage to becoming a woman. Why had she thought it so desirable before? Her stomach clenched again. She cried in spite of the sand-like feeling in her throat, or maybe because of it, or maybe causing it.

Her mother crept into the enclosure frequently to massage her feet and legs, to tip drinking water into her mouth. A couple times a day, she would wrap Maḥtii in a long cloak and take her to where she could relieve herself and where she could bathe.

"I am hungry," Maḥtii said.

"You know you must fast," her mother answered, even as she tucked a tiny piece of dried fish into Maḥtii's mouth.

Maḥtii barely chewed. She groaned and tipped her head back against the wall. Her mother slid a strand of hair off her face, tucking it behind her ear.

"This will happen every cycle of the moon?"

"Yes, but you only have to sit this way this first time."

"It hurts."

"It will not hurt so much after this. You will recognize the pain, and as you come to know it, it will be easier to bear."

"Does it hurt like this when you push a baby out?"

Her mother bit back a laugh. "That hurts far worse, my love."

Maḥtii bit back sobs that turned into whines.

"Compose yourself, my daughter," her mother said.

Another old woman entered, another in a flickering parade of faces Maḥtii would not remember, nor the words they sang. She pressed her lips together, watched their veined feet, and pretended to listen.

~

The bleeding stopped, and she felt drained.

The morning of the fifth day was a blur of preparations with moments of shocking clarity. As she set foot into the creek, the cold reverberated up her body. Two slave girls helped her crouch until the currents curled around her chest, the moving water finding its way into the hidden folds of her body as the older women scrubbed her with fern leaves. Her skin felt new.

Dried and wrapped in a fur-lined cloak, they plucked stray hairs and thinned her eyebrows. They worked soothing tonics and extracts into her face, her neck, her arms, her legs, her stomach. They braided her long hair into two thick plaits, then rolled each braid up to her shoulders, securing them with bands of cedar. The hair bands were embellished with dentalia and fringed with trailing strings of still more of the precious shells. Her mother brought in a woman who pricked her arm with bone, over and over, droplets of blood merging in wave-like lines. The tattooist rubbed a black substance into the wounds, leaving a permanent mark that would be added to later by a man more skilled in the art. Another woman pierced Maḥtii's nose for a bone ornament, and her ears for dangling discs of abalone—an extravagance—the way a chief's daughter should look when she is ready to be courted.

Maḥtii held herself erect as her mother examined her. She felt different, more substantial. Her braided and rolled hair weighed on her shoulders. Her ears and nose throbbed and seemed to announce themselves with the addition of ornament. The fresh tattoo around her wrist glowed red, and she was aflame, filled with the heat of pride.

Her mother nodded her approval and smiled, a smile that faded as she cupped Maḥtii's cheek in her hand.

They walked back to the house. Maḥtii felt taller. She relished the gazes of the other villagers as she walked with her mother out of the trees, across the beach, toward their doorway that faced the sea. She was a woman now, nearly her mother's equal. She wished her father were here to see her and not out trying to find a trading partner. Gray clouds wafted high in the sky. A raindrop fell on Maḥtii's nose, and then she was ushered across the threshold.

Instantly, her stomach rumbled, as the warm scent of flaked fish wafted to her nose. She looked over at the hearth fire in her family's corner, where her mother's slave man crouched with a platter in his hands. A slave woman slipped cooked food onto the platter, and Maḥtii eyed the fish greedily. The man looked over his shoulder at her, and stood, his head tilted in consideration. He smiled at her mother, then turned his attention back to Maḥtii and walked up with the plate of food. He held it out for her to examine.

"I thought the young lady might be ready for some of her favorite foods, if they are still her favorites," he said. He paused and looked to her mother, as if to ask for the approval for which he had not waited.

Maḥtii cared only for the food. Arrayed on the platter were her favorites—smoked bass, seal oil for dipping, and a bowl of fresh berries whipped to a froth with water and eulachon grease. She bounced at her knees like a girl. Maḥtii turned and deflated at the look of concern her mother gave the man. "Oh mother, I am allowed to eat now...?"

Her mother blinked and turned to her, and then flashed a smile. "Of course, my love," she said.

The slave man led Maḥtii over to the fire, where she sat on a fur-lined bench. He held the platter for her as she ate one bite, then a larger hunk, and more. Maḥtii felt she should let her mother eat as well, but her hunger knew no propriety. She licked oil from her lips.

"Are you still hungry?" he asked. "Shall I catch you some fish?" Maḥtii felt heady but nodded.

Her mother took his place on the bench beside her. "Give the first fish you catch to me when you return, then go out and catch more for our supper. I will serve my daughter," her mother said.

"Of course, my lady."

Maḥtii sighed and giggled at the same time, and tipped her head onto her mother's shoulder.

"I feel much better."

Her mother reached around her and brushed her hand up and down Maḥtii's arm. "Good," she whispered. She stroked Maḥtii's arm, up and down, up and down, up and down.

Maḥtii was asleep before the man returned from trolling, and not even the smell of cooking bass made her wake.

~

"Do you want to play?" Tiichswii asked.

The boy's hair was a familiar riot around his face, his smile expectant. A toy canoe dangled loosely by its bow from his finger. He rapped the side of his leg with a carved whale. The toys had long been key elements of the friends' ongoing storytelling game.

But things were different now.

Maḥtii felt the eyes of the other girls on her, and the old woman minding them at the forest's edge.

"Go away, Tiichswii," Maḥtii said.

The boy's smile faltered.

Maḥtii seized on his sorrow, pouring in her own. "I am a woman now. You are a boy. Go away, and play with your toys." She instantly regretted the words. After hesitating a moment, she shoved her carved bear at him. "You may have my bear. I do not need toys any longer." Yet her gaze lingered on her companion of so many years.

Tiichswii looked angry for a moment, then hurt. He turned and walked away. She watched him move through the forest toward their village, noting the firmness that had come to his shoulders and arms—a change she had not noted before—and feeling sad. Tiichswii did not turn back once.

When she went to her bed later that night, her bear lay there, resting atop a fern leaf.

The life of a woman is lonely, she soon learned, and lonelier still for one like herself. Propriety had reduced Maḥtii's circle of friends to two young women her age. One or the other of the girls would accompany her for short bursts of time, but mostly they bathed together at their removed beach, or replaited each other's hair, or sat weaving or cooking in their own houses. Maḥtii looked from afar at Tiichswii, who was free to run about where he pleased and get dirty. Sick of weaving, and angry, Maḥtii took to following an older woman from her mother's home village. Maḥtii shadowed along, until the woman smiled and bid her closer. Over the ensuing weeks the woman taught Maḥtii what she knew about the mundane and hidden things of the forest.

Sometimes they simply walked. "Listen to the wind in the trees." And Maḥtii would close her eyes and hear the sighing of a bough, the swish of a twirling leaf. They crouched by the edge of a stream. "Listen to the water talk." And as the breeze danced across her cheeks, Maḥtii listened to bubbles burbling high, others low, and still others all in between, like a house full of people.

The woman painted her face in particular patterns. Demonstrated how to properly bathe. The woman taught Maḥtii how to make herself ready for the things she would take from the earth.

Sleep was elusive, the night achingly short. Soon, Uhpahs was nudging her awake. Groggy, Amuun'axsum followed her friend outside, blinking at the daylight. There were no words about their spat. They did not talk at all. The women simply stayed at each other's side that day on the beach to wash, cut, fillet, hang. To sea's edge, into smoke, and back to the edge. Over and over again.

Throats raw, the pair took a break and climbed to the top of the island. Over several weeks, this high perch had become a strange source of solace. The wind was always strong, forcing down growth; the women often had to walk hunched over, past spindly trees, flattened patches of grass and clover. But it was as if focusing on walking a straight line helped push aside thoughts of their aches.

Thick walls of fog started to roll in from open ocean. The chill breeze that fronted them slinked over Amuun'axsum's shoulders. Fishermen hurried back in their canoes from the halibut banks. The time to descend had come. There was work to do.

Amuun'axsum closed her eyes for a moment, listening to the hollow tunneling of the wind, the muffled barking of seals and cries of gulls, and to Uhpahs's faint laughter which could be within arm's reach or on the other side of the island. The wind pushed and pulled, tracing its cold fingertips over her face. Standing there, vision dark, her skin prickled. She took the wind's breath deep into her lungs, curled her toes over scrappy bits of clover.

As she opened her eyes, she turned and looked off to the mainland. Against its backdrop, Uhpahs waved from a distance, seeming to stand at the very edge of the cliff—as if, with one tiny step, she would tumble into abyss. Amuun'axsum looked beyond her friend to the rocky and forested cape that grew dark with the approaching fog.

11

IT WAS NIGHT, and the young men's voices and bursts of laughter felt intimate in the canoe that floated on the bay.

A clouded sky shut out the moon and starlight. Rain fell in the wake of a passing storm. A fire burned atop a sand-covered board in the stern, sending flickering light across the smiling faces of the men surrounding Dushuuw. Then a duck squeaked in the dark, and the men hushed, or at least muffled their laughter. Yaq raised a mat behind the fire, cloaking the men in darkness.

The canoe coasted into the congregation of ducks and gulls that floated on the sheltered waters of the bay. When the firelight reached them, the waterfowl blinked and instinctively swam into the shadow cast by the mat, their tail feathers wagging.

Dushuuw and Uhpqoolth together readied a heavy net. The large swath of fine mesh was stretched between two long poles. Dushuuw's smile lay frozen on his face as he held his breath, holding one of the heavy poles aloft as they waited for a few more fowl to swim within reach. The birds' wings agitated as they swirled in a mass. Q̇otsik tapped their shoulders, and Dushuuw and Uhpqoolth reached out with the poles and thrust the net down over the gathered flock. The panicked fowl poked their heads through the holes in the mesh—and were trapped. Yaq pulled the mat back down, sending firelight over the panicked mass of thrashing birds.

Dushuuw shared a satisfied smile with his cousin.

"As fun as you remember?" Uhpqoolth asked.

"Yes, surprisingly enough."

The impromptu hunt had been spurred by Q̇otsik as the storm waned. During such storms, birds often settled on the bay's waters for shelter. Q̇otsik had grabbed Dushuuw, then hauled him around to the other houses to gather up the other young men from the whaling crew.

They pushed through the wind to their uncle's house, and grabbed Uhpqoolth. Then they had gone to grab Yaq—"Yes! You are saving me from death by boredom"—as well as Huh-uuk—"I am hungry, now that you mention it"—and finally, after nearly giving up the search, they found Kweelthup as he emerged from the forest. The young man cringed as he adjusted the hat on his head, but gave a nod.

"I knew you wouldn't be too serious to agree to come," Yaq crowed, and threw his arm over Kweelthup's shoulders as he steered him toward the bay. "And it's good, because we cannot pull this off unless we have the man who has a *tume·nuwis* for seeing in the dark."

Kweelthup murmured something in response, too low for Dushuuw to hear other than to get the impression that it was a firm correction.

"Yes, yes, all right, a 'talent,' then," Yaq said. "A talent for seeing in the dark."

Kweelthup protested again. Yaq stopped and threw up his arms.

"You mean to tell me you cannot see in the dark?"

Kweelthup turned to Yaq and started to launch into a low discourse—the most he had said in one stretch in moons—then caught himself. He walked on. Yaq laughed at his victory, and Dushuuw slapped his friend's back in congratulations.

Kweelthup lived in the great house, though he was not kin, taking up residence beside his father, the elder whaling chief's speaker. Though they shared a roof, Dushuuw knew the man's children better than he knew Kweelthup. Quiet and reserved, Kweelthup was easy for Dushuuw to overlook. He had always thought the man too soft, too weak. After sharing a thwart with Kweelthup in the whaling canoe, however, Dushuuw had started to take more notice. And he was beginning to understand why Q̇otsik valued the man's presence in the canoe. Kweelthup didn't often speak, but he was always watching, observing—and that was most evident on the rare occasions he did choose to speak.

Now, Kweelthup took the end of the net pole for Dushuuw, and Dushuuw smiled his thanks.

Dushuuw and Uhpqoolth wrung the trapped birds' necks.

As they handed the birds to others, a gull flew out of the darkness, skimming the air over their heads. A moment later, Uhpqoolth exclaimed in disgust.

Huh-uuk took one look at Uhpqoolth and started belly-laughing. Uhpqoolth cringed as a thick slick of white excrement oozed down his arm. Dushuuw and Yaq burst into laughter too. Q̇otsik tried to hold back a laugh, but it snorted out. Kweelthup kept silent, but a wide smile crossed his face. Uhpqoolth shot looks at them all, his hands askance.

"You could lick it off," Yaq said with a laugh.

"Stop."

"No, really," Dushuuw said. "I've heard seagull shit has healing properties."

"Stop."

"Oh, come now," Q̇otsik said, his tone coaxing.

Uhpqoolth ignored him, looking straight at Dushuuw. "I suppose you should know."

Dushuuw chafed at the reference to his ex-wife's apprenticeship.

Q̇otsik put a hand on Uhpqoolth's clean shoulder. "Enough. Here." He scooped seawater with a bailer and emptied it on their cousin's dirtied arm.

Kweelthup busied himself with the fowl, mostly ducks and one gull.

Huh-uuk took up a paddle. "Well, let's go roast these dumb birds."

On the way back, everyone remained quiet but Yaq, who flitted from one joke to the next. Q̇otsik's expression was as straight as his posture, and Uhpqoolth's brows remained drawn. Dushuuw caved, countering his friend's bawdy ditty with one of his own. By the time they got to shore, even Uhpqoolth cracked a smile. More important to Dushuuw, Q̇otsik's eyes were alight again.

They hauled up the canoe and set it upside down above the tide line. Yaq and Huh-uuk swung the birds by their legs as they all headed to a large bonfire.

Older men sat on drift logs ringing the fire. A couple of them deftly removed the stiff outer feathers of the birds. The feathers fell to the ground and a breeze sent them skipping and rolling into the darkness like sparks. The men dipped the birds in a box of heated water to loosen the rest of the feathers. When ready, they skewered each bird from neck to groin and held them near the fire. Soon, the mouth-watering scent of crisping, oily skin permeated the air.

Q̇otsik had taken a spot next to their father and spoke to him in fervent whispers. The young whaler's hand moved through the air to underscore some point. The other young men goofed off.

Dushuuw pondered his brother's stubborn efforts to fit him into the whaling crew. Men groomed from birth to unflinchingly sever heads did not make friends easily, if at all. From a young age, Dushuuw could only ever call Yaq a friend. Even as children, he could have snapped Yaq's slight body in half—but Yaq was never intimidated. The lower-born jokester was the only one who saw past Dushuuw's bloody reputation, and the only one besides Dushuuw's mother around whom the warrior ever let his guard down. Even around the war chief, with whom he spent countless hours over the years, Dushuuw always felt a pressure to perform. When Yaq wasn't around, Dushuuw contented himself to the safe company of young children or old women. Dushuuw was beginning to enjoy being included in this group, even if it was at its edges. Getting to know the rotund Huh-uuk and quiet Kweelthup. Even seeing his cousin in action sparked grudging respect. And there was always Qotsik. To be close to his brother again—to be drawn closer by him—filled Dushuuw with a longing to be like them. But such longing was not new. And he wondered when it would all come crashing down again. When his brother would see the truth: that he could never fit in, because he wasn't made for this higher calling.

Buhkweeduuk strolled up. "I would thank you for this snack, but..."

Dushuuw took the meat his uncle offered, and tasted gull. Unfortunately, the duck wasn't ready yet. "I see what you mean."

Buhkweeduuk eyed him. "You ready for our trip south coming up?"

"I look forward to it. You are generous to let me tag along again."

"Generous? I am being selfish. You have shown you have a good mind for trade—and either way, I still need a strong arm to show off. You remember two summers ago..."

Dushuuw's muscles twitched at the memory of the tense moment off their shores, when a northern trading party had aimed to bypass the cape on its way up the strait rather than trade with the cape people first. Word of their intentions had come to Wuh-uhch through a network of marriages and slaves. Dushuuw had joined Wiid and the other fighters in war canoes to surround the group, as his father and uncle tried first to negotiate. They had hoped the show of force would be enough. The Wuh-uhch warriors' faces were painted red and black. Chahbuht had painted his face all black, adding sparkling mica to bolster the grim effect. Dushuuw's hand had been on his spear, ready to attack, waiting for his father's word. He remembered the turning point. The moment where his relief at the foreigners' capitulation competed with his desire to draw their blood. His fingers had twitched on the spear, and they twitched now. That was when being a weapon was all his family had asked of him.

"It is only a matter of time before it comes to violence again," his uncle said. "So our presence at that southern market is vital. The unique items we are able to get there provide us with the variety and the quantity that should make us a northerner's first stop anyway. But beyond that, our presence there also reminds people of our reach, of our strength. Ultimately, it is all about holding this place, the cape." Buhkweeduuk drew crossing lines in the air, as if to chart out what lay large and invisible in the dark—the sweeping line of the outer coast, its intersection with the strait. "We are where everything intersects, the pivot point," he said. "How we control the direction of what enters that space determines our own direction." He tore off another piece of meat, and handed it to Dushuuw. "That often means applying pressure. Maybe it's enough to simply withhold what they most need. But maybe they need a firmer show of our upper hand. A warrior and his club."

Dushuuw tucked the rest of the tough meat in his mouth. He considered his uncle's words as he thought again of the spear in his hand. Did that possibility of confrontation have something to do with why even a trade visit sparked more enthusiasm in him than a whale hunt? Carefully chosen words can carry the same threat as a spear poised to strike.

Yet it was more than the fight for control. There was something else his uncle unwittingly offered him on that first trading mission. He had felt it in his first exhilarative step into the teeming market. It was the ability to walk into the unknown and feel the freedom of being unknown in return—to recreate himself.

Dushuuw sighed and wiped his mouth. The fire bathed his chest in heat and light. The wind off the nightfallen sea sent a chill up his back.

Buhkweeduuk stood beside him as conversations that had begun without them continued on without them. An old man drew one of the roasted ducks from the fire, then set it aside to cool. Buhkweeduuk pinched the last scrap of gull meat from the bone in his hand, tossing the bone to a pile. He shook the bit of meat as if giving it a lecture. "I am convinced each time that bones are all these gulls are good for—and still I wear out my jaw on their meat."

He popped the morsel in his mouth, squeezed Dushuuw's shoulder and rubbed his hands together as he walked to sit by the fire and eat some good duck.

After the bonfire had died down to a cozier blaze, Dushuuw walked around the ring of drift log benches toward Q̇otsik. His brother was looking away, a bashful smile on his face. Chahbuhi smiled broadly.

The old storyteller Hawitsuksh slapped his hands together, jabbing a finger toward Q̇otsik. "I hope she farts in her sleep." The men laughed.

Kuhbuhtup started to sing, and everyone groaned. For a man with such a powerful speaking voice, he could not carry a tune. He persisted off-key through the song about a man courting a woman gently like the little waves along the shore, only to come like a big wave with many gifts for their marriage. He ended it early, and a mixture of heckles and cheers thanked him for it.

"Let me know if you need any advice with what that song is really about," Yaq said, to laughter.

One by one, the older men moved into the houses to sleep. The young men stayed by the fire, tossing in bits of dried wood that sent up splashes of sparks. They boasted, gossiped.

Uhpqoolth shifted his legs on the sand where he reclined against a log and looked up at the others. "Three whales, two of them drift. The elders say Q̇otsik is blessed," he said.

"Takes the pressure off, so we can do other things this summer," Kweelthup said.

"Fall runs are going to be big, too, just watch," said Yaq, stretching his arms as if to get ready.

Huh-uuk wiped greasy fingers down his thighs. "Definitely."

Dushuuw was silent, the familiar tension returning to his shoulders.

Q̇otsik lifted his head but said nothing. He rubbed the top of his nose. This was only his second year leading the hunts. Last year had brought four harvests from spring to fall, an impressive number for his first year in the bow. Most people saw it as confirmation of his leadership qualities, ready for him to marry and be more than the heir apparent. But Dushuuw knew by gestures like this one, and his brother's long absences, that Q̇otsik cared about the numbers—that he longed to hold an oil feast of his own. To begin the real march up the ranks to whaling chief. One that hinged on the number of whales a man brought to his beach, but only because those whales agreed to fall to his harpoon.

The men stared at the subsiding flames. Dushuuw tossed in another large piece of wood that settled and shot up popping sparks.

Uhpqoolth started beating the log that he sat on with a short length of driftwood. He hummed, and Yaq and Dushuuw picked up the impromptu musical cue with smiles.

Dushuuw started in a sing-song lilt.

Q̇ot— Q̇ot— Q̇otsik

Yaq joined him in the chant.

Q̇otsik

They drew out the tones and practically shouted the third time.

Q̇otsik!

They joined Uhpqoolth's humming in a buzzing drone, as Uhpqoolth kept drumming and Huh-uuk enthusiastically accompanied him with smacks to his belly that sent the flesh rippling. Dushuuw and Yaq struggled against laughter as they launched back into the chant.

Q̇ot— Q̇ot— Q̇otsik

Q̇otsik

Q̇otsik!

Q̇otsik raised his hands and urged them to stop, but they ignored him. Even Kweelthup joined in, batting sticks on a flat rock to add to the beat as all the friends now hummed and chanted, hummed and chanted. Dushuuw scrambled to his feet and improvised an exaggerated version of a harpoon strike, moving into a wild spin that kicked up the sand and sent it flying at his friends' shins.

Q̇ot— Q̇ot— Q̇otsik

Uhpqoolth and Huh-uuk beat and slapped in wild staccato.

Q̇otsik

Kweelthup lifted his sticks high, then tossed them away with a grin.

Q̇otsik!

Yaq's and Dushuuw's voices trailed upward to end the refrain, as if to cement the hope they all placed in this man who looked back at them with an abashed smile.

Dushuuw flopped onto the sand and joined the laughter. They took turns shoving and kicking Q̇otsik until he laughed too.

Inside the house later, Dushuuw awoke to a rustling and the scents of fresh water and earthy forest. Dushuuw lay still, pretending to be asleep, as Q̇otsik lay on the bench set against the wall next to his own, smelling of ritual. Their heads lay inches from each other, as they did when they were boys whispering stories back and forth in the night. They were close, yet Dushuuw still felt the distance.

~

Ghost-like sounds spilled from the rocky caverns in the cliff sides, sending fishermen scrambling to return to the bay ahead of the summer storm. But in the building winds, Dushuuw felt like he was already battling a maelstrom.

Scratches lined Dushuuw's arms from the branches and thorns—and fingernails—that tore at his skin in his pursuit of the runaway through the forest. Now, he tightened the bindings around the boy's ankles and wrists, and gave an extra tug to the rope that held the boy to a tree. Gripping the boy's hair, Dushuuw forced him to drink some water. "I will give you more before nightfall." Then he walked away, not knowing or caring if the boy understood. In response, the boy spat toward Dushuuw what water remained in his mouth. The insult fell short of its goal; Dushuuw looked back with a shake of his head.

Blood ran along a cut on the boy's cheek, the same blood that coated Dushuuw's blade. But his effort to remind the boy of his new status—as a slave—was met by eyes dripping with contempt. They had captured him in the raid on the strait village. His uncle said the boy's insolence could take down the price they could get for him at the southern market, unless Dushuuw could tame him by then without breaking him—for the boy was hearty enough to sell for a canoe's worth of goods.

At this point, though, Dushuuw wondered if it was worth it.

The edge of the storm reached the village. Fat raindrops started to pelt down.

Dushuuw called for Yaq. The pair went to go help an older fisherman lift his canoe ashore, when Dushuuw heard a shout come from another arriving canoe.

"Quht-Quht!"

Dushuuw felt a mixture of confusion and dread. He slowed, stopped, and turned toward the small voice.

The boy ran toward him across the beach. His small feet kicked up messy splashes in the surf that blew into mist in the increasing wind.

"Buh-uhs?"

The boy smiled. Beyond, a man from Oosa-ilth waved from a canoe and beached the craft with help from some local slaves. Dushuuw could find no sign of his cousin, Xhud-uck, the boy's mother—the woman he had widowed.

Dushuuw reached out hesitantly and tousled the boy's hair as he used to, gripping the short lengths and pushing on them so that Buh-uhs's chin tilted up. Short hair for a boy his age. Short hair because it had been cut, not so long ago, as a sign of mourning.

"You have grown, Buh-Buh," he said, forcing out the pleasantry. He smiled, but it felt crooked. His fingers, laced through the boy's hair, felt wooden as he looked into the adoring face of the son of the man he had killed. He let go.

Buhkweeduuk and Chahbuht walked over, holding their hats atop their heads against the wind. The chief leaned on his walking stick. The Oosa-ilth man directed the slaves to carry a carved box of belongings from the canoe.

"Mother finally let me come," Buh-uhs said, bouncing at his knees. He grabbed Dushuuw's hand in both of his own, then thrust it outward, lifting his legs to swing. Dushuuw had forgotten this game. He quickly shifted his feet and flexed his arm to suspend the boy above the beach—more difficult, now that the boy was a bit taller.

Chahbuhƚ eyed the box, which the visitor had brought forward and set at the boy's feet. "And how long do we get the pleasure of your youthful company, my boy?" The chief's eyes flitted between the boy and his minder, for the box implied it was not a short stay.

The boy gave a stern look. "I will not leave again."

Chahbuhƚ and Buhkweeduuk eyed each other. "Your mother agrees to this? Your grandparents?" Buhkweeduuk asked.

Buh-uhs dropped from Dushuuw's arm and puffed out his thin chest, hands on hips. "Yeah, I already said that!"

Dushuuw's thoughts were as off-balance as his body, as Buh-uhs dragged at his arm one moment and let it go the next.

"She does not believe me," Buh-uhs said, "but I will stay. Wuh-uhch is my home." He tilted his head up toward Dushuuw. "I want to be a warrior, like Quht-Quht."

The boy's chaperone shrugged, and Buhkweeduuk pulled the man aside to talk as they walked back toward the main house. Chahbuhƚ followed as the rains increased. The boy whooped.

"Can I sleep by you, Quht-Quht? Or is that lady back?"

Touching his own forehead, Dushuuw realized his hand was shaking. He opened his mouth, but no reply came. Already, though, the boy was rushing ahead to voice other thoughts.

"I got my spear you made me. There was a boy who said his was better, but he was just jealous because he knew mine is best..."

"Welcome, little man." Yaq gave Buh-uhs a playful punch on the shoulder as he crouched down to eye level. "The boys are playing the ring game over there." Buh-uhs craned his neck to see the pack of boys racing uphill and down behind the houses, flinging rings toward the crest of the slope to roll back and catch sticks on the way down—the storm winds adding to their thrill. "You still got the touch?"

"Oh, yeah!" Buh-uhs went off running. Boys called out with cries of recognition. One rushed out to meet Buh-uhs halfway, bouncing as much as his friend. Yaq gave Dushuuw a quick, tight smile, then followed after the boys.

Chahbuhƚ and Buhkweeduuk had seen to the chaperone and Buh-uhs's belongings, and now walked back to Dushuuw. "Sounds like the boy is telling the truth, at least as he understands it," Buhkweeduuk said. "His mother says he can come back to her when he realizes he is wrong—if we do not send him home first."

Dushuuw nodded his head in acknowledgment of the conversation, but his jaw was locked closed.

Buhkweeduuk's eyebrows drew together. "Maybe we should send the boy back tomorrow, before he gets his hopes up further," he said. "Who is going to watch over him, anyway?"

But Chahbuhɫ shook his head, and turned his face up to the rain with a grin. "No, the boy is right. Wuh-uhch is his home," he said. He brought his walking stick up and planted it back in the sand for emphasis. The old man's excitement was palpable. "There are plenty of slaves to mind a single boy. Let us see where this leads." The chief's back was straight as he strode away.

Dushuuw forced a smile at his uncle. Buhkweeduuk took the cue and walked away as well. Dushuuw turned toward the bay, intending to watch the heart of the storm pass over. Instead, he propped one foot atop a log, and considered the tangle of seaweed and scraps of wood pushed into mounds at its base by tide after tide, surge after surge.

The boy had always favored his father in appearance, and multiple turns of the moon had only made the resemblance more apparent. For a brief moment, the twisted neck of the dead man rose in Dushuuw's memory with such vividness that he gasped. His foot came down off the log with a heavy thud.

After a time, as the rain pounded and the wind howled—and aware that others would be waiting to see how he would react—Dushuuw gathered his breath and strode toward the house. On the hillside beyond, Buh-uhs lifted his arms in victory at the game. The boy turned and smiled at Dushuuw, waving. Dushuuw slowly lifted his hand in response. A swirl of wind lifted the boy's cropped hair and funneled back to billow at Dushuuw's chest. His feet fought the loose sand until they hit the hardened path.

That night, his grandmother drew Buh-uhs close to her side in the family's house corner. The elderly woman sat with the young boy in the warmth of the fire's heat. Yahbis wagged a finger in Buh-uhs's face. "You must know who you are and where you come from," she said. Her eyes shone with an eagerness to match her voice, and her embrace of the boy was full of the warmth of a grandmother's pride over a child who was where he belonged. "This night I will tell you the story of how we became related to the whales. It is a love story."

The boy groaned, and she poked him on the nose.

"Get used to it," she said, "because this is a story I will tell again. It is a story from a time before time. In that time, there was a girl. She was the daughter of a chief and lived with her family by the sea…"

Dushuuw knew this story well. Indeed, Yahbis had told him the story at least a dozen times over the years. Yet he found himself settling back against the wall, dangling his leg over the edge of his bench, and listening again to the old woman's voice, which shifted into a storytelling cadence to capture a listener's ear and carry them along.

"…She saw the whales, spying and spouting near the shore. She looked out at them, and her eyes fell on one whale in particular. The girl admired the whale's body, its graceful movements. The whale saw the girl on shore, and was taken aback by her beauty. Their eyes met across the waves…"

Buh-uhs groaned, but Dushuuw smiled as the boy ceased fidgeting.

Dushuuw's mind swam through the story, following the whale as it came ashore and turned into a wolf, circled through the forest and turned into a man, seeking after the beautiful girl, again and again, day after day until, one day, many moons later, she was following him into the sea as his bride, turning into a whale at the touch of the sea.

The story showed connection. Dushuuw watched over the small boy and the old woman huddled in the warmth of the fire from his shadowed perch, and wondered about this renewed connection.

~

By the time Dushuuw stirred awake the next morning, Buh-uhs had already left to play with friends. Soon, Dushuuw headed uphill, past the slave boy—still glaring—and to the high ground where his father and uncle were overseeing work on the new winter house. Ọotsik stood with them, watching the progress.

Chahbuhᵗ waved Dushuuw over. "Young Son!" The name rolled off the chief's tongue without malice. No one turned to look. It seemed everyone but Dushuuw was resigned to the nickname, helped along by its years of familiarity. Even Ọotsik had ceased his pitying looks. At least there was that.

His father led him, Ọotsik, and Buhkweeduuk up the path toward the point. "You must hold your uncle to a promise," Chahbuhᵗ said.

Buhkweeduuk laughed and shook his head as he followed.

"No long stays down south this year," Chahbuhᵗ said. "There is more whaling to do this fall, and we need you both back in time for the preparations."

Dushuuw's heart sank a bit. He wondered if this would be the first fall without a war club in his hand. It had been weeks since he had talked with Wiid. With another trading mission, then whaling, would he be able to help plan any raids?

"Do not worry, brother," Buhkweeduuk said, placing his hand on the chief's shoulder.

Q̇otsik put a hand on Dushuuw's shoulder, gripping tight as if sensing Dushuuw's own worries. Dushuuw smiled at his brother, relaxing a bit.

Soon, they reached the open meadow at the crest of the point. Towering spruce ringed the meadow and supported large nests for resident eagles and falcons. In a low spot, cattail swayed in the wind around a pool of water. A group of slave women hefted buckets of drinking water back to the village.

The men crossed the meadow and went down an overgrown trail to the edge of the point, a high vantage that allowed them to see for miles to the south, from the fires of Tsooyuhs to the far seastacks off Oosa-ilth. Buhkweeduuk pointed out the path they would soon paddle.

Suddenly there was a rustling and breaking of twigs from the salal near the cliff's edge. Dushuuw stepped in front of the rest of the group, raising his arm as if to hold them back and wishing he had his club. The bushes rocked back and forth, but still Dushuuw did not see anything. Then out popped Buh-uhs. The boy was naked and scratched, and grinning ear to ear. He held a small hair seal by a noose about its neck, his toy club tucked into a rope around his waist.

Dushuuw's arm dropped. Q̇otsik breathed a sigh of relief, and Buhkweeduuk bent over laughing.

"My, my," Chahbuhɫ said. "Do we have a rookery on the highlands?"

"I climbed!" The boy beamed at each of the men, then faltered when his gaze fell on Dushuuw. "How did I do, Quht-Quht? I did it all by myself!" He held the limp pup out by the rope.

Dushuuw knelt in front of the boy, ignoring the seal as he took Buh-uhs by the shoulders. "Do not do that again," he said. "You could have gotten hurt."

"I would not." Buh-uhs drew the seal back to himself.

"Do not be stupid, Buh-uhs," Dushuuw said. "You will not go out alone again."

"I can take care of myself," said Buh-uhs, glancing in embarrassment at the other men.

"Let me take you next time," said Dushuuw, softening his tone. "And we will practice the way I did, and not on any animals." He loosened his grip on the boy, then placed his hands on his thighs, still crouched low to look Buh-uhs in the eye. "You must learn the right way, yes?"

There was a brief softening, but Buh-uhs's wounded pride resurrected, and the boy dragged the seal toward the trail back home without answering.

Dushuuw ran his fingers through his hair as he watched the boy.

Ọotsik put a hand on his shoulder. "Do not worry, brother. We will keep an eye on him while you're gone."

Dushuuw pulled his hand back to his side and shrugged. He turned back toward the view south, toward Oosa-ilth and points beyond.

~

Early the next morning, Dushuuw loaded the canoes to head out with Buhkweeduuk and the rest of the trading crew, primarily men strong at the paddles. He stood with one of them, counting everything over.

"The baskets." Dushuuw slapped his thigh. "I will be right back."

He went back to the main house for Sawsin's decorative baskets that he had put in the safety of his storage box to trade later—all but the one Sawsin had shown them that night in her father's house. That basket he had given to his aunt, Pikoo, who lovingly traced the basket's design whenever she picked it up. But as Dushuuw, anxious to get underway, approached the partition that walled off his family's living space, he slowed upon hearing his boyhood name. His father and uncle talked on the other side.

"...get his confidence back," Buhkweeduuk said.

"If that were all it took, I would not be concerned," his father replied.

"You think there is more to it."

"I trust Ọotsik's vision. Still, the only whale we have harpooned since he has been in the canoe was a fight we nearly lost."

"I still think..."

Dushuuw slipped back outside, heart pounding. He waited beside the doorway until he heard them drawing near, then entered with a passing greeting and went to get the baskets.

He tried to recapture his excitement, to focus on the trade route ahead. He drew lines in the air. First to the east, up the strait to the inland waters to procure salmon and some more wool-bearing dogs.

From there, south down the sound for soapberries and more salmon, and to an island village that each year prepared giant clams for the Kwidich'chuh-aht. Then the long paddle back north and west down the strait, stopping among allies and kin before returning home to hand off some goods for his father to use in trade in their home waters. From there, south down the coast to barter with households at Oosa-ilth. Then the real goal—powering down to the southern market, where they would stay a few days to hit up all the converging groups. It was a plan that mimicked the previous summer in every way, except one.

Dushuuw drew the baskets from his bench, closed the lid, and set them on top. He bent low, gripping the edge of the bench. He closed his eyes, shoulder blades drawing together as he breathed heavily. Memories of her skin pressed to his, of the shuddering union that had made him feel dizzy, of the euphoria of knowing such a delight. The lie it all was, culminating in the largest lie that started during those many summer weeks he was away from home. When she gave her body to another—how many times, he still wondered.

He stood and shoved memory aside. Shoved aside, too, the sudden urge to crush the beautiful baskets before him. Their tight weave brought to mind the hats the shaman's slave wove. He had seen the woman in passing at Chahdee; he wondered if she had any time there for working on a hat. He wondered, too, at the sense that even a slave—as close to the shaman's side as she was—knew more about the reality that lay just beyond their own, a reality he needed access to but that was closed to him. He brushed a finger over a tiny bird on one of the baskets. With a deep breath, he placed the baskets in a clean box, fixed the lid, and went back to the canoe. He would add distance to his worries, try to leave them behind.

Buh-uhs sat on the edge of the canoe, legs dangled over the edge. The boy swung his legs back and forth to kick the hull over and over. He looked out over the river. The boy furrowed his brows when he spotted Dushuuw, then turned his gaze back to the burial site where small houses marked graves.

"They buried my father over there," the boy said, "after the accident."

Dushuuw's shoulders sagged. He wondered when the boy would be told all the details of his father's death, and what he would think of his Quht-Quht then. Dushuuw wanted the boy to hold on to the good memories he had—of his father, of his Quht-Quht. But he knew it couldn't last, not forever.

"You want to come to Oosa-ilth?" Dushuuw asked. "You can stay and visit your mother. Decide if you want to come back."

"I am staying here," Buh-uhs said. He spat on the ground.

"It is understandable if you wish to change your mind," Dushuuw said, careful to keep his voice low. "I know I miss my mother, and I am a grown man."

Buh-uhs's arms drooped a bit. Then he straightened and looked at Dushuuw as if offended, worried. "I told you," he said. "I am home."

Dushuuw tousled the boy's hair, hand lingering atop the boy's head.

"Will you really teach me how to use a club when you get back, Quht-Quht?"

Dushuuw smiled and dropped his hand to the boy's shoulder. The boy's skin was soft, but Dushuuw felt the first signs of solidifying muscle. "To show you the right way, yes. You were fortunate, Buh-Buh," he said. "Pupping season is a risky time. The mothers are fierce."

"I found it laying alone," the boy said.

"Yes, and you should have left it alone. It was not just the danger of angering its mother. The young must be left to grow, yes? If you had left the pup alone, our sealers could hunt it next year, when it is big and fat, like you." He poked the boy in the stomach. Buh-uhs laughed reflexively.

The boy rapped the side of the canoe with his feet one more time, leaped off and kicked up sand as he ran to find his friends.

Dushuuw joined the paddlers as they moved into the freedom of the water. Bound inside the hull, the eyes of another boy fixed on little else but Dushuuw. And Dushuuw knew it would be that way until they reached the southern market, where the boy would be sold, to be carried off inland to a home neither he nor Dushuuw had ever seen.

12

Summer ended in a shroud. Fog sailed over Chahdee's main beach all day. The chill wind howled as it swirled in and out of a nearby cave.

Working hours were now focused on packing up to return to villages on the mainland. There would be salal berries to harvest and dry into cakes. Fern roots to dig up. Gooseberries and nettle fiber to gather. Uhpahs and Amuun'axsum lagged and spent more time joining common games and watching the men's contests. The urge to ignore responsibility spread like a cough. Men leaped down from ladders, chased laughing women across small chasms.

A feathered target soared from Amuun'axsum's paddle toward Uhpahs's paddle. The piece of thimbleberry stem with feathers attached arced through the air, back and forth. Then a gust of wind cut through the beach and the target took flight. The friends shouted as they gave chase. Spying their effort, Ṫoopuuk dumped a coil of rope from his arm and leaped. His fingers brushed the game piece's feathers before the sea air carried it tumbling off. Amuun'axsum and Uhpahs laughed and groaned in turn, their game cut short just as it began. Ṫoopuuk laughed and smiled with them, then reached down for the end of the rope and began coiling it again.

"My, and now you have to do your work all over again," Amuun'axsum said, holding the makeshift game paddle—a flat piece of driftwood—in front of her face to hide her laughter.

The slave man smiled and shrugged. "There is time enough," he said. "I only wish I were taller; I could have kept your game going for you."

"Serves us right for even trying such a game here," Uhpahs said.

Ṫoopuuk smiled politely, turning his eyes back to Amuun'axsum.

Amuun'axsum looked down and hooked elbows with Uhpahs, steering her friend back to the other end of the beach. "Well, off we go to find some other way of avoiding our packing."

Uhpahs gave her an exasperated look, then brightened and tugged on Amuun'axsum's arm. "And I think I found my happy distraction."

A fisherman helped heft a canoe onto the beach. He paused and smiled shyly at Uhpahs. Uhpahs clenched her friend's arm as if to keep herself from floating into the air. He was, indeed, the same man Amuun'axsum had spied between the houses on that spring day she had helped Uhpahs fetch the salmon roe. Amuun'axsum had learned the fisherman's name was Suu-ahp. This much was shared with her, at least, after she had come upon them groaning and entangled on Uhpahs's bed mat in the middle of an island work day when others were sweaty from far more mundane tasks.

Amuun'axsum glanced at her friend, whose face glowed. A weight settled in her gut. Uhpahs's grip had relaxed, but Amuun'axsum hugged her friend's arm tight. She wasn't sure if the sudden jealousy that fired in her chest was for or of her friend. Uhpahs gave her a look both pleading and exasperated.

Toopuuk appeared beside them.

"My chief, Oodahk, has agreed to a *hala?a·* match on the beach," he said. "A last great entertainment before everyone goes. I am playing. Perhaps you would like to come watch?"

He had glanced at Uhpahs, but his invitation was directed at Amuun'axsum. She did not know how to answer. The man's attentions set her skin afire. She wanted to run away again. He shifted and blinked. Though she had wanted to see how the bone game was played here...

Uhpahs decided for her—"She would love to!"—and wrenched free of Amuun'axsum to skip to her lover before anyone could respond.

Toopuuk smiled at Amuun'axsum, then looked down at the coil of rope in his hands. "You do not have to, of course," he said.

"I am interested—"

He brightened.

"—in the game. I have wanted to see how you all play."

"Walk with me."

"I will see you there, at the game."

He masked his disappointment with a simple nod.

Later, when Amuun'axsum arrived at the gaming area, she spotted Toopuuk beside his chief, Oodahk, and others from Deeyuh. The slave man had not spotted her yet. The chief from Oosa-ilth who had challenged the Deeyuh to the game of *hala?a·* gathered his team. Logs were dragged over for the teams to sit opposite each other.

But Oodahk demurred.

"What would the wager be? I see nothing that interests me."

Amuun'axsum found a spot against the cliff wall behind the Oosa-ilth side to watch. Toopuuk leaned over to his chief and whispered something; they laughed.

The Oosa-ilth team offered wagers—a portion of the losing team's halibut catch, a seal hide, jewelry—but Oodahk rejected each one.

A nobleman from an allied village across the strait spoke from the rock where he lounged. "What if I provide the prize?"

Oodahk and the Oosa-ilth chief both looked over in interest.

"What kind of prize?" Oodahk said.

The visiting nobleman put his arm around the woman at his side and gave her a squeeze. "My wife," he said.

The woman leaned away from him as laughter bounced off the cliff behind the crowd.

"Ah, well, if not my wife," the man said, shrugging, "then that canoe."

A chorus of gasps and exclamations arose from the crowd. The canoe was older and unadorned, but it was well-wrought and in good repair, carved from one of the cedars that made the tribes across the strait famous.

The man's wife leaned away from him again in shock, but he drew her close again.

Oodahk's eyes glistened as he glanced from the canoe to the visiting nobleman. He turned to the Oosa-ilth men. "We have a game."

Those listening laughed, knowing it was not a question of whether there would be a *hala?a·* game, only what it would be played for—and this was now a vastly more interesting contest, with a prize that far outweighed a typical pickup game.

Games like Amuun'axsum's and Uhpahs's paddle-and-target mishap merely passed the time. Games like *hala?a·* were another way of doing business, or making war if someone was found to cheat. And like all serious affairs—hunting the whale, claiming land—its beginning was tracked to the time before time, when humans were animals. The kind of rite that survives the upheaval of complete transformation.

On the Deeyuh side, Toopuuk was one of two players who would hide the game pieces. So that was it. Amuun'axsum remembered their conversation by the fire. A talent for hiding the bones could make a slave very valuable.

The men began drumming a log and chanting their game songs. Oodahk cupped the game pieces in his hands and blew on them before hiding them in Toopuuk's hands. Before Oodahk sat back down,

T̓oopuuk shouted and tossed the bones high in the air. He snatched them back in his hands with smooth movements, crossing his arms back and forth as he brought his hands close to his chest. Amuun'a̱xsum laughed at the audacity of giving the other team such an open chance to see where the unmarked bone fell. Indeed, the guesser for the Oosa-ilth team immediately held out his hand to make his guess. He guessed right, but guessed the position of the other Deeyuh player's set of gaming pieces wrong. One of Deeyuh's counting sticks went to Oosa-ilth. Oodahk held the other sticks with a confident smile.

So it went. Each team hid the bones, drummed, and sang while the other team indicated with hand signals which hands held the marked pieces. Counting sticks traded sides based on whether guesses were correct or wrong.

Onlookers crowded the game, and Amuun'a̱xsum had to leave her place against the cliff wall to get a better look.

Again, T̓oopuuk started a round quickly with surprise, and success.

The teams were well matched, and it stretched into a long game. But no one grew tired. The mood remained jovial. At one point, a nobleman on the Deeyuh side bet a point for an opponent's plate of fish. The crowd laughed, the Oosa-ilth man agreed, and they all laughed again when his meal went over to the other side, a few bites short.

Her view blocked again, Amuun'a̱xsum slipped in front of two men as another round started. T̓oopuuk spotted her; a smile briefly brushed across his face before he was sober again, his attention on the game.

Soon, all but one of the sticks were held by the Oosa-ilth team. The Deeyuh team had the bones. T̓oopuuk deployed one of his trick maneuvers again. Amuun'a̱xsum held her breath as, once again, he tossed his game pieces high into the air. This time, he flicked them so that they spun; the small black dots on the marked piece merged into blurred lines. Crossing his hands in the air, he grabbed the bones on the descent. T̓oopuuk brought his hands together—did he swap the bones as he did?—and crossed and uncrossed his arms, the bones hidden in his clenched hands. It all happened in a few moments.

But the Oosa-ilth team was not fooled by distraction. Their guesser held up his hand to indicate his guess on the placement of bones T̓oopuuk held—wrong—before he turned and made a separate guess for the other bone holder—correct.

The last stick went to Oosa-ilth for the win—and the canoe.

Disappointed sighs and sunken shoulders on one side were answered by upraised arms and cheers from the other. T̓oopuuk handed the game pieces to his chief, then strolled over to Amuun'ax̱sum.

"You were a good distraction," he said. "Unfortunately, it was for me."

Amuun'ax̱sum twisted a toe in the sand and tried to spot Uhpahs.

"Not like the canoe was for me anyway, hey?"

Amuun'ax̱sum faced him, drawing her shoulders back. "Still, if I hurt your efforts, then I regret the loss—for your chief."

Toopuuk merely smiled. He took a step closer. "I would accept a different prize," he said. He slid a hand onto her hip, and gave a gentle, testing tug.

Amuun'ax̱sum's face burned. She pushed at his arm, hoping it would also push away the confusing heat that swirled inside her body. "I need to find Uhpahs," she said.

Disappointment dulled his eyes, but he smiled anyway. "Deeyuh and Wuh-uhch are close neighbors. I look forward to seeing you again," he said. Amuun'ax̱sum kept a straight face and looked for Uhpahs. Toopuuk leaned close enough to whisper in her ear, but did not touch her again. "I am good at many things, and one of them is convincing the most beautiful woman I have ever seen to give me a chance."

He walked away, but not before spying her begrudging smile.

The next day, before leaving the summer encampment, the people of Deeyuh, Wuh-uhch, and Oosa-ilth traded generously with the visiting nobleman, whose wife looked on with a smile. The couple headed home across the strait in another canoe, which was laden with more than the prize canoe's worth.

WEEKS HAD PASSED by the time Dushuuw and his uncle returned from trading, just as everyone else converged at the village from their various summer haunts, at Chahdee and elsewhere.

The cape seemed a smaller place again in the wake of far-flung travels. But this was offset by the familiarity of its waters, the shape of every outcropping and stack. It would take time for Dushuuw's legs to get used to the unmoving earth, for his ears to tune to the sound of his own language instead of a multitude of languages all mixing together. Walking onto the beach, the smells of home struck him at first like a stranger and, in the next instant, an old relative.

Curiosity always drove a crowd, and the traders' canoes were full of objects to draw stares and comments. The women enthused over the dish-sized shells of abalone. Pikoo jokingly held one beside her face like an earring, then held the shell atop young Blubs's head like a hat. Ọotsik smiled as he picked up and set down utensils, carved from the horn of a wool-bearing animal unknown to their area, holding some of them up for Uhpqoolth to see. Chahbuhł examined the slaves—women and children who understood nothing he said—and sent them to one of their own people for further instruction. Thluuch-muup filled a bowl with soapberries, eager to whip up a frothy treat.

Dushuuw handed a basket off to a slave, then noticed Chaiyuhx-ik peeking from the house doorway. From a box, he grabbed a piece of dried meat and went over to his sister, urging her to try a taste. Chai bit off a chunk, and scrunched up her nose. He laughed, took the rest back, and returned to the canoes.

Yaq joined him, leaving the side of a young woman, and punched his friend in the arm as a welcome. He snatched the remaining piece of bison meat from Dushuuw's hand and popped it in his mouth without asking what it was.

Dushuuw nodded toward the woman who stood at a distance talking with a friend. "You are bringing one of your amusements out of the woods?" he quipped. He startled at the flash of anger that crossed his friend's face. But it was followed by another surprise—a blush.

"We shall see," Yaq said. "She has taken a fancy to me, which I suppose cannot be helped."

Dushuuw's grin faded to a smile as he watched everyone go about their normal business on an otherwise ordinary day. Even for his best friend, who returned to his woman. Dushuuw stood awkwardly, trying to figure out where he fit, what to do next. It was like the low after a raid.

Then Wiid approached, casting a glance over the trade items with a nod. He walked right up beside Dushuuw, shoulder to shoulder, leaning his head close to speak in his ear.

"You going to help me procure some fine items the other way?"

Dushuuw smiled at the faint stir in his gut, the urge to fight that had lain dormant on the trip coming back to life.

Buhkweeduuk was at his other shoulder the next moment.

"Well, I fulfilled my promise to your father," his uncle said. "There will be plenty of time before whaling. Plenty of time to prepare, as well as to enjoy—I hear now—a certain wedding. Perhaps your extra deal for Sawsin's baskets earlier this summer nudged things along, hey?" Buhkweeduuk laughed and slapped Dushuuw's back. "We'll make a trader of you yet, my boy."

Dushuuw stared at the beach, feeling the different pieces of himself—including pieces he never knew were there—start to pull apart again. As Wiid looked on, though, with that familiar look of challenge, it was the urge to prove his natural strength that was loudest.

The canoes were emptied. The two older men stood beside him yet, as if waiting for him to move in one direction or the other. But Dushuuw finally spotted his brother, at the edge of the crowd, and the twisting feelings dissipated as he left both the older men to jog up to meet him. Qotsik grinned as they clasped arms.

"Welcome home, brother," Qotsik said. "You've heard my news?"

"I knew it would not take long," Dushuuw said.

"With Sawsin, my prayers for the whale will be complete. Everything is coming together. Can you feel it?"

Dushuuw felt himself tugged in yet another direction—whatever direction his brother was going, and inviting him to follow. But he still felt the other pieces tugging, too, and wondered which would win out.

The girl's face stood out against the clothing festooned with dentalia that otherwise hid her body. She sat in a canoe laden with gifts, held aloft on the shoulders of her male relatives. The sun shone, reflecting off the white adornments. The girl sat unsmiling.

Dushuuw noticed because he was examining the curve of her lips, each subtle parting, and any other part of her he could glimpse. His breath hitched when her tongue emerged to wet her lips, and he prayed for rain to be forever banned to see the sight again. His hungry eyes sought the hidden curves of his bride—his bride!—but all he could see was her face. And so his eyes drank of that, and imbued each smooth patch of skin and jewelry-adorned ear with near-spiritual significance. Her sloped forehead was covered with strings of shells as well as foreign ornaments. Her dress was made of cedar fibers, but so covered in shells that one could not be sure. Dushuuw was sure that he intended to explore what it all hid, and had hidden, in the years since her first blood, keeping her pure—for him. The idea of it still made him heady. She was meant for him. So her first smile would be for him.

This was their first glimpse of each other in their entire lives.

"Try not to drool, brother." Ǫotsik cocked a smile at him that was equal parts humored and concerned.

Dushuuw snapped his jaw shut. "She is… beautiful."

"This is a true statement," his brother said. "Although I wonder if you would say that about a gaunt and gray-haired matron at this moment."

Dushuuw shot a look at his older brother. "You are just jealous that I get a wife before you, oh great one."

Ǫotsik looked out over the procession again. "No, I am happy for you, brother."

Dushuuw deflated, feeling again less a man compared to his brother, who always told the truth.

"It should be you," Dushuuw said.

This, too, was the truth, even if Dushuuw was glad with the turn of events. By normal standards, Ǫotsik would be the one marrying, with Dushuuw following in perhaps two summers. But the lavish naming *ṗačiƛ* his father had held for him the previous year had been an indication of shifting plans. The taint of his mother's lower birth was wiped away, so that he was no longer Young Son but the recipient of one of the most revered names in his father's family. Dushuuw walked taller under the name, felt stronger. Dushuuw was a name of high status, high enough to be married to a woman of stature—a woman whose bride-price also had been lavish. Their father would have to save up again to acquire a bride for Q̇otsik.

But Q̇otsik shook his head. "Not yet. I desire to hunt the whale more than I desire to know a woman. Does it not make me less of a man?"

Dushuuw regarded his brother, who looked out over the procession again with a worried expression. "It makes you more than a man, brother," Dushuuw said. "You are following your *tume·nuwis*."

Q̇otsik shifted with discomfort.

"Many whales will come to you. I know it," Dushuuw said.

Q̇otsik glanced at him, as if embarrassed to accept affirmation of his own beliefs—especially at the expense of their father's leg injury, which had affected his balance in the bow enough to hasten Q̇otsik's ascent.

The procession continued its slow, weaving approach. Gifts were thrown from the hull to uplifted arms—cedar blankets, baskets, trinkets—and the bride remained still, her eyes fixed north as if looking through the cape.

"I envy you, brother," Dushuuw said.

He sensed Q̇otsik's confusion, but did not meet his brother's eyes.

"I envy you, because I cannot be like you. More than that, I am ashamed—because I do not want to be." He recalled the evenings locked in playful but violent wrestling matches with the war chief beneath his roof, the laughter around the fire deep into the night as Wiid praised his battle prowess and celebrated their various sexual conquests. "I want other things more too. My war club removing a man's head. My body sliding into a woman." He glanced at his brother. "These are not higher desires, and I know it. And I am glad for it—to not require the kind of spiritual power you need—because I would never be worthy."

Q̇otsik shifted and shook his head. "You think too highly of me, brother. And too little of yourself."

Dushuuw looked again to the wedding canoe as it neared with the stone-faced young woman, and smiled. "I do not," he said.

Sunlight glinted off the shell ornaments that decorated the bride's body and clothing. Sawsin sat in the canoe with two other men and stacks of gifts, carried aloft by six of her male relatives. They followed the lead of her father—draped in a bear skin, a trio of eagle's feathers stuck to the back of a cedar headband—who played the part of a whale before the canoe. Ḥawith sounded and rose. The men carrying the canoe took shuffling steps. The men in the canoe tossed gifts to the people who gathered on either side with outstretched arms, creating an undulating path to the groom's doorway. The bride sat still, her eyes set on some point of the peak above Wuh-uhch. But a smile brightened her face.

Dushuuw watched that smile, testing it for falsehood. But as the wedding procession reached the doorway of the great house, where Ọotsik waited with a grin, Sawsin's smile only grew to match his own as she was lowered in the canoe to the ground. The couple looked at each other full in the face for the first time, and they remained that way for some time, as if drinking in the sight.

The sky was cloudy, the air warm. Festivities filled the day. The focus was this wedding ceremony. Throughout the day, there was feasting. But with so many groups together, there also were plenty of opportunities to show off. Dushuuw rolled his shoulders, remembering the canoe races. The Wuh-uhch team had nearly won, but was edged out by the group from Oosa-ilth. Though a loss, the close finish had added to the locals' jubilant mood. The reputation of Oosa-ilth, the coast's largest whaling village, was unparalleled in most feats.

Many attendees came from nearby Tsooyuhs. Uhpqoolth's wife, Ootsihd, laughed and welcomed the gentle pats at her pregnant stomach from those of her home village.

Children from different villages eyed each other nervously, then played favored games as if they were cousins. Older men sat on the beach and talked, while older women kept busy with weaving as they shared the latest gossip.

On the beach, a ring was made and the younger men gathered in bunches, brimming with nervous energy, preparing for the first contest of strength. The rounds started with new wrestlers, boys their village elders saw as having talent for battle but who were as yet unproved. There were sporadic cheers for the winners who threw their opponents out of the marked area. Yaq stood beside Dushuuw for these early rounds. They traded observations and chuckled over some of the more amateur mistakes. The winning boys gave the boys they bested tips for next time. Conversations quieted later, as onlookers anticipated the more experienced fighters—men whose skill had been proved in real battles, with blood and with heads.

Huh-uuk, fresh off his win in a boulder-throwing contest, lumbered up to him and Yaq, joining the more serious debates about technique, and making guesses about who would take each match. As one fight followed another, Dushuuw got the tense itch of a nearing fight. His own would be at the end. Chewing on thoughts, he gripped his long hair and folded it end over end to the top of his head, tying it into a knot. The breeze ran fresh across his exposed neck and back. He filled his lungs with the air. He rolled his shoulders.

Soon enough he was in the marked space, facing a man he already knew. He tried to quiet the adrenaline, a heady rush of anticipation and apprehension.

"Good to see you again," said Shuchkuk, the Tsooyuhs warrior. He looked less threatening when not covered in war paint and blood. But he still had the calm, confident demeanor of a man who knows his way around a challenge.

"I am glad to see you as well," Dushuuw said, "but we will see if you still think it a good meeting when I have knocked you across the line."

The two men had started to circle each other as they spoke.

"My father asked me to pick the best fighter among his guests," Dushuuw said. "I could only tell him the truth."

"You honor me," Shuchkuk said.

"I will honor myself," Dushuuw said, "when you are flat on your back."

Shuchkuk gave him a mocking smile in return. "Like you were, just recently," he said, as they lowered into a half-crouched stance, circling still. "I heard you got whupped in a contest down south."

"Ah, well," Dushuuw said, "that was a strategic loss." He nodded toward Shuchkuk's hair. The Tsooyuhs fighter's top knot was decorated with sprigs of evergreen. "I did not take you for the showy type of man."

Shuchkuk's focus dropped for a moment as gave an annoyed grunt. "My wife insists on such things," he said.

"It is good to know someone has already overpowered you."

"Well, while you were busy buying baubles," Shuchkuk said, still smiling, but his shoulder muscles tightening, "I was training for this."

The crowd cheered as the Tsooyuhs fighter made the first move. Dushuuw had read the man's stance and was ready, but the force of the blow still robbed him of some breath. He dug his back heel into the ground and held the man off. Each felt the crowd's festive mood and shifted his bearing to meet it, settling into stances for a long tussle that would show their strengths. The men each gripped the other's top knot—a skilled maneuver banned among the younger fighters, who did not yet appreciate the risk of fatally twisting a friend's neck—then put their other hand on the other's shoulder. The move came naturally, but as soon as the man's hair was in his grip, Dushuuw held his breath, remembering how he had killed a man in such a way. Shuchkuk sensed his hesitation and briefly smiled. Dushuuw forced himself to focus, and he fell into the back-and-forth rhythm of the match. Soon, his spirits lifted, as he reveled in showing off his strength. Aware of Wiid watching, he set himself to the task. To win. To prove he had not changed.

Dushuuw watched the other man's feet and torso, trying to anticipate Shuchkuk's next move, even as he sought to hide his own, knowing Shuchkuk was doing the same. They were well matched. The ring had been marked with sticks, and the grappling men flirted with its edges on all sides. Sprinkling rain became a proper rain, falling in proportion to the rise in the noise of the crowd. The men each tried different maneuvers to leverage the rain and force the other man to slip. If neither could win by brute force, it would come down to sheer skill—to what the other had yet to learn. In these choices, too, the men found themselves well matched. Even the flickers of smiles that turned their lips came at the same moment, and disappeared as quickly. They turned with each other. The many-faced crowd churned in the background.

At times, a voice Dushuuw recognized would penetrate the noise. His brother's or sister's encouragement. The war chief's shouts. Yaq's familiar taunts. But it was the words of someone he did not know, a woman cheering for the Tsooyuhs side, that broke his concentration.

"End it!"

Her voice was light, encouraging. He knew that, if he looked, the woman would be smiling, perhaps raising her hands. Yet the words were enough to make him mentally stumble. Her naked body, the twisted head, her neck between his hands, his fingernails caked with blood.

The Tsooyuhs fighter looked confused, then took the opening. He was late, and Dushuuw was able to recover in time, but his feet slid through the packed sand toward the ring's marked edge. He shouted as he held off his opponent, the cheers of the crowd reaching a crescendo as they anticipated an end, then falling off with exclamations as he managed to twist with Shuchkuk back to the center of the ring. They had each let go of the other's top knot, and now took defensive stances.

Still feeling the blows of memory, Dushuuw for a fleeting moment wished the fight was for more than show. He flexed his fingers, trying to send the rage that weighted his gut into his muscles, tendons, and veins instead. He met the Tsooyuhs man's eyes with all the hatred memory conjured. Shuchkuk saw it, and his own mood shifted as he became offended. He pushed at Dushuuw, and Dushuuw took a controlled step backward, then another—allowing himself to be backed toward the edge of the ring. He no longer watched Shuchkuk's body but the man's eyes, seeing them shift from offense to annoyance. The line came closer and closer, marked by the rising tumult of the crowd.

Then, at the cusp of the ring's edge, Dushuuw let his limbs relax by a fraction. Shuchkuk felt the release and pounced, but Dushuuw redirected the blow and fell to his knees. He braced himself with both hands. Shuchkuk held him around the waist from above, a leg poised outward as leverage to flip Dushuuw over and out of the ring. The crowd roared in anticipation. But in the moment before the flip—as the man took the large intake of breath—Dushuuw let one of his arms slip to the ground between them and rolled free. He sprang to a crouch. The Tsooyuhs fighter was still poised with one leg out. Dushuuw leaped before the man could get his balance, and tackled him out of the ring.

Shouts of surprise mixed with cheers around them. For a moment Shuchkuk looked irate. He sat in the wet sand beside Dushuuw and slammed his hand on the ground. As his anger faded, he looked over.

"'Strategic loss,' you say."

Wiping the sweat and rain from his forehead, Dushuuw smiled and nodded. He plucked one of the now-dangling sprigs of greenery from Shuchkuk's hair, flicking it onto the man's lap.

"All for 'baubles,' you see."

Dushuuw stood and held out his hand to help Shuchkuk up.

"Well done, Young Son," Shuchkuk said.

The Tsooyuhs fighter was genuine; he had not meant it as an insult. But as he strained to keep a smile, Dushuuw shifted the conversation. The two men conferred about the move that won Dushuuw the contest. They practiced a few times by reversing roles. Dushuuw felt good about the win, but robbed of joy.

"Quht-Quht!"

Buh-uhs bounded up to him with adoration.

"I knew you would win!"

The small boy jumped to hang from Dushuuw's arm, and Dushuuw gave him a few short swings.

Rain turned to mist as dusk fell, and the few onlookers who had remained outdoors turned to the great house for more feasting. Shuchkuk headed in to find his family. Dushuuw waited for Buh-uhs, who was distracted by a clam's hole. The boy soon tagged along beside Dushuuw, skipping, his gaze reverent. Buh-uhs stopped again to pick up a piece of seaweed, ripping it to shreds as they walked, but his fingers stilled as they neared the house. The boy stopped again and tilted his head up at Dushuuw.

"Quht-Quht, why do they not call you that other name anymore? That name you had when that lady was in our house."

The last scrap of respite Dushuuw had drawn from the contest wafted away.

"They said it was because you were strong, because you got that name," Buh-uhs said, his eyebrows scrunched in concentration. "But now they don't say the name anymore. Yet you are still strong."

"They do not call me that anymore," Dushuuw agreed. "But you know my name, right, Buh-Buh?"

Buh-uhs looked up at him, his smooth face a vulnerable moon. "Young Son?"

Dushuuw shook his head with a soft smile. "Quht-Quht, of course."

Buh-uhs's face brightened. Then, spying a friend, he smiled up at Dushuuw and ran off.

Pounding drums and raucous laughter poured from the house. Dushuuw paused just outside, tried to settle his mind on the day's win, and entered the house to join his brother.

The food that night was as plentiful and as good as what was served earlier in the day. The wedding came at a time of year when his father could capitalize on fresh resources without diminishing reserves. People reclined with happy stomachs and happy moods.

Two men strode to the center of the house, carrying a large board between them. Standing in the middle of the room, the men raised the board and turned to display it to everyone gathered. It was crudely carved, the ends shaped like bird heads—maybe—and while the guests started to wonder about their sanity, the locals were already holding back laughter. The men took turns speaking with self-importance as they listed off the plank's many supposedly artistic features. They talked on and on, but the list was truly short, as each kept repeating what the other man said, until they were saying the same thing three times over. They capped it all off by proclaiming that only they had the right to display the board, and wasn't everyone blessed to get a glimpse.

One of the Tsooyuhs nobles asked about the board's supernatural origin, and another chimed in right after asking how the men got the privilege. The two men looked at each other over the board, then out at the audience. They each opened their mouths as if to speak in unison, but said nothing. One of the men turned to a woman in the audience. "Wife, do you remember the answer?"

The crowd roared with laughter.

The night deepened, and stories and songs continued. Children fell asleep one after the other on men's shoulders or in women's laps. Slaves came and went through the doorway. Men added wood to the fires, though in smaller amounts, letting them die down slowly. Q̇otsik put his arm around Sawsin's waist. But it was in her gaze at him, not his grip on her, that the seal was made.

Dushuuw walked over to Chai, who was all smiles as she undoubtedly thought of her own potential wedding. Dushuuw bent over and whispered in his sister's ear. Chai gave him a brief look of concern, but nodded, and Dushuuw ducked outside. This celebration would go on for a week. He could miss one night.

The moon was full and eliminated the need for a torch. It cast its light on the sea, painting a glittering, endless path. Dushuuw headed into the scrub for a forest trail, leaving the sounds of the wedding behind. He broke off a small branch from a tree, and jabbed its ragged end into his thigh, keeping time with his tromping steps.

14

BEYOND THE DOORWAY where Amuun'axsum lay sleepless, a full moon lit the waters like a weak sun. Sounds from the wedding festivities at the head of the village occasionally rose on the breeze.

Eekbis had opted not to attend the evening feast. Amuun'axsum had helped the shaman trudge through the forest all the previous day, and the old woman claimed to be too tired to submit her bones to such revelry. She would go the next night perhaps. Amuun'axsum wondered if it had more to do with gossip about a rivalry. Weddings meant contests, and many times that included shamans. Uhpahs had whispered to her about a late-night contest some years back between Eekbis and a shaman from Deeyuh. A dark room. Heavy paint. Elaborate headdresses. Otherworldly sounds. And a meeting of power in the air between them, coming from their mouths. Amuun'axsum was not sure about the particulars, but she was sure Eekbis resented weakness.

Whatever the reason, Amuun'axsum sighed with relief when Eekbis's snores finally sounded beyond the partition.

She tip-toed over to a pile of trash. Carefully, she sifted through the refuse and pulled out one shell in particular. Casting a glance the shaman's direction, she crept back to her bed mat and tried to clean off the dirt and bits of bark clinging to the shell. She lifted it to her nose. The smell of the balm was not quite as sweet.

How the shaman had come by it she was not sure. Amuun'axsum had been careless at some point, it seemed. She hoped the shaman saw it only as trash. Amuun'axsum brought the shell to her nose again. The smell of the balm was clearer this time. She pondered where she should keep it now. If the shaman found it again, she'd realize it meant something to Amuun'axsum. It would be something the old woman could take away.

Outside, the bright moonlight beckoned.

Soon, wearing a light cloak and carrying a small torch, Amuun'axsum was walking into the forest, checking over her shoulder now and then, though nearly everyone was at the wedding. It took her a while to find the spot, especially once she left the trail. Yet she recognized it as soon as the large, fallen trunk crossed her path. She rounded the snag, and stepped inside the hollow, torch light flickering.

Amuun'axsum fixed the torch upright in the ground, then knelt before the hollowed-out hiding spot where a child long ago had hidden his treasures. She removed the piece of bark closing off the hole, intending to remove the broken toy spear and other odd bits—when she saw the wrapped bundle lying atop the pile. The hummingbird. She hesitated, then lifted the bundle, tentatively unwinding strip after strip of cedar to the sand-filled grave she had given the small bird after twisting its neck. It had started to decay in spots, but it was free of insects, and its feathers remained bright—and soft. She left the children's toys in place. Instead, she rewrapped the bird and nestled it back among them, then placed her shell of balm atop the horde.

Already she felt a sense of relief. Searching about, she found a larger piece of broken bark and set it across the hole, like a lid on a box. To be sure, she started shoving bits of bark and handfuls of dirt against its base to hold it in place. Then she sat back.

It was warm inside the snag. Though large, its curved walls captured and held the heat of the torch.

Amuun'axsum looked at the drawings of the animals, made at a child's height. Faded, and smudged. The snipe lifted a wing. The bear had his arms and legs splayed. They wavered in the light of the flame. As if they were dancing on a beach. How old was that child now? How old then? She scraped a section of burned bark away above the drawings, then found a piece of charcoal on the ground. Arching over the heads of the dancing animals, she drew something else: a slithering body, a searching snout, and a protruding tongue that was ragged and piercing. The black lines were dark, looming over the fading animals. She brushed her fingertips over the bear. Charcoal from her fingers scarred its face.

Tears welled up in her eyes, turning the scene liquid.

Amuun'axsum sat among the soft, decomposing debris. Grief settled in beside her. The torch beside her was a small light. And she was alone.

She looked at the Lightning Serpent she had drawn over the animals; the animals now appeared to be cheering—or screaming. Amuun'axsum flinched and knocked the torch over. She gasped and flung dirt over the flames before they could spread. Flustered and afraid in the sudden dark, she scrambled out of the snag into the night. She started to run. Branches scratched her arms and legs. Shafts of moonlight flashed across her face. She found the trail and ran faster.

Then she was suddenly on the ground on her back.

Amuun'axsum held a hand to her chest, groaning. A darkened form above leaned toward her.

"Are you all right? You came out of nowhere," he said.

Amuun'axsum shifted up on her elbows and peered up at the man.

"Why were you running in the dark?" he asked. He held out a hand to help her up.

Nervous but trying to appear otherwise, she placed her hand in his.

"Why were you?" she said, annoyed.

"I wasn't—running, that is." The man lifted her before she was quite ready, and she nearly fell again. He quickly pressed his other hand to her shoulder to help steady her. So close now, she could see his face. Recognition swamped her thoughts.

"Dushuuw…"

The chief's son had started to step back politely, but now he paused. His warm hand still gripped her own. His other hand slid down from her shoulder but paused at her elbow. The tree boughs rustled in the breeze, making openings for the moonlight before closing them again. He dropped his hands to his sides, and she shivered.

Dushuuw bent and picked her cloak up from the ground. He draped it around her shoulders, though still she shivered. He suddenly gripped her harder.

"Is something wrong at home?" he asked.

"No. Something scared me in the woods. I ran. Silly, I suppose. Probably just a small animal."

"Why were you out in the first place?" Dushuuw stood away from her a pace. "Were you running away?"

Amuun'axsum blanched and shook her head. "Eekbis wanted to stay home. I couldn't sleep. I'm going back now, though." She started to step around him.

He put a hand out to stop her. "You are going the wrong way."

"I see…"

He kept his hand raised.

"I would not run away without taking food with me, would I?"

"No, I suppose not."

"I needed some air is all."

"I see…"

He relaxed, and together they followed the trail into the village. The shaman's house drew closer.

"Dushuuw…"

He stopped and turned.

"Do not tell her, please, that I was out."

He looked at her intently. Amuun'axsum held her breath—she only added to his suspicions with that. He slowly nodded, then continued on.

Amuun'axsum crept back into the house. The shaman snored beyond the partition, and Amuun'axsum breathed a sigh of relief. She lay on her mat and hugged her blanket to her chin, still trying to banish from her mind the memories that had assaulted her again inside the snag. She wanted to fill a river with tears, and shoot her fear to the moon. She wanted a bench, not a mat. To own things, not hide them. A home. A voice. A name—to be known.

Exhaustion set in. Amuun'axsum focused on the warmth of the blanket, of a brief touch.

The Long Ago

HEAVY HANDS GRABBED Small One by the waist. Small One's father flung her over his shoulder, and she watched the approaching wall of water. Where was her grandmother? She had never seen the old woman run. She shut her eyes. A roaring sound drew closer, louder. Small One squeezed her eyes further shut. Stories about monsters and her own bad dreams of being chased jabbed her mind.

Small One tasted a salty mist on her lips, even as she smelled the boundary of the forest. This time, Small One knew her screams were real.

Suddenly, her father thrust her toward the sky and she opened her eyes. Her body slammed against a large tree bough. Instinctively, she wrapped her arms over the branch. Her father yelled something she could not make out. She struggled upward, his hand at her foot to give her one last push. She lurched toward the trunk, clinging to the cedar's stalwart girth in a desperate hug, and looked down. But where she expected to see her father's face and outstretched arms, there was surging black water.

Small One watched in horror as she clung to the shuddering tree, the sea surging beneath her drawn-up legs. Planks, bowls, gasping faces and limp bodies—and canoes, some empty and others with families clinging to the edges—all of it rushing past, some of it knocking into the trunk of her refuge before bouncing off and continuing along, so fast.

Soon she no longer screamed as they did. Her throat was raw with exertion and salt, her voice silenced by the grip of unparalleled terror. She felt as if a story was ending before it was supposed to, conclusion surging over tiny imagined scenes of rites and passages before they could be brought to life.

A boy clinging to a piece of driftwood now rapidly approached her tree. He did not scream. His eyes were searching, then found her own. He was nearly beneath her. He shouted over the monster's roar, and shot his hand up. Shivering, Small One held onto her tree with one arm, squeezed her eyes shut—and reached out her hand.

Oh, the people have never seen such a storm. Thunderbird whips his serpent belt. Flash! goes the lightning. He beats his great wings, beats them, beats them—and the thunder is so loud that it shakes the very earth. Even great houses fall as if built from twigs. And such rains fall that the sea begins to overrun the beaches, and it rises and rises and rises still more... So much water that the salty taste begins to go away.

Thunderbird soars over the sea, his great wings spread wide, wide, wide... And beyond, far out at sea, he sees Whale.

Whale is out there, spraying and diving and celebrating, for the people have chosen him, chosen Whale. And, well, there is an old rivalry there between Whale and Thunderbird.

Thunderbird sees Whale. He spreads his talons wide—sharp, sharp talons—and he dives. He lands upon Whale's back, and digs those talons in deep.

Whale tries to dive,
    tries to bring Thunderbird down.
Thunderbird tries to fly,
    tries to bring Whale up.
It is a great battle... Whale trying to dive. Thunderbird trying to fly—and not letting go, those talons digging deep, deep, deeper into Whale's back.

1699
FALL

15

It was like many shifts—quiet. A whisper added to the breath of the wind. A single strain of chill infused in the sunlight. The barest tinge of yellow seeping out of the veins of an alder leaf. A stray drop of rain on the shoulder. The height of a child growing by a length of shadow.

The moon spent in rest—with nothing expected of anyone except to soak up the last sun-filled days—came to an end.

Hunters sharpened their arrowheads, preparing to bring back otter furs and elk hides. Carvers sharpened their own tools and spent their mornings trekking, deciding which trees would be fated for planks and for canoes. Weavers sat against house walls outdoors, soaking up the steadily waning daylight as they wove nets and mats. Fishermen assembled their bait and hooks. Warriors took their private counsels.

The village swelled with anticipation, but most of all for the imminent return of full, fat whales on their passage south. Indeed, the village swelled in truth, as several people followed Sawsin across the strait to Wuh-uhch when she married Q̓otsik. Houses began to fill again. All eyes seemed to follow the young whaler and his bride, waiting to witness what the pair would bring to their shore.

But Dushuuw shielded his eyes from the dipping sun and looked toward the sea for something else. It was low tide, and women wended their way along the bay, pausing now and then to swing a leg in a wide circle as they stalked crabs. Dushuuw looked over the women who circled and bent in silhouette.

"Young Son, come to me."

Dushuuw turned toward his father's voice and meandered to the drift log. They sat facing the horizon. Dushuuw stretched his legs out.

Around them, people wiled away the waning hours. Smoke rose from beach fires where women cooked evening meals. A dog sat in the sand, tongue lolling as it watched boys play with a hoop it could not chase for the leash binding it to a post. The women in the shallows continued their slow orbits, trapping crabs beneath their feet, bending to retrieve them, tossing them into baskets.

"What do you see?" his father asked.

The chief's gaze was directed at the sky and hills, and so Dushuuw sought to identify the signs of the coming weather. "The water is a dark gray, yet the seastacks are still visible," Dushuuw said. "The wind is from the northeast, strong for this early."

Chahbuhł waved his hand for Dushuuw to stop.

"I see almost everyone here," the chief said. "Do you know who I do not see?" Chahbuhł slid a glance to Dushuuw but did not bother waiting for a reply. "I do not see your brother and his new wife. I do not see your cousin. I do not see your uncle. I do not see Kweelthup. My, I do not even see Huh-uuk and Yaq."

Dushuuw dreaded his father's next words.

"If you are to do a thing that is beyond human power, you must have more than human strength for the task," Chahbuhł said.

The pronouncement sat between them.

"I bathe. I pray," Dushuuw said.

Chahbuhł shook his head. "You are careless," he whispered.

Dushuuw worked his jaw as he drew his gaze over the women.

"I had a lot of time to think while you were away," his father said, "and a lot of men whispering in my ear. Qotsik went whispering along behind them, always with a word of reassurance they were meant to hear. In your name, Qotsik will challenge every one of them, every time. Your brother would fight even me, if I took you out of that canoe. Fortunate for you, or not, I believe him. You belong in that canoe. But your brother is wrong about one thing. He believes you already possess the protection that is needed for the hunts. When there is a failure, he takes it on himself—and, truly, sometimes I do wonder," the chief said, "when I see what he can do. So much power contained in one man cannot always be safely contained." He turned back to Dushuuw. "But that is all the more reason you must be properly prepared."

Dushuuw tried to absorb his father's words, but he could not get past his frustration. His brother would fight in his name. But what kind of name was that now?

"And still you fight..."

Dushuuw glared at his father before catching himself. He looked down at his hands, which were balled into fists. He clenched them tighter. "I was born to fight battles for you. I have brought you salmon and slaves and the heads of your enemies." He took a breath. "Why isn't that enough?"

Dushuuw waited for his father's anger, always strong enough to match his own. But instead his father nodded.

"I thought it was enough, before," Chahbuhí said. "More than enough." He looked out to the sea. "Not anymore. Not now." He waved off Dushuuw, anticipating a response. "I take the blame. It seems I should have taught you our ways from the beginning, as your mother always wished when she carried you inside, both of us hoping for a boy."

The sea sliced the sun in half. Wispy clouds burned orange over the men's heads. The women continued to move in their silent transits across the bay.

"You are physically strong, Young Son. A skilled warrior. But this is an old man's reminder that there is danger in every kind of weakness," the chief said, lifting his walking stick for emphasis. "We move along a thin and fearsome line: the physical world on one side, the spiritual world on the other. And if we forget that, we not only lose the power and protection of the stronger world—we invite the destruction it brings. We face forces far greater than anything we could match on our own.

"Do you think you will be strong enough to wield a war club forever? Look at me and see the answer, Young Son."

The sun made its final descent. The women seemed frozen in movement.

The chief turned to him. "With your brother's strength in the bow, we will finish out the whaling season. But first, you will follow me to the peak. I will teach you the way I taught your brother, perhaps what I should have taught you all along. I will teach you how to live—as a man, as a whaler. As my son."

Dushuuw swam through swirling emotions. The bitterness of the implication that he was not yet a man. The terror of the unknown. The claim of fatherhood delivered so late.

"We leave in the morning," Chahbuhí said.

The last shred of the orange sun sank into the sea. The sky glowed. Dushuuw could start to make out the features of the women who backed up the beach as the tide turned. One woman already stood beyond the reach of the creeping surf, her wrist bound with a cedar band. Dushuuw and his father sat side by side awaiting dusk, their eyes settled on different points of what lay before them.

Young Son shouted as he brought down the club, and struck again. The head flew to the ground with a thunk. It was only wood. Yet seeing it fall and roll was satisfying. He looked over at the war chief for approval.

Wiid walked over, his muscles like boulders. "Good, good. You will please your father. You make me proud."

Young Son was happy at the first statement, overjoyed at the second.

The war chief slapped a club against his thigh as he walked. "You would do well to be less eager, however." He slugged Young Son on the back of the head.

"*ʔiškida!*" Young Son rubbed the already growing lump.

"You miss the man who is preparing to strike you if you are so eager to take the life of his friend," Wiid said.

"Yes, chief," Young Son said, still rubbing his head.

"Join the warriors by my fire tonight, hear their stories, get their advice?"

Young Son grinned. "Absolutely."

Wiid waved him away with a smile. "Go make some mischief." Young Son dropped the club and ran to find Yaq.

Yaq sat in the sand, tossing rocks into the surf. When he spotted Young Son, he sprang up. "Finally!"

"The war chief keeps me busy," Young Son said.

"He's always keeping you busy!"

The young men made their way down the long beach, farther from the river and the village, heading toward a cluster of rocks.

"So you have a *tume·nuwis* for killing, hey?"

"*ʔi·*, Yaq," Young Son said, mouth twisting.

"What? Come on, some do. There is nothing untoward in that."

"Well, yes, but…"

"But, but, but," Yaq said, his hands splaying out in front of him in mockery. "Someone has got to bring home the heads. And we both know it will not be me." He flapped his thin arms for emphasis. "Why not you? If not to save a woman's bare ass, at least to save mine." He stopped, held up a finger. "But, if you do, please save at least one woman's ass, and breasts, and—"

Young Son shoved his foot at his friend's backside. Yaq laughed.

They reached the rocks and climbed up, then picked their way back down into a hidden depression. It was low tide, but soon to turn. So they picked up their sharpened rocks that Yaq had stashed higher up and started scraping at the rock before it would be submerged.

After a time, Young Son sat back while Yaq continued dragging his rock back and forth across the stone surface. Young Son dropped his own rock into his open palm and let it sit there. "I like it," he said.

"I like it too," Yaq said, settling back to admire their progress. "But you do not sound like you like it." He looked over at Young Son. "You are not talking about this here, are you?"

"Isn't it wrong to enjoy killing?"

Yaq shrugged and turned back to his carving. "That is what Ċotsik will do, yes? Kill, and enjoy it?"

"No," Young Son said. He firmly shook his head. He felt a twinge of pride, remembering the words repeated over and over to his brother from their father. "That is far different. The whale gives himself to Ċotsik—or will, that is, when father gives him the harpoon." Young Son was pleased with himself, always feeling taller himself when he was able to brag about the young man he could claim as his brother.

"He has not 'taken' a whale yet then. Although, for that matter, you have not taken a man's life yet," Yaq said. "So how do you know you will like it?"

"I just—do. Some things you know, the war chief says."

Yaq sat back against the rock, and tossed his carving tool back and forth between his hands. "I suppose it is something, that we both speak of Ċotsik as having a *tume·nuwis* for hunting whales, though he has yet to lead a hunt."

"Inevitable," Young Son said, sitting forward.

Yaq looked frighteningly close to deep thought. As if realizing it, he went back to his carving. "Even my father talks about Ċotsik's power."

Everyone talked about Ċotsik's power.

"Men like that, my father says, you can keel over and die or be hurt if you get too close to them."

Young Son thought of his brother, of the distance that had grown between them as they progressed through their respective training—he for battle, Ċotsik for the whale. Ċotsik spent considerable time with their two older cousins. Some day, the trio would whale together, all in a line. Uhpqoolth would be right behind Ċotsik. And behind him, Wiikihbis was far into his training to be line-tender, a role his father held before him. Even this lower-born best friend of his, Yaq, was expected to join the whaling canoe, being trained to inherit his father's role as diver. Young Son would not join him. He wondered if that meant Yaq would be too good for him too. He chucked his rock at Yaq's back.

"Hey! You almost made me mess up." Yaq's tongue protruded from between his lips as his etching tool scratched and dragged across the rock. Young Son cracked a smile. No. No worries in Yaq's case.

"Ọotsik will take many whales. I will sever many heads. So what kind of *tume·nuwis* will you seek, Yaq?"

Yaq smiled over his shoulder and gestured with his head at the bisected oval taking shape on the rock. "What do you think?"

They laughed.

"What are you two pups doing?"

Young Son sighed and looked up at the waiting leer of Wiikihbis.

"Nothing that concerns you," Young Son said.

Things had changed since Wiikihbis had married. Wiikihbis had convinced his new wife, a cousin of Young Son's family, to relocate from her family home in Oosa-ilth to join his family and her own relatives in Wuh-uhch. Knowing the boys' jealousy, he lorded his marriage over them as if he had accomplished something. Never mind that his wife was higher ranked than him; so too, their toddler son. Ọotsik didn't mind; he simply shrugged when Young Son complained. But their cousin Uhpqoolth was starting to exude the same smug attitude—reminding Young Son and Yaq that he would soon marry as well, now that his father had given him the name of Uhpqoolth. He bragged about a sexual prowess that would give him a strapping son with just a look at his wife. Young Son and Yaq shared stifled laughs whenever they pretended Pikoo was approaching—and the would-be sexual hero shut up, with a guilty glance over his shoulder to a mother who wasn't there.

As if any of them had anything to brag about. Yaq had beat all of them to that first rite of manhood.

Uhpqoolth popped his head up alongside Wiikihbis, looking to him as if for direction.

"You know what, Young Son? You are common," said Wiikihbis, as he examined their activity with mock disgust. "That is why you hang out with this Yaq kid so much."

Uhpqoolth looked a little worried, but he didn't say anything.

Young Son gritted his teeth and resented the fact that he had to look up to see the men perched on the rock above them.

"You cannot talk about Yaq like that," Young Son said. "Yaq is going to be in the whaling canoe too. Nobody dives better than him." He regretted throwing his rock at Yaq. His hand searched behind his back for another.

"Yes, he is good for that one thing," the young man said. "Just as you will be good for one thing. Just as your mother was good for one thing." He reached down and patted the carving Yaq had been making. His eyes remained fixed on Young Son.

Uhpqoolth shifted. "Wiikihbis..."

Young Son's fingers curled around the rock he had found at his back and he hurled it at the man's head. Wiikihbis staggered backward with a cry of pain and disappeared over the ledge. Uhpqoolth gasped and disappeared to follow. Young Son scrambled after them, scraping his legs and feet as he jumped the ledge and slid down the rock's face into the rising surf, where the injured young man sat with his hand against his bleeding forehead. Young Son ignored Yaq's frantic shouts behind him.

Wiikihbis staggered to his feet, but Young Son slammed him back down. Uhpqoolth shoved Young Son from the side, and a slosh of salt water burned Young Son's throat. But he kicked his cousin in the groin, left him writhing, and threw himself at Wiikihbis again. A fleeting expression of fear ran across the man's face and Young Son smiled. Then the man's rage returned, and Young Son matched it, digging his knee into Wiikihbis's chest and flattening the man's face into the water, letting the sea surge into his nostrils and open mouth. Young Son's arms trembled, tense.

Then strong arms were pulling him away. Wiikihbis spat salt water and coughed, slapping out of the water onto the beach. Young Son tried to fight his way back, but his brother shoved on his chest, pushing him toward the woods.

"Walk away, brother." The voice low but firm. "Walk with me."

At first, Young Son hadn't registered his brother's voice. He balled his fist and lifted his arm. Then his eyes snapped to Qotsik's face, and his arm crumpled to his side, his fingers loose. Young Son staggered, and let his brother lead him. They walked on, his brother's calm hand at his back as if to bank his roiling emotions.

"Do you know what your mother called you when you were a baby?"

Young Son went numb. He wanted to hate his brother, too, for mentioning his mother. But this was Qotsik, and Young Son could not even summon a desire to think an unkind thought about his brother.

"It was not Young Son," Qotsik said. "It was always Uhsahb."

Young Son broke away and sat on top of a moss-covered rock, his back to Qotsik. Song birds chirped merrily against his mood.

"She would tickle your stomach and whisper, 'Uhsahb,'" Qotsik said. Young Son heard him over his shoulder, echoing his mother's whisper.

"She would take you by your face before you went out to play with your toy club and say, 'Uhsahb.'" His voice took on an encouraging tone.

"She would sit next to us at night and stroke your head after one of your night terrors and say, 'Uhsahb.'" His voice soothed.

High-Born Child.

High-Born Child.

High-Born Child...

Young Son squeezed his eyes, fighting the childish tears that slipped through all the same, and sat slumped and silent.

"Maybe you can start acting like it," Qotsik said, without malice, his voice echoing a mother's encouragement. "At least for her."

It was the deep of night, and Dushuuw was in the forest.

Troubled thoughts had roiled through his mind, and no amount of turning from one side to the other brought sleep. So he had moved.

And now, crouched low, he looked upon the face of the woman who called him by name. The slave's eyes were closed, her cloak rose and fell with her breaths, her hand curled beside her head, fingertips tinged black from charcoal.

Here, in this snag—a guidepost on his way to the river pool where he tried to be the man his brother and father wanted—here, the shaman's slave lay sleeping like an answer to a question he had never asked. A small torch flickered in a firebox. The light flickered over the snouts of a simply drawn Lightning Serpent and a wolf, making it seem as if the charcoal drawings spoke to each other.

Dushuuw drummed his fingers on the side of the firebox, to the beat of an ancient dance.

The woman stirred, her fingers gently closing, as if to capture something. Her lips seemed to shape a word.

He reached out, feeling her breaths pulse against his palm, and pressed his hand against her mouth.

SHE WAS DREAMING. The words of her mother's song tried to sing themselves. Already the drum was madly beating. But the voiceless cannot sing. Then suddenly she was in Wuh-uhch's bay, and a wave of seawater shoved the words back down her throat.

Amuun'axsum awoke, consumed by fear—but the cry that came from the dream was held back by a hand pressed against her mouth.

She kicked and struck out at the man's arm.

"Quulthoo," the man said. "Quulthoo…"

It was Dushuuw, she finally realized, and she stopped beating at the chief's son. But with his hand still pressed to her mouth, she was even more fearful. And determined. She bit him.

"*ʔiškida!*" He whipped his hand away, shaking it. "I just didn't want you screaming when I woke you up."

Amuun'axsum scrambled into a sitting position and slid back against the wall of the snag. "What are you doing here?" She drew her cloak tight.

He stood by the opening, blocking it. "What are *you* doing here?"

"I come here sometimes."

"So do I."

"I have never seen you."

"Perhaps you knew better before to stay indoors when it is time for a whaler to pray." His tone was more sarcastic than serious.

Amuun'axsum slumped as she looked up at him. "You should not tell me that."

"You should not be here for me to tell," he said. "But here you are." He gave her a nervous smile as he crouched down, and she looked away. "Does the shaman snore so loudly that you must sneak into the woods at night so often?"

Amuun'axsum's shoulders relaxed with a shaky laugh. She ran her hand over the back of her neck. She had never meant to fall asleep here, so in a way it was good that the chief's son had found her here. And in another way, it was very bad. The dream still clung to her, and she thought of all the things hidden here she had not wanted to share. But she would have to share one, now.

"You have heard of the Wild Woman of the Woods?" she asked.

Dushuuw pursed his lips. "You mean Qaq-owuhtsah-lth—or to many here, Ihsh-kuhs. The Basket Woman, yes? A giantess. Old, and ugly. She carries away children in her giant pack basket to her lair—a story the grandmothers use to scare the little ones into not straying too far." He grinned. "You are not saying the shaman snores like…"

"No," Amuun'axsum cut him off with a laugh. "Yes, there are many names, many stories. But to me, she is Dzunukwa. And she is more than a stealer of disobedient children." Hesitantly, Amuun'axsum moved aside the piece of bark atop her hiding place and reached inside for the wrapped bundle. "She also is a protector of forest things. And, in her wild hair, there nest—"

He rested one knee on the ground and leaned forward, looking at the dry object she uncovered and held out in her palm.

"A hummingbird," he said.

"They fly about her as she walks in the woods. They are a guide," she said, rising to her knees, still holding out the bird's body, "and they bring whalers blessing."

He edged back and eyed the bird in her hand.

"You said you are preparing for the whale hunt," she said. "Take it."

Dushuuw shook his head with a scoffing smile. "It would be wasted on me." He stood up again and looked out the opening of the snag.

"There is no harm in taking it either way," Amuun'axsum said as she rewrapped the bird.

He looked down at her, with that searching expression again.

She stood and held out the bundle.

"Take it, Dushuuw," she said. "Perhaps it will help you."

His expression shifted, and he took the bird. She took a step back and drew a breath. She did not want to give up this place. Now that he had accepted the gift, she tried to gather her confidence to tell him as much. But he spoke first.

"Why do you call me that?" he asked, his voice stiff.

Amuun'axsum said nothing, unsure what he was asking.

He stared down at the bundled bird. "You don't call me… what the others call me."

Amuun'aẖsum stiffened and drew a nervous breath as she realized her mistake. She had rehearsed their names so much, she had not thought to call him anything other than Dushuuw. Had she slipped at all in public? Had she failed to call him Young Son in front of the shaman or, worse, the chief? Then she thought of his tone. She thought of her own name, and how she cringed every time she was called by the slave name she refused to own. Bitterness rose in her throat.

"I call you Dushuuw because it is who you are," she said.

But she feared what questions he might ask next. And so she grabbed her torch, and hurried past him into the dark, hoping it was still a long way until morning, fearing what might happen if the shaman awoke to find her gone.

Spring 1689
Ten years earlier

Maḥtii lay on her back on a bench, looking up at the roof planks. She hummed as she swung her foot back and forth and picked at the shredded bark skirt she had bound around the fat waist of her toy bear.

It had been three days since her father left in his canoe to go catch a whale. She was dreadfully bored.

She flopped her bear off to the side—its nose a bit crooked from where it had been broken and reattached—and rolled onto her stomach. Maḥtii rested her chin on her hands and looked at her mother. Her mother lay on the adjacent sleeping bench, a blanket covering her body up to her shoulders. The woman lay facing the wall, to urge the whale in the same direction, bringing it to their shore. Noblewomen of their line had a special bond with the whale, her mother had told her, forged through ancient pacts and from powers derived as givers of life. That sounded nice and big, Maḥtii thought, even if it only seemed to mean doing next to nothing.

Maḥtii's stomach growled and she looked around for a slave to give her a bite to eat. Then, with a wash of guilt, she glanced at her mother as if caught in a lie. Her mother had not eaten and barely drank since the whalers departed. It would be rude to eat in front of her. But Maḥtii was tired of taking her meals elsewhere.

"Not eating at least makes not moving that much easier," her mother had tiredly quipped that morning.

Not for the first time, Maḥtii wondered if she wanted to become a woman—or, more to the point, a whaler's wife. The baths were bad enough. Her mother was already taking her along on those. Staying in that cold water until her lips turned blue? And her mother chastising her for complaining. "I will not raise a lazy daughter. You will be able to last longer than your man, like me." Bad enough. But not even being able to brush one's hair, for fear the lines piercing the whale and towing it home might snap with one broken strand from her head—no wonder her mother did not dare move!

There were other mysteries that were alluring, on the other hand. Her mother's constant cold bathing was in preparation for secret rituals with her father for his whaling prayers. And there was nothing quite so thrilling as a secret. No one was privy to those details, or at least Maḥtii was not. She gathered only that it involved swimming around and acting like whales, or so Tiichswii claimed. But he was being trained by his uncle to hunt sea otters, so what did he know?

If he was right though, her parents were not great imitators. Or at least her father did not seem to get as many whales as the southern men he tried to emulate, according to the mumbles of the elders. Maḥtii was not sure. She looked at her mother, tracing the outline of the woman's motionless body that rose and fell beneath the blanket. Even laying down, her mother was a picture of poise. Her mother was an exacting woman, good at everything and beautiful besides. Maḥtii picked at the carved eyes of the bear's face with a fingernail. And her father had built them this village by his own strength—a place he had brought whales, even if they were not many.

Maḥtii's stomach growled again. Maybe her parents were just avoiding being greedy. If there were more whales, she would have more friends, she thought, as she flopped to her back again and blew a hair from her eyes. Tiichswii was her best friend, and he was a boy.

As it was, Maḥtii was not allowed outdoors to see a whale when it was brought to shore. Girls, as well as women in the moon of their blood, would work against the whales' good favor. She supposed that might be a reason to be a whaler's wife. Then, as a woman full of the power to give life, she would be free to get up and go outside to greet the whale, which gave them its life. Surges of excitement met her when she was allowed outdoors now. How much more elated would she be if it were to welcome the whale? How important! The last time a whale was carved on their shore, Maḥtii had peeked through the wall boards. She had watched her mother place feathers on the whale in the shape of a crescent moon. No one said she could not look, though she felt a little guilty about it.

She looked over at her spy hole, low on the wall, where a gap had formed between the overlapping planks because of a rotting knot of wood. The shadow of a man passed over the spot, the slave man who was charged with keeping vigil, to let them know when the whalers returned. Out of sight, but always there, charged with protecting them.

Maḥtii yawned and pulled her bear tight in the crook of her arm. She had come into the house determined to train to be a whaler's wife. To lay as still as her mother. To see if she had what it took to become a woman. She could not last until the next meal.

~

She woke blinking to the sounds of talking. She wiped the drool from her chin and levered herself up. At the front of the house, her mother leaned against the wall for support as she inclined her head toward the doorway, talking to someone. A slave girl crouched in front of the noblewoman, rubbing the cramps out of her calves.

Maḥtii perked up and swung her legs over the side of the bench. She hugged her bear. Her father's whaling party must be in sight. He was home! Probably now the slave man was telling her mother whether there was a whale behind her father's canoe. Then her mother would know what to do next.

Leaving her bear behind, Maḥtii scampered over to her mother. She slowed, recognizing the look of disappointment on her mother's face, though the noblewoman tried to hide it. There seemed to be an extra measure of exhaustion weighing on her shoulders; she waved the slave girl away outdoors. Mother and daughter were alone inside the house. The slave man remained unseen outside the empty doorway. The three of them stood together, and yet not, a wall between them. Maḥtii slipped between her mother and the wall, curling her fingertips over the edge of a board, and peeked through her spy hole.

The slave's legs blocked her view. She considered reaching through and poking him. A quick check back at her mother's face, eyes clenched shut, led Maḥtii to think that may not be the best idea just now.

"I will not leave," her mother said.

"There may come a day when you don't have a choice, my lady."

Maḥtii could barely make out the man's soft words.

Her mother took a shuddering intake of breath. "You know that will only ruin everything. I must think of my daughter."

A vision of the sea suddenly opened up through the peephole as the slave man shifted. She blinked as the reflected sunlight momentarily blinded her. She hunted through the wavering dark blue splotches for her father's canoes.

"And what do you believe I think upon every day, Mowach?"

The slave man's voice was not loud, but in contrast to his usual soft tones it was loud enough. That was not the only reason, however, that Maḥtii shifted her vision to the side, seeking the slave man who would call her mother by her given name.

Maḥtii's arm was wrenched upward as her mother pulled her back to their benches in the corner of the house.

"Please," the slave said, his voice soft again. "You must consider it…"

Her mother said nothing.

Maḥtii winced as her mother pulled her tight to her side. The noblewoman's face twisted on itself as tears wet her cheeks. Maḥtii was frightened.

"Are you in pain, mother?"

Her mother nodded but did not speak. Her mouth parted, though she restrained the cry.

"Shall I rub your legs, mother?" Maḥtii was already kneeling in the dirt as she asked the question. She cupped her hands around her mother's calf. The taught muscle was rigid against the girl's fingers, which seemed incapable of affecting change, though she kept trying.

Her mother took a long, deep breath. She gently patted away the tears from her face. She stared straight ahead, running her palms along the sides of her head to smooth her hair. Her back was straight, and soon she looked as if nothing upsetting had ever happened. She transformed before Maḥtii's eyes. It was a familiar regal look. This was the first time, however, that Maḥtii found in it a reason to be scared. It was as if her mother put on a mask. How many other times had she affected the same change? Her mother looked down at her. "Come, Maḥtii. Sit next to me."

Maḥtii hiked herself up onto the high bench beside her mother. She smoothed her hair, though she wondered if it did any good.

"What are we doing, mother?"

"We await your father."

Maḥtii looked up at her mother, whose face was set with determination—chin lifted, eyes forward. It was the look she always wore when Maḥtii's father returned without a whale, frustrated and accusing. This was the first time, though, that Maḥtii would face her father beside her mother and not just eavesdrop. Would he still greet Maḥtii with his wide smile? Would he still pick her up and swing her toward the roof? Could she run to him?

Perhaps her mother was deciding that it was time for Maḥtii to begin her own path to womanhood. A woman does not giggle. A woman keeps her feet firmly planted. A woman is strong, even when she is not.

Maḥtii heard the sounds of the canoes coming onto the beach, the whalers calling to family and unloading gear. She took a long, deep breath, fixed her eyes toward the open doorway, and lifted her chin.

17

AFTER THE SLAVE had left, Dushuuw stayed at the snag for a time, trying to sort through all that happened. Wondering if she were up to no good, he sifted through the small items in her hiding spot and found bits of rubbish: a broken toy spear, pebbles, a perfumed shell, a small scrap of otter fur, a tiny fragment of abalone. He eyed the woman's charcoal drawings: the slinking and soaring serpent, the open muzzle of the wolf, the crude snipe, the bear. He regarded the small bundle that he still cradled in his palm, and his skin prickled. Why did she come here? Did all these small bits connect into a whole? The shaman seemed to trust her with things, unusual for a slave.

After a time, he realized that, while he still felt as unsettled as he had when he had left his sleepless bed at the house, the feeling had shifted. She left something behind, in this place. He had been heading toward the river pool for a reason: to get away. Now, with this tiny bird in his hand, he might be equipped for the pool's purpose. He spent the rest of the night at his river pool, going through the rituals for supporting the whale hunt as his uncle had taught.

The night passed. The time neared to meet his father. The pre-dawn air was cold across his head, his hair and skin damp from the river.

A cloak flapped over the branch where he had hung it, and Dushuuw raised the corner to wipe his face. His feet squished in the muddy bank, and the river rushed. As he rolled his shoulders, his back faintly smarted from where he had scrubbed with hemlock branches. Absent the muddy feet, he could not be any physically cleaner. He had thought that would be enough—to rid himself of his human stench. A pouch lay on a rock below the cloak. He picked it up, reached inside, and brushed his hand over the bundle, itching to see the feathers the wrappings hid, feel them beneath his fingertips.

Dushuuw took the cloak down from the branch and swung it across

173

his back. The fabric enveloped him in warmth as he pulled it close.

It was nearly dawn. Dushuuw hurried back to the house. When he arrived, he entered softly so as not to awaken anyone. A fire burned in the far corner, where his father looked up at his approach. Dushuuw saw the shifting of his father's expression. From anger at his absence, to surprise at the sight of his son's wet hair and the cloak. The chief nodded in approval. Behind the chief, Um-iiqsu looked over at her stepson and smiled; she draped a heavy cloak over the chief's shoulders, and gave Dushuuw a look he knew to mean: Take care of this man.

Chahbuhi took his walking stick, leaning on it as he stood. He handed Dushuuw a small pack and a rolled-up bear skin, then led him back out the doorway without a word. Dushuuw glanced at Buh-uhs—who slept under his blankets near Dushuuw's bench, mouth open—then followed his father out the doorway.

~

Night had fallen by the time the men pushed through the trees to the pinnacle. The wind caught Dushuuw's hair and whipped it about his head. A wide swath of light arched overhead, like the sea-churned wake of a canoe. Compared to the dark forest, it was like stepping into the dawn of a new day.

Chahbuhi spread the bear skin on the ground and Dushuuw helped him lay down. Dushuuw remained standing, his face turned upward. His gut growled. He tamped down his body's calls for food, circulating the spit within his mouth. This part, at least, was a familiar form of preparation for him. The fasting, the long nights—all things he did to prepare for the rigors of battle.

A wolf howled from the deep ravine below. Salal rustled as suspicious eyes glowed among the branches. The stars seemed so close, as if they might reach down and touch him.

"This is where it begins," Chahbuhi said.

Dushuuw startled at his father's words, the first since they had spoken on the beach the previous day. He waited for more. But the exhausted chief pulled his hat over his face and fell asleep.

Taking the cloak off his shoulders, Dushuuw spread it on the ground beside his father. He lay down, and closed his eyes to sleep beneath the ancient and watchful night sky—the only night, he sensed, where sleep would be allowed.

They were up well before dawn. Dushuuw awoke to the crackles of a fire.

Chahbuhⱡ placed containers of ocher and mica between them. Dushuuw hunched his shoulders. The old whaler dragged his fingers through the paint and applied it in striped and dotted patterns on his face. Dushuuw dipped his fingers in the paint, and copied the patterns onto his own face. Then they set off.

By the light of torches, they descended partway down the peak by a different path—if it could be called a path. Soon, they walked among alders. The mottled white bark brightened the forest above a creek, which bounced its way through a steep-sided ravine. Father and son followed the creek's path from knotted overhangs. The creek's babbling turned to a rushing, then a crashing. The ridge they followed suddenly ended with a sheer drop. Dushuuw peered over the edge, in the growing twilight of a blue hour, and watched the waters swirl in a large pool at the base of the waterfall. Their destination. He followed his father down a narrow path.

Tucked among trees near the pool's edge was a moss-covered structure. Its cedar roof sagged with rot. Inside the shrine, the empty eyes of carved figures and bleached skulls looked out at the pool. They watched as Dushuuw trudged behind his father into the water.

As the sun rose, Dushuuw followed his father in prayer, shaking a rattle and singing, on and on. His wrist spiked with pain from shaking the rattle, something he had never done. His feet grew numb and his legs ached from lack of movement. And he knew this was merely a prelude.

Dushuuw dragged stinging nettles along his skin.

Rubbed his back and arms with hemlock.

Dipped beneath the pool waters and rose again, over and over.

Day into night into day, and again.

Deprived of sleep, food, and any drink other than the waters that slipped down his throat, Dushuuw began to see only what was in front of him, the edges of his vision growing black. His father was pushing him to new limits, and Dushuuw fought to keep the black unknown at bay—defending himself against the fear it sparked.

A canoe approached him. It was filled with masked men, who stood in the canoe that moved without paddles. Their lips moved as if singing a song, but he could hear nothing. The canoe bore down, its hull slicing the water—and cleaving his body in two...

Dushuuw awoke with a gasp, arms flailing over the rocky ground.

It was mid-morning. The scent of smoked fish awakened his senses with a jolt. He rolled over, joints stiff as he rose to a sitting position by the fire. His father handed him the food. Dushuuw barely chewed the fish in his hunger, and relief.

Birds called. Flies buzzed about. A spider skittered over a rock.

"I have taught you all that I can here for now," his father said. "The rest must wait for another time."

Dushuuw did not want to know what that meant. He was happy it was over. For now. He considered the hunk of fish between his fingers, poised before his mouth. He placed the food in his mouth and luxuriated in the taste. As he ate, he studied his father's face, seeking a sign that he had passed whatever test he had been given. He wondered if he had failed as soon as he had taken a bite of the fish. It was as if eating had awakened other forms of hunger. If there had been a hidden source of spiritual strength he was supposed to have attracted, his father would be disappointed; that was as elusive as the nightmare's song.

They prepared to leave. Grabbing his cloak, Dushuuw spied the pouch that he had hidden beneath it—he had forgotten about it in the haze of unending ritual. Opening the flap, he thrust his fingers past wrappings he had already loosened in search of the smooth feathers beneath, feeling a sense of reassurance at their touch, and a spark of something more. The idea that, maybe, he already had all he needed.

18

THE SHAMAN HAD SENT Amuun'axsum outdoors for the afternoon. The old woman worked on something she needed to keep secret.

Sometimes Eekbis seemed to treat Amuun'axsum like an acolyte, showing her things like the burl. The old woman never gave Amuun'axsum the full story; she stopped short of that. The shaman teased—or perhaps coaxed. At times, Amuun'axsum felt like prey, as if the shaman were stalking her, waiting for her to slip—or laughing, having already sprung her trap. Amuun'axsum kept her own secrets; and she would not give them up for the likes of a burl of wood. In the end, she knew what the old woman truly thought of her, despite her mothering moments. In the shaman's eyes, Amuun'axsum was a slave. And Eekbis gave her far more slave's errands than workbench lessons.

Today, Amuun'axsum found she did not mind. The shaman's house was lonely, remaining empty even after Sawsin's arrival. And given a whole afternoon to collect firewood, Amuun'axsum decided to wander to her heart's content. She forded the river, and meandered toward the far hillside. As she entered its forested flank, she gave a satisfied sigh.

She was humming to herself, walking under and among swaying tendrils of green, when she heard splashes and singing. Quickly, she ducked behind a tree. As the sounds continued, she slipped from tree to tree, closer and closer to their source. The sky opened above a lake. And on a small, pebbled shore stood Sawsin, a rope in her hand. The young noblewoman's voice was clear and as beautiful as the fine dress she wore. Her posture was erect, her expression confident, her eyes on the end of the rope, which disappeared beneath the surface of the lake.

The rope moved about as Sawsin sang about a whale. Amuun'axsum could not make out all of the words, but she recognized several of them from her mother's own language. The rope snaked closer and closer toward shore, toward her words. A figure rose from the water, a band of branches about his head. It was Q̇otsik, the rope tied around his waist. He blew water from his mouth toward the center of the lake, then grabbed hemlock branches and scrubbed his body as he circled Sawsin, singing his own song in his deep voice as his wife turned with him, linked together by the rope. They traded songs again as he slipped back into the water, submerging with barely a ripple.

Amuun'axsum turned away, back pressed to the tree. Sawsin's song carried over the water. Amuun'axsum fought to tamp down the jealousy that rose inside, that wished it were her, standing by the lake, rope in hand, singing a song she had the right to sing—a woman with power. But greater than her jealousy was her fear. For she was trespassing—in far graver ways than for a burl of bark.

~

Amuun'axsum dumped her hastily gathered firewood on the beach. The afternoon was not done yet, so she built a small fire and took some fish to prepare for the shaman's meal. She replaited her hair in the cool breeze as she waited for the fish to finish steaming. She had stopped looking over her shoulder some time ago, but her fingers still twitched on the strands of hair.

A gull meandered her direction over the beach, cocking its head toward the fish, feigning nonchalance. Amuun'axsum tossed a rock, sending it flapping.

A young boy suddenly plopped onto the ground beside her. Buh-uhs gave a very loud, very disgusted sigh.

Amuun'axsum looked around, but saw no one accompanying him.

"Quht-Quht says I have to sit here until he comes," the boy said, glowering.

Amuun'axsum opened her mouth, paused to search her memory for a moment, then shook her head. "Who?"

Buh-uhs eyed her but seemed hesitant to explain.

"Oh, now I remember." Amuun'axsum nodded at the boy. "Quht-Quht—yes, of course."

He breathed a small sigh of relief.

The boy jammed a twig in the matted sand and ground cover between his outstretched legs.

The twig was as thin as a hummingbird's beak, and snapped.

"What else did Quht-Quht say?"

The boy's eyebrows went up, and his lips twisted mockingly, as he

178

jabbed a bigger twig. "Just that I have to be *patient*, and he will be here *soon*." He paused, looking at her sideways. "And also that you should give me some of that to eat."

Amuun'axsum stifled a smile. She lifted the leaves and plucked out some of the fish, which was starting to flake. She broke the piece in two and handed him one of the hunks. They folded the bites into their mouths and shared self-satisfied smiles, a tiny conspiracy.

Feet settled between them and they looked up in unison from under their hat brims at Dushuuw. The chief's son went bareheaded. His hair lay matted against his back in the rain.

Buh-uhs scrambled up, then fell back onto the sand as Dushuuw gently kicked the boy in the back. "There you are," Dushuuw said.

The boy looked up at him aghast. "You told me to come here!"

Dushuuw looked nervously at Amuun'axsum.

She fought her own nerves. "You should have a better hat to protect you from the rain," she said.

He ran a hand over his wet hair and crouched between her and the boy. "I do not mind," he said, picking up bits of wood and tossing them into the fire.

"These hats take time. But with yours, I also am unsure about the design," she said, eyes flitting between the fire and his face. "There are different ways to represent a successful whale hunter."

Dushuuw dropped the bits of wood that remained in his hand. "Well, any way you choose, at least I can look the part," he said. But unlike the grimace in the snag, his expression this time was different. Self-effacing. Perhaps hopeful.

"Are we getting dinner now?" Buh-uhs slumped as if he had gone for days without sustenance.

The chief's son reached over and shoved the boy to the ground again with a smile. His expression toward Amuun'axsum was serious, however. She tried to work him out. He looked at the fire like it held the words for which he searched. "Perhaps we could discuss the design of the hat later," Dushuuw said. "Just as we—as we discussed designs before?"

Amuun'axsum was puzzled.

"The Lightning Serpent, for example," Dushuuw said.

"And the wolf, yes," said Amuun'axsum, remembering the charcoal drawings. "And the bear."

"But not the snipe," he added, finally cracking a smile.

Amuun'axsum laughed and flushed. She needlessly poked at the fish, as if its ogling eye could tell her how to respond. People walked past them up and down the beach, and the inside of her chest went cold. What was this about, really? Was she safe? Yet she couldn't shake a small thrill at the back of her mind. A chance, after all these years...

"A discussion," she said.

Dushuuw batted away Buh-uhs's attempt at a tackle and looked flustered. "Yes, yes," he said. "Just some—ideas, maybe." He wrapped the boy up against his chest as the boy kicked.

Before she could change her mind, Amuun'axsum assented. She offered a steaming chunk of the cooked fish.

A smile started to brush his lips, then he took a gangly elbow in his stomach from Buh-uhs. The boy snatched the fish from her fingers and shoved the morsel in his mouth, nearly spitting it out with his laughter. With a grunt, Dushuuw flung the boy over his shoulder, grabbed the boy's hat, and stood.

"Right then," he said.

"Finally!" the boy cried.

Amuun'axsum watched him stride away with the boy still flopped over his shoulder. The boy laughed as Dushuuw swatted him on the backside with the hat, the boy twisting as he tried to grab it back.

Under the brim of her hat, Amuun'axsum glanced around but no one paid her mind. The shaman's door remained blocked with the hanging hide. Amuun'axsum lifted the fish onto a platter. But she was too flustered to eat any of it now.

Had she understood his hints? Emotions swirled and chased each other inside her chest. Confusion. Curiosity. Fear. And a spark of hope, as if the hand she had been waiting for to lift her out of this life might finally be reaching out.

~

The shaman was in one of her talkative moods. Anticipating meeting the chief's son, Amuun'axsum did not respond or add to the conversation. She simply listened, trying to hurry the shaman to sleep. Yet night had fallen, and still the old woman buzzed from one topic to the next.

"The family cannot always help sing a song over the sick..."

Eekbis protected her knowledge. But she was also an old woman who hungered for conversation. Mostly the shaman focused on safe topics—the uses of plants, certain seasoned tidbits as to their more hidden uses. When she could, Amuun'axsum would reciprocate. She would share the rituals the old woman in her home village had taught her in the forest.

Once, the shaman had tried to coax more than face-paint patterns.

"You were once noble," said Eekbis, with a flippant gesture at the hidden, scarred tattoo. "Do you retain anything from your mother or father? Knowledge. Rituals. Songs?"

Amuun'axsum remembered freezing up as she briefly considered sharing the song with the shaman. Her heart thumped. She could prove her worth, perhaps impress the old woman enough that Eekbis would understand and help Amuun'axsum find whoever remained of her family. But her mother's words of warning kept the words inside. So she stuck to the lies foisted upon her that fiery night. "Nothing," she said. "I was young. And we were poor." It was not completely a lie, after all.

"What is your opinion?" the shaman asked.

Amuun'axsum startled back to attention and turned to see Eekbis smiling at her in a coaxing way.

"Are you listening?" the shaman asked.

Amuun'axsum forced a flustered smile. "I am sure I have no opinion on that topic." It did not matter that she had not heard what the shaman said; it was how Amuun'axsum always responded, unwilling to risk losing the woman's favor.

The shaman looked at her skeptically, then shook off her annoyance with a smile. She pinched Amuun'axsum's arm. "You are a dear girl to listen to an old woman prattle."

Amuun'axsum smiled back, relieved the night seemed to be ending.

"So, then there is also the matter of which song..."

Or perhaps not.

~

The shaman's snores were a long time coming from beyond the partition. At least Amuun'axsum did not have to worry about falling asleep herself; she was far too worried. She waited a good while longer to be sure Eekbis was soundly asleep, then shoved aside her blanket, pulled on her cloak, and grabbed a small torch and the unfinished hat.

She hurried through the forest, stepped off the path, neared the fallen tree, and almost ran into Dushuuw.

He laughed as he put his hands on her arms, steadying her. "At least we did not collide this time," he said. His hands were heavy and warm through her cloak. She stepped back, drawing the cloak snug.

"I was going to go back," he said. "I figured I had not made myself understood after all."

"The shaman was in a talkative mood," she said, shrugging. "Though I was not sure I understood either."

Dushuuw's eyes were bright with eagerness as he beckoned her back to the snag. Inside, she set her torch inside a firebox and sat down on the mat she had left on her last visit. She held the hat in her lap.

He sat across from her, the firebox between them. He looked nervous and eyed the hat in her lap.

"I did not really want to talk about the hat," he said.

Amuun'axsum gripped the weaving.

"The hummingbird," he said, placing a hand on a pouch attached to his hip. "I carry it now, when I go to pray. I plan to take it with me in the whaling canoe."

Amuun'axsum's hopes lifted on a surge of joy. He had kept it. He valued it. Her mind raced as she tried to think of what to say to bolster the connection.

"What are you?" he asked.

Amuun'axsum blanched, caught off guard. She looked toward the way out. Was it all a trap? She wrapped her hand around her band-covered wrist. But Dushuuw's face was alight. He shifted closer to the firebox. His gaze flitted to the base of the snag off to her side.

"You know things. You see them," he said. He looked at the bark wall behind her, his eyes gleaming.

Amuun'axsum glanced over her shoulder to the charcoal drawings of the Lightning Serpent and a wolf—images she had drawn as she had thought of her mother, of the song—and to her hiding spot, where she kept her childish but coveted reminders of her worth. She looked back and he was staring at her with a look of determination.

"That is why Eekbis has you," he said. "The shaman would never let a slave get so close, not unless you meant more than physical labor."

Amuun'axsum blinked rapidly, rubbing her thumb over her wristband. She had thought the shaman treated her differently, but to have a nobleman agree dispelled any doubt. At the same time, fear moved her to be cautious. The shaman coaxed, as if waiting for Amuun'axsum to share some measure of power. It seemed Dushuuw was no different. He saw in her the same shadowy potential for his own gain.

Except there was nothing more she could give him.

What connection to the spiritual world did they think she possessed, that they would hold their breath and watch her like a deadfall? And was she the trap, or the prey? Or both. Once exploited for what she possessed, would she be turned out—or worse? All she had was the song, and that was not something to share.

A sense of dread filled Amuun'axsum. This was the hand held out, but she did not know what to put in it. He would have no use for rituals to gather clover. This was dangerous territory. Yet she was as close to a chance at redemption as she had ever been. It was only a hope of a chance. But hope was enough. She would not give up her hunt. She drew a breath, and raised her chin.

"You have aided your uncle as a trader," she said.

Dushuuw looked a bit perplexed, but nodded.

"Then you know that things of value do not come free," she said.

He sat back with a smug smile. "What about the hummingbird?"

She shook her head. "An exchange. You have not told Eekbis about my ... nighttime strolls. And you did not tell me to give up this place," she said, gesturing around them.

He leaned forward. "Then I suppose all I have to do is threaten both of those things, unless you give me something else."

Amuun'axsum mentally stumbled, cringing at herself. Of course. To him, her noble past was just that: the past. In Dushuuw's eyes, she was a slave—his father's slave at that, even if she served the shaman. Dushuuw could threaten a lot more than a revealed secret. As a warrior, he would not hesitate. Hope faded as her gut sank. Perhaps this was a trap after all.

"But I wouldn't do that." He gave a reassuring smile. "After all, how could I trust the information you gave me then? It could be worthless."

Amuun'axsum gave a hesitant nod.

"The better question," he said, his expression suddenly unsure, "is whether you have anything more of worth to offer at all."

Amuun'axsum looked down at her lap in case her face betrayed her thoughts, for she was not sure what she could give him either, beyond what was required of a whaler's wife—and she was no romantic partner. From what she had witnessed at the lake, it was clear the whalers of Wuh-uhch already knew those rituals anyway.

Then she thought of the charcoal drawings, and of the things hidden beneath layers of bark—about the secret that this snag had become itself, to protect and nourish the secrets she kept about herself.

"I can help you," she said, screaming in her mind for it to be proved true. "But, Dushuuw, they are things I must do unseen, here in this place. You would have to agree to that, to trust me."

At the sound of his name, he had glowed. And when he solemnly gave his approval, without pausing to consider, she knew what had truly drawn him here. The same thing that had drawn her here. A place to be all the things they were told they were not. A man with respect. A woman with power.

"And you must give me something in return," she said.

"What would it be?"

"I will tell you when we are done. When you have proof of my help."

Dushuuw nodded thoughtfully. The wavering light of the dying fire played across his broad chest which, like the rest of him, was taut skin over hard muscle, an ideal of physical strength whose only evidence of weakness was not in the scars, but in the mixture of sorrow and uncertainty that always haunted his eyes—always there, even when joking with Yaq or playing with Buh-uhs—a troubled look that she had dispelled with a single word, a simple word if it were not bound up in the power of a name. Now he looked across the fire at her with flames of confidence and determination dancing in his eyes.

She had already given him the gift he needed.

"You are already stronger," she said, before she could catch herself.

They were true words. But as he sucked in a breath and regarded her with undue formality, running his thumb over the layers of material hiding the hummingbird, she could see he ascribed that truth to her contributions and not to any efforts he might make himself. This attitude worked to her advantage, if all went well. But she felt a pang of sadness on the heels of a sudden sense of distance. For a moment, she had reveled in the feeling of someone looking up to her, as she had so longed to feel again. Now, she realized that elevation could leave behind the same feeling as someone looking down on her: loneliness. A damp kind of loneliness, a loneliness that settles coldly into the marrow.

DAWN AT SEA was not marked by the sun but by the moon. Bands of coral and ocher colored light laid themselves bleeding atop the distant line of an endless horizon. The canoe rose on a swell, and Dushuuw watched the moon fade over the shoulders of the men seated in front of him.

Waves pulsed all around the canoe. They licked the sharp-nosed bow. They sucked at the cedar hull. They tugged at his paddle. Dushuuw's stomach rose and fell with the canoe over each crashing swell. Sea otter teeth, embedded in lines along the hull, spat trailing drops of saltwater.

The previous afternoon, spotters on the point had called out whale sightings. Elders who sat on the beach every evening reported the weather would be favorable. And so they had paddled all night in the direction of the herd, the first hunt of the fall migration. On and on, they had shoved more of the sea behind them, their broad shoulders and taut arms following a rhythm they had each known since they were boys.

The harpoon lay over the thwarts. Dushuuw drew his gaze down its vast length. The thick yew shaft crossed over the hull spaces that were laden with floats and lines, then came to rest between the ears of the prow. The harpoon's mussel-shell point jutted out over the expanse. In the bow, his brother stood alone beside the harpoon, a hand resting against one of its grips. Q̓otsik's posture, like that of the canoe, was alert to what lay before him, as he sought the whale who also sought him. From his position, it seemed to Dushuuw that his brother and the harpoon and the prow were one.

A petrel skimmed the air over Dushuuw's head, its wings outstretched. The sea bird was rarely seen, though whalers spoke of the bird as a friend. Dushuuw shoved his hat off his head to follow the bird's flight, and a wide spray of water burst skyward in the far distance.

"We have spray," Kweelthup called.

From the stern, Buhkweeduuk steered them on a slight shift south, then started a chant to set a faster pace. Dushuuw adjusted his paddle and joined the song. Wind tugged at his hair. Some strands pulled loose from the top knot and flicked in front of his eyes.

Q̇otsik leaned over the prow, scanning the barnacle-encrusted backs that arched in and out of view in the distance. His gaze passed over the ones followed by calves, and over the smaller whales.

In the midst of the herd, a whale rose. Its massive jaw reached toward the sky. The tiny hairs on the back of Dushuuw's arms and neck stood on end. A whoosh of the whale's warm breath turned to mist in the cold air. The whale lingered, taking breaths, then dove again to feed. The other whales moved on, but the large one lingered.

Q̇otsik motioned underhand for a steady pace, and they followed the chosen whale's shallow wake. Dushuuw stiffened in anticipation. His mind went to the small bird hidden away at his hip.

On and on, they followed the massive shadow beneath the water under the rising sun's glare. Wind filled their ears. Cold droplets of sea spray gathered on their necks and dripped down their backs.

Q̇otsik wrapped his hands over the harpoon shaft.

As the ridges of the whale's wake drew closer together, Buhkweeduuk shouted—"Come on!"—and the men paddled furiously as he steered the canoe to come alongside the whale.

Q̇otsik rose and planted a foot on the edge of the canoe. He held the harpoon out in front of his body at an angle—one hand high and behind his head, the other close to his chest—maximizing power and balance.

As the whale's back broke the surface, Uhpqoolth gave the order.

"Now strike!"

Q̇otsik lifted the harpoon high with a loud grunt and drove the mussel-shell point into the whale. The jointed sections of the harpoon shaft drove the point deeper. Barbs of elk antler kept the point in place.

The shaft disengaged and Q̇otsik lifted it free. Four fathoms of the prized sinew line were thrown over the edge of the canoe, following the harpoon tip lodged deep inside the whale. Uhpqoolth tipped over the float attached to the line. The float was sucked beneath the waves.

The rest of the men paddled the canoe backward, giving the whale distance. The injured whale raised its tail from the water, higher and higher, and the men paddled in time to Buhkweeduuk's chant, faster and faster. The whale's tail came down with an angry slap. A great surge of water lifted and pushed the canoe. Dushuuw and the other men on the support side fought against the oncoming waves, shifting their bodies over the side to lean into the surge and drive their paddles deep, thrusting the water under the canoe.

The canoe settled, rocking gently.

Ҫotsik signaled to the support canoes that his quarry had been struck: "*hya·ʔo·!*"

They shifted to the next phase of the hunt.

With only a paddle to mind, Dushuuw found himself paying closer attention to the other men and their roles. Buhkweeduuk's chant marked a quick but measured pace. Kweelthup called out changes in the whale's condition, marked by its movement. Leehuuk's apprentice line-tender tied on the next section of cordage. Uhpqoolth tied on seal-skin floats, one after the other, emptying the hull space in front of him. Directly in front of Dushuuw, Huh-uuk brought the spool of a flattened sealskin to his mouth, and started inflating the float to refresh Uhpqoolth's supply. And already Yaq was taking deep breaths, thinking of the dive to come when he would lash the whale's mouth shut, for Ҫotsik's aim was true and, despite its angry slap, the whale already started to slow.

Ҫotsik stood in the bow, one foot again braced on the canoe's edge. He hung on to the line, letting the whale tow them into its wake. He looked over the path of the submerged whale.

"Whale, you have what you wished for. My good harpoon."

This was no taunt, but a prayer—an acknowledgment of an agreement fulfilled.

"Now whale, turn towards my fine beach. All the young men will come down to see you, and they will say to one another, 'What a great whale he is! What a fat whale he is! What a strong whale he is!' And you will be proud of all you hear them say of your greatness."

Ҫotsik began singing, singing to comfort, singing to encourage the whale toward their home, where his wife Sawsin lay prone in quiet and stillness, facing their small mountain, drawing the whale to herself.

Soon, the whale rose to take a growling breath. Several of the floats that had followed the whale down were now pressed against its body, tangled with the lines. Ҫotsik drove a second harpoon with a float into the whale's back, then continued his singing. The support crews approached from the other side and added their own harpoons and floats as the whale dipped below the surface again. The surface of the sea churned with blood. And the blood arched across the water as the whale twisted and thrust—and turned toward the cape.

A breath, a wound. A breath, a wound. Each time the whale

surfaced, another hunter would drive in a harpoon. As the numbers of floats in the canoes grew smaller, the animal moved slower, the time between its breaths shorter, and the haze of land closer. The buoyant seal-skin floats dragged at the dying whale; it plodded along at the surface. Lice skittered across its skin, seeking its blood.

More harpoons, more floats—and Qotsik sang on.

The sun sank toward the horizon, growing larger in its descent, gorging itself on light.

Atop the whale's back, mucus and condensed breath slid around the holes of its nose. Blood pooled. Short breaths came in wet shudders. The whale groaned and crawled. Qotsik sang quieter, then he took up a short spear and, after the crew brought the canoe alongside the weakened whale, he lanced under its arm to its heart.

The voices of the paddlers rose in exultation that Qotsik and Sawsin had brought the whale so close to land as to see the smoke of Wuh-uhch's fires. Dushuuw added his own voice to the song. The canoe was turned about by the waves as the men rested their paddles on their laps, and Yaq dove into the water. Dushuuw reached inside the pouch at his hip, and brushed his thumb over soft feathers as the canoe spun about to face the blazing line of the horizon. A broad smile crossed his face, then faded as he regarded his brother's silence. Qotsik's back was still turned to the others, his head inclined toward the whale, listening for a voice no one else could hear. Qotsik stood over the prow against a circle of fire.

~

Weeks of whale hunting followed. The men barely paused to sleep before they were out on the water again. Fair weather held day after day. The whales were easily found. The captures, when they came—one after the other—were swift before Qotsik's harpoon and drawn close by Sawsin's prayers.

People arrived at Wuh-uhch in droves to help with the workload. Payments became larger—first a tongue, then a tongue and a section of meat, then a bladder of oil besides. The cape glutted itself on Qotsik's success. Perhaps there would not be a long wait for an oil feast after all.

Dushuuw moved back to line-tender, eager to take up the role again, to his cousin's surprise and his brother's approval. He found himself entering a heady cycle through the periodic fasting, the long days and nights moving a paddle, then hauling at the tow ropes to bring the whales ashore. His vision seemed to change—daylight took on a lustrous sheen, as if the world was painted with water. His body was raw from the cuts and scrapes incurred from hemlock and nettles and the rocks on the river's bottom. It was the kind of physical exertion that propelled him to stretch and beat himself further. He moved his feet and arched his back to ancient steps, adding the dance alongside his prayers. He pummeled himself to an ancient beat, making music of the pain. Because it all finally seemed to be coming together, just as his brother said, but on the strength of tiny wings.

It was as if he were holding his breath.

After each whale hunt, he would wait impatiently for night to fall. When everyone was gone or asleep, he would leave the house, and go first to the snag.

Sometimes she was there, weaving. The hat grew by degrees, and soon she was adding the design. Each time he saw it, something new took shape—a canoe, a man, a harpoon—figures drawn with grass around strips of cedar.

Other times she was not there. Then he would seek out the other signs—a canoe, a man, a harpoon—drawn in charcoal around the snag.

Another hunt, and another visit. A hunt, a visit. He would round the curve of bark and see her lift her face to him, or he would brush his fingers over lines of black, and he would breathe and start again.

In between, he caught himself looking for her even when not in the forest. He would spot her among the rocks or on the beach. Laughing with a friend. Handing a meal to the shaman.

Tiny feathers loosed from the hummingbird. Tiny bones cracked beneath the weight of his hand as he sought it out time and again.

20

THE AIR WAS TAINTED with smoke. Cranberries picked, the people in neighboring Tsooyuhs were now burning the bog. The burning beat back the encroaching forest, which would allow the cranberry and medicinal leaves to grow in profusion the following year, which would in turn draw elk and bear within easy reach of hunters.

Clouds of smoke from the fire reached over the bay, invading Amuun'axsum's senses. The fires, now in their second day, were timed to the weather and carefully monitored. But a ridge full of smoke and a flame-brightened night sky held its own meaning in her memory, and she quaked in her bed, afraid to sleep.

The fire was not the only reason she missed sleep, however.

Amuun'axsum went to the snag every night following the shaman's snores, trying to keep up with the whalers' pace. If her errands for the shaman took her into the forest, she tried to make trips during the day as well—though not entirely for Dushuuw. She continued to work on the hat, which she planned by first sketching her ideas in charcoal. It was the closest she could get to a ritual that might benefit him somehow, though she worried her exhaustion may lead to another botched job. Still, the visits to the snag were even more for herself.

At first, she simply added to her cache. She dug out more dirt and bark to make the hiding spot bigger. To her growing collection she added a chipped piece of dentalia, an eagle feather, and a little girl's discarded rock, its surface scratched to resemble a smiling face.

Some nights, she was still sitting among the warm detritus by the firebox when Dushuuw came to the snag. She would look up and see his face, alight with victory and relief. They never spoke. He would look over her, over the hat. He would smile, and she would smile back, and he would go off to pray. Amuun'axsum did not feel she had anything to do with Dushuuw's newfound success in the whaling canoe. But her own success hinged on Dushuuw's belief that she did. And so she continued to linger longer each time, anxious to see him round that corner and break into a smile, clinging to the promise that smile held.

In between, she caught herself looking for him at other times. She would spot him emerging from the forest or stepping out of a canoe. Giving food to old women. Playing with children.

Whaling would soon end. Then it would be time. He would ask her what she wanted. She shuddered with excitement, and tried to remember what she had been told about her mother's home village, the place Amuun'axsum was to go if disaster ever befell their family. Somewhere, there was a man and a woman who thought their daughter and granddaughter were dead. Would they recognize each other? Did they share anything by which Amuun'axsum could be known?

Of course. The song...

For the first time in too long a time, Amuun'axsum pondered again the words of the song that her mother had given to her on the day their world collapsed into ashes. Slaves were not allowed to own songs. But she was no slave. And there in the snag, there was no one to tell her to be silent, to tell her she could not sing.

The first time, it was just the sounds, a tremulous *hu, hu, hu* to signal the coming chorus. She came to the first line, and sang—a testing whisper, to prove she remembered the words.

Daylight is found on the mountain

She whispered that single line, over and over.

The second time, she added the second line, still whispering.

Daylight is found on the mountain

feathers dance on the echoes of wolves

The curve of the snag sent her voice back to her, and she stopped, overwhelmed by the flames that still hid her mother's smile.

But the third time...

hu, hu, hu...

The shaman was secretive and sent Amuun'axsum outdoors. It was daylight, which usually made Amuun'axsum reticent. That day, however, was a wonderfully sodden day. The wind moved in bursts. The earthy smell of the forest was enhanced and, inside the snag, it was warm and dry. Her fingertips were black with charcoal as she drew on the smoothed sections of bark. Other animals had joined the ones she had drawn, as if Dushuuw offered a greeting. She smiled at his crude depictions of a fish, a club.

As she drew, she thought on her attempts to sing the song in the snag, why it had felt at once so familiar and yet somehow foreboding. Then it dawned on her.

"The words..."

The words were not her father's language, but not quite her mother's language either. A different language, from a different beach. This beach—or one like it—the language of Wuh-uhch and the rest of the Kwidich'chuh-aht.

The charcoal hovered in the air, trapped by Amuun'a⎵sum's fingers. Her skin tingled, from her scalp on down the back of her neck. In words this people understood best, coming from the mouth of a scorned and foreign slave, they would claim she had stolen the song.

"The song is mine..."

Heart beating fast, she scratched out a new drawing. Over the whale and the Lightning Serpent, she drew a bird with massive wings, wings powerful enough to create thunder. She thought of the drum, which was as much a part of the song her mother gave her as the words. She drew in the last of Thunderbird's talons. Then, if only to counteract her pounding heart, she started rapping the side of the snag with her fists. She closed her eyes in concentration, softly singing...

Daylight is found on the mountain
feathers dance on the echoes of wolves

The snag cupped her words, sent them back, making them a touch louder than a whisper, though her mind was still on the drumming. She opened her eyes, preparing for the lift of the final line. The drawings glowed in the light of her fire.

we touch lightning

A hollow roar swept over her head as a sudden wind sailed over the top of the snag. The torchlight flared. And a charred wooden feather of the Thunderbird fell to the ground.

Amuun'a⎵sum stumbled backward. She slid down and leaned against the snag, staring across the firebox to the drawings that moved in the flickering light.

Drip, drip, drips of rain started to patter the forest canopy, then built in intensity. She dumped dirt into the firebox, then fumbled out of the snag. She clutched her basket of weaving supplies and hurried toward the path. Rain pelted her arms. Her feet kicked through the dirt that was turning to mud, flinging it onto her calves in murky globs. The breeze tugged at her hair, drawing it loose.

21

Q̇OTSIK CALLED AN END to whaling after taking another humpback.

Top feeders, the whales were tastier than grays. They also produced far more oil, especially after a summer feeding.

They found the whale near a shallow area, where a group of humpbacks fed in a tight pack beneath a swarm of gulls. Beneath the water, one of the whales blew a spiraling cone of air bubbles, trapping fish. The net of bubbles churned on the surface of the sea, then broke as the whales rose in unison, mouths open as they took synchronous gulps. Time and again, their massive bodies rose high in the air and came crashing down, sending up waves of water that rippled out to the canoes, where the men watched from a distance.

Yet not all the whales took part. One whale meandered apart from the frenzy. The whale's throat was deeply lined, like scores from a knife.

The men crept around the plodding whale, following it as it left the feeding group farther and farther behind. Q̇otsik thrust his harpoon deep, the heart of the whale gathering the point to itself.

~

Processing the massive humpback would take nearly a week. The stench would last longer.

Early into the process, however, in the dark of that first night by the light of fires, the workers were surprised to be joined on the beach by yet another whale.

The gray whale, its sides gashed by tooth marks, was the third drift whale to come to the beach that year. Everyone looked to Q̇otsik. The old whalers knew the young man did not pray for his harpoon alone, and this third drift whale confirmed his power to call whales to shore without even getting in a canoe. Sawsin scattered feathers over the whale, singing a song of gratitude.

More help was called in from the cape's other villages to ensure none of the two whales' bodies went to waste. And in the following days, murmurs coursed through the crowds like tidepools touched by high tide. Talk of oil feasts and power built and spread, while Q̇otsik stood apart, Sawsin at his side.

Early one morning, Q̇otsik gathered the young whalers together on the beach with older whalers, discussing what to do next. As the older men spoke, a watcher came running from the point and loped to a stop in front of the group.

"Spray, from gray whales, the closest to shore this season."

The elders smiled, but Q̇otsik was sober as he looked to their father. Chahbuhⱡ waited in silence with the others. Q̇otsik thought for a moment, then drew himself up and looked around the group, his eyes settling on each of the older men in turn.

"The whales greet us, singing their songs," he said. "We will sing back, and bid them well on their journey. They have gifted as chiefs do—generously. We will show ourselves generous in return."

There were weeks of mild weather left, weather conducive to whale hunting. But the Wuh-uhch whalers would not be among the hunters.

Dushuuw felt the workings of constant preparation and paddling dissipate from his muscles and, as the day dragged on, he wondered what to do with himself. The other young whalers were equally restless. Songs done, they searched for something to occupy their twitching arms and restless minds. They helped with butchering. They delivered fresh meat and blubber to the older men and women of the village in their houses. Still, a heaviness weighed on Dushuuw, and by Yaq's frown—a rare thing—he knew he was not alone.

Finally, Dushuuw pulled Yaq along toward the wide beach that fronted the bay across the river. Here the full force of the sea made itself known as soon as autumn deepened into winter. Driftwood lay in a jagged, heaped line just above the high tide mark. In storm season, the beach could be a lonely place. But on calm days, and when enough children could be put on extra tasks like clearing bladderwrack, it was a popular spot for food gathering, companionable strolls—and games.

"What are we about?" Yaq asked, eager.

"Something Q̇otsik has no power to do," Dushuuw quipped. "Something only the likes of you and me could think of right now."

Coming to a marked spot at the upper reaches of the beach, he began to dig. Yaq smiled, and rushed to help dig out the ball.

Dushuuw gripped the ball, testing it. Curling the fingers of his other hand into a loose fist, he knocked on Yaq's head. "Passes my test: as hard as that head of yours."

Yaq batted the fist away with a smile, and took the ball. The ball was made of gristle from near a whale's arm, preserved from Q̇otsik's first take and buried to cure since then.

"Should be good for a few games at least," Yaq said, tossing the ball between his hands.

Uhpqoolth walked up to see what they were doing and relief washed over his face at the sight of the ball. "Is it ready to play?"

Yaq chucked the ball at Uhpqoolth's chest, and Uhpqoolth tested the ball's strength between his palms. His smile grew.

By now even Q̇otsik had wandered over and, spying the ball, called over a slave boy to help him mark off the *huʔu·* game field.

Uhpqoolth drafted other young men into the service of his and Q̇otsik's team. The recruits included Huh-uuk, whose girth provided its own tactical advantage but also belied impressive strength, as proved at the most recent rock-throwing contest.

"I see how it is," Yaq said. He pointed at a lean but muscular young man, known to haul in copious amounts of lingcod and halibut. "We claim Suu-ahp for our team," Yaq shouted over his shoulder as he ran to retrieve the bats, leaving Dushuuw to recruit others.

By the time they joined Q̇otsik on the wide beach, two lines were already dug into the sand, spaced far apart. Q̇otsik called for the ball and set it halfway between the goal lines. Yaq ran up with the bats. He divided the two kinds of sticks—one slightly curved at the end, the other with a scoop-like hook—and the teams dispersed to their starting points on the goal lines.

Dushuuw and Uhpqoolth each took one of the straighter bats, then stood at the center of the field over the ball.

"Strike it like it's your sworn enemy's severed head! Protect all our buxom women!" Yaq shouted in mocking drama, his arms raised.

Dushuuw shook his head. Uhpqoolth lobbed a shell at Yaq's back.

Yaq went to enlist a slave boy for the rather hazardous job of throwing the ball up in the air to start the game. The strikers stared at each other over the ball, swinging the bats as they waited. Dushuuw thought of the last time he faced his cousin in defiance, when they were stuck in a canoe. How long ago that now seemed. How much had changed. Dushuuw cleared his throat. "You know, the people who live far inland say this is mostly a women's game."

Uhpqoolth stood erect and let his gaming stick flop by his side. "*ha·tqa·d*," he chided. "Nobody cares what they do. Besides," he said, slapping the stick on the sand and getting back into a ready position, "we play it the right way."

The slave boy tried to keep the rest of his body far from the two men as he reached in for the ball. He shot the ball upward and bolted.

Dushuuw reacted too late. Uhpqoolth got to the ball first, smacking the ball so hard that Dushuuw barely slipped to the side out of harm's way. He fell to one knee. The ball boy's frantic escape kicked up sand into Dushuuw's eyes. Dushuuw growled, scrambled up and ran, chasing down his cousin. He rammed Uhpqoolth to the ground before the man could reach the ball again. The pair tumbled as their teams converged on the ball with shouts.

"You are going to pay," Uhpqoolth said, smiling and breathing hard as he reached for his bat from beneath Dushuuw's weight.

"Not today," Dushuuw said. He laughed, even as he tried to catch his breath. He used his bat to nudge his cousin's bat farther away, bolted up, and ran in the opposite direction, trailing Yaq.

Yaq slid his hooked bat over the sand, running the ball down the field, then snatching it back after a bad hop over a hunk of driftwood. Teammates flanked him. They butted and tackled the opposing players who tried to cut in front. Huh-uuk and the fisherman Suu-ahp seemed locked in a personal battle up the field. Dushuuw drew up alongside the ball. Yaq passed it over. Dushuuw swung his bat from a sprint and sent the ball soaring across the goal line.

The slave boy leaped—his excitement now surpassing his trepidation—and scurried off to retrieve the ball.

A couple of cheers went up from the top of the dunes, where a handful of onlookers had gathered and chosen their favored sides.

"First game is ours, cousin," Dushuuw said.

Uhpqoolth's pursuit flagged into a lope. His look of disgust gave way to a smile—and Dushuuw felt a sudden whack on his backside. He pitched forward, nearly dropping his bat in surprise. Q̇otsik ran by waving his runner's bat in answer, and Uhpqoolth laughed.

"Enjoy the accolades, brother," Q̇otsik called. "They are the only ones you are going to get today."

The games continued until near sunset, the young men trading bruises and wins. Cheers were loud for both teams, as more people finished their work and gathered to watch, both from shore and at anchor in the bay. Young boys clustered in a group, most of them pulling for Q̇otsik, while Buh-uhs remained faithful to his beloved Quht-Quht. On track to tally his team's fifth win toward the end of the series, Dushuuw nearly gave the boy bragging rights. But then Yaq's run suddenly flagged into a jog and Dushuuw overran the pass. The ball went skidding toward the surf before it was snatched by Uhpqoolth's bat and driven the other direction.

When Dushuuw raised his bat in question, Yaq's lopsided grin and nod toward a cheering young woman was answer enough. With a groan, Dushuuw stuck the end of his bat into Yaq's stomach. "ʔa·dwa?" Yaq shrugged, and flipped his bat in the air. Dushuuw shook his head, snatched the bat from his friend's grasp as it fell, and hefted it over his shoulder with his own.

As the sky colored toward night, the young whalers trudged back toward their houses, tired, battered, and happy. Dushuuw rolled his shoulders, shook his hair down. He followed Q̇otsik and Uhpqoolth as they strode shoulder to shoulder. On the high ground, the winter house loomed, nearly complete. Soon they would spend their winters under its single, massive roof. For now, they followed each other through the doorway of the great house at the bay's edge, the surf shushing. And the carefree moments of the game wafted away.

In the middle of the house, a fire burned. The light played off the glossy slab of whale flesh slung over a pole near the fire, a stubby fin pointing toward the roof. Curling billows of smoke wafted over the flesh, away, and back. Downy feathers studded the tip of the fin. Other feathers were arranged into thin, crescent moons, decorating both sides of the slab. The family's crests were painted in ocher-colored curves. On the other side of the fire, over another pole, a flat slab of a different whale hung with its own decorations, dripping oil into the trough below, drop after drop after drop.

Q̇otsik handed his bat to Dushuuw, then walked to the fire. Sawsin drew her hand away from the fin, a feather in her hand, and Q̇otsik rested his forehead against hers.

Dushuuw's father and uncle stood with other elder whalers, waiting for Q̇otsik by the fire in their full regalia. The old men took turns according to where they sat in their whaling canoes, chanting their prayers of the whale. As he sang, Chahbuhɫ shook an elk-horn rattle filled with pebbles. The feathers that decorated its handle shuddered.

The rapid rattle.

The slow chant.

As the elders sang, Q̇otsik fed more wood to the fire, which fed the smoke, which spilled over the slabs of whale and filled the air. As night deepened, his fire was the only one left burning.

When the last song was finished, the old men withdrew, and in the light of the flames Q̇otsik moved in silence around the poles on which hung the slabs of whale—as well as the whales' eyes and the coil of sinew line—first one fin, then the other, around and around the fire. He arced and rose, sounded and spied, circling the whale flesh that flickered in the firelight as if in memory of movement.

No rattle.

No song.

Dushuuw watched from the shadows of his bench, a small bundle laying in his open palm. He gently unwrapped the bird. Its green feathers reflected the firelight. Its eyes were tiny caverns.

On the low platform next to Dushuuw's bench, Buh-uhs awoke and raised himself on his elbows atop his sleeping mat. He yawned, and rested his chin in his hands as he watched Q̇otsik.

After his fourth pass, Q̇otsik sat down between the pieces of whale. He would stay all night—as he had the previous two nights, as he would the following night—keeping the fire burning, paving the way for the spirits of the whales to return to their homes in the sea, to enter the bodies of yet other whales, to reveal themselves to the whaler once more, to give themselves up again.

Buh-uhs's mouth hung open as he fell asleep again, his head still propped up on one hand.

Like the boy, Dushuuw had watched this ceremony many times from the outskirts. But, though the distance between he and his brother was still great, Dushuuw was more affected by the ritual this time. Maybe it was because the hunting season was done and this would be the last such ritual for moons. Maybe it was the contrast with the simple joy of a good ball game with friends. And maybe it was something else. Dushuuw tucked the hummingbird back in its pouch. Then, just as gently, he eased Buh-uhs back onto the mat, cradling the boy's head and stroking the boy's hair, which was becoming long again.

~

The gray clouds had held back their rain all morning. And so an outdoor feast was held, with each household in Wuh-uhch invited to eat. The flesh from around the humpback's fin—the choicest meat—was cooked, and everyone but Q̇otsik indulged in at least one bite. There also were fresh cranberries, smoked halibut, and strips of whale blubber that had been cured and broiled to a sizzle.

Men pounded on plank drums, as women moved their hands up and down like the sea's waves. With their hands and with their words, the people gave the whale its human voice.

i come to your beach

i cannot walk

but i am human

Knives creaked as men and women cut through thick meat. Near the shoreline, sand fleas crawled over the bones. The air smelled of sea and of oil. As more feasting got underway, a light rain started to fall, but it went unnoticed amid laughter, conversation, and the good taste of whale meat and oil.

Dushuuw stood flanked by greatness, his father at his left and his brother to his right. Qotsik had brought in ten whales since the beginning of the spring hunts, in spite of the early setbacks and delays. Even with three being drift—no, especially—it was an extraordinary number for a single whaler. And, in their family, a responsible limit.

The day started to fade, and the rain increased. But songs continued to fill the air. Buh-uhs cavorted with the other children in the surf. Older women smiled as they chatted, the shaman hunched over among them, her gnarled hands atop a cane. And standing at the edge, Dushuuw spied the woman who seemed separate from it all on a normal day.

The woman's hair was simply plaited. She wore only a shabby work skirt, its clumps of thin strands blowing about her legs. But she stood with straight back, chin raised. Eekbis beckoned the woman over, gripped the woman's proffered arm, and the pair walked away.

Dushuuw startled at the soft touch on his arm, and he turned to find his grandmother at his side, bundled in hat and cloak.

"So far away I must pull you back," the old woman said. Her tone was chiding but her mouth tilted up in an amused smile. "Help an old woman to her bed, Young Son. I need a nap."

Dushuuw clenched his teeth, then took a deep breath at realizing the spark of anger he still felt at hearing his childhood name, a spark never directed toward the elderly woman before. Though he doused the spark, and she smiled up at him still, he escorted the stout woman more gently than she needed.

22

Eekbis slapped at Amuun'axsum's hand over the work surface.

"We want to hide it, not obliterate it, child!"

Amuun'axsum blushed and poked at the wet mass of herbs.

The shaman grunted and batted her aside with her ample hip. "Go fix the meal," Eekbis said. "I will get this."

Amuun'axsum put down the pestle.

"And do it the right way," the old woman added with a mutter.

"I will be outside," Amuun'axsum said, gathering cooking tools.

Eekbis grunted in response, and waved a hand over her shoulder.

Amuun'axsum pulled on a hat and walked out into the rain. The shaman had protested that it was ridiculous for her to keep cooking outdoors, given how much space they had indoors. Amuun'axsum knew it would not work much longer. In truth, it was a terrible day to cook outdoors—certainly no one else did. Yet she longed to avoid the smothering confines of the walls. Let it rain.

The wind whistled and fought her attempts to start the fire. Finally, the jerking flames were strong enough to heat rocks. At the creek, she filled a box with water. Back by the fire, she added to the box fish heads, herbs, and the heated rocks to make it all boil.

Ironically, it was walls she longed for most. More than ever, she wanted the comfort of a noble home. More than ever, that goal seemed possible. If only Dushuuw would say something, now that the hunts were done. Yet he had not even glanced her direction. Perhaps he never meant to give her anything in return after all.

A young voice grew louder at her back. She turned and saw Buh-uhs, trudging beside Dushuuw and Yaq. They passed her fire, and the shaman's house, and Dushuuw did not look over. Her heart sank. So that was it, then.

She lifted the lid on the box, letting the steam envelop her face as she stirred the mixture.

"What is in there?"

Buh-uhs stood over her, biting his lip as he tried to spy the contents of the box.

"Broth," she said.

He licked his lips.

"But it is not done yet, I am afraid." She set the lid back over the rim.

His eyebrows and mouth dropped into the scowl mastered by boys.

When he didn't leave, Amuun'axsum patted the ground next to her. "You are welcome to wait impatiently with me," she said.

He shrugged, and settled onto the ground.

"How is the little whaler?"

The boy brightened a bit, then sighed dramatically. "Hungry," he said. "But I guess I came over for a different reason. I guess I am sent to tell you that you are taking too long on Quht-Quht's hat." Amuun'axsum raised an eyebrow and flicked a glance at Dushuuw's receding back. "He said he has had to wait too long to hear an update from you."

"I see," she said, aware of the annoyed edge to her voice.

The boy leaned forward on his elbows, chin in his hands. "I don't know anything about hats. But I know this broth takes too long," he said.

Amuun'axsum smiled as she took a calming breath, opened up the basket of unused foodstuffs and rooted around inside. She pulled out a dried berry cake and handed it to the boy, who smirked his pleasure.

"Tell your Quht-Quht that I share his frustration, and I will work on the hat tonight." Buh-uhs nodded absently as he broke the cake apart. "Those words, now," she said. "I will 'work on it tonight.' I know I can trust a young nobleman like you to deliver an important message."

The boy sat up, offended. His lips were stained blue. "Well, of course I can," he said. He stood and turned to go, only to spin back. "I can still have broth, right?" With her assent, he ran off to catch up with the men.

Amuun'axsum watched as the boy sidled up to Dushuuw, who looked down as the boy gave his report. He looked over his shoulder at her. She could not see his expression through the haze of rain, but it was enough of a confirmation. She turned to the broth, trying to tamp down her smile, fingers fluttering with nerves.

~

A fire already glowed inside the snag. It was inviting, but Amuun'axsum stopped at the threshold, gripping the stump's ragged edge. The

Thunderbird wavered in the light, charcoal lines broken at the wing.

Dushuuw leaned against the back of the snag, hair tied in a knot as if he were preparing to hunt or to fight. But when he saw her, he took an excited step forward. He eyed her wrist. She had not worn the cedar band. The scarred tattoo stood out against the skin, lighter than her sun-darkened forearms and hands.

He gestured to a mat on the ground. He had added an extra mat, folded on top for more cushioning. She smiled as she sat on the soft padding, and he seated himself on the bare ground on the other side of the firebox.

Neither of them seemed sure what to say or do next.

After weeks of secret smiles and stolen glances, now to be sitting here alone again—it was like meeting him for the first time. Dushuuw looked at the drawings over her shoulder. Amuun'axsum entwined her fingers in her lap, wishing she had indeed brought her weaving.

"You were successful, with the whale hunts," she said.

"My brother is blessed," he said.

"And you—you moved up in the canoe," she said.

"With your help."

Amuun'axsum studied her hands in her lap again, taken aback again by the fervency of his belief.

"So what can I give you?" he asked. "Furs? Jewelry? Food? Anything—"

"I want to go home," she said.

This was not the answer he expected. That much was clear.

"You said I could ask for anything," she said.

"Yes, but..."

"I want to go home," she said, drawing her shoulders back. She had practiced these lines, but was frustrated to feel her face flush. "I am sure when you find my family, there will be a large ransom. It should be enough to appease your father, and to give Eekbis a new slave to—"

"You want to leave..."

So afraid of his reaction, it took Amuun'axsum a moment to realize that Dushuuw seemed disappointed. But he shook it off.

"Well, you need to talk to Eekbis, or to my uncle," he said. "This is only something my father—"

"No! No one can know, not until you find my family and make the arrangements yourself—"

"Wait." Dushuuw leaned forward and yanked at his top-knot in frustration. "Find them... You don't know where they are?"

"I know you are a man of your word, Dushuuw."

He looked over at the sound of his name, but was offended at having his honor even implicitly questioned.

"You ask the impossible, I think," he said, his tone hard. "And if I am to do this on my own, you ask for something dangerous as well."

"I kept my promise. And if you do not keep yours, you will simply confirm what they all perceive us to be: a chief's disgraced son, and a slave on a leash."

She was tempting his rage. It burned in his eyes.

"That shame was wiped away," he said.

"So by what name do they call you, Young Son?"

"What name do they call you, Quulthoo?"

"A lie!"

Amuun'axsum tried to rein in her fury, but his own had sparked the fire. Frustrated, she held back tears and stood so she could pace in the tight space. She trembled from head to foot.

"You have nothing to fear," she said. "Who can take away all that you have?" She threw up a hand toward him. "Do you know what it is like to have to pretend to be what they say you are? To keep everything of value that you own hidden away? To pretend that it does not exist? It is as if I am dead."

Amuun'axsum clutched her cloak to her chest. There was no stopping her tears now, as she swung between grief and fury.

"You believe I have power. But in this, I am lost. And it is killing me."

She hurried past him and out the snag, running, thoughts tumbling as her feet slapped onto the path. Amuun'axsum tossed her torch in the river, pushed aside the hide in the door, and lay down on her bed mat. The house was so quiet she could hear her blood thrumming in her ears. Her mouth opened in silent screams as she held in her sobs. She clenched the blanket, trying to bar her mind from the horrible memories that pummeled through her defenses. The shaman's snores started up, and to that familiar sound, Amuun'axsum wore herself out.

HEAD ACHING WITH THOUGHTS, Dushuuw crept back into the house.

"Hey, where were you?"

Dushuuw startled. Q̇otsik sat on Dushuuw's sleeping bench.

"I—I went to my prayer spot," Dushuuw said, matching his brother's whisper. He stepped over a sleeping Buh-uhs and sat beside his brother.

Q̇otsik nodded absently. "I cannot sleep either." He drew a knife over a piece of bone in some shapeless carving. He nodded toward the partition that now divided their beds every night. "I did not want to wake Sawsin. I hope you don't mind."

Dushuuw dragged his hair out of its top knot. "Thinking about the oil feast?"

Q̇otsik was confused, then raised his eyebrows as if remembering the most important milestone of his life as a whaler. "Oh, that—no, not that. But trying not to think, really."

Dushuuw felt more unsettled. What had his brother awake in the middle of the night, whale hunts done, at the pinnacle of skill?

"I am thinking about our visit soon to the home of Ḥawith," Q̇otsik said. "That Sawsin..."

Both Buh-uhs and Sawsin shifted and sighed in their sleep, and Q̇otsik shook his head.

"Do you want to go on a walk tomorrow? In the forest." Q̇otsik threw out the question. "We can check on the canoe's progress. Or wander. I do not know. I just do not think I can sit still for another day."

"I do not think I can either," Dushuuw said.

Q̇otsik sighed with relief and returned to bed. Dushuuw laid on his side to face the wall. Past the partition, Q̇otsik was soon breathing evenly, asleep. Dushuuw lay awake with his own troubled thoughts about a woman.

The air smelled of wet earth and wood shavings.

The brothers had trekked to one of the forested flanks of the peak above their village, and they now stood in a cleared area laden with the trunks of fallen giants. One of the previous year's series of windstorms had ripped through this area and left behind a crisscrossing pile of downed cedars. The newly fallen lay over and among older windfalls that sprouted tiny trees and shrubs. The mud-encrusted roots of a massive cedar towered over the men's heads.

"I tell you, I about had an orgasm when I saw it," the carver said.

The carver's brother shook his head, but he too smiled at the memory.

The woodcarving brothers the year prior had split the cedar in three parts for three canoes and roughed the segments out where they lay. Now, they were digging out the hulls. A fourth canoe was further along.

"This one came from a tree we had already identified for a canoe last year," the carver said. "We felled it in spring, and roughed it out. Then I had them take it here. I like to work in one spot."

Qotsik approached the canoe and slid his hand along the hull.

"This will be your new whaling canoe. Solid, and true," the carver said.

The carver put one hand on the inside of the hull and one on the outside, running his hands down its length. He took up his adze and drew it along the wood, shaving off one small chip at a time. The tool's handle was carved into the shape of a wolf; its snout reached toward the carver's own nose, nearly touching as the man hovered low over his work, intent.

The carver smiled up at Dushuuw, who had come closer to watch.

"Nobody else is allowed to use this adze," the man said, not breaking his rhythm. "Small differences in how a blade is hafted can affect results. This one I have adapted over a long time, adapted to fit the rhythm of my heart, help me work on and on to its beat."

"And the Wolf? I suppose it adds power to your work," Dushuuw said.

The carver laughed, but didn't break rhythm.

"That is so some dullard knows this is mine and to keep his hands off!" The carver's face was alight, but his eyes grew intense on his work as he continued. "Maybe it adds power. But more it reminds me of power—that it exists, that it's stronger than me. With every draw on the tool, I bring this reminder close, of my role, of my responsibilities, of how to behave."

"And he definitely needs constant reminders," his brother said.

The carver finally broke rhythm. The tool stilled as he stood upright and jabbed a finger toward his brother. "Who needs a crest when you have an older brother to tell you how to live?"

The pair laughed riotously. Dushuuw cracked a smile, all too aware of Q̇otsik, standing at his side.

His attention was drawn to another canoe—off to the side of the clearing, cast in the shadows of living trees, but the missing prow piece and the split down its hull unmistakable. He turned to the younger carver. "Why has that one not been repaired yet?" he asked.

The adze stilled in the carver's hands, then picked up its rhythmic work again. "The time will come," he said, without looking up.

"But it can be repaired, right?"

The carver glanced up, and nodded before turning back to his work.

Dushuuw crept backward, rejoining Q̇otsik who had gone to wait at the forest's edge. Q̇otsik was looking back at the new canoe taking shape.

"It will be a good whaling canoe," Dushuuw said. "And I will be glad to send Leehuuk his canoe back. Father will be even more pleased—the sooner, the better."

"And soon, we will have two whaling canoes to his one," Q̇otsik said.

Dushuuw wasn't sure what good that would do with one harpooner. But Q̇otsik had already hoisted his bow to his shoulder and was walking off. Dushuuw hoisted his bow and followed.

The path to the clearing had been long, but now Q̇otsik took an older path that would lead them back to the village on a more circuitous route. They walked in silence for a good while before Dushuuw spoke.

"What about the trip to see Ḥawith has you worried?"

For a time, Q̇otsik said nothing, looking up, down, and around as if searching for his words. "Sawsin will go too."

Dushuuw slowly realized what his brother was getting at and smirked in disbelief. He was not used to seeing his brother worried about anything—and his sleepless night had been about a woman? His smile faded. No, it was yet another sign of his brother's superior wisdom.

"What if she wants to stay there?" Words started pouring out of Q̇otsik. "I know our union is for an alliance. Yet I want Sawsin to know that an alliance is not the only reason, not in my eyes." Dushuuw glanced back at his brother, noting that the renewed pace helped Q̇otsik calm his nerves, speak more plainly. "I am so enamored of her, brother," Q̇otsik said, and he gave a short laugh. "It would pain me, should she decide not to return home with us."

Dushuuw sank within himself as memories of his ex-wife flared. He had been enamored. She had not. Dushuuw flexed his hand in and out of a fist. He sneered to himself, about to tell Q̇otsik not to worry—that Q̇otsik was immune to such failures. But a glance back showed Q̇otsik was digging his eyes into the ground again. The man actually thought it possible that he would experience the same kind of humiliation. Dushuuw rolled his shoulders to release more of his tension. Like always, grief moved in to fill the space left by anger. No matter how much he hated the woman's betrayal, he could not banish the feeling of her skin, her smell, her smile, and the way she looked so happy when she laughed—how he tried so hard to be the one to make her laugh.

"You are right to worry," Dushuuw said. Tracks of a bear joined the path, and they looked fresh. Dushuuw pulled the bow off his back. "To ache for a woman is a dangerous thing, for any man."

The birds had stopped singing over their heads. Dushuuw slipped the arrow loosely in place against the sinew cord. "The more you are drawn to a woman, the greater a mystery she becomes," he said, bringing his voice low. He started taking shorter, more careful steps. "The tests her father gives you to prove your strength and worth—perhaps she believes such tests don't end at the betrothal." Scratch marks in bark above. More paw prints in the mud. "I suppose the only thing to do is find the thing that proves your love and captures her own, a thing only you can give." He faltered, unsettled by his own words.

A tall rock hovered over the path. Dushuuw led the way around the back side of the rock, and they picked their way to the top. They sat, high above the trail, and waited to see what might come or not come.

"So, what you are saying," Q̇otsik said, his voice sinking into a whisper, "is that I am quite doomed."

A grin bloomed on Dushuuw's face. The brothers shook as they tried to contain their laughter. Then a bird shot into the sky. The brothers looked toward the sound of its beating flight, from the undergrowth down the path.

The black bear and her cubs melded with the shadows as they lumbered down the trail, heading toward the rock. The men crouched and kept still. Q̇otsik raised his bow, arrow poised. Dushuuw nocked his arrow as well, ready to follow his brother's shot with his own.

The bears' rumps lolled as they foraged. The mother bent her wide forehead, brown snout sniffing out insects from a fallen log. Her cubs followed close behind, mimicking their mother's movements. The mother's black fur clumped, its course outer layer topping the dense underfur that was so prized for winter clothing. She sniffed and grunted as she pried open the decaying log with her claws. One of her young ones balanced on his hind legs, eager.

Dushuuw remained still, muscles as taut as the bow line.

The sow growled softly as the wood gave way and a cub dug his snout into the forest's feast bowl, humming his pleasure. Then she blew out a breath, teeth clacking, and rose on her hind legs, looking in the direction of the men.

Dushuuw drew a breath and brought back the arrow a hair farther, ready to shoot. The sow's chest with its beating heart was turned toward them, vulnerable.

But no arrow flew.

Qotsik sat at ease, his bow laying unused atop the rock, his eyes on the bear. He was calm, confident. Dushuuw relaxed the string as he lowered his bow, turning to watch the sow and cubs as well.

The bear was back on all fours. The cubs continued eating. The sow was silent, and looked up toward Qotsik. One by one, the cubs toddled away from the meal, bellies satisfied. One cub nuzzled its mother, who tucked her head to its head, taking her eyes off the men without worry. Mother and cubs ambled on their way, melding back into the shadows of the forest's underbrush.

Qotsik took a deep, satisfied sigh. He looked at Dushuuw, his face lit with wonder. He smiled and nodded confidently, looking back to the spot where the bears had disappeared.

"I had a vision before my first whale hunt," Qotsik said. "In it, I met the Whale People in their house in the undersea world. The Whale told me that I would see success if I always passed over mothers with calves."

Dushuuw's heart pounded as he looked at his brother.

"As at sea, so on land," Qotsik said.

He led the way down the rock and back the way they came, in the opposite direction of the bear.

Dushuuw shook his head and followed. "And you worry," he said.

"Hm?"

"You worry about securing her love? You, Qotsik, the man to whom whales and bears alike offer up their spirits."

"Those I understand, somehow. But a woman, a woman like Sawsin..." He was nervous again and he picked up his pace in his agitation. "Our parents prepared each of us for what must be done for the whale. I worry, though. Not that she would neglect her role, but that she would see it only as that: a series of required tasks, and not the partnership it truly is. I am not all-powerful, brother. I need her in many ways." He looked lost in thought. "You said to give her something only I can give her. That is good, that is simple enough. A gift..." And he brightened again.

Dushuuw opened his mouth to object, to say that a gift was not exactly what he meant. His gifts of furs and jewelry to his ex-wife were proof of that. But his brother had the look of an excited adolescent and Dushuuw did not have the heart. What was there to worry over anyway? His smile soon faded, though, for he remained locked in a constant battle between bitterness and acceptance.

His brother sensed his despondency.

"That woman was a fool to give you up," Q̇otsik said.

Q̇otsik turned about and walked backward down the path, facing Dushuuw.

"She did not see what is inside you," Q̇otsik said.

Q̇otsik continued his backward amble, not even stumbling as he stepped over roots and eased around curves. Dushuuw began to get angry. Was there a *tume·nuwis* for seeing out the back of one's head? Did this man have so much room for power that he could even afford space for a ward against stupidity?

"You do not believe it," Q̇otsik said, with an incredulous laugh. "How can you not see what you have inside you?"

Dushuuw's anger stirred. Was it not obvious? He gently shoved past his brother, taking the lead—if only to set Q̇otsik facing forward again. The backward walking was making his skin crawl.

"The bear responded to you as well," Q̇otsik said. His voice was confident, as if making a proclamation.

"I think not."

"Two men with bows who did not shoot at her? She respected us. She sees the generosity and strength inside you."

"You, brother—she was watching you."

"She marked both Q̇otsik and Young Son for—"

"No! In your light, brother, I am quite certain I was invisible."

Q̇otsik started to object, but Dushuuw cut him off. He turned around, walking backward for about two steps before he stumbled over a root. He stopped and closed his eyes in frustration. Prayers meant nothing. Charms meant nothing. He was still Young Son, as if it were permanent. He raised his hands against Q̇otsik's renewed attempt to speak. He looked his brother in the eye.

"It is a good thing to go unnoticed, brother. I would be satisfied with that," Dushuuw said. "Do you not see? Each weight of power you have, seems to require a lack thereof on my side. For one such as you, there must be one such as me."

Q̇otsik looked sober. "I know what they say, but they are wrong. And you are wrong too. You should see that by now. Your prayers have made you strong in the canoe."

Dushuuw blinked and looked away. So the other men did still think he didn't belong in the whaling canoe. And what would Q̇otsik think if he knew it was not his own prayers but the prayers of a slave woman that had made the difference? He would lose even his brother's stubborn respect. Dushuuw turned and started walking down the path again, his breaths coming fast.

Q̇otsik's voice dogged him. "Brother..."

"Why can you not let me be?"

"You are a son of Chahbuhł."

"I am the son of a woman with nothing to her name," Dushuuw said, feet pounding onward. "And I am only—as all now certainly know—the Young Son."

If Q̇otsik were trying to respond, Dushuuw would not know. He strode ahead, arriving back in Wuh-uhch on legs fueled by anger.

24

AMUUN'A<u>X</u>SUM FOLLOWED Uhpahs into the thick woods, to a rise far above the river, too far from the sea to even hear it whisper. Uhpahs kept an eager pace, pausing only to pluck at curls of fern leaves she had tucked into her hair.

"When will you tell me what we are doing?" Amuun'a<u>x</u>sum said.

Earlier, Uhpahs had pulled Amuun'a<u>x</u>sum away to run some kind of big errand for Thluuch-muup. The shaman agreed and sent her off for the afternoon.

Uhpahs slowed to a stop and turned to Amuun'a<u>x</u>sum with a beseeching smile. A guilty smile.

"Uhpahs..."

"You would not have come if I told you why," she said.

Over her friend's shoulder, Amuun'a<u>x</u>sum saw a man approach from the other direction. "Is that Suu-ahp?" she whispered.

Uhpahs grabbed her hand and gave it a squeeze. "Do you realize how long it has been since we were at Chahdee? Quick meetups are not enough," she said. "I have kept your secret. Now you keep mine."

"This is a far different secret, Uhpahs," Amuun'a<u>x</u>sum said, blushing.

Uhpahs dropped her hand. "Well, let's bring another man out here for you, and we can share a secret for once," Uhpahs said. She did not smile, and Amuun'a<u>x</u>sum did not laugh. Uhpahs grabbed her hand again. "Please, my friend. Thluuch-muup would never approve of a marriage—at least, not yet. I must take what I can get, when I can get it."

Amuun'a<u>x</u>sum regarded her friend's neatly plaited hair with sprigs of fern. She sighed and patted Uhpahs's hand. "What did you tell Thluuch-muup?" she asked, managing a smile.

"That the shaman gave you an errand that was far too much for one person and you needed my help." Uhpahs gave an ingratiating smile.

Amuun'a<u>x</u>sum gently shoved her friend. "Go to him."

Uhpahs laughed and lifted Amuun'a͟xsum's hand, kissing her fingers. "We will not be too long," she whispered, and ran toward her lover.

Time, though, passed on and on. At the first sound, Amuun'a͟xsum had lingered, curious—and confused, jealous. Blushing, she hurried farther away from the sounds, sat down, and absently gouged at the dirt with the foraging stick Uhpahs had insisted they needed. Well, she needed it now. Thoughts of Uhpahs. Of her father and mother. Of her father and other women. Thoughts of a man's hand on her cheek, of another man's hand cradling her elbow. A hot rush heated her from the inside out. "Stop it..." She flung dirt this way and that. Her face burned.

Amuun'a͟xsum flung the foraging stick aside, then peered inside the tiny pit she had created. A root. A pebble. A clam shell? Amuun'a͟xsum grabbed the foraging stick again and dug a bit more, and found another clam shell.

Later, she stood over the filled-in pit, one of the clam shells gripped in her palm. She did not hear Uhpahs approach.

"Here you are," Uhpahs said. "Burying something?"

Amuun'a͟xsum dragged herself back to the moment. She reached out and plucked a dangling sprig of fern from Uhpahs's hair.

Suu-ahp passed them, casting an abashed look their direction as he headed back toward the village. He and Uhpahs shared satisfied, longing smiles. But Amuun'a͟xsum paid them no mind.

"You are not so mad at me, are you?" Uhpahs asked.

"No, I am not mad," Amuun'a͟xsum said. "I am confused..."

"I know you have never been intimate with a man," Uhpahs said, as she hooked their arms and tugged Amuun'a͟xsum toward the path. She twirled the fern leaf between her fingers. "But surely you understand what happens when—"

"No, not that," Amuun'a͟xsum said with a laugh. "No, there were clam shells up here, lots of them." She showed Uhpahs the one in her hand. "Why would someone drag such a load so far from the sea?"

Uhpahs shook her head. "I would say maybe they had a canoe. But the river does not rise this far, not even when it floods."

"And why here anyway? Was there an encampment here before?"

Uhpahs swept the air with the fern. "A question for one of the local old folks. Now hush about meaningless mysteries. You can only ask me questions about what it feels like to be—"

"You can think on that alone, friend." Amuun'a͟xsum tossed the shell.

"You are no fun," Uhpahs said. She unhooked her arm and gave a luxuriating stretch, before spinning as she walked. "I will endeavor to talk about something boring, then. That should please you."

Amuun'axsum grinned. "Please, bore me."

"Well, they will be going across the strait again soon, and Thluuch-muup will want me to come with her," Uhpahs said. "You never know how long these visits will take. But with Sawsin along, seeing her family again, this one will be no quick visit. Thluuch-muup was also trying to convince the chief to make more courtship plans in the area." Uhpahs gave her friend's arm a squeeze. "That I will be gone for so long was one reason I needed to take such a long errand."

Amuun'axsum shook her head. "Did you say courtship?"

Uhpahs looked skyward. "I am so glad you and I do not have to bother with time-consuming traditions. I am free to just say yes, yes..."

Amuun'axsum shoved her dreamy-eyed friend, if only to cover up a sudden sense of worry she did not quite understand. "It will be the chief's younger son, I suppose," she said.

Uhpahs snorted. "His reputation up against theirs? No, it would be Buh-uhs. Can never start too early, you know."

To her surprise, Amuun'axsum felt a twinge of relief.

When she entered the shaman's house, the woman was putting items into a pack basket. Amuun'axsum forgot all the questions she had about clam shells, and her pulse raced.

"Are we to go across the strait as well?"

Eekbis turned to her with a questioning look.

"Uhpahs told me they are going," Amuun'axsum said.

Eekbis turned back to her packing. "No, I do not make such long trips anymore if I can help it. But I do pack for a trip," she said. "They cannot leave until Buhkweeduuk is back. And Buhkweeduuk has urgent business in Deeyuh to attend to first. He asked if I would come along, as I may be needed for proper—convincing."

Amuun'axsum's enthusiasm snuffed out.

"Am I to go to Deeyuh as well?"

Eekbis paused, as if she were still trying to decide. "Buhkweeduuk would say yes. But I say no," she said. "No, I need you to stay here. There is a long list of things I need you to do for me before winter, things my old bones cannot take. And with these rains, I do not dare take a break from the work." She spoke as if trying to convince someone.

"How long will you be gone?"

"A week, most likely," she said.

Amuun'axsum's skin prickled anew with anxious, hopeful thoughts.

"Now," Eekbis said. "Here is what I need you to do while I am away."

~

Amuun'a̱xsum's mind churned. The shaman gone for a week. Dushuuw soon gone across the strait. Winds picking up already. Time running short. Her home somewhere across that strait. And a question still unanswered.

She strode toward the bay, basket and knife in hand to join the other women gathering among the intertidal rocks.

Several small canoes had landed on the beach. Dushuuw stood in the water behind one canoe, helping take gear from two sea otter hunters. He held a quiver of arrows, their bone tips menacingly barbed.

Amuun'a̱xsum resisted the urge to reach in and run her hand over the plush fur. She curled her hand against her chest, and caught Dushuuw's eye as she stepped beyond the canoe. One step. Two steps.

"How is the hat coming along?" he called.

Amuun'a̱xsum sighed with relief and turned to him.

"I would like to see it," he said.

She struggled to keep her face impassive, aware of the hunters and the other people who surrounded them. She fixed her gaze on his own and nodded, then turned again toward the still-exposed tidal pools. Bent among the rocks, she swiped away excited tears and smiled as she pried loose an urchin from its crevice.

DUSHUUW ARRIVED at the snag as the sun set. On either side of the firebox, he set a round of wood he had lugged from the high ground worksite. He eased himself down on one and waited, looking over the drawings she had made, drawings that still made him faintly uneasy.

A rustling skirt and sweet scent drew his attention to the snag's opening.

He stood. "You are early."

"The shaman is gone to Deeyuh." She dusted off the other round of wood, sat down, and settled a basket on her lap. The cedar band was missing from her wrist again. He wondered now about the story behind the tattoo, marred by scars.

Dushuuw tried to figure out what to say.

"I brought the hat to show you," she said, breaking the silence, "even if it was not really of interest to you." She dug into the basket. "I am afraid I must admit that I made a mistake."

Dushuuw thought of the sagging knob on the other hat, to which he had grown strangely accustomed. "I am cursed," he quipped.

"Or it is me."

"Or both of us."

She smiled. "I think I like this mistake, though."

She pulled out the hat, holding it by its knob, which did not sag one bit. The bottom of the hat had yet to be finished off. But she had started the grass-woven design—the familiar whale, tracked by a canoe in which a hunter stood with a harpoon—created with short, black lines. A dotted line of red linked the whale to the canoe, representing blood from a successful strike.

"The mistake is here." She pointed to a red line that crossed the man's body.

"Ah," he said, holding his side in mock pain. "That hurts."

She shook her head as she laughed. "I was distracted. I did it wrong. But I like it. I think I will repeat the mistake as I make the pattern again on the other side." She brushed her thumb over the errant red line. "It is you. You carry your wounds with you. They make you strong."

Dushuuw regarded the hat for a moment, deciding not to point out that the geometric figure could not be him—since that man held a harpoon. Instead, his eyes shifted to her wrist.

"You carry your wounds with you too," he said.

She looked down at her scarred tattoo.

"You want to go home," he said. "I keep my promises, but you have to know this promise may not be one I can keep. If I cannot even tell—"

"This must be a secret, Dushuuw," she said. "You can keep that one promise. And if it should be that there is no way to give me what I want, or that the rewards are not enough for you... I would understand."

She sat with back straight and did not meet his gaze.

Dushuuw abruptly stood and turned away as he dug his fingers through his hair. She was leading him into dangerous territory. Yet they already were in dangerous territory. All he knew was that he felt pulled to stay. Something tugged at him that he could not pin down.

With a sigh he turned around and felt a different kind of tug. Though she quickly returned to that self-assured posture she so often presented, he had seen the stark fear written across her face.

"Tell me what I need to know," he said.

Tears shone in her eyes, though she blinked them back. Drawing a breath, she smoothed the hat in her lap.

"The day I became a woman was the day my father was beheaded," she said, voice cracking. She looked aside for a long moment. "In truth, there is no home to return to—they made sure of that."

"Who?"

The woman shrugged. "Neighbors. Helped by northerners. Men like you, with clubs and spears and arrows." A look of hate flashed across her face. She held up her tattooed wrist. "My mother's slave scarred me—scarred my tattoo like one already turned over to slavery—in order to hide my noble status. Otherwise, he said they would kill me too."

Interest overcame his trepidation. This kind of total war was rare. Only the worst need for vengeance led to killing off everyone who might some day pose a threat of reclaiming the land. Dushuuw rubbed his chin. If what this woman said were true, he would be in trouble with a lot of people if he knowingly offered her aid.

"Why would they do that? What did your father do?"

But the woman looked away again, chin raised. She gave a little shrug. "How should I know? They just did. My mother was killed also. The slave was supposed to take me to my mother's family, far to the south, but—we did not get far, and he was killed too."

Dushuuw listened as the woman told him what she remembered of the few descriptions of her mother's family and home village. There was not much to go on, and even those scraps of memory took a long time for the woman to get out as she paused regularly to gather herself. She rocked back and forth in her seat.

"It has been so long," she said. "I have not been able to tell anyone this before. I didn't think it would be this hard."

"We have time," he said. "You said Eekbis will be gone for the week. We can meet again tomorrow. It is getting late, after all."

She crunched the hat in a tight grip again. He reached over and placed his hand over her own. "Rest." For a moment, her guard was down again, and the look in her eyes was one of gratitude. He was suddenly aware of the warmth of the dying fire, the warmth of her skin. He quickly drew his hand back.

Chin jutted out once more, the woman nodded, and lay the hat in her lap, trying to straighten out the crease she had made.

"Tell me... tell me about something you enjoy," she said. "About anything. I want to fill my head with something else—something good—or I'll never sleep."

So he did. About how he liked to get out on the water to fish with only his best friend for company. Spend the night under the stars, being rocked to sleep with a firebox to keep warm. The sense of peace. One thing fell out of his mouth after another. Things he had never told anyone before.

"You are often out at sea," she said.

"It is home as much as here on land," he said. "I hate winters."

She laughed. "Well, then it is good that there are stories to tell in wintertime."

"Like about the Wild Woman?" he said, remembering the hummingbird, wrapped again and tucked away in his storage bench.

"And stories we haven't been told a thousand times by nagging grandmothers," she said.

"Plenty of Q̓watee stories out there, enough to never repeat the same one twice," he said.

"You Wuh-uhch people and your Q̓watee stories," she said, shaking her head.

"Ah, you are after weightier stories," he said, and looked over her shoulder to the drawings that skipped over the ridges of bark. "More serious stories, about Thunderbird..."

She didn't volley back, and when he looked over, she was yawning.

"I should go back," she said. "I am tired, and the shaman has given me an extensive task list." With a look of annoyance, she stood and gripped her basket, another wide yawn forcing her to pause.

Dushuuw grabbed the torch from the firebox. "I will walk you back."

They walked in silence and paused at the edge of the forest. They looked out over the dark houses, the winding river, and the bay. A light rain fell. Clouds hid the moon and stars.

She slipped away, angling between walls toward the shaman's empty house. Dushuuw walked out from under the trees and toward the great house. As he crossed over the creek, he dipped the torch in the burbling waters, releasing a faint hiss and stream of smoke. The surf pounded onto the shore of the bay, retreated, and pounded again.

26

THEY MET THE NEXT several nights. Amuun'ax̱sum remembered a bit more each time, frustrated it was so much harder to share than she had expected. She was grateful for the time they had to get through it all.

More time was spent in telling stories, though, and trading explanations of words in each other's languages. These discussions helped Dushuuw to recognize the general area of her father's village, farther north than he had ever traveled. She did not give him the village's name, unsure if it would be wise.

During the day, Amuun'ax̱sum experienced the same kind of tiredness she had felt when keeping vigil during his whaling. But their new reason for meeting filled her with energy. She looked forward to each night—and not only because each night brought her closer to finding her family.

Each night, there was something new inside the warm confines of the snag. Mats padded her seat the second night. The next night was tossed with wind, and a fur-lined blanket over her lap added a layer of warmth. He laughed as she kept petting the sea otter fur, and as she gave in and buried her face in its softness. Another night, he brought a dish of salmon roe, and she covered her tongue with the briny orange orbs. She regretted eating them, because it meant they were gone.

During the day, she kept busy with the tasks Eekbis had given her that took her into the forest, up along the creek, and banging around inside the empty house. She hurried to finish the tasks so that she would have time to sift through the shaman's boxes and baskets and shells, taking a bit of this and a smidge of that until she had a balm mixed. She brought the shell from her hiding spot and filled it to the brim.

She went to the snag early that day, and pulled aside the piece of wood over the hiding spot to replace the balm. But there was something new. Amuun'ax̱sum brought out the small circles of abalone, with their sunrise hues. It took a long time to work at the old holes in her ears. Drops of blood dotted her fingertips, and her lobes burned and ached. She reveled in the weight of the earrings, feeling them move as she turned her head from side to side.

Skin softened with leaves and perfumed with the balm, earrings swinging, Amuun'axsum draped the fur-lined blanket around herself like a cloak. She raised her arms and danced, watching her shadow quiver over the bark of the snag. As she turned, she came to a sudden stop at the sight of Dushuuw, who watched from the entrance of the snag, twirling a fern leaf between his fingers.

"I was hoping you would not notice me," he said.

Amuun'axsum gave a flustered laugh and spun in circles toward him, eyes closed. She felt the moment of proximity, that invisible boundary where the heat surrounding one body meets that of another. She stopped, and opened her eyes. She had to bend her neck to look up at his face.

"Why is it," he said, brushing the fern over her arm, "that there is no dance where a man and a woman touch?"

Heat crept up her neck. She counted the beats of her heart.

"Eekbis will come home tomorrow," she said.

Dushuuw looked at his feet, and they each shuffled to their seats across the firebox from one another.

They reviewed the details that Amuun'axsum had been able to scrounge from her memory, about her mother's family and home village. Her mother's stories described a place far, far to the south of where Amuun'axsum's father took his bride. Amuun'axsum's mother would describe dancing on a narrow sandy beach beside whales and sea lions that drifted there moon after moon, like offerings. Amuun'axsum recognized her mother's native tongue among many of those who lived at Wuh-uhch, including Um-iiqsu and Thluuch-muup and Uhpahs. In that case, the village would be closer to Wuh-uhch than to where she grew up in her father's village, which was good.

They stayed up all night. Sharing memories of their mothers. Of favorite childhood friends and favorite toys. Dushuuw lay on the ground, propped up on an elbow. Nestled inside furs, Amuun'axsum looked down at him, absently entwining the fern leaf into her hair.

"Where is your favorite place to be?" he asked.

Amuun'axsum wilted a bit at the question, her first thought going only to the place she could not yet be.

"I suppose the forest," she finally said, looking up into the darkened canopy above them.

She told him about the old woman who taught her how to bathe and pray for the smallest of plants. Who revealed the many layers of the sodden landscape that rose in spires around them. As she spoke, Amuun'a̱xsum reached out a hand to the bark of the snag, brushing her fingertips over its ridges, and tipped the edge of the fern to her nose. "There is something about the scents of the forest—of cedar and spring flower buds, even the rotting remains of a fallen tree, the sour smell of hemlock crushed against skin, the dirt when you dig into it... There's a damp quality that leaves you feeling clean, a fullness that makes you feel safe." She smiled self-consciously and looked around at the snag. "In a way, I suppose I feel like I am home out here."

Dushuuw had slid up into a slouched position against the bark while she spoke; he leaned his head back against the snag with a soft smile.

Amuun'a̱xsum cleared her throat. "What about you?"

He sat up, as one suddenly alert. "The sea," he said, without hesitating.

But instead of elaborating, Dushuuw pushed his tongue in his cheek as he looked away. When he looked back at her, he had a mischievous gleam in his eye.

"Would you like to go fishing?"

~

Soon Amuun'a̱xsum found herself in a small canoe as Dushuuw paddled them into the bay, before the village awoke. She lay in the hull of the canoe. Dushuuw narrated what she could not see, noting the old men stretching in their doorways.

"They are wondering, I think, how a young man could beat them and be the first to drop a line," he said.

She laughed up at him. His face was in shadow against the still-dark sky, yet she knew his smile.

Her stifled laughs gave way to nerves, however, as he maneuvered the canoe farther into the bay. The waves rushed underneath her, and the hull seemed a thin margin between her and the sea.

"Do you trust me?"

Amuun'a̱xsum drew her hands away from the canoe's sides, where she had braced herself, and held them at her chest. Her life already was in his hands.

Dushuuw's posture became more alert as he powered the canoe

through the bay with strong, smooth strokes. He no longer joked, but concentrated on the waves. The canoe suddenly lifted high, then sank in a steep dive. Amuun'axsum felt as if she was falling, and it took everything she had not to scream. She trembled and kept her eyes squeezed shut.

"You are all right," Dushuuw said, using a normal volume. His tone carried the hint of a smile again.

His paddle strokes got longer. The swells rolled, calm when compared to the single-minded push of the waves closer to shore. After a time, he stopped and held out his hand. Amuun'axsum rose from the hull, and saw the silhouette of land over his shoulder. Gray light started to sketch its curves. The waves sloshed against the canoe, and the canoe started to drift and sway. She gripped his hand tight as she eased herself up onto a thwart.

With an embarrassed clearing of the throat, she let go of his hand to let him maneuver the canoe. He took them a bit farther out, then slipped the paddle under the thwarts. He dropped an anchor by its long cord, then baited a weighted line to toss into the water.

Amuun'axsum tucked her hair behind her ear, though it only blew free again. Seals swam nearby, their spotted heads and necks bobbing among the waves. Far off, a flock of gulls circled above unseen fish.

Dushuuw scooted back and reclined against the stern.

The gray light turned white, and the sun started to edge above the peaks behind Wuh-uhch. There were only a few wispy clouds; the morning came cold and clear. Holding the fur blanket close with one hand, Amuun'axsum shielded her eyes with the other and scanned the area. The village's houses were barely visible, still tucked into the shadow of the small mountain. There were a few tiny plumes of smoke to mark the place, but only because Amuun'axsum knew where to look. Mist floated over the river, and wafted between the trees on the hillsides.

Dushuuw was looking beyond her, a smile across his face.

She twisted about on the thwart and took in the view—the sea, in all its vastness, extending to an endless horizon.

Amuun'axsum felt her world shift even further. A prickle of fear moved through her, as if the sea would swallow her whole. Instinctively, she closed her eyes and listened. The slosh of water against the hull. A pitter-patter of drops of sea spray falling back to the sea. The wind sliding, whistling. A distant gull's cry.

"It's beautiful," she said, eyes still closed.

Behind her, Dushuuw shifted closer; his breaths echoed the gentle pulse of the sea, in and out, up and down.

"This was one reason I wanted to take you out here," he said. "To see Wuh-uhch as I see it."

"From the sea, your favorite place," she said, opening her eyes and turning back toward him.

A flood of words followed as Dushuuw described the collision of sea and strait, the great eddy that churned up anything and everything, the strong tidal current that hurried canoes to the best fishing spots or sped a long journey to see friends. There were the waters nearer to shore, too, where he had his biggest battle with a writhing bass. From his knees, he described the catch for her, waving and thrusting his arms, and then gripped the wooden seat on either side of her, rocking her back and forth over imaginary waves.

She laughed—a loud and skipping laugh, fueled by lingering elation and nerves—and grabbed onto his shoulder as she started to tip.

He steadied her with an apologetic look. "You will not go overboard."

A flush heated her cheeks as she pulled her hand back.

Amuun'axsum looked away to the north, beyond Chahdee toward the still-dark smear on the horizon where, somewhere along a vast forested and mountainous coast, was her home. She massaged the twin lines of her tattoo— both undulating like sea waves—which spoke of her father's village and, in a way, of all the villages that set their doorways toward the sea. She could not feel the lines of the tattoo, which were part of her skin. Neither could she feel the scars that erased them, which also were part of her.

Dushuuw sat again on the edge of the thwart ahead of her, so close that their knees nearly touched.

"I will try to find them, as I promised," Dushuuw said. "Yet you have to know that the information you have given me is still not enough."

Amuun'axsum looked at her wrist.

"To find one family among thousands, on one beach among hundreds," he said. "You have not told me everything I need to know."

Amuun'axsum was silent.

"A name," he said. "The name of your father's village. Your name—I must believe your grandparents would know your name. And I am guessing your name is not Quulthoo."

He was trying to jest, to encourage. But she held still. A gull swooped low, a whisper in its feathers.

Amuun'axsum raised her chin. "As a girl, I was called Maḥtii. That may be the name they know me by still. But when I became a woman, I received my new name. My father had built our village from nothing, and called it Amuun," she said, folding her hands together to cover their shaking. "When I became a woman, he tied me to the place. My name is Amuun'axsum."

As she spoke, she had grown rigid, as if bracing herself. She worried so long that mentioning these names would spark violence. Instead, there was ignorance. Dushuuw gave no reaction, and this proved worse. As if her past really were a nightmare. Something that only happened in a cautionary tale.

Dushuuw attempted to repeat her name. He failed, and shook his head with a laugh. Her own laugh hitched in her chest, even a botched pronunciation causing her to hold her breath, for fear of losing it.

The next time, his eyes directed at their feet, he got it right: "Amuun'axsum."

Amuun'axsum could not restrain the sobs that dug their way from her throat. The stifled cries came out in gasps as she fought to choke them back, to make her body submit to her will.

Seven years a slave. Seven years her name banished from speech. And now, on another's lips—a whisper may as well be a shout. It was one thing to give her name. It was quite another to have someone give it back.

"Did I say it wrong?" he asked.

He shifted closer, bracing an arm on the side of the canoe beside her. She gave a shaky laugh and shook her head.

"Amuun'axsum," he said, encouraging her to speak.

She squeezed her eyes shut as more tears came, and held onto his arm as the canoe rocked.

"Amuun'axsum," he said, soothingly.

His hand slipped over the lines and scars of her wrist.

"Dushuuw..."

Then his other hand was cupping her face, the canoe rocking as he leaned in and pressed his lips against her own. Amuun'axsum swam through the emotions coursing through her body. Surprise rose and broke into greed. She gripped his shoulder and his hair and pulled him closer, eager to taste his words and meld them with her own. Sparks popped inside her head, and she shuddered as a feeling coursed upward through her body in what could only be described as a song. A groan pulsed through Dushuuw as he knelt again in front of her, this time slipping his hand beneath the blanket onto her back, and pulled her against him. Her flesh met his flesh. The blanket slipped from her shoulders, and in the cold shock Amuun'axsum suddenly heard only the sea and the wind and Dushuuw's deep breathing. The sensation of singing was silenced by the cold open. Her eyes shot open and she tore her mouth away for a breath, shoving him away.

She twisted on the thwart, grabbing her blanket back up as he returned to the other thwart.

Dushuuw put his hands to his head. His eyes were closed and his face twisted into a confused expression. Abruptly, he pulled up the anchor and the fishing line with its empty hook, picked up the paddle, and turned the canoe about to face land. It was still early, but light enough that the bay was dotted with the canoes of fishermen.

Amuun'axsum curled up at the bottom of the hull, pulling the blanket up to her chin. She stared up at the wisps of clouds. The canoe rocked against each movement of the paddle, first on one side, then the other. They sped forward. The sound of the rushing water against the hull was joined by the distant chatter of people, the scent of salty air joined by woody smoke. The sound of the water quieted as it pushed them along in a smooth current. The hillsides rose on either side of the canoe as Dushuuw took them upriver. Branches sliced across the sky.

Dushuuw brought the canoe ashore beneath the overhanging branches of a copse of trees. He helped her to shore through a small pool, and she kept her eyes down the whole time.

"The snag is over there." He dropped her hand. "You can see my trail."

Amuun'axsum took off the blanket and folded it against her chest.

"I should not have..." He didn't finish.

She swayed on her feet, though not from being on the water. She didn't even try to keep the tears back this time.

"In my mind, I am still what I was before," she said, stroking the folded blanket. "A woman of worth, who should be draped in furs and adorned." She took out the earrings, one by one. "But until I am redeemed, this is pretend play."

"I want to get it all back for you," he said.

Amuun'axsum's heart pounded as she looked up at him. Dushuuw stood before her, his eyes pleading.

She hugged his gifts close and closed the distance between them before she could tell herself it was foolish. She rested her face against his chest. He folded his arms around her and buried his face in her hair. They stood there for some time, and Amuun'axsum wondered what it would be like to fall asleep nestled against him. She wanted that now. Even if it meant pretending. Her head swam and her blood raced, and she had to force her mind to cold logic. To put aside the want. To focus on the need. She gripped the earrings in her fist, feeling them prick.

As she stepped back, his hands slid down her arms. She pressed the fur and the earrings against his chest.

"These are so beautiful," she said. "Worthy of a bride."

ONCE MORE, DUSHUUW wandered down the rocky beach of Ḥawith's village, watching people as they worked or visited. His mind churned. They had paddled here across the strait days ago. He had yet to discover the answer he needed, and time was running out. But he wasn't sure how to even broach the topic—the secret that Amuun'aẋsum had entrusted him with, just as she had the secret of her name. He held one secret close, while contemplating how to strategically reveal the other.

On the beach near a house corner, a carver worked on a long trunk, stripped of its bark. Dushuuw wandered over to watch. The man was carving a totem.

Unlike the cape peoples, these villages used totem poles in profusion. Each house had at least four poles outside its walls; Ḥawith's boasted nearly a dozen. Each branch of a family who had the status and the wealth contributed a carved pole, the animals and crests varying between them. Dushuuw watched as the carver chiseled the wood at one end of the pole. The form was tiny, insignificant somehow. Not the Eagle, nor Bear, nor Elk.

The carver looked up at Dushuuw and saw his questioning look.

"It is Mouse," the man said.

Dushuuw raised his eyebrows.

"Do not disparage the small creatures," the man said, smiling as he took in Dushuuw's bulk. "Sure, this totem will have the Thunderbird, and the Lightning Serpents. They will remind us to teach our laws to our children and that, when we strike our enemies or our prey, we must strike hard. But we do not ignore the small voices, the quiet voices. They have much to teach us, too, if we are willing to make ourselves small enough to listen."

The man turned back to his project. Curls of bark fell to the ground, as the man chanted to the wood.

Caught up in watching the master carver work, Dushuuw was surprised when the man stopped and put away his tools. Night was falling already. Dushuuw helped cover the pole, and carried the man's box of food and water for him. They headed into the great house, which was already loud with feasting.

Dushuuw paused in the doorway, watching Ọotsik rub his nose as he stared across the room at Sawsin, who laughed and chatted with the relatives and friends she had left behind when she married. Dushuuw shared a knowing smile with his stepmother. He walked over and punched his brother in the shoulder, drawing him back to focus on his family—and stop worrying.

The festivities had already commenced. Memories of the wedding were still fresh, and each side seemed charged to present their best side. Ḥawith's people were loud and well-synchronized, bringing out their best singers, dancers, and dramatic sleights of hand. Food was laid in front of the guests in astonishing quantities. Dushuuw struggled to restrain his appetite at his father's quiet insistence—and later understood the need for self-control. The local villagers kept the show going until the late-night hours, then opened up the floor to their guests. Tired from the journey across the strait and with a full stomach, it would be difficult to match their hosts if he had stuffed himself with their food.

It was agreed on the journey over that Ọotsik would not dance or sing that night. Um-iiqsu said remaining off the floor would help her son stand apart, as a whaler and man of status. Her sister was more blunt. "If we aim to show our best," Thluuch-muup said, "Young Son is better at dancing, anyway."

So now he donned a cedar bark headband and an ornamented cape, grateful he had listened to his father's advice over his stomach's rumbling protests, and strode to the center of the house. He took a cleansing breath and passed his eyes over the sea of chattering faces surrounding him. He stopped.

She was there.

Among a group of neighbors that had arrived late, she stood in a one-shouldered wrap, a baby balanced on her hip. She looked at ease as she waited for a man to prepare a cushion for her to sit on. Her hair was neatly braided, and she wore her favorite earrings. Before she sat down, she looked at Dushuuw. His ex-wife held his gaze, then pointedly gave her hand to the man beside her and sat down.

Dushuuw looked at the floor and forced himself to step forward. The house swirled with laughter and conversation. Only a moment had passed, but time shifted beneath his feet. He looked back at his family. They had noticed. Chai chewed on her bottom lip. Q̇otsik gave him a worried look before turning back to the conversation he was having with one of Ḥawith's relatives. His father sat erect, staring somewhere at his chest, waiting for him to begin. Dushuuw looked over to the drum, where his uncle sat. Buhkweeduuk gave him a look of challenge, then struck the drum.

The plank sounded. One beat. Loud.

Dushuuw thrust out his arms, holding the cape taut by its edges. He pinned his eyes to the floor. The drum sounded again. And he began to stamp his feet. A beat. A step. A beat, a step. Then both in unison, marking time together. One high step for one beat—another, and another—in a tight, leaning circle.

The dirt floor spun. The sounds of the crowd rotated around him. His body moved by memory, but his mind twisted within its own storm. He thought of a woman, with soft skin. Tears streaming, and a plea.

The drum began to beat more quickly. His feet responded. He bent over, battering the dirt with his soles. He traced over his own footprints.

Light shining off unbound hair. Mouth parted in oblivious slumber. Soft lips against his own.

The drum beat fast. He opened his eyes and met it, spinning. The people became indistinct—ovals for faces, rectangles for cloaks.

Her hand in his hand in the dark of night.

The drum beat up and down, on and on. He moved with it, spinning faster, faster. He whirled, round and round about the axis of his body and of the room, faces and colors melding into a blur. His cape flew behind him, slicing through the smoke-filled air.

Perfume. Scars. A name.

Faster. Faster. Faster still.

The drumming stopped—a last, deep note, lingering. He stopped too—and bowed low with the fading beat. The tightly held cape billowed behind him in resistance, wanting to spin—its fluttering descent the only remaining sound.

Whispered conversations and an old person's cough punctured the silence. Dushuuw waited for the drum to cue his rise, to resume the dance, to spin the world and its doubts away again to a sweet blur. To think again on the woman he left behind, the woman who haunted him in ways that made him want her to spin closer, closer, closer.

The last beat sounded. Dushuuw remained low to the ground, waiting for the feel of the dance to fade. He focused on the dirt, regained his balance. People resumed their conversations at normal volumes. Slaves wended through the house, offering more food. As he stood, he found himself smiling—with pleasure, with defiance.

The smile remained as he faced the portion of the house where his ex-wife reclined. She looked at him, her eyes bitter. Then he turned his back, to find the beaming face of Tluulth, the local chief's younger daughter, who smiled from the edge of the crowd in response to his own. She lowered her chin, but brazenly held his gaze. Her smile held the hint of challenge. Dushuuw hesitated, worried about the message she assumed he sent. Then he thought of the woman to whom he turned his back, of her betrayal. He inclined his head toward Tluulth as he made his way back to his family.

"I'm not sure that will help us, brother," Q̇otsik said in a low tone.

Dushuuw flopped down beside him on the low bench and dug his fingers into his hair in annoyance. "I know. It was impulsive, and stupid. I was just so…"

"Yes, I saw." Q̇otsik glanced in the direction of Dushuuw's ex-wife. "Still, I am trying to stay on my father-in-law's good side, you know."

"Brother, you really have nothing to worry about. Do you not see the way your wife looks at you?"

"She has not looked at me all night. Her attentions are all for others. I have never seen her look so happy."

"Well, I have—on your wedding day."

But Q̇otsik wasn't listening. He shifted and angled his head closer. "I have something to show you." He took something from a pouch. "I took your advice. Do you think she will like it?" His voice was strained.

Dushuuw held the object in his palm. It was a carved bone comb. The decorative accessory was a bit crude—rough where it should be smooth, nothing like what one of their craftsmen would produce—though the painted design was precise.

Q̇otsik sensed Dushuuw's question. "I made it," he said. "It is no good, is it?"

Dushuuw did not think it possible for Q̇otsik to lack talent at anything. As he watched his brother—this legend on land and on water, now mooning about and spending in secret what must have been hours on making a personal touch to a ritual-laden political marriage—he realized this effort was perfect too.

"She will not like it," Dushuuw said, handing it back. Q̇otsik pursed his lips and nodded. "She will love it," Dushuuw said, giving his brother a friendly shove. Q̇otsik offered up a nervous laugh.

~

By morning, Dushuuw's careful avoidance of Tluulth was paying off. Now if he accidentally looked her way, she was sure to turn away in a huff. By contrast, his brother and Sawsin were arm in arm again. Sawsin reached up to pet the comb she had put in her hair and smiled up at her husband. Both encounters made Dushuuw slightly sick to his stomach.

He felt more sick by the conversation he was about to have. But his family was getting ready to depart. He was out of time.

So he stood on the beach beside Ḥawith, as the clouds parted.

Ḥawith held the dagger and turned it back and forth in admiration. Sunlight glinted off the shiny foreign material that made up the blade, fashioned by southern hands and mounted in a haft by a toolmaker of Wuh-uhch. He nodded at Dushuuw.

"This is excellent," Ḥawith said. "Where did you find the material for the blade?"

"Embedded in a bit of driftwood," Dushuuw said. "I could have had one of the craftsmen from Oosa-ilth pound it into shape. But the people they have down at the southern market are better at the job. I didn't want any cracks. So this has traveled the length of the coast and back to come to your hands."

Ḥawith nodded thoughtfully, then smiled at Dushuuw in a knowing manner. "A sharp blade to soften a father's heart."

Dushuuw scanned the beach with a shrug. "Certainly not." He looked back at the man. "That's what the vat of whale oil is for."

Ḥawith laughed amiably and admired the dagger again.

"I wonder if I might ask you a question?" Dushuuw asked.

Ḥawith's smile relaxed, but he nodded. Dushuuw brought up the lie he had prepared before he could second-guess himself.

"Do you know of a village called Amuun? Someone on my travels south asked whether I knew a friend they had there—the village chief's wife, I believe—and said she lived north of here. But I have not heard of Amuun, which I find odd."

Ḥawith's brow had furrowed as Dushuuw talked. The chief's eyes remained on the blade.

"Someone said that name?" the chief asked in a low voice. He looked away before Dushuuw could think of an answer. Ḥawith shook his head, grew stiff. "No such village exists."

The chief considered what to say next. Dushuuw held his breath, resisting the urge to bring up the next in his string of lies.

"I should tell your uncle about this, you know," Ḥawith said. "There are some who, if they found out that name was brought up here, would make me a target. I would point them directly to you." Ḥawith worked his jaw, as if chewing on his words before deciding whether to speak them. "If you see this contact again, advise them to remain silent. The friend they seek is... gone. And if he goes to her people in Loḥta, he would be wise to pretend she never lived up north at all."

Dushuuw twisted his hands behind his back as he nodded. His skin prickled. His gamble had worked—barely. He ran the village name over and over in his head, committing it to memory.

Ḥawith turned toward the house, where Ṫashii called to him.

"Duty calls," the chief said, his voice relaxing. He raised the dagger again in admiration, balancing it in his palm in a weighing manner. "Remind me of your name?"

Dushuuw turned from the chief's calculating gaze. The man was testing him; Ḥawith would already know the truth from the gossip that traveled the coast faster than a northeast wind. "A question best asked of other men, I am afraid, or a name also best left unmentioned," Dushuuw said. "There is a reason that it is my brother's name shouted from the rooftops and not my own."

Ḥawith looked at him for a moment, then gave a bemused smile, followed by a regretful shake of a head, the type of which Dushuuw was becoming well-acquainted. The chief strode off.

Dushuuw rejoined his family by their canoes.

"I will have to watch out," said Ġotsik, with a light laugh. His whole mood had changed from the nights spent by the fire; he seemed a head taller. "Young Son might bargain Sawsin right out from under my nose."

Sawsin let go of his arm only to swat it. "I am quite content with the husband I have."

Dushuuw smiled at the joking, though he did not join the laughter.

"You know, it is a common practice in many places for brothers to marry sisters," Buhkweeduuk said. "And it seems, if my eyes are not mistaken, that Young Son is already finding approval from a certain young lady."

Dushuuw tried to shake off his apprehension. He really was getting himself into trouble.

"She is indeed young, uncle. Too young, I should think, to rob her parents of her company just yet," Dushuuw said. "And perhaps my brother would wish to follow in our father's footsteps—I certainly would not be the one to rob him of such an opportunity."

Buhkweeduuk did not laugh. In fact, he seemed to frown before catching himself. He offered a tight smile. "I see your meaning," he said. "But you should be careful. An eldest daughter holds her father's pride. But a youngest daughter holds her father's heart. And you do not toy with a father's heart."

Dushuuw recalled his brazen look the night of the dance. "Yes, uncle."

Buhkweeduuk looked at him as if he was going to say something more, but instead patted him on the back with a smile and turned away.

Soon, they were on the water, singing their farewells, and Qotsik sat next to Dushuuw on the thwart. "You held up well, brother, given the unexpected guest that first night. We all worried when we saw her there. You seem to be doing better, yes?" He did not wait for a response. "Do not worry. You will get a wife soon enough, one worthy of your attentions."

Dushuuw cupped his hand over the end of the paddle, then dipped the blade into the water. "I do not worry, brother."

For once, it was the truth.

The woman he found he desired still required careful bargaining, but of a kind where there was no set ritual to follow. This was something outside the charted waters of propriety. And those were waters Dushuuw knew well.

They entered the cold mist of a small bank of fog. Dushuuw's skin prickled. The land was sucked into obscurity behind them. All was shrouded in gray. But he smiled, as if seeing something for the first time.

~

The travelers were quiet as the men paddled the canoes across the strait in loose formation. The sound of water dripping from the paddles was amplified by the low cloud cover. An occasional gull squawked high above. The paddlers were attuned to the sea's currents, swells, and sounds. When they got beyond the strait's middle, bits of conversation popped up here and there—a guffaw at a joke, a grumbling about the misty weather.

Chai shivered on the thwart in front of Dushuuw, and he rested his paddle over his legs while he wrapped a cloak over his sister's shoulders. She looked back at him and smiled appreciatively.

They paddled ahead for the shorter route, splitting the gap between the mainland and Chahdee. Hulking spires of rock rose above their heads, looming. Streamers of fog hovered over the water.

A gull flapped out of the low clouds suddenly, its feathers grazing heads as its surprised calls trailed away. Uhpqoolth vigorously rubbed a hand over his head. Dushuuw and Q̇otsik burst into laughter, which echoed off the rocks. Uhpqoolth drew up his shoulders and started to turn to respond.

But Q̇otsik suddenly held up his hand for silence, his posture alert. Dushuuw and Uhpqoolth gave him their silent attention. From the stern, Buhkweeduuk passed the signal to the canoes spread out behind them. Paddles were held on laps. Conversation stopped. The women grasped their cloaks. The waves lifted the canoes, set them back down, up and down. A wooden bailer knock, knock, knocked against a hull until someone picked it up.

Q̇otsik shook his head in warning at Chahbuhṫ, carefully rose in the canoe, and turned back, facing the gray haze over gray waters. He scanned the area. Dushuuw twisted to follow his brother's gaze, edging up from his seat to get a better view. The heads of other crewmen swiveled.

Then Dushuuw heard it too.

A fast wake.

A prow shot through the fog in the distance. For a moment Dushuuw thought it was one of their own war canoes. But the foreign battle cries quickly dispelled that notion.

Q̇otsik and Dushuuw shouted as one for a quick retreat. Outfitted for traveling, they did not have adequate weapons to repel an unexpected attack—not quickly. The enemy canoe surged toward them. Loaded down, the Wuh-uhch canoe seemed to crawl.

Arrows met the water around the canoes. One arrow lodged with a thunk in the hull beside Dushuuw. The women screamed and huddled as low as they could manage. Thluuch-muup's slave girl curled up beside the woman in the hull. Chahbuhṫ gripped the edges of the bow.

Dushuuw looked over his shoulder. He saw the warriors now, in their elk hide tunics.

But the warriors were turning their canoe away.

"Why give up so soon?" Uhpqoolth asked, voicing Dushuuw's thought.

In the next instant, a red prow shot through the fog from the other direction—bringing with it the whirling whine of a spinning rope.

Dushuuw shouted a warning. Blood pounded in his ears. His paddle seemed to move through mud.

The raiders sent their stone weapon sailing through the air by its rope. The stone crashed into a canoe at the rear of the traveling group, a smaller one with men and most of their supplies. The hull split with a loud crack. Dushuuw turned and watched as the crew of the struck vessel went into a panic. Most of the men dove into the water. One man remained, eyes wide, jabbing his paddle into the sea even as water poured in around his feet. Another stone canoe-breaker came in high, and the head of the paddler sprayed blood.

Heart thumping, Dushuuw turned away. Behind him, the dead paddler's body splashed into the water.

A foreign war cry thundered. One Dushuuw did not recognize. Another cry went up in another direction, meaning there were more enemies on the hunt.

The timing was horrific. Wuh-uhch was too far to signal for help. But so were any of the nearest redoubts, if they could even spot the party in all the fog. Dushuuw searched their surroundings, then shouted above the din a moment before Ǫotsik gestured in the same direction. An arrow spliced the air by Dushuuw's ear. Another arrow sailed past on his other side. The women screamed. Chahbuhł bent lower, gripping the sides of the canoe as if to urge it faster.

The paddlers powered into one of the inlets that pierced the cape. The cliff walls towered above them, amplifying the wind and the shouts, and funneling out fog in curling clouds.

Dushuuw shouted out directions, steering their crew around the rocks he knew were hiding beneath the waves. They headed for the arched stone entry of a cave. It was a narrow gap, best threaded by those who already knew it—the group's one advantage. Ancient rock splayed out into the water all around them. Stone at their sides and ahead, the enemy behind, there was nowhere for them to go now but with the building waves toward the cave's entrance, where there would be no other exit. Water broke against the cliff walls in towering sprays.

They had played in this spot. As young teens, Dushuuw and Ǫotsik had camped at the upper reaches of the cave's hidden beach, balanced atop rocky ledges as high tide ate up all the sand. Small canoes. Two scrambling boys. Now, as the sea crashed and droned off the rocks, Dushuuw wondered how he could lead two large canoes full of travelers into its narrow confines.

There was no choice but to try.

As he shouted directions, guiding the canoe into the narrow entry, the stone walls came closer and closer together. Their paddles and his shouts came to nothing. Stone amplified the sounds of the sea—and its power. The canoes lurched on the swells. The sea pulled them backward. The men dug deep, forcing their way. The entire world seemed to shrink into one dark point.

Then everything flipped in an instant. Dushuuw's shouts and the women's screams blasted. The canoe surged forward and skidded onto the small beach. Dushuuw nearly lost his paddle as he lurched forward, only to rock sideways as the second canoe skidded alongside their hull. The men leaped from the canoes, splashing into the water, and pulled and pushed the canoes as close to the rock wall abutting the tiny beach as they could.

A hole above let down a beam of daylight. The wind and waves howled beyond the cave, as if the entrance marked some invisible barrier. Here, the water swayed languidly. Rock surrounded them, so that in most places the men had to stoop. Dushuuw helped his stepmothers, sister, and Sawsin out of the canoe, one at a time, leading them to a tall rock ledge. Shocked by their own amplified screams, the women now sat tight-lipped, afraid to whisper. The dank surroundings echoed with drips and drops.

Outside, the enemy's war cries built to a fever pitch. Still, as Dushuuw had hoped, the attackers did not approach the cave entrance. They would not risk their canoes or lives in unfamiliar territory so far from home.

Dushuuw patted his sister's leg, looking up at her with a reassuring smile. Chai took a deep breath and squared her shoulders, nodding down at him.

The women would be out of reach when high tide came. But nothing else would be.

Behind him, the men started talking over one another. Qotsik helped their father to sit on the beach. Buhkweeduuk strode toward them. Uhpqoolth grabbed a bow from the supplies stored under one of the canoe thwarts. He waded back into the water and faced the cave's entrance, ready to pick off anyone who may decide to try and enter.

"We need to get rocks for throwing," Uhpqoolth said, "and find anything that can be carved into a spear." He spoke with authority as he lifted his knees high to slosh through the water. "Gather the weapons we do have and, at tide's turn, make our move."

Dushuuw's hand slipped off his sister's lap as he turned toward his cousin and shook his head. "It will not work. They would pick us off as we came out."

At the edges of his vision, Dushuuw saw Q̓otsik trying to get his attention. But Dushuuw waded into the water and cut Uhpqoolth off before his cousin could respond.

"A rising tide helps them more. That is exactly what they are waiting for—to drown us out," Dushuuw said. "We need to get help."

The bow and arrow in Uhpqoolth's hands dropped to his sides, his face twisted with disbelief. "What kind of help do you expect, Young Son? The Sea Cougar to rise from the deep and cut them down for us?" He raised the bow again, and turned back toward the entrance. He raised his voice over his shoulder. "Better expect our heads would come off too waiting for that kind of help. We need to act."

"We need to act—but not like fish on a hook," Dushuuw shouted back.

"We are on a hook!"

Gulls suddenly fluttered high from hidden roosts in the crags.

"Young Son!"

Q̓otsik's shout silenced them both. Dushuuw turned back toward his brother, who sat beside their father. Of course his father would judge between them. It would be Dushuuw's right to make battle decisions here. But much had changed since he last helped drive heads on pikes, and he wondered whose side the chief would take. Around him, the other men exchanged nervous glances. Some had edged toward the cave's rocky ledges to start fetching rocks as Uhpqoolth ordered. Now they waited. Dushuuw took an angry breath and prepared his argument.

"Father, you must know—"

Dushuuw stopped.

Q̓otsik and Buhkweeduuk crouched on either side of Chahbuht̓. The older man hunched forward, leaning against his older son. He was pale. The women clung to the ledge, trying to stifle their sobs. Chahbuht̓ held a hand to his chest, near his heart. Bright blood ran between his fingers.

"We have to get it out," Q̓otsik said.

But he said it in a pleading way, his face strained with helplessness.

Dushuuw soon understood why. He looked in the bow of the canoe where their father had been sitting. A thin shaft fletched with woodpecker feathers rested in the hull. But there was no sign of an arrowhead. The weapon had worked as designed—a point loosely fixed to its shaft, so that it could not be easily removed from its victim. A warfare favorite of the strong people of the strait. Their father had been able to tug the shaft out of his body. But the barb was buried beneath his bleeding skin.

"Even if we could get it out, that barb would rip apart whatever piece of his body it's stuck in," Buhkweeduuk said.

Dushuuw fetched a mat from the canoe and helped Q̇otsik ease their father onto his back. Buhkweeduuk gestured toward the remains of a small fire pit left in a rocky cavity near the women; Sawsin was climbing down from the women's perch. "Get me ash," Buhkweeduuk said, to no one in particular. Sawsin's feet thudded to the beach and she scooped some in her hands and brought it over. Q̇otsik's eyes darted between his wife and his father. Taking the ash, Buhkweeduuk spit into it and stirred it in his palm with his finger. "For now, we can at least do this much..." He rubbed the gray mash around the wound. Chahbuht̓ winced, then went lax again; he was silent, focused on breathing.

"There, you see. We need to act now," Uhpqoolth said.

Dushuuw rose and shook his head. "I know a way—"

"Everyone start gathering rocks," Uhpqoolth said, sloshing through the water. "Search the ledges. Pry them loose. Look under the water. What about that one?"

"I can slip out and—"

"We make our move as soon as the weapons are together. We can get over the waves if we unload one of the canoes and all dig hard."

"Just give me until—"

"Let's move!"

"Stop!"

"Silence!" Buhkweeduuk's order boomed off the rock walls. Thluuch-muup's whimpering cries filled the silence that followed.

Buhkweeduuk looked between the two young men. "Keep your voices down, unless you want to hand the enemy our plans—not that you two have been able to agree on one." The older man looked at his brother. It was not clear if Chahbuht̓ registered all of what was going on around him, but Buhkweeduuk knelt beside him and spoke to him with the same tone of respect he always bore when giving his brother advice. "We find rocks. We prepare to fight. But we wait until the tide starts to turn, to give Young Son a chance to find help." Sweat dotted Chahbuht̓'s face as he looked up at Buhkweeduuk with tight lips. The chief gave a short nod.

Now that it was decided, Dushuuw stifled a rising panic.

Uhpqoolth started pointing and grabbing at rocks. Dushuuw shook off his fear and sprang into action as well. He strode over to the fire pit, and started to rub ash over his body.

Q̇otsik placed his father's hand in Sawsin's, then came over to help. Dushuuw had him cover his back with ash.

"I will go with you," Q̇otsik said.

"No. I need you to stay here and make sure Uhpqoolth waits. You remember our signal?"

Q̇otsik nodded, but drew close. "Brother, I worry you cannot hold your breath long enough. And the ash? This will not hide you from them—it will wash off as soon as you go down."

Dushuuw stood and faced him, the whites of his eyes standing out against his blackened face. "Not down," he said. "Up."

Q̇otsik registered his meaning, looking more worried. Dushuuw watched as his brother came to the same conclusion as he had. He wished Yaq were there. Diving and taking a long swim beneath enemy hulls would be the direct route. But Dushuuw did not have that kind of lung capacity; and even if he did, nobody had the endurance to swim so far—and as fast as was needed.

His brother followed him across the small beach toward a narrow cleft, nearly invisible high in the rock. Dushuuw jumped up and picked his way along a narrow ledge leading to the dark fissure.

"It looks a bit more cramped than I remember," Dushuuw said.

"We were boys," Q̇otsik said, drawing a palm down his face. "Always on our little adventures. But this one was one of the more stupid."

Dushuuw remembered being frightened and trying to hide that fear from his brother when they entered the cave through this crevice from the other side, their small canoe anchored and bobbing offshore.

Stealing a glance at his brother, he saw he had not been alone. But he would be alone now. And there would be no friendly canoe waiting.

Q̇otsik put a hand on Dushuuw's leg. "Do not fail, brother."

Dushuuw slipped inside the crevice. Immediately, the sounds of the men and women inside the cave vanished. Instead, his ears filled with the hollow drone of air moving between the narrow rock walls. He squeezed his body through the passage, hoping the thick layer of ash coating his skin would remain. Salty, mineral-laden rot filled his nose and snaked down his throat. He reached a low, tight point and had to tilt his torso and force his body through. Rocks scraped his chest and back. He ground his teeth and stayed silent. He was close.

He broke through the other side into a crash of sound. The silence of the passage gave way to squawking hordes of roosting gulls and to the battering and sucking surges of sea. Mist wet his ankles.

Dushuuw scanned the immediate area and saw no one. The rocky point that he had passed through blocked his sight of the enemy canoes, though he heard their shouted jeers. Wind whipped at his hair, tugging more of it free from the top knot. Dushuuw scouted his possible routes, shifted and started edging out along the rocky outcrop toward the main cliff wall farther in. He gripped the rock and pressed his body as close to it as possible, choosing his footholds carefully. Sprays of sea reminded him how close he was to the surges.

The general chatter of the men in the war canoes ricocheted off the rock walls and sounded closer than they really were. Dushuuw still could not discern what language they spoke. He froze as the cliff walls echoed with a sudden war cry. He waited until he was sure the shouts were aimed at intimidating those inside the cave, then picked his way along the rock face again.

Soon he paused and sighed in disgust. Any farther inland and he risked being spotted. Urgently, he shifted his path upward. He looked up, trying to trace a path over the mottled black rock. Flattened against the cliff wall, though, his vision was severely limited. He took a breath. There was no time to find the best path. This was the way up, ideal or not. He found the first rocky grips for his foot and hand, and heaved himself up. Another spot, this one big enough for the side of his foot. Another, only a big toe. Again, his fingers finding purchase on the slightest of holds.

He did not allow himself to hesitate. Grip. Heave. Grip. The movements passing into and over each other as he continued in a meandering, upward trajectory. He did not look down. He pressed his body against the rock, separating himself from its cold embrace only far enough to slide upward. The churning wind grew colder and more forceful at his back.

Suddenly he lurched downward as a pebble-like outcropping broke beneath his foot. Dushuuw winced as he gripped all the more tightly with his fingers. He steadied himself with his other foot. He paused there, one leg dangling. Listened with eyes shut in a panic. Sure they would have heard the rock fall and come for him. End his chance.

When all he heard were the gulls, Dushuuw opened his eyes. He wanted to take a full breath—take air in and expel it in a rush—but his tenuous grip would not allow even that shift in balance. So instead he held his breath. He found better grips, and he continued to climb. He reached a shelf of rock that supported both his feet and his full weight. Finally, he took a deep breath. He rested his forehead against the cliff, breathing in and out. He opened his eyes, taking in the mottled colors and specks of lichen and guano. He pressed his hands against the cliff and shifted his head to the side. A dizzying rush of adrenaline threw spots up in front of his eyes. He was higher than he anticipated. He forced himself to evaluate his position.

The back edge of a war canoe peeked beyond the farthest edge of the outcropping of rock he had traversed. The canoe still faced the cave entrance. Dushuuw watched for a moment longer. The canoe did not move, which meant they were still at anchor. They were not making a move, not yet.

The fog was dissipating. It still offered him some cover, along with whatever ash managed to remain on his skin. But his time was limited.

Dushuuw carefully turned his head again, shifted slightly, and looked up as best he could. Without leaning far back, there was no telling how far he had yet to go. He pressed his forehead against the rock again. It did not matter how far. There was still more to go. He gave the weeping scrap of rock in front of him one last glare, then grabbed for the next hold even as he looked for the next one above it. His feet left the last bit of safe edge.

28

AMUUN'AX̱SUM SAT on the ground of the noble house, running a hand over her weaving. She had not woven much in the past several days, even though the work sat on her lap more often than not. Instead, her attentions shifted left and right, tracing the movements of myriad slaves, studying weavers at looms, smiling at the children, and gazing at the adornments that filled Buhkweeduuk's corner.

Eekbis was eating and sleeping in the trader's house while the travelers were away, having finally given in to Pikoo's repeated requests. And Amuun'ax̱sum had lived inside a dream ever since. A dream that might soon become reality.

Nearby, Ootsihd held her hand against her stomach, feeling the baby kick. Pikoo sat next to her daughter-in-law, bouncing her own son on her lap. The older noblewoman gossiped, unaware of little Blubs's efforts to get a morsel of food in his mouth. With each bounce, the toddler's pudgy fist bounced off his chin or nose, missing his open mouth.

"Quulthoo, bring me my cape," the shaman said.

Amuun'ax̱sum set the weaving aside and crossed the house to a bench set against a wall. She sifted among the shaman's things. The cape was right there, but she wanted to drag out the time, closing her eyes for the thousandth time to luxuriate in conjured images of living in such a place, dressed in furs, bedecked in jewelry, a new tattoo wrapping her wrist that outshone the old. A crash interrupted her reverie. Nearby, Buh-uhs rushed to replace the contents of a box. The boy normally slept beside Dushuuw's bench. Amuun'ax̱sum tilted her head, imagining Dushuuw there, ruffling the boy's hair, striding over to her...

"Quulthoo!"

Amuun'ax̱sum jolted and started to rush back to the healer, realized she forgot the cape, whisked back, and returned again, her neck and face flushed by embarrassment—though not only over her forgetfulness.

"My next slave will be more well-versed in the practical arts of following simple instructions," the shaman said, the words grinding.

Pikoo and Ootsihd both laughed.

Amuun'axsum lifted her chin and said nothing. But she didn't have to. Eekbis gave her a knowing look—and not a pleased one.

"I do believe it is not raining for once," Eekbis said. She spoke to the others, but the lift of her voice let Amuun'axsum know the words were meant for her.

"Indeed, quite a wonder," Pikoo said. "Though I think I shall keep myself and Blubs near the warm fire indoors today. I am wiping away more mucus than usual from his little nose."

The boy touched his lips with his fistful of food, but as soon as he got a taste, his face crinkled up, and he sneezed the soft morsel out.

The shaman grabbed Amuun'axsum's arm. "I am low on ocher. Since it is not raining, go get a box—and spend the rest of the day filling it."

Amuun'axsum shuffled off to get a box, grimacing and dragging her feet. But as soon as she stepped outside, she smiled and traipsed up the path to the hillside. A whole day to let her mind wander? Easier to indulge when alone on a task of drudgery than with constant demands beneath a great house roof.

She thrummed the side of the empty box to the beat of the song. She had practiced the song more and more since she started meeting Dushuuw under the glow of a promise. She was eager to bring the song to life among her people. They did not know her, but they would know her by the song, this song that tied them to ancient power. She would claim her seat among them. Worries that Dushuuw would not find her mother's home village crept up often, but she pushed those nagging thoughts aside.

The winter house loomed. More and more wall planks were strapped in place every day. A couple men worked on it now, tools knocking. She wished it were raining and the men were gone and she could spin about inside the house and imagine a piece of it to be her own. Instead, she passed the house and knelt to the soft ground behind it, grabbed her digging tool, and set to work.

Amuun'axsum lost herself to the rhythm of digging ocher, her mind free to nurture scenes that became increasingly opulent. Soon, her knees and hands were coated in brown dirt and red dust. She scooped ocher into the box. Taking a break, she drew a hand across her forehead, leaving red streaks. She took a drink of water.

Glancing around, she did not see anyone. The men had gone down for a bite to eat. And so she imagined herself inside a large house—in the center of the floor, a drum beating—and sang her song in whispers.

Daylight is found on the mountain

She scooped red earth into the box.

feathers dance on the echoes of wolves

Wind droned over her ears, tossed her hair.

we touch—

Amuun'axsum stopped. Something crashed through the forest, drawing closer and closer. Amuun'axsum reached for her digging tool, her hands and forearms coated in red.

A man rushed out of the forest. His skin was gray; bloody streaks ran down his arms and legs. A wild-looking man.

As the man rushed past, Amuun'axsum cried out and shuddered—with fear, then relief, then with building trepidation. Heart hammering, she grabbed her supplies, tucked them against her body and ran after Dushuuw down the hill.

Amuun'axsum skidded to a stop at the edge of the great house, facing the bay with its distant shushing. Fires were left untended on the beach. Fishermen paddled for shore. People ran about, crisscrossing paths in a frenzy of movement. A baby cried in his mother's too-tight arms as she fled toward the forest. But a voice carried above the throng. Wildness still clung to Dushuuw as he shouted orders, but it was controlled, strong. Gone was the man who was desperate and unsure, seeking answers from a slave. Gone was the man who brushed his hand down her arm, breathed on her lips, stroked her hair, who wrapped her in furs, and watched her dance toward him.

The war chief Wiid helped direct the men as they raced toward the canoes. They carried bows and arrows, clubs, and spears. Several men rushed by in pairs, lugging between them the planks used as drums. Still others emerged from houses carrying women's cutting boards, or from the sides of houses with large pieces from the drainage ditches—bones. They carried large whale bones. Two men passed her hefting shoulder blades, wide and thick.

Amuun'axsum found herself backing up, until the wall of the great house loomed at her back. She pressed herself against the wall, then slumped to the ground, the terror of that long-ago night racing through her veins. She hugged herself, unable to move from this spot in the middle of all the activity, but unable to look away.

A shadow fell over her. Dushuuw towered in the doorway, tucking his war club and dagger into his belt. The whites of his eyes stood out against his skin, streaked with black. He was fearsome, but she saw the fear he tamped. Not for the fight, but for what he was fighting to get back. He ran toward the canoes.

The sea hurled itself toward the beach, and drew back to heave a bigger blow. Tide was turning.

~

these words will help you heal...

Eekbis sang as she hurriedly prepared ingredients, not bothering to hide her methods from Amuun'axsum.

Amuun'axsum placed more wood onto the building fire in the shaman's small house, nudging rocks closer to the heat, then raced to fill a box with water.

your hand will move...

Amuun'axsum came back with the water, set it near the fire. Using two sticks, she lifted a hot rock and slipped it into the water with a knock and hiss, then added two more. Bubbles raced to the surface.

to show the power is working...

Stiff green leaves and clusters of shriveled black berries fell to the ground and into the flames as Amuun'axsum slid her fingers over the length of bark, stripping it. She broke the denuded stem in half, did the same with several more branches, then twisted them together and tucked the bundle into the box of boiling water, capping it with a lid.

Eekbis pressed a clutch of dense elderberry roots against her bench. She pounded one end to a mash, put it in a cup and stirred in hot water. She set a segment of another root next to the cup.

There were shoots from a spruce tree steeping. Tiny leaves and stems from a woodland flower waiting to be mashed.

"We will need the brown lichen that grows on rocks for Young Son," Eekbis said, searching through her boxes.

Amuun'axsum remembered the scratches and bruises that marked Dushuuw's body, but she wondered if there would be worse injuries upon his return. Dushuuw's hurried descriptions to Wiid of the enemy made it clear who held his family captive in the cave: a northern slave-raiding party. Northerners were deadly foes, but particularly at sea—a battlefield where they excelled.

"And hopefully we will need nothing more," the shaman added. The woman dragged her hands down the front of her dress.

Amuun'axsum ran back to the bay's edge, anything to keep her body moving and her mind from lurching again to her own memories of a northerner attack. She pushed back at the bile rising in her throat, the haunted taste of smoke. The sun was sinking. It brushed golden bands across the sky. It sparkled on the bay, and hid anything else from view in its eye-level glare. There was no sign of them yet. Amuun'axsum entered the trader's house to retrieve more of the shaman's supplies. The other women all paced. Waiting. Watching. The old grandmother Yahbis sat on a platform in front of a bench, hugging a fur-lined cloak closer, though it was already pulled tight.

Ootsihd padded over from the far corner. Her eyes were bloodshot. She stroked her stomach. "You still have no sign either?" she asked.

Amuun'axsum shook her head.

As Ootsihd turned back, Yahbis came and placed a hand on the pregnant woman's arm. "You should join the others in the forest," the grandmother said.

"And not you?"

"I will see my son."

No one left.

Supplies in hand, Amuun'axsum went to the doorway. Something moved in silhouette against the sun over the bay. "They are here!"

Amuun'axsum flew toward the bay, the other women close behind. Slave men rushed to help take the canoes onto the beach. The warriors looked haggard. Several clutched at wounds. Blood coated the skin of several of them. But he was alive—Dushuuw was alive. With a guilty start, Amuun'axsum found Uhpahs and rushed toward her friend, then helped the other women out of the canoes. The women were stiff, as if they had not moved in a moon. Sawsin moved more easily, and rushed toward the great house. Chaiyuhx-ik clung to her mother, Thluuch-muup, as they made their way up the beach. But Um-iiqsu waved off Amuun'axsum's help and went to her husband.

Dushuuw and Ǫotsik shuffled forward, propping up their father's limp body between them.

Keeping a few paces away, Yahbis stood with a hand over her mouth. The old woman restrained a cry at the sight of her son.

Sawsin reappeared, her arms full of a cloak that she draped over the old man's shoulders.

Amuun'axsum ran ahead of the group toward the shaman's house, feet pounding over sand and dirt and the wooden bridge. She rushed up to the shaman, panting. "We will need more medicine."

Eekbis pushed down on an aged headdress—a wild mass of feathers, shaved bark, and wool—that seemed to illuminate her face, even as it cast shadows. She started to drone in a dream language, then cut off as the men entered. Her countenance briefly fell at the sight of the chief. Even powerful shamans traveling the spiritual plane could not bring back all souls to their bodies. Some wounds go too deep. But there may also have been a spark of fear in the shaman's eyes. There had been times a shaman, whose healing efforts failed, was accused of putting an evil spirit inside a person who died.

The men eased Chahbuhḋ down on the pile of mats the shaman had arranged near the fire. The whaler coughed, and the dirt floor at the edges of the mats grew dark and smelled of urine.

"We rubbed an ash poultice around the wound," Buhkweeduuk said. He sounded tired, strained. "And before leaving, I laid him in the tide, to open the wound and draw out the bad blood."

Eekbis betrayed nothing in front of the men. Standing rigid in the headdress, the diminutive woman cut an imposing figure. Amuun'a̱xsum studied the shaman and saw that her fear was gone. The chief's wound was grave. If the shaman could point to a well-intentioned but ultimately misguided attempt to help, however, she could foil any accusations of blame should the chief die.

The shaman droned on again, posture erect, words precise. Her gaze grew distant, but retained its hard and focused edge. Powerful shamans were known to bring men's souls back from the brink of death. There was always a chance. Paint caked the wrinkles of her forehead; her gray-flecked hair tangled in a nest beneath the lengths of swaying eagle feathers stuck on end. Eekbis moved, and the family came to attention.

The shaman eyed Dushuuw as she strode around the fire toward the chief. Amuun'a̱xsum swallowed against the tightness at her throat. Dushuuw was coated in blood, at least some of it his own; a nasty cut sliced his arm. His face was pale, and thin from a day spent in extreme physical exertion with no food.

"Young Son, you should sit," the shaman said.

"Focus on my father," he said, not looking at the women.

"I am," the shaman chided. "But you will do no one good hobbling around, threatening to pass out on top of him. Sit."

He blinked at the old woman and plopped down, hugging his knees.

Eekbis took Buhkweeduuk's proffered arm and lowered herself to the ground beside the chief. She moved slowly, but her gaze was swift as she scanned the chief's body for other potential wounds, seen and unseen. She motioned for Amuun'a̱xsum to bring the box of tincture water. Amuun'axsum brought the warm box over and lifted the lid, releasing a ripe smell. The shaman took a clump of soft lichen, dipped it into the steaming liquid, and pressed it onto the chief's wound. The man's breathing sounded wet.

The shaman sang.

these words will help you heal

Buhkweeduuk held his brother's head in his lap.

your hand will move

Amuun'axsum put a different cup of steaming medicine to the chief's lips.

to show the power is working

More liquid dribbled down Chahbuht's chin than went down his throat at first; but soon his chest heaved, his arm rising slightly.

"What are you doing?" Qotsik said.

Buhkweeduuk was less surprised and, at the shaman's nod, he rolled the chief onto his side again so he would not choke on the vomit.

Amuun'axsum set the cup down—she glanced at Qotsik, who glared at her—and placed a bit of hot root in the chief's mouth, to soothe his stomach after the emetic. The root lay in the man's cheek. His face was mottled purple, his body slick and stinking with sweat and bad blood.

"Why is she touching my father?" Qotsik pressed.

Eekbis did not answer. The shaman blew over the chief's chest and placed her mouth over the wound.

"The slave caused him pain," Qotsik said.

The young chief was no longer asking questions, but making pronouncements. His voice was low, heavy with the danger of a man with power made scared. Pikoo pulled at her nephew's arm and whispered soothingly. Amuun'axsum ducked her head.

Eekbis continued to work, sucking at the wound and spitting what came out into the dirt. She placed a shell, filled with a poultice, over the chief's wound, then directed Amuun'axsum to hold it in place. Eekbis took out a wooden ring strung with palm-sized shells. She drew out the last word of her song and started to shake the rattle.

"Qotsik, get your father's power objects," she said. "Buhkweeduuk, cover your brother with that blanket. I need him to sweat."

The rattle clacked and clapped. The fire popped. The chief's breathing struggled to meet the rattle's even beat.

Buhkweeduuk drew blankets over the chief. Qotsik did not move.

"Not until that slave is sent out." Qotsik's strained voice cut through the loud rattle, and the prayer it called for. "We don't know what she puts inside him. She should not touch him. Send her away."

Amuun'axsum kept her eyes on the ground to hide her anger, and to pretend she did not hear—to see what the shaman would do.

"She lends power to my work," Eekbis said.

Amuun'axsum's eyes widened, but she tucked her chin closer to her chest. Her palm, holding the shell against the chief's chest beneath the layers of blankets, was hot with sweat—her own, the chief's.

"If it is a power, then I believe it is an evil power," Qotsik said, taking a step forward. "You saw what happened when she touched him. You see what happens now."

Amuun'axsum glanced at the shaman as the chief moaned. She could tell the old woman wanted to argue with the young man, point out the benefits of an emetic—that expelling the black things that gnawed inside the chief's body was part of it all—but time was running out. And this was Qotsik speaking.

"We need to keep singing," Dushuuw said from where he sat hunched on the ground. "Do not stop singing. We need to keep singing."

Eekbis gestured for Amuun'axsum to leave, directing Buhkweeduuk to hold the shell in place instead.

As Amuun'axsum walked through the doorway, the family formed a tighter circle around the sick man.

Night had fallen, and the air was cold with autumn chill. Amuun'axsum thought of searching for Uhpahs, but instead she turned the corner of the house and leaned against the back wall.

Needles and roots and leaves, steeped and pounded and mashed. There was power in the forest, but everything had its limits. Tears ran down her face as she listened to the singing and to the shaman's rattle. She could make out Dushuuw's voice. Words of healing. Tones of begging. Singing to reverse course. There was even more power in a song, but to what limit?

THE SHAMAN'S HEALING power seemed to be working. In a lucid moment, Chahbuhⱡ motioned for his whaler's hat, which was among the objects drawn close as the shaman and family sang. The chief gripped the hat's brim. He stared up at the roof, mumbling. The shaman changed the dressing on his wounds again, wiping away more of the pus that had replaced the blood.

Suddenly, the chief pitched to his side, trying to get up. Dushuuw and Qotsik struggled to lay him back down. The frail man regained the strength of his youth. Words pounded from his mouth off the walls.

"We must get back..."

The chief was in another place.

"We must get back to the mountain." His body strained against their hands as he tried to crawl away.

His shouts overpowered the song of healing, which Eekbis and the other family continued to sing—all except Yahbis, who pursed her lips and pressed her eyelids shut, digging her fingers into Chai's arm. Chai sang on, unblinking. Thluuch-muup sang the words at a too-high pitch.

Soon, the chief stared slack-jawed at the roof again, his raving spent.

Dushuuw and Qotsik relaxed their grips on his arms.

The shaman started to rub the chief's chest. She sang a new song, alone. The first tone was prolonged and urgent—searching, appealing. She rubbed and rubbed, then passed cedar-bark rings over the chief's body, and rubbed and rubbed again—searching for the chief's soul, appealing to it to stay.

Once again, the shaman's power seemed to enter the chief's body.

Chahbuhⱡ brushed the whaler's hat against Dushuuw's arm. The man's lips moved, thick saliva extending between them. Dushuuw knelt close to hear his father's words over the shaman's voice. Qotsik stood nearby, shaking a rattle.

His father whispered about whaling. "Just a moment, father," Dushuuw said, and he started to stand to get his brother's attention.

But Chahbuhi tugged Dushuuw down.

"You know what to do with me," he said.

"Father, I am not Qotsik..."

His brother looked over at the sound of his name. But Chahbuhi tugged at Dushuuw's arm again. A heavy film covered the chief's eyes. The odor of his breath caused Dushuuw to flinch.

"You know what to do with my body," the chief said.

Dushuuw looked over at his brother in a panic. But Qotsik was shaking the rattle and could not hear.

"You know..." The chief's fingers dug into Dushuuw's skin.

"Yes, father. Yes. But I am not—"

"I am proud of you, son."

The chief's grip loosened, though he still clung to Dushuuw's arm with one hand, and clutched the hat with the other. Dushuuw pressed his lips together, not knowing what to believe, but knowing what he wanted to believe.

"We want to stay on the mountaintop," Chahbuhi murmured, his gaze going back to the planks above his head, "where everything is—so clear." A hint of a smile formed on the chief's face, then faded. The brim of the hat folded in on itself as the dying man tightened his grip. Then it fell to the floor.

Several moments passed in silence, as they waited for the shaman to confirm the truth.

In the corner, Thluuch-muup released the cries she had dammed in hopes of saving her husband. Her piercing wail filled the house. Yahbis closed her eyes, as if to accept what she must. Chai absently rubbed her arm, eyes like stone. Um-iiqsu fell to her knees beside her husband, caressing his face. Qotsik knelt on the other side of the body, the rattle set aside, and the brothers each held one of their father's hands. The shaman took off her headdress, and held it at her side.

They were still there, like that, when the earth rumbled beneath their feet. Pieces of the shaman's loom vibrated against the wall. Herbs hanging from a rafter swayed. The fire in the hearth settled on itself with a smoky hush.

The rumbling stopped almost as soon as it had started. Everyone looked at each other. Eekbis took a tiny step back. Smoke twisted out the hole in the roof.

30

AMUUN'A̱XSUM WAS STILL sitting against the wall when she heard the end. The end of the song. The end of a life. The earth trembled in response, and Amuun'a̱xsum felt a deep-rooted fear bloom and grow. The words of a story sprung from memory, as if bidden.

On that highest mountaintop...

In the dark, when the family had left—bearing the body in an ornate box brought for the task—and the shaman had left with them, Amuun'a̱xsum crept back inside the small house. She went to the spot where the chief had lay. Pungent odors lingered. A log in the fire settled with a crack.

Amuun'a̱xsum shook her head as if moving through a dream. She dug a hole, then knelt to the ground and shuffled on hands and knees to clean the vomit, the blood, and the sweat, burying them under dirt. She fed the mats to the flames.

And still the old story ran through her mind.

Bones

      bones

          bones.

The Long Ago

SMALL ONE AND THE BOY had reached for each other over the churning sea. Now, they sat high in Small One's tree atop branches on either side of its trunk, reaching toward each other. They clung to each other as they clung to the tree, a desperate embrace. Time surged and slowed, but the sea was incessant.

The boy spoke, his teeth chattering.

Small One peered at him through her long hair, matted to her face.

"We were visiting," he said, trying again in her language. "My father... he is a whaler."

"My father," she said, trying to speak in his language. But she could not say what she wanted to say. She tried in her own. "My father..."

She sagged. The boy grabbed at her arms, bringing her back close to the thick trunk of their refuge.

Small One felt the rough bark, his rough hands. This tree did not feel a part of anyone's territory anymore. The whole world was unmoored from ideas like ownership and usage rights. Things that had seemed so solid were in fact fluid. Who could own the sea?

"Do you think they..."

She could not finish.

"I do not know," he answered.

Small One wilted.

"But we are," he said quickly. "We are still here." He shifted on his branch, drawing up his legs, readjusting his grip on her arms.

Out of the corner of her eye, she saw a canoe spinning in the flood waters. It drifted toward them. The boy saw the canoe too.

"We must go now," he said.

Time seemed to stretch, but they had only a moment. She put her hand in his. Together, they dropped into the hull. Small One held her leg, face twisted with pain. He hugged her, arms akimbo as if unused to making such a comforting gesture.

There were no paddles in the canoe. There was no bailer. They were at the mercy of the sea. They spun and surged and drifted amid the sounds of screams—of trees, of people. A woman spun near them, then slipped under. Small One looked at the boy. Even his eyes were scrunched closed now. She joined him in the dark. They hugged each other as true darkness fell, the boy's arms wrapping her tighter.

In time, the canoe lurched to a stop, wedged into the boughs of a large tree by the receding waters.

In the dawn light, Small One and the boy managed to climb down and make their way over piles of debris, like stepping stones. And in fear of what may be lurking, dark and growling, waiting for its chance to snatch them up again, they hurried—higher, and higher still.

For days, Small One and the boy wandered in the highlands, a lonely pair in a barren world where only the highest peaks were unfazed. They were weak with hunger. They intertwined their fingers, and the boy led Small One onward, keeping them moving, moving, moving—toward what? Only up, and up. The only way to be safe, safe. Finally, when she could go no farther, they reached a summit and she collapsed, crying. He joined her on the rocky ground, and they slept.

At the start of the next day, they twitched awake in the growing light atop the mountain, a mountain much like the ones in whose shadows Small One had grown up. Small One slowly stood, facing the east. For the first time in her life, she saw the sun rise in all its pink, blazing glory. The boy stood beside her, head tipped at an angle. Their faces were bathed in light, their chests filled by it, as the sun was lifted higher and higher.

As the day faded to blue, then gray, Small One and the boy continued to sit on the rocky ground, listless. Until calls drew their attention skyward.

A hawk squeaked as a raven cawed. The raven chased the hawk in tight circles, the raven only silencing its battle cries to jab at the hawk with its beak. Around and around they went. Until finally the hawk retreated. The raven alighted on a branch, crowing its victory over the giant. Small One watched the story unfold. In the distance, the feeble howls of wolf pups were echoed by that of their parents in a different direction, the calls drawing closer and closer together.

The boy continued to look up at the raven in the treetop. But Small One's attention was drawn to their feet. There, on a rock... She clutched at the boy. The boy looked down, then tucked her behind him. He reached toward the rock and what lay there, but not in fear. In expectation.

Their battle is so great, so fierce, that it sends up a large wave that sweeps over the land. The water rises and rises and rises still more. Many people die, by that wrath, in that fight that continues on, and on...

Until at last, Thunderbird, talons deep in Whale's flesh, carries Whale high out of the sea and flies with him to the topmost peak

—to the mountaintop,

so high the sea has come.

1699

WINTER

1700

THE WINDS HOWLED, and the bay roiled in response. Surges of water crashed against the point with towering sprays and swept up the beach. The sea thrust entire trees ashore with ease. River watchers kept an eye out for particularly dangerous surges, ready to send warnings upstream. Clouds filled the sky and rain fell in droves, and everywhere the Kwidich'chuh-aht turned their minds toward the long succession of short days to come.

They would turn their backs on the cold shoulder of the outdoors and turn toward the warmth of the fires within cedar walls. They would mark the long nights by telling stories, by dancing—by welcoming the spirits drawn to their fires. Old men started speaking of wolves. Old women started speaking of the forms that humans and animals took before the transformation, of the glimpses they soon would receive of that time before time. Older children started whispering excitedly to younger children, masking their own lack of knowledge and its accompanying fear behind a veneer of confidence.

Though they would for several years be in official mourning of the chief, the people of Wuh-uhch were nevertheless ready as always for the mix of levity and secrecy that came with the winter ceremonies.

Plenty of work remained, however, before they could fully withdraw indoors. Canoes were turned upside down against house walls. Harpoons oiled and stored. Materials gathered that, over the course of a season, would be fashioned into coiled lengths of rope.

Dushuuw trudged back from the stockade at the cape's point. He had helped Wiid reinforce the redoubt following the attack at sea. Dushuuw finished his watch and installed the new sentries before heading back to the village. Extra sentries manned all the redoubts among the cape's allied villages. Messages about the attempted raid were sent before Dushuuw and his fellow warriors paddled out to save his family. Weeks had passed, and the northerners had not reappeared in their waters. "They will think twice before showing up in our waters again," Wiid said. But Dushuuw was only starting to relax, now that the sea was too storm-churned for travel.

Even so, his gaze on watch had more often strayed toward the enemy up the strait than to the enemy that lay far beyond it.

"Stay alert," he told the sentries. "No matter how much chop you see."

It had taken time to unravel what had happened.

They confirmed that the canoes with towering red prows which had cornered the travelers in the cave had been a northerner slave-raiding party. Perhaps the raiders had come for them specifically. Far more likely, the raiders saw more convenient prey on their way to another intended target. Either way, to have beat them off was a blessing. War at sea was a different field of battle, one at which the northerners excelled. The Wuh-uhch warriors had Wiid's experience to thank for their success. That, and the element of surprise, thanks to Dushuuw's brazen rescue mission up the face of the cape and down its flank. They used whale bones and drum boards as shield walls, absorbing enemy fire until they could move within range for arrows to be useless, for the fight to come down to spears and rocks and brute strength. Even so, they fought the incoming tide and swirling waters as much as the northerners. The sea's own twists and feints had added to Dushuuw's desperation.

Dushuuw rubbed the back of his neck, recalling his impulsive leap into the middle of one of the enemy canoes, the desire to draw their blood and end the fight surging through him as he fought left and right with club and knife. They were two Wuh-uhch canoes against three enemy canoes, but they bought enough time for Shuchkuk and his Tsooyuhs war party to arrive and secure their win. The surviving enemy retreated, chased by the nonsensical taunting of Tsooyuhs warriors.

"Your breath smells like a woman's bleeding!"

"Your fighters are as limp as jellies!"

"You run like slugs!"

It was a moment of euphoria, a heady victory. Laying in exhaustion at the bottom of a canoe beside the body of a man he had killed, looking up at the sky, Dushuuw had smiled. He had done it.

But it had not been enough.

Dushuuw broke through the tree line to the meadow and freshwater spring. He knelt to cup water to his mouth, then he was off down the trail on the final stretch toward home. Water dripped from his fingers, and he remembered the sight of blood dripping from his father's wound.

That arrow—that arrow that had pierced his father and ultimately killed him—was no northerner arrow. It had come from that first canoe the travelers had encountered in the fog, the one that had fled when the northerners arrived. Strait warriors. If the Wuh-uhch travelers were victims of convenience for the northerners, they were certainly the intended targets of that initial attack. The strait warriors probably didn't set out to find and target the chief himself—killing anyone from Wuh-uhch could have sufficed—but by now their messengers and spies would have known it was their arrow that killed the great whaler. In their minds, the balance was achieved. In the minds of Dushuuw and his family, though, it stirred further vitriol and a desire to take more heads. "We have all winter to get creative," Wiid said, grabbing him by the neck.

These feuds could last years.

Dushuuw clenched his fists as he heard the muffled sounds of village life under the rain. Despite his rage, the time for reprisal would have to wait. It was not a season for war. But more, there had been enough to rattle the village without adding a rushed counterattack.

The earthquake had been so minor that the elderly and young children who had been sleeping at the time did not wake. But its timing, at the chief's death, lent extra urgency to the men's discussions and to the village's winter preparations. Old men tied their long ropes to canoes, then dragged the ends of the ropes into the forest, wrapping them around elderberry. When asked why, the elders said it was what should be done when the earth shook. Strong cords. Deep roots. No other earthquake had followed, but the old men and women were uneasy, their steps careful, their eyes trained to the sea, their stories tilting to Thunderbird and Whale, to mountain spirits.

"Beware..."

So the focus shifted, from reprisal to reassurance.

With singing and gifts, Dushuuw and Ọotsik had interred their father's body with his sacred objects in a box that they secured high in a cedar tree, its bark draped with the same soft lichen that was among the shaman's healing efforts. Then Buhkweeduuk bent the heads of the leaders of other family groups toward the heir. The highest responsibility, of leading their whale hunts, had already come to Ọotsik. Now the family's remaining patriarch ensured there was no question that this winter, Buhkweeduuk himself would be staying in a house under the arm of Ọotsik.

Dushuuw approached the back of that massive house. Tools sounded in off-kilter beats. Some men worked to fell a tree, while others stood atop a house and locked roof planks together. Children chased each other around the outskirts of the meadow. Women lugged piles of blankets and other goods.

Men had rebuilt a few houses on the high ground, transferring them board by board from the low ground. Now the women filled them with belongings. The vast winter house overshadowed them, dominating the ridgeline that overlooked the bay. The house had been built for two brothers. And even after the chief's death, it remained a house for two brothers. Ọotsik and Dushuuw both admired the formidable structure, which would be worthy of the ceremonies they would continue in their father's stead.

Most homes remained on the low ground. Part of the reason was for space. And generally, they were already far enough back to be safe from winter storm surges. Lower-class workers and slaves also found it more convenient to be near their daily fishing and intertidal gathering duties.

Dushuuw rounded the corner of the winter house. The wind off the bay whistled through small trees and grasses at the cliff's edge. The shore crashed on the rocks far below. He paused at the doorway to let Thluuch-muup pass through in a huff, shoving her slave girl ahead.

"You pay no attention anymore. Useless!"

Dushuuw felt sorry for his stepmother. The loss of his father had placed Thluuch-muup in a difficult situation. Um-iiqsu was content to be a grandmother alongside Yahbis. But Thluuch-muup was young enough to not want to be considered a matronly elder like their mother-in-law. Still, if she remained at Wuh-uhch, it would be as an unmarried woman. Buhkweeduuk was hesitant to offer marriage, not wanting to diminish Ọotsik's status, if he had any desire for a second wife in the first place. Should Thluuch-muup return to her home village across the strait, the family would lose access to valuable resources. But Ọotsik's marriage to Sawsin brought similar access. Dushuuw understood why his stepmother could suddenly switch between tears and shouts. For all her bluster and demands, Thluuch-muup had found a home with his father. For now, Ọotsik assured their stepmother that her and Chai's place remained beside him and Sawsin in the honored corner of the new house. Dushuuw hoped they would remain, or at least that Chai would until her marriage was secured.

Since the attack, Chai had been quiet and distant. He kept an eye on her, but there was nothing to say.

And there was nothing to say about his father's final words, either. Were they for him or for his brother? He and his father had had a fraught relationship. But deep down, Dushuuw had always wanted to please him. Now, he was left wondering if he had. Now, despite their distance, he was left with a strange gap. One the renewed closeness of Wiid could only partially fill. What would his life be like without his father? What possibilities did it hold?

Dushuuw lifted aside the deer hide that hung in the doorway and walked inside. The winter house was built to fit both large households under one roof. But when everyone was settled inside, it did not feel vast or impersonal. If anything, it felt more cozy, with more young children running from hearth to hearth and more adults keeping busy at weaving, carving, cooking. Q̇otsik presided with Sawsin over the back right corner of the house, its seat of power. In the back left corner of the house was Buhkweeduuk's and Pikoo's domain. Partitions marked off living spaces against the rest of the walls, for relatives and favored advisers. Just as many slaves lived and worked under the roof as well, and most would sleep by the draft-prone doorway.

Dushuuw tried to bring some order to Buh-uhs's heaped belongings beside his own bench, then walked over to his uncle's house corner. Pikoo held Blubs by his fingers as she walked him around their new space and named the various landmarks in their tiny journey. Dushuuw crouched in front of the boy, poking at the toddler's belly. Tension left his shoulders. He was glad to have his uncle under the same roof this winter. Glad he did not have to seek these comforts in another building.

"Uncle comes back soon, yes?"

Pikoo nodded with a smile. "Never soon enough, of course. But," she said, with a diplomatic lilt, "it was important that he go. We may have to partner even more with Deeyuh now. We're still not quite back to where we were. And now your father is gone."

Dushuuw deflated at the reminders of his wrongs, but his aunt shushed him, knowing his thoughts. She picked up Blubs and pushed the little boy into Dushuuw's chest. The boy tugged at Dushuuw's hair.

Ootsihd emerged from an adjacent living space, where she had been arranging belongings for she and Uhpqoolth, including a new cradle board. "I am just glad he didn't bring Uhpqoolth with him this time," she said, joining the conversation. Ootsihd placed a hand at the small of her back. "I cannot help but feel this baby wants to come soon."

Her mother-in-law smiled sympathetically as she placed her hands at the young woman's sides, speaking sweet nothings to the life blooming inside.

Pikoo sat back and watched Dushuuw play with her boy. "With

Q̇otsik and Sawsin together, I wager this house next winter will be filled with more little feet." She added hot stones to a box of water. She brushed her hand down Dushuuw's arm as her boy fought against him to try and reach the hissing bubbles. "I hope that soon you shall have a family and a corner of your own as well, Young Son," she said. "You will know the joy of having a child. A child is a gift for the present and a promise for the future." She placed her other hand on Ootsihd's stomach. "A living inheritance."

"A stinky inheritance," Dushuuw quipped, as Blubs pinched his skin and tried to break free.

His aunt laughed and held out her arms.

Dushuuw let the boy go to his mother. He wondered about the baby who had hung on his ex-wife's hip. An invisible hand seemed to squeeze his heart. Whose future would that baby carry on? He shoved his toes into the still-soft dirt.

"I wonder if a nobleman must marry for alliance," Dushuuw said.

His aunt looked off to the side in thought. "Sometimes a bride comes from closer to home, while still bringing valuable access of one kind or another," she said. She poked at a mussel steaming in the cooking box, checking to see how far it had opened. "Like our son's fine wife, with her father's salmon fishing."

"It is nice to be so near my family in Tsooyuhs," Ootsihd said.

"And with my husband's frequent trips to Deeyuh, I would not be surprised if he sought more than to pave the way for Chaiyuhx-ik's marriage. There are whalers' daughters there too, with good names." Pikoo handed her boy over to her daughter-in-law, and scooped out the cooked shellfish. "Though, from what I hear," she teased, "maybe it will be the sister of Q̇otsik's bride for you."

Dushuuw shifted and bent his legs. He plucked at a thick nub of grass. "What about a woman who is not noble?"

Pikoo had been digging out the flesh from a mussel shell, but her hands stilled at this comment. "You know I loved your mother, Young Son. She was a good friend." Her eyes flitted between her work and his face. "You have someone in mind, nephew?"

Dushuuw shook his head and sat up straight. She half-smiled as she worked on another shell. "I would be glad if you do, you know. You deserve to start again," she said. "And yet—"

Dushuuw waited for her to speak, as did Ootsihd, who clung to Blubs as the boy squirmed and started to bawl in her lap.

His aunt finally continued, her tone tilting back to the diplomatic. "I know men will find ways to fill the sexual needs they have, as we women do," she said. "Yet I would caution patience, Young Son. Many eyes are on our village. We are well positioned with Q̇otsik leading the hunts, and my husband at his side to offer counsel. Sawsin adds to Q̇otsik's strength in the whaling canoe, as do my son and his wife, and they will bring us heirs." She looked with affection again at her daughter-in-law. "But it is all just that—positioning our village for an ascent after a time of lows."

She shoved the pile of shells toward a slave girl to toss outside the door. "If you do feel your culpability in these matters and want to make amends—"

Dushuuw sucked in a breath.

"—then you must realize that, at this stage, every choice is critical. There is no gain for yourself if it is not also a gain for the community. And in marriage, a man's goal must be first to maintain and increase the family's prestige." She brushed her hands together and faced him again. "You would diminish our value if you did any less."

Pikoo took her tearful boy in her arms; he folded himself against her shoulder and sniffled. Ootsihd shuffled back to her living space.

"Marry again for family first," his aunt said, patting the boy's back. "Then, if you yearn for a lesser-ranked woman, you could take her as a second wife, even if she deviates from a noble line, as long as you give your first wife her first rights."

"Even a slave, perhaps," Dushuuw said, keeping his tone casual.

Pikoo laughed, then shook her head. She pursed her lips into a knowing smile. "If it is merely under a woman's skirt you seek to get, a slave is convenient enough—though you may still risk the marriage you just obtained."

"But I mean a marriage. My mother had no high status, yet married my father. I am now of high rank. Why can a slave not be elevated in the same way?"

Pikoo's laugh was short but loud. "You have an outsize idea of the power of a man's penis." She shook her head.

Dushuuw took a risk and continued on. "But to say it has never happened seems unlikely," he said. "For most people, marriage is as simple as agreeing to share a bed. And a divorce is as simple. This all seems much more fluid than—"

"Do you mean to insult me, Young Son?"

"No," he said. "But I—"

"You speak dangerously," she said. Her son started to whimper again in response to her anger.

"I am sorry, aunt. I did not mean... I was just asking."

She closed her eyes and took a deep breath. "I know," she said. "I know. And I can grant you one case that I have heard, of a noble man and a slave woman coming together in a marriage. But the boy had to give up his place and leave his village. In effect, he became a slave himself. The marriage meant nothing, for he lost everything. And even then, it was only because his father capitulated—he had been planning to kill them both after discovering the tryst."

"Killing them seems a bit harsh..."

"Not at all," Pikoo said. "He should have at least killed the girl straight away and solved the family's problem right there."

Pikoo looked down at her tight hold on her whining boy and loosened her arms. She set him down to toddle along the floor, and he sped happily away. Her face was drawn. "What do you have my mind on now, Young Son?" She shook her head as she watched her son. "Even for those who are fortunate enough to be redeemed, slavery is a stain that never goes away. That shame is permanent."

She took Dushuuw's hand. "Pray that you and the other men of this village continue to protect us. We were close, you know. Especially your sister, your stepmothers, your brother's wife." She gripped his hand harder. "You running into the village that day... If it had not been for your warning, they could have made it here too. Brought those canoes to that beach down there, to our beach..."

Dushuuw stroked the back of her hand.

Pikoo stood and rubbed her cheeks. Dushuuw stood as well.

"I do love you, Young Son, and want the best for you," she said. "I suppose that is why I needed to make sure—to make sure you understand your position. You cringe at being called Young Son now, I see that. And that is good. For it will not be forever. It was your father's place to give you back your name—I know he thought on it, my husband says so—and so you must give it more time. All the same, you also must continue to live up to that name if you are to receive it again, and keep it clean. And if your children are to be equal to my own, you would appreciate more seriously the wife we seek for you. Do not throw away their future for selfish desires."

Dushuuw worked up a smile for her. She nodded, then walked across the house, plucking up her son as he reached the doorway's blanket of light.

32

AMUUN'AX̱SUM'S FINGERTIPS struggled with the tough twine, numbed by the repetitive work. Creating a fine-mesh dip net took a great deal of time and energy. The spun nettle fiber needed to be protected from rot—and there was no day without rain this time of year. So Amuun'ax̱sum worked indoors, day after day. The net mocked her as she willed her fingers to operate properly, to feel like human flesh again.

"All for a minuscule fish," she grumbled.

Time seemed to be unraveling. She had such hope when Dushuuw left across the strait, bearing her secret. That hope was distant again. She had seen him the day after the interment. The shaman had him come to her house to look at his arm—the red wound had started to pus, the danger of bad blood increasing—and Amuun'ax̱sum had knelt on the ground, applied the shaman's special treatment, wrapped the wound. He did not look at her once. He was rigid. She told herself it was his grief, that in time she could ask her selfish questions. Now she wondered if it was something else.

The old whaling chief had been largely ignorant of her—a blessing, she now realized. She had captured the attention of the new whaling chief—and Q̇otsik was hostile. Dushuuw was willing to help her before. But had that changed?

Amuun'ax̱sum folded the net for storage.

The shaman said she had calmed the new chief. Amuun'ax̱sum was not so sure. And if Dushuuw had abandoned her cause, there was little hope left. The world itself would have to be upended.

Trying to dodge such thoughts, Amuun'ax̱sum sought the rain and cold air. She took the edges of her cloak and lifted it to the top of her head like a hood. The cloak billowed behind her in the wind. She ran her hands down the edges, pulling it back close beneath her chin.

Men and women went about their work, their faces shadowed by the conical hats they had rouged with a waterproof coating of crushed elderberries. Amuun'a̱xsum crossed the bridge over the creek, its rain-fueled waters surging toward river and bay. Rain joined the dun ripples of the sea.

Amuun'a̱xsum sighed with relief as she spied Uhpahs returning from the exposed rocks with a basket of mussels.

"Can I help you? I am tired of weaving," Amuun'a̱xsum said.

"It would be nice to have the company—and the help," Uhpahs said.

Uhpahs was thin. She had trouble sleeping since the attack, and helping a distraught Thluuch-muup wore away at what energy remained.

Amuun'a̱xsum eyed what remained of the great house fronting the bay. The old whaling chief's house had been largely disassembled to help construct the winter house. A good portion of Buhkweeduuk's house also had been repurposed. Now, slaves and household members from both households moved in and out of what remained, ferrying belongings up the hill. Amuun'a̱xsum stopped as she and Uhpahs neared the uphill trail. The winter house loomed above. Q̓otsik would be there, as would Sawsin. The man who hated her, and the woman she envied.

"Can we cook out here instead?" Amuun'a̱xsum asked.

Uhpahs eyed her through the rain that dripped off the rims of their hats, but ultimately relented, too tired to argue. Uhpahs led the way around to the back side of Buhkweeduuk's old house, where they could at least sit behind the wall, out of the wind. The rain slid down the roof planks and dripped onto the ground behind them. The women started a small fire, added stones.

"We are a sad village these days," Uhpahs said, as the flames died down and the rocks sucked at their heat.

Amuun'a̱xsum thought of the chief's death, of Q̓otsik's needling distaste, of Dushuuw's silence. The unsettled feeling that followed the earthquake, everyone on tip-toe. The two widows in mourning, and Chai turned to stone. Of rain falling, seas churning, hope fading.

She covered the stones with leaves.

"Do you ever dream of running away?" she asked.

Uhpahs picked up the basket of mussels.

"No," Uhpahs said. She poured the shellfish onto the bed of leaves. "And neither should you."

A flattened rectangle of earth lay beyond where they sat. A half-built house once under construction had been disassembled for parts for the winter house.

Buh-uhs ran down the hill toward them. He cut across the old house space, and sped past the women as he squawked. He disappeared, splashing through the water channeled by the whalebone ditch.

Dushuuw descended after the boy. He plodded along, eyes on the ground in front of his feet, no sign of the usual playfulness when he was around the boy. His face was still thin, but his skin had regained its normal coloring. The bandage around his arm was clean.

Aware of her friend, Amuun'axsum hurriedly looked down and adjusted the mat covering the steaming shellfish.

Buh-uhs's voice bounced off the walls as he sloshed through the ditch back toward Dushuuw. "I have got it for you, Quht-Quht," the boy called out, straining.

Uhpahs leaned forward to look around Amuun'axsum toward the boy. Amuun'axsum looked again to Dushuuw. He saw her this time, then his eyes flitted to Uhpahs, and he turned his attention to Buh-uhs.

"I think even strong little warriors need help, Buh-Buh," he said.

Buh-uhs lumbered forward, tongue stuck out between his lips. He tried to hold multiple weapons at once, a spear's end dragging in the dirt behind him. A basket of knives flopped across his back, so that he stopped every two steps to shove it back out of his way.

Dushuuw took his war club and held it above their heads. Buh-uhs looked up, forlorn.

"Now, take care with that spear," Dushuuw said. "It's very valuable."

The boy held the spear with both hands, looking at it with new eyes.

The pair walked back uphill. Dushuuw rested the club on his shoulder and rested his other hand at the boy's back. The boy looked up at him with a smile. Amuun'axsum conjured a fleeting image of herself walking the path, looking up at Dushuuw over the child between them.

Uhpahs put a hand on her arm. Amuun'axsum startled, and looked over at her friend's concerned face. She poked inside the box.

"Do not tell me you still nurse foolhardy notions, Quulthoo," Uhpahs whispered. "Of any kind."

Amuun'axsum stiffened and shook her head. "No. No, I do not."

Uhpahs's hand hovered over Amuun'axsum's arm, then drew back.

~

Soon after sliding into sleep, Amuun'axsum awoke gasping out fragments of lyrics, choking on imagined smoke. In the dream, it was her mother's slave who mouthed the words of the song—her mother's voice coming from his lips—as blood dripped from a line about his neck.

Amuun'axsum stood up, heart racing. She fought the urge to flee to the shaman and cling to her, to beg for the old woman's comfort.

Instead, she sat on her bed mat and drew up her knees. The song blew through her mind, diaphanous. A breeze pushed through the doorway, and she startled. Dushuuw stood there, holding back the deer hide. He looked relieved to find her awake, then concerned by her tears.

Elation filled her. She stood and walked to him, then hesitated. She searched his face for the answer she hoped was there, but he had the same unreadable expression as his sister did these days. Guilt at thinking of herself instead of his loss dragged at her chest.

Dushuuw eyed the partition, beyond which Eekbis loudly snored.

Amuun'axsum grabbed her cloak and followed Dushuuw to the snag. She stared at his back as they walked. His shoulders seemed weighed down. At the entrance to the snag, bits of leaves and moss cluttered the ground. Inside, sand had leaked from a corner of the firebox. A corner of a mat was chewed back.

Dushuuw set the torch in the box, twisting the handle absently.

Amuun'axsum sat opposite him.

The silence stretched on.

"Your father was a great man," she said.

Dushuuw stared at the fire as he nodded. Fear crept into his eyes.

"Qotsik will be a good chief," she said.

Dushuuw let go of the torch and sat back, his gaze still on the flames. "Yes," he said. "He will."

More silence. Amuun'axsum burned with questions. And Dushuuw looked anywhere but at her. He bent forward, arms on his legs.

"Qotsik is gone, to make himself clean for all the duties that lay before him," Dushuuw said, looking out the snag. "I couldn't sleep, so figured I should do the same. There are plenty of things for which I should make myself clean. Maybe too many to ever be clean enough, because I couldn't even stay away from your doorway."

Heat flooded through Amuun'axsum.

Yet he still did not look at her.

"And there you were, awake," he said, with a shrug. "Will you stay here tonight until I am done?" He finally looked at her, his eyes haunted, as if he expected to be turned down.

"It would bring me honor to do that for you," she said.

A wave of relief moved through his body, and with a quick nod and averted gaze he walked into the darkness toward the river.

Amuun'axsum felt disjointed with confusion and ignorance. Desires warred within her, mind pitted against body. She itched to make demands, to know if he still searched on her behalf and if the hope to which she had clung since he had left across the strait was still alive. At the same time, her heart grieved for his losses, knowing that drifting feeling of loneliness. And it was the loss of his strength that made her most worried and shocked. She wanted to run to him, hold him tight, kiss all the unseen wounds, and make him come alive.

So she softly sang. She sang the song, the one sign of power she still possessed—a gift he had given back to her, without ever knowing it. She had only started singing the words again during those long weeks of whaling, when she finally had hope of finding her way home. Sweat dotted her forehead and slipped down her face as she sat on the ground next to the firebox, drumming its sides to the beat that wanted to take over and throw off her words. She had to close her eyes tight to hold both—the drum that sought to overtake the words, the words that won in the end. The curved enclosure of the snag cupped her words and sent them back to her, and at one point she swore something flew inside her to spur the last refrain even higher. It felt like something small but fast, surging through her blood to her heart, beating it like a drum, and lifting the words up her throat and over her tongue.

After that she stopped. She worried the feeling was a figment, that it would not return. She worried more about Dushuuw hearing. Maybe one day the song would be something she could share, safe within the confines of noble authority and protocol. Until then, she would not risk losing the words. So she turned instead to the charcoal drawings. With a warm bit of blackened wood from the edge of the firebox, she went over the lines of the Lightning Serpents and the whale, darkening their shapes and making them stand out again. She went over the lines of the Thunderbird, filling in his broken wing.

There was a rustling behind her, and she turned to see Dushuuw. He stood erect, shoulders back. His skin was damp, his hair wet. The faint scent of hemlock hung in the air. And though he still looked worn and tired, there was a life in his eyes that had not been there earlier. She smiled, then wondered how she must look, smudged with sweat and dirt, fingers black with charcoal. They stood across the snag from each other, and she wondered if he was also fighting the urge to close the distance. Then the haunted look returned. His poise remained intact, but he looked away like someone facing a demand he knew he must fulfill, but didn't want to meet.

"This isn't right," he said.

A chill crawled inside Amuun'axsum.

"I've been selfish, robbing you of so many nights," he said. "I will not need you anymore for this anyway."

The chill descended through her, pinning her to the ground. So he had not found her family. He could not keep his promise, so he released her from her own. Her hope was gone. The charcoal dropped from her fingers and she wanted to be held, comforted. To press her face to his chest and feel his fingers in her hair. But she also wanted to throw embers in his eyes and beat his chest. She didn't know what she wanted to do. But she knew he wouldn't move toward her. He was clean now. She was not. She struggled to summon her mind to work. He could try again in the spring. One visit could not be enough.

"It's all right," she said, voice catching. "I suppose I knew it was not possible to find them in so short a time."

He looked at her with faint surprise, and stepped forward. "I've been selfish," he murmured again, but as if for the first time. He dug his hand through his hair. "Lohta. The village's name is Lohta."

Amuun'axsum was stunned. She could not move or speak.

"I cannot do anything until spring. The journey would not be safe until then, and I must come up with some kind of excuse," he said. "We have never visited that village. That could be excuse enough, but I will need to be careful not to offend those we do deal with who live nearby."

Amuun'axsum had to remind herself to breathe. It felt as if she rocked on waves. Breathe in. Breathe out.

"Once I find them, I can speak to them. Lay the groundwork. Then lay the opportunity before my brother, ready for his final word."

Amuun'axsum put her trembling, blackened fingers to her forehead, not caring she was making herself even more unkempt.

"The village is closer than my stepmothers' home," he said. "We could probably see it from Chahdee. It will not take long to get there."

Amuun'axsum put her fingers to her mouth, startled by her own laugh. Atop the island with Uhpahs all summer, and her mother's home village had been part of the view. She wanted to swim there now. Perhaps someone from the family had been at Chahdee; she'd be giddy if it had been one of their slaves. Taking a deep breath, she forced herself to calm down, to slow down. There were still many steps between now and then, and Dushuuw's comment about his brother formed an ominous shadow that she shoved to the back of her mind.

"Well, then," she said, beaming, "there is a lot of time before spring. Many nights. I do not mind—I do not mind spending them out here with you, if you still want me."

The troubled look came over him again. He leaned toward the opening of the snag. "I will not come out here any longer for all that," he said. "My father left me with certain expectations. My brother will finish showing me what it all means, and that will happen far from here. It would be best if you... If I did not... I am to do this part on my own."

Amuun'axsum nodded as if she understood, but the rejection stung. Of course she had not lent anything to his prayers. If anything, being released of that expectation was a relief. But she had felt close to something when she had been trying. She knew he did too. More than that, she had thought he had come to see her as more than a charm.

She had pushed him away before. Now he pushed her away.

She was getting what she wanted. But she was heartsick.

"You said you didn't want to pretend," he said.

Amuun'axsum looked up.

"I don't want to pretend either," he said. "I want to be worthy of what's expected of me. I owe my father that. I owe my uncle that. I owe my brother that, above all. And I owe you that. All those nights like this one, with you here and me at the river or out at sea," he said, gesturing around them. "It's as if we are trying to do separate what we are meant to do together."

Amuun'axsum felt both frozen solid and as if she were floating.

"I want to stand before you, and your family, as a man who can take care of you on his own strength. To pile up gifts outside your doorway. To bring you back here and have your help with honor. Not use it carelessly, like I have tonight and on so many other nights—as if I had a claim on you already."

Amuun'axsum felt lightheaded. She stared at him, wanting him to look back. But his head was still averted, his brow furrowed.

"I want all that. So much that I am ready to do whatever it takes to get it. But I cannot, unless I know you are waiting for me at the end," he said. "That you would want me to ask them for you. That I'm not just—a means to an end."

Amuun'axsum could not help but laugh again. She was incredulous. Dushuuw whipped his head up, and she realized he thought she was laughing at him. She drew her black-smudged finger down her lips and smiled at him.

"I will always be looking for you," she said, "and waiting at the end."

33

DUSHUUW LAY ON HIS BACK by the pool, exhausted. His mind was wrung out. How many days had he been out here with his brother? In the pocket of night sky visible above the pool, streaks of light clawed the sky. The splash of the waterfall made it seem as if the stars crashed. The moon was at its turning point, preparing to rise higher in the sky on its slow march toward summer.

"Is this how you claimed your *tume·nuwis*, brother?" Dushuuw asked, still trying to find his breath.

Q̇otsik lay on his back beside him, panting as well but looking as if he had far more energy than was reasonable.

"I did not, though I tried," Q̇otsik said. "So much praying, and going through the rituals as I was taught, as father taught you, and as I have now finished for him. Year after year. Craving it. Wanting to be like those whalers of old. I did my first fast in pursuit of that power when I was five years old."

Dushuuw was startled. Buh-uhs was older than that. Yet this was Q̇otsik, of course.

"And, year after year, those efforts were not wasted. Just as other forms of training were not wasted, be it the physical training of lifting and thrusting the harpoon, or the precise aiming—going from shooting ducks, to gulls, then hummingbirds—or knowing every role in the canoe, from steersman on up. But I did not claim the power," Q̇otsik said. He laughed as he shook his head, turning his head toward Dushuuw. "It claimed me, as I understand others were claimed by their own *tume·nuwis*. I will say that, when such power does finally come, it is usually when you are alone, and on the longest nights—nights like these." Awe tinged his voice, as he tipped his face back toward the sky. "Keep seeking, brother. Make yourself clean, inside and out."

"No power has ever wanted to claim me."

"It will—I know it," Q̇otsik said. "And father knew it too. Even if you are not sure, you cannot discount its possibility, and so you cannot stop trying. Even diminutive grandmothers pray before they pick weeds. You would let them be more worthy than you?"

"I would like to see an elderly woman do all this."

"Oh, you would be surprised," Q̇otsik said. "Some come close. They do. The shaman might put us to shame. My wife certainly does."

Dushuuw drew his palm down his face to hide his scowl.

They pushed themselves up with twin groans. A fire burned near them on the rocky ground, but Dushuuw felt he must be as immune to its heat as he was to the cold waters of the pool by now. A hard shell had formed around him.

Q̇otsik looked over the pool. He had grown thin since their father's death. Lines often creased his brow as he thought. But his exhaustion could not shroud a new determination, one born out of pain and the increased mantle of responsibility. A determination that seemed to grow with every gentle touch from Sawsin. Q̇otsik took a deep breath, and nodded in the same way he had after they had encountered the bear.

"This place is for you for now," Q̇otsik said. "Stay here, at least one more night. More, if you can stand it. Then come back again. I will use the other place I prepared for my prayers with Sawsin, beyond the river."

Dushuuw felt as if he were falling, falling down the line of the waterfall but never to feel the pool's cold embrace—just falling.

But Q̇otsik did not sense his worry. Decision made, he was already walking away. Dushuuw was alone. A thin wisp of smoke trailed up from the waning fire, and he got more wood to build the flames back up. He did not want to stay, in this place where he now felt all the more a stranger, or an intruder. But for his brother, he would do anything. And for the path that led to Amuun'axsum.

~

Daylight and the sounds of twittering songbirds. Wasn't it night? Stars wavered on the water. No, snowflakes, melding into the surface. One melted on his arm. What if it had been a star? He was standing in the pool. The fire had burned low again. The vacant eyes of whalers past stared out from their shelter.

And it was night again.

Dushuuw's body moved of its own accord. Diving and sounding, expelling water to take a breath. Seeking, and not finding. Carrying the weight of expectations of dozens of better men who watched over him. Images flashing across his vision—real, imagined, or remembered—of severed heads, of bloodied faces, of lifeless skin pressed against his body. In fear he cut more deeply into his skin, hoping to satiate whatever maw sought to swallow him whole.

It was only when he felt his head would split—submerged in the pool, holding his breath longer than ever before—that a thought embedded itself in his mind. He was fighting against something he would never understand unless he gave up, opened himself, and let it fill him. Staring up at the wavering surface—the stars, or snow, or pinpricks of light fading away—the urge seemed reasonable. And so he started to open his mouth, then jolted.

Dushuuw broke the surface of the water, blowing out a mouthful of water with a heaving gasp. It was not intended as mimicry of a whale's breath, but it was a desperate act to live all the same. He was afraid of what he had been about to do. More than that, angry with himself, to be capable of such weakness. He shook his head roughly.

He collapsed on the ground by the cold hearth, then shakily restarted the fire, built it up to a roar, took his first bite of dried fish since leaving the village, and tumbled into sleep under a blanket.

He dreamed, of a canoe and masked men, of a soundless song. He was drowning. And then...

He was hungry. His muscles ached. He was lonely.

Waking, he brought the dried fish that still lay in his open palm to his lips. What all had happened here? He could no longer keep track. Day and night were meaningless. He didn't remember pulling a blanket over himself. A song, there was a song. Words, indistinct. Indistinct like the song he thought he heard one night by the river, far, far away, yet somehow moving in time with his dancing feet to an ancient drumbeat. No. A dream. That was a dream.

Winter 1690
Nine years earlier

Young Son's mother rubbed her hand over her swollen stomach. The skin was pulled so taut over the baby inside that dark stripes sliced across her skin like scars. Young Son found himself resenting the child inside his mother—a parasite causing her pain.

"Again," she said.

Young Son's shoulders slumped. "Again?"

"Again."

He grumbled and shuffled into place. He lifted his hands halfway up and let them flop down toward the ground.

"Young Son!"

"Mother, I have done this since morning. I am hungry."

"You can eat when you have done it correctly."

"Why does it matter?"

Young Son instantly regretted his words. His mother's pained look this time was not from the baby growing inside her.

"I didn't mean it, mother."

She looked at him for a moment, as if inspecting the thoughts inside his head. "No, you did not. You know better."

He tried to dig his big toe into the compacted dirt floor of the hut his father had built at his mother's request, for practicing things like dances, out of the way of prying eyes and ears. He was ten summers old. Soon, he'd go upriver to start training in earnest under the war chief, who already was giving him special lessons now and then. He would learn to really move like a warrior, as his parents had planned since his birth. He was eager—but fearful too. He liked being in this hut, alone with his mother, spinning and reaching and diving. It's just that he didn't think of it too much when he was outside its thin walls.

"Your father gave you this dance."

"I know."

"His most valuable dance. The most ancient."

Young Son almost said the next phrase in the familiar refrain for her, then thought better of it.

"It is a precious possession. And you shall not besmirch his name—nor mine—by giving it half an effort."

"I know, mother."

She cringed at another pain, and Young Son took a concerned step toward her, unsure what to do. She panted and looked at him, then softened.

"Come here, my Uhsahb, sit by me."

Young Son sat as close to his mother as he could. She put her arm around him and pulled him even closer to her side.

"Another fight?"

He nodded.

She sighed. "You must be careful, son," she said.

"It was his fault."

"Then it is yourself whom you must fight against—your urge to strike back."

Young Son scowled, and drew up his knees.

"Isn't fighting what I'm supposed to do?" he asked.

"You are also a whaler's son," she said. "You must be better than the common boys."

His mother winced and moved through another of her pains. Her hair hung in front of her face as she bent her head, waiting for the wave to pass. He rubbed his hand over her stomach, trying to take away her pain, trying not to think of how he wanted to punch the thing inside her that made her hurt.

She caught her breath. "You must be better than the other noble boys too."

He looked up at her in question.

"They think less of you because of me," she said.

"They are wrong."

But more than anger, fear crawled over Young Son's skin. His mother had never talked of herself this way. In their home, her birth was an unspoken thing—like the men who obtained visions and refused to speak of them so as to not diminish the power they brought. And now, the word given, his strong mother was weak, hunched over in pain.

"Nevertheless, you must prove yourself," she said. "You must see everything as a contest to be won—the best dancer, the best wrestler. Yes, the best at taking an enemy's head and mounting it on a pike, all bloody and ogling for bird food." She poked him playfully, drawing a smile. "Give them no excuse to shove you to the side. Be stronger."

Young Son sat up, feeling foolish for his sniveling. Like a baby.

"Do they shove you to the side, mother?" He hated how his voice cracked when he said it, as it was prone to do these days. It was the reason for that morning's fight, in fact. When she did not answer, he balled his fists. "I can make them respect you."

Another wave of pain came over her. She turned her head aside with a wince, even as she shifted to hold him by the shoulders. "You can never make someone respect you, Uhsahb." She caught her breath and gripped him tight. "You earn it by your actions. By giving them no reason to think less of you."

He sighed. "How long will that take?"

Her gaze bored through his own as if entering his body, seeing the deepest parts of him. "You can never stop."

Face softening, she released her grip and stroked her taut stomach.

"I sometimes wonder if I put this conflict inside you," she whispered. "I put you out in the cold to sleep between stones. I pricked you awake. I put a war club in your tiny little fists. I took away your blanket. But before all that—before all that, I placed your afterbirth on a mat, sprinkled it with feathers, and spun a top over it." Sweat dotted her face, but she smiled. "Your future was marked with dancing feet before it was buried in that cold swamp."

Suddenly, she cried out, face contorting. Sweat slid down her brow.

"Mother?"

"Get the midwife," she said. Her gaze retreated from him, inside and out. "It's too soon. Get your father—"

Her last word broke off in a loud cry of pain.

For a moment, he stood frozen in place.

"Young Son!"

He bolted out of the hut and down the river's edge—tripping, falling, getting up again—past houses, past slaves working on the beach, the great house at the bay only seeming to get farther and farther away.

He always wondered later: If he had not hesitated, would she have lived? And if he had not wished the thing inside her dead, would she have escaped its same fate?

The glimpse of his mother's blood-covered legs, a lifeless mass on the ground between them, would haunt him.

The dead are not to be named. But "mother" is more than a name. As they buried her body with that of her stillborn girl, he tried to carry her memory—reverse her death—by putting his full effort into the dance. He could never do it well enough. His father praised his dancing. His father told him his self-criticism was a sign of understanding—that their ancestors spoke of a song that had once accompanied the dance, a song long lost. In dancing, he was feeling that loss, so his father said. But Young Son felt the weight of lack within himself, the dance forever linked with his own loss, and his guilt.

34

THE TIME OF THE WOLVES neared. The village waited for the brothers to return. In the pair's absence, the mood of the village was light, anticipatory. Soon there would be guests to entertain from neighboring villages. A chance to reunite and show off strengths.

Amuun'a<u>x</u>sum helped with the preparations. She walked to get water from the spring at the point, and gathered more food to serve the dancers who practiced their precisely timed, tight movements to a woman's song tied closely to the Tlukwaali. The practices were held each night in the shaman's house. Amuun'a<u>x</u>sum watched from the far wall. Only the most highly skilled danced to this song. It was a rite to which she was no longer welcome—not yet.

Each day she watched for Dushuuw's return, then settled down to another night without sight of him. The brothers were gone so long, she began to wonder if he and his brother had trekked to Thunderbird's roost in the white-capped mountains.

Finally, on a clear day, she saw Q̓otsik. She was filling a box with water from the creek when he appeared. He returned from beyond the river, not from the hillside above the village where the brothers had headed when they had left two moon phases ago. Q̓otsik strolled across the beach with a soft expression that shifted to a hard-edged gaze when he noticed her watching. Amuun'a<u>x</u>sum looked down at her feet. She listened to him tromp over the bridge that crossed the creek, then watched as he headed uphill toward the winter house. Scratches marred his back. He was thinner. She searched the way he had come, but there was no sign of Dushuuw.

Now, standing against the wall inside the shaman's home, she watched the dancers, moving in ways she had memorized watching her mother long ago. In her mind's eye, she danced with them in the circle as they bent and turned and dipped, but without ever moving their feet.

my wings are tucked inside...

Their voices followed the drum. Then the drum beat on its own, until their voices met it for the final refrain, high and prolonged, taking Amuun'aẖsum's yearning heart with them in their dream of flight.

~

It was daytime, and Amuun'aẖsum headed uphill with a large basket to gather in the forest for the shaman. She held the basket to her side to better see where to put her feet on the steep slope. She skidded every few steps on the slick earth. Rain had already melted the dusting of snow, and now rain fell again.

She reached the top and strode past the winter house, across the meadow, still watching her steps in the rain, until she reached the forest's edge. Anticipating the sheltering boughs, she relaxed her grip on the basket, and when she looked up, Dushuuw stood in front of her on the trail.

A cry of surprise escaped her lips, in part because she almost had not recognized him. He was enveloped in a cloak, his cheeks sunken, and the skin beneath his eyes dark. She started to look around, but her body pitched forward as Dushuuw drew her close for a kiss. Her hat fell from her head, hanging by its string about her neck, and flailed back and forth across her back in the wind. She started to drop the basket, caught herself, and pulled away.

"Dushuuw..." Her whisper was angry, but her smile was not.

He was already stepping beyond her—giving a smile that was mischievous, if tired—to head toward the winter house.

Amuun'aẖsum tried to tame her breathing as she kept her back turned to him and closed her eyes. Anger at Dushuuw's brazenness competed with the thrill of being kissed again, and she hoped his confidence was a sign of some personal achievement with his brother. They would need that more than ever soon.

The rain became thick, as if to remind her of her errand. She skipped into the woods, letting the hat dangle by its string, and was smiling to herself when she glanced up and saw Uhpahs.

Uhpahs stood on the trail and regarded her coldly. A basket hung against her back. The rain was a muffled roar beyond the tree trunks.

"Gather much today, Uhpahs?" Amuun'aẖsum shifted her basket.

"So, you do still imagine yourself to be something you are not," Uhpahs said. Her face was shadowed by her hat; a drop of water fell from a branch and ran down its rim.

Amuun'axsum clenched her teeth and brought her hat back atop her head.

"You imagine filling those empty holes in your ears."

"Uhpahs, please—"

"A noble man proclaiming his love, claiming your virgin bed."

"Uhpahs!"

"Oh, right, you appear to have a noble man between your legs already—though he is awfully silent."

"That is not the way it is."

"I do not know how else to get through to you. I have been trying for so long. It is not going to happen, Quulthoo. You are a—"

"I am not a slave!" Amuun'axsum shouted over her friend and the rain and the wind, and it was the language of Wuh-uhch that spilled out.

Uhpahs was unvexed. "You can keep on saying it," she said. Her voice was low and Amuun'axsum strained to hear. "You can even believe it. But all you will ever be able to give that man are slave babies—like me, like you." Uhpahs sighed and took a tentative step toward Amuun'axsum. Her voice grew softer. "Soon enough, he will leave you behind for good, as silent about you as he is now."

Amuun'axsum smiled. "But you are wrong, my friend," she said. "Walk with me. Let me tell you—"

"I don't want to hear it, Quulthoo," Uhpahs said. "Whatever promises you think he has made to you, they will go unfulfilled."

Uhpahs looked at her with pity, which Amuun'axsum returned with anger. Uhpahs moved to walk past her, but Amuun'axsum grabbed her by the arm.

"Do you really think it is wrong? Or are you just angry that I did not tell you?"

Uhpahs yanked her arm free and continued onward.

"Or is it because you are jealous?"

Uhpahs stopped. She turned and looked at Amuun'axsum. She said nothing, and she did not have to, because Amuun'axsum immediately felt ashamed.

~

Two nights later, Amuun'axsum walked through the chill night to the warm glow of the snag. Dushuuw looked up as she approached and smiled. He came toward her, but she walked off to the side.

"What troubles you?" he asked.

Amuun'axsum tried to smile, but Uhpahs's exhortations had churned up doubts that she had tried to bury.

"Your brother hates me. You think he would accept me under his roof in your bed as your wife? What if he does not agree to ransom me? Or worse."

"Qotsik does not hate you."

"You are blind, Dushuuw."

"Qotsik is a great man, a great chief—"

"The greatest," she said. "A man worthy of following. And you—you follow him closer than anyone else. You go where he leads, as you should. You follow him out to sea. You follow him up a mountain. And you will follow him when he puts a knife to my throat."

Dushuuw swept over and grabbed her by the arms, his rough grip betraying frustration. "My brother showed me many things up there," he said. "Things that are meant for great men. Things that should bring a man power. And I felt that maybe I was close, Amuun'axsum. As close as I ever have, even if it was barely a glimpse. But it still passed me over. There was one moment of elation that came over me—and it was when I saw you, my own little hummingbird." His grip relaxed. Abashed, he massaged her skin. "I want to feel everywhere else what I feel when I am with you. That I am enough as I am. That I am not worthless."

"You are not worthless—"

"You say that, but... If he does not agree, or if I cannot secure your ransom—if I fail—would you still want me?" His question was asked in challenge. Dushuuw dropped his arms and stepped back.

"I want you to be enough." She took his hand. "But if it is as a slave—a secret kept in darkness, or a stain openly born—I do not think I could survive the shame, Dushuuw. I would not just be your bedmate. I would be your full partner, a noble wife who sings and dances and helps you bring in a whale."

He pulled her to him, and raised her hand, kissing her palm. "Then trust me," he said. "For I want that as well, and I will make it happen."

Warmth flooded her body, urging her to make other demands, demands that threatened to drown out her mind's protests. "And for now?" she said.

"For now, over the winter, I will focus on becoming the nobleman and whaler my brother expects," he said. He kissed her palm again, her tattooed wrist, her neck. "And it is good that it will mean much prayer and fasting, for I do not know how I will be able to wait otherwise."

Amuun'axsum forced herself past the headiness that made her body tingle and pushed him away. She smiled at him as he shuffled backward.

"The winter is long," he groaned, but he forced a smile.

"Then let us tell stories," she said, leaning against the opposite side of the snag and drawing her cloak tight. "It is good to tell stories on these long nights."

Tree boughs blocked the rain. Clouds moved overhead, further shielding the stars that spun in the sky over a spinning world, as they traded some of the stories they knew. He with tales of the alternately irascible and heroic Q̓watee. She with tales of the otherworldly Thunderbird. They shared the different versions they knew of other stories. The power of Day captured inside a box. People falling into drums and contracting diseases that made the ground shake. Thunderbird fighting with Whale.

"One day, Whale becomes jealous," Amuun'axsum recited.

"Whale tells our people that we must decide, decide forever who is greatest," Dushuuw continued.

Amuun'axsum's skin prickled.

"Whale or Thunderbird?"

"Thunderbird or Whale?"

They laughed, and Amuun'axsum wanted to see if it would continue.

"And the people, they are afraid..."

"...afraid of making Whale angry..."

"...afraid of making Thunderbird angry..."

"Afraid of them both," they said in unison.

They stopped there, and the greater part of Amuun'axsum was relieved. She was curious if their story endings were also the same, and the lessons that followed from the storytellers. But the story always brought to mind her mother's song, which was so often paired with the tale. And the young friend she lost so long ago. She hugged herself tight.

She cleared her throat. "And the Tlukwaali?" she asked, with a hint of challenge. "Your headdresses are rather small. I have seen headdresses so large they required multiple men to hold them aloft."

"Oh really?" Dushuuw said. "Well, we will have to see about that. Yaq and I have big plans, you know."

She laughed, then turned thoughtful, knowing that although slaves could join that secret society—where rank was set aside—the doors had still been closed to her so far. She would not see whatever Dushuuw and his friend had in mind.

"They are practicing the Deer dance in Eekbis's house," she said. "I remember the lightning dance too; it was my favorite."

"You shall dance them again," he said.

She smiled at him, and wished she were not so impatient.

"Here is a word," he said.

He had shared many words from his language. Mountain. Club. Kiss.

"It means to reenact a bad dream, so that it does not come true."

Amuun'axsum looked away, knowing that her worst dreams came because they had already come true.

"And here is a word for you," she said.

She had taught him words in her father's tongue. Rich. Steal. Promise.

"It is the hurt you feel, when you lose someone close."

Around and overhead, night sounds punched and drifted through the air. Rustles. Hoots. Sighs.

"Then there are the languages no one really knows," Dushuuw said, brow furrowed. "The ones of dreams."

"And of desire," she said. There was an ache in her heart, a bitter taste on her tongue.

"I don't know," he said, crawling over to her. He set his hands on the bark at either side of her face, leaned in, and burrowed his face into her neck. "That one is pretty straightforward." His breath and his tongue were hot on her skin. She slipped her hands around his neck.

All at once, a shower of bark fell from the top of the snag. Swooping wings fluttered over their heads as an owl halted its dive with a screech, talons gripping the bark. A small mouse skittered beside them and squeaked in response, burrowing itself into a pile of leaves, though the owl had already flapped away.

Amuun'axsum gasped and pressed her hand to her head.

Dushuuw shifted away.

The owl called from the forest, and Dushuuw shuddered, though he tried to hide the reaction. The leaves trembled over the shifting mouse.

Amuun'axsum straightened and plucked at one of the leaves atop the mouse. "The owl does not bring death every time." Her voice was shaky. The mouse burst out of the pile and skittered out of the snag.

Dushuuw edged closer again, but angled his head to look upward.

"Daylight will soon find us and send us scurrying too," he said. He smiled, and gave a shaky laugh.

They walked back to the village, drawing closer together the farther they got from the snag. The backs of their hands brushed against each other, until finally their fingers intertwined. At the outskirts of the village, he kissed her deeply as he drew his hand away.

~

Amuun'axsum moved the deer hide hanging in the doorway and slipped back inside the shaman's house. The smile on her face fell away. There was a fire burning high. She peeked around the partition. The shaman sat on the floor, holding out her hands to gather the fire's warmth.

"You are up early," Amuun'axsum said, clearing her throat. "Let me go see if any fishermen are up yet, and I'll cook you a meal."

"Where were you?"

"Out relieving myself."

"All night?" The shaman's face was unreadable.

"I suppose I should tell you," Amuun'axsum said. "I have a place I like to go, to be alone."

"Because this house is so crowded..."

Amuun'axsum pressed her lips together, waiting for the shaman's discipline. She would take it, and keep away from the snag until the old woman forgot.

"Buhkweeduuk was right," the shaman said. "I should have brought you to Deeyuh straight away."

Amuun'axsum looked on in confusion. But Eekbis did not offer any further explanation. Instead, she rubbed her hands together.

"It will be light enough soon. Get us a small canoe, Quulthoo. You are taking me upriver." The shaman looked over. "No questions."

Amuun'axsum's mind was so filled with confusion and worry that she had the small canoe borrowed and at the water's edge before daybreak. Soon, Amuun'axsum was paddling them upriver. She remembered the last time they had taken this route, when green leaves were in profusion and the sap running.

"To Deeyuh...?"

"Not yet," the shaman said. "For now, take me to the place you took me before—around the bend."

Amuun'axsum let up on the paddle. "There will be canoes coming down from Deeyuh for the gathering," she said.

"You need not worry about such things any longer," Eekbis said. "I have the proper words, as you were so concerned about the last time."

Amuun'axsum steered them into the small crook of land.

"He gave you gathering rights?" she asked, dropping the anchor stone over the side of the canoe.

"Here and all the way up the hillside, and extending all the way up the river to its end at their village's back. All in exchange for you."

Amuun'axsum was still looking over the land when the shaman's words sunk in, and for a moment her senses went numb. The old woman spoke, but it was as if she spoke through water.

"...better end of the deal. I think the man does not understand quite what all lays hidden in this area. The Deeyuh shaman derives strength from other areas."

Amuun'axsum groped through her mind, trying to resurface.

"If Buhkweeduuk had his way, you would be in Deeyuh already. I still hold some sway, if not as much as I did with his brother. I at least got them to agree that I can keep you until spring. By then, I expect to have a new acolyte from Oosa-ilth. Relations there have thawed enough, and Buhkweeduuk is eager to renew strong ties."

Amuun'axsum tried to sort through the string of ideas pummeling her. "Do not send me away. I can do more. I will work harder..."

The shaman snorted. "The girl who puts on airs now begs to remain my slave?"

"You wanted me. You said I lend power to..."

"Come now," the shaman scoffed. "I merely tried to cool the young chief's anger. He was blinded by grief. I do think it possible you could hide something from that so-called noble past of yours. But thus far, your 'power' has provided about as much help to me as a bad bout of indigestion. Or perhaps the young chief is correct, and you do send evil power against his family. I could be convinced of that now."

"I did not send anything into his father's body."

"Of course you did not," Eekbis said. "I would have known, and killed you myself. I do not even think Qotsik believes it—he knows how bad his father's wounds were, how much time was lost. If there is anyone to blame, he knows it is someone closer to him. And that's exactly why he turned on you. But I am old enough to know which battles are worth fighting, especially when it involves a young man with the power to speak things into existence—or out of it."

Amuun'axsum tried to rein in her panic.

"How long until...?"

"As soon as the sea is navigable for the men to bring me my apprentice from Oosa-ilth. When they set out, so do you—if I do not send you away before then."

"Isn't there anything I can do to stay?"

The woman sat forward and leaned her elbows on her knees. It seemed a strangely youthful position. Amuun'axsum had one of those incongruent moments, seeing a semblance of what Eekbis must have looked like as a young woman, and she wondered at the cold strength that must have been under that wrinkled skin and gray hair all along. At ease, Eekbis simply looked at her.

Amuun'axsum gripped the sides of the canoe. "I will run away."

Eekbis gave a look that was part pity, part disdain. "You will not. Or you would have long ago with that pride of yours. Where would you go? Nowhere better than where you are already headed."

Amuun'axsum bristled and grabbed for the thoughts flying through her mind. "We can convince Buhkweeduuk to give them another slave."

"They asked for you."

Amuun'axsum looked over at her in shock.

"You are knowledgeable, you know. And I think that half-rate shaman expects you to be a little spy, reveal all my secrets." Eekbis sat back. "He does not well know me. But there was another reason too. A slave of Oodahk's took a liking to you. He must be a valuable one, to receive you as a wife."

Amuun'axsum felt as if she were being stuffed inside a basket, its walls being woven higher around her as she tried to climb out.

"You have to talk to Buhkweeduuk," Amuun'axsum said. "I—I know how he can get much more for me if he just waits until spring. I do still have noble family, family who will redeem me. I have a friend, who has located the village and just needs to—"

Eekbis looked increasingly perplexed, then nodded with understanding and cut Amuun'axsum off mid-sentence. "You mean Young Son," she said. "I am starting to wonder just how long you have been slipping out to these all-night excursions to 'relieve' yourself..."

Amuun'axsum was numb.

A smile snaked its way up Eekbis's face. "You are only good at lying to yourself, child. Always have been," she said. "You are fortunate I only recently informed Buhkweeduuk of my suspicions. You certainly must be removed now. And you are fortunate it should be in trade. There are more straightforward ways of removing problems like you. You are especially fortunate if, as you claim, there is now some family who would redeem you; though I find that doubtful. A man will often make grand promises to get what he wants. Either way, you lose nothing. It can be for Oodahk to decide if he wants ransom for his slave."

Amuun'axsum gripped the sides of the canoe.

"Does Dushuuw know about all this?"

Eekbis narrowed her eyes at that name. Amuun'axsum winced at her slip. The shaman took a deep breath, as if debating how to answer.

"Do you know that I love that boy? Watching him grow up, become a warrior—dance," Eekbis said. "Even through his mistakes, I have still believed that he would find his way. Buhkweeduuk secured all this access for me because he thought it was the only way I would give you up, and he needs to strengthen that alliance. I suppose he wasn't wrong, but I soon had a much bigger reason to agree. This is not about a soggy bit of land so much as it is about saving that boy from himself. If it became known that he was willing to give up everything he had left for one such as you..."

The shaman cut off the response forming on Amuun'axsum's lips, and folded her arms. "No, Young Son does not know. And he cannot. Maybe you are fine with stripping him of his rights and privileges, not to mention what remains of his self-respect, but we are not. You two are blind. The truth is that with every act of seduction you make, you stab him yourself. So," she said, placing her hands on her knees, "from this moment it is ended. You no longer belong to Wuh-uhch. I merely borrow you. Oodahk will arrive soon for the Tlukwaali with his household, and even here your obligations are first to him—and you will obey.

"You will obey, and you will ensure that Young Son no longer finds reasons to seek you out. Do these things, and you will both be saved. Do not, and you will be exceedingly fortunate if all that happens is your early transition to Deeyuh. And I do not think that more favorable outcome likely."

"It does not have to be this way," Amuun'axsum whispered.

Eekbis looked offended. "It absolutely must."

They spent the rest of the morning paddling up and down the river. The shaman surveyed the area, pointing out thin trails where Amuun'axsum could later gain access to the land. She ticked off a long list of things for Amuun'axsum to seek out and gather. The woman was eager to exploit this new open resource, and she would ensure Amuun'axsum worked all through each of the still-short days that they had remaining to them after the Tlukwaali.

"You will have no trouble going to sleep at night," Eekbis said. "Though if you do, I will know."

Amuun'axsum paddled the canoe back and helped the old woman to shore. Inside the house, she stoked the fire and prepared a meal. She accompanied the shaman house to house on the old woman's visits and errands, something she had not often been required to do before. Eekbis would indeed keep her close. Amuun'axsum would be lucky to be alone to truly relieve herself.

Late in the afternoon, the two women trudged up the hill toward the winter house. Eekbis leaned heavily on Amuun'axsum's arm, but maintained a tight grip even once they were on level ground. Guests had been arriving from surrounding villages all day. Large groups of older men congregated outdoors. Children ran about in crowded games. Slaves walked to and fro on the path to the point to gather bucket after bucket of spring water.

Eekbis led the way into the great house. Dushuuw was the first face they met. He was laughing with Yaq and clutching a bag, his eyes bright with merriment. Amuun'axsum felt her insides fold and she tucked her chin to her chest. She was relieved when Dushuuw followed his friend outdoors with only a passing greeting for the shaman. Eekbis tugged her toward the back corner, stopping to speak with acquaintances from other villages along the way. Amuun'axsum looked over her shoulder, trying to catch a glimpse of Dushuuw, but he was gone.

Amuun'axsum sat down close to a wall to work on the dip net for the seventh time that day while the shaman went to join a circle of chatting women. Amuun'axsum dragged the end of the net out of the basket. The net had changed little since her first round of work on it that day. Half the time, her fingers remained frozen around the lengths of twine. She made a poor spider. She felt tied up and numb.

Eekbis pulled Buh-uhs close, patting the boy's head and whispering in his ear. The boy looked at Amuun'axsum expectantly, as if he thought she would bring him food, then laughed at whatever the shaman whispered. The shaman moved on and poked little Blubs's stomach as the boy sucked on a piece of blubber, getting grease marks all over Pikoo's legs. She remarked on Ootsihd's pregnancy, and settled down between Um-iiqsu and Thluuch-muup, joining in the exchange of gossip in the circle that also included Chaiyuhx-ik and Sawsin. Amuun'axsum sat apart and listened, making a knot in the net.

"Young Son was up to something," Eekbis said.

"He and Yaq apparently have plans for some great display of theater this winter," Um-iiqsu said.

"That sounds exciting," Sawsin said.

Um-iiqsu laughed. "No. That sounds familiar…"

"Yes, they always have plans," Chai said. A rare smile flashed across her otherwise sober face.

"And always secret," Pikoo added.

"Secret plans they never reveal," Thluuch-muup said.

"Because it always needs more planning," Chai said.

Knowing smiles crossed every woman's face in the circle.

"Yes, they will be out all day, as far away as they can get from us," Pikoo said, bouncing her boy on her legs. "And by the time their great display is ready, Blubs here will be grown and a whaler—and they will decide they need to incorporate him into things. So that, after all this secret and careful planning..."

"...there will be a need for more planning," Um-iiqsu and Pikoo said in unison. The women tumbled into laughter.

Amid the levity, Eekbis motioned Amuun'a̱xsum over. "Go out and get more firewood," the shaman said.

Amuun'a̱xsum left the net behind, swinging a basket tumpline into place as she walked out the doorway—and nearly ran into Uhpahs. Amuun'a̱xsum froze. Uhpahs acknowledged her with a look that was as full of disappointment and pity as the day she caught her with Dushuuw.

So that was it. That was how the shaman found out.

Hurt and anger swirled inside Amuun'a̱xsum as she made her way to the trail. She wanted to beat Uhpahs with her fists, scratch her face, tear out her hair for her betrayal.

The loud chatter surrounding the houses faded as Amuun'a̱xsum marched into the woods. She wandered off the main trail, switching side trails until all was silent around her except the damp rustle of ferns, until she was all alone except for the animals who knew to stay hidden. She stumbled down to the packed dirt and leaned against a tree.

For a long time, she cried. She cried for a lost friend. She cried for lost love. She cried for her mother and for her father, even for the slave man who had helped her live by ending her noble life. She finally cried because of the sand-like feeling in her throat, so in contrast to the forest where she sat, once a place of refuge, and now a damp prison.

She fixed her eyes on the point where the path disappeared into the deeper green of the forest, where fern and salal wavered, where shadows lengthened and shortened in response. The path led somewhere, deeper into the forest, away from the village. Amuun'a̱xsum looked to the ground. A silvery path crossed her skirt, shimmering in the dappled light. Within arm's reach on the path beside her toddled a tiny shell, moving so slowly that it seemed at first not to move at all. The snail marked its path. Having encountered her as an obstacle, it forged ahead.

Amuun'a̱xsum ignored her hunger and thirst. She ignored her errand. She went to the snag. She stood at the ragged threshold looking over the tiny symbols of a shared life. Makeshift seats, torn blankets, cracked bowls. A rotting house. Signs of power drawn in fading black lines, streaked and broken. A sodden hole in the ground to house tiny and unwanted things.

She took a deep breath, forcing herself to see this place as it was.

Amuun'axsum ran her fingers across the charcoal lines of a Lightning Serpent, smearing the lines further. At one point in the canoe, she had almost offered the shaman the song. Anything that might make the woman change course. The words were on her tongue. But it would change nothing. And it would only risk the last thing that kept her connected to her mother, and to the mountaintop from which she was descended.

Whether Amuun'axsum liked it or not, the shaman was right. It was for the Deeyuh chief to decide now, and so it was to the Deeyuh chief that Amuun'axsum would focus her efforts. She was moving again, but not far, and this time she had more than hope alone. The name flew around her mind: *Lohta.*

Amuun'axsum.

She fell back against the snag wall for support, and closed her eyes as she tugged close and then pushed away the memory of the voice that had brought her both names. The lips that had touched her own... She wanted...

"Lohta," she said, curling her fingers into fists.

There were her roots. There lay her past and her future, a pivot point for her fate. There she could sing full-throated to the blasting beat of a large plank drum, cedar walls amplifying her voice for all to hear. She could get anything she wanted, as long as she first got that back. Anything.

So why did she feel as if she were losing everything all over again?

With eyes closed, Amuun'axsum listened to the wind over the top of the snag, the calls of distant birds, the creaking of boughs that bent so they would not break. She remembered the windswept island, a starfish's silent hunt, a song of longing, a brush of heat down her cheek, a gentle tug at her waist. Fleeting moments, she had thought. But instead, small signs of the big shift to come. Amuun'axsum stood away from the bark wall at her back, hearing pieces of it crumble to the ground as she stepped out of the enclosure without looking back. She returned to Wuh-uhch, a load of firewood strapped to her back, the line of the path reeling her in, her chin raised, her hands trembling.

IT WASN'T JUST the long days and nights at the pool with Q̇otsik—nor the long night spent with Amuun'a̱xsum at the snag—that seemed to throw Dushuuw off balance as the village commenced the winter ceremonials. With his father gone, and their house in official mourning, the Tlukwaali this year would be given by Leehuuk in his house at the upriver end of the village. The vast winter house instead became another place to sleep for the guests pouring in from the other cape villages.

Leehuuk had been growing richer. His eldest son now lived down at Oosa-ilth, married to a whaler's daughter there, bringing shared rights to premier whaling and sealing grounds that direction.

"It is said Leehuuk found a piece of rock that contained stars, which brought him these riches," Yaq said.

With a rare calm day, Dushuuw had escaped with Yaq to fish on the bay. They had no intention of actually catching anything. The idea had been to discuss their plans for the dances and, more immediately, the children they would steal later that night. Now, though, Yaq was sober.

"You and Q̇otsik will need to watch him closely," he said. "He did some things while you both were gone."

"What do you mean?"

"Leehuuk approached Kuhbuḣtup and said he and Kweelthup should bring their families to live under his roof—become his speaker, and the watcher on his whaling crew. Promised them a corner. Kuhbuḣtup refused, of course."

Dushuuw fumed, trying to match his admiring memories of the nobleman with what he was hearing now. "No one would leave Q̇otsik."

"That is what Kuhbuḣtup said," Yaq said. "Still, Leehuuk was bold enough to ask. Some of his new partners at Oosa-ilth used to live under your father's arm, you know."

"How did I miss this?" Dushuuw mumbled.

"He is shrewd, friend," Yaq said. "And you have been—distant." He pulled his fishing line out of the water, plunking the empty hook into his hand. "Though there were some who wondered if you would even care."

Dushuuw looked over. "That feels like ages ago now," he said. "Father and uncle had been finding more and more ways to keep me from that end of the village. I just didn't see it, before."

Thoughts churned in his mind. If Leehuuk was shrewd, his cousin Wiid was even more so. All this time, had the war chief been trying to steer Dushuuw away too?

Dushuuw took deliberate care putting his own hook back into a pouch. "So, we take Leehuuk's youngest son tonight?"

"And his daughter." Yaq smiled as he looked at Dushuuw. "Maybe the wolves will be a bit more rough than usual with the boy, hey?"

Dushuuw laughed but ended up shaking his head. "That would goad Leehuuk too much, I think."

"Ah, you are getting soft. But *this* wolf's claws are not blunt."

Dushuuw smiled.

"Your uncle said Buh-uhs is not to be initiated?" Yaq asked.

"Do not look at me," Dushuuw said, bristling a bit. "If that is what my uncle says, that is the way it is."

Yaq shrugged.

"It is good he is not," Dushuuw added. "He is too young yet. Other things come first. And it is not our place."

He did not say all he was thinking. The Tlukwaali was only one kind of initiation for a boy, and Dushuuw was not sure he could hurt Buh-uhs in the way required leading up to it. He argued against the notion that he was prolonging and exacerbating the inevitable. Surely the boy would return to Oosa-ilth at some point. Maybe being penned indoors for several moons would take away the boy's desire for living here. Dushuuw shook his head at himself. It was not his decision anyway.

~

The young people woke with frightened expressions.

Sticks rattled over the wall boards like rain. Footsteps thudded on the roof planks over their heads like thunder. Moaning sounds came from all around like the wind. Flaming torches were dipped through gaps in the roof, then pulled back up, like lightning flashes.

Dushuuw had slipped through the open doorway and stood against a wall, waiting and watching. Painted black with charcoal, he blended with the shadows.

A boy sat up straight on his mat and looked over to his grandfather. The old man bent low and whispered, "It's the Wolves."

Men streamed and leaped into the house. Dushuuw rushed toward the boy as the other men rushed to steal other sons and daughters identified by their parents for initiation. Wreaths of hemlock boughs ringed the men's heads, waists, wrists, ankles. A man slipped through the doorway, the whites of his eyes bright against his blackened face.

There were shrieks and whistles and howls.

Dushuuw wrapped the frightened boy up in his arms and carried him out into the dark, moonless night as the boy's grandfather looked on with a smile.

Dushuuw blew through a whistle hidden in his mouth as he escorted the boy into the forest where the other boys were being taken, to be taught by older men. The girls were taken to another spot by women. Dushuuw gripped the boy by the arm. The boy tried to say something, and Dushuuw slapped the back of his head to silence him. Dushuuw remembered his fear when he had been initiated. He believed the men to be real wolves in human form. He thought he was losing his family and community forever. But he spared no pity for the quaking boy in his grip. He was old enough to handle worse. And Dushuuw also remembered the return, with the ceremonies, and the puffed-up feeling of belonging to something important that erased all earlier fears. That was the lesson: to leave the fear behind in the forest, and never bring it back into the village.

A small fire marked the gathering point in the dark folds of the forest. Dushuuw relinquished the boy to the older members of the society. He remained at the outskirts, with his brother and cousin and the other younger men from the whaling crew. The group stayed in the forest day after day, the older men teaching the younger ones important lessons, before they all returned to the village—and gathered in Leehuuk's house to commence several nights of celebration. The house was filled with society members and the young initiates. Each family took its turn singing and shaking a rattle. Dawn came before everyone had taken their turn.

One evening, Dushuuw donned a Wolf mask and joined a procession entering the house. He crouched low with a dagger in each hand. Yaq and Kweelthup held him back from the crowd by cedar cords. A shrouded man stood against the wall, wearing a white mask with deeply set eyes. A wild figure, he represented the spirits of the drowned and kept destruction at bay with a constant, monotonous chant. At one point, the singing came to an abrupt stop. A man snarled and howled, then was joined by the entire assembly, which together gave a howl so loud it seemed to pushed against the cedar boards. Beyond the house walls, real wolves answered with their own distant howls.

In the morning, the young initiates were assembled on the beach. Society members, noble and commoner alike, even some slaves, milled together, the usual attentions to rank deliberately set aside. In this, Dushuuw and Yaq were finally on equal ground. And everyone would be cut. Blood seeped from fresh gashes on their arms, made by an expert cutter. In some cases, seasoned society members had slaves bleed on their behalf.

Q̇otsik surveyed the group of initiates and called forward two boys together. One boy was cut, then the other. They each pressed their mouths closed, eyeing each other with shoulders back and chins raised.

Soon it was Leehuuk's daughter's turn. Her father and mother gently shoved her from behind. "I do not want to," the girl whispered. Leehuuk glanced at the crowd, and tugged the girl forward. She whined and started to cry.

Sawsin left her husband's side and crouched in front of the girl.

"Leave your fear behind, little one," Sawsin said. "Remember? Come, let's do it together."

Sawsin remained kneeling in the sand, closer to the girl's level, and held out her arm to be cut. The girl watched Sawsin's face, and admired the fine jewelry that adorned the woman's ears and nose and dress.

"You see? It is over quickly. Can you be brave?"

The girl stood up straight and carefully positioned her arm at the same angle as Sawsin's. She held her breath, then smiled with pride when it was done. Sawsin put their arms together to admire.

"Now for the worst part," Sawsin whispered.

The pair washed their arms together in the sea's salty bite.

The Tlukwaali continued, with dancing and masked processions. In one dance, fires were built higher and higher as the initiates were chased by a Wolf, round and round until buckets of water doused the fires and the house was cast in darkness, and exhausted silence. Another night, they masked themselves as animals, their motley shadows marching along the exterior walls. As they slid into the house, each one was caught and unmasked—a final taming of the Wolf spirit.

Dushuuw was the last to be tamed. The Wolf headdress was tied securely, its long snout extending out over his painted face. He was free of ropes. Instead of being held back, he danced in a rapid pace low to the ground. Whirling, like a soul in a shaman's hand. Crouching, like a wolf on the prowl. Springing up, but with bent legs, like a man trying to break free and stand. Dancing, dancing, dancing, until finally the mask was torn from his head and he stood tall, and still, and quiet. Human again.

And at daybreak on the final day, it was Q̇otsik who stood atop the roof of Leehuuk's house with other men, a long cloak fluttering at his back in the restless wind. He stood at the edge of the roof, looking out over the shuffling assembly below, wearing a headdress representing Thunderbird whose beak extended so far out that it shadowed his face.

Drummers struck long planks set up outside the front of the house. Two other men took turns tipping up either end of a long box filled with tiny rocks, creating a sound like a downpour.

Q̇otsik spread the cloak like wings as he danced. After the final drum beat, he leapt from the roof. And for a moment, suspended in the air with caped arms outstretched, Dushuuw believed his brother really would fly.

~

A steady rain soon developed into a downpour.

It was evening, and the Tlukwaali had officially closed. But there were many societies. And there were many men from the surrounding villages who were eager to keep meeting. A group of deer and elk hunters, who each year estimated the herd counts and came up with a responsible take, led the way.

Everyone packed inside Leehuuk's house.

"I thought we were going to have the Elk dance," one man called.

Leehuuk looked uncomfortable.

"That is a beach dance," he said.

"I have come a long distance, and I brought my mask all this way," another man called.

"There is no room to…"

"When the first human was transformed into the elk, a man sawed off the elk's horns and made a whale harpoon," said Oodahk, the whaling chief from Deeyuh, who had been staying as Leehuuk's guest for the Tlukwaali. "Because of Elk, we eat and clothe our families."

Leehuuk pursed his lips. His gaze darted about the room.

Dushuuw shared a look with his uncle. Buhkweeduuk appeared equally interested in where things would go next. Leehuuk had just closed a days-long celebration with a display of his wealth. Now his generosity as a host was questioned. Deny the men their dance, and his expensive purchase of prestige would be blemished.

"Of course, I would not deny anyone the Elk dance," Leehuuk said. "I myself enjoy the dance. Let's return to the beach..."

"You would put us out in that downpour, Leehuuk?" Oodahk said.

A look of frustration flashed across Leehuuk's face. The nobleman quickly smiled, but it was clear now that Oodahk was digging into him on purpose. Of course, no one cared about rain.

"If no one desires to dance in such a small rain..." Leehuuk trailed off with an inviting laugh, but no one spoke up.

The nobleman swallowed and nodded his head. "Then let's not waste time. We will dance now—every man who has his Elk mask and antlers with him."

Yaq was suddenly at Dushuuw's side, handing him black strips of deer hide.

"You were in on this?" Dushuuw whispered. "Why didn't you tell me?"

"I just found out too," Yaq said. "That slick little whale watcher of ours has been hauling in masks and antlers ever since Oodahk spoke up."

Dushuuw turned toward the doorway and spotted Kweelthup handing out masks and antlers to their owners with help from Huh-uuk. Dushuuw ducked his head to hide his smile.

To his credit, Leehuuk was the first to tie his mask around his forehead and strings of deer hooves around his ankles and wrists. Soon, more than four dozen other men were similarly attired—about half the usual number for an Elk dance, but clearly far more than Leehuuk expected to be ready. Strips of darkly dyed deer hide banded Dushuuw's eyes and fell down the sides of his face. The hooves at his wrists and ankles clacked together as they moved. The dancers held antlers aloft against their heads, and drummers started striking sticks.

There was no choreography to the Elk dance. No song. The men simply moved about the room. At first their steps were a haughty prance. Soon one or two men were locking antlers with others, Yaq and Dushuuw among them.

Onlookers shoved partitions and belongings aside. Those who lived in the house frantically stored items away. Mothers with young children made their exits. And the people who remained pressed themselves against walls to be out of the way.

Dushuuw feinted a charge at his old mentor, and was pleased to see Wiid flinch. Dushuuw danced back over toward his brother.

No one was sure who shouted the word; Dushuuw had his suspicion, looking at Yaq. But when someone shouted the word for Elk, the mayhem started.

Dancers swung their antlers about, urged on by the crowd—both the laughter of men and the shrieks of women. One man flailed about so wildly that he lodged his antlers by their points between wall boards. As the rack quivered, Leehuuk appealed for calm. But the antlers had found their mark in the crowd's mood and, soon enough, some hidden voice called out the animal's name again. The frenzy renewed.

Eventually, Leehuuk's shouts could not be heard. Bowls were scattered, holes ripped in cedar mats, hanging baskets toppled, the mob given over to the glories of happy destruction.

THE SHAMAN'S HOUSE was empty except for Amuun'axsum.

All who were allowed were in Leehuuk's house upriver. Many of those not allowed inside nevertheless followed to listen in and spy what they could of the newest celebration—which sounded like it was getting more boisterous.

Amuun'axsum drew a cloak around herself and welcomed the relative silence of the empty house. She walked across the dirt floor, eyes on her feet, wending between dark drops and streaks of dried blood.

The days and nights of the Tlukwaali had dragged by one after the other. Amuun'axsum had walked as if on broken shells, so afraid the next step might bring her face-to-face with the Deeyuh chief or his slave—her owner, her husband. She had seen Toopuuk from afar, always following closely behind the whaling chief Oodahk, whose back he guarded. They never strayed far from Leehuuk's house, where the festivities were centered and where Oodahk stayed with his family as honored guests. With the Tlukwaali concluded, she wondered if she could stop looking over her shoulder. Surely they'd simply return home. But then the visitors remained, and her unease persisted.

In some ways, it was a familiar unease. Over the years living as a slave, Amuun'axsum had become inured to being shut out from the Tlukwaali—never being in one village long enough to take her own place in that society. She took part in the ways she could. She peeked through cracks in wall boards, and watched the beach dances from afar, curious of the ways different villages marked this highest of ceremonies. Mentally, she collected the most attractive of the outsiders' traditions, envisioning how she would be able to help her family elevate their own celebrations when she was restored, turning her exile into treasure. But over this Tlukwaali, fear of running into Toopuuk overpowered her curiosity; she avoided all the places the Wolves gathered—except one.

It had been held here in the shaman's house. A meeting of the Tlukwaali. There were no dances to go with the meeting. No feast. Yet in some ways it was the crux of the entire series. And the final dances of the final day did not take place until the meeting was over.

Hidden around a neighboring house corner, Amuun'axsum had watched as Dushuuw followed his family and other local society members into the shaman's house. Yaq was there. Even Uhpahs. They were sober faced. Other members of the Tlukwaali streamed through the doorway, including Oodahk with his wife and eldest son. Amuun'axsum retreated farther into the shadows as Toopuuk followed, his gaze going left and right, searching. She heard no laughter. She saw no smiles. Only straight postures and determined looks marked those who prepared to make important decisions for the health of the community. For those pulled through the doorway for the pack's judgment, it was dread.

A quarreling couple emerged from the house with carved pieces of bone piercing their arms—the pain and blood would give them something worth their disruptive complaints.

A girl wiped away tears as she bore the shame of having the front of her hair cut at a diagonal, marking her as a liar.

A boy caught in lies was treated more harshly. His mother dragged him into the house. Soon he screamed. His screams continued, drawing the attention of everyone outside the house. When they left, the boy followed his mother meekly, his hands trembling near his head. The scent of scorched hair lingered.

Eventually mingled songs flowed from the house. Different men sang their Tlukwaali songs, often two or three at a time, singing right over each other. Song blending into song blending into song.

Amuun'axsum shook herself from her reverie, and realized she was staring at one of the hot stones near the fire. Hair was attached to it by a bit of scalp. With a stick, she flipped the hot stone over and nudged it into the fire.

Hugging the cloak close, she ambled to the far corner of the house. A corner reserved for prestige now sheltered a pile of dead leaves and dust.

Shouts sounded from the distant gathering, then suddenly died off.

Amuun'axsum stood in the corner and closed her eyes. She imagined herself in the corner of another house, one destroyed by flames. She did not bother to reconstruct it accurately, but instead let a flood of images fill her mind of what the living space would contain if it were her own. A warm fire. A carved plank. Painted capes. Piles upon piles of soft blankets, bowls overflowing with delicacies, a bed hidden from prying eyes by tall partitions, the weave tight.

Eager footsteps ran past the shaman's house toward the unseen spectacle upriver, the revelers' laughter trailing behind them. In her mind's eye, even the wind funneled itself toward the gathering. But she remained in this empty corner.

She found herself swaying to the movements of a dance she had nearly forgotten. The cloak slipped off her shoulders and slid across her back as she wended her way about the room, eyes still closed, gripping the corners of the cloak, arms lifting and lilting, one after the other as she twisted in the Spirit of the Songless. A dance with no song. No drum. A dance that needed only silence.

"It's beautiful."

Amuun'axsum spun about and looked toward the man's voice.

Beyond the house's walls, distant shouts sounded again from the gathering.

"Toopuuk..."

The Deeyuh slave smiled and stood straight.

The din from upriver built itself up in intensity again.

Amuun'axsum drew the cloak back atop her shoulders.

"Please, I didn't mean for you to stop."

She hugged the cloak tighter.

Knocking and striking sounds joined the shouting upriver. The noise did not subside as it had before, but grew louder, seeping between the chinks in the wall at her back.

Toopuuk drew nearer. She ducked her head.

"You were told?" he asked.

She nodded. There was the din, her pounding heart, and the back of Toopuuk's finger caressing a line down her cheek.

"I wanted to come sooner. Next winter, you'll be at my side in those rooms, gathering with the pack," he said.

Her breath hitched. He placed his palm against her other cheek.

"Are you happy?" he asked.

Amuun'axsum tried to hold back her tears. She couldn't deny the spark ignited by the picture of the future he drew—though she wanted so much more than a momentary reprieve. She managed a nod. He tugged gently at her waist. And the stark reality of her situation dawned on her, the moment that would come next. Even so, the choice was life or death. And she would choose to live, though she felt dead inside. She rested a hand on his bicep, brushing her palm over his skin. She lifted her other hand to his face, and gently traced his scar with her fingertips.

Ṫoopuuk made shushing sounds as he bent and kissed her tears, one by one, before moving to her neck and behind her ear, his hands loosing the ties that held up her work skirt. He sang the song he had first sang to her beside the fire at Chahdee. She tried to find the pleasure that she had experienced in the words before, as she tucked her head to his chest and he stroked her hair. But her heart beat wildly, as if guilty of betrayal, with the fear of one facing judgment.

On the ground, her cloak spread beneath them, Amuun'a̱xsum closed her eyes and tried to send her mind upriver as Ṫoopuuk's tender whispers were drowned out by the sounds of a house being torn apart.

Summer 1686
Thirteen years earlier

"I am going to be your husband."

Maḥtii looked at Tiichswii, her hands wrapped around the girth of the wooden bear.

"Why would you do that?"

The boy looked stumped, or perhaps disappointed. He held a wooden figure, tiny harpoon in hand, over the bow of a tiny canoe that rode waves of sand. He looked at her askance.

"Well, I suppose so I can keep playing with your bear," he said. "It is a very nice bear."

"That makes sense," she said, wagging her foot back and forth. But she did not give up her bear. It was smooth, polished wood. It shone in the light. The grains of wood roiled like fur over its stomach. She rocked it left and right. It looked back at her blankly as it bounced off one of her knees, then the other. The leaf she had placed atop its head for a hat floated down.

The children sat on the damp mixture of dirt and sand, in a spot between the splashing surf and the houses spouting smoke. Sand dusted their cheeks. Dirt dusted their knees.

"Hey now, look at this," he said, crouching on all fours by a log.

Maḥtii set aside the bear to join him.

Tiichswii picked up his wooden whale and held it alongside the green-yellow slug, spotted all over with black.

"It is a perfect fit," Maḥtii said.

"Meant to be," Tiichswii agreed.

Indeed, the slug's slurping foot clasped onto the whale's wooden back quite capably. Tiichswii held them aloft, rocking them in the air.

"It is Thunderbird, plucking Whale from the sea," he said with glee.

She laughed and stole the pair, continuing their favorite story.

"Thunderbird drags Whale higher and higher," she said, flying the slug-glommed whale to Tiichswii's head. "To the top of the mountain!"

"Oh, hey, Maḥtii!"

She fell back to the ground laughing. "Thunderbird wins!"

Tiichswii worked his hands above his head, trying to separate slug and whale and hair. "The mountain loses." But he laughed with her.

They doubled over again as Maḥtii tried to describe the rigid flame of hair that stuck up from his head.

Then she gasped. "Bear!"

Her toy bear had been shoved against a rock during their fun. Its snout was now blunted; bare wood gleamed against its stained face. She picked it up, and looked at the broken piece in her palm.

"Do not cry, Maḥtii," Tiichswii said.

She blinked. She had not realized she was crying until he said so.

"I can fix it," he said, gently taking it from her hands. "Do not worry."

She sniffed, dragging the back of her dirty hand under her nose. She watched as he earnestly sized up the project, holding the snout in place so that the break was nearly invisible.

"Well," she said, with a sniff, "I suppose I could be your wife if you did that."

He kept his eyes on the bear, but he smiled widely. He bit his lips then, and looked at her placidly. "Perhaps we are both just interested in the bear, after all."

She giggled. He smiled. And the next moment felt suspended in time, as if they were on the cusp of glimpsing their future selves.

Distantly, Maḥtii heard her mother calling for her. But she was still swimming through the clouds in her mind, trying to come up with the thought left behind.

It came to her. She leaned toward Tiichswii. "What does lightning feel like?"

His eyes flicked over her shoulder at the adult searching her out, then snapped back to her face—intent, urgent. "I do not know," he said. "But I am going to find out."

Tiichswii leaned forward and placed his lips against her cheek. She wondered at the softness of his lips. He smelled even more like a boy this close, all dirt and sweat and salt water. She tilted her face to see him. He smiled at her, then gathered up the toys and bounded away.

"Maḥtii!" her mother called.

Maḥtii breathed out. Her hands felt empty without her bear. She stood and walked over to her mother.

"ʔe·ʔe·, that face," her mother said. She licked her thumb and scrubbed at Maḥtii's cheek. The girl groaned. Her mother licked her thumb again and went for her other cheek, but Maḥtii stopped her.

"Not there, mother," she said.

"Mm, so he has stolen it," her mother said.

Maḥtii twisted her face in confusion. "No, he is going to fix it."

Her mother raised her eyebrows. She tapped the girl's chest. "There is no fix for the heart, my girl."

"My heart?" Maḥtii looked down at her chest. "How can a heart be stolen, mother?"

"A heart can be stolen as easily as food, as slaves. As land. The things we hold closest to our hearts too—even they are not completely safe."

Maḥtii perked, remembering an earlier lesson. "Like the song!"

But her mother looked sad, not proud of her daughter's answer, and when her mother finally looked back down at Maḥtii, it was only to brush the backs of her fingers down the girl's cheek where the boy had placed his kiss.

"Yes, that is right. Words can be stolen too. Though they are the most resilient. If we are diligent."

She knelt and took Maḥtii by the shoulders. "Think of your heart like a song. They cannot steal what they do not know, what you do not offer."

Maḥtii felt prickles of fear at her mother's intensity. She nodded, and answered as she always did. "Yes, mother."

She held her mother's hand as they walked back toward the house. Maḥtii worried this was a lesson she would never fully understand. She tried, though.

"I did not give him my heart," she said quietly, almost in question.

Her mother smiled at her wistfully. "I wonder," she said. "And it would be better if you did not." Her voice took on a flat quality. "That boy could rise above his station. But your father and I will find a suitable partner who is your rank or better from another place. You will help us add to our strength by marrying well."

"And I will give that boy my heart?"

She wondered if she imagined seeing tears in her mother's eyes as the woman stared ahead. Maḥtii crept closer to her mother's side, straining to hear the answer. But her mother only opened and shut her mouth a few times, as if testing and discarding ways to answer.

They reached the doorway, and her mother stopped. The breeze made her mother's earrings swing, and tendrils of hair float as if held up by water. "Passion is a danger. A kind of greed. It leads to trouble." Her mother's palm was cold on Maḥtii's flat chest. "Keep your heart."

The creek clamored. Frost snatched at anything green. Muddy furrows were transformed into ragged, unyielding spires. It was early morning, and the light was blue as ice. Amuun'axsum's breath came out in clouds, and she trembled, though she would have trembled beside a fire. She scrubbed at her body again. There was no dirt or blood left to clean, but she scrubbed harder.

The shaman had not returned at night. Amuun'axsum slept in Ṫoopuuk's embrace near the fire, and at dawn he had filled her with himself again. She had still been pulling on a skirt when Oodahk walked through the doorway, unheeding. The nobleman listed off orders for Ṫoopuuk in preparation for their departure for Deeyuh. He spotted the still-unfinished whaler's hat among Amuun'axsum's weaving, and picked it up admiringly.

"As soon as you finish this one, make one for me," Oodahk said. "And after that, a version for my wife." He did not look for her reply, certain that it would be done. Setting the hat back down, the nobleman strode toward the doorway. "I will send your husband back in a moon or so. He can bring my hat back with him."

A wind blew over Amuun'axsum's wet body and drew her mind back to the creek. She dropped the branches, splashed out of the water, and pulled a blanket on. Her lips and toes tingled.

Eekbis was leaving the house as she returned. The shaman gave her a quick appraising look, head to toe, and nodded.

"There is fish inside for you to prepare for our morning meal," Eekbis said. "I will be back soon."

In a daze, Amuun'axsum pulled out the flat fin bone of a whale and set the fish's body atop it. She angled the knife and slit its flesh. The cut went ragged and she let the knife fall to the ground.

Wafting plumes of steam and charred smoke curled into the air from the meat when Uhpahs walked into the house.

"Oh, Quulthoo, you will not believe it!"

Uhpahs skipped over and knelt beside her on the ground.

Amuun'axsum tensed, and reached for the knife.

"Thluuch-muup decided she will return to her people after Chai's marriage, and she is willing to let me stay behind," Uhpahs said. "Suu-ahp talked to the young chief, arranged it all. Come spring, he will purchase me for a wife and— What's wrong, Quulthoo? You look sick."

Amuun'axsum cringed as she gripped the knife. "Go away..."

Uhpahs reached out, and Amuun'axsum jerked away at her touch, raising the knife between them.

"How could you?" Amuun'axsum said.

"Quulthoo, I did not think you could still be so angry with me, not over a few little words. I had thought enough time had gone by, that we could go back to how we were before, like we have each time we've had a spat." Uhpahs was perplexed, and she gently laid her hand on Amuun'axsum's wrist, drawing the knife down. "How could I not share? Aren't you happy for me?" She coaxed the knife out of Amuun'axsum's hand, and set it on the ground out of reach. "No joke about the vetch...?"

"Was that why you did it?" Amuun'axsum said through tears. "To see me given to a slave so that now you, Uhpahs, could marry a commoner and claim some kind of rank over me, even if it's stolen?"

"What are you—"

Amuun'axsum raised her hand, ready to strike with a knife that was no longer there. But one look at Uhpahs's wide-eyed face, so empty of malice—exhaustion overwhelmed everything else.

"Why did you tell her, Uhpahs? Why?"

Uhpahs tilted her head in confusion.

Amuun'axsum realized the truth. "You didn't tell her..."

"My friend, please, what happened?"

Slowly, Amuun'axsum shared about the healer confronting her, the trade deal with Deeyuh, the night and the morning with Toopuuk.

As she spoke, Uhpahs took over the cooking. The meal was done as the story was finished.

Uhpahs looked on her with sympathy. "I am relieved, I will not lie." Uhpahs waved off her forming protest. "You live. You are safe. But I already am missing you, my friend. And your hurt is my hurt."

They clasped hands, and sat together for a long while. Amuun'axsum had expended her tears, but Uhpahs cried for her.

DUSHUUW STOOD AT THE EDGE of the cliff in front of the winter house. His breath formed clouds as he looked over the bay. In his hand, he weighed one of the smooth sticks that had been used in drumming during the Tlukwaali. He reached back and hurled it over the precipice. It spun through the cold air with a whirring sound. Other men threw their own drumming sticks toward the sea. The splashes far below were silent.

Q̇otsik was not there. The young chief had left before dawn, heading over the river. Dushuuw knew that meant he must head up the mountain, even if there were other things he desired.

It had been a late night. The riot during the Elk dance was relatively short-lived but produced a moon's worth of damage. Most of it was put back in loose order. But one pair of antlers was left where it had lodged in a wall, and perhaps was there still.

After they had returned to the winter house, Buhkweeduuk and the shaman bent heads with Oodahk. Thluuch-muup joined them, and Dushuuw surmised a marriage for Chai with the Deeyuh chief's son was being arranged. Dushuuw had planned to ask his uncle about the late-night gossip he missed, catch up on the back-and-forth exchange of knowledge and goods. But he forgot, and now a desire to sleep stifled any further curiosity. The only other motivating thought, now that the distraction of the ceremonies was done, was Amuun'axsum, and she was frustratingly absent.

Neither desire could be satisfied. Q̇otsik had gone to pray, and Dushuuw was committed to shadowing his brother on the path to regaining his name—and a life with Amuun'axsum. He set out toward the forest.

First, he went to the snag. She was not there, of course. Still, he paused there, walking around its interior. He lifted a leaf from a pile against the back of the snag, half-expecting the frightened mouse to still be hiding. The remnants of a torch sat blackened in the firebox. He picked it up and started to draw on the wood, adding his first picture to the charcoal-drawn menagerie. It started with the first thing that came to mind and a sensually curved line. Catching himself—neither Amuun'axsum nor whatever power he tried to seek might appreciate that—he changed his angle and turned the drawing into a wild face.

The face seemed to laugh.

"Yes, you are right," he said, tossing the blackened stick back into the box. "I am no good at this either."

He looked about the snag. The feeling of Amuun'axsum's body against his own was seared to his memory by virtue of its fleetingness. But despite his urge to create childish graffiti, he longed for more than her flesh. He brought to mind her voice, forced his thoughts past her lips to the words that had made this dead, hollow cedar a warm haven.

He drew a breath and looked again at the charcoal-lined face. Taking up the torch, he added a sinuous tongue, extending it impossibly on—down the snag wall, then outside, wrapping around to the outer side where the charcoal line skipped over the outer bark, largely disappearing except where it crossed bright green moss. He added a forked end to the tongue. It pointed in the direction of the peak. He tossed the blackened stick aside, and followed the course he had set.

~

From the depths, Dushuuw watched the dark hull of a canoe approach.

The men with no paddles sang a song with no words. What left their mouths floated on the surface of the water like spots of color. The words rippled over the wake, wavering and soundless. His lungs burned, but he dared not breathe. He reached for the words, chest tightening, blood pounding an accelerating beat in his ears. Yet just as his fingertips drew close, the hull reached him, slicing him in two. He was consumed by the darkness. It was cold, so cold...

Dushuuw awoke with a start, clutching his chest and gasping for breath. Water splashed as he reflexively kicked. He slid out of the pool, drawing his legs out of the icy water with effort. His feet were numb. He looked up at the morning sky, reorienting himself with annoyance. Mist floated over the surface of the pool and billowed with the water at the foot of the waterfall.

Rubbing his feet to bring feeling back, Dushuuw studied the burn marks on his arms from the nettles, the cuts from hemlock. Branch and vine lay in a circular tangle, shining with frost. He moved closer to the warm embers of the hearth and shakily added wood to coax back flames. A shudder moved through his body, and he was grateful when it also moved through to his toes. Stumbling up, he began to warm himself with movement. He hobbled to the shrine and took up the stiff bearskin cloak. The skulls' vacant eye sockets stared through him. A fresh mound of dirt, topped by its carved whaler totem, was starting to sprout grass. He pursed his lips, drew the fur tighter and turned away, wishing to be gone from this place that turned his mind to seafoam.

At night, he reentered the village with no elation—and no sign of Qotsik. A dog barked before he even broke the tree line. Sawsin stood at the cliff's edge, gazing across the river to seek a sign of her husband one last time before returning to the winter house. Dushuuw groaned, but he could not bear the thought of the long return to the pool in an attempt to match his brother step for step. Instead, when he spotted Yaq and Kweelthup by a fire on the beach, he trudged downhill to join them. The fire was small, but gave a heat that felt to Dushuuw like a raging bonfire. He stepped close, letting the warmth blaze against his skin and beat back the ice.

Kweelthup lay on his back, head propped on a piece of wood as he looked up at the stars and rubbed the blanket-covered back of a sleeping child who lay on his chest. Yaq greeted Dushuuw with a smile, then turned back to winding a long rope.

The rope was thicker than Yaq's wrist, and fathoms in length. Old men had taken the tapering limbs of cedar and the fibrous roots of spruce and twisted, steamed, reduced, twisted, and spun them into a cord so strong it could tow a whale home. The rope was unfinished, but the old men were done for the day and had gone in for the night.

Dushuuw looked beyond the fire to the sea. The clouds above moved away like surf, revealing the celestial sea, where Whale, Halibut, Skate, and Shark plied the darkness. Dushuuw huddled further into the bear skin, which had finally lost some of its cold stiffness.

Yaq coiled the line more slowly.

"Think I should try a fancy mask again for some of the dances this winter? My first attempt was perhaps less solemn than what I was aiming for," Yaq said, with a hint of humor. "I want to inspire what they talk about with so many bated breaths about those northern folks. Talk of hidden pits underneath the walls. Giant bird on strings. Men sleeping on hot coals? I am starting to think they are exaggerating."

Dushuuw believed there was no trick to that last one.

But the pageantry Yaq referred to reminded Dushuuw of Amuun'axsum's memories. Masks so large, a second person had to help the dancer keep his head aloft. Twirling mechanisms had topped others, throwing off feathers with each turn of a dancer's body—bringing to mind the snow that had started to dust the peak and the hills surrounding the cape.

Dushuuw opened his cloak a bit, trying to capture the fire's heat. He smiled. "I don't know, that first fancy mask of yours was quite powerful," he quipped.

Yaq had brought out the new mask during a night of dancing. The mask—if it could be called one—was an oblong piece of wood crudely carved to resemble Mink, or so Yaq claimed. Yaq had cut the mask in two pieces, and he scampered around the house holding both pieces in front of his face. Then he stopped and dramatically "opened" the two halves of the mask to reveal—his own face. Laughs and heckles went up as Yaq gave a look of surprise and pretended to search the floor for his lost ancestor.

Dushuuw wanted to laugh at the memory, but his chest was frozen.

Yaq stopped coiling the rope and grew animated.

"Hey now, here we go," Yaq said. "We take a mask and break off its lower jaw, attach it back with wooden pins and work it like this..." He moved his hand up and down on an imaginary pole and opened and closed his jaw with exaggeration, then leaned toward Dushuuw as if to bite his head off. Dushuuw succumbed with a wheezing laugh, and Yaq sat back with a satisfied grin. "Now that will scare the shorties!"

Dushuuw reached out from under the bear skin to poke his friend, who sat bare-chested in the winter air, carrying the sun inside him.

Kweelthup remained quiet, but a soft smile brushed his lips.

"Wasn't that the same night we convinced that pack of boys they were supposed to play the part of Raccoons? Climbing all over the place, dropping through the roof. And you and I going around pricking people like Bees while they were distracted," Dushuuw said, warmed now to the company and conversation. "Father was so angry."

Yaq tried to hold in a laugh but ended up snorting instead. Dushuuw did the same in reaction, and the pair leaned forward with spurts, trying in vain to be quiet. The child stirred on Kweelthup's chest.

"He was more upset that night than when he saw our rock-carving prowess," Yaq said.

Dushuuw's shoulders shook, pent-up laughter pushing tears out his eyes. "No, no, father. It is, uh, a stone sinker, you know. Nothing more."

"Nothing I would want to sink myself into," Yaq said.

The more they struggled to contain their laughter, the longer it lasted, until finally they sat back again, their mirth spent. The friends eased into another silence, warm and full and forgiving. Kweelthup caressed the child's back.

Dushuuw's chest ached as he gazed out at the bay. Starlight and moonlight wavered on the shifting sea. The horizon, as always, lay unreachable. Dushuuw closed his eyes as he swayed and sank briefly into darkness, feeling liquid. He forced himself to take a deep breath and open his eyes.

"I had a dream," Dushuuw said, dragging the words out. He pulled the bear skin tight, trying to trap the heat of the dying fire. Tendrils of warmth slipped over his skin and out the gaps.

Yaq looked at him and his smile disappeared.

"Out with my father. Then with Q̇otsik. And again, on my own," Dushuuw said. He kept his face turned toward the sea, his eyes tracking a wave as it flowed toward and succumbed to the shore, avoiding that distant line. "Never had such a vivid dream. Or one so—" He clenched his teeth. "There was a song. But I couldn't make out the words. I knew they were important—in the dream—but I had to get away. Doesn't matter how close I get anyway; they remain silent and out of reach."

"They came back before," Yaq said. "They will come back again."

Dushuuw raised his eyebrows and gave a small shrug. He dug out a broken shell from the sand and brushed his thumb over its ridged exterior, its smooth interior. "It's probably just a nightmare. Or just my mind trying to create what I want to have, you know? Taking up bits and pieces of what others have experienced, and tossing up my own version. Like any of those fancy masks or dances—stories, too. Different versions of the same old thing. Just echoes." He snapped the shell in two ragged parts. "And who were those people? The ones who had it all figured out. Who were the people who first danced a dance, sang a song, or told a story so long ago but we still pay witness around our fires? I always wonder what they saw. The real reason for those cryptic words, movements. If we could go back to the beginning, see it as it happened through their eyes, maybe everything would make sense."

"Friend, I can barely remember what I ate this morning, much less get a clear vision of my own past. Can you?" Yaq laughed. When Dushuuw didn't respond, he shifted and coughed. "My point is, maybe they didn't even quite know. Maybe it was a mystery to them too. Maybe people—them, us—are not the point, you know?" He wrapped a length of kelp around his fingers. "The thing that comes out, it is its own thing. Doesn't have to make sense."

Dushuuw sat up from his slumped posture to hurl the shell fragments, first one, then the other. The world was a spinning disc beneath a starry sky. The shell fragments reached for a constellation, then fell into the starry reflection in the water below, first one, then the other. "Then I may as well settle for the joke rather than the real thing."

Yaq had resumed coiling the rope. He lay the end atop the pile.

"Yaq is right and wrong, I think," Kweelthup said. "The people matter."

Dushuuw had nearly forgot Kweelthup was there.

Kweelthup adjusted the blanket on his sleeping child, then nodded toward the rope. "I see those dances and songs and stories—maybe your dream too—as like ropes. They stretch out over time and the other in-between places. One person grabs on to the rope, then another, each helping to carry it on and on, maintaining that link to the source, to what really matters—towing it along through time, to keep strong."

Dushuuw stiffened, as if vacant eyes watched him from afar, as his mother's voice snaked through his memory. He flexed his fingers, grasping at air. His head swam again, vision splotching with exhaustion and hunger. He clenched his jaw. "So what if I cannot reach it?" he asked. "Or what if I let go?"

Yaq sat forward, tearing a piece of kelp into chunks as his eyes alternated between his hands and the sea, his mouth half-open in thought. Kweelthup looked at the stars. The child shifted and sighed. A foamy surge of water crept up the beach, trickling over pebbles.

~

Dushuuw lay on the ground, as if asleep.

Yaq stood over a bucket of water and pretended to piss into it. Dushuuw cracked his eyelid, to make sure Yaq's "piss" was as fake as his own "sleep."

Laughter percolated from some of the men in the crowd who sensed what was coming. Yaq picked up the bucket. As he neared Dushuuw, the rest of the crowd started to laugh. Dushuuw squeezed his eyes closed and flinched in anticipation. Those near enough to notice guffawed. Yaq dumped the bucket of water over him, and Dushuuw sat up with a bluster. He stood up, shaking off the water like a dog. The crowd roared with laughter.

It was an oil feast to fete his brother's whaling success. Dushuuw used the opportunity to turn his own failed roles in those hunts into comedy. There was no erasing the shame of those actions, but he could dispel its power by accepting it and sparking laughter.

"You are brave, brother," Q̇otsik said as he handed Dushuuw a fur.

Dushuuw patted the water from his skin and sat beside his brother.

"If I am brave, it's only because I can afford to be with everyone's stomachs so full with your halibut and whale," Dushuuw said. A man gestured at him appreciatively, and Dushuuw smiled back.

"You should give yourself more credit," Q̇otsik said. "I am not the only one who has noticed your increased discipline."

Dushuuw fought a reflexive urge to search the room for Amuun'axsum. Of course, she would not be there. He caught himself, and smiled at his brother. "I can only hope to prove myself to you."

Q̇otsik looked away with a smile. "You have nothing to prove to me. I am glad you are proving it to yourself," he said. "I wish father were here," he added. His voice was low, amid the loud rumbles of conversation around the vast house.

Dushuuw looked at his hands in his lap, then looked over. "I do, too."

The oil feast was lavish by design. Q̇otsik had brought in ten whales by hunt and drift, and nothing would delay the kind of celebration that must follow.

Slaves wove through the crowd with platters of dried halibut, dried whale blubber, and dried whale meat. Others kept wooden dipping bowls filled with rendered whale oil, glossy white and greasy. No plate was left empty for long. Guests knew they could eat their fill and still take more home with them. Q̇otsik would retain only enough food stores to get his people through the winter.

Q̇otsik led Sawsin out of the house to prepare for the next ceremony. He squeezed Dushuuw's shoulder and Sawsin smiled. Dushuuw felt his chest fill, and noted other men smile in his direction. He acknowledged each and relaxed in the glow of acceptance, even if it was based on a laugh. He wondered if there would be a day when he could erase the shame of his father's death, some act that could turn desperation and blood into a story of daring and strength.

Dushuuw scanned the room. Wiid sat with Leehuuk on the other side of the house. The war chief tried to catch Dushuuw's eye, but Dushuuw kept scanning. He still wasn't sure what to think of his old mentor after Leehuuk's attempt to steal men away from Q̇otsik. The betrayal stung.

A contingent from Deeyuh sat nearby in a place of honor. Oodahk had been invited along with his wife, their sons, and their attendant slaves. Dushuuw knew his father had planned to forge an alliance with the whaling chief by marrying Chaiyuhx-ik to the man's eldest son. Buhkweeduuk had begun paving the way again, but it would not hurt for Dushuuw to make friends himself. Especially since the man looked dangerously bored.

Sidling up to Oodahk, Dushuuw struck up a conversation about fishing, then shifted to battle stories when he saw that topic spark more interest. Dushuuw shared with Oodahk one of his closely guarded preparation practices for war. The man from Deeyuh smiled widely, his boredom giving way to eagerness. It was wise to be generous not only with food, and Dushuuw did what he could on his brother's behalf. Most of all, he did it for Chai.

As they spoke, Dushuuw snatched moments to scan the room. Since it was winter, only the closest neighbors were represented. Oodahk was the most noted guest, from Deeyuh. A healthy contingent from Deeyuh's neighbor, Bih-ihd-uh, also was in attendance. From Tsooyuhs, he spied the fighter Shuchkuk and his mind jumped to questions he wanted to ask the man later. Dushuuw spotted the shaman near the doorway, and a glimpse of Amuun'axsum just outside made his wandering eyes stop. The two women spoke, Amuun'axsum nodding to some instruction before her attention was diverted. A man appeared in the doorway facing Amuun'axsum, his back toward the house. Dushuuw watched as she looked up at the man and nodded. As she started to turn away, she noticed Dushuuw watching. Her lips parted for a moment, then she disappeared into the darkness, the man's hand at her back.

Dushuuw startled as Oodahk placed a hand on his arm. He turned his attention back to the man with a tight smile, trying to determine the value of the hunting advice the man had given him in return for the tip he gave. It was a gift he would never be able to use because he had not listened. Either way, he erred on the side of exuberant gratitude—and tried to think up an excuse to leave without offending the nobleman.

But the drums started beating.

More than a dozen women glided into the house in a line, led by Sawsin, her glossy hair loose about her face. The women ushered in Ọotsik, who sounded and spied.

Dushuuw edged past his grandmother as he returned to his seat.

A group of men followed Ọotsik, a canoe hoisted on their shoulders. They set the canoe down in the middle of the house, propping its hull so that it remained upright. Men and women filed in after them, hefting boxes and bladders full of whale oil. They dumped the oil into the canoe, one after the other, on and on.

Dushuuw sat down, his gaze going once more to the doorway, though all he could see was the unending line of men and women with vessels of oil.

The canoe was filled with oil until it overflowed.

Qotsik dipped a box into the oil. He poured oil over his wife. Over his mother. Over his sister. He anointed each of the women in the long line with oil as they approached. Streams of oil flowed. The women's slick skin reflected the light from the fires that, this night, had been set in the farthest hearths. Oil dripped off the ends of their hair, their fingers. Oil pooled at Qotsik's feet.

That night, when the festivities had ended and he could leave the house without causing offense, Dushuuw slipped into the forest and waited at the snag. He waited a long while, cutting off bits of the rotting enclosure with his dagger and tossing the bits into the firebox, imagining Amuun'axsum's body dripping with oil. His gouges in the wood became deeper. She did not come. He thought about seeking her out as he had before, then thought better of it. The shaman's house accommodated some of the guests and slaves from Deeyuh. And surely that was the warning inherent in Amuun'axsum's avoidance of him. A reminder of his promises. An urge to be patient. That they needed to be careful. He twirled the dagger, then let it fly to lodge in the bark wall.

~

Several mornings later, Dushuuw walked with Buh-uhs over the creek to seek Amuun'axsum's cooking fire. They would beg a bit of food again for the boy. The last of the guests had left the day before. The shaman was visiting with his stepmothers. Still, as they stepped inside the house, Amuun'axsum seemed skittish when she saw them. She looked as if she had not slept.

"I look forward to the warmer winds of spring," he said. He wanted to coax, to comfort—to remind.

She looked off in the direction of the shaman's living space.

"Yes," she said, as if remembering something. "I should be finished with your whaler's hat in time for the spring hunts, Young Son."

Dushuuw looked away for a moment. "That is good," he said. "You do fine work, Quulthoo."

Buh-uhs tugged on his arm, but Dushuuw kept his eyes trained on

Amuun'axsum. She did not look up. She took the cooked meat from the fire and then stood there, as if unsure what to do next.

"I am not feeling well," she mumbled. "Excuse me."

Concerned, he started to follow her out the doorway. She left behind her hat. She did not even take a cape.

"When can I see your progress on the hat?"

Amuun'axsum stopped and turned to him, though she looked off to the side. Her body was rigid. "I am afraid the moon has hold of me at the moment," she said. "You understand."

Dushuuw was startled silent. He rubbed the back of his neck.

Buh-uhs tilted his head. "I don't get it," he said.

Amuun'axsum rushed uphill. Dushuuw stood dumbly.

"I don't get it," Buh-uhs repeated.

Dushuuw cleared his throat and led the boy away without answering him.

"What about the food?"

Amuun'axsum was far ahead, and by the time they reached the winter house she was already on her way downhill again, with an empty basket this time.

As they reached the winter house, Dushuuw shoved Buh-uhs ahead of him through the doorway and got his stepmother's slave to give the boy something to eat, if only to silence the boy's questions about why they had walked so far for a snack only to come back to where they started. As Dushuuw watched the slave, he recalled that she was a friend of Amuun'axsum. The two often were together. He eyed the woman. Did she suspect? It would be another reason Amuun'axsum might avoid him. As if sensing his thoughts, the slave darted a glance his way, then turned back to her tasks for Thluuch-muup.

As the boy smacked his lips, Dushuuw left the house again into a light rain to clear his head. He strode to the cliff's edge and looked down. Amuun'axsum was there, among a group of women gathering. He watched as she navigated from rock to rock. He wondered if he had misunderstood her rebuff.

Amuun'axsum had said the moon had her in its grip. With plenty of women in the house, Dushuuw had long known what that meant. Sullen attitudes. A distinct stench. Wads of plant material soaked brown in blood. Two or three baths during the day instead of the usual one. Still, other than turning away fresh fish to eat for a few days, women in the moon of their blood were free to go about their normal tasks and interactions with family. None of the exceptions applied here—first blood, a salmon or herring run, bringing in a whale. So why did Amuun'axsum use it as a reason not to meet him?

Dushuuw watched Amuun'axsum from above. She tucked some intertidal find into her basket. Her back curved as she bent for another. Her knee poked out from the shreds of her skirt, then her thigh as she knelt lower. The sea wove its way between the black rocks all around her, rising and falling as it moved closer and closer to land.

The sea responded to the moon in ways he understood. But the moon called in hidden ways to a woman's body, leaving him baffled and intimidated.

As a boy, watching his stepmother leave with his father, Dushuuw sensed this mystery of womanhood was part of the reason for the elaborate husband-and-wife rituals that accompanied a whale hunt. A wife lent power to the hunt, tying together all those things that feel the push and pull of the moon. Yet he also remembered sulking, for despite being a woman and a wife and a giver of life, his own mother was never a partner in his father's highest prayers.

The sight of Amuun'axsum adorned like a noblewoman in the snag had moved Dushuuw. He wanted to give her that noble life in full, and in turn draw upon whatever power the moon bestowed inside her cyclic body. Strength added to strength. Yet as she stepped over the rocks, edging toward shore with the tide, he found himself equally captivated. It was in these ordinary movements that he found her most beautiful—the smooth skin of her neck when she turned her head, the way her fingers drew up a length of cedar when weaving, the way she unconsciously tipped up one side of her mouth when he traced her cheek with his thumb. He loved being the one privy to the past chronicled in her tattoo—but also to the constellation of freckles above her knee. To be the one who called her by name—but also to hear her say his name. To trace the scars on her hands, because it meant he was holding them. To know how her skin smelled, to breathe in that mixture of flowers and earth and fiber.

And yet all these tiny bits of knowledge did not add up to a whole. He still did not know her.

Women were a mystery, and that would persist, both confirmed and compounded as it was by lore. Snot Boy, after saving his sister, had climbed his rope of arrows to the Moon for a bride. If Dushuuw could go back into those mists of time before time, he would corner the boy and demand more than vague colorings. Not about the traps the boy had eluded to get the woman. But what the woman had been like when once she was held aloft, and how she had changed in her descent—whether her face was full and illumined with her husband in her new home, or whether she instead slowly faded before his eyes. What language was spoken in the Moon? Perhaps the Moon, all this time, was trying to pull his daughter back, like some cosmic contest of strength that must be played out every cycle of the moon. The boy would never be done proving himself. Because maybe it was never about the Moon's daughter. Perhaps the boy, all along, was intent only on linking himself with the Moon. A tie of marriage to replace a ladder of arrows.

Dushuuw turned away from the cliffside and its view from above of Amuun'axsum. He would take her cue, and tread lightly. He would watch for traps. But he did not know for how long he could refrain from seeking her out in a hollow of earth by moonlight.

~

In the days that followed, though, Dushuuw sent Amuun'axsum silent messages—a glance here and there, a comment in her hearing about looking forward to spring. He trolled for rockfish when he could, and prepared fishing lines when he couldn't. Showed Buh-uhs the lines used in the whaling canoe. And retreated with Yaq to refine dances and songs that they then reenacted in performances at home and in the homes of their neighbors, even if not quite to the level of their daydreams.

He learned Q̇otsik's patterns, then made sure he left before his brother on those nights spent in prayer and training.

Some days he would go to the shrine even if Q̇otsik did not go to pray. Those were the days Dushuuw left because he worried that he would forcibly carry away Amuun'axsum to make her his own, as he did so many times in his dreams—sleeping and waking—jerking to consciousness when her voice took on another's. Dushuuw found a tortuous comfort in ritual those nights, beating his body into submission, not even bothering with prayers, the sting of nettle and flaming lungs from holding his breath carrying its own petitions. Every icy dip and shudder-inducing breeze across wet skin making his yearning for spring and a fresh start that much sharper.

If he could not expend his efforts on her, he would redouble them on the other side. He would show her that he intended to keep his promise. He cradled the bundled body of a bird.

And so, the nights passed.

Until one clouded and cold winter night.

Dushuuw waited near the doorway inside the winter house, a cape over his shoulders. Ọotsik had been feeling their father's absence acutely that day. Dushuuw could tell, not because his brother said anything about their father—he did not—but because of the dance his brother asked him to give. There were no guests to entertain. No alliances being forged. There was not enough food for a feast anyway. Just a clouded and cold winter night with family resting near the warmth of their fires, whiling away the hours until sleep.

Uhpqoolth drummed for him. It was no background beat, this drumming. It did not mark the steps of the dance but its own incessant path. Uhpqoolth did not pound so much as batter the plank.

Dushuuw measured off time in his head to an entirely different count—no easy feat beneath the noise—then crouched low to the ground and took his first light step. Against the loud pounding of the drum, Dushuuw's body seemed to disappear into itself. He crouched low to the ground, wrapped in the cape with his arms tucked inward, his back arched upward. He moved, but with such small, feather-light steps that the movement almost went unnoticed. Gradually, he rose from his hunched position, moving all along in light, small steps in a tightening spiral. Until he was upright, at the terminus of the spiral, and—the loud drum still blasting—he thrust his arms outward with the cape, revealing a ceremonial club. The pose lasted only a moment. In the next, he thrust the point of the club into the ground—a movement as fast as the initial dance steps had been slow.

The drum did not change. It kept up its incessant march. And Dushuuw resumed his crouched, hidden pose, taking his small, feather-light steps, building up to the climax. Over and over, they continued. The drum beating loud. The dance rising to meet it.

Then nothing.

The dancing and drumming both stopped. The room pulsed with the echoes of the drum. Dushuuw did not dare budge for several long moments, did not dare breathe. It was the most ancient of his family's dances, tying them to the mountaintops of the mists of time. It was the one thing he could do that had drawn his father's full approval. Yet it carried the ache of loss, an ache that only seemed to grow.

38

A MIXTURE OF RAIN and snow swirled in driving winds. Waves pounded the cliffside and surged up the river, spilling over the banks. Amuun'axsum sat against a wall next to the shaman in the winter house. People from all houses in the village had made their way to the great house, bundled up against the storm, and now kept warm with stories and songs around the fires.

Laughter still bounced around the room as an old man, his flesh sagging in folds, preened in the middle of the room. White patches of hair floated from the sides of his head. His front teeth were missing, the gaps exposed by his large grin as he began to sing.

of all the things that come with old age

i look like a tufted puffin

He gestured at his white hair and proudly circled the room, pointing to the young men in the gathering.

try to become old as quickly as you can

He wriggled his hips.

i look so handsome

Groans and guffaws met the comedian's gyrations, as he shook the various parts of his body and flapped his arms.

Across the room, Buhkweeduuk stood and sang loudly in response.

stop singing

they are beginning to make fun of you

Amuun'axsum's laughter joined that of the rest of the crowd. The old man shook his fist at one and all, and shuffled back to a seat, a grin still stretching across his face.

The shaman took a lid off a box at their feet. Amuun'axsum's smile morphed into a grimace. The forceful scent of boiled urchin seemed to smash her nose up into her forehead. When would this sudden impulse to recoil at the smells of good food end? Eekbis eyed her knowingly. At least the old woman had lightened up on the duties she gave Amuun'axsum. It was a rare day she had not been sent into the forested flanks all the way above Deeyuh with a burden basket, no matter the weather. Amuun'axsum leaned her head against the wall, convincing herself it was cooler. She brushed her hand over her stomach.

Clumps of children scrambled about the house. Forced indoors, the children's energy multiplied. They fed off each other. Now, the gray-haired storyteller Hawitsuksh gathered them all in the middle of the room. His myriad grandchildren were the first to plop down on the ground at his feet.

Hawitsuksh rubbed his hands together, and gave a preamble. "Q̓watee could do everything." He shrugged. "Sometimes he was a layabout. But when it got down to it, he would be the one to save us." The story of Wuh-uhch's most famous cultural hero may have been for the children, but Hawitsuksh spoke in a way for all to hear. The storyteller's voice was trained to rise above the rustling and chatting, to banish all other noise to the background for those willing to listen.

The storyteller leaned forward, raised his eyebrows, and held up his palms toward the children who held their breath, eyes widening with the storyteller's, waiting, waiting, waiting. Then Hawitsuksh clenched his hands shut, and began.

"There was a sea monster living under Chahdee. Nobody could go out and fish, because the sea monster would come out and swallow them up, canoe and all. So Q̓watee got ready. It took him a long time. He made mussel-shell knives. He dug a hole, poured in water, and threw in fire-hot stones. He bathed in the water, training, until the hot water burned off all of his hair. Then he was ready. He went out in his little canoe. He could tap, tap the side and it would go. He attached spikes all around. He went up to the monster, singing,

> *i am not afraid of you*
> *i am not afraid of you*

"The sea monster swallowed Q̓watee, canoe and all, just as Q̓watee knew it would. The spikes on the canoe made it lodge in the monster's throat. Q̓watee could feel the sea monster's heart, thumping. He took his bag of mussel-shell knives and started cutting toward the heart, to cut it out, going through knife after knife until the last one broke. He used his teeth for the last cut, and the sea monster was finished off. The monster drifted onto the beach. The people were so hungry—the sea monster had kept them off the water, so they could not eat. They were so hungry that they immediately began cutting into it. It was like a whale, but covered in hair. As they cut it open, a little man walked out."

The children laughed and exclaimed. A boy flopped his arms and pretended to be covered in sea monster bile, earning a disgusted slap on the arm from a girl, who nonetheless fought off her own smile.

Hawitsuksh wended his way from one Q̓watee story to another, until he grew tired. But the children's energy was not satisfied.

"Another story! Another story!"

Hawitsuksh laughed and shook his head. He promised to tell another story after others had their turns. Day slipped to night as people traded songs and stories. Amuun'axsum tried to keep her eyes open as she listened to Beaver's song that floods everything, of the birds that distracted Deer with their dance, of a trapped bird with no wings to fly away because she was now human.

His voice rested, Hawitsuksh was back at the center of the room, to everyone's pleasure. His next story started with Woodpecker, who lived with his wife at Wuh-uhch.

"One day he told his wife to get ready and they would go over to visit the neighboring village. They traveled there, and Woodpecker took his wife to a little tree, made her get up in the high branches, and cut off all the lower branches so she could not get down. He went home and left her there."

Eekbis cracked open the urchin. Amuun'axsum pulled aside a mat that hung behind her, seeking the cold draft it blocked.

"His wife had nine brothers, and the next day they went to the ocean to shoot ducks. One of the men shot a duck and it went toward the shore. They followed it, and when they came near the shore, they heard a woman crying and singing."

Amuun'axsum opened her eyes and looked back toward the storyteller, who shifted from flowing prose to a broken and halting song.

o brothers,

here,

he has put me in the treetop

The storyteller moved seamlessly back into the story, his voice falling to its normal register.

"The men in this canoe recognized their sister's voice. The men came ashore and found red strawberries growing around the foot of a tree. The oldest brother tried to climb the tree and reach his sister, but he could only go up two steps. The next-to-oldest tried. The third brother climbed one step higher, and the fourth brother went up four steps. The fifth, sixth, seventh, and eighth brothers climbed five steps and slipped back. The ninth brother was a hunchback, who loved to eat strawberries all the time, and he seemed indifferent for he was busy eating the strawberries. The oldest brother told him, 'We do not expect you to succeed, but you must try.' He threw the hunchback against the tree and the little fellow made a chattering sound with his lips and took the form of a squirrel."

The storyteller's voice bounced, singing to a simple rhythm.

my ƚume·nuwis is the squirrel

He called for everyone to join him after the first time through, and again between each phrase. "Sing! Sing louder!"

Children joined their voices to that of the adults, giving the squirrel-hunchback the voice of a giant. Amuun'a̱xsum's added her quiet voice, smiling.

The storyteller held up his hands to shush them and continued, leaning forward and looking around at the young ones who still wiggled with pleasure.

"The woman was hung between two trees, one hand tied to each tree—and the strawberries that the hunchback ate were her tears. When he untied the twisted cedar boughs that fastened her arms, she was stiff and helpless. So, he put her across his shoulders and brought her down in that way. When she had been healed, they told her to return to her husband, and to wait, for they would find a means of revenge..."

A tear rolled down Amuun'a̱xsum's cheek and slid between her lips, salty sweet.

Uhpahs brought more food from Thluuch-muup to give to the shaman. She gave Amuun'a̱xsum a gentle, searching look. Amuun'a̱xsum gave her a weak smile but looked away. She reached into her basket of materials, and drew out the knob she was weaving to get a start on the Deeyuh chief's whaler's hat. She tried to concentrate on the tight weave as the night wore on and on. She was so tired.

Despite her excuse to Dushuuw days earlier, the moon for her bleeding had passed with no blood. She kept carrying her wad of absorbent plant material in her work baskets, in hopes of feeling the familiar cramps. It was for naught, and each wave of nausea pushed through her denial.

Amuun'a̱xsum held up the knob of the hat again, but the fine weave taunted her clumsy fingers. Instead, she took up a fish net no one had requested but that she had started to make anyway. She twisted and wrapped strands of nettle fiber in a stranglehold. Inside her midsection, she felt only a familiar tension. When she looked up, the shaman was staring at her hands. The old woman's eyes shifted to meet her own.

"How do you fare, Eekbis?"

Both women looked up to find Dushuuw standing over them with a lopsided smile. Amuun'axsum flushed, and hoped the people surrounding them would take it for the heat of the house. She looked down at her work as the shaman and Dushuuw traded pleasantries.

"Was there something you needed, Young Son?" Eekbis asked.

"I was hoping your slave could set aside whatever she is working on at the moment and fix this for me," he said. "I would like it done tonight."

Dushuuw held a hat out—that awful first hat, with its wilted top.

Her eyes shifted to the shaman, then down to her lap again. "I know it has taken a while," she said. "But I will finish your new hat soon…"

"Yes, I am sure it is looking fine." He cleared his throat. "However, in the meantime, you can fix this one—tonight. You see, the band is loose."

The shaman took the hat from him. "Of course she will, Young Son." She slapped it against Amuun'axsum's shoulder. "Get to it, Quulthoo."

Dushuuw turned to other guests nearby and struck up a conversation. He would not stray far. Amuun'axsum was mindful of the shaman, who had shifted closer to her on the bench. As she fumbled with the band—which Dushuuw had clearly loosened himself—Amuun'axsum spied Uhpahs, who looked between the three of them before returning to her own tasks. Amuun'axsum finished the fix and handed the hat to the shaman.

The shaman and Dushuuw conversed for a time. Amuun'axsum focused on folding up the net twine. Soon, Dushuuw moved on.

"He was supposed to stop seeking you out," the shaman whispered, her words curt.

Amuun'axsum allowed herself to look at Dushuuw's back as he walked away; the shaman could say nothing against that. As she watched, Buh-uhs bounded up and hopped on Dushuuw's back, catching him unaware. Dushuuw flipped the boy over his shoulder and held the boy by the legs, walking through the crowd so that the boy had the floor for a roof. The world seemed to spin for Amuun'axsum as well, as she gave the twine a long, spiteful tug. Why couldn't the baby inside her be his? Now, no matter where the baby was born—in Deeyuh, or Lohta—the baby's slave-born father would seal a lower status.

Unless…

Dushuuw turned, his face in profile, smiling as he looked down at Buh-uhs; he set the boy on the floor. Amuun'axsum's hands stilled, and the twine unfurled to her feet.

DUSHUUW SWATTED BUH-UHS away and sat beside Q̇otsik as the storyteller finished his tale. It was a risk to approach Amuun'axsum in public, but it had been weeks since he had last been with her alone. He felt the old twitch of anger at her repeated rebuffs of his signals to meet; worse, he was beginning to worry. When he had turned away, he noticed his stepmother's slave girl watching them—Amuun'axsum's friend. Or once-friend?

A yawn passed over several of the children like a wave, one starting up after the other. The very young already were asleep in their mothers' and grandmothers' laps. Even Buh-uhs fought heavy eyelids, and laughed when the adults laughed. Pikoo cradled Blubs in her lap as Buhkweeduuk leaned against her and stroked their son's hair. Pikoo put her face alongside the sleeping boy, her lips moving in whispers. Even in his sleep, the mother spoke for the boy, imbuing him with dreams of success and love.

Nearby, another small boy—the only one who remained wide awake, back straight as a spear—tried to match the storyteller's singing.

Dushuuw nudged Q̇otsik. "Listen to him get the words wrong."

Q̇otsik smiled and shrugged. "He sings because we sing."

Dushuuw thought about the snag, and the hours of darkness that stretched ahead before the adults would finally call it a night. He searched for a distraction. Several benches away he spied Sawsin, visiting with other women. She brushed her fingers over the decorative comb in her hair, turning to smile at her husband.

"Are you still worried about losing her, brother?"

Q̇otsik gazed at his wife a beat longer, then turned to Dushuuw with a smile. "No, I do not think I am worried about that anymore."

Dushuuw shoved his brother with his shoulder.

"Are you—disappointed at all?" Q̇otsik asked. "That I married before you marry again? You joke, but I wonder sometimes."

"I am glad it is you," Dushuuw said. "Besides, I could never draw the kind of look from a woman that Sawsin gives every time you appear."

Q̇otsik smiled, and he looked a bit relieved. "But you cannot tell me, brother, that there is no woman you do not have your eye on." He lowered his voice. "If your forays into the woods were not so long and so full of scars, I would wonder at the real reason."

Dushuuw wished Yaq were there for that one. Instead, he swallowed the joking reply. Better to focus on being the matured brother, the humbled brother—which he was finding, with each night of prayer, to be possible in truth.

"I am finding that I can be more patient than I thought," he said, with a touch of wonder.

Q̇otsik shook his head. "And you are avoiding the question, Young Son."

Dushuuw's smile disappeared at the sound of the name. Q̇otsik sensed his offense, and the pair sat for a time looking about the house.

"You know," Q̇otsik ventured, "men often change their names when they marry or accomplish some big goal, like an oil feast. I decided I would not. Not yet, anyway. Still, I think it would be the right time for a naming. So that, when the first whale of spring arrives, it is with a crew where my brother is again called Dushuuw."

The skin on Dushuuw's arms tingled.

Q̇otsik sensed his next question. "You will need to use that patience awhile yet, brother. We are not the only ones still getting used to father being gone. But before the first whale hunt. That, I can promise."

Words still refused to come to Dushuuw's mouth, so he simply grabbed his brother's shoulder.

Their aunt walked past, cradling her boy's head against her shoulder as she headed to their partitioned space on the far end of the winter house. The space was near Amuun'axsum, and as Dushuuw's famished gaze rested on her she gave a slight nod, then turned to the weaving in her lap. He was unsure he saw correctly, but his heart sped up, adding to the euphoria of his brother's promise. Another storyteller had started up, however, and he would have to wait to find out.

~

Dushuuw reached the snag and shivered as he waited. He tried to rid the space of its pervasive feeling of disuse. He dislodged spider's webs, brushed leaves and dirt from the mats. He turned at the sound of her footfalls. A small torch lighted her face. She looked tired. He took the torch from her to put in the firebox. She looked about the forest with searching eyes.

"It has been too long," he said, drawing her into the snag.

Amuun'axsum didn't exactly resist the gesture, but she was rigid.

Dushuuw started to let go, but she held onto him, popped up on her toes, and kissed him. His greed to have her, fueled by the long separation, clouded his head. He felt her cloak shift away, but was unsure if he had pulled it apart or she did. Her breasts crushed against his chest. His body responded, and she pressed herself closer, the shredded lengths of her skirt parting for him. She was insistent, and she was silent.

Dushuuw groaned and, with effort, shook his head, agonizing over his mind's and his body's opposite demands. In a fumbling effort at gentleness, he pushed her away to gain distance.

"Amuun'axsum..."

"I do not want to wait anymore, Dushuuw," she said. Yet her face told a different story. She tried to hide it by resting her head against his chest. Her breath came in hot bursts. "I cannot wait until spring."

Dushuuw again fought the urge to abandon thought and focus only on the permission she was giving him. But he knew her better than that. He was both proud that he knew, and worried as a result.

"What is wrong, Amuun'axsum?"

Her body constricted, as if she were sick. But her hands caressed up his thighs. Dushuuw fought off the fuzziness taking over his head. He grew angry.

"Stop," he said. He gently pushed her away. "First you tell me I would well nigh kill you if I took you while you are considered a slave. Now you throw yourself at me."

Her shoulders slumped and she placed her arm over her chest.

Dushuuw put her cloak back on her shoulders. "What is wrong?"

She shook her head, unable to speak. He thought about waiting, but remembered the good news. The type of news that enabled him to be more patient than he could ever have believed himself capable.

"I have something to share that will comfort you," he said. "If you could have heard my brother. Everything is heading the right direction for us. A little longer, and I shall be able to redeem you myself, as a man should." He wanted to kiss her again. He didn't trust himself to, and instead caressed her cheek. "You will be my wife, and everyone will call us by name. I will drape you in finery, and we will have a whole brood of children who will be the best warriors and weavers the coast has seen."

But she shook her head at each one of his words. "Even so, make me your wife now," she said, placing her hand over his at her cheek. "Just for us." She held his hand and touched the tip of her tongue to his palm. Her breath made hot pulses on his skin.

For a heady moment, Dushuuw indulged again in the idea of doing as she asked. Then he took a deep breath and held both her hands down at her sides. "On any other night, I would flatten you in my eagerness to meet that request," he said. "But you are not yourself, Amuun'axsum. You do not look well. I should not have made you come out here. Go back, and sleep. We can talk, maybe tomorrow night." He rubbed his thumbs over her hands, and gave them a squeeze. "Winter is almost over. Spring is near. Everything will change then for the better."

She stared at his chest, saying nothing. He pressed his lips to her forehead. When he could do that and stay calm, he bent and allowed himself to kiss her neck to breathe in her scent. He kissed her lips, and she raised her face in response, so that the kiss deepened.

Dushuuw pressed his forehead to her own. "Do you still trust me?"

Amuun'axsum looked up at him with eyes as wide as moons, glistening. "I am leaving soon," she said. "I am being sent to Deeyuh."

Dushuuw went cold.

"A trade deal. I go in the spring, but I already belong to Oodahk."

"I will talk to my uncle—"

"No. It is done. And you promised to say nothing about me."

"But—"

"Don't you see? I do not need your help anymore. I am afraid this means the ransom will be Oodahk's instead of yours. I thought I could at least give you..."

Dushuuw fumbled to grab the word flying about his mind: "Stop."

"...one night, in thanks for all you have done for me."

"Stop."

"Take your fill of me. It costs neither of us anything."

"*Stop*—"

If she were sad, she did not show it. Her chin was raised, though she did not meet his gaze. Countless questions came to his head, but strongest was the one he feared most.

"You were using me all along?"

"No..."

"Do I mean anything to you?"

"Yes..." She lowered her cloak and tried to press herself to him again.

Confusion boiled up into anger, and he wrenched her away by her wrists. He was hurting her, but he could not seem to loosen his grip.

"Farewell, Dushuuw. I have no further use for this place. It is yours," she said. "And do not speak to me again—unless it is at Loḥta. ... I will still be waiting for you at the end."

He made himself release her, barely hearing her last words, which she had whispered. He fixed his gaze on the snag wall, to the smeared and broken images in charcoal.

"I need you to trust me too," she said.

When he looked back, she was gone. She had taken her cloak, but had not bothered to take the torch. He strode to the opening of the snag, then stopped. He wanted to follow her, refuse her demands to stay away. He wanted to drag her before his uncle, and pay for her that night—whatever price his uncle asked. Even though he knew that price. He would give up his place in the family to take her and go, to find their own way to Loḥta, or to a place to which neither of them had any ties, to make a new life. But it was this thought that made him stop. Because it was a price he could not pay.

His brother's promise still pulsed warmly at the back of his mind. The name. The name returned would mean a life in good standing returned. He could do anything then. He could buy her back under his own power—be it at Deeyuh or Loḥta. He had learned to be patient.

Anger still filled him, though. And he did not know where to aim his rage—at her, at his uncle, at himself. Even his sister crossed his mind, since undoubtedly Amuun'axsum's sale had been part of the ongoing effort to see Chai married well. Dushuuw groaned as his emotions warred within him.

And there was still a lot of night left.

So he did not follow her. Instead, he turned away and went to the waterfall and the pool. The air was already cold, heavy with the earlier storm, and grew more frigid as he ascended; but his mind whirled with other thoughts and worries and desires.

At the edge of the pool, he tilted his head to look up to the hole of sky. Bunched-up clouds gave way and made their own hole to the farther reaches of the night, where a dim blanket of stars wavered alongside a waxing moon. Dushuuw closed his eyes and tried to draw the spare moonlight to his mind and blot out the needling thoughts of uncertainty and confusion. He thought of his brother, and of the honor he was forging for himself here in this place. He drove the torch upright into the sand for a light, discarded his fur-lined robe, and stood before the shrine.

He painted his face as his father had taught him, spoke the words as his brother had taught him, then waded into the icy pool. Looking up at the stars, he sank backward and submerged. He stayed underwater until his lungs burned like fire, drowning desire and doubt. He stayed at the pool, until he could send his anger away and focus on hope.

~

In the morning, he woke with a start. Shadows of dead men and a murderous wake pierced his mind, as the cold and fresh wounds pierced his body. He winced and propped himself up on his elbow, reaching out with his other arm to add wood to the fire. Birds twittered and cawed as the waterfall-churned pool lapped at the gravel. Morning frost clung to salal leaves. He winced, and laid back again, taking in the shrouded sky, trying to determine what took him out of the dream this time.

A dark form crossed his peripheral vision. Dushuuw remained on his back, trying to keep his body still, and slowly turned his head to the side. A small, dark bird hopped about in random short bursts. As it squeaked and sputtered, the bird kept its slender wings raised—as if still gliding in the air—and kicked up rocks and leaf and dirt with its webbed feet. It raised and lowered its forked tail.

Dushuuw finally placed the bird after several moments, his memory dulled by ritual and context. He had seen the dark bird rarely, but always—always—far out at sea, gliding over the water on its way to the same shots of spray as men in whaling canoes.

"There is no whale here, friend," he murmured. "This is no sea."

The petrel made a guttural drumming, as if to contradict a weak human's puny assertions. The bird flew in a circle over the pool four times, bobbing up and down over its surface, and then went up, tracing the waterfall's downward rush, and flew away.

A black feather fluttered near Dushuuw's head. It stuck out of the mud at an angle, left behind.

40

SHE HAD TO RETURN to the village. She started to—but had he listened?

So Amuun'ax̱sum didn't leave, but lingered among the trees, looking back on all that had been. The top of the snag shown with torchlight. Dushuuw stood in its ragged opening, blocking the light. He faced her general direction, but they were lost to each other in shadows. The set of his shoulders against the light showed he warred within himself, as she warred within herself. Would he count the cost, as she did? What path would he choose?

He should leave by another path. But she wanted him on her own.

She thought of everything she should have said to him in the snag, everything she would say now if he came after her. About the man who would be her husband. The persistent ache she still felt for Dushuuw in spite of the dangers. The need to have him take her now, to have first claim on her body as he did her heart. She would tell him again how, if he still wanted to seek her out in Lohta despite his family's rejections, she would be waiting. Because there was a cord binding her to him, and she felt its persistent tug. She would tell him everything—except that there was a child already growing inside her body. Time would pass, and when her stomach started to protrude, he could believe he had implanted the seed. He would want her all the more for the child. And they would live in their corner, with a son or a daughter to whom they could pass on their wealth. Songs. Dances. Names.

The light moved as Dushuuw left the snag, torch in hand. He paused, then turned toward a trail that led uphill and away from the village.

Amuun'ax̱sum fought the weight that wanted to drag her to the dirt as she watched him weave away among the trees.

In her fatigue and desperation, she had taken a direct approach, counting on his passion. She should have known.

The goal was accomplished. But not the dream.

Dushuuw became harder to track, his torch a tiny, wavering star.

A line from an old story ran through her head.

Deep, deep, deeper...

The tiny light guttered out.

Trembling, she made her stumbling way back to the village. She entered the shaman's house.

Eekbis sat waiting.

Amuun'axsum paused in the doorway. Then she pulled on an old blanket with one edge trimmed in squirrel hides—a gift left by Toopuuk—and came near the fire.

"It is done," she said.

Eekbis breathed a tired sigh of relief, and nodded her approval. But the old woman remained stiff, and wary.

~

Once again, Amuun'axsum was glad for work, this time for all the ways she could prevent herself from looking for Dushuuw.

The wind off the bay whipped through her skirt as she walked toward the surf, a bundle in her arms. Fishermen trolled for spiky-finned rockfish. The fresh meat, along with shellfish, offered some variety to the standard winter diet of dried whale, dried halibut, dried berry cakes—what remained of it, that is—all eaten in the dry, contained air of fire-warmed houses.

Amuun'axsum delivered her completed net to a surprised fisherman, picked at random at his beached canoe, then poked around for periwinkles where the higher rocks were no longer blasted by splashes of sea. The shaman desired the winter treat, which was hard to come by. Amuun'axsum also sought clams for Uhpqoolth's wife at the shaman's request. Ootsihd, large with child, had been having pains of late. The baby would come soon, and the new mother would need rich milk to feed the child. A dark line bisected the woman's pregnant stomach, and Amuun'axsum dreaded what lay in store for her own skin. Already, it was as if her body were no longer her own. Pains cramped her gut. She wondered if the *tibu·t* root she ate—like fire on her tongue—was doing its awful work.

A dog whined and ran in distressed circles on the beach by the bay.

"May I gather here with you?"

Amuun'axsum looked over and saw Uhpahs. Her friend held out a periwinkle, a tiny offering. Amuun'axsum slowly reached out and accepted the shelled delicacy. Uhpahs smiled, and each lifted a periwinkle to her mouth. Amuun'axsum sucked out the briny, smooth flesh. She gave Uhpahs a tired smile. Uhpahs sighed and looked as if she wanted to ask questions. Amuun'axsum shook her head, tired of even thinking about all that lay ahead.

A man waded in the water near them, returning from fishing. Uhpahs stood up straight and waffled between turning to him and keeping herself focused on her friend. Suu-ahp smiled at her shyly, and she beamed in response before turning back to Amuun'axsum and trying to dampen her joy.

"I am glad to see the vetch worked," Amuun'axsum said.

She made herself smile, to reinforce the truth, and to see it reflected on her friend's face.

DUSHUUW BROKE THROUGH the forest line at midday. The day was spring-like, a lie that came between cold snaps. The mild weather drew nearly everyone outside. Dushuuw searched for Amuun'axsum. On the walk back from the shrine, he had decided to ignore her demand to never speak. He would be careful. But he would get answers that satisfied him. He did not see her, but he did spot Yaq.

Yaq eyed the large cloak Dushuuw used to hide the fresh signs of ritual, but tactfully said nothing.

"We are getting ready to put in the support poles for Qotsik's new house," Yaq said. He nodded toward the clusters of men who dug large pits near the existing support posts of the deceased whaler's old house. The winter storm had shoved a number of large drift logs onto the beaches, and men had identified ones large and strong enough to serve as house posts. Come spring, the high ground's large winter house could be re-created on the low ground too. Qotsik and Buhkweeduuk would remain under the same roof.

"I will lend a hand," said Dushuuw, grateful his friend sensed his need for distraction. "Give me a moment."

He went up to the winter house. Qotsik was in the far house corner. The whaler's shoulders shifted as he worked at some unseen task. Qotsik turned at Dushuuw's approach, looked him up and down, and smiled. Dushuuw scanned the bench in front of his brother. Supplies were laid out. Though few, they indicated the whaler was preparing to leave—and not for a short while.

"It is certainly cold out," Qotsik said. He slapped Dushuuw's back, and smiled as Dushuuw gritted his teeth to avoid wincing. "Just checking." He slapped his brother harder.

Dushuuw shook his head, but basked in his brother's pride. "And you. Going 'fishing,' I see," Dushuuw said. He swapped out the fur for a lighter cloak, pinning it in place.

Q̇otsik gave him a knowing smile and hoisted the strap of the small basket—too small even for fishing tackle—to his shoulder. A faint rattle sound came when it settled against his side.

"You have been doing so much 'fishing' yourself, I find I need to keep up," Q̇otsik quipped.

Q̇otsik gave Sawsin a lingering kiss. Then the brothers walked together downhill, and Q̇otsik continued on, fording the river, then trekking into the forest beyond to the small lake where he had been building up his and Sawsin's prayer spot.

Dushuuw looked down into one of the empty pits that would hold a new house post. Yaq hopped inside to measure its height. He flopped his elbows over the lip of the hole that reached his shoulders. Huh-uuk toted over large rocks that would help hold the posts upright. Kweelthup paced off the length of a planned wall. From their perch on a nearby drift log, Buhkweeduuk and Kuhbuhtup consulted each other and, shaking their heads, sent Kweelthup a few paces closer in from his last mark.

Hawitsuksh ambled over to join the group and admire the progress. "I wonder what Q̇otsik will have carved on the house posts," the storyteller mused.

"Oodahk put in a support pole that is carved—from ground to rafters—into a man holding up the sun, with the moon under his feet," Buhkweeduuk said. "And that was just one of them."

"What I want to know," said Yaq, heaving himself out of the pit, "is why we cannot have a buxom woman for once?" He cupped his hands in front of him, as if massaging a woman's breasts. "There's a vision to go to sleep to on those late nights, hey?"

"A wooden woman is all you can hope for," Uhpqoolth said.

Yaq smiled as the men laughed, but for once had no adolescent comeback. Instead, his response was remarkably serious in tone. "Not anymore, my friend."

The group reacted with a mix of amusement and bafflement.

Dushuuw's heart sank a bit as he looked over at his friend. "You married? Who?"

Yaq was disappointed. "You've met her," he said.

Dushuuw looked off at the beach and maintained a fake smile, finally recalling a woman who had indeed been at Yaq's side more often than not since the summer trading trip.

"I suppose Huh-uuk will be next," Buhkweeduuk said.

Huh-uuk wiped his brow, having finished his pile of near-boulders.

"No," he said, his mouth lifting to one side. "I sort of like being chased. They bring me lots of treats."

"You are the wisest of us all," Hawitsuksh said.

The wind shifted, and carried a distant, pained cry down the cliff.

Uhpqoolth paled and glanced uphill.

Hawitsuksh walked over to the expectant father and rested his hand on his shoulder. "Your wife is strong. Your baby will be too."

Dusk made its swift passage, bringing the winter cold back with it, but many people remained below, away from the birthing woman's cries, enjoying the otherwise quiet night. Small children ran about at the frenzied pace that comes before fatigue. Buh-uhs raced other young boys. They kicked at each other, threw rocks, pulled hair. Girls shrieked and skipped, or strolled with bent heads to mimic the marriageable girls they admired.

One girl's shriek rose above the noise as she pointed at a line of mice skittering into the forest. A little boy sucked noisily at his fist, in denial of being sleepy, and dragged a shriveled length of snake skin.

42

IN THE DARKNESS of night, the woman's chilling cries of pain met Amuun'axsum before she lifted the flap to enter the small hut.

Ootsihd's birth was not going well, and the shaman had been called to help. The cries of pain were normal; all birthing women struggled. Yet the look the shaman gave Amuun'axsum—the fact that the shaman had summoned Amuun'axsum at all—confirmed something was amiss.

The hut was small, with thin walls made of woven mats. But there was a fire, and it was warm.

Ootsihd sat on the small, heavily padded birthing bench, and leaned back against its pole backrest. Her mother, who had arrived from Tsooyuhs earlier, wiped her sweaty brow. Her mother-in-law gave her a drink of warm yarrow-infused water. A slave girl added a fresh pile of shredded cedar bark to the ground beneath her legs. The air smelled of discharge and urine.

Eekbis held a frond of lady fern. As she stripped the leaves from the stalk with a swift downward motion, the shaman prayed for the baby to slip as easily. Pounding the stems, the shaman turned to Amuun'axsum. The old woman kept her voice even, soothing. "The special oil I keep, to ease a child's passage out of the mother's body—it is in the small bladder container above my storage box."

"And on your way back," Pikoo added, "go to the winter house and find the bowl I left out on my storage bench. It has been used in many successful births, and will hold the oil well."

Amuun'axsum left the hut, crossed the small patch of meadow, and hurried downhill, torch in hand.

Above the beach, several men were still working on the placement of new house posts by the light of a bonfire, the birthing woman's nervous husband among them. Though her task was urgent, Amuun'axsum felt her eyes tugged toward Dushuuw, whose arms drifted at his sides as he watched her pass. She chastised herself for looking at him—he must not see any messages that could not be sent—and tore her eyes away as she picked up her pace. Her feet pounded across the bridge over the creek.

The shaman's house corner was a jumbled mess, and Amuun'axsum was glad the oil was easily found among the hanging items in the rafters. As she stretched high to untie it, she thought of Ootsihd, and felt as if the life inside her own body swelled in response. The fiery root she had eaten continued to fail. She wondered if it was because some part of her did not want it to succeed. No prayers had been said.

Rather than risk seeing Dushuuw again, Amuun'axsum went back uphill by another path. Her feet slid in the mud, but she kept her footing.

Inside the brightly lit winter house, Blubs toddled across the floor in search of his mother. Thluuch-muup lifted her nephew and deposited him back near her own living space—where Sawsin stretched out her arms for the boy—only to watch him toddle away as soon as his feet touched the dirt, starting the process over again. Not even Yahbis could keep the little one's attention. Uhpahs chased the boy this time, tossing Amuun'axsum a smile as they encountered each other in the corner where the boy normally took his naps.

"You have been called to help with the birth too?" Uhpahs asked. Blubs fussed against her arms.

"Yes, we hope these will help," Amuun'axsum said, tipping the oil from the sea lion stomach into Pikoo's bowl. As she started to cross the house, she sighed—it would have been far quicker to take both to the hut and fill the bowl there. As it was, she now had no free hand for the torch. At least the hut was close. She walked carefully, so as to spill none of the oil.

Thluuch-muup placated the still-fussy boy in Uhpahs's arms, waving a drumming stick in front of his face. Blubs giggled and reached for it, and proceeded to bang out a hapless tune on a cutting board.

Amuun'axsum skirted a hearth and neared the doorway. A shudder ascended through her body. The oil in the bowl quivered. She gripped the bowl more securely. But the oil trembled more, shuddering up the edges of the bowl. Amuun'axsum stopped and gazed at the liquid, perplexed. Ripples of sound seemed to reach her ears through her feet, and she looked about the house.

A wooden loom rattled against a storage bench. The top of the chief's large ceremonial plank slapped against the wall boards, as if the Thunderbird struggled to take wing. Amuun'axsum's legs went from a dull shudder to a stumble. Blubs paused his drumming to intone loudly, marveling at the way his voice vibrated without any special talent on his part. His prolonged tones were stymied by his giggles. Yet the boy's giggles soon turned to tears as the earth shook more strongly. Amuun'axsum was pulled to the floor near a hearth. She cried out. The bowl toppled from her hands. The oil spilled, touched the fire's edge, and flared into a rivulet of flames.

Paddles and spears toppled. Feathers puffed through clouds of dust and dirt. Sealskin floats spun wildly from the rafters, casting dizzying shadows. The women's faces became pictorial reliefs, flashing in and out of view—their eyes like plates, their mouths dark boxes. Blubs cried for his mother.

Water sloshed over the edges of a bucket. Amuun'axsum crawled over and clumsily tipped it at the oil-fueled flames. The oil only flared further and spread. She dropped the bucket and grated her fingers through the dirt, trying to fling it over the flames. But the ground was compact as stone, and she could not stay upright even on her knees. The boy's cries grew louder.

And still the earth churned.

A dish of oil fell into the fire near the chief's corner. Flames flashed, illuminating the wings and black eye of Thunderbird, and the horrified face of Sawsin. On the ground, Blubs cried beside the prone body of Thluuch-muup.

Again, a line from the old story struck her memory.

By that wrath...

Her breaths chased over top each other. She was transported to another place. Flashes of fire, rattling walls, shouts and confusion, loved ones disappearing as she hid inside a cedar box, fear clawing—

She screamed, and crawled toward the doorway.

The earth still shook. She both felt and heard the thundering shudders coursing through the house, cutting a vibrating path through her body as she dragged herself to the doorway and clung to its edge. She drove her fingernails into the thin grooves of the wood. In front of her, a portion of the cliff's grassy edge broke off and disappeared. It wasn't much, but enough to change the view. The smooth blackness of the sea appeared to grow before her eyes, as if coming for the high ground itself.

The sea had come...

"The sea is coming."

So high...

A loud rumble coursed through rock and dirt, tremble upon

tremble. A series of tremendous crashes sounded as a portion of a neighboring house collapsed. Some of its roof planks bounced and skidded down the hillside. A wave of screams went up. The shadowed form of a man staggered from the wreckage, hands on his head—before he disappeared over the cliff.

Amuun'axsum cried out, then squeezed her eyes shut. The earth crumbled further. Trees creaked in strain; some collapsed with cracks. Her fingers scraped down the doorway. "The sea is coming..."

By that wrath...

Thunderbird stirred up his storm because the people had chosen another. Amuun'axsum opened her eyes and glared at the darkness.

Fight...

She dug her fingers into the doorway's edge again and started to drag herself up despite the earth's protest.

Until at last...

The earth stilled. There was silence for a moment. Then gasps and exclamations. Behind her, Blubs's wailing filled the room.

"The sea is coming," she whispered. Not part of the story, yet somehow the story's most essential part. Were they the storyteller's words? Were they part of the lesson that followed? It was as if she were remembering someone else's experience of the world, the memory too small a shard to grasp.

Rises and rises and rises still more...

Amuun'axsum's throat burned with the rising sense of expectation—of something coming, something unseen, her mind flashing with images of blood and smoke. Danger. And like all dangers, there was one response: Run.

But she was unable to move her legs. The skin under her fingernails stung. She released her grip on the wooden planks at the edge of the doorway; splinters remained lodged beneath her nails. She slid to the ground. Behind her, the house was in shambles. Partitions and boxes and floats and clothing and food and blankets and dishes were strewn about the ground or half-falling from the rafters. Darkened patches of dirt still smoldered. Uhpahs folded up Blubs in one arm, and tugged with the other at her mistress who remained on the ground, a weight stone from the roof near her head.

The vast winter house remained standing around them; its supports went deep. Outside, men worked their way over the wreckage of the other house. The birthing hut...

Amuun'axsum stumbled up and limped around the outside corner of the house. Relief coursed through her at the sight of the women crossing the meadow toward her, the two mothers supporting Ootsihd. The trio stopped as the pregnant woman worked through another wave of pain. Beyond them, across the meadow, the hut lay in a smoldering ruin; its flimsy walls had been no match for the prolonged shaking. Men beat at the flames with blankets. Eekbis rushed ahead and grabbed at Amuun'axsum's arm.

"I can only be glad we had the sense to get out in time," Eekbis said. "That shaking…"

"We will have to deliver the baby in here now. Come with me…"

"But that shaking—we must go…"

"Go where?"

The story ran through Amuun'axsum's mind. "As high as we can."

Recognition filled the shaman's eyes, as if she remembered the same story, its lessons. But, peering back at the pregnant woman, she shook her head and dug her fingers into Amuun'axsum's arm. "This will have to be high enough. Getting that girl this far is going to be all we can do. At least here we have a roof." The shaman cast a glance at the shorn cliffside, the remains of the neighboring house. "This house can survive whatever might follow. If anything does follow."

"Thluuch-muup is hurt…"

The shaman closed her eyes and breathed out. "Then we will have even more to do. Come."

Amuun'axsum looked once more over the wreckage outside. Men walked around it, light flickering from their torches. She wondered how the other houses had fared, the ones—downhill.

"The men! Down below…"

"Caring for everyone down there, and they will know what to do."

Amuun'axsum turned to see Pikoo, who supported Ootsihd on one side. The noblewomen gazed toward the hillside; but with a deep breath, Pikoo steered them to the house. "We must focus on our own duty right now," Pikoo said, patting her daughter-in-law's hand. "Our husbands will join us when they can."

Amuun'axsum took over for Pikoo. As she helped Ootsihd to the far corner of the house, she tried to quell her worries. She reminded herself that Dushuuw knew the same story. He would know the same lessons. He would get to high ground. Whatever dangers lay out there in the blackness, she knew the story's lessons were for everyone—not even the strongest were exempt.

Ootsihd cried out in pain, gripping Amuun'axsum's hand so tight she thought the small bones threading out from her wrist would break like a bird's. Amuun'ax̱sum spoke soothing words, hoping they remained untainted by her billowing dread.

DUSHUUW SWIPED the burning coal from his arm and tried again to stand as the earth convulsed. Yaq shouted—Dushuuw could see his friend's mouth open wide—but the two men may as well have been a thousand leagues apart.

Remembering the last earthquake, Dushuuw mentally ticked off what he would do once the shaking stopped. Check on the winter house. Then find Amuun'axsum at the snag, where he was certain she had wanted to meet. Trees already weakened by rains had fallen in the last quake. He worried about more of the same. But these thoughts soon drifted away. For the earth continued to shake—and shake, and shake. House walls creaked. The beach turned to slurry, swallowing a fire.

Dushuuw tried to quell the fear rising in his throat. He searched the darkness. That shadowy form was Yaq. Beside him, the hulk of Huh-uuk. That man on all fours was Kweelthup; and beneath his arm, a young boy who might be Buh-uhs. And there, the one outstretched on the ground that moved like the sea... Dushuuw scrambled up, trying to get to the man. As he tripped and wove, he remembered it could not be Ọotsik. His brother had left long ago, to prepare for the coming hunts. Dushuuw would need to set a watch for his brother's return.

But getting anywhere was fruitless. Dushuuw was tossed to the ground as soon as he managed to stand. Sand coated his hands and bristled on his tongue. Dirt clung to his eyelashes. Even kneeling he could not hold himself steady amid the shaking. He started to tip into a forming sinkhole. Fought his legs free. Gasped as he looked at the swaying sky. Clumps of clouds allowed small windows of light from the stars and the thin shard of a waxing moon. For a moment, Dushuuw believed they shook too. Panic and confusion clawed at his throat.

Women screamed from above. Men cried out from below.

Yaq shouted again, as if calling for the blood of their enemies.

Dushuuw crawled over to him, having to free himself from the soft soil's greedy bites with every movement. Yaq bent over Uhpqoolth, who lay on the ground with his arm pinned beneath a house post they had been maneuvering into the pit when the quake struck. Dushuuw remembered how it took all of them to heave that large post. Now it pinned his cousin to the ground. Uhpqoolth strained to get free. But his screams were for his wife—he did not seem to understand why he could not move. Dushuuw knelt beside his cousin.

"Ootsihd is fine," he shouted. His voice seemed unnaturally loud. The earthquake had subsided. "Ootsihd is fine," he added, more gently. He hoped he spoke the truth.

All around them rose the grunts, moans, and cries of the wounded and the scared. Far out to sea, a sound like thunder cracked.

Uhpqoolth looked at his arm that disappeared under the pole. His eyes were rounded, his lips pursed as he breathed hard and fast. Dushuuw shoved at the post, but it wouldn't budge. Yaq put a hand on his shoulder to stop him, then called for help.

Kweelthup shoved the boy he had been shielding away, urging him toward the hill with other people. Buh-uhs gave a disgruntled retort.

The three men arrayed themselves around the end of the pole. At Yaq's mark, they heaved the pole upward, straining. Dushuuw roared, and the men together took one step forward, falling with the post as it rolled. Uhpqoolth cried out in fresh pain, but his arm was free; he grit his teeth and blew out loud, deliberate breaths.

Dushuuw looked around at the shifting shadows of men and women, and a few children. He grabbed a piece of still-flaming wood from a remnant fire and held it aloft. Fearful faces moved in and out of light. They coalesced onto a path that led to the high ground.

A flicker of memory: her smiling face, eyes full of recognition in a shared story. A story that for him was always followed by messages of safety—to get to high ground. But she was at the snag. Waiting for him.

Dushuuw stepped forward. A huddle of young boys cut off his path. The tallest held a torch aloft. Hawitsuksh chased others from behind—"*waha·k!*"—throwing small rocks at the backs of the slowest until they ran.

The older man saw Dushuuw. "Get your cousin to high ground."

Dushuuw's head swam as he turned back. Uhpqoolth tried to stand, then fell back to the ground with a fresh cry of pain. His arm and hand were swollen and discolored. Yaq searched the ground for something with which to bind the arm.

Dushuuw felt competing urges—to lift his cousin, to go to the snag. He froze. "I need to go find Q̇otsik."

"No." The storyteller was firm. "The earth shakes like this, you go to high ground. He knows that. If I understand, he is already on high ground, yes? He would be wise to stay there—as you would be wise to stay and help here."

But Dushuuw still worried. A weight shifted and hung inside his chest. He looked upriver, over the wreckage of houses and shifting shapes. Would Amuun'axsum know what to do?

"Go on uphill," Dushuuw said. "Yaq and I will—"

As he spoke, Kuhbuhṫup ran up, huffing. "Where is Uhpqoolth?"

They angled back and let the speaker have a view of the young whaler, who leaned against Huh-uuk as Yaq used a rope he found to immobilize the man's useless arm against his chest.

Kuhbuhṫup swallowed his shock. He held himself straighter, as he would if he were about to speak at an assembly. "Buhkweeduuk is trapped, and I cannot lift him free. Maybe you younger ones will be able to do something working together." He did not sound hopeful.

Uhpqoolth winced. "Show me," he said.

The men made their way to the wreckage of what had remained of Buhkweeduuk's house, the only winter house Uhpqoolth had known until the one on the high ground. Even in the poor light, it was clear that should they free his father, it likely would not make a difference in the end. The posts remained upright, embedded in the ground in their rock-lined pits. But the roof and most of the remaining walls had collapsed. Planks crisscrossed each other in tilting masses, tangled up with whatever had been hanging from the rafters. Buhkweeduuk's legs were pinned beneath the pile. One of the large weight stones, which had held a roof plank in place, pinned his pelvis to the ground. The end of a thin pole stuck out from his torso.

Buhkweeduuk's breathing was ragged and wheezing. As Uhpqoolth fell to one knee by his father's side, the other young men evaluated the debris pile. This was not a lone piece of wood. Shifting one piece could cause a greater collapse.

"I tried to pull him out," Kuhbuhṫup said.

Buhkweeduuk wheezed, and shakily lifted a hand as if to wave them away. His hand fell back to the ground. "Go..."

"Do not worry, father, we will not leave you," Uhpqoolth said.

Buhkweeduuk looked angered. "Go." His voice sounded wet.

Dushuuw turned to the older men. "Get the others uphill. We will try again."

Hawitsuksh touched Kuhbuhṫup's arm. "Our strength would add nothing to theirs," he said. "We can find any stragglers as we go."

Kuhbuhṫup nodded his agreement, but he hesitated and put his hand on Kweelthup's shoulder.

"What do you think is coming, father?" Kweelthup said.

"Hopefully nothing," Kuhbuhṫup said. "But we can speculate when you are safe uphill with your family."

As soon as Kuhbuhṫup left, the young men tried pulling Buhkweeduuk free. Buhkweeduuk sputtered. Flecks of blood dotted the corner of his mouth. Uhpqoolth dug at the ground around his father's hips with his good arm, sweat sheening on his face. Dushuuw went to the other side of his uncle's body and dug there. Buhkweeduuk grabbed at his arm, though, and looked at Dushuuw as he tried to speak. Dushuuw brought his face near. Buhkweeduuk gripped Dushuuw by the hair hard. His body trembled as he glared at his nephew, his eyes full of fire. "Go..." Dushuuw fought back tears as his uncle's hand slipped away from his hair and fell to the ground with a thud. The man's eyes went blank. A small orb of blood slipped from his mouth to his chin.

"We need to go," Dushuuw said.

Kweelthup and Huh-uuk were already standing aside.

"We will come back later with more men and get the body," Dushuuw said.

Yaq stepped forward and put a hand on Uhpqoolth's back.

Uhpqoolth slapped him away with his good hand and resumed digging. "No."

The other three looked at each other.

"Go on," Dushuuw said to them. His mind went in the direction of the lake beyond the river, then in the direction of the snag in the forest. He could only choose one. Yaq, Huh-uuk, and Kweelthup still hesitated. "Go on!" After one more glance at Uhpqoolth, the three men turned and left for the hillside.

Dushuuw pulled at his cousin's arm. "Come..."

"You leave my father here, after all he did for you—for you." Uhpqoolth spit out the last words with bitterness. "You would be nothing without him."

"I know."

Uhpqoolth set his dirt-covered hand against Dushuuw's leg and shoved. "I will do it myself," he shouted. "Go on, yourself. Do nothing but run away. What you're good at."

Dushuuw's own anger flared in response to his cousin. He stomped out of the wreckage, faced the bay, and tried to gather himself to decide the direction he should take. He heaved a breath. He took one last look back at his cousin. His mind told to his body to move, to follow the path he had already decided on, for there was never any question where he would go—

He took a step.

The clouds sailed across the sky. The white light of the forgotten crescent moon shone down. There was the wreckage of the house. There was the frightening pallor of his uncle's body. There was Uhpqoolth staggering toward him, rage in his eyes. There was the dark forest behind them. There was the river, glinting in the sliver of moonlight, emptying into—nothing.

The bay was being sucked dry.

A canoe grounded itself against a rock with a creaking shove.

"Cousin..."

Uhpqoolth stomped toward Dushuuw, then pulled up short alongside him.

"What strange tide...?"

Dushuuw stepped forward as he regarded the retreating waters, then looked up again to the moon. This was a time for a minor low tide. But rocks that had only been exposed at the lowest of tides were being revealed. He shook his head.

"Not a tide," Dushuuw said.

Like the earth's continued shaking, the water continued to fall, and fall, and fall. Rocks that he knew to navigate around in a canoe only by experience were now exposed. They could walk across on sodden sand to the wide beach across the river—and several young people had already done just that. They held torches aloft as they chased each other, flirting and playing with the unusual tide line. Happy to be unharmed and alive. "This is no tide."

It was as if the sea were drawing itself inward, in order to—to what?

Cries from the hilltop ascended in an eerie chant. A song?

Dushuuw walked into the dry bay, seeking an answer. He stopped. A shadow ahead moved. The moon shone. A boy romped among the rocks in a spot where the water should be above his head. The boy skipped, his short hair bouncing, then bent over a flopping fish.

"Buh-Buh..."

From the hilltop, the chant gained volume. A warning.

The sea...

The sea is coming…

Beyond the boy, out to sea, the moonlight glinted off a white line, like the foamed top of a wave—but a wave that stretched across the horizon.

Uhpqoolth made a choking sound. Then he cried out and ran back toward his father's body.

Yaq shouted as he ran toward Dushuuw.

His uncle's lips still shaped his last word: *Go*.

Dushuuw sprinted toward Buh-uhs.

His feet crushed wet ripples of sand.

The white line on the horizon grew closer.

A cloud passed over the moon. Its shadow passed over Buh-uhs, over the exposed sands, over Dushuuw's pounding feet. A roar filled the air—or was it his pumping blood?

Buh-uhs turned to him with a laugh and held up two surfperch, giddy with excitement. "Come fish with me, Quht-Quht! They are so easy to catch like this!"

Dushuuw slapped the fish out of the boy's hands.

"Hey! That's not fair!"

Dushuuw ignored the boy and pulled at his arm, turning him toward land. Buh-uhs wrestled out of his grip and slapped at Dushuuw. "You are not my father!" The boy turned to run away.

"Buh-uhs—"

But the boy had already stopped. He stood with his arms at his sides and stared at the approaching horizon. There was a smell of urine as Buh-uhs trembled. And the roaring grew louder. Not the sound of a pulsing sea, nor a storm-fueled wind—something monstrous. On the ground, a thin layer of seawater surged landward. Its foamy front cut around their feet.

"Quht-Quht?" The boy's voice faltered. "Quht-Quht, the sea is coming."

That thin layer of seawater did not ebb. There was only flow, layer upon layer adding to the next. The sea pushed, and pushed, and pushed. Dushuuw hoisted Buh-uhs over his shoulder.

"I want to go home." The boy's voice trembled with fear. "I want to go home."

Dushuuw ran in splashing steps, hoping to beat the incoming flow of water. They were in trouble. He frantically scanned the shore ahead. There was no way they would make it to the uphill trail—no way they would make it to the beach.

Then he spotted the canoe.

The canoe was wedged against the intertidal rocks. But the water was climbing the rocks, and the canoe squeaked against them as the water started to lift it free. Dushuuw reached the canoe as it broke free. He pried free Buh-uhs's terrified grip on his neck and rolled the boy into the canoe, shouting for him to hang on.

Dushuuw remained in the water, guiding the canoe through the rising flow, aiming the craft for the river's mouth. If they could reach the river, they could move with the current and be better able to navigate the surge and maneuver to shore. Buh-uhs screamed and Dushuuw heard echoing screams come from other places. The roar built behind them with crashes.

The canoe touched the river and rushed onward, pushed by the incoming sea. The pace far outstripped Dushuuw's sloshing steps, as he tried to hoist himself over the side.

Dushuuw gripped the edge of the canoe as the water reached his chest. His feet lost purchase with the rocky surface beneath. He looked back, and almost lost his grip. A dark mass stalked them—a towering wall crowned with white, like the jaws of a mythical beast. Inhuman screams popped through the air. The river rose, and rose, moving faster, and faster. Buh-uhs's frantic screams continued. Dushuuw felt foolish. He clung to the side of canoe. His legs were sucked underneath, trying to take the rest of him down with them. There was no navigating whatever they were in—they could only hang on, and hope.

The canoe jerked.

And suddenly there was nothing surrounding Dushuuw but roaring water. His grip had been ripped free so fast he did not have time to heave a final breath.

44

THE TIME HAD BEEN so short, between the quaking earth and the approaching sea. Shorter than a children's story. Too little time to escape the monster that loomed. Amuun'ax̱sum had screamed with the others, sending out their warning to anyone still below. Now, they were all silent. Amuun'ax̱sum watched in horror at the approaching darkness that was deeper than the night sky.

Around her, others left the cliff's ragged new edge to run into the forest and join the rest of the village, as if fleeing an invasion. They shouted about the sea as they ran. Amuun'ax̱sum remained behind, not only for the birthing woman inside the winter house.

She was transfixed.

The sea moved in a dark, roaring surge. She expected it to stop when it smacked into the point. But the massive hunk of ancient rock meant nothing. The earth shuddered under the impact, and Amuun'ax̱sum nearly fell to her knees. Sea spray shot above the cliff's top and cascaded back down. Surely the sea would stop when it reached the shore—a surge, from some distant storm—a surge as bad as ever she had known, but that would ebb like any other. There were screams. The roiling darkness kept surging. The shadow of the sea consumed everything in its path, like an unfurling blanket of night sky. Pinpricks of firelight and torch light winked out one after another. The screams continued and built in volume. Trees—it was the trees that screamed, torn asunder.

Amuun'ax̱sum searched the darkness below in vain for some sign of Dushuuw. She argued with herself—perhaps he had mimicked his brother and went to pray; perhaps he was making his way down the peak to see about all the fuss. Maybe he was among the men herding the children up the hillside—he would be with Buh-uhs, certainly.

A mournful refrain rose from the winter house. A birthing mother crying for her husband. A young boy sobbing. A daughter keening over her mother and calling for the shaman.

"Quulthoo!"

Amuun'axsum hurried back inside at the shaman's frantic call. She stumbled toward the far house corner, her hands shaking. In the middle of the house, Thluuch-muup remained prone on the floor, rolled to her back now. One of the noblewoman's arms curled against her body. The hand was twisted at a strange angle. No amount of tugging straightened the limb, though Chaiyuhx-ik kept trying. Uhpahs knelt next to the young woman as she helped Sawsin wrap a bandage around Thluuch-muup's bleeding head. Nearby, Pikoo held her crying son to her shoulder, bouncing him back and forth.

The shaman shouted for her again. Amuun'axsum ran to the corner.

Ootsihd leaned back against her mother atop a mat, skin shining with sweat. Ootsihd leaned forward as she gave a deep-throated bellow that built in volume as she sank farther and farther forward. As the contraction passed, the woman whimpered with exhaustion. Her mother held a damp rag to her forehead.

"Another pain will soon come," the shaman said. She directed Amuun'axsum to take the mother's place at Ootsihd's back. The woman gratefully traded places, rubbing her sore arms before kneeling at her daughter's side, wiping the birthing woman's brow and holding her hand. Amuun'axsum sat behind Ootsihd, bracing her legs on either side of the woman. She slipped her arms under Ootsihd's armpits, bringing the woman's hot, sweaty back against her chest. The woman groaned as the pain started anew.

"Push now," the shaman ordered. "The baby is close. Push."

Amuun'axsum flattened herself against Ootsihd's back as the woman cried out and pulled against her grip. Amuun'axsum closed her eyes and thought of the black surge of sea. Was it the ground that trembled up through her body, or the shudders of the birthing woman?

"Push!"

Ootsihd grunted, then relaxed limp in Amuun'axsum's arms again. The shaman shook her head.

"Get ready to try again."

Ootsihd shook with sobs. Her mother wiped her face.

The next contraction came quickly. Amuun'axsum pulled back as the woman flung her body forward.

"Push!"

The birthing woman lifted her face up and screamed.

"Come on!"

Ootsihd sagged.

The stench of blood and urine filled the space. The cushion of fern and leaves was sodden. Beyond this corner, a daughter cried over her mother, while down below the sea surged and surged. Amuun'axsum squeezed her eyes shut. She tried to hear her mother's voice, the slave man's drum—wanting to seek what was lost, wanting to bring it home.

Ootsihd shifted as another contraction came. Amuun'axsum dug in her heels, using her strength to prop up Ootsihd's weakness. She shoved back her fear, and brought forward hope and gratitude to help Ootsihd and her baby push through. The shaman leaned closer, palms open as if in welcome. Amuun'axsum felt Ootsihd gather up and bear down. The woman's voice deepened to an animal-like call. The shaman drew closer. "Nearly there..." Ootsihd's shout resounded off the roof and the walls. Flesh pressed against flesh, Amuun'axsum felt the movement of the cry—as Ootsihd drew it up from her gut and released it with what power she had left, marking a path for the little life inside her to follow. Amuun'axsum's pulse quickened.

The earth did tremble then, though not like a quake. Perhaps another hunk of the point succumbed to the sea's brute force. The salt-stirred air was spiced with the scents of downed trees. A baby's feeble cry floated beneath.

Ootsihd panted, hanging from Amuun'axsum's arms. The shaman cooed as she cradled in her hands a slick black head and tiny purple body. She smiled at Amuun'axsum over the new mother. Already Amuun'axsum was impatient to return outdoors, to search the night. But she kept her arms under the new mother, propping the woman up.

"See? Look on him—your baby boy."

Ootsihd barely glanced at the infant. Instead, she cried as another contraction wracked her body. The shaman's smile faded. She gave the crying baby to the new grandmother, then bent to examine the mother.

"We are not done," the shaman said. She looked at Amuun'axsum, or perhaps Ootsihd, or both. "Brace yourself."

COLD, DARK, AND ALONE. No up or down. Dushuuw struggled to resurface, but what little breath he had in him was nearly—

His body slammed into something and he opened his mouth in pain. The water reached through the gap in his defenses, sliding over his tongue and down his throat. Dushuuw reflexively grabbed on to the object he had struck, even as his body was being sucked under it. His fingers found a branch. He pressed a leg to the bark and pulled himself above the surface of the water with a gasp.

Dushuuw clung to a tree that extended nearly horizontal over the churning water. The tree was in the process of falling. But somewhere in the darkness its roots hung on. The rushing water still tried to suck Dushuuw under the trunk by his legs. The surge was so fast and roiling that it created a breeze; the branches in the tree swayed in and out of his view. All around were shrieks, cracks, shatters. Objects swept past, some of them battering him. Dushuuw needed to get out of the water. With a burning grunt, he pulled himself higher and managed to straddle the trunk. He pressed his naked body to the tree among its branches—his clothing gone, ripped free. He coughed violently until he vomited a stream of brackish water.

"Buh-uhs..."

He tried to shout the boy's name, but his throat felt as if it had been scored by knives. He could only whisper. He clung to the tree as the sea surged on and on below him. Not daring to move, his muscles cramped and grew stiff.

After what seemed like ages, the tree suddenly shuddered and dipped; it groaned as its roots finally began to break away from the deluged earth. Dushuuw tightened his grip. The tree fell into the water with a splash and rotated, sending Dushuuw toward the water again. He hurriedly switched his grip and pulled himself atop the trunk again. The tree rocked and spun on the water. Its crown of roots rose high as it was pushed upriver. Dushuuw clung to branches, squeezed his thighs against bark. A jolt, and he shifted his body to remain aloft. Another jolt. A shift. Jolt, shift.

When he was not sure he could move himself again, the tree jerked to a stop, then swung around in a wide arc as if anchored at one end. It was tangled up in some kind of towering mass. Floating pieces of wood—drift logs, house posts, boxes, tools—bobbed and turned in circles, bumping up against his tree. The tree bobbed on the churning waters, but it no longer moved upriver. Slowly, Dushuuw lifted himself to get a better look, but he was still disoriented. He recognized nothing in the dark. A ragged silhouette of what must be tree tops seemed to signal a shoreline. The question was how to reach it.

Dushuuw no longer trusted his perch. The pile of debris loomed over him. More and more objects crashed into his tree, lodging it further into the pileup. He turned and searched the shadows. Swimming was not an option. So instead, he started to pick his way down the tree's length toward its roots. Perhaps he could get close enough to land to risk a few strokes or find some other means of getting out of this nightmare. The tree bobbed under his weight as he picked his way down its length. The water churned and splashed.

He had gone as far as he could, when he realized his mistake. He was no closer to land. Instead, he had moved farther into the body of water he was trying to escape. His heart sank. The tree trembled beneath him as objects continued to bounce off it, some joining the pileup, others meandering away. He was about to try and turn around, when he realized the general flow of water was now going the opposite direction—headed back out to sea. The pile of debris acted like a dam, but it was an incomplete dam that did not block all of the sea's flow. Dushuuw was near its end, where smaller items broke free and joined the swift movement downriver.

Frantic, he eyed the debris floating past him. None of it was as stalwart as his tree. But his tree was stuck. And Dushuuw had no wish to be stuck with it, especially if that great pile truly broke apart. Gathering his nerve, he squinted at one piece of debris after another, then leaped onto what appeared to be a piece of driftwood, pale in the moonlight. But it was a house post—shaved smooth, unadorned—and in the sudden pull of the sea he again fell. His hands slipped one over the other, trying to keep hold. His fingertips made one last brush against the post. Then his mouth filled again with brine.

THE CRY OF A SECOND CHILD rippled through the house. The girl's cry was stronger than that of her twin brother, as if she were offended to have to wait so long to greet the world—only to find it was this world.

Amuun'axsum leaned back against the wall, her own skin sheening with sweat now. Ootsihd had been moved to lay on a pile of furs, pale and spent. Uhpahs came into the corner and gave the new mother a drink of water.

"It is not much," Uhpahs said. "Most of the containers fell over."

"I will go to the spring," Amuun'axsum said, grabbing at a reason to get out of the house.

Ootsihd took the babies in her arms and counted each of their fingers and toes. A smile played across her lips, then faded. Ootsihd looked between the two small lives in her arms, then up at the shaman. "Where is my husband?"

Eekbis cut the others a look of warning. "Uhpqoolth is probably helping set things back in their places after all that shaking," she said. "Quulthoo will see that he knows. And you," she added, turning to Uhpahs, "you go find Buhkweeduuk. The men will need to build a hut—with walls more substantial than mats."

Ootsihd started to cry. But the shaman shushed her as she guided each baby's mouth to one of their mother's breasts, helping them to latch on. The young mother looked down at the pair of tiny heads, their hair slick.

"Two to feed," the mother said. "Two..."

"Never mind that now," the shaman said.

Everyone but Ootsihd, her mother, and the two babies left the corner and closed the tiny family off from the rest of the house.

In the center of the house, Pikoo still clutched Blubs to her body, his head draped over her shoulder. The boy finally slept, but she did not put him down. She stared down at Thluuch-muup, whom Chaiyuhx-ik had covered with a blanket to keep warm. But as soon as she spotted the shaman, Pikoo came over and whispered in the old woman's ear. Thluuch-muup stared up at the ceiling. Her arm remained twisted against her chest; it rose and fell with her breaths. Amuun'axsum shuddered, and left the scene behind as she grabbed a water bucket and headed outside. Uhpahs followed, holding a torch aloft.

But neither turned toward the trail that led to the spring. Amuun'axsum strode forward until she stood near the edge of the shorn cliffside. Her heart beat in quick time as she searched the darkness for a sign of Dushuuw. Nearby, Sawsin knelt near the cliff's edge. The whaler's wife rocked on her knees as she gazed out over the black expanse. Her hand trembled as she wiped her eye.

The broken moon shone down on a black blanket of surging sea that covered the world below. Uhpahs joined Amuun'axsum, and they looked down into the murky, flowing darkness. The blanket was being drawn back to sea, sliding back over deforested hills and rocky banks like a dancer's trailing cloak.

"There are no more fires," Uhpahs said.

Off to the side, men started shouting from the direction of the collapsed house. Torches moved this way and that. Several started to pick their way down the hillside. A crowd formed and split apart. Uhpqoolth appeared at the top of the hill, one arm bound to his side.

Sawsin cried out and ran toward the men.

Amuun'axsum followed her at a distance.

Yaq and Kweelthup came behind Uhpqoolth, followed by Huh-uuk, who hugged a struggling and sobbing Buh-uhs tight to his broad chest. Amuun'axsum dropped the bucket, her hands clinging to the edge of the cloak at her throat as she ran closer. The men were dark in the shadows, dark with mud. Amuun'axsum searched face after face, man after man.

Sawsin clutched at Uhpqoolth's good arm.

Buh-uhs's cries turned into screams, calling for his Quht-Quht.

"I keep trying to tell him," Uhpqoolth told a man. "He is gone. Gone."

Amuun'axsum looked toward Yaq. But Yaq looked at the ground in anguish and added nothing.

Sawsin tugged at Uhpqoolth.

"I'm sure Qotsik is fine," the nobleman said, wincing. "He was on high ground. He would know what to do." Sawsin still clutched him, burying her face in his chest. He brushed his hand over her hair. "He is strong. He is smart."

Inside the winter house, the babies cried feebly. Uhpqoolth looked up at the sounds and stumbled away from Sawsin toward the house, wincing in pain.

"The world is upended," Uhpahs whispered.

Amuun'axsum stared into the darkness downhill toward the spot where the men had appeared. Beyond, the sea rushed on. The moonlight and starlight illuminated the world from above, but the waters below reflected nothing back.

Still, people who had seen the men and the boy emerge at the top of the hillside felt a spark of hope. They started shouting the names of those still missing—daughters, sons, brothers. As the sea retreated, a few men started to pick their way down to search with torches. There were scattered urges to stay, in this high place where most trees and a vast house remained standing. But they would not wait. Buh-uhs tried to follow, a young boy demanding to be a man, even as he shouted for his Quht-Quht.

Amuun'axsum tried to cling to the same hope. She returned to the cliff's edge, searching. A bucket was in her hands again, though she could not remember why. Uhpahs took it from her and disappeared. Amuun'axsum knelt and stared over the edge of the cliff. She trained her eye on one spot, where the tip of a rock was exposed by the retreating water, a rock that had no business feeling air. She stared at that rock for a long time, and she was staring still when she saw the sea's dark return. The swift filling of the box. The rock, submerged. The water, roiling.

The ground shuddered beneath her knees and palms. Darkness poured in below. Monstrous. Relentless. More screams filled the air, and they were not trees. The surge was not as big as the first. But it still hit against the point with a force that sent up sprays of water, misting Amuun'axsum's face. She remained on her knees at the edge, uncaring. The sea was black, black with the earth it had consumed, black beneath the cover of an indifferent sky that rolled out its clouds again and blocked the moon. The clouds amplified the sea's roar, like a lid on a box of boiling water. The sound of the sea drowned the called names, drowned the weeping, drowned the moans of pain, drowned the shouts of still more lost men, drowned the terror she once felt—coating her instead with a dark numbness.

Amuun'axsum pinched her eyes shut, and Dushuuw's face appeared as if in a dream. Mouth agape. Filled with water. Skin transforming, drop by drop, to a white and ogling mask that sank into darkness.

A cry curled up her throat and spilled into the night. The cold air washed over her. She tugged at her cloak and forced the wail into a signal to sing instead. The land beneath her shuddered, on and on, from the relentless sea, a relentless beating. She hurled her song out over the waters that engorged the earth.

Daylight is found on the mountain

She no longer cared if anyone heard, who might demand these precious words. They were words for dark places. They were words to seek what was lost. They were words that remembered the mountaintop. She sent her words flying out over the sea, to drag up whatever they found to grip.

feathers dance on the echoes of wolves

A light rain started to fall. Only a passing shower, but thin drops congregated into fat ones on her hair and skin. As if the land were not submerged enough. As if the tiniest remnants of life must taste water.

we touch lightning

Amuun'axsum let the rain roll down her skin, fresh drops absorbed by salty drops—of sea, of sweat, of tears. The black water threatened to flow through her veins. The loss she felt was an old loss. The sea's relentless power had ripped his hand from hers long ago. Before he kissed her. Before she told him her name. Before darkness and mutual longing had them stumbling into one another. Before she came to the shaman. Before she came to Wuh-uhch. Before the fearful transport of rocking canoe after rocking canoe. Before a night of flame and blood.

The sea withdrew again. Amuun'axsum sang on. The sea surged over the land again, and Amuun'axsum sang on. The sea withdrew, returned. Out, in. On and on, throughout the long night. Amuun'axsum's voice built, rising in expectation, fell again, her palms in the dirt vibrating with the earth's relentless beat.

Those missing loved ones kept calling out the names of the lost. They all tried. Eventually, they all went silent. Amuun'axsum kept singing, though her voice grew hoarse, though her hands slipped through the mud. She grew unfeeling in the cold, splattered with earth, facing the sea. The rain moved on. The moon and stars shone down in the breaks between clouds.

Dawn stretched its golden arms behind the hills.

Amuun'axsum sang one last refrain, the last words rising with the sun. A curl of light seemed to spill out of her mouth, a curl of light that might have been the sun's first stretching ray.

In the silence that followed, the birds eschewed their morning songs. They called in lonely twits and caws, seeking each other out.

THE SEA PLAYED with Dushuuw like he was a girl's cedar bark doll. He flailed his arms, kicked his legs, grabbed at whatever was near.

Then, he stopped struggling.

He was stunned by the thought—not that this was the end, but at the comfort of being so certain of the end. He stopped fighting. Let his arms drift upward. Lights, of red and purple and green, hovered and chased each other in front of his eyes. His arms floated up, as if reaching, reaching for those tones—

A sudden swell pushed him up. His head pierced the surface of the water. He blew the water from his mouth and took in gulps of rain-soaked air. Gasping, he focused on the nearest object. He slid his hands over the smooth wood. He held on to it with a desperate grip.

The sea continued to carry him. His legs were scraped by whatever he was dragged over, then were pulled along through nothing but water. His body pulsed with pain, and with one last exhausted grunt he managed to pull himself atop the plank. He lay prone and gripped the edges. The rain fell across his skin. The clouds hid the moon. And then it did not matter if he opened or closed his eyes—everything was black, as if he or the world or both no longer existed. The sea slid beneath him. Waves rocked him. He tasted salt on his lips, felt seawater draw stinging constellations as it traced his wounds.

He tried to call out. For Buh-uhs. For Q̓otsik. For Amuun'ax̱sum. For his uncle, his cousin, and his best friend. For his father, for his mother. His voice did not work. His throat was raw from brine and vomit. The sea was louder, stronger.

48

THE SEA STOPPED its assault. But it remained a stranger. It did not surge or retreat. But neither did it ebb or flow. It simply shifted, thick and close, wrapping around the trees that remained and smothering what used to be a village.

Amuun'axsum held on to the rope handle of the bucket with both hands as she trudged down the path from the point back toward the winter house. Branches were strewn everywhere, like after a strong winter storm. The box knocked against her legs, and water sloshed over the sides, washing away some of the mud that still clung to her shins. She had not slept, and even fetching water from the spring proved difficult. Her limbs felt as if they were filled with rocks. But she was grateful. The need pushed aside the desire to grieve. And she was not ready to grieve.

A boulder had rolled over the path. Amuun'axsum took a long step over the path it carved, then rested against a tree. She set the bucket down, adjusted her cloak. It was a chill morning, but she looked up at a blue sky with a sun that blazed bright, oblivious to what lay below.

As she approached the back of the winter house, another wave of people emerged from the forest on the opposite side of the meadow. More and more of those who had fled to the forest were making their way back. As one of the few structures still standing on high ground, and the largest by far, the winter house became a gathering point. Plumes of smoke curled upward through gaps in the roof, acting like signal fires—here, they said, here is life. Amuun'axsum did not reach the house before she was approached by the newcomers, who only had eyes for the bucket of water.

A mother tugged her disheveled daughter close. Amuun'axsum recognized them; they lived in the house two away upriver from the shaman. Those houses were gone now or at least flooded. The shaman's herbs would be ruined. The bed mats and partitions gone. What had this little girl lost? Mother and daughter both looked pallid. Amuun'axsum set the bucket down. The mother lifted the dipper of clear water to the girl's lips. The girl shook her head and refused to open her mouth. The woman looked at Amuun'axsum, her shoulders slumping.

"We tried to drink from the creek," the woman said. "It was no good. So full of sea and filth. Dead fish, everywhere. She was the first, and she was so thirsty. She took in too much. It made her vomit."

The mother pressed the dipper against the girl's mouth, pressing her other hand to the back of the girl's head so she couldn't turn away. "Taste," she said. "You see? It is good. Sweet and cold."

The girl licked her lips, looked between her mother and Amuun'axsum. Amuun'axsum gave her a tired smile, and the girl finally took a drink, then a deeper draught. The mother took a quick sip as well, took her daughter by the hand and moved away so others could have a turn. So that, before she reached the house, Amuun'axsum was out of water. She turned around and trudged back up the trail to the spring to fill the emptied bucket. She let her mind go numb.

By the time she returned, the vast winter house was filled with people, all of them tired, hungry, and most of them now without roofs. She spotted several households who had lived on the lower ground along the river. As she walked around with the bucket and dipper, she heard their stories.

"We did not dare light a large fire after that," a woman said.

"Maybe that is what happened across the strait," said a man, recently returned from the cape's highest lookout. "A whole ridge there is on fire. The smoke is towering."

The woman rubbed her throat.

Amuun'axsum moved to another part of the room.

"They got in their canoe. But it wasn't tied to anything, you see. Where could they be now?"

She passed out water, listened, and moved again.

"I tell you, if I can get a hold of a bow and quiver, there is plenty of game for the taking," a man said.

"Oh, you would not believe the noises, the howls," his wife said, turning to another woman. "It was as if every animal on the cape were with us. You could see their eyes, glowing." She shivered. "I tell you, I did not sleep a wink."

"If we do not, the Deeyuh hunters will snatch them all up," the man continued. His voice went lower. "Did you see a bow around here?"

Amuun'axsum looked at the bottom of the bucket and sighed at the little water that remained. She hugged the bucket close and worked her way to the far corner. Peeking behind the partitions, she spied the shaman still singing and praying over Thluuch-muup with help from other women. Um-iiqsu looked on her sister's vacant expression with fear. Chaiyuhx-ik knelt at her mother's side, silent. Sawsin looked over at Amuun'axsum expectantly, only to close her eyes and turn back when it was clear Amuun'axsum did not bring the news she craved. She sang again with the shaman. Amuun'axsum slipped away.

At the opposite house corner, she edged the partition aside. On one side of the space, Uhpqoolth held his crying baby girl in his good arm. The baby boy slept in a nest of furs. Ootsihd leaned over a box of steaming water, trying to coax more milk to come to her breasts as her mother rubbed her back.

Ootsihd looked up, hope sparking in her eyes. "Do you have clams?"

Amuun'axsum shook her head. The young woman had no clear picture of the outside world. "There are no clams," she said.

"Then why are you here?" Uhpqoolth said, his voice hard.

Amuun'axsum avoided looking at him and took a step toward his wife, handing her the dipper full of the last of the water.

Pikoo sat on the other side of the living space and spoke up. "Did you take my husband's spirit?" A chill descended on Amuun'axsum. Pikoo stroked Blubs's head as he sucked on his fist. She had not let go of the boy since taking him in her arms following the quake. Now she eyed the dipper in her daughter-in-law's hands as if it were the next source of danger. "And what of Qotsik? And Young Son?" the woman said. Her eyes were red from crying. "And what of Thluuch-muup? Do you intend to take..."

The woman's voice broke.

Amuun'axsum took a step back.

"Qotsik said you put evil inside his father to rob his soul. They say it was you, singing that song, and now none of our other men are here."

Amuun'axsum did not dare speak—to correct the older woman's timing, nor to defend her intentions. She would not be heard. She would not be understood.

Uhpqoolth stroked his mother's back as he looked down at his wife and son. Ootsihd handed back the dipper.

Amuun'axsum put the partition back in place and paused to catch her breath.

"They should not be here," a woman whispered.

The woman's companion grunted in agreement.

"Twins. A good sign or bad? Neither, as long as they remain here," the woman said. "And besides, that space could be well used by others."

Amuun'axsum hurried toward the doorway. A woman snuck a piece of dried fish into her child's mouth, eyes darting. Amuun'axsum looked the other way.

The stock of food in the winter house was largely intact. Only a little bit of dried fish was lost after falling into a fire during the earthquake. The problem was that there was so little food. The whaler's oil feast had left the extended household only enough to get through the winter. Now their numbers were at least doubled, and likely to remain that way for some time. Normally there would be fresh fish and mussels to vary and augment the winter diet of dried fare. Now...

Amuun'axsum stepped outside, trading the smells of a full house—body odor, smoke, soiled mats—for the building stench of the wrecked world outside—putrid, burned, and rotting.

Near the forest's edge, a group of men built a hut for the shaman to continue her work with the injured noblewoman.

Farther into the woods, other men built a more substantial hut for the family of the twins. The workers' striking tools resounded, unseen.

On the hillside, still other men continued to pick apart the wreckage of the neighboring house. A human-shaped lump lay on the grass, covered with a blanket.

Amuun'axsum turned toward the cliff. Where the earth had sheared away, the ground burned red with exposed ocher, as if the earth bled, wounded. Amuun'axsum found herself once again at its edge.

Dark water shuddered everywhere. The familiar curve of the river, the familiar beaches—everything was hidden beneath water. Only a few stalwart trees rose from the mire, lonely sentinels. Debris collected at the edges, and formed haphazard paths out to sea. Closer in, the rocks where Amuun'axsum would normally gather clams were completely submerged—at low tide, at high tide. There was no tide. A tangle of broken wood, fragments of rope and mats, tree roots, and dead fish butted against the cliff wall. But that was not all. Amuun'axsum caught her breath and squeezed the bucket to avoid dropping it. She closed her eyes, but in her mind the image persisted of the pale human limb shifting amid the debris. She took a few shaky steps backward, tasting bile rise in her throat. There had been burial sites below, with their carefully tended houses. Perhaps what she had seen—perhaps they had already been long dead. But many people had been down below when the sea came. Many still remained unaccounted for. And Dushuuw as among them. Amuun'axsum turned dizzily toward the trail. Stumbling, she dropped the bucket and vomited in some bushes.

Uhpahs was at her side. "Are you all right?"

Amuun'axsum stayed on the ground. She began to cry.

"Here..." Uhpahs held up the dipper from her full water bucket.

Amuun'axsum sat up and took a small sip. She started to cry again and shook her head.

"Come now," Uhpahs said, rubbing her friend's back. "I would very much like for my child to be friends with your child. It would be a shame if my fat little one could not find his friend because her mother did not feed her enough to appear more than shadow."

Amuun'axsum felt her chest constrict. "You are pregnant?"

Uhpahs put on a smile, pressing her palm to her stomach. "I think so."

Amuun'axsum looked down, ashamed. "I tried to..."

"I know," Uhpahs said.

Amuun'axsum pressed her palm to her own stomach, dragging it across her skin. "It still lives."

"Yes, and so do we."

Uhpahs helped Amuun'axsum up. "They are getting a canoe ready. They will go out and search. If Buh-uhs was saved, I have to believe there are others. Even at Tsooyuhs—their high ground may have been close enough. It must have. And like Buh-uhs, others certainly got in their canoes. Maybe anchored to something like elderberry, like his, by someone else who listened to the elders' stories. They are just waiting for us to show up." She spoke as if trying to convince herself as well.

She pushed the bucket into Amuun'axsum's hands. She hooked their arms together and led the way up the trail. In the winter house, Eekbis's voice rose, singing a song over the woman with the bent arm.

The earth shook.

The friends went to their knees. They spread their palms against the dirt. The mud sloughed farther downhill. The temblor was weak, and it was over nearly as soon as it began. But Amuun'axsum and Uhpahs remained on the ground for a long while, nerves wound tight. Inside the house, the shaman droned on in her song.

"Well...," Uhpahs said, her voice shaky.

"Yes."

Later that night, a runner returned with news from Deeyuh and what he observed along the way. The cape was indeed an island once more. In Deeyuh, the sea came from two sides—the strait, and the river.

A great pileup of debris showed where the currents met, downriver toward Wuh-uhch. As at Wuh-uhch, those who were already living on the high ground at Deeyuh and those who retreated there after the quake all survived. Nearly everyone who remained on the low ground had perished. A few had made it to their canoes; but for those unanchored, it was unclear what their fates had become.

"Not all of them made it," the messenger said, his voice low and pained. "We saw a canoe lodged in a tree..."

Amuun'axsum listened with half an ear, wondering if her husband was among the living or the dead. Her husband. She had not thought of Ťoopuuk until now, and wondered if she should feel guilt over that.

There was little time to dwell on such questions, however. Amuun'axsum and Uhpahs were kept busy. The winter house was overflowing. When it came time for sleep, the friends were pushed outdoors with the rest of the slaves.

The air stank of rot. A lone owl hooted somewhere in the dark. Beyond the cape, distant wildfires glowed in the dark night sky, like a stubborn sunset, a moment of transition postponed. And there was no sound of shushing surf by which to fall asleep.

IT WAS TIME TO GET UP. Gulls called. Sunlight tickled. Someone rocked him by the shoulder. But Dushuuw resisted, kept his eyes closed. He was so tired. He wanted to sleep. He felt like a stone. He lay on his stomach, face pressed against cold wood on one side, faintly warmed by sunlight on the other. Someone must have moved the roof plank aside. Gulls cried and the sea sloshed. He smelled salt and cedar. For a moment, he started to relax into the lulling, rocking motion...

As he opened his eyes, the rest of his body opened to reality in a rush. The pain flared, and he groaned. But that was all he could manage. The plank beneath him dipped, taking on a surge of seawater. The salt water found his wounds and clawed them deeper. He grit his teeth and sluggishly drew up on his elbows. A drop of water fell from a clump of hair hanging in front of his face.

"Buh-Buh..."

His throat was still raw. He barely got out the boy's nickname. Nausea came over him in a wave. He was so thirsty. He was so cold.

The raft swept up on one swell. A drop of water fell onto the plank. The raft dipped into a trough. The drop slid down a groove. Dushuuw followed the path of the droplet in an attempt to send his mind past the pain and work through his confusion. He soon found himself predicting the bends and turns of the groove in the wood. It would bend left now; and it did. It would make a sharp turn here; and it did. Dushuuw edged up farther, to take a wider view.

The slab of wood was half a dance screen. It depicted a Lightning Serpent at one end and, with a glance toward his feet, its twin at the other end. Beneath his body was Thunderbird, wings outstretched. The serpents aimed their pointed snouts, bared their teeth, hunted the prey that had broken away. Familiar depictions. A familiar scene.

Keeping still to avoid the stinging pains on his back, Dushuuw lifted his eyes to examine his surroundings. Before him, he saw nothing but horizon, sea leading to sea. White-tipped swells. Dark blue water. Dull sunlight, glinting. A gust of wind blew, reminding him of his wet skin, and he shook. His fingers had a bluish tinge, his feet were slightly numb. A gull flew over him. He heard it squawk behind him. Dushuuw brought himself to a sitting position. The bird remained perched on a floating piece of debris and squawked again, as if asking him what he was doing in so poor a canoe. Then it flew away with beating wings. He followed the gull's flight—toward land.

Rivers of debris wended from the distant shore to his makeshift raft.

As he scanned the scene from left to right, the landscape looked both familiar and foreign. The stone house of Chahdee seemed unchanged. But the cape was somehow diminished. He tried to pick out familiar landmarks where the land had met the bay. But it was no use. Either they were gone, or his low position left him unable to see them. He looked for the houses of Wuh-uhch. He saw spires of smoke from the cliffside. He thought of the snag, and of a small boy in a canoe. He thought of his brother, and he looked in vain for the slight opening of trees that would mark the creek that spilled from a lake on whose shores the whaler prayed. He could see no spire of smoke to point the way.

The peaks were still there, crowned by trees, unmoved.

Dushuuw dragged his finger through the smooth groove of a carved feather. Already shivering, now he trembled. He was alive, born aloft by symbols of power. He had to believe the others were safe as well. Certainly nothing could touch Q̇otsik.

Still, he felt besieged—by confusion, awe, uncertainty, and panic, all of it wrapped up in one giant ball in his gut. His throat burned as he tried to call out. He craved water to drink. He could not drink, but he also could not stop the craving.

Dushuuw turned to face the horizon. At least for a moment, the world could look familiar—even if the waters that stretched out before him no longer were.

THE CAPE WAS STILL an island. Water continued to pool and swirl in restless eddies. But in some places, the seawater had drained away, leaving behind wastelands dotted with the carcasses of dead fish. Amuun'axsum searched for signs of life. Almost everything that had sprung from the ground had been scraped away, even the roots—of grass, of trees. The ground that emerged often was meticulously flattened, as if carved by an adze and polished by flame. The bay's once-turquoise waters were a clogged brown. The denuded low ground made the forested hills rising above stand out in stark relief. The green trees were vibrant, a life-filled answer to the devastation below.

Yet even on the high ground people moved about in distrust of the land and sea. In some cases they distrusted each other as well. They gave Amuun'axsum—the shaman's strange slave woman at the cliff's edge—sidelong stares. In the winter house they lived cramped together, and once outdoors they moved around each other in wide circles. Elders and family leaders wove among and through them, reminding them of their ties to each other, the strength they drew from each other in challenging times.

Amuun'axsum stood at the edge, still searching.

A baby's cry pulled her away.

The birth of the twins added to the unease. In their passage into the world, the boy and the girl had lived among the Salmon People. Uhpqoolth would now be required to live with his wife and the babes in the hut being built in the woods. He was expected to spend his time in near-constant fasting and prayer to call not only the salmon, but herring and whales as well. But with a river and bay choked with debris and seawater, would there be anywhere for them to return?

The boy still struggled. Things that would help Ootsihd stimulate milk flow—clams, a certain seaweed—could not be found. Most rocks where they would be gathered were still underwater. Those that started to emerge were as stripped as the land. Old women sang prayers for the baby's strength, for the mother's milk to be sufficient for two.

Uhpqoolth wore a cedar bark band knotted at the forehead. He held his injured arm as he watched other men gather building supplies for the makeshift shelter. The men used whatever was available. Scrap from the collapsed house. A broken roof plank. A paddle set upright. A whale scapula to fill a gap.

The people were silent around Uhpqoolth. Their hope in the twins' supernatural ability to bring them food was balanced by the sobering reality of effectively losing yet another in their hereditary line of leaders. In a few days, Uhpqoolth and his wife would move with the twins into that forested hut and live there, apart from the rest of the village—and remain there for as long as two years. His job was to pray. No fresh meat could touch his lips. No ceremonies. The feast doors would be closed to him, unless only dried foods were served. No whaling. The headband he wore marked his dedication, but also his uprooting.

Uhpahs walked into the forest after the men, bringing a box of dried salmon and a basket of roots for the family's meals. More than a few people in the winter house had grumbled at the larger portions when there was so little to go around.

Among those helping to build the hut was Leehuuk, the nobleman from upriver. His house was lost, and so now his family lived in the winter house. Amuun'ax̱sum watched the nobleman from the corner of her eye as she returned from the spring with a bucket of fresh water. Leehuuk remained energetic and optimistic, perhaps to lift the general mood. But earlier she had come across him speaking to several heads of households while Uhpqoolth was out. Leehuuk had urged the posting of guards at the spring. He advised that only select people should draw and apportion the water. And no one argued otherwise. The nobleman had moved his family into the center of a wall near the house's highest-status corner, a corner where now only Sawsin, Um-iiqsu, and Chaiyuhx-ik came to nap or eat. More often, the women were at the shaman's hut, helping sing and pray over Thluuch-muup.

Tools rang out from the forest where the men finished the twins' hut. Others planned temporary shelters, which they would construct in the meadow behind the winter house.

For now, when it wasn't raining, the old storyteller would gather young ones around him in the meadow to tell humorous Q̓watee stories. Older people sat on logs set against the house's back wall and listened in.

Several women approached the cliff's edge, looking over the sea.

The body of a dead slave lay outside the winter house doorway. At some point, some man would be called to take the body, to hurl it over a far cliff into the sea. But the corpse did not yet stink too badly. So they focused first on caring for the living.

Earlier, the community's higher ranked individuals had gathered separately to talk. It was decided that Yaq and Kweelthup would set out in a canoe to see what, and who, they could find. The people craved knowledge like they craved fresh meat. Was there anyone alive down there? Did anyone from Tsooyuhs survive? Before they left, Sawsin had stood at the edge of the cliff with the men, pointing across the swollen river, guiding them in their coming search for her husband.

Soon after they left, a family arrived in a canoe, speaking a language only a few in the winter house understood. They had drifted in their canoe out to sea during the deluge, then paddled back toward land and found themselves in Wuh-uhch territory. They had seen the tiny search party, and through gestures and trade language indicated at least one person had been found alive.

The news sparked a fresh wave of hope. But no one returned that night. Another day was nearly done. And the good news did not ease the myriad challenges the community continued to face.

Amuun'axsum entered the winter house and flinched. The house stank of unwashed bodies and the faint whiff of diarrhea, that not even the resinous sweetness of spruce-needle tea could mask. The vast majority of people had come through the event without any injury. But the wounded sat along the walls, watching their wounds worsen. Cuts and scrapes were turning into festering sores on some people, particularly those that had washed only with contaminated creek water.

People fixed their gazes on the bucket she brought around. Trapped by salt water, it was fresh water that dominated their focus. Mothers took the tumblers and served their dehydrated children. Fathers washed their loved ones' wounds.

Amuun'axsum flicked a glance toward the corner of the house, where Uhpahs had attended Thluuch-muup for so many years and where Amuun'axsum had run her fingers across the ornamented bench. Thin mats still partitioned off the sides of the space, though they had been moved inward to create more room for guests. Leehuuk's family was closer to the corner. If he wanted to, the nobleman could stretch from his bed and touch the boundary, could push it down. Sawsin sat motionless there, staring at the nobleman's things so near her own. She held a comb in her hands, waiting.

Her bucket empty, Amuun'axsum sighed with relief and escaped the gloom and stench of the winter house. She should go get more water. But as had become ritual, she first went to the cliff's edge. She was not alone in this habit. The boy, Buh-uhs, had dragged over a piece of wood and sat there, surveying the water like an elder river watcher.

Amuun'axsum sat beside Buh-uhs, and looked out with him.

Below, an injured gull rested atop a pile of brown debris. The bird raised a wing, as if trying to remind it how to work.

"He is alive, right?"

Amuun'axsum looked at the boy. His face had lost much of the childish fat, and probably not all due to hunger. The line of his face, from brow to chin, formed a stern profile. He turned toward her. "Dushuuw is alive?" he said.

Amuun'axsum blinked. "Do you mean Quht-Quht?"

The boy looked back out to sea, then faltered. His shoulders slumped, and his face twisted in frustration as he tried to hold back tears. "Do you think my mother is still alive?"

Amuun'axsum placed her hand on the boy's shoulder. "Your mother is alive," she said, "and she is thinking of you."

He nodded, as if her words confirmed what he already believed.

They both looked out again. The boy's skin was warm and smooth.

"He is alive, too, no matter what they say," Buh-uhs said.

Amuun'axsum's skin prickled, and she withdrew her hand. "You are good to be strong for your mother," she said.

After one more glance toward sea, she took up the water bucket.

Buh-uhs sat up, turning his gaze inland to the flooded river valley.

"Look!"

He tugged at her cloak. "Amuun'axsum, look!" He jumped up and started shouting. "They're coming! They're coming! Look!"

Amuun'axsum was dizzy, however. A buzzing filled her head as it did so long ago in the hull of a rocking canoe. She looked up, but Buh-uhs was off and running toward the sloping hillside. He was pointing and shouting. People gathered as near the cliff's edge as they dared get, blocking her view. But she wasn't trying to see the water anymore. The boy. She stumbled as she tried to get to Buh-uhs, stopping and dodging around the people running across her path.

"Buh-uhs..."

"Look!"

"Buh-uhs!"

Loud exclamations and sobs rose up from the others. One woman's wail rose above the others. Still Amuun'axsum could hear the boy, shouting in joy. She tried to call for him, but her voice—still hoarse—was lost in the chorus. She worked her way through the crowd until she was finally able to clutch the boy's arm and tug him close. She crouched in front of him.

"Look!" he said, twisting.

"Buh-uhs..."

"Don't you see?"

"Buh-uhs! How do you know my name?"

The boy looked at her directly—not as a distracted child, but as an equal. "Dushuuw." He pointed in triumph to the canoe pulling up to land from across the valley. "Dushuuw!"

Amuun'axsum gripped the boy for support as she swayed. Her hand encircled his bicep, he was so young. But he was stronger than he looked. He did not falter.

A man with many wounds stepped out of a canoe onto a makeshift platform of remnant planks. The man held a limp body.

Cheers did battle with wails of grief among the crowd as Dushuuw carried the dead man toward them.

Sawsin screamed and went to her knees.

Amuun'axsum studied Dushuuw's face as he trudged up the muddy hillside, refusing to relinquish his brother's body. His expression was a knot of pain, and anger, and grief. Still, the sight of him alive filled her with joy. Amuun'axsum brought her other hand to Buh-uhs's arm. The boy placed his hand atop hers and they took a step forward together.

"Quulthoo..."

Amuun'axsum stopped, and the boy tugged at her hand as he continued forward. He looked back with a smile. Those that surrounded him looked back with suspicion. Amuun'axsum dropped the boy's hand. He continued to smile as he turned away and ran onward. Amuun'axsum turned back with an effort toward the shaman's voice, her heart running after the boy.

Eekbis glared from outside the hut. Her headdress flared above her wizened face. Amuun'axsum moved toward the shaman, as the crowd parted and surged around and behind her. Sawsin's grief filled the air. Amuun'axsum dragged herself forward and stopped short of Eekbis. The shaman reached out with her walking stick and rapped the side of Amuun'axsum's bucket.

"They need water, child," the shaman said.

Amuun'a̱xsum felt the crowd drawing closer at her back again, forcing her to take a step closer to the shaman, whose skin shone with sweat. The crowd moved by them toward the winter house. Amuun'a̱xsum cut through the human stream, and headed toward the trail to the spring. The reminder to obey, the looks of suspicion, the boy's smile when he left her—these things floated at the edges of her mind as she followed the trail. Though her heart screamed at her to turn around, she moved up the well-worn path in an automatic trudge. The view in her mind remained of Dushuuw's face as he crested the hill—unseeing, consumed by the death of the man he held in his arms.

DUSHUUW TRUDGED up the hill cradling his brother's body in his arms, a body that grew heavier with each step. The crowd moved back as he moved forward. They stepped on each other's toes, checking over their shoulders as they fumbled backward in their attempts to not stumble, to keep their eyes on him and his awful load.

In the crush of faces, Dushuuw registered two of them. Sawsin, on the ground, ripping at her cloak, face tilted up in anguish. And Buh-uhs, full of joy, who did not retreat but instead rushed closer.

The boy's expression fell briefly with a shuddered look at the body, but returned to curious rapture as he looked up again. He stayed close to Dushuuw's side. Dushuuw choked on sobs born of the emotions that warred over his heart—gratitude for that young face, grief for the damaged one that lolled from the limp body in his arms.

~

Before he had found his brother, he had been found.

Laying on the plank once more, drifting in and out of sleep, he heard the calls of strangers. A small canoe approached, carrying a bedraggled family. The man spoke a language Dushuuw couldn't fully understand. But he did understand their offer of help. Dushuuw managed to sit up again, but it was about all he could manage. The man helped roll him into the canoe. The couple draped a fur cloak over his back and brought their firebox close. The woman rubbed his feet. Dushuuw slowly warmed up, wincing at the spikes of pain. When he could control his movements better, he held the edges of the cloak around the firebox to better cup the heat. The child with them handed him a container of water, and he drank deeply. They gave him dried meat to eat. Tears clouded his vision as he gestured his thanks.

The man pointed toward the winter house's spires of smoke, and Dushuuw smiled. The man and his wife dipped paddles into the water, to head for the cliff.

But before they crossed the bay, Yaq and Kweelthup reached them.

Dushuuw tried to match his friends' enthusiasm, but his throat was still raw and he felt weak. He looked forward to reaching the winter house—to embracing Buh-uhs, who was alive, and to lying on his bed for a hundred years—until he heard his friends' next stop.

"Qotsik has not returned?"

"He was on high ground. Should just need help getting home. He didn't have a canoe. Didn't need one—before."

Dushuuw scanned the shoreline, seeking the creek that spilled from the lake tucked into a forested hillside where his brother prayed.

"I'm coming with you."

It took time to convince his friends to let him join them. It took many more gestures and words from the trade language to decline the family's invitation to join them on the last leg of their journey to the cliff. But soon he was sitting between Yaq and Kweelthup, still wrapped in the fur, which the family gifted him.

His friends paddled the canoe through the debris toward shore.

The wide, sandy beach was gone.

As his feet touched a scraped bit of land, Dushuuw went to his knees. Somewhere in this area, they had played the ball game to celebrate the end of the whale hunt. Somewhere, lovers had chased each other in the night, convinced that danger had passed. Now, trees by the dozens, planks, baskets, and myriad ropes lay tangled with seaweed, driftwood, and the stinking carcasses of fish and crabs. In the distance, the forested hillside remained untouched; but most of the shrubs, grasses, and understory trees that had filled the low ground between its rocky flank and the sandy shore had been ripped out. The debris field extended on and on. With a deep breath, Dushuuw pushed aside his shock and struggled up.

It took a long time to make their way to the mouth of the creek. As Yaq helped him pick his way over the mud-coated debris, Dushuuw's attention moved past the larger objects to the smaller ones. A knife. Gaming paddle. Wooden doll. Soggy fur cloaks. Fishing hooks.

He stopped his mental inventory when they came to the body. A swollen, pallid arm extended from beneath a pile of debris. Black marks covered the skin. The palm lay open, as if asking for help. Feminine. His mind went to Amuun'axsum, and he started to scramble toward the spot. Yaq placed a hand on his chest to stop him, and with Kweelthup uncovered the body. Like Dushuuw, the woman had been stripped by the sea and he averted his eyes from the scarred flesh. His hands shook at the edges of the fur cloak as Kweelthup brushed her hair, clumped with mud and seaweed, from her face.

It was not her.

It was no one they knew.

As they ascended the hill, the terrain regained familiarity, and they soon found the trail that traced the creek's zig-zagging path over earth and basalt. The going was easier, though Dushuuw was still slow. His friends flanked him, Yaq going ahead and periodically calling for Ọotsik, with Kweelthup on Dushuuw's heels in case he needed help. As they walked, Kweelthup updated him on more of the village's status. Who was gone. Who else had come to seek shelter. Thluuch-muup's illness. The birth of the twins.

With the trees now blocking the view of the seaside landscape, it appeared nothing had happened. The lake when they reached its edge looked normal too—at first. Cattails rose from the blue waters, which sparkled in the sunshine. Birds sang. Dushuuw scanned the area, half-expecting to see fishermen at work, and he looked for his brother's shrine. But as they wended their way around the lake, they saw it had been affected by the event too—the shoreline showed signs of inundation. Dushuuw stepped through a puddle near waterlogged grasses, eyeing the trail of pond scum that extended down into the lake. It was as if someone had cupped the lake like a bowl and given it a good shake, letting the water slosh over the rim. Here and there, trees lay toppled or leaned at precarious angles.

Yaq and Kweelthup paused to point out observations. But Dushuuw spotted his brother's shrine and picked up his pace. From a distance, the shrine appeared smaller than the main shrine on the peak above their village. There was no sign of Ọotsik, at least not yet.

Renewed, he trudged on toward the shrine, hearing his friends follow. Then he slowed to a stop.

The sloshing water had reached here as well, putting out the fire his brother had built and soaking a fur cloak that lay folded on the ground. But that wasn't what caught his eye. It was the aged tree that lay across the encampment, extending from its dirtied root ball near the water's edge into the middle of the lake. And in the shallows of the lake, pinned between its bed and the tree's girth, was a body.

~

They camped there for a night and a day. Yaq and Kweelthup freed the body and laid it out on the ground well away from the lake, where they built a new fire. Dushuuw collapsed beside his brother, pulling the fur cloak over both of them before finally succumbing to sleep. He slept a full day, waking into a haze of dehydration, pain, and grief. Yaq convinced him to drink and eat. Dushuuw only agreed so he would have the strength for what he must do next.

His friends carried his brother's body down to the canoe.

They slogged their way through the tumid waters. And it took a moment for Dushuuw to realize it was not the bay, but the swollen river they crossed toward the hillside.

When they made landfall, he would not let them touch his brother's body again. This was a load he would bear, on this last stretch home.

All the monumental power that his brother had possessed—so much power that it had threatened to overflow the banks of his brother's spirit and wreak havoc upon those with less spiritual strength, which was everyone—all that power did nothing to save him. Dushuuw could not understand. He understood only that his brother would have been somewhere else if it had not been for him. He understood that the flesh in his arms was unresponsive. He understood that the man destined to lead was dead. And the one who should have died was left holding on.

~

Now, as he walked toward the winter house, his friends propping him up and helping him on, Dushuuw held the body close. At the doorway of the winter house, a familiar face waited in expectation. Kuhbuhtup reached out and touched the shoulders of both Dushuuw and the body in his arms.

Dushuuw followed the old speaker inside. He was shocked by the crowds and for a moment wanted to run away. Kuhbuhtup helped hurry him to the house corner. Um-iiqsu appeared at his side. His stepmother's lips trembled as she looked at the body of her son. Yet she cleared a bench, and Yaq helped Dushuuw lay the body atop it. Um-iiqsu held shaking hands to her mouth as she sobbed. Sawsin stumbled into the space and collapsed again on the ground beside her husband. Yahbis edged close on an adjacent bench and with a shaking hand stroked her dead grandson's hair, as if he were merely asleep.

Dushuuw sat next to his brother's body, and pain washed over him with fresh vengeance.

"You need to drink, Young Son," Kuhbuhtup said.

A woman approached and knelt in front of him. Her scarred wrist dipped low into the bucket and brought up a cupful of clear water. She looked up at him, and Dushuuw felt again out of time and place. For a surreal moment, none of it had happened, and she was kneeling before him in the warmth of the snag. It was the water touching his lips that brought him back—water so clear, so pure, sliding down his throat. He took a shaky breath, and realized his hand was over hers on the dipper. She helped him to drink. He closed his eyes as he drank the water and felt her warm skin. So full of life. He took his hand away, turned aside, and stared at his brother's body. He listened again to the cries of Sawsin, of his stepmother, of his grandmother.

Dushuuw heard the speaker send Amuun'axsum away for medicine and rags. The older man sat down beside him. "As soon as you are clean, bandaged, and get some sleep, we will update you and discuss what to do next."

"No." Dushuuw looked at the body. "Yaq and Kweelthup already filled me in on the basics. I've had rest. We can talk now."

Kuhbuhtup sighed but did not argue. He left, returning with Uhpqoolth, who fell to his knees beside the body of the young chief.

Yaq remained at Kweelthup's side. The pair stood with arms crossed, each of them watching with unease as another man entered the space. Dushuuw watched Leehuuk approach the bench, hands clasped behind his back. Wiid followed close behind. They looked down at the body. Leehuuk stepped back, posture rigid as he angled away and looked askance at Dushuuw.

Kuhbuhtup straightened and confronted the nobleman. But Leehuuk cut him off. "If there is to be talk of next steps, you know we should be part of the conversation."

"This is not the time," Kuhbuhtup said, "and this is not your house."

"And who do you speak for anymore, Kuhbuhtup? This is not your house, either. And right now, we all live under this roof."

Anger rose inside Dushuuw, fueling him.

"You won't even wait." He glared up at Leehuuk. "You would dishonor my brother by trying to take his place, already?" Black spots swam in front of his eyes. He wanted to stand. He hated staring up at the nobleman. Hated being weak before the war chief. But he didn't dare try to move. He gripped the edge of the bench with both hands.

"You think so lowly of me, Young Son? I mourn with you. But we mourn many others as well. You may have returned," Leehuuk said, shuffling back a step, "but there are many others who will never return. The people who mourn them and love them have been waiting here for direction. And as one whom they trust, and a man of rank, I deserve a voice in the decisions made from here, same as any other head of household."

"The people of this house do not follow you," Yaq said.

Leehuuk acted as if Yaq had not said anything at all. "I have taken certain measures, of course, with your own household otherwise—greatly—preoccupied." Leehuuk slid a glance toward Uhpqoolth, who still knelt with bent head beside his cousin's body and said nothing. "People were starting to get their own ideas. Driven by fear and worry. Finding weapons. Hoarding water."

Kweelthup dropped his arms to his sides and stared at the dirt. Kuhbuhtup was silent. Dushuuw worried over their responses. How bad had things gotten in so short a time? It was more than the loss of homes. It was more than the holes left by his uncle's and brother's deaths. More than the strange mixture of people, as many unfamiliar faces as familiar. This place did not feel like home. He was suddenly aware of the smells of sickness and rot, of his friends' tired postures.

Leehuuk stepped to the side, then back. "I've had Wiid post sentries at the spring. They make sure water is portioned out appropriately. I have one of my own men in each group that wants to go hunting, to make sure the Deeyuh do not take what we claim."

"And yet you are not making a move for our territory," Dushuuw said. He did not voice the other thoughts in his head, which told him those were wise moves. They knew from the fight generations earlier what could come from allowing people to share land that did not belong to them. Soon, there was no getting rid of them, except by force. But the same thing was happening now. Leehuuk would gain control simply by being the only one left who could care for the community. They would come under his arm without a fight.

Leehuuk sensed his thoughts and paused in his steps, holding out his hands. "I merely help keep things moving along in an orderly fashion until Uhpqoolth can take over."

"So you would do this for how long?"

"As long as it takes."

"And then you would just hand things back over. How magnanimous."

Leehuuk shook his head, as if dealing with an unreasonable child.

In his head, Dushuuw felt relief mixed with his anger. At least it was Uhpqoolth to whom people looked.

Amuun'axsum reentered the corner, slipping between the men with eyes down. She carried a box of steaming, woody-smelling tonic. Dushuuw suppressed the urge to send everyone away, to curl up in her arms and mourn. Beside him, his cousin shifted beside the body. Dushuuw put his attention back on the rich nobleman and ignored Amuun'axsum, keeping his mind on his brother.

"You know you will need my men to make any kind of whale hunt this spring," Leehuuk said. "You already did when you had everyone you could get."

The faces of those who would not be in the whaling canoes flitted across Dushuuw's mind. His brother. His uncle. Even his cousin, for now.

The nobleman held Dushuuw's eyes. "Your family needs to work with me sooner or later."

"With you, always," Dushuuw said. "But not for you."

Dushuuw suddenly winced as a wet rag touched his back. The tonic seeped into the gashes on his skin. He pushed back the urge to voice the pain. Amuun'axsum sat behind him and touched his back in a brief apology. He shrugged her off, welcoming the pain now that he knew it was coming.

"We are all men of Wuh-uhch," Leehuuk said. "The decisions about this house do not belong to you alone."

"Yes, they do," Uhpqoolth said, stirring. He stood and turned to the nobleman.

Leehuuk's eyes flicked with worry and he held up his hands. "I merely meant that the rights belong to both of you now, of course."

"Well, at least you agree that they are not yours," Uhpqoolth said. "I was beginning to wonder."

Kuhbuhtup stood and moved as if to send everyone away.

But Dushuuw interjected. "How is the food supply?"

Kuhbuhtup turned in surprise at the shift, then lifted his hands in resignation. "We had enough for the household to last the rest of winter. But the timing is poor," the speaker said, his eyes flitting toward the body. "Supplies run low this time of year anyway. But we were even lower following the oil feast."

"And now there are more mouths to feed," Kweelthup said, his voice soft. "And more people arrive every day."

Dushuuw held back a grimace as Amuun'axsum moved her rag to

his shoulder. "The mussel beds?" He thought of women like her who went out daily with their baskets, even in winter.

"Even if they weren't submerged, I doubt there's much of them left," Kuhbuhtup said. "We've seen what happens in bad storm surges. This..."

Leehuuk's eyes glinted with eagerness. He was about to speak. But Dushuuw was not sure he could take much more of the man's voice.

"You said more people are coming," Dushuuw said.

Kuhbuhtup nodded. "This house is the largest of the houses that remain intact. That alone has drawn those who did not fare as well. Besides those on our low ground, like Leehuuk's household"—he flicked a glance at the nobleman and his cousin—"we have some folks coming out of the forest from Deeyuh."

"They are building more shelters on their high ground," Yaq added. "But in the meantime, a roof is better than no roof, especially in winter."

"And then there's that family that drifted here in their canoe."

"If they found us, others are likely to as well."

"And we still have to check on Tsooyuhs..."

Dushuuw slumped and turned his mind to the lessons his uncle had taught him. "We will need to get inland, hit the trade routes," he said. "Groups farther inland may not have been hit, at least not as hard. They will have food." He sat up straighter with the thought, plans already bustling in his mind. But the movement stretched the gashes across his back. That alone hurt, but the tonic from Amuun'axsum's rag also sank in further, and this time he could not stifle a choked grimace. Latent exhaustion swept over him, black spots hovering in front of his vision again. He hunched back down and flung out his hand to brace himself, finding nothing. He heard the women gasp. But Uhpqoolth was there and grabbed his arm, helping him sit back up.

Kuhbuhtup raised his hands. "All right, that is all for tonight."

Dushuuw rubbed his temple, trying to understand how it was night already, trying to understand where in time he was now.

"What Young Son says is good. But we have other things to do first," Kuhbuhtup added, his tone softer.

The other men looked at the body of the young chief.

A fresh wave of guilt washed over Dushuuw. He should have discussed memorial plans for his brother. Instead, within moments of promising himself a life of self-denial, his mind had gone to the familiar aches of anger and hunger.

Uhpqoolth still gripped him. He made sure Dushuuw was steady, then released his hold. Dushuuw grabbed him back, and squeezed his cousin's arm. "Give my greetings to Ootsihd and the children," he said.

Kuhbuhṫup walked over and urged Amuun'axsum to finish. "Do a thorough job—we do not want infection—but get it done quickly so he can rest and you can return to Eekbis." The older man turned to Dushuuw. "Get some sleep, Young Son. We will talk tomorrow..."

"I am sick of talking," Dushuuw said, slumping further in on himself.

"There is plenty to do," Kuhbuhṫup said, understanding. "Tomorrow. After sleep. For now, I will have someone lift your brother into his box..."

Um-iiqsu looked over in a panic. She clung to one of her son's hands.

"No, I will do it," Dushuuw said. "Tomorrow will be soon enough."

Soon, of the men, only Yaq remained. Amuun'axsum brought her rag to Dushuuw's other shoulder and started to clean the wounds there. She was gentle, but it stung worse than nettles. Yaq gave one last worried look, then left as well.

Um-iiqsu brushed her fingers against his cleaned shoulder. "I must wash my son," she said. "Make him clean."

Sawsin ran the back of her hand under her nose. "I will help you."

The pair left the corner in search of what they needed.

Yahbis stood to follow. His grandmother paused in front of him, looking down on him from tear-filled eyes as he sat there, too tired to move. She brushed her palm across his cheek, then turned away.

For a short time, Dushuuw and Amuun'axsum were alone.

Furs lined the benches. The fire was warm. In the flickering light, opercula shimmered from their artful rows on the wooden box. The plank bearing Thunderbird and the whale leaned against the wall. And his brother's body lay beside them, beneath the carved wings.

The house was filled with voices. Scents of sweat and sickness permeated the air. A child cried.

Amuun'axsum stopped washing his back. His wet skin burned. She came and knelt in front of him, dipping her rag in the steaming tonic to wash the wounds on his chest. She looked up at him, tears streaming down her face. He grew weak as he struggled to keep his emotions in check. He gripped the edge of the bench as he leaned forward. Her breath came in warm bursts against his skin.

"I sang for you," she whispered. "I sang for your return."

The words filled him with cold dread, and he leaned away.

"You should not have." His voice was deep, full of rocks. Still, she drew close and washed his feet. "You should have sang for him," he said. She looked up at him from the floor, gaze full of hurt and longing. As if she had prayed for this world, a world upended with his brother gone.

Dushuuw closed his eyes, wanting to shake her, wanting to kiss her.

Um-iiqsu and Sawsin returned, cloaks rustling. Dushuuw looked at Sawsin, her face drawn and stained by spent tears. She carried a steaming box of water and a clean rag to the bench where the body lay. Dushuuw looked down at the bowl beside Amuun'axsum and the pile of rags beside it, everything tinged pink.

Dushuuw bent over and took Amuun'axsum's hand between his own, cupping the wet rag and guiding it back toward her bowl. He stood and took the bowl from Sawsin.

"We will do it together," he said.

Sawsin looked at him and nodded. She dipped a corner of her rag in the bowl, then traced it around her husband's eye. Um-iiqsu's hands trembled as she dipped a rag in the bowl, and caressed her son's cheek.

Dushuuw dipped another rag, and held it above the bowl, letting it drip. Behind him, he heard Amuun'axsum leave the space.

Rag dripping, Dushuuw stood there for several moments, looking at the body that fell in his shadow, the fire both warming his back and inflaming the wounds. Blood started to pool again near his wrist. He reached out. A drop of his blood fell onto his brother. He dragged the rag across his brother's skin to wipe it clean.

COULD SHE EAT after the sight of Dushuuw's scored body? And yet the scent of roasting deer meat taunted. Her stomach roiled with yearning.

Hunters had returned, jubilant, after a long day tracking a stranded doe on the peak. But it was one carcass for a precipice full of people. No meat for a slave. Not much food at all for a slave. The life inside her made offended demands.

She was tired of the groaning people.

She was tired of lugging bucket after bucket of clean spring water.

She was tired of traversing the same short paths.

It was maddening, to be so confined.

Eekbis bristled at her angst during a brief respite from praying over the noblewoman, whose condition had not improved. "Perhaps I should send you to Deeyuh now. One less mouth to complain as well as to feed."

Amuun'axsum folded in on herself. She still wondered if Toopuuk had survived. With Dushuuw returned, she did not want to find out, so she did not ask. Even if Toopuuk were dead, he was part of her now.

The world was upended. How had Lohta fared? She would have to be more patient. Even if her family had piled up their canoes with treasures as they escaped the flood, they would need them for immediate needs. They likely would have to save up to buy Amuun'axsum back. But now... The world was upended. Dushuuw could take his brother's place. He could reside in the house's seat of power, and she... She was no longer certain of her goals. But she knew, washing his torn skin, that she would need to be patient for him too.

Amuun'axsum trudged once more toward the spring, bucket in hand.

She was tempted to hold her nose as she hurried up the trail. From down below, the putrid scent of dead fish radiated everywhere. But she slowed as she neared a couple walking ahead. Each of them wore fur-lined cloaks. The woman's ears dangled with clicking strings of shells.

A feather hung by a cord from the pointed knob of the nobleman's hat. It was Leehuuk, who walked with his wife, who carried a water bucket—though it seemed weighed down already.

Amuun'axsum slowed to let the distance grow between them again, until at last she lost sight of them in the wooded curves of the trail. When she reached the spring, however, they were not there. She looked around, but she saw no sign of the couple. She filled her bucket. She briefly met the glance of one of the men from Leehuuk's household, a man tasked with keeping an eye on the spring. Amuun'axsum almost asked him about the couple, then changed her mind.

Before heading back downhill, Amuun'axsum set the bucket down and trudged through the salal, following a path to the edge of the point. The sea wind was strong at the edge. Amuun'axsum craned her neck. A chunk of the cliff had fallen away in the earthquake. It sat heaped atop smaller chunks, that had themselves fallen away years earlier, perhaps in some other earthquake. Amuun'axsum thought about the rocky coastline, wondering about the other changes that must be out there.

Before she headed back, she took one last look south across the bay—and saw smoke. A large, managed plume. Excitement coursed through her as she jogged back up the path to share the news.

As she neared the edge of the salal, however, Leehuuk and his wife emerged from the trees on the other side of the clearing. She stopped, and peered out from behind a spruce. The noblewoman handed the sentry her bucket. He filled it with water, handed it back, and returned to the stick he was shaving with a knife to pass the time.

Amuun'axsum waited until the couple had gone back down the path toward the village before returning to the spring to retrieve her bucket.

"I went out to the edge of the point," she said.

The sentry nodded, noncommittally.

"I saw a signal from Tsooyuhs," she said.

The man straightened, sheathed the knife, and ran toward the path.

Amuun'axsum watched him disappear, then set down her bucket and ran to the spot where Leehuuk and his wife had emerged from the forest. It did not take long to locate the spot where they had lingered. Amuun'axsum turned back to the clearing to retrieve her bucket. She contemplated who to tell about her discovery, or whether to share at all.

She was halfway down the trail when the sentry jogged past her. But as she neared the winter house, she slowed and came to a stop beside the man. They would both have to wait to deliver their news. A gap had been made in the back wall of the winter house. A few of the younger men, including Dushuuw, walked through with a canoe hoisted on their shoulders. Songs of mourning spilled out behind the procession, flowed beneath the canoe, carried it along on a current of grief.

THE AIR WAS COLD. The ground was cold.

The shadows were deep, and the tree boughs creaked in the wind.

Uhpqoolth rested his hand on his injured arm, which was bound to his side. Brow furrowed, he stared into the forest floor. His face was wet with tears, though his mouth was pressed shut as if denying their existence. He looked far up, his eyes finding the spot where the young chief's burial canoe rested high on a platform set across the strong branches of the cedar tree, ropes holding it fast. Was Uhpqoolth thinking of his cousin—his best friend? Or of his father's lost body—interred in whatever haphazard way the sea saw fit?

Dushuuw looked up to the hull of the canoe. The canoe was Dushuuw's demand. Others argued that they needed every intact canoe they could get. But there was no box grand enough for his brother's body; the canoe was the right thing to do. The vessel that had saved Buh-uhs, bound to the earth by a strong rope and wise hands, would now anchor the body of the whaler aloft.

In the tree, Yaq and Kweelthup perched on sturdy branches and finished lashing the canoe to the trunk—as they had done weeks earlier for his father's burial box. Dushuuw glanced at that box. A patch of white bird dung marked one side. Moss had already crept over the corners. It had shifted in the quake, but remained aloft. They left it alone.

Across the backs of Dushuuw's hands, dark veins bulged, branching and snaking their way up his arms. He peered at them, wondering if the blood they housed really was flowing—or if it was as still as it looked from the outside, and as still as it felt inside. Bruises and cuts crossed his body, red with the threat of infection, but he could bear that pain.

Far above his head, a cedar box and a cedar canoe sat among the branches of a cedar tree. Two deaths that could be traced back to him. Would this be the moment? Would the men standing with him on the ground finally surround him, close in, hold out their ropes and lash him to this tree to die as well? He would let them. He squeezed his eyes shut, even though it called up the darkness that now haunted him, the monster at his back. The men moved past him, silent with respect.

~

The sentry from the spring had reported the plume of smoke from Tsooyuhs, and Dushuuw and a few other men now prepared to paddle toward that smoke. Dushuuw was still twitchy, and getting into that water again was a mental hurdle. But he had learned long ago what to do with fear of that kind: he fought it back. And taking action would do more for his spirit than lying on his bed.

But they could not leave yet. The grandmothers forced food on them before they left. Dushuuw tried to wave it off.

"There is not enough as it is," he said.

Yahbis looked at him as if he were both a fool and a disappointment.

The once-stout woman had lost weight since the disaster. Mirth had left her face, leaving age behind. Dushuuw did not like the frailness that snatched at his grandmother's bones. But her forceful voice dispelled him of that concern.

"Do you have no pride?" she said.

Dushuuw fumbled for words. "Of course, I—let the food go to those who need it more."

Yahbis huffed. She tried to draw her short frame taller. Instinctively, Dushuuw leaned back, but he was too late to avoid the blow. She poked him in the ribs—pointedly aiming for one of his more pronounced bruises—and he winced. He put his hand over the spot, if only to protect it from more pokes.

"I, for one, know that you are not invincible," she said. She gave a stiff nod, as if the statement answered all the universe's questions.

Dushuuw looked to the clouds despite his better judgment. "I know that too."

The old woman opened her mouth to say more. But she stopped when she saw his face.

Dushuuw turned his gaze down to the ground. "Do you not think that I know," he whispered, "that it should have been me in a burial box—if not lost altogether, out to sea?"

Yahbis inhaled long and blew out a quiet breath. She brushed her hand down his arm. "My boy, my boy," she whispered.

Kweelthup walked up. "You about ready to go, Young Son?"

Yahbis glared up at the young whaler, who was even taller.

"No. He needs food," she said.

Kweelthup put up his hands and turned. Unlike Dushuuw, he knew when to back out of a fight with an elderly lady. Dushuuw was just glad the interruption had brought the woman's mind back to food. At her direction, a slave shoved a box into his hands. He looked inside. It was not much—strips of dried meat, a length of kelp stem filled with oil, dried berry cakes—but it was more than enough for their journey.

Yahbis read his mind. "Who knows how long you will be out there? But there's also no telling what shape they will be in, the people you find," she said. "And how many can you bring back with you in two small canoes? This will help you feed those who may need it more than us—and I won't feel as guilty eating my own share."

Out on the water, the familiar rhythm of paddling soon took over. Dushuuw and Kweelthup took a woman's canoe; it served their purpose. In a larger sealing canoe in front of them, Yaq and Huh-uuk powered ahead. One canoe had been saved by a rope tied to a tree. There had been only minor damage, which other men had fixed earlier. The other canoe had been stored on the high ground for the winter. As they crossed the bay, Dushuuw saw another canoe lodged high in a tree, tilted awry. A large hole pierced its side.

The men set their sights on the plume of smoke, piercing the sky. Dushuuw's hope was tempered by caution. Only one person was needed to light a signal fire.

Tsooyuhs was their closest neighbor down the coast, occupying the south end of the same wide bay into which Wuh-uhch launched its canoes. A small, low point stuck out into the bay, marking a halfway point between the two villages. But that landmark was invisible now; it made the distance seem greater.

The men tried their best to ignore the things that their canoes pushed aside as they started to cross the bay. The body of water might take half a day to cross in its clogged and altered condition. About a third of the way across they passed the engorged creek mouth that extended from the unseen lake higher up, the lake where the young chief had died during his prayers. Dushuuw forced his gaze again toward Tsooyuhs. Farther on, the canoes glided over the rocks of the submerged point, passing the halfway point. As the Tsooyuhs territory came into view, they all stopped paddling. Kweelthup muttered under his breath. Dushuuw gazed landward in disbelief.

Tsooyuhs sat on low ground. The village faced the sea head on, forested hills rising far to its back.

They had seen what the sea did to their own houses on the low ground. And they could guess at the scene at Tsooyuhs, even when it was out of sight. They knew. Yet to see it up close was a different matter.

During visits, they had requested a landing on a broad beach. Homes had followed the curve of the shoreline, flanking a small river. Small trees had provided shade and a natural barrier around a broad prairie, which reached inland to sharply ascending hills.

Only the hills remained. Everything else was brackish water.

With wavering hope, the men paddled toward to the high promontory. They drew close enough to see the movement of the smoke, curling above the treetops. The promontory was cut off from the mainland by the flood waters. Dushuuw looked inland toward the other high points, but those were farther away and there were no signs of other fires. Whoever had made it out of Tsooyuhs in time, they would be found on this outcrop.

Anticipation filled the men as they drove forward.

Kweelthup spotted the man first. The man stood on a rocky ledge, waving his arms to make himself visible within the shadows of the trees.

Another man appeared from the shadows. Then a boy. A woman.

Dushuuw and Kweelthup pulled up alongside the other canoe. Yaq and Huh-uuk looked over with wide smiles.

"The old ladies back home are going to have a lot more stomachs to fill," Yaq said.

Dushuuw smiled back. But his smile faded as he thought ahead. There was not enough food for the mouths they already had to feed.

~

They brought as many survivors back with them as they could. Back at Wuh-uhch, the sight caused an excited stir. Crowds rushed to help the elderly or care for the injured. An older man of Wuh-uhch took out his skin drum, and sang a song of celebration.

People with relatives in Tsooyuhs asked about loved ones.

"Did you see my sister?"

"Anyone from the north side of the river make it? My wife's aunt lived there."

And they asked about others as well.

"What about Oosa-ilth? Do you have any news from there? My

great-grandmother's side is down that way."

To each question, Dushuuw answered that he did not know yet—even if he did. Whose news was sad or good could wait, or come from another's lips.

But the rush of questions confirmed for him the need to get out to more villages. He worked through his idea with Kuhbuhṫup. Soon, the older man was helping him convince a Wuh-uhch family to give up two seal hides for the refugees. Dushuuw asked for a third to take himself.

"I am keeping this one," the woman said.

"I am asking you to give it," Dushuuw said.

"We are not the only family with extra furs."

"And I am asking them as well. Do you know what we need?"

"Food, of course."

Dushuuw nodded. "And that is what I aim to get. But it will require your fur."

The woman looked down at the soft hide in her hand, caressed it one last time, then handed it over to Dushuuw.

"There will be more hides soon enough, and I will make sure you get more than you gave," he said.

"Oh, now, that is not necessary."

"I know."

He smiled. She returned the smile, then shook her head and bent down to the child tugging at her skirt.

Kuhbuhṫup grabbed his arm as they walked away. "I do not think you need me to speak for you," he said. "I never would have thought that gossiper would part with anything."

"Only because you were by my side," Dushuuw said.

"But I did not say anything!"

"Sometimes it is not words that are needed," Dushuuw said.

"I do not need to lend you authority. You have it, especially now."

Dushuuw bristled and turned to the speaker. But he could not come up with the words to express his thoughts.

"You have it, whether you want it or not," Kuhbuhṫup said, sensing what went unsaid.

The old man straightened and looked about the winter house. "I will go work on Leehuuk over there, see what he can contribute. He cannot say he lost it all in the flood. I know my old friend too well."

Dushuuw called Yaq over. "Is the other canoe ready?"

Yaq nodded. "As soon as the repairs were done, the men loaded it up with blankets and left for Tsooyuhs. They should return before nightfall."

"When they do return, you and I are going to start loading that canoe up again, but not for Tsooyuhs."

"Where do you want to go?"

"We'll wait for the runner to come back from Deeyuh with the latest news there. But probably up the strait. The inland villages will be our best chance for finding food," Dushuuw said. "We'll send out other canoes to check on our relations in the closer villages. I think Kuhbuhtup is best to go seek Ḥawith and our other contacts across the strait. Leehuuk can go to Oosa-ilth. They can each take another man with family ties, but I think only one each—we cannot load down those canoes too much, and everyone is going to want to go."

Dushuuw was aware that he was speaking rapidly, but he was afraid the thoughts would disappear if he didn't get them out.

"There is plenty of work here to keep their minds off things," he continued. "The able can help take more people in from Tsooyuhs and deliver supplies to those staying there at the redoubt. The waters are starting to recede, and there's plenty of cleanup to do. We'll need to clear new overland trails too."

"I don't know, friend. People don't have much energy, not with the rationing we've already been doing. And now, with more food going out the doors..."

"I know. That is why we need to leave soon."

Yaq nodded. He started to walk away, but hesitated.

"It is good to have you back," Yaq said.

Dushuuw watched his friend go. It had been just the two of them so often, gallivanting off for some fishing or pranks.

His thoughts were interrupted as Amuun'axsum crossed the house. She noticed him but focused on taking water to the guests and the wounded. He never saw her without a water bucket now. The slaves were not getting meat. She was thin, but solid from the work. He trusted she saw the work as he did—a welcome distraction. Seeing her still stirred guilt over his survival, and confusion over what kind of power seemed to tie her to him. He wondered where their relationship stood. With each other. With the community. With the world.

Right now, it was the world that concerned him most. How many were left? He intended to find out.

# 54

AMUUN'AX̱SUM SAW Dushuuw in the winter house. Earlier she had passed right by him, but he was deep in conversation and did not notice. When she returned with water for the Tsooyuhs guests, she caught his eye for a moment before turning back to her task.

She had never seen him so driven. He acted as if he were among those in charge.

The dipper clacked against the side of the empty bucket.

He was...

"More water, please?"

Amuun'ax̱sum looked down at the girl at her feet. The girl's chin was wet from where the water had spilled in her eagerness to gulp it down.

"It is so good," the girl smiled.

"Of course, little one." Amuun'ax̱sum smiled back, grateful for the sign of courtesy, even if it was from a child. She leaned down and gave the girl a wink. "I will go get some more and give you the first taste—it's always the best."

The girl giggled, and ran her hands down her splinted leg.

Amuun'ax̱sum moved around bed mats. She passed the spot where Leehuuk had taken up residence with his family. The nobleman stood with his wife, who held their daughter by the hand. The nobleman spoke to Kuhbuht̓up, the man who had served as the speaker for Dushuuw's father and brother. Amuun'ax̱sum slowed her steps to eavesdrop.

"I am happy to help, Kuhbuht̓up," Leehuuk said, spreading out his palms before folding them in front of himself again.

"We lost so much in the flood," his wife added. "But take anything you see, of course."

Kuhbuht̓up took the few offered items, then gestured toward the woman's ears. "How about those?"

She reached up and clutched one of the earrings. She opened her mouth as if to protest, but was at a loss for words.

"As you say, you have lost so much already," Kuhbuhtup said. "This will help feed the children, including your own."

The noblewoman flushed, gaze flicking to her husband as she pulled out the earrings and placed them into Kuhbuhtup's open palm. Leehuuk looked at the ground.

Amuun'axsum followed Kuhbuhtup out of the house. Her stomach fluttered, but she forced herself to speak. "Excuse me, Kuhbuhtup?"

Kuhbuhtup turned with a look of surprise.

"If you would come with me up the hill, to the spring—"

"I have more important things to do then help you fetch water, girl." For proof, he lifted his arm, which was slung with a fur, and held up his hand holding the earrings.

"There is something you should see," Amuun'axsum said, taking a step forward. She raised her chin and dropped her voice. "Something that would help you fill your hands, considerably so."

Kuhbuhtup looked at her with interest. He passed off the goods in his arms to a slave boy. "Lead on, then."

They walked up the hill toward the spring. The sentry passed them along the way. The men gave short greetings. As they approached the point, Amuun'axsum turned to the older man. "We will have to veer off a bit, into the forest." He looked skeptical but kept walking beside her, so she picked up her pace.

As they entered the forest's edge, she worried she would not be able to find the spot again. But the rich couple had been lazy, and she quickly found the small mound covered in fern leaves.

"Rather odd pile there, don't you agree?"

He eyed her.

She tried to maintain a normal pace as she left him there to go fill her water bucket, though her heart pounded. She clutched the bucket to her stomach. As she neared the forest's edge, she heard a sound of exclamation behind her—and smiled.

55

CHAI LOOKED OLDER, her usual effluence a memory. She had become quiet following their escape into the cave and their father's death. Now, with her mother's strange illness lingering on, she barely ate. She kept to the hut where the shaman prayed and sang over her mother's twisted limb. She came to the winter house only to sleep. In early mornings, Dushuuw would see his sister clutch the hide hanging in the doorway, cinching it in her hands, back straight, as she set her eyes toward the sea, as if looking for a return. Dushuuw mourned this change in his sister. Yet he also noted the fierce bravery that lingered beneath her grief. She was less frivolous. Chose her words carefully. Moved like a noblewoman beyond her young years.

Now, she faced him with open hands.

"I remember uncle saying one of the inland peoples always pay well for these," she said, handing him her most luxurious fur cloak.

"And I have no more need for any of this," she added.

He took the box and looked inside at the earrings, pendants, cuffs, and myriad other accessories. He spotted one particular earring near the bottom. The small plate of copper retained its iridescent sheen. It was tiny, and without a mate. A lonely bauble. It was what remained of her finest gift from their father. He remembered how she had cried when she had lost its match.

"You should keep this one," he said, placing the earring in her palm. A mix of emotions crossed her face. "I will not be able to use it; it would need a match," he lied.

"Of course," she said, clutching it with poorly hidden relief. "How silly of me."

"Not silly at all," he said. "This is more than anyone else has given, Chai. It is a generous sacrifice that will be repaid to you tenfold."

She looked up at him, flustered. "You must not think that is why I—"

"I know," he said. "And that is why it is true."

She looked down again, and bounced her closed hand against her side. "I hope it does some good."

Dushuuw drew her close, placing his forehead against her own as he looked in her eyes, waiting for her to return his smile, then walked over to the group of men waiting for him in a partitioned corner of the house.

His eyes fell first on Leehuuk, and he stifled the grimace he wanted to give. The nobleman sat beside Uhpqoolth. On his other side was Wiid, and Dushuuw felt uneasy over the bright glint in the war chief's gaze. Part of him regretted avoiding the man, if only to know what plan cooked in his mind.

Dushuuw focused on his cousin. "How fare the twins?"

Uhpqoolth lifted one shoulder in a shrug. "Their mother needs more good foods," he said. "Not producing enough milk."

"We will get her what she needs."

Dushuuw launched into the guts of the plan, identifying destinations, goals, and who should go where with what trade items they had gathered.

Leehuuk glanced at Uhpqoolth, who sat without comment.

"I wonder, Young Son, why it is you who seems to have all the answers," Leehuuk said.

Kuhbuhtup turned to the nobleman. "What do you mean by that?"

Leehuuk held out his hands. "I simply mean that many of us have questions about succession now that both the men who built this house are gone." He bowed his head at Dushuuw. "I mean no disrespect. But most of us presumed Uhpqoolth would be determining how the resources are spent. On the basis of names alone he is highly ranked while your status is... questionable."

Dushuuw slid a glance at his cousin and remained quiet, because he could not disagree.

"I mean, Young Son brings in a lowborn friend to conversations meant for noble heads of households," Leehuuk said, gesturing toward Yaq. "What's next?" He looked at Dushuuw. "Slaves, I suppose..."

Dushuuw felt a response rise as rapidly as the heat on his face.

But his cousin spoke first.

"You go too far, Leehuuk," Uhpqoolth said.

Disgust tinged Uhpqoolth's retort, and Dushuuw realized he had nearly walked into a trap. He tried to push Amuun'axsum from his mind.

"And this is a waste of our time," Uhpqoolth continued. "We are deciding who goes where. And my cousin is right. Kuhbuhtup to the north. You to the south. And you to the east," he finished, looking over at Dushuuw. Uhpqoolth stood up, running his hand over his injured arm. "As for whose roof we are under—for the time being, you sleep under my cousin's arm." His voice was resigned. "Aside from having only one at the moment, my arm is reserved for my wife and children; and my time, for prayer."

Kuhbuhtup watched Uhpqoolth leave and turned to the others. "The village will be in capable hands while we are gone," he said.

Leehuuk sighed. "And yet how good, with a bad arm, if others would come here while we are gone, intending to take what we have?"

Wiid turned toward his cousin, his skin flushed. "I would answer them," he said, "with full force."

Confidence rose in Dushuuw, banishing his fears and worries. "We have our warriors. But that fear is exactly why we need to get out on the water," he said. "It's not just to get food. It's to show that we are still here, and that we remain strong."

"As we beg for food...?"

"We will pay handsomely." Dushuuw shook his head. "And they will not know it is everything we could pool together."

"Oh, not everything, Young Son," Kuhbuhtup said. The old man smiled. "I almost forgot." He pulled out a box. "I found these..."

Dushuuw marveled at the trove. He thought he recognized some of its contents, too, though he wasn't sure.

"Where...?"

"Oh, laying out in the forest. Hidden a bit, actually. But certainly within the family's territory. There was no question about that."

Leehuuk bolted upright, his posture as stiff as his voice. "I shall go ready our canoe for the trip south." A look of disappointment flashed across Wiid's face, but he stood and followed.

Kuhbuhtup and Dushuuw shared a knowing look, and Dushuuw glanced at Yaq, who stifled a laugh.

When the other noblemen were out of the house, Kuhbuhtup spoke again. "Leehuuk may have a point, though, about Uhpqoolth."

"That's his throwing arm," Yaq said, keeping his voice low.

"I know," Dushuuw said, "but my concerns are closer to home."

"You think Leehuuk will make a move while you all are away."

"I think it's possible. Wiid is up to something. Perhaps it's because of all that has happened..."

"He lost his sister," Kuhbuhtup said. "And her son, his nephew."

"But that means he'll be itching even more for a fight," Dushuuw said. "That's why I already spoke to Shuchkuk over at Tsooyuhs."

Kweelthup bunched his brows in thought. "The one who stayed at the redoubt there. The one you bested at the wedding?"

"And the one who fought with us up the strait, and chased off the northerners," Dushuuw said. "He will camp here, along with most of their men who can fight. It will leave the Tsooyuhs encampment diminished, but only for a short time. And what is left there to raid? Any strike would come here first.

"I've also enlisted some of their best paddlers," Dushuuw continued. "They know we're getting information and supplies for them as well."

Kuhbuhtup looked full of thoughts; but if so, the speaker kept them to himself.

Kweelthup shook his head, looking at the partition as if he could see his wife and children on the other side. "I worry about the journey."

"A moon has passed since the deluge. The women would normally be back on the water already. And we will stay as close to shore as we can manage," Dushuuw said.

Yaq rubbed his neck. "But what will those shores look like?"

"There's only one way to find out," Dushuuw said. "And we cannot wait for spring."

THE FIRST BATCH was done and deemed good enough. Now Um-iiqsu sat with Chaiyuhx-ik and showed her how to make a second batch of the black cod broth. Amuun'axsum handed the young woman a tray holding the remains of the few smoked fish they had been able to find among the house's stores. Amuun'axsum's fingers were covered in bits of the meat she had pried from the bones; she ducked her head to lick her fingers.

"Fresh would be better," Um-iiqsu said. "But this should work."

The women knelt in the house corner to work. The shaman had shooed even Chaiyuhx-ik away from the hut for a time, so Um-iiqsu sought to distract the young woman from her mother's lack of improvement. The partitions had been drawn closer to make more room along the walls for still more refugees seeking shelter from the winter cold. Nearby, a child complained of hunger. Deep in the forest, two infants cried for the milk that did not come plentifully enough from their struggling new mother who cried with them.

Um-iiqsu sighed and reached for a container. The skin beneath her eyes was dark, and her face was thin. The noblewoman still cared for others, but there was an edge to her moods. She filled the container with the steaming broth that had simmered for most of the morning, then handed the container to Chaiyuhx-ik.

"She won't like the taste," Um-iiqsu said, "but she will drink it."

Chaiyuhx-ik left to deliver the drink to Ootsihd in the family's woodland hut.

Amuun'axsum lingered near Um-iiqsu, knowing there would be some other task but also not wanting to go near the hut where the shaman droned on for the injured woman.

"I hope it helps," Um-iiqsu said, stirring the remaining broth. "But what helps most is the good news about the rest of her family at Tsooyuhs. Perhaps her mother will convince them to move here, now that she has grandchildren here. I wonder why they would want to rebuild that village anyway, why they cling to a beach that is no more."

Amuun'axsum said nothing. The tales coming from Tsooyuhs had captivated Wuh-uhch and Deeyuh. Everyone had related the stories they'd heard at least five times over. Um-iiqsu, though, seemed to be talking for the sake of talking.

"No food for them there," Um-iiqsu continued. "They take more of ours, and ours is nearly gone too. So why not bring the rest of them over? What do they guard there? They should come and build up our numbers while our men are gone in those canoes, working for the good of all of us." She took a deep breath and readjusted the cloak over her shoulders.

"Chitons," Amuun'axsum said.

Um-iiqsu looked up at Amuun'axsum, as if realizing she was not speaking only to herself.

"They're eating chitons, at Tsooyuhs. It was all they could find." Amuun'axsum looked down at her hands in her lap. "They eat them here, too."

Um-iiqsu wrinkled her nose. "Only once have I ever had to eat that rubbery monstrosity." She gave Amuun'axsum a wry smile. "I think I would rather starve."

Amuun'axsum smiled back, enjoying the black humor. Chitons did taste awful. They didn't have much nutrition either; her thinning arms were evidence of that. But something in the stomach was better than nothing in the stomach.

"There is also plenty of salal," Amuun'axsum said, in a searching tone, unsure if she should try to extend the humor.

Um-iiqsu laughed. "Indeed, we can all be warriors on the trail." She pumped her fist in the air. "Actually, I have never eaten salal leaf. Perhaps it is quite tasty."

Amuun'axsum scrunched up her nose and shook her head.

"You have tried it?"

Amuun'axsum looked at the ground again as she nodded. "Too many times," she said. Just thinking about it brought the sensation to her mouth. She had pinched many a waxy leaf from a salal bush during hungry winters as a child, and many times in the past week. A folded leaf, ground between her back teeth—but only if she had something to occupy her time, to keep her mind off that acerbic bite. The taste assaulted the tongue as the leaf broke apart into tiny bits, filling the mouth like thistle fluff. It relieved you of hunger only because you had no desire to put anything else in your mouth again for a long while.

Um-iiqsu hummed over the expression on Amuun'axsum's face. "Right, scratch that also from the list of foods I would eat in the most dire of circumstances." She stood and hugged her fur close. "An extra robe, I should think, will be the preferred way to bring back my figure."

Amuun'axsum smiled and stood up as well. She thought of other foods to eat in times of hunger. Fronds of deer fern. The tips of hemlock leaves. Not for the first time, she wondered about the relative poverty of her noble childhood compared to a village like Wuh-uhch.

"Speaking of food, I set aside a bit of dried whale and a dish of oil," Um-iiqsu said, her voice low.

Amuun'axsum's stomach grumbled. An eager rush filled her—until she realized the noblewoman did not mean the food for a slave.

"Eekbis is not eating enough, and working so hard. Bring this, and urge her to eat," said Um-iiqsu, handing her a small box.

Amuun'axsum stifled any sign of her sinking disappointment.

As she left the house corner, though, Leehuuk's wife bustled over. She was one of the few women who had not lost the sheen to her hair, the plumpness to her cheeks. Amuun'axsum surmised the cache of jewelry was not the couple's only hidden treasure.

"Where have you been?" the noblewoman said to Amuun'axsum. "We need more water in here. Why should my slaves do all the work?"

Amuun'axsum bit back the reply that wanted to race from her tongue to put this woman in her place.

But then Sawsin was at her side. The young noblewoman drew herself up. "I do agree we could use more water... Quulthoo, after you have done what Um-iiqsu has asked, find our other attendant slaves. You will join Leehuuk's slaves as they go to the spring." Amuun'axsum stared at the young woman's profile, taken aback by her renewed strength and conviction. A simply carved comb decorated her hair. She was slight, and younger than Amuun'axsum. But she more than held her own before the older noblewoman. The smiles they traded were not friendly. Amuun'axsum hid her own.

Soon, Amuun'axsum and Uhpahs were walking up the trail, trading insults about Leehuuk's wife at a safe distance from the other slaves.

"As useful as a mussel shell for a bailer," Uhpahs said.

"A heart as dark and stinky as a soiled diaper."

"A tongue as bitter as salal leaf."

"A head as full as my stomach," Amuun'axsum said, with no smile.

The women filled their buckets at the spring. The watch now consisted of two sentries, who looked less bored than in the past.

Tensions and altercations were growing more frequent across the cape near clean water sources. Wuh-uhch's was plentiful and reliable, and word had gotten out. But no matter how productive, it was not bottomless. The two women said nothing as they filled the buckets under the men's watchful eyes and trod back down the trail.

They had been the last to leave and were on a shady stretch of trail when Amuun'axsum saw him. She nearly dropped her bucket. An icy splash slid over the rim and drenched her skirt.

Toopuuk walked up the trail toward the women, his eyes on Amuun'axsum. She wished she could stop her body from trembling. Emotions warred within her—relief, fear, confusion. The Deeyuh slave cast a quick glance at Uhpahs in acknowledgment, then stopped in front of Amuun'axsum. He held up a dead hare by its legs like an offering.

"You need meat," he said.

"I'm fine," she said.

"I'll cook it for you," he said.

"There's no need."

"I'll prepare it. She'll eat it, I'll make sure," Uhpahs said. Amuun'axsum looked at Uhpahs as her friend took the rabbit from Toopuuk. Uhpahs gave her a pleading look. "Do not look at me like that, Quulthoo. Your baby needs it, even if you don't. So does mine."

"You can share it," Toopuuk said, nodding eagerly.

"It will only get us in trouble," Amuun'axsum said, her voice rising as she turned back to face him. She started to march down the path, but he held out an arm and stopped her—gently, but firmly.

"I take care of my own," he said. "I take care of you—and my child." His voice lifted with his grin.

Amuun'axsum blanched as he placed his palms at her sides and crouched, kissing her stomach. "I will make you a lullaby," he whispered.

He smiled up at her. "The shaman told me about the pregnancy when I came to find you to give you this," he said. "She understands that the meat must go to you first. And you need it. More than I knew." He stood and tucked her hair behind her ear. "I was pleased to hear you were unharmed. I worried. And that was before knowing about the child..." He cupped his palm against her face.

"I will make sure she eats the meat," Uhpahs said. "We do have to get this water back to the winter house though." She took a step forward.

Toopuuk shoved the bow further up his shoulder and held out his hands. "Let me carry the buckets for you."

Uhpahs handed hers over. So Amuun'axsum did as well.

Toopuuk smiled again, causing the scar on his face to shorten. In a flash, Amuun'axsum saw what he would look like as an old man, wrinkles and sagging skin reshaping that scar even more. Eyes dancing when they looked at her. She looked aside, hooking her arm over Uhpahs's elbow and propelling them downhill. Toopuuk kept up a steady monologue.

"I was lucky to catch that hare," he said. "The flood flushed a bunch of them out, but I'm not alone out there. I strayed a bit beyond the boundaries, but with everyone else doing it... By that point, I figured I may as well keep walking here."

Amuun'axsum winced at a stitch in her side but did not slow down.

"I left the rest of what I killed behind that hut of your local nobleman, the one with the broken arm. I would get some nasty looks if I brought it any closer to hungry eyes. It was bad enough with a single hare. But the rest is for Deeyuh. I've spent enough time away. Oodahk will be expecting me."

At the forest's edge, he handed Uhpahs back her water bucket, and placed Amuun'axsum's on the ground. Toopuuk drew Amuun'axsum close, caressing and kissing, then knelt in front of her and kissed her stomach. Amuun'axsum felt a pang, a surge of warmth, and the familiar confusion. As he left, he walked backward for a time to keep looking at her, humming his song.

Amuun'axsum took the hare and the bucket and followed after Uhpahs. In as isolated a spot as she could find outside, she cleaned the hare. Skinned it. Roasted it. Then, though the meat was still scorching hot, she hacked it in pieces and put the meat in a bowl. The intoxicating scent trailed after her like a long, slinking tail. Heads turned, faces full of longing. Children bounded up to her begging for a taste. Amuun'axsum swallowed the gathering saliva in her mouth, and pursed her lips.

She walked past the winter house to the hut where Eekbis sang over the noblewoman. Thluuch-muup looked frail, her arm still twisted against her chest. Chaiyuhx-ik knelt once again beside her mother and swayed, though Amuun'axsum sensed it was not because of the music.

The shaman glanced at Amuun'axsum as she sang, dragging an eagle feather down the length of the woman's side. Any healthy person would have at least twitched at such a tickling touch. Thluuch-muup lay still.

Amuun'axsum held the tray of meat up, giving the shaman a questioning look. Eekbis looked at the meat, a gleam in her eye. Amuun'axsum walked around to Chaiyuhx-ik and put the tray of meat on the floor beside the young woman; she gently touched her arm.

Chaiyuhx-ik looked up as if wondering where Amuun'axsum had come from, then glanced at the meat. Amuun'axsum left the hut, and she wouldn't know if Chaiyuhx-ik ever ate any of the meat. But the shaman's song turned to humming for a time.

TRADING DONE, THE MEN headed down the strait, back toward the sea and home, in a state of disbelief.

Dushuuw's canoe had eventually converged with others at a large winter village that sat high atop a ridge overlooking the inland waters and waterlogged islands. He got more food than he had hoped, thanks to good trades and their host's generosity. The Wuh-uhch crew's quick timing—and their surfeit of valuable goods—worked to their advantage over other tribes coming to the high ground for the same reasons.

Multiple people groups were present, including the strait group Dushuuw and his warriors had attacked earlier. Dushuuw eyed those men warily, but the war went unmentioned.

The various groups traded stories as they traded goods. Massive whirlpools had churned the seawaters into maws with teeth of froth. Canoes came down in trees, or broke free of their lines and floated away. Whole villages succumbed to the quake and deluge, while others survived in canoes only to wash up on faraway shores. Rivers flowed with salt. Valleys were submerged. A rock slide obliterated one village.

Here at Hibulb, the area's main village site, more houses were being built for families coming to stay under the local chief's arm. A woman sat spinning wool, its fluffy white fibers twisting and swirling around the whorl. Down below, the waters spun and shifted, creating new patterns in land and sea.

Dushuuw shared bits and pieces, running his fingers through the wool of one of the local dogs that had survived on the island where it was kept, a dog that could be a cousin or brother to one of their own.

In truth, the information was all bits and pieces—no one yet had a vision of the whole of what had happened—but in combination with what he had seen for himself, it was enough to set Dushuuw further on edge. Despite the pleasure of a warm house and full stomach at Hibulb, he longed to get home. If it was this damaging headed inland, what would Kuhbuḥtup and Leehuuk have found on the other parts of the outer coast? So he made the visit short.

Now, they passed the same scenes they had seen on the way up the strait. Forested sections of hillside scraped bare, like supernatural claw marks rending a garment. Floating islands of debris that shifted and moved with the currents. Rivers like bloated tongues, trying to unblock their airways. A blue sea made black and brown, mixing with the earth even as it tried to spit it out.

They made their way down the strait. They pushed on to Deeyuh, and stayed the night there, sharing some of the food they had bought. They entered one of the houses clustered on the hillside. Flood waters had receded from the low ground, but no one was eager to rebuild, not yet. Cleanup would take many more moons anyway.

Oodahk rested his hand on Dushuuw's back as they walked to a fire.

"People around the cape have been looking forward to your return," the Deeyuh whaler said.

"For the food, you mean."

"Obviously."

"Did the other canoes come back?" Dushuuw asked.

Oodahk nodded. "A runner told me when Kuhbuḥtup's canoe was returning, and I went over to Wuh-uhch to hear the news. He was able to locate a few key family folks, with help from Ḥawith."

"Ḥawith is alive then."

"They were hit hard," Oodahk said, shaking his head. "All those little inlets and places for the water to send itself—and it did, about as far as you can go in a canoe, and then much farther."

Dushuuw nodded, thinking of their river that had become a strait, and of swollen creeks that for a time more closely resembled rivers.

"I heard of strange patterns," said Dushuuw, recalling nights around the Hibulb fires. "One village wiped out. Their neighbors almost untouched."

"Our people are blessed, to have as many survive as we have, from here to Oosa-ilth. We have the strength of our elders. Our high points. Our canoes and our ropes. Our leading men too." Oodahk rested his elbows on his knees, and leaned toward the fire. "I hear Leehuuk is doing some good things back your way. Making some good decisions."

"Where he is allowed to make them," Dushuuw said.

Oodahk laughed and ran his tongue over his teeth as he eyed Dushuuw. "You can help us on a whale hunt in the spring."

"Or you can help us," Dushuuw countered with a smile. "So you are not worried either, like the others?"

"I don't worry, no," Oodahk said. "We're hungry. But we're usually hungry this time of year. And we all have our stories remembering famine and hardship. Even this is not so unusual," he said, sweeping his arm over the view below. "We are called Deeyuh for a reason; this isn't the first time it's all been underwater. Those stories wouldn't be told if they hadn't survived to tell them. And of course, they taught us how to survive them as well. It may be a bit harder this time. We mourn, and will mourn with every feast, every dance that reminds us of who we lost. But this struggle with hunger, shelter—it will pass. We'll regroup. You had the right idea, getting out there. You showed them strong men working paddles in a canoe, and they will figure there are more of the same back home."

Dushuuw nodded. "That was part of the idea."

"Still," Oodahk said, "it was a risk. You know what happened to Q̓watee when he went after that sea monster—he got swallowed."

"Then he cut his way out and provided a whole meal for his starving people," Dushuuw added.

"Got vomited out, more like! And what you have in your canoe is hardly a sea monster's worth of food," Oodahk said, shaking his head. "You went a long way for a little. People are going to get real hungry again soon enough."

Dushuuw looked down at his hands. "I know."

"Well, if you manage to lay a feast, I won't be the bird who was too busy preening to arrive on time." Oodahk squeezed Dushuuw's shoulder with a smile.

Dushuuw appreciated the chief's light tone. But he knew Oodahk was right. And so did the men listening in. The elation they had felt returning home with a full canoe now fled as they thought of all the mouths that would soon make it disappear. Dushuuw had bargained only for a delay of the inevitable, and a short delay at that.

When they reached Wuh-uhch the next afternoon, Dushuuw sought out Kuhbuht̓up.

"How did H̱awith and the others survive there?"

"In their canoes, much like Buh-uhs," Kuhbuht̓up said. "The elders had pointed to worrying signs the day before, like mice moving in droves in daylight. So they anchored their canoes to sturdy trees, and loaded them with food and water. As soon as that quake hit, most people fled up trails as high in the mountains as they could get, or they got in those canoes. Ḥawith had thought the old people were being too worried. He listened anyway, and was glad for it. But not everyone listened."

Dushuuw was suddenly submerged again. He felt the sea's frigid grip, the churning, the battering—and the far greater pain of holding his brother's body in his arms. He had to force out his next question.

"You told them...?"

"I told them about your brother, yes. They're in no shape to travel yet. But Ḥawith will come when he can to take Sawsin home."

The loss of the marriage alliance did not hurt Wuh-uhch in the short term, but it could prove a significant loss for both sides as they moved into a time of uncertainty. The loss paled, though, against what Sawsin must be going through. Her marriage was about more than an alliance, as it had been for his brother. He hoped she'd find peace with her family.

"Any other news?"

"Not much more than what Oodahk probably shared with you. Many dead, but many living. Villages wrecked, people drifting here and there. At least one village was completely wiped out that I heard about—the land and all its people. Their neighbors watched from the hillside above as the land gave way and the sea tore away what was left," Kuhbuhṭup said. "Everyone was sleeping. They had no chance."

Dushuuw sat back with a shake of his head. "Who was it?"

"None of our relations, and no one we ever did business with," Kuhbuhṭup said. "I believe the name was Loḥta."

Dushuuw's stomach dropped.

"You know the name?"

"I've heard of it." Dushuuw put his head in his hands, then pulled upright again. "I had hoped to go there in the spring. On a—rumor. A rumor of a good trading opportunity."

"It's strange to think about," the elder said. "A whole people, gone in a moment. More than flesh and blood is lost. Songs, dances, crests, stories, names... A whole world with its history and its future, gone in one breath. Nothing left to even bury."

Dushuuw thought of all Amuun'axsum hoped to regain. She had survived her first village being wiped from existence. Could she survive knowing the last one was wiped away too? He could not tell her. Not yet. He had to see where things stood with Deeyuh, and how things stood between them after she knew the truth. Would she still be waiting for him, if the gifts he piled up were the price to purchase a slave?

He looked down at Kuhbuhṭup, realizing he had stood up.

Dushuuw looked beyond the corner of the house to the tight groups of people. He had released a first ration of the new food stores. A young girl smiled up at Sawsin, who handed her a bit of dried salmon. The girl chomped away, her leg held out straight in front of her between wooden splints. The rest of the food was stored away in boxes in the corner of the house. He was aware of the hungry gazes that kept flitting his direction.

Like many of the men, Dushuuw did not eat. They were used to fasting. As Huh-uuk had said, patting his now-flat stomach, "This fast will just last a bit longer." But Dushuuw noted that several noblewomen, including Um-iiqsu and Sawsin, also passed up their portions.

"I will go find Yaq to come sit with you," Dushuuw said.

Kuhbuhtup nodded his understanding—that they could not leave this area unattended while it stored food.

Leaving the house, Dushuuw found his friend and sent him off to the winter house. He couldn't remember what he had said, nor Yaq's response, only that what he wanted done was being done.

A canoe full of food, nearly gone already. A risky search for a family, now gone in a flood. Frustration and disappointment built inside Dushuuw, threatening to turn into despair. Instead, he turned to his anger, and steered it uphill. Fists clenched, he charged toward the forest. He walked past two women, bickering over the food they had received. He walked past a hunter, who averted his gaze as he adjusted his bow over his shoulder, hands empty of game. He walked past a hut, hearing the cries of a daughter for her mother, then passed another hut, hearing the cries of a mother mixed with the feeble cries of two babies.

He walked until he faced the stalwart trunk of a cedar. Standing there, he looked up its length until his gaze was arrested by the canoe and by the box, two wooden vessels for two men empty of life. But not empty of power. He pressed his hands against the trunk of the tree, then walked on.

~

Dushuuw did not sleep. He was late coming to bed, and too agitated to relax. So, in the early morning, through the pounding of rain, he was among the first to hear the loud wail.

Others awoke as the piercing cry went on and on.

Buh-uhs sat up from the mat on the ground beside Dushuuw's bench. He looked around, trying to find the source of the wailing, and looked to Dushuuw.

"What's wrong?"

"Your auntie has died."

Dushuuw swung his legs over the side of the bench and headed toward the sound of Chai's cries. Others roused as well. In the light of the low fires, they moved toward the outdoors. Children rubbed sleep from their eyes, propped up on elbows.

Outside, the early hour was made darker by the heavy rain. Dushuuw rushed across the meadow toward the hut at the forest's edge. The shaman took the hide down from the doorway, anticipating his arrival. He crouched under the low ceiling and fell to his knees beside Chai, scooping his wailing sister into his arms. She clung to him, and her body shook with sobs. Their grandmother sat against the back wall, tired from singing with the shaman. Sawsin stroked the old woman's arm. Um-iiqsu leaned over her sister's body, her fingers playing with the dead woman's hair. His stepmother's rigid body lay on the same mat as before, the arm still twisted against her chest. The shaman came back inside, her exhaustion apparent as she struggled to take off the weighty headdress.

Uhpqoolth slipped inside. Dushuuw nodded for him to come closer. He nudged Chai against their cousin, and tapped his stepmother on the shoulder. Um-iiqsu reluctantly sat back, running her hand down the side of her face. Dushuuw slipped his arms underneath the dead woman's body and lifted her up. He left the house, hearing his sister's wails reach a new pitch as she rose to follow.

Others came outdoors, many holding torches. They moved as one, as if drawn by the grieving young woman—all their loss and grief coalescing around this one loss and grief.

Dushuuw was halfway across the meadow, rain falling down his hair, when Chai was suddenly at his side, tugging at his arm.

"Do not take her away from me!"

She moved in front of him and dragged at the body. Dushuuw tried to absorb the shock of her hysterics. He knelt to the ground to avoid dropping the body or seeing Chai hurt. She sat on the muddy ground and held out her arms.

"Give her to me," she begged.

Dushuuw felt as if his chest were cracking. He placed the body onto his sister's lap, easing the head into the crook of her arm—as if passing off an infant.

Chai rocked and cried over her mother.

The crowd grew. The people formed a circle around daughter and mother. The rain pressed Chai's hair to her face. She rocked back and forth, the body limp across her lap. The dead woman's arm lay on the ground, lax. The palm collected rain, as if to drink.

Uhpqoolth stood over them, urging the crowd to give them space. Pikoo cut a path through the onlookers, with Um-iiqsu on one arm and Yahbis on the other. Sawsin followed close behind. The women came to Chai's side.

Dushuuw helped his grandmother kneel beside the keening young woman. The elder noblewoman's self-assured presence drew Chai's attention, though his sister's wails did not diminish.

"You should not bear such grief," Yahbis said. "We should not let your mother's death be marred by such tears."

Chai bent over her mother's body, as if her heart were trying to rip itself from her chest. Yahbis leaned toward her, brushing her wet hair from her face. "Let the grief fall on someone else," the old woman said. "Then you will gather the rest of the things that should also go into the earth with your mother."

Dushuuw watched as a change came over his sister. She continued to cry, but tried to restrain herself, her body twitching with stuttering sobs. She straightened and had a look of cold self-assurance. She nodded, looking to Yahbis now instead of the body in her arms, keeping her eyes on their grandmother.

Yahbis held her hand out to Dushuuw who helped her to stand. She gripped his arm, not letting him go, and he gazed down at his sister's upturned face, wet from falling rain and tears; Chai glared at him, making her unspoken demand. Holding her mother, she had never looked more fragile nor more imposing. He nodded at her and, satisfied, she dipped her head again toward her mother. Her shoulders rose and fell in the uneven rhythm of her renewed sobs.

Rain dripped off the ends of Chai's hair, falling onto the dead woman's face in drops that traced her cheeks, as if to cry on her behalf. Yahbis pulled on his arm, a reminder. Dushuuw patted his grandmother's hand, and gave her a curt nod.

AMUUN'AX̱SUM AND UHPAHS had given up on sleeping beneath the lean-to, which only magnified the sound of the rain. Instead, they built up a fire and cozied up to its edge, huddled inside the same large blanket. Uhpahs smelled of smoke and a sweet kind of sweat.

"Do you think our children will be best friends?" Uhpahs said.

Amuun'ax̱sum nuzzled up against her friend, thoughtful. She wondered where she might be when her baby was born. Deeyuh. Loḥta. Wuh-uhch. The first was most likely. She still clung to the other two hopes, though. If it were Deeyuh, at least she would be near Wuh-uhch. Amuun'ax̱sum laced her fingers through her friend's and held on. Whatever path Amuun'ax̱sum took to nobility, losing this friendship as it existed now was nearly certain. Amuun'ax̱sum pushed away a sudden urge to cry, and focused on the moment, the warmth of her friend beside her. "If we remain close, how could our children not also be close?"

"I think I am going to have a boy," Uhpahs said. "For he is already giving me indigestion."

Amuun'ax̱sum laughed with her, then answered Uhpahs's unspoken question. "A girl, I think. But for the same reason!"

The women sat together, warmed by the fire and each other. The amiable silence was interrupted by a woman's wail.

Uhpahs looked up. "Do you think..."

"Yes."

"Poor Chaiyuhx-ik..."

"Yes."

Amuun'ax̱sum was relieved, however, that the sick noblewoman was done lingering. The woman had suffered in that eerie silence for too long. Now she was at rest, and hopefully her daughter and sister could find some rest as well, freed from the confines of that death-scented hut.

"Are you sad?" Amuun'ax̱sum asked.

"Of course," Uhpahs said. "I was with her so long... this does not quite seem real. And yet, my mind and heart had already left her side, as soon as she agreed to let me stay and marry Suu-ahp. And of course, there is Chaiyuhx-ik to serve."

"Does she know you are pregnant?"

"I've told no one except you. Not even Suu-ahp. You know how pregnancies sometimes end themselves. And who else needs to know?"

Uhpahs hugged Amuun'axsum's arm.

"Will you need to go help now?"

"Oh, I suppose I should. There will be plenty of cleaning to do, and making sure Chai eats," said Uhpahs, as she tilted her head onto Amuun'axsum's shoulder. "But if so, I will wait until they call. I don't think I am ready to see her that way."

The fire had grown low, and they did not build it back up. Dawn light pierced the gray, wet film of the sky. Amuun'axsum leaned her head against Uhpahs's, and they stared at the shortening flames. They shuddered in unison, and stifled their laughter.

"Uhpahs..."

They looked up at the slave who spoke. For a moment, Amuun'axsum felt like she was caught—that they had committed some crime by finding a happy moment in the midst of another's pain.

"They need you," the slave said.

Uhpahs gave Amuun'axsum a small smile and leaned against her friend. "So I will serve her one last time..." She stood, shivering as she let her side of the blanket fall to the ground beside Amuun'axsum. Uhpahs groaned against the cold, but smiled again to show she was fine. Amuun'axsum knew better though. Uhpahs's identity had been wrapped up in the noblewoman for many years, and she couldn't hide her sense of uncertainty. So although Amuun'axsum was reluctant to leave the warmth of the fire, it was the fleeting warmth of her friend pressed to her side that she wanted more.

"Wait," she said, standing. "I will come with you."

Amuun'axsum held up the corner of the blanket and Uhpahs ducked back inside. They wiped the smiles from their faces as they hobbled toward the open meadow, following the other slave. Once or twice they had to catch their steps, and once Uhpahs stepped on Amuun'axsum's toes. Under the blanket, they each slipped an arm around the other's waist to better time their steps. Left, right. Left, right. The rain still fell, and a heavy mist rose off the warming ground. A songbird trilled a short tune, as if testing the verity of the day.

The slave looked back at the pair and gestured at Uhpahs as they drew near the crowd's edge. Uhpahs gave Amuun'ax̱sum's waist a squeeze before slipping out of the blanket again. "Wait for me before you go to the spring for water. I will come with you if I can," she said. Uhpahs's eyes shone with tears as she smiled once more, then she turned to follow the other slave through the crowd of people, who turned aside to make a path. The mist swirled upward as Uhpahs swished through.

Amuun'ax̱sum tried to remember where she had left her water bucket, then paused. The people who had parted for Uhpahs remained where they were, watchful. All of them—even the slaves—focused their attention on what lay in that clearing. Amuun'ax̱sum glanced beyond the crowd to the hut where the shaman had ministered to the dying woman. The doorway gaped black and empty.

Holding the large blanket close, Amuun'ax̱sum started to follow her friend. The lines of people on either side of her drew together to a point ahead, Uhpahs's small frame at its center.

In the clearing, a sodden Chaiyuhx-ik knelt with the dead noblewoman in her arms, rocking her mother's body as she clamped her mouth shut, only for it to open again with sobs. Uhpqoolth stood behind her, his arm bound to his side. The other noblewomen looked on. Dushuuw stood off to the side next to Um-iiqsu, his hands behind his back, and they all watched as Uhpahs approached with gliding, confident steps, as ready to serve as ever.

The bottom of the blanket dragged through the wet grass as Amuun'ax̱sum approached the inner edge of the crowd. People filled in behind her.

Um-iiqsu motioned Uhpahs over, then turned her toward her dead mistress. Dushuuw drew up close behind, looking over Uhpahs's shoulder toward the body in his sister's arms.

Amuun'ax̱sum crept beyond the inner ring of the crowd.

Chaiyuhx-ik raised her face to her brother. Um-iiqsu's hand tightened on Uhpahs's wrist. Uhpahs pulled back, only to step into Dushuuw's embrace. Dushuuw was slipping his hand up her neck, grabbing her hair, and bending her face up toward his own as he reached up with his other hand.

Amuun'ax̱sum shuddered to a stop. Her fingers loosened on the blanket; it slipped from her shoulders.

And Uhpahs was falling too. Her body crumpled to the ground amid a spray of blood as the blanket crumpled around Amuun'ax̱sum's ankles.

In his other hand, Dushuuw held a knife, both hand and knife wet with blood. The sun burst through a gap in the dripping clouds.

Um-iiqsu looked at Dushuuw and nodded.

A man broke through the crowd, collapsed to his knees and sobbed.

But Chaiyuhx-ik no longer cried. She looked up at her brother as she brushed her mother's hair, back and forth, as if coaxing the dead noblewoman to sleep.

The dead woman's arm lay on the ground, her tattooed wrist exposed. The fingers reached toward those of her slave, whose arm lay on the ground, wrist still red from Um-iiqsu's grip. The dead slave looked up at the sky, blood spilling down her chest. Um-iiqsu nudged the slave's arm aside with her foot.

A piercing cry rent the air. A moment later, Amuun'axsum realized it came from her own mouth. She was rushing forward. Um-iiqsu stood over the body, and turned. Amuun'axsum fell upon the noblewoman, bringing her to the ground. Amuun'axsum watched her hands as if they were not her own. She was scratching at the woman's face. The noblewoman was looking up at her with terror. Amuun'axsum blinked away tears, each blink bringing a new face into view beneath her hands—a face with more wet, red lines with each blink, as if Amuun'axsum were painting the woman for a dance.

Then Amuun'axsum was floating away, the noblewoman's body becoming smaller beneath her, as strong arms pinned her own and swung her away. She screamed. Warm breath whispered a familiar name in her ear, pleading, but she sobbed in response and turned her head away. One of his hands was wet, still warm. "How could you?" she cried. "How could you?" She tried to reach him, but could not. So she scratched her own face.

The circle that had surrounded the grieving daughter closed in. Um-iiqsu's cries shuddered with pain and anger. The circle drew tighter, people standing shoulder to shoulder. One man knelt at their feet—a fisherman crying for lost love—his mourning drowned by shouts and accusations.

"Evil! She sends evil into me!" Um-iiqsu clutched at her stomach.

"Yes, she sends out evil—she has done it before!"

"We all saw it!"

"She was jealous..."

"She took things from the noblewoman's corner and buried them."

The last voice was that of a boy—a boy who so often begged food, carried messages, who knew her name—and she crumpled further.

Dushuuw had dropped the knife when he grabbed Amuun'axsum. Now, Uhpqoolth grasped the hilt in his good hand and stood before Amuun'axsum—held tight by Dushuuw—and raised the blade.

"No," Dushuuw said, and Amuun'axsum was jerked to the side as he twisted her away from his cousin.

Amuun'axsum wrenched from his loosened grasp and fell to her knees beside her friend. "Please be alive," she whispered. "Please be alive." Her fingers trembled around her friend's face.

The young woman looked up at the brightening sky, but there was no sparkle in their black depths. Her mouth was turned downward in confusion. Blood dotted her cheeks and chin and spilled from the deep gash that rent through tissue and muscle and cartilage. Amuun'axsum muttered denials as her shaking hand went to her friend's cheek—the warmth already gone—and she tried to wipe off the blood. The bloody drops grew into bloody swaths, stamped by her own fingerprints.

Amuun'axsum leaned down and put her cheek against her friend's stomach, even as her hand continued to caress her friend's face, mourning both the life and the promise of life that were gone.

Above her the arguments raged—but she paid them no heed.

"A slave?"

"...not your call."

"Your duty..."

"...enough death."

Amuun'axsum thought of her friend and thought of the unborn baby. She thought of her mother's last step and her father sliding into darkness. She thought of the slave man and his hand slipping from her own. She thought of a boy whom she had loved, a family still lost, a hope that was getting harder and harder to hold.

"...mother's blood?"

"Go back..."

Amuun'axsum tried to remember a lullaby. What had she heard as a child? She could not remember.

"...evil magic."

"Your father..."

"Your brother..."

"Traitor..."

She remembered snippets of some soothing song. One that her mother's slave man would sing in his and her mother's language, and it was Amuun'axsum's favorite. He had sang that song so many times, when she was a girl and, even later, whenever she asked in whispers while her father was away and her mother lay praying for a whale that rarely answered. And maybe it was never the words, but the soothing tones of the slave man's hushed voice. Amuun'axsum started to whisper what she could remember of the lullaby, adding whatever other words came to her, singing as she stroked her dead friend's hair, trying to ignore the other voices.

"Responsibility."

"Blood."

"Unacceptable."

Amuun'axsum petted her friend's hair as she pursed her lips. She already forgot the words she had sang. It may have been a farewell song.

"If I may say something..."

A woman's voice rose above the others, and Amuun'axsum recognized it as the shaman's—the woman who sang songs of comfort over her when she woke from nightmares. Now, she awoke from another nightmare. Amuun'axsum finally looked up. Dushuuw looked defiant, and alone. The people watched him with confusion, distaste, unease. A few looked at her, in horror. She twirled a lock of her friend's hair around her finger. She sensed what would come next—what Dushuuw would learn. And the broken parts of her welcomed it.

"I make no claims on this girl," Eekbis said. "Yet your uncle did trade her to Oodahk. I was allowed to keep her with me through the winter. She is, however, already the man's property and she is to go to Deeyuh in the spring. Oodahk will expect fulfillment of the payment."

The old woman's shuffling steps rustled through the grass.

"So it is true," Dushuuw murmured.

The shaman ignored him. She spoke more for the ears of those around them.

"Perhaps the leaders and elders should meet to discuss this further," she said. "If the girl must be punished, so be it. If it is determined she must die, I make no claims. However, you should know that you would not only be killing her."

Amuun'axsum put her hand on her friend's forehead.

"I don't understand," Dushuuw said.

As she closed her friend's eyelids, Amuun'axsum willed that vacant look to enter her heart for what she was about to do. She spoke up.

"I am carrying a child to serve Deeyuh," she said.

She looked up to meet Dushuuw's shocked look and held his gaze as she stood, back straight.

"My husband—favored slave of Oodahk—waits for me there."

She watched him struggle for composure. She drew a breath, arming herself to meet his gaze. The look of hurt he gave her nearly prompted her to fold. She wanted to tell him there was no other way. She wanted to tell him she was drowning in grief. She wanted to urge him again to take her hand and run away. And she wanted to beat his chest for killing her friend. Instead, she raised her chin in an echo of the regal. She focused on the body at her feet.

"It is right that a man sees the child he has placed inside a woman."

Dushuuw looked away, but Amuun'axsum pressed on.

"A slave child who will be a strong worker for his chief."

He turned and glared at her.

"A chief who is one of your few remaining allies."

Even the shaman raised a hand to her wrinkled throat, as Dushuuw stomped up to loom over Amuun'axsum. But this is what it would take.

"Put me out of Wuh-uhch, Young Son," she whispered, so that only he could hear. "Send me to my chief, and my lover."

As the last word left her lips, he cracked. Dushuuw gripped the knife in one hand and grabbed Amuun'axsum by the back of the neck with the other. She winced. He steered her away and pushed her ahead of him through the crowd toward the tree line. Her heart pounded as she registered the faces they passed—curious, expectant, indifferent. The early morning sun did not yet reach the trunks of the trees that loomed ahead; they were bathed in bluish light.

"What happened to Lohta?" he whispered.

She said nothing.

Dushuuw stepped into the cover of the trees. The forest's edge seemed to hold people back, a barrier.

"I will tell you what happened to Lohta," he said.

He turned her around and slammed her against a trunk, jabbing the knife into the trunk by her head. She gasped in spite of her promises to remain impassive. Her back scraped against the rough bark.

"Lohta is gone," he said. He grabbed her chin and forced her to look at him. "The sea took them all."

It was her turn to feel again the weight of shock and confusion. Amuun'axsum wanted to sink in her despair, but he held her there. The knife stuck out of the tree at the edge of her vision.

The final wave of loss pushed through, relentless. It overwhelmed all previous losses. It overwhelmed her fear, her grief, and her longings with its mocking. For what is a song, when there is no one left to sing it to? This loss was a spreading darkness, but it helped her to face what was coming—perhaps what her quest had been leading to all along. For everything had changed. But nothing had changed.

Dushuuw gripped her arms. The air was cold, but his body near hers was warm. She smelled his skin, its many shades of water. His eyes gleamed wet, pooled with hurt and with questions. As sure as a knife, she had slashed the cord that bound them—the only way for either of them to hold on to what they each had left. But now, she had nothing left. Now, she needed that knife in his hand, for one more slice. She told herself to hate, to act like the anchor stone she felt herself to be, in the dark bed of the sea.

"I did sing for your brother," she whispered. She lied, seeking to sever the final thread. Seeking an end to the pain. "I sent my power out over the waters. I sang that he would die."

His fingers dug into her flesh as he cried out and grabbed the knife. She gathered a last desperate breath, giving despair its wing.

"End it," she pleaded.

He groaned as he let go. He gathered up her hair, and yanked her head back against the tree. He held the knife. She looked up at the swaying boughs. She felt the breeze across her neck. The knife came down. She closed her eyes, waiting, a tear finally slipping through. Her body was loosed from its moorings. She fell to the ground at his feet.

And scattered around her were lengths of hair.

Confused, she lifted herself from the ground, and put trembling fingers to her neck. No cut, no blood. Her hands went to her hair, following the ends that fell in front of her face—shorn by the knife at a ragged angle.

The mark of a liar.

BITS OF AMUUN'A̱XSUM'S HAIR stuck to the slave's blood on the knife.

Dushuuw listened to the footsteps coming closer behind him as he stared at the knife. The hazy image of Amuun'a̱xsum hovered beyond the blade—huddled on the ground beside her shorn hair. He was unable to shake the look she had given him. Her eyes that shifted from wrath to barrenness.

Uhpqoolth stood to his right, his angry breaths pulsing in time with Dushuuw's own. Yaq stood to his left, silent and expectant.

It was over… Dushuuw would do what he had to do.

"I want her tied to a tree, out of sight," he said. "Send for Oodahk. When he arrives, we will bring her to us and discuss her fate."

The shaman hobbled forward.

"It is a long way to Deeyuh and back in these times," the old woman said, as much to the rest of those gathered as Dushuuw. "It is winter. And the forest these days is restive."

Dushuuw avoided the old woman's eyes, avoided his friend's eyes, avoided his cousin's eyes, and above all avoided looking at Amuun'a̱xsum.

"If she dies, then we know which way the negotiations must go," he said, speaking quickly.

Yaq took Amuun'a̱xsum by one arm, and Kweelthup took her other arm. They hauled her up and walked deeper into the forest.

Dushuuw started to follow, but Kuhbuhtup grabbed his arm. The speaker whispered in his ear. "There is something far more important you need to do. Your family needs you."

Dushuuw closed his eyes at the man's words, feeling the tug on his heart from his family that warred with the tug from another cord that—even frayed by betrayal and a knife—refused to break. But when he opened his eyes, Amuun'a̱xsum was gone, and he did not know where the men would take her. It did not matter; he had already started to turn back toward the meadow.

Um-iiqsu knelt on the ground beside her sister's body. Sawsin sat beside her, holding a rag against the woman's scratched cheek. Chai's hands still stroked her dead mother's hair, but her gaze was set upon the dead slave, a calm look on her face. Uhpqoolth walked over to Yahbis, helping her send away the crowd. They each turned as Dushuuw approached—his cousin with a glare, his grandmother with relief. The fisherman Suu-ahp remained bent over among them, his face buried in his hands as he wept.

A few onlookers still lingered at the backs of the winter house, watching. Leehuuk and his wife stood off to the side. For once, Wiid looked subdued.

Dushuuw knelt before his sister. She looked at him with a small, sad smile. Her eyes were dull. He slid his arms under his stepmother's body, looked his sister in the eye, then lifted the body away.

In the winter house, he lay the woman's body on a bench in his family's living space. Yet another to mourn, and he was not sure he could handle any more death. He stared at the swaths of blood that remained on his hand. Uhpqoolth joined him, and after closing the partitions they walked over to the large storage box his stepmother had used. They unloaded it of its goods for Um-iiqsu to sort—what to add back for the burial, what to set aside for Chai, what to give away—then Dushuuw lowered the body into the box.

"What is left of our family, cousin?" he whispered. "What is left?"

Uhpqoolth glared at him, as if challenging him to a fight he was sure of winning. "What is left? You. Me. Your sister. Our mothers and grandmothers. Our children." He stressed the last one.

Dushuuw clenched his fist, thinking of his ex-wife, and of the woman in the forest. "You mean your children."

"Buh-uhs is your child. Your charge," Uhpqoolth said. "He was under the arm of your father, then your brother—but he was yours to adopt the moment he arrived."

A pang of jealousy flared against Dushuuw's chest as if, in realizing the truth about Buh-uhs, some force was already trying to steal the boy away again.

"Good," Uhpqoolth said. "So no talk of what is lost. We are here. We are strong. And we still have what's important."

Dushuuw nodded as his cousin turned back toward the box.

"Is it big enough for both?" Uhpqoolth asked.

Dushuuw looked down at the lifeless noblewoman. The box's tall sides cast the body into shadow.

"It will be big enough," he said.

Outside, in the meadow, Dushuuw looked down at the corpse of the slave, her neck and chest still coated with blood. Children played quiet games, and slaves hauled water, and old men and women ate some of the food bought in trade. Dushuuw bent down and slid his arms beneath the body and lifted it. He carried the body into the forest, then down a path to the creek, where he washed away the blood. Setting the body on the ground at the edge of the creek, he wrapped the torn neck with a strip of cedar. Back at the winter house, he lay the slave's cleaned body next to that of his stepmother in the box. He looked down at the pair. The slave's body on its side, shredded bark skirt still damp, breasts pressed into the side of the finely dressed noblewoman, who lay on her back, arm beneath the slave, as if comforting a daughter.

He had lessened his sister's grief. He had given his stepmother a companion in death. He had done as he must. But he had lost someone else in the process.

The older men had murmured their approval of his decision—to both consult more experienced men, as well as to leave the life of a woman suspected of harboring evil before the justice of fate. Wisdom, they called it, to bind the slave in the forest, exposed. What had stayed his hand? For despite the elders' belief, it was not wisdom. Her claims had pummeled him; so too her cold, indifferent gaze. He had nearly cut her throat there at the forest's edge, to end her hateful words, to rip them out. Then the two words that followed—"end it"—spoken to him yet again from the lips of a woman he had loved, that he had thought loved him in return. Those two words nearly won again.

So, what had stayed his hand?

Perhaps he wanted her to suffer. This time, the woman he had held and thought his own would feel shame. And so he marked her for what she was and banished her to the forest. No one questioned that slice of the knife. But, now, it was the only question that mattered to him. For she was a liar. But was the lie to him—or for him? Because he began to see. The hidden hand of his uncle, the coaxing words of the healer.

Wisdom, the old men had called it. If only they knew the truth. He was a coward to the end. But perhaps it was because he had wondered, even there at the tree, with his knife raised and poised to pierce her throat... *End it*. Those two words, those two words inviting the blade, had not been spoken in spite.

~

Dushuuw trudged through the woods, trying to find the path Yaq and Kweelthup had cut. But he could not determine where they had gone. New paths crossed old paths, many hunters chasing too few prey. Finally he headed for the place where he had always sought her out. To the broken tree in which they had tied themselves together.

He had known the route in the dark before. Now, it took him a bulk of the afternoon to find only the general location.

It was gone.

So near the river, the swath of once-forested land was now a tangled waste. Ferns and salal and saplings were buried in mud, where they weren't stripped away altogether. Old nursery logs were gone, replaced by denuded trees. Only the largest healthy trees still stood. Treasures and blankets and a firebox—everything they had shared there, everything she had hidden—were gone or buried with the snag itself.

What had he hoped to find? He had known he would not find her there. But perhaps confirmation, conviction? Perhaps some remnant of her power that might point where to go. He did not feel any of that. He felt only the tug. A painful yearning for her that would not let go, that he refused to let go.

He walked on, tracing the river's edge as he picked his way over piles of driftwood and other debris shoved up against the hillside or scattered on soggy exposed ground. The river was still a muddy mess, trying to find its new path. He tried to picture where he had traveled that terror-filled night in the dark. But it was a useless exercise. Coming around a bend, on the approach to the back of Deeyuh territory, he stopped and took in the sight he had been aiming toward.

A wide mound of wreckage rose above the water. This appeared to be the spot where the surge from Wuh-uhch met the surge from the Deeyuh side. Everything pressed together in a great pileup. It was likely diminished from the mass that had loomed over him while he clung to a tree. But it was still a large conglomeration of large things. There were trees, house pieces, even boulders, with smaller things wedged among them from the reports he had heard. He had no wish to get close enough to see the details. Likely his body would be wedged there as well, if not for that stubborn, dangling tree. Or maybe there was another reason, one he didn't understand or couldn't see in the dark. Or no reason at all.

Dushuuw lay awake in the winter house, fighting off the fatigue that wanted to put him under. The house was stifling, so many clustered together under one roof. When only the soft sounds of slumber surrounded him, he got up and took out his fur-lined cloak, a flask of water, and a small basket of food. Before leaving, he looked down at Buh-uhs. The boy had grown; he was lean, but strong. In a way, the boy had already passed his first test of manhood by coming out of that deluge alive. It would make his next tests that much easier to endure.

Outside, in the crisp moonlight, he walked across the dark meadow to the edge of the shadowed forest, toward the spot where he had brandished the knife near her face.

But a small fire stood in his path.

"Do you come to join me," Yaq asked, "or are you going elsewhere?"

Dushuuw looked down at Yaq, who whittled a stick.

"I go to pray," Dushuuw said.

Yaq eyed the bag of food Dushuuw held, then looked at him.

Dushuuw searched the darkness before meeting his friend's eye.

"Where is she?"

Yaq merely returned to whittling, his mouth a tight line.

Dushuuw felt the familiar rage rise inside. "Was it you that turned her over to be traded away?"

Yaq remained silent.

"Where *is* she?"

Yaq let his hands hang loose as he looked up at Dushuuw. "Let me tell you a story you never heard."

Dushuuw looked away.

"Once there was a beautiful girl who lived across the strait. Her family made an agreement with the leading whaling chief of Wuh-uhch for a marriage alliance. The girl was the perfect age for the chief's youngest son. But his oldest son saw the girl, heard her family's songs, and he fell in love. And he did the one selfish thing in his life by asking his father to let it be him to marry the girl. So the younger son married early to fulfill another alliance. And the older son waited."

Dushuuw felt a weight in his stomach.

"And when the younger son's marriage failed? The older son took all the ensuing blame aimed at his brother and bore it on himself."

"Stop," Dushuuw said, but could only manage a hoarse whisper.

"The older son tried to help his younger brother. And others sought to help too. The young man was put in the whaling canoe. Taught to pray. Given the tools to direct the future of the village's trade empire."

Dushuuw fought back tears. A mixture of resentment and grief and confusion threatened to consume him.

"Friend, even I joined in, trying to coax you back with willing ladies. And we thought it was all working. You finally seemed to focus more—and all that praying." Yaq's tone dipped low, tinged with bitterness. "When Buh-uhs started spouting off to one of his little friends about how he snuck up on two adults in his old hideout, do you know how lucky you were it was me who overheard him? This is Buh-uhs. Who else does he follow everywhere?" Yaq smiled up at Dushuuw with exasperation. "At first, I was glad, you know? You were finally letting yourself move on. A little romp in the woods—*šuwa*, I was happy. I waited for you to tell me about it. I'm still waiting."

Dushuuw's throat burned. "Yaq..."

"So we try to help you again. Clean up the problem for you by simply making it disappear. And I wish the shaman had given her up right then and there."

"Where is she, Yaq? Tell me."

Yaq shot up. "Does a slave mean more to you than your father? Your uncle—more than your brother?"

"Don't you dare—"

"Because if this village loses you next, it's done," Yaq said. He stepped forward and shoved Dushuuw in the chest. "You're handing it over to Leehuuk, and all the good names carried by your family will turn to dust. Nobody will even remember."

"And so what if I am handing it over?" Dushuuw found himself shouting, and brought his voice back down. His tone was tight. "You said so yourself; I cannot get anything right on my own."

"You don't understand. We all see it in you—even if you don't. You've got access to power, my friend. You always have. You just haven't grabbed onto it. That woman didn't just hurt your pride when she cheated on you. She stabbed something in your heart. But you're the one letting it bleed out," Yaq said, his voice swinging between sympathy and frustration. "Do you know how many people look on you as some kind of Q̓watee-like Wild Man, coming out of that disaster like you did? You've got Leehuuk on his heels so scared that he's losing what hold he had. That's why he's been pounding on you. And it's working. Because you're giving them the best reason of all to dismiss you."

Dushuuw was quiet for a moment. His friend spoke truth. Still, he did not believe everything. The one with true power had been put in a canoe and tied to a tree. No one would deny that.

"I am with you, my friend, in everything," Yaq said.

Dushuuw shot him a look. "Except this…"

"Especially this."

Dushuuw started to walk away, clutching the basket tight in his fist.

"What will you do if you don't find her?"

Dushuuw looked back at his friend. "I did pray, you know."

"And your dream. Did you finally hear the song?"

Dushuuw looked down, and walked into the forest.

He did not find her. He thought about finding the tree where his brother and father had been interred, but what he wanted was not there. Instead, he sought the company of the shrine. He sat before the unblinking gazes of better men, their skulls joined by the remains of a tiny bird and the feather of a bird that did not belong.

60

THE SCENT OF A LIFE lived by the sea surrounded her. Cedar cords wrapped her cedar-clad body, binding her round and round to a cedar tree beneath the hulk of a cedar box and a cedar canoe. The scent had run along the length of her life, from noble youth to scorned slave, and now it bound her here at the end.

In the dark, Amuun'axsum rubbed her already scratched face against the bark again. The effort brought fresh cuts, but she kept going. The cord keeping the cedar gag in her mouth was strong and resisted her attempts. She could not tell if she was making progress. It did not matter. The effort kept her mind off what she could not see—the dead chiefs above her head, the glowing eyes flickering all around her—and off the cold that bit into her flesh despite the cloak they left her.

She had thought hunger would bother her, but it was the isolation that took the greater toll. A winter day had never lasted so long. She noted the calls of birds that made their nests nearby, and of the invaders whom they chased off with loud twits, chits, and chatterings. Twigs broke, and ferns rustled, but she had seen nothing from her seated position except swaying ferns and shifting shadows. Once her attention had strayed toward the dead men above her, drawn by the squirrels that raced over the ropes binding the young chief's burial canoe to the tree. She quickly looked away.

More often than she could stave off, the image of Dushuuw came to keep her company. The vision cycled through the progression of his expressions—hurt, rage, absence—and back again. She whipped her head back and forth, shouted against the gag in her mouth, kicked out at the dirt. The ropes across her chest deepened their red grooves.

It had been a gift, her offering of hate. If she could not have life on her own terms, she would have her death. And he could live free of her stain. But she had cut too deep. There was no slit to the throat, no quick bleeding out. No slave fate for her... This—

Something slid across her legs in the dark. Her scream was a strangled gasp.

~

Amuun'axsum awoke just past dawn. The cloak had shifted further askew in her struggles. Shafts of sunlight pierced the forest but remained far from her cold skin. The dampness of the forest dotted her shoulders and wet her purple lips. She had tried to stay awake through the night, moving her body in what meager ways she could to keep the blood flowing. Now...

Cuts stung with the salt of her sweat, which fear produced despite the chill air. She twisted her hands and feet to bring back feeling. Her jaw was locked in its gagged position. It ached. Rubbing her face against the tree, she sucked at fresh pain, trying again to fray the rope.

A second day marched on. and she rubbed away at the gag to stem her panic.

Ants marched in a line over the crown of her foot. Beetles alighted in her hair. Spiders traced over the sweaty crooks behind her knees and up her thighs, leaving bites she could not itch.

She screamed, though her throat ached and the gag stuck. She kicked, though her legs tingled with weariness. Black spots hovered at the edges of her vision, and she groaned.

She awoke again in the afternoon to a deer's wet tongue cleaning her face, likely drawn by the blood or sweat. She thought at first it was the shaman dabbing at her wounds with a cloth. When she jerked awake, the deer startled—a snort of warm breath bathing her face—and bounded off. Her heart leaped after it. She wanted to call the deer, beg it to come back.

Amuun'axsum resigned herself to rubbing her face against the bark again. To her shock, the rope broke free. She tried to spit out the gag. Finally she was able to dislodge it. For a time, she could not close her mouth. She worked her jaw side to side, realigning tooth and bone. She tried to speak. Her screams had sounded so loud in her head when they were muffled by the gag. But her voice would not rise above a whisper. She leaned against the ropes and cried. She would welcome whatever came to eat her alive. Just let it end.

Then, a rustle in front of her. She looked up and saw the heads of two small boys above the ferns. They poised a toy bow and arrow and a tiny harpoon point at her in their trembling hands, eyes like clam shells. Amuun'axsum opened her mouth to ask for water, but her voice was hoarse and unintelligible. The boys tumbled into one another as they turned and ran back, their loud voices calling back to each other. Amuun'axsum felt the burn of sadness at the back of her throat. How she must have appeared to them. Streaked with reddened lumps, dried blood, grease, and sweat. Shorn hair standing out at odd angles from being raked against rough bark. Smelling of urine and sweat. Disheveled and fearsome as Dzunukwa, as Qaq-owuhtsah-lth, as Ihsh-kuhs—as the Wild Woman, the Basket Woman—as many identities as stories, all of them fraught with warning.

"Water?" she croaked.

She started to laugh. At the sheer absurdity of it all. At her lack of concern. She was drowning.

~

The woman was hazy before her.

Daylight is found on the mountain

It could be her mother's voice. But her mother's pampered skin and clicking shell jewelry were lost in mist.

feathers dance on the echoes of wolves

The song followed its set path, down into valleys, up into hills, a path it followed no matter the voice.

we touch lightning

But something was missing.

Amuun'axsum opened her eyes to see the wrinkled face of Eekbis. She blinked away confusion, then felt the persistent tug of hope. She leaned against the ropes, dragging up her knees. The shaman walked aside, took off her fur cloak, laid it over some bushes. Amuun'axsum smelled food. Her stomach growled. But she longed even more for the shaman's words of comfort that would tell her this was only a bad dream. Yet the shaman stood back, hesitant, glancing up into the tree.

"You came for me," Amuun'axsum said. Each word took effort.

"I wasn't going to." The shaman's eyes were still trained upward, then she looked at Amuun'axsum with a sigh. "I couldn't. I didn't know where they took you, until those two boys came out of the woods looking for all the world like they escaped an ogress with a basket. I got them to tell me where the monster was." She gestured at Amuun'axsum with the wave of a small dagger in her hand.

Amuun'axsum ached for the shaman to bring the knife closer, to cut the ropes. "I go to Deeyuh?"

The shaman shrugged.

"Back to Wuh-uhch?"

The shaman shook her head, and took one step closer.

"Oodahk has not arrived. So they have no decision yet. Maybe they will kill you. Maybe not," she said. "I don't know, so I needed to find you now."

"Cut these ropes."

Eekbis's gaze kept flitting up to the burial containers above their heads as she knelt on the ground, face twisting in disgust as she drew close enough to smell Amuun'axsum. The sharp tang of smoked salmon somewhere nearby taunted Amuun'axsum; she watched the dagger with expectation, but the old woman set it on the ground.

"I was right to keep you around a bit longer," Eekbis said, not meeting her eye. "There was something you were keeping from me after all. Words you knew. Words you told me you didn't have."

The shaman brushed her fingers over Amuun'axsum's lips and then curled them into a fist, as if capturing something and holding it tight.

"The fools thought it proof of evil—that you are a witch," Eekbis said, picking the dagger back up and waving the point around in a circle. "But I know. I know a song's power."

The shaman's words fluttered around Amuun'axsum's brain as she tried to make sense of them.

"And now I know the words," Eekbis said. "But you must give them to me, you see." The dagger shook in her aged hand. She held its point flat against Amuun'axsum's lips, as if to mark the source of the words. "This is what I have come to see in the time I have fasted and prayed since they took you away, in the times I fasted and prayed since you arrived in my doorway." The words were certain; her tone was not.

Worry fluttered in Amuun'axsum's chest. She pressed herself against the tree. She dragged her cheek against the bark. The dagger followed.

"You are a slave, child. You can do nothing with the song. Worse, I cannot have my rival in Deeyuh discovering the same secret—nor have you betray my own secrets to him," Eekbis said. She cast a frightened glance above their heads. "But if they spare you—what then? It is not for me to decide..."

The old woman began to sing.

Daylight is found on the mountain

Amuun'axsum stilled at the words.

The old woman slipped her thumb and finger into Amuun'axsum's mouth and tugged at her tongue.

feathers dance on the echoes of wolves

Amuun'axsum's eyes widened. She shook her head in an attempt to break free, but the old woman was stronger than she looked, and Amuun'axsum was weak. Eekbis brought the dagger up beside Amuun'axsum's cheek, holding the tongue out, ready to slice.

we—

Amuun'axsum dug in her heels and pressed herself against the trunk of the tree as the edge of the blade slid across her lips. An initial sting, as from a bee—the pain traveling through her tongue, sliding down her throat—and then the knife and the tree and the ground and everything began to violently shake. The old woman looked up and screamed. Amuun'axsum's scream was shoved back down her throat—

~

How long she was out, Amuun'axsum was not sure.

Eyes still closed, she moved her aching head and curled her fingers, confused by what she felt. Her cheek lay in soft dirt instead of against rough bark. Her body felt only the imprint of the ropes. She brought her arms out, and they moved freely. Bracing her palms against the ground, she opened her eyes, and found herself staring at the spilled contents of the burial canoe.

A cry caught in her throat as she rolled away. She tried to get up, but her shaking and weakened limbs wouldn't allow it. Her voice would not come. Her fingers scrambled to her mouth, seeking. She tasted the dirt and salt from her fingers as they found her tongue, tinged with blood and saliva. Amuun'axsum crawled back toward the base of the tree, and looked up.

The platforms above were empty, except for a few dangling pieces of rope. The young chief's burial canoe lay propped against the trunk; when it fell, its hull split the ropes that had bound her. On the ground lay various objects—a cloak, a rattle. The burial box of the older chief lay nearby, tipped on its side and spilling more objects.

Amuun'axsum's gaze darted around the forest. She cried out, but it was a whimper. Someone groaned, and for a split second she was convinced it was a ghost. She pressed herself flat to the ground and curled up in a ball, her hand scraping against something sharp. A sharpened mussel shell tip. The dagger. She remembered Eekbis. The old woman holding the blade, singing stolen words. Amuun'axsum's fingers closed around the hilt, and her insides burned as soon as she touched it.

She crawled toward the shaman.

Eekbis lay on the ground, groaning. A sizable bump formed on her forehead. She managed to roll to her side. Amuun'axsum sat apart, gripping the dagger with both hands against her chest. The old woman registered her presence and her eyes grew shiny with fear. Her mouth shaped soundless words.

Amuun'axsum forced words through her own raw throat. "If you had only ransomed me or helped me find my family in the beginning," she said, "Perhaps I would have shared the song with you, like an auntie—or a grandmother—if only you had been one to me."

She wanted to collapse to the ground then. But she gritted her teeth and crept forward. The old woman lay back, her eyes fixed on the dagger.

"Then, home at last, I would be dead now, pulled out to sea with the rest of them, and the song would be yours alone. But it was not meant to be that way, was it? As it is, you never had my song." Amuun'axsum uncurled one hand from the dagger in order to pound the ground in a rapid burst next to the shaman's head, baring her teeth. The old woman squeezed her eyes shut with a gasp. Amuun'axsum's fist rested against the ground. Her cut lips stung as they stretched to allow her to speak. "It was never the words alone."

Her fingers trembled around the dagger.

A rustling came from the underbrush, and Amuun'axsum met the gaze of a wolf. The animal remained frozen—one leg lifted, snout lowered, ears perked, yellow eyes penetrating. Amuun'axsum remained still, but her grip on the dagger grew lax. The wolf looked away from her to the shaman, a rippling twitch sliding up its lean haunch. A slight shudder moved through the old woman's body as she noticed the animal. Amuun'axsum crawled backward. As she inched away, the wolf took its own tentative steps forward.

Creeping backward, Amuun'axsum gradually came to a stand against the tree. The wolf hobbled toward the women, favoring a front paw. The shaman dragged herself upright and looked at Amuun'axsum. There was no fear in the old woman's gaze, only expectation. She reached inside her pouch, and turned toward the wolf. Beyond her, the bushes from which the wolf had emerged swayed.

Amuun'axsum let the dagger fall, heart ramming in her chest. She slid around the trunk, turning her back on whatever was coming. The cloak lay on the ground, but she left it behind. She walked away slowly, moving farther into the folds of the forest down a thin path. With each step, she feared she would hear the sound of paws racing up behind her. She felt pursued, the strong sense of something at her back. She did not dare turn around. Loud breaths. Cracking twigs. She started to run. It was a hobbling gait, riddled with pain. She tripped, fell, scrambled up again. The thin path began to fade. Salal and fern and tangles of nettles clawed and swiped at her legs. Panting breaths. Pounding feet. Soon, the trees thinned, and she was running through mud, the path barely visible. Rain pattered, and she emerged at the edge of a cliff. The sea battered the rocks far below, reverberating up through the stone. The wind blasted, curling its icy grip around her skin. A gasp. A howl.

There was nowhere else to go. A fearful cry ripped from her throat, and she took a step forward as if to flee. But the cliff's edge waited.

Rain slipped down her face and her arms as she wept, cold. Amuun'axsum held her arms out, letting the rain wash away some of the blood and the grime. Somewhere through the mist and clouds that stretched out beyond the cape was the place she used to call home, beneath the sea now. So, too, the place hidden by the mountain and forest at her back, a place that also had been a home and now was flooded. And whatever pursued her crept closer, pushing on the wind.

Amuun'axsum looked down at the black rocks that reached out like giant talons into the surging sea. She crept forward until her toes curled over the edge of the precipice, bits of rock falling away. She held her trembling palms in front of her, closed her eyes as she lifted them toward her face, felt the sea winds circle about her waist, and tug her close.

THE AFTERSHOCK had been brief but strong. Baskets, looms, and other sundries had toppled and spilled. A few people tripped. One woman rubbed at her head where the end of a paddle had struck when it fell. Mostly it was nerves that were rattled. Some of the children still cried.

Oodahk and his slave had arrived as the quake struck. Now the Deeyuh chief sat across the fire from Dushuuw, along with other people of high rank. The group sat quietly, waiting for Yaq and Kweelthup to return with Amuun'axsum.

The Deeyuh slave stood near the doorway, looking out in obvious anguish. Dushuuw tried not to look at the man. But his gaze kept going to that doorway, waiting for a glimpse of Amuun'axsum, hoping she was unharmed by the short exile which had stretched on longer than he had wished. If her hate of him was feigned before, it would be real now. He ached. And he hated the slave man, who would be the first to see her when she was brought out of the forest, who had been the first to... Dushuuw stiffened, his hands forming fists. He wasn't sure who he was angry at the most.

The wait continued.

Um-iiqsu's anger had cooled—she no longer fought the idea of negotiations—but she also did not join the nobility for the talks to come.

Oodahk was disgruntled, but mostly for show. The man sensed talks would go his way. He was not wrong. The group would find a simple solution for complicated times. And Dushuuw would figure out a new way to get Amuun'axsum back when enough time had passed for tempers to cool—or stand up in front of them all, take her hand, and go.

The nobles shifted in their seats.

Eekbis would normally be among the faces around the fire. But the shaman had gone missing, and it added another layer of uncertainty. The old woman had cared for Amuun'axsum's welfare. Perhaps she knew where Amuun'a̱xsum was bound; brought her food, water. Perhaps his friends would not even find Amuun'a̱xsum; she may be free and making her way—somewhere. These were his wild hopes.

A slave girl moved around the circle, offering dried meat. Uhpqoolth waved the food away. The others did the same. Dushuuw did not look at the platter when it came around.

They all looked up as Yaq and Kweelthup entered the house and approached the hearth. The shaman leaned on Kweelthup's arm. A dark bump rose on her forehead.

Dushuuw stood and rushed toward them.

Yaq rubbed the back of his neck and looked around the circle, avoiding Dushuuw. Kweelthup was quiet. The shaman spoke up. "The wolves took her away."

"What do you mean?" Oodahk asked.

"So you did go to her," Kuhbuhťup said.

The old woman nodded. "I tried, anyway."

The old speaker gestured toward her bump. "And you got that...?"

"When the earth shook, yes. I fell. Then these fellows found me."

The Deeyuh slave approached. "You said the wolves took her?"

Yaq nodded. "There was no sign of a struggle. The burial box had fallen. It could have fallen right on top of her..."

The burial box. A forbidden place no one would normally approach.

Dushuuw sat back down, nauseous. He bent forward and put his head in his hands. He searched inside himself, seeking that strong sense of connection he had felt.

The Deeyuh slave fled the house, and the nobles began to talk over each other. Dushuuw remained with his head in his hands, numb.

One voice rose above the others, commanding attention.

"I think I can offer an acceptable solution," Leehuuk said.

There was a hint of triumph in his voice, as if the nobleman had been waiting for his moment. Dushuuw tugged at his hair, fighting the urge to leave.

"I am listening," Oodahk said.

"Wiid and I propose a war party up the strait," Leehuuk said. "Quarters have gotten tight around here, certainly for my growing household. And the people there have a productive river, a river that has survived, a river we need."

Uhpqoolth started to protest, but the nobleman cut him off.

"I don't mean to diminish your prayers, Uhpqoolth. I only mean that, if we're honest, our river has never been the richest anyway. Neither has

Tsooyuhs's—or even Bih-ihd-uh's—and their rivers are as changed as ours. We could use another reliable source of fresh food—especially now," Leehuuk said.

"We are not river people," Kuhbuhtup said.

"Whales come into the strait," Leehuuk countered.

Dushuuw sat up, fuming. But his cousin beat him to the retort.

"We're outside-coast people," Uhpqoolth said.

But across the fire, from a village with a toe in the strait already, Oodahk looked intrigued. "What does this have to do with my loss?"

"There would be slaves, of course. You would have your pick," Leehuuk said. "Better than that, though, you would gain security and a better trading partner."

Oodahk was not quite convinced. "You would need my warriors."

"Naturally."

Dushuuw's anger billowed. "We should not do this."

Wiid stood and faced him. "Would the spirit of your father, dead by their arrows, agree with that, Young Son? That is the only reason we truly need to attack. We won't even need help, if the report you gave about their weakened position is correct." The war chief looked to Oodahk. "They would easily fall."

Dushuuw stood and drew his old mentor's attention. They faced each other, eyes level. "It is not the right decision," Dushuuw said.

"Nothing is gained without shedding blood," Leehuuk said. "You know that better than most."

Wiid's eyes were dark with challenge. "You are my best warrior. A warrior," he added, " who had been itching for this fight."

"Then maybe you will listen to what I have to say," Dushuuw said. "You could take their village, settle the area. Then what? They are a strong people. One weak moment doesn't take away that character. They will remember. They will wait. They will prepare—maybe for years—and one day they will come back for it all, strong again, more than enough to win and stick your graying head on a pike."

Wiid clenched his fists, but the armor of his gaze cracked, revealing a hint of sadness.

"You are one to talk," Leehuuk said. "You brought the war…"

Dushuuw broke away and looked at the nobleman. "That war is mine to finish. And I have no intention of starting a larger one."

Oodahk looked sober, and Dushuuw knew the man was making calculations in his head. Was it worth risking the lives of some of his best warriors, when their villages were in a weakened position too?

"By contrast," Dushuuw continued, "a man could secure a lot of quality trade goods from a weaker partner by promising to hold back his war clubs—and to protect them from the war clubs of another man he knows intends to strike."

Leehuuk and Wiid flushed with anger.

Even Oodahk looked taken aback.

"You go too far, Young Son," Leehuuk seethed. "You grow distraught over the death of a mere slave. You should get some air."

Dushuuw turned his back. He did not want to give in to Leehuuk. But at the mention of Amuun'axsum his mind clouded with confusion and remorse. He strode away from the group, not knowing what to do or say—afraid of what he might do or say.

A voice called out. "Who of you has harpooned a whale?"

Dushuuw stopped and turned toward Kuhbuhtup. The elder used his speaking voice. His words resounded off the walls. Conversations around the house stilled, faces turned toward the gathered nobility. Leehuuk opened his mouth to answer, then thought better of it.

"Knowing how or having someone do it from your canoe is not the same thing," Kuhbuhtup said. "Only one man around this fire has ever harpooned a whale—Oodahk."

Oodahk sat back and regarded the speaker.

Dushuuw turned back toward the doorway. He thought of his brother. He thought of his father. He thought of his uncle, his cousin, the man he had killed. How much loss could a canoe contain? How much loss could a heart absorb before it broke? He thought of the woman in a rotting snag, weaving her prayers for a whaler at sea. He took another step toward the doorway as Kuhbuhtup continued to speak.

"No matter how rich you are, no matter how many salmon runs you take, no matter how good a warrior—it is the whale that keeps this village alive and prosperous. It is the whale that tells us who we are."

There were murmurs of agreement.

Dushuuw stopped short of the doorway. Buh-uhs came bounding in, his cheeks red from running. The boy's hair reached past his shoulders now. He looked around at the adults, and grew still with silent questions.

"And who will throw the harpoon for this house?" Leehuuk said.

Dushuuw gazed down at Buh-uhs, who looked up at him with a wide smile.

"Where are you going?" the boy asked.

Dushuuw looked out the doorway to the changed sea, and the dark clouds gathering above. "Up..."

~

The day started to warm as he held a scrap of clothing in his hand.

The scrap was covered in the same grime and blood that soaked the paw-pocked ground at the base of the tree, where Yaq said she had died. Nothing remained of her except this scrap of dress—a tiny thing belying a bigger story to which only the trees were witness. There likely had been more signs, but his friends said they had cleaned up the area, to bring honor back to the site.

Dushuuw paced. It was by his hand that she died. But the fatal strike came long before he sent her to the forest. It was not a blow to the head or the fangs of a wolf. It was a hand over a mouth, a name pressed to lips.

Her blood joined his brother's blood. His father's.

Dushuuw dropped the scrap, and pulled out his knife. He dug the blade across his forearm, slicing the skin once, twice, three times. As the blood trickled down his arm to his fingertips, he made his way up the mountainside. He went to the pool. Dushuuw dragged his legs through the water. Fists clenched, he let the water turn his blood to ice. He turned and fell on his back into the water, looking up through the clearing to the sky. The silhouette of a bird circled above him. He kept his eye on it as he slowly stood up to hear its call. The gray loon circled on open wings. A short, soft call—searching. A long wail, rising and falling—like a mourning woman. Then it beat its wings and flew away.

A scream traveled up from his gut, propelled by all the building fear, anger, and grief he had carried with him since he was a boy facing his first day without his mother. The scream was propelled by those feelings, but it did not expel them. So he screamed again, a kind of prayer. But the forest was silent in response. And he was still alive.

Using nettles and hemlock, Dushuuw reopened old wounds and made new ones, trying to mark any patch of smooth skin that remained. He dove and sounded. At the whaling shrine, there was a new hill of earth and a new wooden statue, one he had added himself. Arrayed there were generations of whalers, a group of witnesses that now included the very best of them. He prayed under their gazes. The weight he carried threatened to pin him to the bottom of the pool, with its call to be stronger, to live. He was finishing something. Visions and hallucinations ran across his mind. His mother sang a lullaby. A faceless body was drenched with blood. A woman turned into a bird. And a dead whaling crew sang its soundless song as it cleaved him in two.

Afterward, he did the only thing he could do next. He went home. Maybe it would be to come under the arm of Leehuuk, or a confederation headed by Oodahk. Maybe it would be paying homage to Shuchkuk and his Tsooyuhs fighters, who could take Wuh-uhch without shedding a drop of blood by simply staying in the houses Wuh-uhch had opened to them. Maybe their friends from across the strait would club them to death to claim the land. Maybe the northerners would return to finish the job, going village to village, north to south, making slaves of them all.

He started back at first light. It was his third night without sleep; he had spent even more without food. He noticed things as he worked his way down the mountain. The air smelled of change. Green buds sprouted from reedy canes and thin branches. A cluster of greenish-white flowers dangled over the creek, which trickled and babbled. A light breeze blew. A hummingbird buried its tongue inside a bloom, darted in, darted out, darted in and out and sped away.

As he neared the village, Dushuuw heard shouts. He chafed at yet another argument. Or perhaps another loved one had died. He almost turned back, if only to stroke the feathers that remained on the hummingbird that now lived in its bundle at the shrine. He longed for the hollow stump.

The meadow on the high ground was empty. So was the winter house. The shouts came from down the hill—in celebration. Dushuuw's fatigue was overtaken by his curiosity. He followed the sounds toward the new beach that had been methodically cleaned, bit by bit, as the sea slowly released it. The crowd was thick, obscuring whatever lay at the center of their attentions.

"There he is!" Buh-uhs shouted. The boy tugged at Kuhbuhťup's arm.

Kuhbuhťup looked Dushuuw up and down. His gaze flicked to the forested peak above them and back. "A whale has drifted to our beach," the speaker said.

Dushuuw reached the edge of the crowd. Uhpqoolth emerged, and stood in front of him, a considering look on his face. Then he turned toward the crowd. "My cousin's prayers have brought us this whale!"

A cheer went up again, and Dushuuw swam through his confusion.

"Come on," Uhpqoolth said. "You know what to do."

His cousin and the speaker, followed closely by Buh-uhs, cut a path through the crowd and led Dushuuw into the shadow of a great hunk of rock—one of the pieces of cliff that had fallen in the quake. Children stood atop the rock and looked down at the sleek whale, its pointed mouth gaping. Dushuuw looked down its massive length to the curved dorsal fin and thickly set tail stock. A chill ran through his body, from his palm, through his arm, down his torso and legs to the soles of his feet, as if he were in the pool again. It was a finback, a species of whale that was far too fast and too far offshore for their men to hunt. If they ever processed one, it was only by drift—like this.

Uhpqoolth held a knife out toward him. He took it, in a daze.

Dushuuw paced alongside the whale, running his hand down its long, streaked body. When he reached the hooked dorsal fin, he stuck the knife into the whale's flesh at an angle and started to cut through the tough blubber, down to the red flesh. The people crowded in close, eager. The first cut done, he stepped back to let other men come forward with their blades and mark their own sections to take home. Other men would finish the hard work of carving the whale. Dushuuw hoped the meat was not bad. But even if it was, they could eat the blubber. They could render the oil.

Women already were setting up vats. Their chatter filled the air. Young boys helped the older men haul over the sections of whale.

Dushuuw watched the work, swaying from lack of sleep and too little to eat—and more—but unwilling to lie down. An idea was forming, and it would not let him rest. He caught Kuhbuhtup's eye and motioned the older man over, along with Uhpqoolth and Hawitsuksh, to tell them what he thought they should do.

The men looked thoughtful, and called over other noblemen, including Leehuuk and Wiid. They spoke, each in his turn, until darkness fell. Dushuuw said nothing more than what he had at the beginning, and soon a consensus was reached. His idea was accepted as wise.

"Nothing is prettier than the sound of the paddles and the voices when singing a song of invitation," Kuhbuhtup said.

Only then did Dushuuw collapse onto his bed. He did not fall asleep right away. The excited sounds of work continued on the other side of the wall. There was laughter and the hot scent of grease. Inside, his grandmother sat nearby with Buh-uhs, hugging the boy close.

"You remember the story of how we are related to the whales?" the old woman asked.

"Yes, grandmother," the boy said.

The sticks in the fire settled.

"There is a second part to the story," the old woman said. "Of how the whales returned to help their human relatives in a time of famine. This was when we became whalers. But first, we had to learn an important lesson..."

Dushuuw swam through the story, following the small bird who was the friend of the whale as it showed the man the truth: how the berry and the worm gave themselves to the bird for food, and it was grateful; and how the cedar and the elk and the yew gave themselves up for the man, and yet the man...

As he succumbed to sleep, a thought floated across Dushuuw's mind, something that had not registered until his mind was being emptied—at the cedar, when he had looked up into its branches, something had been missing...

When he woke in the middle of the night, the whale's dorsal fin was draped over a pole and set near the fire. Oil drip, drip, dripped into a trough. The smoke swept over the gray flesh, swirled upward, and curled toward him, beckoning.

~

Fresh foods, like herring and rockfish, were in meager supply. Delicacies like urchin were, by all indications, wiped out. Shellfish beds could take three years, at minimum, to regain harvestable size—but not just in isolated storm-surged corners as in the past; this time, the damage was widespread.

Yet inside the winter house at Wuh-uhch, there was a feast unlike any that came before.

Not the largest.

Not the most lavish.

Out of sync with familiar seasons and occasions.

Not a first, and not the last, but a feast that occupied its own moment in time, for its own purposes.

Every village of the Kwidich'chuh-aht confederacy was present. People from Tsooyuhs were already there and were now joined by those from Deeyuh and Bih-ihd-uh. A contingent from Oosa-ilth was there, too, and Buh-uhs sat in a corner speaking to his mother. Xhud-uck kept putting her hand wonderingly to the boy's face and tugging at his growing hair.

There were others, too.

Hawith sat in a place of honor with his wife and their family. Sawsin joined them and wore her sadness like a cloak. Tluulth was like

Chaiyuhx-ik—both young women were made older by the events of the past months—and they sat close like old friends.

There were more than friends, too.

Also among the guests were a few households from up the strait, including the village they attacked the previous spring. Their distant relations directly across the strait, whom they had beat back generations earlier and raided for salmon. Even a family from Oosa-ilth's southern neighbors, with whom strife went back generations.

Dushuuw sat beside Uhpqoolth, who would make appearances at the feast, but leave when the fresh meat was served. Uhpqoolth hid his injured arm under a cloak when he was around other people. Ootsihd remained in the hut with the twins. A woman from another village who had lost a young child in the deluge now stayed with Ootsihd and helped nurse the babies. In return, Dushuuw granted the woman's household access to choice halibut areas and an open arm to live at Wuh-uhch as long as they desired.

Kuhbuhtup stood before the house full of guests. The crowd quieted.

The speaker reminded them all of the territory that belonged to the whalers of the house under whose roof they sat and whose food they would soon eat. He remembered the litany of names that afforded them these rights—all but two of them. It was too early yet to speak the names of Dushuuw's brother and father, two names among hundreds that were absent from this room, silenced by earth or by sea. Dushuuw looked down at his lap, listening to the speaker bring memory to life, listening to the sounds of the full house.

"We are all related," Kuhbuhtup said, "we who call the sea home."

The house grew warm—from a fire, the number of people, the conversations—and everyone had their fill of meat and blubber and oil, plus what little remained of the stores Dushuuw had purchased in trade. On more than one face, young as well as old, a layer of relief gradually softened the hard edges of sorrow and determination.

Dushuuw did not eat. He sat on the ground and held Blubs, handing the boy one bite at a time. He could not look away from his cousin's face, at the little mouth working long and hard over each morsel, stout legs bouncing with glee, pudgy face free from worry.

As appetites slowed, Dushuuw returned to his place and nodded toward Kuhbuhtup. He had given the man some words to speak for him. Now that he had given them, he found it hard to breathe. He hid his nerves behind a frown.

Kuhbuhtup approached the center of the room and waited for the guests to quiet a bit. The speaker looked around the crowd, at the questioning faces, let the anticipation linger.

"The first canoe that our people made," he began, continuing to scan the room, "was a canoe for war." He took a few steps farther into the center of the room. "But it is the same canoe in which we visit your shores in peace, to invite you to feasts like this, to share in our blessing."

Kuhbuhtup gestured, and slaves came forward to distribute gifts.

"We have all lost people. Where we can, we carry on their spirit. We carry on their rites and privileges. We continue to make their songs speak, their dances move, their drums beat."

Dushuuw ran his hand over the trio of new scars on his arm.

Gifts were few, but distributed by rank. A slave. Bowls, platters, jewelry. A spinning top. Scraps of a partially woven whaler's hat—a piece cut from that same hat was tucked inside Dushuuw's storage box; on it was the figure of a man, whaling harpoon in hand, his body marred with red.

The greatest gift went to the guest of the highest rank. The new whaling canoe—made from that massive windfall, held safely out of reach by the forest—would touch Hawith's waters rather than those of Wuh-uhch. Hawith had lost far more material goods than they had. And it seemed right for the canoe to follow Sawsin home. More, their family would be tied to Wuh-uhch for many seasons and for many reasons because of that gift.

The people shared their words of gratitude for life. They sang their songs. And late that night, Dushuuw closed the gathering with the ancient dance.

He stood behind a screen as his aunt painted his face black—whether to mask his identity or to prepare for war, he would let the hearts of the onlookers discern. Emerging from behind the screen, he took a blanket and placed it over his shoulders like a cape. As he approached the center of the room, he looked back toward Yaq and nodded. Yaq took up a box of oil and poured the oil over the fire burning in a well-cleared section of the house. An extra-large opening had been made in the roof above the hearth, and now the guests would see why. The flames gorged on the oil, surging high with a flash. It was as if the roof planks were gone, filling the house with daylight.

At the same time, Kweelthup joined Uhpqoolth at a plank drum, adding his strength to the injured man's to help create an even louder, incessant beat.

Dushuuw crouched, hidden inside his cape where it was dark and humid with his breath. He slowly rose in his tight spiral. He flung his arms wide and jabbed the club to the ground. The fire flared as Yaq poured on another box of oil. Dushuuw crouched and turned, spread his arms wide, and struck the ground with a flash, over and over, while the drum pounded on and on. The room filled with heat and light as more oil was poured onto the fire—as if to say he had so much, he could afford the waste. He had nothing, yet he had everything. He gave away all he had, yet he was rich. It was a transaction, as was every action. And what Dushuuw sought in return had nothing to do with food or flesh.

When he was done, he remained in the center of the room. He took his dagger and pierced his body—his cheek, his lip, his chest, his arm, his thighs—over and over, here and there, until the blood flowed and coated his body. Scars were reminders. He already had plenty. From war. From ritual. From surviving the deluge. Dushuuw now fed the rumors of being impervious to pain. He did not even groan. But the pain was there. Scars were reminders, and the scars that carried a pain to outweigh all others were the ones he had sliced into his skin with no one as witness.

The Long Ago

SMALL ONE AND THE BOY were found dirty and shivering among the bushes, delirious in their isolation, and unnerved by the constant rumblings of the earth that seemed to threaten further disaster. The boy clutched the thing in his fist and would not open his fingers to reveal it to anyone except Small One.

The foragers brought them into their group, and they slowly descended the mountain. Small One stayed close to the boy's side.

All around now were the persistent cries and smells of death. Now and then, a man or a woman would take Small One by the shoulders and examine her face, only to turn away. It was the same with the boy. Now and then, another child's body would be found lodged in high branches. Here, an old woman coughed as she leaned against a tree. And an old man could no longer open his eyes. There, a mother held her infant, still against her thin breast.

No food. Little clean water. After a long time—taking a path the boy insisted they create—the foragers came upon a whale's carcass, far from the sea, rising out of the draining waters in a new, salt-tinged lake. Much of the whale already was spoiled, but the people feasted nevertheless. Many fell sick, some did not. The boy held his fist to his chest, watching as Small One filled her stomach.

It was a new world.

Small One and the boy had drifted far to the north from her village. The boy grew excited when he heard people speaking his home language, and they joined that group for a time. They urged the boy to stay. But he refused. And Small One—who had no family now but this boy—followed him onward.

Always, the boy kept them trekking south—the sea to their right, the forested peaks to their left. They wove in and out, up and down, blisters forming, then shredding, staying here to eat, there to sleep—but always moving south. They walked, hand in hand, wandering among strangers, moon after moon, the boy always seeking, always asking after his father, who seemed to be there but not there. The people he approached who spoke strange languages, all mixed together in their drifting canoes by the deluge, could only shrug. But even those who shared the boy's language, which the girl now well understood, could only shrug. There were so many lost. So many gone. But, yes, some knew that name. A strong name. Perhaps over the next hill, the next bay, the next rocky outcropping slowly reappearing from the draining morass.

Small One was still holding the boy's hand when, nearly a year later, his questions finally found their answer. They had reached the end of the vast island and faced a strait. They wondered if it marked the end of their journey. But word had gone ahead of them. And on a rocky, ragged beach, the boy's father was welcomed ashore to meet his son.

The boy's father wrapped him in a crushing hug. The girl felt the boy's impulse to let go and clutch at his father with both hands. Instead, his hand tightened around her own, and his back straightened as he stood over his kneeling father, ready for whatever came next.

They went home.

It was a new home, but not only for Small One.

New villages formed, and others consolidated. People groups split, settling in the places to which they had drifted. But the boy's father had emerged as one of the constants, a leader people clung to in those days of uncertainty. He held on to the cove the boy called home, held onto it as fiercely as he had the belief that his son was alive. And the first thing the old men of the village did following the deluge was to sit down, face the sea, and begin the long work of making a rope, a rope strong enough to tow a whale. For the place would not truly feel like home again until a whale was pulled up onto its beach. A whale, for a feast, to welcome his son home.

So on that first day, Small One walked onto the beach, hand in hand with the boy, into a cacophony of singing and dancing and feasting that lasted into the night. And on that first night, they were still holding hands as they lay down, bellies full, facing each other until their eyelids fluttered into exhausted slumber.

The chief took Small One under his arm. He treated her like a daughter. Even if he had not, she would have remained in the boy's shadow. It wasn't so much that they were inseparable, Small One and the boy. It was that something in the deluge had bound them with a force no mere man could challenge, especially a chief.

That first night, stars fell from the sky in streaks, burning.

On that highest mountaintop, Thunderbird finally sets down the great carcass of Whale.

On cold stone, Thunderbird uses his sharp talons to rip Whale's flesh.

He digs his great beak into Whale. Thunderbird devours Whale there, until all that is left is an immense pile of bones.

Bones

    bones

        bones.

1700
SPRING

DAWN AT SEA was not marked by the sun but by the moon. Bands of coral and ocher colored light laid themselves bleeding atop the distant line of an endless horizon. And the moon, broken and yellow, fell toward them, to be consumed for a greater light.

Chihṫup-uh watched the moon fade over the sea.

Land was long lost in distance and in mist.

Waves pulsed all around the canoe. They licked the sharp-nosed bow. They sucked at the cedar hull. Chihṫup-uh's stomach rose and fell with the canoe over each crashing swell.

The whale was close now. A petrel skimmed the air, its wings outstretched, heading to the same one, and Chihṫup-uh's gaze followed the path of its flight. A black feather was tied onto the grip of the large harpoon in his hands. He ran his thumb over the feather, the feather of a seabird he had been gifted at a pool on a forested peak, where a hummingbird remained to guide it home.

Chihṫup-uh crouched in the bow. The waves came on strong. But he focused on the whale as it rose into view. He gripped the long harpoon—three times his height—in front of his body. Shifting his torso, he anticipated the canoe's rise and fall as it crested each swell and fell into each trough. The canoe's knife-like hull cut through the water on the descent, preventing splash. His toes gripped the canoe's rough bottom. They glided through the water. Gulls screeched in the distance. The wind shushed.

The whale rose to breathe and to meet him.

Scars traced Chihṫup-uh's body. Each one led to this moment. They carved pale paths—burned by fire, smoothed by bone, polished by stone. Before this moment, he too had been beneath the waves and risen to take breaths that each may have been his last. He had survived and returned—by fate, or perhaps a woman's song; by choice, or perhaps the one she made for him—so he would be here, in this canoe, with this harpoon, keeping his family name alive. He had shown his thanks in his preparations for this hunt. He did not go up to the pool, however. Instead, he had waded into the sea and swam out to one of the new rock formations caused by the quake. He had dragged his body across its jagged girth, back and forth, over and over, the salty sea swirling the blood away. In time, barnacles and shells would populate the rocks and add further pain to the ritual—and maybe it would be enough.

The sea turned black, like a night sky under the sun, as the massive gray whale broke the surface. A soft but firm voice sounded behind Chihtup-uh—he had been listening for it, and he was ready. He took a great gulp of cold air and twisted his torso, lifted the harpoon above his head, then thrust its point into the whale. Heavy yew and a jointed construction added the shaft's strength to his own strength. The mussel-shell point penetrated the tough layers of skin and blubber and flesh and bone. The impact shuddered up the harpoon, up his arms.

The shaft came away. Blood spilled into the water. The whale cried.

The seven men behind him in the canoe shouted as they paddled to build distance, to avoid the whale's angry tail. Chihtup-uh—who had once been called Dushuuw, who had once been called Young Son, who had once been called Uhsahb—released a breath.

"Whale, you have what you wished for—my good harpoon."

But he had missed its heart.

It was his first time harpooning a whale; still, he mourned the pain the strike caused everyone. The whale was large, and now it was fueled by anger. It fought and dodged, and what strikes they got in were made far apart. Thrust after thrust. Float after float. The sun completed its circuit in the sky, as the disc of the world spun and dipped in its endless dance. The men lit torches and continued their pursuit through the night. Dawn colored the water and colored the rank breath that came as a mist from the whale's blowholes. And still the whale pressed on. The crew maneuvered close again.

Chihtup-uh saw the tired men in the canoe. He saw the distant smudge of shore where they must tow the whale. He saw the whale, recalcitrant; growing sluggish, but fighting on. And the sea, everywhere else the sea, moving to its own beat—a beat that could break at any time. He looked at the rope that trailed from the canoe into the whale's flesh, the rope that, severed, would let the whale go free. He looked at the whale. The seabird was now perched atop its head, ruffling its feathers as it tilted an eye toward the hunter.

"Whale, you must turn towards that fine beach," he murmured. He bent down, retrieved a short spear; its long blade was not a shell, but the gray and rigid material they sometimes found embedded in driftwood—sharper, stronger. He had prayed over it during its transformation into this lance.

"All the young men will come down to see you," he said, placing his foot on the edge of the canoe by the rope, "and they will say to one another, 'What a great whale he is! What a fat whale he is! What a strong whale he is!'"

He ignored the exclamations behind him as he jumped from the canoe onto the whale's back.

The whale's skin was rough and cold. The barnacles that clung to the whale for life scraped Chihtup-uh's soles and forearms as he straddled its startled, rocking body, grabbing hold with one hand to the blessed sinew rope that disappeared into its flesh.

"And you will be proud of all you hear them say of your greatness."

The whale heaved. Chihtup-uh took a shouting breath, raised the lance high, and drove the blade into the whale's brainstem just as they submerged.

Chihtup-uh listened to the water rush over his ears. It mixed with the whale's final song, loud in the sea it ruled. Waves of vibration passed through Chihtup-uh's bones. Still they plunged on the whale's last burst of momentum. Chihtup-uh clung with one hand onto the rope, the other on the lance's hilt. His hastily trapped breath started to burn in his lungs. Blood thrummed in his ears. He looked up.

The dark hull of the canoe passed above them. Paddles pierced the water. The other whalers spoke or sang but, like the world above the surface of the sea, the sounds wavered, indistinct.

Then the whale was still, and they ascended. Its fighting at an end, the many floats now tugged the whale upward.

Chihtup-uh broke through the surface on the back of the listing whale and sucked the air. He worked the blade out of the whale's body, then pressed his hand against the spot. As he tipped his head toward the Daylight above, he spread his arms wide, so filled with gratitude he felt he would burst.

Suddenly exhausted, Chihtup-uh turned toward the canoe. Yaq reached out, the worry on his face giving way as a corner of his mouth tilted up in a smile.

"You cannot have my job," Yaq quipped.

Chihtup-uh smiled back as he took his best friend's hand and hauled himself back into the canoe. "Would not want it," he said.

Yaq dove into the water to tie the whale's mouth shut.

Chihtup-uh nodded at the other men in the canoe.

The old storyteller, Hawitsuksh, sat in the stern as steersman, happy to have his arms largely freed from paddling.

On the thwart in front of the old man, a strong young man from Oosa-ilth sat quiet after helping call out songs and chants to keep the men calm and working together. Since the feast, the young man had lived under Chihtup-uh's arm while his young wife helped nurse Uhpqoolth's twins. He fit the crew well, and Chihtup-uh hoped he and his wife would choose to stay after the twins were weaned.

Beside the young man sat Suu-ahp, a fisherman who still mourned the loss of a slave woman he had loved. Chihtup-uh hoped this new role would help to pull Suu-ahp out of his inward state, as it had for Chihtup-uh.

In the middle of the canoe, Leehuuk's apprentice line-tender worked, and would continue until Buh-uhs could be trained to take over his father's old role. Beside the man sat Huh-uuk, who was shockingly lean, but no less effective at inflating the floats—or flinging boulders as they cleared their new beach.

Yaq sat again in his usual spot, and beside him was Kweelthup, whose quiet voice had come to Chihtup-uh's ear over his shoulder the whole long journey, leading to the signal to strike with the harpoon.

Chihtup-uh had thrust the harpoon, but he had only been able to do so with the guidance and support of all the men behind him, and the ritual support of their wives and lovers. They had become as one. Chihtup-uh watched a small support canoe speed off toward the cove, to bring the good news to the women—so they could prepare to greet the whale they helped call to their shore.

With the whale's mouth sewed shut, the men attached the tow lines to the thwarts. They started to tow the body home.

Chihtup-uh slipped his paddle into the sea and shoved the waters back. He sang a song to help them keep time. It was a song more of sounds than of words. Tones that droned and pulsed. A dream language—from a dream just completed, while he was awake, alive, and whole—or maybe some long-forgotten language that refused to be silenced, coming to whoever it pleased, searching and demanding, the only language in which to weep, to beg, to exult in one tumultuous burst. But even without words, the song carried meaning, at least for Chihtup-uh—about the path of a whaler, watched over by those who came before him and by those who come alongside him—a meaning tied to a specific time and space, yet free of time and space. And it was perhaps his greatest struggle yet to sing through the joy that overwhelmed his heart.

The men's arms and shoulders ached. They were exhausted from the hunt, from the many days of hunger, and from all the spiritual preparation that had led up to this moment. But their people would eat. There would be oil to sell. And Chihtup-uh would sing to the spirit that still lived inside the whale, so he could seek that spirit in another.

He felt part of the story that his grandmother had told him over and over as a boy—a story he had not truly understood until now. Like the man in the story, it took him a long time to learn the lesson of how to properly live. Too long to understand and appreciate the many things that willingly gave up their spirits to his use. Too long to open up a heart to the cleansing power of gratitude. He had to lose everything to see how rich he was, and how to protect that wealth. He repeated the whale's words now, the words his grandmother had carried and seared into his memory, as they had been seared into her own.

"You have to pray and be strong. You have to open your heart..."

Euphoria and grief intertwined in his heart. Blood and necessity. Pray. Listen. Strike. Nothing more. But when the adrenaline and fear subsided, there was space for relief. Anything more could wait, could wait for the retelling on a winter's night.

Dushuuw was walking straight with a clean heart now. He had found his power. Held it all along—just had to open his hand to let it go.

~

Before the men had rebuilt the houses, they had rebuilt the canoe runs.

Now, the whaling crew rode the tide between rows of rock, up into the cove's embrace. Children joined men on shore as they prepared to pull the whale onto the beach by the ropes.

Chihtup-uh ran his gaze over the canoe hull beneath his feet one more time. The crack was barely noticeable. The carvers had repaired it masterfully, but its deeper damage was one he had to take care of on his own. He released a breath, relieved. The proof of healing lay behind him in the shallow water, tangled with lines and floats.

The whalers stepped out of the canoes onto rocks and shells and sand. Chihtup-uh's guts pulsed and swayed as if still at sea. He stood in the surf and looked up to the great house on the beach, its doorway that faced the sea. He waited for her to appear. When she did, her hair was brushed back, and shell ornaments hung from her ears, reflecting the sunlight. His wife leaned in the doorway, smiled at the whale, and waited as he approached. The side of her face was still creased from laying on her side atop her cedar mats during the long hunt. She stroked her rounded stomach. As he drew closer, Chihtup-uh's eyes went to her wrist. Jagged, mountain-like lines, intricately tattooed over smooth skin.

Many at Wuh-uhch had thought that when he married again, he would retake the name of his grandfather, Dushuuw. But Chihtup-uh had left the last vestiges of his former self behind when he leaped rocky chasms and ran between walls of fire to drive a spear through a flaming plank to reach Sawsin on the other side, attired in wedding finery. He was not his brother. But he was no longer Dushuuw either. A name of such high rank belonged to one who proved a worthy match. But he also could not hear that name without hearing the voice of a woman he still grieved. So instead, he had chosen a new name, tying himself to the drift whale, the one drawn to the beach by the strength of his prayers. Or so they said. Even in that, the whale came to his brother's spirit, a power so strong that death was no impediment. The fin tip had been dried, and Chihtup-uh had added it to his brother's string. His own prayers—his prayers had been for guidance. The whale, as always, pointed the way.

No, when the time was right, he would give the name that evoked strength to another. Dushuuw was a long line of noble men, his grandfather among them. Dushuuw was a man he was for a time. And Dushuuw would be the son he was sure grew inside Sawsin—his brother's last gift. The name did not belong to any of them, but to the first of them—the ancestor who ascended a mountain and brought power back down with him.

"It is a good whale," Sawsin said.

They were the same words she used at that feast of the drift whale—at the feast he had held, when they were all still wondering where the deluge might deposit them. The same words, followed by her subtle invitation to continue their family's alliance by marriage. Savvy and calculating—that was Sawsin—greater in rank than himself, to be sure. If she could not give him the same love as she did to his brother, she did give him the gift of willing partnership. And that made him stronger, in every way. She was what he needed, now that the circle of people for whom he must care had grown from one to hundreds.

Sawsin held a bowl in her hands, and they walked down to the beached whale whom she had helped bring to their shore. She scattered soft feathers over the whale and sang a song of welcome.

Casting his gaze to the cliff top, Chihtup-uh spotted the support posts of the winter house that stuck up like denuded trees. He could not see the hut where Uhpqoolth and his wife still lived with the twins, now deeper in the forest, but he hoped his cousin heard and shared in the joy of their success. Upqoolth's arm was slowly healing, and the cousins often talked late into the night about the future. It may be years yet, but Chihtup-uh looked forward to seeing his cousin in the bow, whaling harpoon in hand. And while Chihtup-uh's war club would not go cold. perhaps he would start on the path of a whaler again then, too, as his brother so passionately pushed. He would spend the years it would take to fully learn each role in the canoe, moving up and over until he served behind Uhpqoolth, be the voice over his cousin's shoulder. And they would carry his brother's strength between them.

He pulled his gaze down the hillside, where he had carried his brother's body uphill so long ago now. The sounds of people at work and play filled his ears again.

It had been difficult moving the winter house back down to the low ground. There were many who chose to stay on the high ground, at least for now. They no longer trusted the sea. The houses they did move down were not put in the same spots as before—they couldn't be; those old house spots were gone. The river's slow drainage seemed to have stopped, despite the men's daily efforts to unclog blockages, and toward Deeyuh the river melded with the prairie and became sodden and salty. A good place for salmonberry was now muddy marsh. A copse of trees where ravens roosted was now open to the sky, not even a stump for a nest. Near the shore, one of the trees that had survived the deluge testified to the height of the waters with mud extending two-thirds of the way up its trunk; its branches grew sick from the salt water at its roots. The ground had lowered in other places—high tide now reached farther, surrounding the bottoms of small trees. And in still other places, the sea's pushes and pulls built up new ground. The mouth of the river had shifted farther into the bay. The wide beach they enjoyed in good weather was even longer.

To the south, no fires yet burned at Tsooyuhs. The course of the river there had been altered entirely, and the water still seemed to be figuring out where to put itself. For now, most of the Tsooyuhs families stayed near Wuh-uhch. But Chihtup-uh sensed it was only a matter of time, and he was grateful. Shuchkuk and others from Tsooyuhs swapped stories daily about their home—about burning the prairie, about the halibut bank they could see from their doorways. They noted every sprig of green that reclaimed the mud. Tsooyuhs was part of them, as Wuh-uhch was part of him. They would not stay long.

Food sources that survived in Wuh-uhch's territory were still carefully cataloged. Women had to go farther and farther to find surviving pockets of shellfish beds, scrambling over rock slides. Among the rocks, they came across more dead fish than starfish. Yet for every loss, there was a tiny scrap of hope.

Chihtup-uh's eyes fell on Buh-uhs, who crouched by a felled cedar that, for now, was left to sit where the sea had dumped it. Men had hacked away its roots to get a glimpse of its base, to see what purpose it could serve. The carvers said it could be a canoe. Buh-uhs ran his fingers over the cut, counting its many rings.

They no longer called each other Quht-Quht and Buh-Buh.

Chihtup-uh took part in the boy's initiation into manhood, and he had been harsh on Buh-uhs, nearly as much as his uncle had been harsh on him. He couldn't keep Buh-uhs a boy, afraid of the man he would become. Buh-uhs was no more his father than Chihtup-uh was his own father. Buh-uhs must listen well, then act as he must. And he must learn early on that it would be painful.

Children ran around on the beach, stomping on fleeing whale lice. They only stopped this game to rush to the whale's side and jump around, jabbering for the fatty bits from beneath the whale's papery skin.

Sawsin returned to the house. Chihtup-uh took off his hat—the same old hat, with its stilted knob—and saw Yahbis motion for him. He went and helped his grandmother sit on a drift log near a beach fire. Her gray hair was still short. It clouded around her head as the wind tossed it about. Yahbis looked around at the children playing and smiled, then began to softly cry.

"Are you all right, grandmother?"

Chihtup-uh clutched his hat in one hand, and held the old woman's hand with the other. He was not sure how she could stand so much loss. Her husband. Her sons. Her grandson. But when Yahbis turned to him, she wore a determined smile. She started to shakily sing.

all my hair is gray
my home is still beautiful

She moved her veined hand in sweeping motions, her hand still dancing, even if her feet were no longer able.

Chihtup-uh let his hat fall to the ground so he could reach over and caress the hand he held. Her blue veins rose above the skin like inverted rivers; he gently rubbed his thumb over them, imagining the blood flow. He faced the sea, listening to the bustle of work and play around him, sitting in the shadow of the rocky heights, a circle of fire bathing him in its heat.

Winter 1687
13 years earlier

Young Son bit down on the stick in his mouth. Blood trickled down his back. He balled his fists.

The boys, most in their seventh summer, were lined up, their bare backs turned toward his uncle. Young Son remembered how happy he had been to leave his mother and the hot beach to follow his uncle into the cool forest. His father had said simply, "Uncle is going to teach you something." Now, the moist air was rotten. He hated the version of himself who had eagerly thanked his father and ran off with a skip toward some new adventure.

Another burning slash fell.

Young Son flexed his back, fingers still curled into his palms, and he waited for the next whipping from the bough. Instead, he smelled a fetid odor, and the next moment warm liquid spilled over his back and seeped into the fresh cuts. It burned like fire.

A fury welled up from Young Son's gut and he spun around with a shout. He took the small stick from his mouth and pummeled the box from in his uncle's hand, sending what remained of the stale urine splashing over the man's arm. The bowl clattered against a tree and thumped into the dirt.

Young Son felt the focus of the entire forest center on him. Only his heavy breathing could be heard, until his uncle grabbed him by the arm, spun him around and shoved him toward the creek bank. Buhkweeduuk told the other boys to get into the water and wash themselves. Most did this eagerly. One was more timid in his approach, so Buhkweeduuk gave him a bit of help, sending him in with a splash. But Young Son was kept at the creek's edge.

Buhkweeduuk put a large stone in the boy's hands. "Hold this. Watch them. Don't move."

Young Son's arms ached. His back stung.

Small smiles flickered on his cousins' and friends' faces as they washed—maybe because the initiation was over for them, but maybe out of pleasure over his suffering. He longed for that cold water.

The other boys were well on their way home by the time his uncle approached him with a bucket. Young Son flinched as his uncle lifted the bucket over his head, then sighed with relief as the creek water washed away some of the grime. Water dripped off the ends of the his long hair.

At his uncle's word, Young Son finally dropped the stone, and his head, but his hands quickly made tight balls again at his sides.

"Still you are angry," his uncle said with a tenderness that surprised Young Son, who peeked up at the man. "These tests, Young Son, they are to teach you—discipline, focus in the face of the unexpected, perseverance through pain." His uncle put a hand on his shoulder and gave it a gentle squeeze. "But I can only teach you if you listen."

Young Son felt ashamed.

His uncle drew a breath as if to say something, hesitated, then spoke. "Come, and place your arm here."

The boy walked over to the boulder and placed his arm across its moss-covered surface.

Buhkweeduuk probed the boy's forearm with his fingers, then took out a thin bone awl. He placed its point against Young Son's skin, then pressed down.

Young Son watched the awl disappear into his arm. He ground his teeth together, longing for the stick he had so carelessly thrown away, but he willed himself to be silent. He blew great breaths out his nose, nostrils flaring.

The awl passed between his bones and flesh until it struck the rock.

Sweat dotted Young Son's upper lip. He peered up at his uncle.

Buhkweeduuk looked at the awl, but his gaze went beyond the rock. When he eyed the boy, he seemed uncertain—perhaps afraid.

"You will be a strong man someday," he said.

He pulled the awl out.

Young Son yelped in surprise and, more so, offense.

"Someday?" He raised his fist to display the blood on his arm. "How can you say I am not strong now?"

"That is a sign of the strength that will follow you," his uncle said. "But you do not have it yet."

"Well, then how do I get the strength?"

"You wait."

Young Son blew out a breath and brought his arm back to his side, fingers still clenched in a fist.

"Not the answer you wanted to hear?"

The boy looked up at his uncle with a blank look.

"I didn't think so." Buhkweeduuk leaned down, looking the boy in the eye. "But you want it."

Young Son breathed deeply and nodded.

"How much do you want it?"

Young Son balled his fists again, his heart still pounding from all that came before, his mind racing like the blood in his veins. Blood seeped from his arm. He thought of all the times he felt powerless, the worst feeling he could imagine. "I want it more than—more than everything."

"Good," said Buhkweeduuk as he stood back up. "Because that is exactly what it will take."

THE OLD WOMAN dragged her fingers over the slave's face. A curving line of paint, tracing the eyebrows. Dashes down the forehead, descending toward the line. A wide arch, from cheek to cheek over the nose, with dots pressed at the ends of the line.

Eyes closed, the slave listened with her skin, bringing to mind the pattern as it was made.

She smiled.

"Clover," she said.

The old woman grunted in confirmation. The woman's milky eyes looked through the slave.

In the cool mist of the next three mornings, the slave led the blind woman by the hand to the creek, and followed the old woman's lead through the prayers. They bathed, and rubbed themselves with tied-up bundles of branches. They drew the story on their skins and acted it out so that it may come true—the roots be found quickly, to spring from the ground of their own accord beneath the women's digging sticks. That the gathered roots, when steamed, be sweet in flavor, rich and thick.

They fasted during the days. And though the old woman could not, the slave stayed awake on her behalf through the nights.

Now and then, the slave would pause to place her palm against her swollen stomach as the life inside stirred. Always moving, it seemed, when she was moving.

The icy sea wind had wrapped her by the waist that day and tugged. Her toes had scraped the hard scrabble at the edge of the precipice. Then it was as if the baby spoke—a whisper of a feeling from that tiny scrap of life clinging to her insides—and she had stepped back in wonder. It felt like the brush of wings. She froze, waiting for the baby's movement again. As she waited, she realized she was alone with that life growing inside her; when she turned around, there were no signs of wolves. Even as she followed the thin path back into the forest, seeking warmth, there were no signs of a pursuing pack; only a single paw print, pressed in mud atop a salal leaf at the trail's edge.

It was only when she had returned to the spot where they had bound her to the tree that she could be sure it had not all been her imagination. The shaman stood in the same spot where she had fed the wolf. As the slave wrapped herself in the discarded, stained cloak, she approached the old woman on shaking legs. The shaman slowly lowered her hands from her face; her eyes were rolled up so high that only the whites showed. She exited her trance, her sharp gaze meeting the slave's. The slave showed her the leaf.

It was then that Yaq and Kweelthup arrived. The two men held back, taking it all in. The shorn ropes. The fallen burial containers. The two women. The fresh wolf prints.

Yaq looked to the shaman. "He looked for her."

The slave closed her eyes and swallowed. "He will never stop."

They stood in their wide ring, birds fluttering overhead and boughs bending with creaks in the wind. The ground beneath them felt charged.

It was Yaq who decided the plan.

He and the other young whaler lifted the young chief's burial canoe and carried it. The slave followed them to the soggy remains of what had been a summer encampment on the outer shore. They started a small fire and left drinking water. She guzzled all of the water down without thinking and vomited. She refilled the container from a creek and drank again, ignoring the salt and the silt mixed in. She waited all that winter night. When the fire went out, she slept dreamless under the canoe, the stench-filled cloak wrapped tight. The following morning, Yaq returned by sea in another canoe and towed her out in the burial canoe beyond the breakers. He got her around the cape. Then he cut the burial canoe loose. From there, she would be alone. It was her and the canoe. No blanket. No food. No water. No paddle. Just shifting waters that could churn up anything, everything.

He left, disappearing among the seastacks.

The burial canoe rose and fell on the swells. She was adrift.

Left to the whims of currents, she lay prone in the hull and stared up at the sky. She waited for the next flutter of wings from her womb. She sang her mother's song as she rapped her knuckles against the hull for a drum, singing to the child, singing for the child, singing over the child. She heard a rush beside the hull, like the movement of paddles. Above the canoe's sides, tall black fins rose high, then disappeared.

She was rocked and pushed, and then the sea changed. She sat up. The canoe drifted closer and closer to land. First it was a distant gray smudge. Then outlines of trees. Wavering plumes of smoke.

The things that wash up on a chief's shore belong to him.

She was drift.

The shore of this village was rough, pocked with pebbles and bits of broken shell, and more like the beaches she remembered as a child compared to the sandy beaches of Wuh-uhch. A high promontory hovered over the cove. Around a small bend lay a scarred scrap of beach. Once the tiny beach was white with clam shells, the locals said. Now it was as much a mix of rock and mud as the rest of the shorelines. Like elsewhere, this village was rebuilding from the earthquake and flood. They prayed and dug out a garden to which the clams could return.

The slave was back to weaving fine-mesh dip nets for tiny fish—tiny fish that would save many lives in such lean times. The day the herring arrived, the people celebrated as if it were a whale. Women swiftly paddled canoes forward, adding to the force of the heavy rakes their husbands held below the waters. The men brought the rakes up, dozens of tiny fish wriggling on the spikes. They roasted the fish. They boiled the fish. They ate it raw. Plenty more were hung to dry, along with lengths of kelp bearing their roe. But all this came only after honoring the first herring catch, their bodies laid out before the chief and covered with feathers and prayers, their bones carefully deposited back in the sea.

Now, sitting against an outside wall—hungry from fasting, and tired from staying awake—she adjusted the loose weaving on the lap of the old woman, her constant companion.

Soon after she arrived, they put her in charge of watching over the frail old slave woman. The old slave woman was blind, and a treasured possession. The woman had foretold the quake, they said. Perhaps her ears were hyper-attuned to the movements of tiny things, like mice. Perhaps her tongue was fine-tuned to alterations in taste, like water. Perhaps it was vision of a different kind. Her warning had saved many lives for those who listened. But her warning could not reach everyone.

A neighboring village collapsed in the sand and then was washed to sea. The old slave had just moved from there with her owner, a chief's daughter who had married a son of a chief here. The daughter of the chief had wept bitterly for the loss of her family, they said, and her elderly slave absorbed that sorrow.

And now the younger slave absorbed the old slave's sorrow—for the name of the village had been Loḥta.

It was dark when the earth shook and the sea came. But it was darker still for the blind woman. Once she had been a stubborn and tough old bird, they said. Now the old woman floated through her days, as if elsewhere. Her fingers, knobby and arthritic, fumbled as she mumbled words no one could understand. She would sit cross-legged and pat her hands on her thighs, swaying forward and backward. Now and then, she would tilt her unseeing face toward the sky or out toward the sea, as if listening.

The slave corrected the blind woman's fingers on the fat strips of cattail, what weavers used to teach young girls when they started out. She guided the woman through the simple warp and weft.

The slave's blind gaze kept straying toward the sea.

"So blind," the old woman mumbled.

The young slave watched other people at work—steaming salmonberry, roasting fish, paddling out in search of shellfish beds, remaking a canoe run.

A group of children lifted carved birds on poles at the direction of two adults, learning a new dance. The birds mingled among the children's heads, as if bobbing on waves.

A carver worked on shaping a new canoe. The man drew his adze across the wood—scrape, scrape, scraping—his back bowing in time with the blade.

The old woman started to lift and drop the weaving in her lap, lift and drop, lift and drop.

"So blind, both of them," the old woman muttered. "Told him he risked everything. ... My only child. I worked so hard to keep him, and then he goes. ... Who can I sing the song to if he leaves? In secret, in secret. You won't tell, no. ... But blind, so blind. He follows her away, away from me, says he has a plan, that they both of them have a plan. A plan for the song, he says. To make it safe forever. ... So blind in faith. So blind in love. ... Now gone, both of them. Gone. And the child." The old woman's voice dropped a register. "My grandchild, whom I would never see, even if only with my hands. Long gone. With both of them. Swept away—like my lady's home. My lady's home, swept away by the sea. My grandchild's home, swept away by men."

The slave started to weave slower. The slave had spent hour after hour with the old woman, day and night, and she had never heard the woman speak so many coherent words at a time. What noble life did this old woman imagine? The slave was quiet though; she listened, curious and grateful for a break from the boredom.

The old woman slapped the loose weaving against her lap more rapidly, swayed harder.

"So the song born of disaster will die with me in disaster," she said, her voice shifting from chant to lament.

The slave stopped weaving.

"A secret, a secret," the old woman whispered. "No one can know."

The children lifted the birds, high, high, higher.

The carver continued to bend over his adze, scrape, scrape, scraping.

The old woman swayed over her weaving, slap, slap, slapping it down.

The sea shushed.

A gull cried.

"I would have given it to that child, that child they gave my name. Child is gone. Long gone. A secret, that child. No one can know. He would give her up, give up everything, to save that song, to save that child." The old woman's arms were a flurry of movement.

Slap, slap, slapping. As if drum, drum, drumming a beat. A familiar, incessant beat. The slave's heart began to beat in time. Blood pounded in the slave's ears, drowning out the children, drowning out the adze, drowning out the surf, drowning out the gulls.

The old woman grunted under her breath, breathing out, and out, and out. *hu, hu, hu...*

The slave turned toward the old woman and sang the first line of the song, in a whisper.

Daylight is found on the mountain

The old woman perked up as she swayed over the weaving. Her milky eyes widened and glistened. The old woman's lips parted in a smile as she shakily added the next line.

feathers dance on the echoes of wolves

The two women joined together for the third line. The slave's pulse and the old woman's flimsy drum pounded in time. The slave's whisper and the old woman's vibrato amplified each other.

we touch lightning

The slave's breath rushed up and out of her mouth with the lifting of the tone. Flashes of color sparked behind her closed eyes. She heard sticks strike a plank drum, her mother's voice. She waited, suspended and weightless, listening for the next prompt. But it did not come. The lengths of cattail sat still in the old woman's lap. The weave, already loose, started to fall apart.

The children extended their flightless birds as high as they could go.

The carver stopped his adze to wipe his brow.

The old woman hunched over, gripping the scraps in her lap. She twisted the thick lengths of grass, bending them.

The slave tried to coax the old woman. Whispered the words of the song. Took the old woman's hands and guided them in the beat. Came to the last line.

"Up, up you see," she whispered to the old woman. "To show expectation."

But the old woman's eyes were submerged again.

The slave cried, then smiled, then cried and smiled. She kissed the old woman's hand; she stroked the feathery white tendrils of loose hair behind the old woman's ear. The old woman, she had learned, who called herself Maḥtii.

~

Amuun'aẖsum did not sleep that night. Toward morning, the old woman awoke agitated and more confused than usual. Amuun'aẖsum stroked her grandmother's head until the old woman fell asleep again beneath a mountain of blankets. Then she took a gathering basket and crept out, followed the creek out of the village, and trudged along its winding shore farther and farther uphill until she got to a wide, level spot.

Tossing the basket aside and throwing off her garments, she strode into the burbling current. The cold water sent shock waves up her body, and she lifted her face to the sky and wailed the last tone of the song, sending it up, up, up.

Birds shot out from their branches and flapped away.

Amuun'aẖsum fell to her knees in the water and cried. Bumps dotted her skin. The tiny hairs on her arms lifted. She sat down, shoved her legs out, and caught her breath. The water curled around her body as if she were a rock. She clenched her mouth shut, breathing deeply, in and out, in, out, and slowly laid down. She turned her eyes to the gray lid of sky as the moving water found its way into the hidden folds of her body. She submerged, blowing a tiny breath into the watery thickness. The view was obscured by rippling waves and bubbles of breath. Her arms floated loose beside her. Her crooked hair, still too short to braid, tugged at her scalp in the current.

Amuun'aẖsum lifted her face just above the surface and breathed.

She watched the gray sky, and took another breath.

Tracked a drop of rain as it fell from a branch, and took a breath.

Traced the path of a wren as it flew to a twig, which sagged beneath its thin legs, and took a breath, as the water filled her ears with the rushing of its current and the amplified exhalations of her breathing.

She closed her eyes, and felt the baby swim inside her, felt it roll and push against its confines.

Daylight is found on the mountain

She whispered, but the words were as loud as a shout to her submerged ears.

feathers dance on the echoes of wolves

She felt the baby grow still, as if listening.

we touch lightning

The song would live on. The song that had lived on multiple beaches, maybe starting with one near the beach she had just left. The song of her mother. The song of the slave man who had followed her mother, who had drummed so confidently, who had looked at her so fondly, who had clasped her hand and saved her life. The song of the old, blind slave woman, his mother.

But the name would live on too—Amuun'axsum—though she knew it now to be as foreign to her blood as she had thought a slave's moniker to be. She would preserve the memory of its intended blessings and give honor to the man who imbued her with nobility, even if it didn't last. And, perhaps most of all, she would keep it to preserve the memory of another man's whisper, his lips soft against her own, sealing the name and the worth it gave.

This was not the end she imagined. The face of the old slave woman was not the one she thought she would encounter as a changed woman, though it filled her with a grievous joy. She could no longer be waiting for Dushuuw at the end. There was someone waiting for her now. A child, who at the right time would receive gifts of precious words.

Sunlight dappled the branches and highlighted the rain that fell in scattered drops, striking her face and the water.

"I know now what it feels like, dear friend," she whispered, thinking back to a boy with an unruly crop of hair who furtively kissed her cheek, "to touch lightning." Tears slid down her cheeks to join the creek. She thought of the bear he had fixed for her, and of the heart he would never fix. "It hurts," she said with a laugh. Droplets of creek water would carry her tears into the sea. She imagined them sink, sink, sinking to the home of the drowned, and to the home of the spirit of Whale. "But it transforms you, into something stronger."

The earth would continue to shift, subside, lift. The sea would surge, fall, rise. But words survive, her mother told her once. If the keepers are careful, words survive long after the earth falls away and the sea consumes. Made of spirit, they move from one vessel to the next. Made of spirit, they carry their own strength, on and on and on.

A pause here.

A beat there.

A final tone, rise, rise, rising—in expectation.

Amuun'axsum rose from the creek, water dripping. She went to the shore, and readied the bundle of sticks. She painted her face with longing and with hope; she scraped her body and bathed, pleading for a tiny sign of life.

Spring 1686

14 years earlier

"No, Maḥtii, like this," her mother said.

we touch lightning

"Up, up you see. To show expectation."

Maḥtii nodded and tried again. Her mother nodded approvingly. Maḥtii fidgeted and turned. The slave man smiled.

There was no drum. They sat atop a fallen log in the forest outside their village. Mother and father had fought again, and now mother had decided it was time to start teaching Maḥtii the song, the very special song. The slave man followed them to this secluded place, protecting them, and he beat the log with a large stick, watching them, watching her especially closely with his kind eyes whenever she turned around to see him, this now-familiar presence perched behind her. Compared to their village's plank drums, the log was comically quiet. She wanted to laugh at the peculiar slave man. But he only smiled.

Maḥtii waggled her new toy bear back and forth.

"I will have Tiichswii perform with me as drummer," Maḥtii said. "He's good and loud."

Her mother drew the kind of breath that Maḥtii recognized meant she said something that was not acceptable for a noble child. She blew at her hair, and waited for the reproach.

"You do not perform this song. It is never a performance," her mother said.

Maḥtii lay her bear down to sleep on its leaf mat and looked up at her mother in surprise, having expected a different correction.

468

"What do you mean?"

Her mother looked over her head, to the slave man who sat behind her. He still drummed. Beat, beat, beating the moss-covered bark.

"This song contains such power, Maḥtii. You don't realize that now, learning it. It is the song that speaks. You must be very careful, when you give it its voice."

Maḥtii shuddered a bit, but also felt a bit of a thrill. You have to be an important person to have such an important song, she figured.

She looked up at her mother, eager for the next instruction.

But her mother had a faraway look in her eye. She gazed somewhere over Maḥtii's head. And the next instruction came from behind Maḥtii, from the slave man, as he drummed on, incessant.

"You hear more than the voices in that room. You hear more than the drum in that room. That's when the song starts to speak," he said.

Her mother spoke up again. "This is a song for dark times. A song that remembers the power of Daylight. A song that calls on that power to light the way home," she said, as if reciting. Her voice grew softer. "To find what matters most."

She looked down at Maḥtii. And the slave man spoke again, his words coming to Maḥtii unseen over her shoulders to her ears as he beat, beat, beat, and she could not decide without seeing his face if he was sad. "The song is bigger than us," he said. "It was here long before us. It will be here long after we're gone."

The Long Ago

THE LAND SURROUNDING Small One's new home had shifted as much as its people groups. What had once been a rocky and forested island became linked to the mainland, water imperceptibly draining from a saltwater bay into something more closely resembling a river. Whole settlements had been permanently abandoned, their beaches gone. Piles of weighty shellfish hulls, discarded where women had dug out the briny flesh from inside, were all that were left behind among the barnacled rocks, to be hidden, buried beneath layers of sand and dirt.

Small One still shadowed the boy when he was not out learning to be a man—to fish, to whale, to fight—and they each often went alone to secluded places. He, with an uncle. She, with an adopted aunt.

She sang the song that came to them on the mountaintop, a time they had mistaken at first for being lost. A song of the earth, and of the sea. The last note rose high, to meet the power they shared.

Yet he was restless as always. And as she sang, he bowed and twisted before her, dancing a dance that transformed him into a bird before he pierced the earth with a swift strength that evoked storm and hunt alike.

The song and the dance were the only ways they could understand what had happened. Still, there was a lingering sense that their efforts were unfinished. Until the boy, brows furrowed and fists clenched, looked up one day and pointed to his uncle, and told the man how to beat the drum. No marker of time, this beat. No familiar thrum. It was loud. It was insistent. It was relentless. And it drove the boy in his dance and the girl in her song to focus on each other to get the steps right, the words right. Hearts beating their own panicked rhythms, the drum imbued in them that sense of desperate need, a need that drove them to meet at the height of that remembered mountain and reclaim the power that had been gifted.

Those times, when Small One sang and the boy danced together against the drum, the sun or the fire seemed to burn brighter all around them, wrapping them in light. They spoke to each other through the dance and the song, each making the other stronger. They spoke to each other in this way more and more, frustrated more and more by the inability of mere words to convey truth. They imbued the song and dance with the power, but also sorrow, love, longing, and a hope just strong enough to heave them from the cold depths of feeling adrift.

"We will never be lost," he whispered, trying.

"Even when we are lost," she whispered, trying too.

Perhaps the closest that words, simply spoken, came to the truth were in their new names...

Some time after coming home to the cape—when the cedar walls of their houses smelled familiar again, when life had carved familiar grooves of routine, when they ventured out regularly as the people who live among the rocks and seagulls—the chief held a feast. Small One's hair was brushed, braided, and decorated with flowers, with shells. The chief offered her an encouraging smile as he slid his hands under her arms and hoisted her high, setting her feet atop a bench set in the sunshine—the forested peak looming above, the passive sea glittering beyond—setting her high, in the middle of it all. A naming ceremony.

The gifts were small, there being so little time since all was lost, but the chief was lavish with what he had. A wooden comb, a small stomach of oil, a doll's woven blanket—gifts given on her behalf, to anyone who repeated her name, fixing her in their collective memory.

They had done the same thing the summer before with the boy, now deemed a man, now called Dushuuw. The name evoked strength. And despite his slight frame—the weeks of hunger never quite giving up their hold—the name was well suited, to one so full of spiritual strength.

Small One had chosen her new name, though she did not realize it.

Many afternoons, the chief would find his young adopted daughter playing with her toys, laying her wooden doll in a tiny cradleboard with cedar-mat scraps, gently taking the yew baby out again, rocking it in her arms, whispering stories in its ear in the language in which they were remembered—of Basket Woman, of Woodpecker, and of Thunderbird, of the Moon's house, the Whale's house, the Wolf's house, of a grandmother who rubbed a girl's hair during story time, of a mother who could dance like the stars, of a father who fought back monsters in the night. "'Don't worry, Mother. Stop crying,'" she would say, holding a shell on the beach. "'I will find her. I will bring her...'"

Maḥtii stood silent and still as the villagers approached her, one after the other, and she heard in their myriad voices not only a name but a collection of memories. She shifted her feet, fingered her skirt, longed to retreat to a corner and play with her doll and the smooth mussel shell painted her favorite color.

Late that night, the house filled with the warmth of flame and flesh, the chief looked down at the still-small girl sitting beside him. "Maḥtii, my daughter," he said, "why don't you tell us a story?"

Maḥtii looked up at the chief, then around the small circle at the faces of those who had slowly become familiar. She took a breath and, surprising herself most of all, started to speak in words that made sense—and new words, at that. The voice that rose from her slight frame silenced the nearest of the onlookers with its strength.

"You know of the great Thunderbird." She brushed her finger absently along her painted mussel shell, back and forth, as she looked for the boy, addressing the gathering but speaking, as always, to only one. "Thunderbird beats his massive wings, and the beating makes a drumming sound in the sky…"

Beyond the swaying singers, the beating drummers, at the outskirts of the sonorous gathering, she saw him, standing watch.

"One day, Whale becomes jealous…"

The rest of the people in the house drew still, turning to listen to her words. The boy held her gaze, anchored her amid the wave of human movement as, one by one, each person turned toward her voice, which was her own and was not her own. The story welled up inside her from the mists of memory—all of it there, then suddenly broken apart, little scraps flying around—like when you wake from a dream. She pieced them back together.

"Their battle was so great, so fierce, that it sent up a large wave of water that swept over the land…"

They would drift apart, she and the boy. They would marry others, have children, who in turn would have children… Their descendants would live on many beaches, but gaze through doorways at the same sea. Disasters would strike, again and again, and her line would nearly be lost. One day there would be no tugging memory of a dance, only the driving urgency to keep a song safe. The girl sensed the edges of this future as she looked upon the boy. He was becoming like the horizon, that ethereal line that slips away and slips away, no matter how far you paddle. But they were bound together, like a strong rope tied to deep roots. They would drift apart, but they would always meet again. In the dance. In the song. In the drum that thrust them together. They would always meet again, two cords intertwined, secured to a mountaintop, where they derived their shared power.

"On that highest mountaintop, Thunderbird finally sets down the great carcass of Whale…"

The story, though—the story would be for everyone. To help them find their way too.

There on the mountaintop Thunderbird remains.

There are now many images of Thunderbird, of Thunderbird carrying Whale to that mountaintop.

Reminding us of how to survive...

The Here & Now

THEY SIT IN THE CANOE, surrounded by water, land hidden in the dense fog that settles over the rocking sea.

Marina's heart pounds, her knuckles white on the paddle, her shoulders and her back killing her. *Every stroke we take is one less we have to make.* She snorts at the adage, only to take a breath and shove more sea behind to keep pace with the woman beside her and with Aaron, whose broad back in front of her looms large. She could touch him, they are so close. He feels miles away.

The canoe full of pullers, some younger and some older, makes its way through the water, though not as fast as a Makah crew could really go. The fog is unnerving.

The journey is what we enjoy.

Not for the first time, Marina's eyes prick. They call it a canoe family, but to Marina this one is missing a member. She oscillates between grief and anger. The red paint she impulsively pressed across her face with an open palm is meant to bring Jen on this tribal canoe journey with them, but it isn't working. Hadn't worked the other times she had done it in the past year either, while at home or from her dorm room a coast away. Putting up posters. Haranguing the sheriff's office. Organizing sit-ins. Hadn't worked when news came of a drowned body found.

"You see that?"

The edge to the woman's voice makes Marina sit up.

She turns and sees the skipper tense, flicking a look to the woman in the bow. On cue, a walkie-talkie crackles with the voice of the support boat captain, his voice urgent. Marina's hand goes to the inflatable life vest strapped to her torso. It has never felt so light. The two leaders stop paddling, and Marina looks where they look.

An unnatural wave of water—a long, unbroken line of white-tipped froth—barrels toward the canoe out of the fog. Marina sucks in a breath.

"Go! Paddles in!"

Marina braces herself, and digs deep.

The wave surges toward them. They paddle forward to meet it.

The pullers follow the skipper's shouted instructions and, working together, hit the wave at an angle. The prow of the canoe slices the water to either side, like a knife. They shoot upward, then slam down. Water drenches Marina.

But they are through.

There's a pause, everyone holding their paddles still and upright, waiting for whatever might come next. It was a wave sent up by one of the unseen freighters, the skipper explains, and there might be another. Alert, Marina squints through the fog, seeking disaster. But none comes. Just small ripple-like waves that rock the canoe and then are gone. Throughout the canoe, shoulders relax. Heads swivel. Sighs burst. Then the celebration.

Aaron laughs and cheers with the others, raising his paddle above his head. He twists around and catches her eye, a smile on his face like she hasn't seen in—a long time. She tries to remember when. Aaron had been withdrawn long before Jen's disappearance, before her naked body was found tangled with fishing line on rocky bit of shoreline around the point back home. He has more reasons to grieve, to be angry. She wonders if it is OK to smile now. And as these thoughts cascade through her mind, her heart still beating with adrenaline, his smile fades and he turns back.

This is the first time either Marina or Aaron has helped pull a canoe.

Marina's parents and grandmother had impressed on her the need to go, talking about the healing the journey could bring. She thought that was what the song was for, the song her grandmother was teaching her in secret. "The song is like your Native name. It is for you," her grandmother said. "But this is something you can do to honor your friend." When Aaron showed up at canoe practices, Marina surmised he must have received the same lecture from his uncle. In years past, there had always been requests for the trio of friends to join the crew, at least as relief pullers. Young, strong arms were coveted for the journey of hundreds of miles, up to ten hours a day, for the better part of a week to join the massive celebration at the end with dozens of other tribes. But they had always had something more pressing to do. Vacations. College searches. Jobs.

Here we are, Jen, Marina thinks. She can't say the name aloud. But it rings in her head. The mist of the fog joins the wet salt of the sea, of her tears. She is no closer to whatever healing she is supposed to feel. She feels cut open, her guts splayed out for all to see. The smell of stage makeup fills her nostrils like a rebuke. *Fake, fake, fake.*

It's time to pull again. The fog persists. And there's still a long way to go to their first stop, where their usual and accustomed waters will give way to another's. Marina's shoulders protest, but she slides the paddle into the sea.

One less.

One less...

~

There is singing and the official welcome to shore at their first stop on the journey. But Aaron wants to find a shower and his sleeping bag. Maybe skip the shower.

Marina disappears into her tent as soon as they haul the canoe up above the high-tide line.

He pauses outside her tent, wanting to—knock? Do you knock on a tent door? He doesn't want to call out. Lately, something seems to lodge in his throat every time he even thinks about speaking to Marina. But, then, why is he standing here? He hears sniffing inside her tent, and he shuffles away. What would he say, anyway? What could he say?

The loss of Jen hangs between them. You'd think it would have brought them together for support, but instead it sent them drifting apart, farther and farther. Aaron feels maybe he knows why. He wasn't there when the body was found. Wasn't there when all the aftermath set in. Wasn't even there for the funeral at summer's end. He was on a boat. On a boat. On a boat.

Aaron has nearly reached his tent when he sees the man standing off by a tree, emerging from the fog like a spectre.

"Uncle?"

"Nephew!"

The old man uses a cane—no, not a cane. A staff? A staff, like he's friggin' Gandalf—and hobbles over the uneven ground.

"Hope you have room in that tent for one more," he says.

Aaron stares, unsure which question to ask first.

His uncle looks between him and the staff. "This? Yep, a new addition. Balance isn't quite back to normal yet after the hospital visit. Claire gave it to me. Her nephew carved it. Look at that eagle feather. Almost looks real. Pretty slick, ah? She was going to give it to me as a gift for being a witness at something or other coming up. But she said it looked like I needed it now. I just have to give it back to her so she can officially give it to me at whatever-the-whatever. Talk about a re-gift."

He gives a gruff half-laugh, and turns his gaze back to Aaron.

"Right," Aaron says. "Um, why..."

"...am I here?"

Uncle Pete purses his lips, looks beyond Aaron toward the other tents. He puts a hand on Aaron's shoulder and gives him a brief smile. "Thought you could use some support." His voice cracks a bit. Aaron wonders if it's a lingering effect of a long hospital stay; his uncle's hand is thin and knobby, but still broad and warm on Aaron's shoulder. An image of a trawler dwarfed by a rogue wave rears in Aaron's mind, interlaced with memories, already fading, of his father's face, weathered by elements, by life choices; and threaded through all of that the fresher memory of Jen's lopsided smirk, her smoker's voice, the blown kiss she sent her two friends as she backed away, into mist. "And to kick your ass," his uncle says, pulling him away. "You look like you need a swift one. Forget why you came out here?"

A wind comes through, sending the fog swirling away.

~

It's morning. Sort of.

Marina grimaces as she sets her feet into the still-wet clogs. She stumbles around, trying to figure things out in the dark. Excited chatter fills the air as crews prepare to leave for the next stop. Headlamps and flashlights send crisscrossing beams across the beach. One man drums and sings. Another woman holds up her hands in prayer. Flags flap over canoe sterns in a predawn breeze. When the tide goes out, the canoes go out—even if it's three in the morning.

"Hey."

Marina jolts against the canoe. It's Aaron, but it's an apparition. His face seems shrouded by more than the dark. She squints.

"Did you...?"

"Yeah."

A red handprint covers his face. A finger crosses his eye. The palm engulfs his mouth and cheeks. Her hand lifts, about to—what? She tucks it back at her side.

"They were going to the supercenter for something. I asked them to bring me some of this stuff." He vaguely gestures toward his face. "I thought I... I don't really know if..."

His voice trails off and he doesn't finish. It is the most they have said to each other in months. He's looking at her, and she's looking at him, but expressions are lost in the darkness. Her heart seems to want to follow the path of her hand. She pulls it back.

"Hup!"

Their heads swivel in unison toward the call to lift the canoe. Aaron's already bending down. At the count of three, they all hoist the canoe up to their shoulders and carry it to the water line.

A man with a booming voice sings a farewell song in his language. Far out on the water, they can still hear him.

Another day begins.

Smoke from distant wildfires casts the day in sepia, turns the rising sun molten.

~

The crew sits in a ring, most in camp chairs, a few on the ground. Aaron perches on a cooler.

"I'm grateful to be here," says one man, flopped in a chair across from Aaron. The man's leg sways back and forth. He recently returned to Neah Bay to live on the reservation. "And I don't just mean here on this journey. I mean here, here at all. And to be here with you all—doing what our ancestors did on the waters that belong to us—is real good. I wasn't in a good place before. And this time has been good, healing. I'm working my body, building myself back up again. It's medicine."

They go around the circle, sharing what brought them to the journey and what they are grateful for.

Some go every year. One guy was born on a tribal canoe journey; his necklace is crowded with colored beads, each marking a journey.

Others are looking to connect to their culture in a new way, taking a break from their lives in New York or Illinois to take part.

One works in research at a university. They talk about the need to heal the sea and see the journey as a way to give that scientific goal a spiritual foundation.

"When I'm out there on the water with you all, I'm not thinking about rising sea levels or acidification; I'm feeling the sea all around me. It's humbling, you know? And that's what our world needs. It's the only way we're going to solve the problems that keep me awake some nights." They pause for a brief moment. "Not that I'm having any trouble sleeping these nights!"

A few other young people have joined for this leg of the journey as relief pullers before heading back to their day jobs in Port Angeles, Sequim, Seattle. Their remarks are brief.

"And I guess you all know why I'm here."

Aaron lifts his head at the sound of Marina's voice.

"I'm doing this in her—" Her voice catches and she looks angry. "In her *memory*. But I don't like saying it like that. I'm bringing her in the canoe with me. This is supposed to show how so many of us have been silenced," she says, gesturing toward the handprint on her face. "But it's not always that. Sometimes we're speaking a lot, but no one's listening." She shakes out her hair and sits up. "I like being on the water. It's scary, but it's beautiful too. Powerful. You called it medicine." She looks at the man who spoke earlier. "I think that's right. I feel like I'm kinda still waiting for this medicine to kick in for me. But I'm getting—perspective. Working things out in a way I never could before." She folds her hands. "I'm glad I came. Grateful to pull this canoe with you all."

They continue around the circle. His uncle sits next to him in their camp chair, nodding his head to everything being said. Aaron's gaze keeps returning to Marina.

"I'm just here for the free food."

His uncle's comment pulls Aaron back to his place in the circle. As everyone laughs, Aaron rubs his hands over his thighs. His uncle looks at him expectantly.

"Right," Aaron says. "Well, you've seen my 'war paint' here." He gestures toward his face, then across toward Marina. "I joined Marina in that, for the same reason. We lost someone who mattered, mattered a lot. But, um, that came as part of the journey. My uncle talked me into joining as a puller, for training." He shoots a glance at his uncle. Uncle Pete nods for him to continue. "Some of you know I joined the whaling crew." A quick glance Marina's way shows she did not. Aaron looks at his feet, runs his hand through his hair, long enough again to keep flopping in his face. "There's a lot of preparation that goes into that. I've been on the water a lot. But being on a trawler is a lot different than being in a canoe. So there's the physical preparation. But also the spiritual preparation. And this is part of that; it's both, really. I'm grateful for the opportunity. It's been different. Been good. Real good, actually. Guess that's all I have to say."

Aaron trains his eyes on his feet, not wanting to see Marina's reaction.

~

It's morning, and the last leg of the journey is about to begin. The summer sun shines bright. There is a relaxed pace around the camp as everyone looks forward to the final beach, the final greeting to shore, the celebration to come—to the sugar restrictions being lifted.

When Aaron's uncle leaves, leaving the tent door flapping behind him, Marina draws a breath and strides over.

"Ready or not, I'm coming in."

"Holy—!" Aaron jolts upright, fingers digging through his hair. He's shirtless; and from the knee that pokes out of the mess of a sleeping bag, he's not wearing much else either.

"What, like I haven't seen you without clothes on before?"

But it's different, finding him this way in his bed rather than taking an impromptu swim in the frigid bay back home in more carefree days, the three friends stripping down to their underwear and splashing each other. She remembers how he grabbed her from behind in an embrace, ready to dunk her, then hesitating and simply holding on a few beats more before abruptly swimming away, splashing Jen as he went. Warmth had filled her, only to be replaced by the sea's chill when their bodies separated.

She masks the sudden heat that floods her face with more bravado.

"I'm doing your paint today. You suck at it. So get dressed and come on out. It reeks in here."

Soon he's outside, dressed in shorts and a T-shirt. "Good morning to you, too," he says, his voice still raspy from sleep.

As he pulls his hair back, Marina coats her hand in red paint. He brings his hands down to his sides, and she steps close. She raises her hand, brings it toward his lips, then pauses.

"You called it war paint."

Aaron grimaces. "I'm sorry. I shouldn't..."

"No—no. That's not what I meant."

She drops her hand and takes a step back. Aaron waits.

"We could use more warriors, you know?" She looks at the blaze of red on her palm. "This isn't for you." She presses her painted palm to her own face instead. "We'll do something different for you," she says.

Aaron sits in a nearby camp chair. She kneels in front of him, arranging her supplies on the grass.

"Working in the museum over the summer, I got to see some of the records they had on face-painting. Things they used to do—maybe some still do, I don't know—in preparation or in prayer for specific things."

"My uncle would love that kind of thing. Since they put me on the whaling crew, we've been doing a lot of the old spiritual preparation practices. For whaling, but also other things. He's teaching me a dance and stuff. I don't think he knows much about face-painting, though."

Marina brings her paint-dabbed fingers up toward his eyes. He closes them in anticipation. She falters, then presses the paint to his skin, which is still warm from sleep and his pillow. One thing she does not note is that the face-painting was most often done between lovers, the wife helping her husband, adding her spiritual strength to his own. She pushes the thought aside.

"They have anything on this for whale hunting?" he asks.

"Probably. I'll look."

"You have time before going back to college?"

"Some. I fly out right after Makah Days. You'll be there too? Not out on a boat?"

"With this canoe journey, the timing didn't line up." He shifts in the seat. "But, maybe I'll go anyway."

His face clouds over, and she knows he is remembering his father.

"I could catch a flight now and join up with whoever's got room," he says. "I'm missing out on some good pay already." He stands up abruptly, his face half-painted. Marina grabs his hand to pull him back.

Aaron opens his mouth as if to shout, but they both became aware of others in the camp watching them. He looks down at their hands, and sits again. She quickly lets go.

"You shouldn't bother with this," Aaron says in a low voice, gesturing toward his face. "I'm no warrior."

"Yes, you are. You're the strongest person I know, Aaron. Coming through your childhood like you did?"

"I have my uncle to thank for that."

"Sure, but it takes more than that. Your uncle couldn't forgive your father for you. Couldn't shake his hand for you. Couldn't choose the path you've chosen for yourself, working hard and helping others. My grandmother being one of them. Don't think I don't know who fills her freezer. You are strong, Aaron. And *I* don't think you're running."

"What do you mean?"

"What do you feel when you're out on the water, on the boat?"

"Tired."

"Besides that."

He thought for a moment. "At home."

She starts painting his face again. "The sea has the power to take away. But it also has the power to heal. Grandma told me that. I guess I'm starting to understand that for myself now too."

~

There is a twelve-canoe pileup as they wait for their hosts to welcome them ashore. Flags flap. Pullers chant. Throngs of people who arrived earlier crowd the canoe-lined beach half a mile in each direction. Speakers amplify the voices of the various canoe skippers asking for permission to join them.

"We bring you our medicine. We will sing. We will dance. And we will feast together."

The familiar refrain, and a dozen variations, repeats over and over. Drums and singing welcome them.

Feast. A feast sounds really good to Aaron. Maybe they could skip to that part. But more than hunger, Aaron feels alive. Like the midfield celebration after a Red Devils win in football. The record-breaking halibut he'd helped pull from the depths. He has done this thing. And he finds he wants to do it again. Makah Days has canoe races. Maybe there's time to join. And maybe it's the face paint. But he feels badass.

Finally they are ashore. Aaron splashes into the water with the other younger pullers, guiding the canoe the last few feet. Marina is at his side.

"We did it," he says.

"We did it."

Suddenly, an excitable mutt is barking and circling their legs. It shoves its nose toward Aaron's hand.

"Max?" Marina looks down at the dog, which belongs to her grandmother. The older woman, Claire, walks toward them over the sand, her hand resting on his uncle Pete's arm as the older man uses the staff she gave him to navigate the uneven ground.

Aaron crouches down and lets the dog lick his face. "Good boy, good boy. Yes, be a deer and get rid of all that salt for me." The dog's hindquarters sway back and forth rapidly—his tail alone insufficient to express his exuberance—and his wiry but strong frame barrels into Aaron, forcing him to his knees. He laughs and scratches the dog's head.

"Well, aren't you his best friend," Marina says. "Didn't think that dog liked anyone except Grandma."

"We, uh, spent a lot of time together over the winter," Aaron says, in between dog kisses.

"There's my drumming whaler!"

Claire leaves his uncle and comes up to him, putting her hands on either side of his face as she looks over his paint. "And a warrior, too, I see," she adds in a low voice. "Good. Very good."

"Grandma?"

"Yes! Marina, my sweet girl, come here." The pair embrace. Claire leans back, holding Marina by the arms. "How did it go?"

"Um, good. Really good. I don't know if I found what I was looking for, but I feel better. Stronger."

Claire nods and holds back tears.

Aaron stands up from the dog to greet his uncle.

Marina looks back at her grandmother. "So," she says, extending the word out. "Your 'drumming whaler,' huh?"

"I guess I forgot to tell you," says her grandma, whose memory is impeccable. "Last winter, after everything that happened and this boy here didn't have a boat to work on—well, I thought Max and I could provide some good company."

Uncle Pete chimes in. "She invited herself in. Didn't even knock."

"I did so knock. I just didn't wait for your old ass to come let me in; because if I did, I'd be waiting all night."

"Bah."

"Max and I take our walks past their house routinely. But one day Max asked if we could pay a visit. And so I obliged him."

"She was snooping!"

"We waited quite a while for our knock to be heard."

"We were busy with something very important—"

"They were drumming."

"—something that was none of your business."

"I had to enlist Max to help me, have him bark and howl to add his own music—"

"Secret stuff!"

"—superior music, I must say, to finally get their attention."

"Spying!"

"After that, of course, we became regular callers."

Aaron draws his shoulders together, uncomfortable at where the conversation might go—they had not only been drumming—but more uncomfortable with the attention.

"Whaling crew. Drumming. My grandmother's dog's new best friend. Guess there's a lot I don't know about you anymore," Marina says.

Aaron senses the hand of silence descending again.

"You were away..." Of course she was away. Hitting the books at some elite Ivy League a coast away. A different sea. Way to state the obvious, dumbass.

But the skipper is calling for action. The older people make room, and the crew lines up along the sides of the hull. Aaron crouches down, getting ready. Marina falls in behind him. "Guess we have a lot to catch up on," she says. "Maybe we can start tonight." They lift on the count of three, and Aaron smiles.

~

There is, indeed, a feast. Thousands of people dine on smoked salmon and sides. Marina savors an ice cream bar. Aaron downs a Coke. And made full again, the tribes dance and sing and exchange gifts.

Each canoe that made the journey is given time on the floor, with those who traveled farthest going first. It could be days until the Makah have their turn. In the meantime, they watch others from the bleachers, grab late-night snacks, and catch a few hours of shuteye in their tents during lulls in the action. With so many tribes taking part, the protocol will be carried on nearly 24/7.

"Have you been practicing?"

Marina glances at her grandmother, who sits beside her on the bleacher. She knows her grandmother is not talking about the dances they're bringing to the floor here.

"Not during the journey, but otherwise yes."

"You do so when I suggested?"

"Before I go to sleep. When I wake up."

The words of the song snake through her mind. In her imagination, they are complete and spill out from her mind's voice with ease. On paper, they are even mostly intelligible. But when she brings the words of the song to her lips, especially without any aids, they still feel foreign.

hi·dawal ƛisi·q̓ak ʔiyax̌ duči ʔi·ʔiq...

She took Makah language classes as a kid, and she's taken refreshers since starting work for the museum. But they are still a struggle—all those pauses and pops, the shape of the throat. Like it isn't her speaking at all. Like she's speaking with someone else's voice.

"You go back to college soon?"

"My flight's the last day of Makah Days. Mom will drive me."

"You will come home in November, though, for every Native's favorite holiday?"

Marina snorts. "Yup."

"We will do it then."

Marina feels her heart lurch. "You mean..."

"Formally give it to you, yes."

Though Marina has practiced the song with her grandmother often, the idea of the song belonging to her gives her a thrill—or perhaps it's fear. Marina looks around the vast building, at the hundreds of people who dance, drum, sing, cheer. The dances and songs brought to the journey floor are ones that can be publicly shared. Marina wonders how many of the tribes here have families like hers, who fiercely guard other dances and songs, possessions that never go beyond familiar walls.

"Family only?"

"Mostly. But we'll do a run-through with a smaller group."

"You, me, and Uncle Bill again?"

"Actually, I was planning on Aaron and Pete."

Marina jolts and her head whips around toward her grandmother.

"What?" Marina struggles to bring her voice low, aware of those around them. "I thought this was the big family secret."

"I have my reasons," her grandmother murmurs.

An annoying smile appears on her grandmother's face, and Marina gives up. Besides, they're waving her over to get ready for protocol.

Marina's already dressed in her regalia—a tunic-style dress threaded with shells and beads that click as she walks toward the large group. Red crests and designs are emblazoned across the black fabric. She carries her cedar hat, and drapes a cape over her arm to don later. Large beaded earrings dangle over her shoulders, a long-ago birthday gift from Jen. She runs her fingers over one.

Aaron and the other crew members stand at the head of the gathering. Other Makahs have traveled out to join this particular part of the journey, and they line up in droves behind them.

At the sight of Aaron, a wave of embarrassment moves through Marina. What is her grandmother's angle? Is she trying to set Aaron and Marina up? That would be awful. So awkward. Aaron would not appreciate that. Or, worse—the thought pops into her head—were Grandmother and Pete...? No. No, she would not let her mind go that direction. Must absolutely not think about that.

"You look constipated," Aaron says.

He wears silver basketball shorts and a black vest over his bare chest. Circles of abalone shells line the vest, which has a red crest appliquéd on the back. His hair is pulled up in a knot. A headband made of woven cedar bark circles his head like a crown, sprigs of evergreen tucked into the knot. His feet are bare.

"Grandma told me her plans for you," Marina says. "What you'll be doing with us this fall?"

"Oh, the drumming? I just learned about that myself from Uncle."

"I'm sorry she's roped you into this. You don't have to, you know."

"I don't mind."

"I don't know why she's doing this. Up until now it's been, like, this big state secret. And now she's—no offense—letting an outsider in? I'm not sure what her game is, to be honest."

"I think she feels a little guilty about sitting in on our own practices."

"For what?"

"Remember me and Max being best buds? All the drumming your grandma and he had advice for my uncle about? We were working on a state secret ourselves. Ever since my dad passed, Uncle's been going on and on about our culture and stuff. There's a really old dance he's working on giving me. One dad was meant to have, but had beat his body up too much to be able to move in the right ways. Anyway, that's what your grandma walked in on. Honestly, I am in awe of your grandma. Only she could talk my uncle into hanging around—much less offer unwanted advice!"

Marina groans. "She has a way of getting what she wants. It doesn't matter what other people want, apparently."

"But I do want to," he says. "Drum for you, that is."

Marina looks up at him.

Aaron rubs the back of his neck. "Do you have your paints? I'd like to, you know, bring her on the floor with us, like we did in the canoe."

Marina feels like smiling and crying at the same time. She chooses to smile, and flags down her younger sister, sending the girl running to their tent for her supplies.

Soon, she and Aaron are standing off to the side. There's an air of anticipation hovering over the group, as the other tribe finishes their time, exchanging gifts with their host. Makah dancers spit out their gum and adjust their regalia. Marina applies the paint to Aaron's face. Then, as the Makah drums start to pound, and a man sings a soaring entry song, she presses a red palm across her face and rubs her hands clean with baby wipes. Aaron joins the men at the front of the procession. Marina joins the women.

The dancers fill the floor, winding and looping, finishing one long dance and then starting another. Children follow more experienced dancers. Babies are strapped to their mothers' or grandmothers' chests. Elders sit in chairs watching over everything. Marina dips and bends around the dance floor.

The Makahs end with a war dance. Marina stands with other women on one side of the floor, as the men enter in a long, serpentine line. The women gaze at the floor, but Marina sneaks glances at Aaron now and then. His expression is focused behind the paint. They have been out here for over an hour already. But he performs the crouching dance with precision. Some of the men are dramatic in their movements, swiping at imaginary enemies with gusto. Others, the youngest ones usually, are more slow, their eyes following the more experienced dancers in front of them. But Aaron is simply steady. He thrusts his ceremonial spear toward the rafters in controlled, quick strokes—formidable.

Do you see us, Jen? Do you see us dancing for you?

Marina waves her hands, the shells on her dress clicking as she sways, both echoing and amplifying the sounds of other clicking shells, beneath the beats of the drums, and the deep calls of the singers.

~

It's an unseasonably warm November night.

But that's not why Aaron drips with sweat. His skin is on fire. He's pretty sure he might pass out. He wants to escape the steaming shack. But hell if he'll let the old man stick it out longer than him.

"This is what it takes, Nephew!"

Aaron laughs, unable to resist his uncle's continued enthusiasm for his role on the whaling crew.

"You've got to be clean," Uncle Pete always says, "not just on the outside. Clean that lens between your spirit and your body."

So here he is, sweating out the uncleanness through every orifice of his stench-filled humanness across from a laughing old man.

"You know what would be good to practice right now in here?" his uncle asks. "The dance."

"OK, I give up."

Aaron throws open the door and runs naked across his uncle's yard and Front Street to the beach beyond, yelping at the barnacled rocks under his bare feet. Rain pounds down. Someone cheers from a passing vehicle and honks their horn. Aaron plunges into Neah Bay's cold waters, not so much diving as falling beneath the surface. He comes up for air with a yelp, then breathes heavily, tasting salt on his lips. The air's warm for the time of year—and they say the ocean has never been warmer—but Aaron's body rejects both scientific claims. The suffocating heat of the sauna is forgotten; he shivers, ice-cold. But he dunks below the water once more—sinks to the bottom and stares up at the dark, wavering surface, feeling the rocks poke his skin—before staggering upright and bolting back to his uncle's house.

Uncle Pete stands at the stove, bare ass still red from the sauna, heating water for Indian tea. Aaron pulls on a robe and socks, and cups the proffered mug close to his face.

"Enjoy the atmospheric river?"

"It's not raining too bad, actually," Aaron says.

"Well, if those things are going to keep visiting us, the least they could do is drop some salmon. I mean, it's called a river, right?"

"We got a tropical sea turtle that one time."

"Yeah, and they named it Surf Smelt Beach."

Aaron smiles. The turtle was named Shi Shi for the beach where it had been found on Makah lands. It was taken in a helicopter like the dialysis patients, dropped off at the Seattle aquarium to be nursed from the brink of death. Apparently, it had been even colder than Aaron feels at the moment.

"Did it survive, do you remember?"

But before his uncle can answer, there's a knock at the door, and a moment later it's opened—also before his uncle can answer.

Marina's grandmother stands in the doorway. Aaron's uncle stands where he is, making no move to cover himself, and sips his tea.

"Pete," she says in greeting.

"Claire."

"Making sure you know what time."

"We do."

"And where."

"We do."

"Good." And she shuts the door and goes on her way.

Aaron shakes with cold, shakes with laughter. He has to set the tea down, so he doesn't spill it. His uncle joins him, until tears spill from both their eyes.

Later, as he showers and gets dressed, Aaron laughs again to himself over Marina's grandmother. Marina only got into town that morning—after a long flight, and a long drive from the Seattle airport—but her grandmother was firm on having their first practice tonight. They'd waited long enough, she said. She was excited, for sure. Aaron might share the sentiment, except he doesn't know what he'll be drumming. "Oh, you'll pick it up quick," was all Claire said. He hopes it's a simple beat. He finds he's glad for the old woman's tenacity, though. It has been a long wait for him too.

They would hold the practice session after hours, in the model longhouse inside the museum. To get the right vibes going, her grandmother said that morning.

Marina winced at the added pressure Grandma's plan would bring, but she knew better than to disagree. "Aaron probably doesn't even want to do this, you know," she mused instead.

"Oh, you might be surprised," the old woman said.

Now, later than she thought her grandmother might ever be able to stand, Marina fishes out the spare keys she still has to the museum. Grandma already got permission for the scheme. Now she adjusts the fluffy blanket over her shoulders, anxiously watching Marina's fingers fumble at the lock.

When she was a girl, Marina's classes had taken numerous field trips to the museum for cultural lessons and story times. She loved the exhibits from the start. The game paddle. The loom. The carved chest. All pulled from the mud of a buried village. They walk past the objects now, and beneath the skeleton of a gray whale that hangs suspended from the ceiling. The skeleton is large, but she imagines how much bigger it was with its blubber and flesh and skin, extending all of its thirty feet, weighing all of its 600 pounds, feeding a gym full of people three times over.

Marina flicks on lights, including the ones for the fake fires of the fake hearths inside the model longhouse. Other than that soft red glow, and the fluorescent lighting that pools in through the open doorway, there's no other light inside the replica longhouse. It is dark, dusk-like. The mock dirt floor dips and rises under her feet. Another doorway opens to the "outdoors"—a mixture of real sand and driftwood for a fake beach that abuts a wall painted to look like the sea. For good measure, she also flicks on the speakers that pipe in sounds of crashing surf. The walls and plank roof, however, are all too real, fitted together as their ancestors had done.

Soon, Aaron tromps through the doorway, his uncle close behind. Aaron's hair is even longer, and he seems to walk with less of his usual slouch. He seems more solid, and his steps match. His uncle Pete totes his own blanket, a musty crocheted thing, and sits across from Grandma on another wooden bench and puts the blanket over his legs.

"There's my dancing-whaling-drumming warrior!" Grandma claps her hands.

Marina looks to Aaron for an answer.

"She's been coming to Uncle's house again for a lot of the dance practices, watching me learn," he says, lifting one shoulder.

"Don't know why I let her talk me into it," the older man grumbles.

"Kept coming back for more. Couldn't help myself."

"And all she does is chuckle to herself—chuckle! Over one of the most ancient dances of—"

"Max says Aaron is doing a fine job, and I agree. Now, let's get started, shall we?" Marina's grandmother shoves a drum notation sheet into Aaron's hands. "Bill wrote that up for you. It's based off his own know-how, but also an old copy from the museum's files. An ancestor of ours got it down on paper with some anthropologist years upon years ago—insurance. Don't worry, you'll pick it up quick," Grandma says. "And remember. Like I tell Pete when he's drumming for you. You got to go full-board, play really loud."

With drum in hand, Aaron settles into a dark corner under a rafter sporting racks of dried fish. The drum is a tanned deer hide pulled taut over a round, wooden frame. The mallet twitches in his hand, as he looks to Grandma for the signal to start.

Marina is nervous too. She hasn't sang the song in front of anyone besides Grandma, and Uncle Bill when he drummed for them—and even he, a professional musician, struggled with the rapid-fire beat.

"Fair is fair," Pete says. "Let's hear this song. It's my turn to eavesdrop on family secrets."

Marina's grandmother just smiles, like she does know a secret.

It takes a few false starts to get the song going. Aaron has to prop up his phone flashlight to see the notations. Distracted, Marina requires a prompt for when to come in.

Still unsure of her grasp of the language, Marina's voice is timid at first. She tries to calm her nerves by thinking on the meaning of the words that confound her tongue.

Daylight is found on the mountain

Grandma instructs Aaron to drum louder. It pounds in Marina's ears, louder and more insistent than ever before. She closes her eyes and tries to hear her own voice in her head.

feathers dance on the echoes of wolves

The sounds bounce off the cedar planks. The drum threatens to take over. Her voice tries to find the right path—its valleys, its hills.

She prepares to raise her voice.

we touch—

Suddenly, Aaron stops.

"I'm sorry," Marina says, growing increasingly frustrated. Everything about this is awkward. If her grandmother had hoped the longhouse would inspire instant understanding, some spiritual link to their ancestors, who probably did this every waking moment of their lives...

Aaron holds up his palm to her. He looks pale in the dusky confines. His uncle has the same pallor, his blanket on the floor at his feet. Grandma laughs uproariously, flapping her blanket like a crazed seagull.

Aaron walks over and thrusts the drum into his uncle's hands. "You heard that too?"

His uncle nods.

They address her grandmother at the same time. "Did you...?"

Grandma gets sober quick and shakes her head, cutting them off. "No. It's the drum that goes with the song. Older than the hills. Back into the long ago. The real thing."

The old man jabs the air with his finger. "Because if you..."

"No, Pete. No. I would never do that."

The old man nods, but is still clearly unsettled. He shifts the drum in his hands. "They always said, in passing, that there was a piece..."

"Missing," Aaron finishes.

"A dance for the boy. But something..."

"For the girl."

Aaron finally glances at Marina, and she sees fear there. Why does it feel like it's her that he's afraid of? Her grandmother has grown still, all levity gone as she listens intently to the men. Her eyes sheen. But Marina doesn't get a chance to ask what's going on. Aaron nods at his uncle, who starts to drum.

It's the same drumbeat as Grandma's song, without the aid of any notation. Loud. Incessant. Somehow, old Pete knows it. And in his confident hands, the drumbeats reverberate throughout the space. He and Aaron share looks of concentration. Her grandmother raises her hand and tells him to stop.

"Play it like it should be played, Pete," she says, pointing to a large bentwood box that's part of the exhibit. Two fat sticks rest on top. "I gave it a rap the other day. A little test. It will do."

The older man leaves the skin drum behind and strides over to the far side of the box, lowering himself on arthritic knees, and gives the wood a mighty thwack with one of the sticks. The sound is far louder than the skin drum. It bounces off the cedar wall behind him and echoes through the empty museum. Marina jolts, realizing how stiff she has become with trepidation. The old man looks up at Aaron and nods.

"I don't..." Marina struggles to express her confusion.

But her grandmother has scurried over and is shoving the old man's blanket into Aaron's arms. And now Aaron strides to the center of the room, his body black in silhouette against the doorway open to its painted sea. The recorded surf makes its shushing sounds. The red light of electric embers pulse. The old man starts to drum, loud and incessant. Marina hunches her shoulders and almost covers her ears.

Aaron draws the blanket over his back. He crouches low to the ground, as if to disappear into himself, wrapped in the blanket-cape with his back arched upward. He moves in a circle, with such small, feather-light steps that Marina doesn't notice at first. Gradually, he rises from his hunched position, moving all along in light, small steps in a tightening spiral. Until he's finally upright, at the terminus of the spiral, and—the loud drum still blasting—he thrusts his arms outward with the blanket. In one hand he grasps the skin drum's mallet, like a weapon. The pose lasts only a moment. In the next, he thrusts the mallet to the ground—a movement as fast as the initial dance steps were slow.

Grandmother motions at her, urging her to sing, and she—

Daylight is found on the mountain

Aaron has resumed his crouched, hidden pose, circling.

feathers dance on the echoes of wolves

He slowly rises, spiraling upward, opening his arms.

we touch lightning

He slams the mallet to the ground.

But the drum pounds on, threatening to overwhelm Marina's voice and throw off Aaron's measured steps.

Over and over she sings and he dances. The drum beats loud. The dance and song both demur beneath its insistence, then finally meet—one rising as the other falls—and overcome its power.

Marina finds it easier to sing as she watches Aaron dance. The struggle with the drum recedes. His movements are perfectly timed to her words. She has to remind herself what round they are on. She aches with longing, now that the song is nearly done.

On the last round, Marina hits the last tone clearly, her voice rise, rise, rising—as if asking a question. The word resounds off the ceiling and walls and seems to shoot out and bounce off the drum itself. Then, at the same moment, the song and the drum and the dance stop. The air vibrates, pulsing with the arrested sounds of song and drum and the shadowy afterimage of a caped figure. The space loses its dusky quality; for that moment, all seems ablaze with a real and fiery light.

~

Aaron and Marina walk onto Hobuck Beach in the dark, quiet.

Neither of them had wanted to try to sleep, when they knew sleep would not come. The older people hadn't talked at all. Pete had waved off Claire as he left the museum in a rush, saying he needed to think. The levity had gone out of Claire, who was all tears—"tears of gratitude, of thanks"—until they took her home too.

Aaron spreads out a towel and sits down, and Marina joins him. She pulls close the fluffy blanket her grandmother used, while Aaron shrugs on his uncle's tattered one. It's cold with the wind. But the sky is clear, as if the night has been swept clean for a dance floor of stars. Orion the Hunter remains frozen, poised to strike. A waning crescent moon hangs bright and flickers its broken streaks across Makah Bay.

"Where did that song come from?" Aaron asks.

Marina hunches her shoulders. "Can you keep a secret?"

"Um, yeah, I guess."

"Can you keep *a secret*?"

"Fine. Yes. Of course."

"Grandma has been sort of cryptic about it. But she says slave blood still means something, and she's not going to advertise it."

"You're kidding me."

She shakes her head.

"Marina, you were a Makah Days queen. Your grandma is a respected elder. She was on the council for how long? What the hell would anyone care if the song came from a slave?"

"You can't tell—"

"Of course not, I won't. I just don't think it's a big deal."

She arches her brows skeptically, then her mouth tilts up in a smile. She leans against him in a shove. A cold wind comes off the sea, and she leans against him again. Her body is warm against his side.

"Well, we know now it wasn't slave stuff," Aaron says. "It couldn't be. Not if it's been a pair with that dance all along."

"And the dance? What do you know about where it came from?"

"Uncle says it goes way back, to a time long ago. There was a great flood—probably a tsunami, we think now. Anyway, whoever was the first to have the dance obtained it then, when he got his power on a

493

mountaintop. There was a girl, too. But that's all that can be said. There's got to be more to the story, but it's been lost."

"Makes you think..."

He turns his head toward her and becomes aware of mingled smells, of her hair, her skin, the old woman's blanket.

"Exactly how far back do that dance and song go, I wonder," she says. "And how did they ever get separated? Grandma says so many songs were lost."

"Dances, too."

"And words—we're not a hundred percent on the meaning of all the ones in this song. But if you say the dance was obtained in a flood, maybe the line about a mountain was about how people survived—getting to high ground? I dunno."

The waves crash on the shore. The scent of seaweed fills the wind-fueled air.

She wonders if he feels as daunted as she does about this responsibility they're being given.

He wonders if she felt what he did in that longhouse.

"You have a Makah name, right?" she asks.

He shifts with embarrassment. "Uncle gave me a new one when they had me join the whaling crew. My great-grandfather was the last one to have it—Dushuuw."

"What does it mean?"

"Something about being strong," he hedges, though he knows exactly what it means. *He Is Strong*. He isn't sure he can claim that. "What about you? Now that you're no longer She-Of-The-Massive-Belch?"

She growls and pokes him in the ribs.

"Ow! Now, come on. Blame your dad!"

"Amuun'axsum. It is now *Amuun'axsum*."

"Doesn't sound like a bodily function. Also doesn't sound too Makah."

"Grandma says it has something to do with that song, that they were passed down as a pair. But no one knows what the name means exactly. Maybe *A Woman From...* but from no place anybody's ever heard about. Definitely not Makah, though the song is. Another mystery."

Aaron pulls up his knee and drapes an arm over it.

"So, what is it like, being on the whaling crew?" she asks.

"Harder than I thought."

Marina doesn't say anything, but he can feel her looking at him, wanting him to say more.

"It's weird... Your song was never written down. But it survived over centuries. Everything now, though—it's like, if it's not written out, notarized, initialed..."

He doesn't finish, but Marina knows what he means.

"They sensed that then," she says. "When they signed the treaty."

Aaron gives a mocking laugh. "No shit. You lose seventy-five percent of your people to a mysterious disease. You're under the gun to sign papers you can't read. But you make damn sure whaling is part of those words before you give them your X. Badass."

"I always marveled at how they were able to convince the government to change that treaty template. Because it wasn't with words. They didn't speak the same language," Marina says. "They took them out in canoes. To show them what they wanted, to show them it wasn't just about land."

A gust of wind blows through. A particularly large wave crashes to the beach, which is shrinking.

"I'm starting to understand what the old folks say," Aaron says, "that our real strength—in the courts, or before some commission or whatever—comes from other things, you know? And yet... You remember what they did with the halibut hooks? Recreating the ancient design to show how it's better than the modern hooks at limiting bycatch and all that?" he asks. "Well, the whaling crew worked with the museum to try something similar. We spent a year trying to recreate one of the whaling harpoon heads, to see what those guys knew. And we couldn't do it, not really. The mussel shells now are too thin. You hold one up against one of the old ones, and it's like rings on a tree. They were stronger then. Ours break."

Marina slips her hand over his arm. "But they stopped using shells ages ago. Once they got steel—"

"Sure, but I mean... It's been so long. So much has changed. Are we enough? Are we too late?"

"It's never too late," Marina says, pulling on his arm. "How many times did it seem there'd be no whales left, no sea lions left—shit, no *us* left? Like they say. We bend a little—maybe more than a little. But we don't break. Because we hold on tight to what is left and take care of it."

"And now you sound like a little old lady."

"Don't joke, Aaron." She shifts away. "You felt it too, didn't you?"

Aaron's throat closes up as he looks away. He puts his face toward the sea as his mind returns to the dance, remembering the way he felt bigger than life as he slowly opened himself up and dove back down—like everything inside him was expanding, to meet and connect with something greater. And dancing to the sound of Marina's voice, he felt alive—not knowing the words she was singing, but feeling the truth of them through the movement of his body that seemed made for her voice. He was no longer alone.

"It felt like, I dunno, remembering a piece of my future self," he says.

"Yeah," she says, with a short laugh. "Yeah, exactly."

He misses her warmth against him. Wind off the bay pierces the space between them.

She shivers. She misses his warmth against her.

"A lot of the old stories are about that, I think," she says. "They're memories, often passing on how to survive, how to stay connected to what matters—even if they never say it outright."

"You've been studying the stories," he says.

"Well, yes. The summer internships at the museum have been pretty awesome." She fiddles with a thread on the blanket. "Filing. Writing grant proposals. Boring stuff"—and here, he knows she's lying, because she loves the boring stuff—"and telling stories to groups of kiddos."

"What stories do you tell?" he asks.

"Lots of Q̓watee…"

"Obviously."

"And Thunderbird stories, like how Thunderbird taught us to catch whales. Snot Boy, of course—but including the part where he travels to the Moon's house to marry his daughter, watching Moon's fires for signs, and dodging Moon's attempts to kill him in order to win her hand…"

"The hero Snot Boy, kids, who saves you from ogresses and gives valuable dating advice."

"Shut up!" But she laughs. After a moment, she continues, her tone still eager. "Most of the stories these kids probably already heard, maybe a thousand times if they're like our families. So I also found a more obscure one. About a flood caused by a fight between Thunderbird and Whale. Seemed like a good way to reference the tsunami evacuation plans and how we're relocating a lot of things to higher ground."

Aaron thinks of the stark blue-and-white signs that mark evacuation routes to assembly points at safe elevations. The elementary kids haven't just ducked under their desks during earthquake drills. They've jogged up Diaht Hill, as fast as their stubby little legs can go, holding hands in a wending line.

Fragments of a story about his dance and her song go through their minds. A flood. A mountain. A boy, and a girl. An overwhelming drum beat. And a vast distance of time and space, closed now, by a boy and a girl sitting on a beach in the wake of generations of losses and victories.

Aaron thinks on his own losses, of a father and a friend. He thinks on the canoe journey, the purposes it held. His uncle's description of the sea: "life-taker, life-giver."

Marina fights tears as she thrusts her head onto Aaron's shoulder as they look out over Makah Bay—with nothing but sea to the far horizon, and beyond that more sea. Waves swell and rush in the moonlight.

He holds his breath, hoping she won't pull away.

She slides her hand over his arm, hoping he won't turn her aside.

Aaron closes his eyes, his chest welling with a warmth he struggles to identify. He feels like he did in that moment at the end of his dance and Marina's song, as if he is in a place suspended between what was and what is. A place of what could be, that *wanted* to be.

"Dushuuw, the Whaler," she says.

Does she know her smile has a sound? That resonates to his bones.

"Amuun'ax̱sum, the Queen," he returns.

Does he know those words have a taste? Both bitter and sweet on her tongue.

Grief and gratitude seem to war over their hearts.

Aaron presses his eyes closed and tries to find the right answer. When the battle continues, he opens his eyes and faces the sea. The waves flicker and dodge in the moon's glow. He keeps his eyes on those cold flames, wary, as he slides his palm against hers, intertwines their fingers, and holds on tight. Maybe the answer is to let both sides fill him. Maybe they aren't at war at all. Maybe the strength he needs, housed in that thin line like a horizon, has been there all along—he just hasn't reached out for it, thinking it unreachable. Marina turns her head toward him, pressing her forehead into the crook of his neck. Her breath is warm through the thin fabric of his T-shirt. Her tears are hot on his skin. She lifts her head, gaze fixing on his own.

His blood races, as if dancing.

Her lips part, as if to sing.

The tide shushes, and the sea creeps higher and higher.

"I want the sea. That is my country."
— Ċaqa·wiƛ, 1855 treaty talks

"Each song has a purpose,
and a beginning
— and hopefully no end."
— Wade Greene, Makah

Character List

A written form of Makah—a member of the Wakashan language family, primarily found among their Nuu-chah-nulth relatives on Vancouver Island's west coast—was not formalized until 1978. The language includes sounds not found in English. In this book, I use English phonetic approximations of Makah and other Wakashan words to at least get your reading mind close to the actual pronunciations. Qʷidičča?a·tx̌ thus becomes Kwidich'chuh-aht and means the "people who live by the rocks and seagulls." (The name Makah is a derivative of a Salish word applied to them during treaty times. It likely describes a people "generous with food.")

Names are sacred in these cultures. Like songs and dances, they often are owned property and passed down in families. To avoid accidentally using owned names, most of my character names will be laughable to Native speakers. In a few cases, my thanks go to language teachers who helped craft richer names. Unless otherwise noted, words are Makah.

Find an audio guide at melissaslager.com/reader

Characters

It was common for people to take multiple names throughout their lives, particularly the noble-born. The two main characters give a taste of that.

Dushuuw — dašuw (dŭ-shoo), "he is strong"

    a.k.a.   Young Son (I use English for diminutives in this book)

           Quht-Quht (nickname) — short for qała·tkʷ (qŭ-lthŏtkh), "younger brother or junior line cousin of a male"

           Uhsahb (nickname) — ?asa·b (ŭ-sŏb), "high-born child"

           Chihtup-uh — čitap?a (CHĭ-Tŭp-ŭ), "whale by the rock"

Amuun'axsum — Amun'axsam (ŏm-oon-ahX-sum), Kwaḵwala-like construction to mean "a woman from Amuun" (but note that Amuun is not a real place)

    a.k.a.   Quulthoo — qułu· (qoolth-hoo), "slave"

           Maḥtii — maḥtii (mŏ-tē), Nuu-chah-nulth for "house"

Other characters

Buhkweeduuk — bakʷi·duk (bŭ-kwē-dook), "to trade, barter"

    Dushuuw's uncle

Buh-uhs (Buh-Buh) — baʔas (bŭ-ŭs), "house, or nation"
Dushuuw's young cousin
Chahbuhł — ča·baɫ (chŏ-bŭT), "chief, wealthy, rich"
Dushuuw's father; Wuh-uhch whaling chief
Chaiyuhx-ik (Chai) — ča·yaxʔik (chī-yŭx-ĭk), "fond of berry picking"
Dushuuw's half-sister; daughter of Chahbuhł and Thluuch-muup
Eekbis — ʔi·x̌bis (ēXH-bĭs), "important"
Wuh-uhch shaman
Ḥawith — ḥaẇił (hă-wĭth), Nuu-chah-nulth for "chief"
whaling chief of an allied village across the strait
Hawitsuksh — ha·wiċaqš (hŏ-wits-ŭksh), "story"
Wuh-uhch storyteller
Huh-uuk — haʔuk (hŭ-ook), "eat"
member of whaling crew, inflates floats
Kuhbuhłup — kabaɫap (kŭ-bŭ-Tŭp), "know (something as a fact)"
speaker for Wuh-uhch whaling chief
Kweelthup — kʷi·łap (kwēlth-hŭp), "misty"
speaker's son; soft-spoken member of whaling crew
Leehuuk — li·xuk (lē-xhook), "cheap"
rich Wuh-uhch chief who lives at upriver end of Wuh-uhch
Mowach — muwač (moo-wŏch), Nuu-chah-nulth for "deer"
Amuun'ax̱sum's mother
Oodahk — ʔuda·kʷ (oo-dŏk), "have, own"
Deeyuh whaling chief
Ootsihd — ʔucx̌id (oots-XHĭd), "to marry"
Uhpqoolth's wife; grew up in Tsooyuhs
Pikoo — piku· (pĭ-koo), "trinket basket"
Dushuuw's aunt; Buhkweeduuk's wife
Qaq-owuhtsah-lth — Qaqʔawaca·ʔł (kŭk-ow-ŭ-tsŏ-lth)
Makah name for the Basket Woman, ogre-like story character
Q̇otsik — q̇aċik (Kŭ-TSĭk), "artful, talented, expert, versatile"
Dushuuw's older brother; harpooner on whaling crew
Q̇watee — Q̇ʷe·ti· (Kwă-tē)
name of trickster-like Makah story character
Sawsin — saasin (sŏ-sĭn), Nuu-chah-nulth for "hummingbird"
Q̇otsik's love; Ḥawith's older daughter
Shuchkuk — šačkak (shŭch-kŭk), "sharp"
Tsooyuhs fighter and wrestler
Suu-ahp — suʔa·p (soo-ŏp), "to catch"
Uhpahs's love interest; fisherman

Ṫashii — łašii (Tă-shē), Nuu-chah-nulth for "road, path, trail"
Ḥawith's wife; mother of Sawsin and Tluulth
Thluuch-muup — łuučmuup (thlōoch-mōop), Nuu-chah-nulth for "sister"
Chahbuhł's youngest wife; mother of Chai
Tiichswii — tiičswii (tēch-swē), Nuu-chah-nulth for "survive"
Amuun'aẋsum's childhood friend
Tluulth — ƛuł (tlōolth), Nuu-chah-nulth for "beautiful"
Ḥawith's youngest daughter
Ṫoopuuk — łu·puk (Tōo-pook), "happy, glad"
Deeyuh chief's slave
Uhpahs — ʔapa·s (ŭ-pŏs), "cute"
Amuun'aẋsum's best friend; slave
Uhpqoolth — ʔapqu·ł (ŭp-kōolth), "bold"
Dushuuw's cousin; Buhkweeduuk's son
Um-iiqsu — ʔumʔiiqsu (ōom-ēk-sōo), Nuu-chah-nulth for "mother"
Chahbuhł's first wife; mother of Ḳotsik
Wiid — wi·d (wēd), "raid, war, wage war"
Wuh-uhch war chief
Wiikihbis — wi·qibis (wē-kĭ-bĭs), "bad weather, unpleasant atmosphere"
Buh-uhs's father; killed by Dushuuw
Xhud-uck — xadʔak (xhŭd-ŭk), "woman, lady, female"
Buh-uhs's mother, Dushuuw's cousin
Yahbis — ya·bis (yŏ-bĭs), "love (noun)"
Dushuuw's grandmother; Chahbuhł's mother
Yaq — ye·qʷ (yăkh), "best friend, bud, partner (male)"
Dushuuw's best friend; diver on whaling crew

Key places in Kwidich'chuh-aht territory
Wuh-uhch — Waʔač (wŭ-ŭCH), Waatch
Deeyuh — Di·ya (dē-yŭ), Neah Bay
Oosa-ilth — ʔUse·ʔił (ōo-să-ĭlth), Ozette
Tsooyuhs — Ċu·yas (TSōo-yŭs), Tsooes (or Sooes)
Bih-ihd-uh — Biʔidʔa (bĭ-ĭd-ŭ), Bahaada
Chahdee — Ča·di· (chŏ-dē), Tatoosh Island (lit. "land on water")
Huuqoo — Huqu· (hōo-kōo), Hoko (Hoko River)

Acknowledgments

I am grateful for the repeated gifts of time and expertise from a multitude of generous Makah and First Nations individuals. However, this assistance does not imply their or any tribe's endorsement of this work, nor does it imply that other individuals enrolled in their nations would share their perspectives. Any and all mistakes, in fact or in spirit, are mine alone.

u·šu·yakš?alic to Greg Colfax, Linda Colfax, Robert Dennis Jr., Dan Greene, Daniel Greene, Wade Greene, Janine Ledford, Gisele Martin, Joe Martin, Micah McCarty, Polly McCarty, Spencer McCarty, Walter McQuillen, Keely Parker, Meredith "Mer" Parker, Maria Pascua, and Melissa Peterson, as well as Branndi Bowechop and Evan Bowechop, for the time and care they gave to this project over the years.

Many thanks to archaeologist Gary Wessen and ecologist Timothy Wootton. And special thanks to Brian Atwater, Curt Peterson, Alex Dolcimascolo, and Daniel Eungard for helping me understand Cascadia subduction zone earthquakes and tsunamis, and especially the 1700 event and its impacts. I am also grateful to the many survivors of tsunamis, from Crescent City to Bandeh Aceh, who shared their stories with researchers for books and brochures that help communities worldwide learn how to survive similar disasters.

Big thanks to my non-Native beta readers: Beth, Briana, Cally, Danny, Gale, Jesikah, Jessica, Julie, Krista, Marci, Marisa, Robin, Sarah, and Stephanie. Special thanks to Allison Braden.

As I write this, the Makah tribe was at long last preparing to get back on their waters to hunt whales. I fully support this treaty right, though it's important to note that not all Makahs approve of the hunt. Culture is not a monolith.

I hope this book inspires people to learn more about the traditions and beliefs of the Makah and their neighbors. One of the best ways to learn is to visit. Take in the Makah Cultural and Research Center in Neah Bay, Washington; the Huu-ay-aht First Nation's Kiix̣in tours near Bamfield, British Columbia; and the traditional lands of the Tla-o-qui-aht Nation near Tofino, British Columbia, with a stay at the nation's Tin Wis Resort. Although not a focus of this book, the U'mista Cultural Centre in Alert Bay, British Columbia, which preserves the cultural heritage of the Kwakwaka'wakw, also is well worth a visit, as well as the Carnegie

Museum in Port Angeles, Washington, operated by the Lower Elwha Klallam Tribe with a focus on that and other Olympic Peninsula tribes.

There are many more "people of the sea"—wherever you go on the coast, get to know those who have called its beaches home since time immemorial.

Work on this book spanned 14 years and, honestly, could go on for a lifetime. (The more I know, the more I appreciate how much I don't know.) The list of books, articles, dissertations, interviews, research papers, and other sources are too many to detail here, though a short list is posted at melissaslager.com/reader.

But some notes are important to make here.

Songs: Songs serve different purposes, but many are the cultural property of individuals or families, and they remain that way even if they appear in books in the public domain. As such, the majority of songs in this novel are fictional, including the song Amuun'axsum inherits. Exceptions would be the humorous exchange where an old man sings about the particular joys of looking like a tufted puffin, and a friend urges him to sit down, both comedic songs described in my much-thumbed copy of Frances Densmore's *Nootka and Quileute Music*.

Dances: Dances are like songs. And so here, too, dances are largely fictional, including Dushuuw's inherited dance. The dance Amuun'axsum observes near the end of the book refers to Huu-ay-aht songs and dances that went with a pair of Thunderbird masks and a set of thirty-seven wooden birds on poles—on display in the nation's facility near Bamfield—the "original tsunami warning system," as Robert (Wišqii) Dennis Jr. put it during a personal tour.

Stories: Nearly all the stories that characters tell in these pages are shared in Makah circles. A bulk come from Densmore's book (a classic that goes well beyond music). For the storyteller's version of Q̓watee and the sea monster, however, I drew directly from the telling Spencer McCarty gave me one cool afternoon overlooking the Waatch River. And the story the grandmother tells Buh-uhs at different points to help him know who he is and where he comes from is a family story shared by Walter (Kloo-Athl) McQuillen, as presented at a 2020 public event in Port Townsend, and used with permission.

The key exception here is the braided "Thunderbird and Whale" story introduced in sections throughout the novel. This my own stylized version of stories about Thunderbird fighting Whale found in Quileute, Hoh, and Makah oral traditions. Stories like these offer instructions on how to survive on two levels. First, they warn about failing to maintain a balance between the physical and spiritual worlds. Second, they often are followed by practical advice, such as to move to high ground when the sea retreats or a large earthquake strikes. As Makah elder Helma Ward told a Seattle P-I reporter in 2002: "The stories say this has happened before and will happen again."

To everyone who is still reading, *ƛeko·!*
—Melissa

šu.

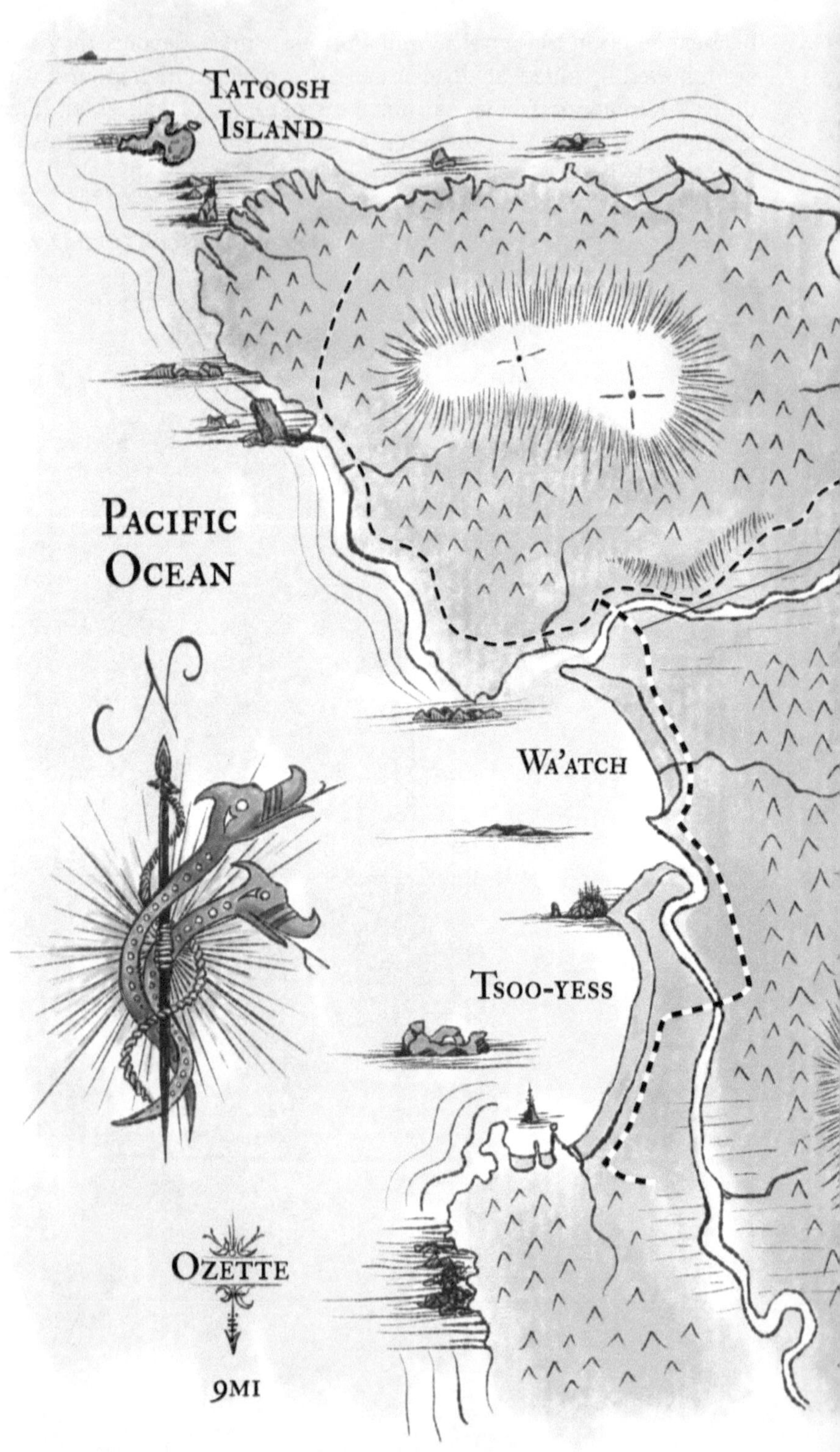

TATOOSH ISLAND
PACIFIC OCEAN
WA'ATCH
TSOO-YESS
OZETTE
9MI

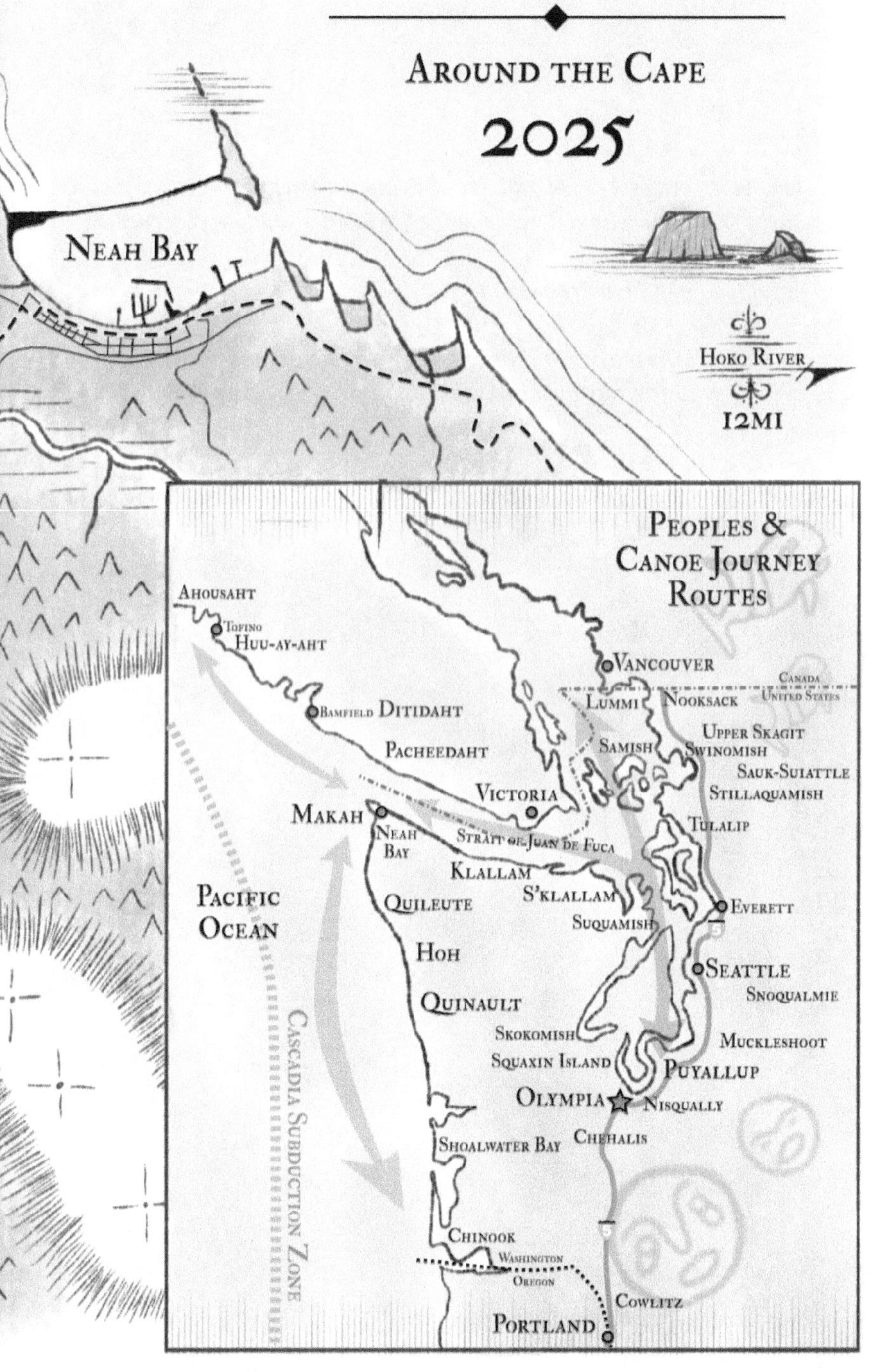
MAKAH
LANDS & WATERS
AROUND THE CAPE
2025
NEAH BAY
HOKO RIVER
12MI
PEOPLES &
CANOE JOURNEY
ROUTES
AHOUSAHT
Tofino
HUU-AY-AHT
Vancouver
CANADA
UNITED STATES
Lummi
NOOKSACK
Bamfield
DITIDAHT
UPPER SKAGIT
SWINOMISH
Samish
SAUK-SUIATTLE
PACHEEDAHT
STILLAQUAMISH
VICTORIA
TULALIP
MAKAH
Neah
Bay
STRAIT OF JUAN DE FUCA
KLALLAM
S'KLALLAM
EVERETT
PACIFIC
OCEAN
QUILEUTE
SUQUAMISH
SEATTLE
HOH
SNOQUALMIE
QUINAULT
MUCKLESHOOT
SKOKOMISH
SQUAXIN ISLAND
PUYALLUP
OLYMPIA
NISQUALLY
Shoalwater Bay
CHEHALIS
CASCADIA SUBDUCTION ZONE
CHINOOK
Washington
Oregon
COWLITZ
PORTLAND

Melissa Slager is a journalist and writer living with her family in Everett, Washington, surrounded by volcanoes, seawater, and evergreens.

Learn more at melissaslager.com

Please support the author and this book by leaving an honest review on your favorite bookish websites, apps, and stores.

www.ingramcontent.com/pod-product-compliance
Lightning Source LLC
Chambersburg PA
CBHW022012300726
48970CB00003B/852